Theft of Decks

Book Two

Lars Machmüller

CONTENTS

<u>DEDICATIONS:</u>

This is the fifteenth time I write a thank you note for a book.

Fifteen books! It would be easy to surmise that you'd run out of heartfelt *'thank yous'* after the first couple of books. Kids, wife, dear friend, maybe a grandmother if you're feeling nostalgic, and hey presto, we've run out. That is, of course, patently untrue.

I feel ashamed for not having thanked you yet. You've stood by my side ever since the start. You've pushed me when I needed pushing, been with me through lack of sleep, illness and brain fog. You've had my back through emotional turmoil, the highest joys, successes, flops and the everyday grind.

Thank you caffeine. You are my only friend.

-Lars
11/12/2024

RECAP OF THEFT OF

DECKS, BOOK 1

"I told them. They should have listened." There. That is our most likely epitaph, as well as my formal complaint that this task falls to me. I have informed them that, in the case of our demise, the odds that any of these notes, jotted down in a tome about Lightborn heroes through the ages, will be of any use to anybody, is not likely. Yet, they insisted. Too important to let die, apparently.

Let it be said that there were four of us: Liam, a Lightborn; Chase, a Darkborn; Kith, Furyborn; and I, Cilia, a much-maligned blend of Liberator and Darkborn. All poor, all cardless and bereft of prospects, growing up in the chaotic pool of poverty on the Waves in the frontier town of Isarn. Yet, we tried to make more of ourselves. Tried, and failed. The story should have ended there, really, with the four of us fated for a brief and violent end as indebted fighters in a Lightborn army.

Yet, fate had other plans for us. While the Lightborn army was in turn overwhelmed, encircled, beaten, and defeated, we managed to escape with three relatively important items: our lives; a new companion, Sera, a Lightborn healer; and a vaunted Deck of Darkness, thought lost for centuries.

Complications ensued. We found a temporary refuge, laid plans, adjusted said plans, scrambled to complete them, walked the Steps and grew in power. Yet, when things were finally starting to look up, we were forced to flee again, this time with a growing certainty: We would need access to Light cards to ever build a life in peace. Any Lightborn would kill to get our Deck of Darkness, and we would need a likely cover to be able to hide. Hence, Light cards.

Due to this, we decided to sneak into *the* Lightborn stronghold in Isarn, the cathedral of the Church of the Circle, and steal Light cards for ourselves. In case we don't make it out, my above epitaph will stand for itself. If we actually do make it out, I'm sure it will still be relevant for the future. Because they never *do* listen. Especially Kith.

CHAPTER 1

"Earth's Ward. The home of Elementals. The stronghold of our race. The safeguard against all aggressors." That's the subtitle? They sell it pretty well, I'll admit that much. (Page 1.)

"That's enough dawdling, people! We need to enact the plan and get the Pits out of here. Any picks that can help you, make them now. Otherwise, save it for afterward when we can think it through properly. That seal isn't going to hold forever." Chase's words rang out over the inner sanctum of the cathedral of the Church of the Circle in Isarn, rousting his crew into action.

They were in a bit of a bind. Okay, that might be a bit of an understatement. They were in serious trouble. They'd barely survived a desperate fight with an inquisitor, knocked out a high priest, and robbed a Deck of Light. Now, they were caught in the center of the inner sanctum, with enemy forces pounding on the doors, eager to flood into the place and slaughter them all. They were all tired, overwhelmed, and bloody. Not a single one was entirely unhurt.

Luckily, they'd planned for this.

It was the one element that had made their choice in attempting the heist in the first place.

Serafine Valerian, erstwhile noble and healer apprentice, had spent a good deal of her life inside this very church. She knew about the security and the rooms. She'd also known about the single opening into the room—the balcony placed high above the inner sanctuary, looking down upon the Deck of Light and the innermost, sacred chamber right above where the deck itself used to be. Until today, they hadn't been aware exactly what it was for. However, they'd realized early on what it could mean for them. An alternate exit, if things didn't go as they planned.

Liam was spooling out their secret weapon: a grappling hook, set on a long rope. He was far enough away from the two side entrances that none of the defenders would be able to see what he was up to. With a few swings, the grappling hook tore into the air, aiming for the balcony above.

Three attempts—and two suggestions from Kith that he would do a better job—later, the hook clattered past the edge of the balcony. With a triumphant cry, Liam slowly pulled the hook back with a calm hand to ensure the hook didn't fall over the edge. It caught, and stuck.

The big Lightborn slowly let his weight fall on the rope, testing its strength. The man, tall and wide, with impressive shoulders, didn't look like a thief. In fact, his bright-blue eyes, short-cropped blond hair, and handsome features made him look every bit the epitome of all that a Lightborn should be. Handsome, strong, and near angelic. That he was also genuinely a great guy would have been infuriating...if he wasn't so damn nice.

"Let me. You don't have the Agility for this." Kith shoved Liam aside and started to climb up the rope in fits and starts.

He made it nearly ten feet into the air, when a massive crack from above ruined their plan. Kith let go of the rope and landed, scampering backward to avoid the crumbling rubble of the ruined edge of the balcony falling down. Wide-eyed, he stared at the wreckage tumbling down right in front of him, then turned to the others with a snarl.

Kith's colorful eyes sparkled as a drop of blood ran down from a cut on his scalp. The Furyborn was almost the opposite of Liam. Where Liam was tall, Kith was low-set. Liam was pale; Kith's skin was the color of the soil.

His eyes were always bright. Like all Furyborn, the sclerae of his eyes were aswirl with colors. Some said you could tell the mood of a Furyborn from the colors in their eyes. With Kith, you never needed to get that close. He never hid how he felt. The powder keg of a person looked every bit your classic Furyborn, lower-set than usual, with a solid, powerful build, and his tall, curly, near-orange hair standing up, like a vivid warning: "Here be tempers."

"Light sear me. That almost killed me!" He spoke the shocked words and launched into a long series of cursing.

Cilia spoke, her words cold and to the point. "Stop acting up, Kith. We are going to get out, and we are going to make it through that opening. Now, shut up, so I can figure out how. The rest of you, start thinking." A bright light showed her engaging her Heart card, drowning out the rest of the world, allowing her to mute the noise around her.

Cilia was a rarity. Not just in the fact that she actually enjoyed solitude and silence, something that Chase would never understand, but in her being a rare mixed breed. On top of that, she had the questionable fortune of her provenance being very clear to see. She was part Darkborn, as showed by her near-grey skin complexion, even darker than Chase's. On top of that, she was part Liberty, evidenced by her thin nose, blue tinge to the skin, and slightly tapered ears. Cilia would never blend in in a crowd. Chase would never want her to, either. She was perfect just the way she was.

Sera moved forward and took a cloth to Kith's forehead, checking the damage. She still wore the rough woolen servant's robes they'd all worn, trying to sneak in. Even so, she'd have trouble hiding anywhere. Her heart-shaped face, friendly smile, and blonde curls framing her face clearly made her out as a Lightborn, and her beauty would make her stand out anywhere. Her looks did manage to hide that she was no wilting beauty, that her body was not that of a soft noble but belonged to somebody who'd pushed herself to excel since childhood. The bright-blue eyes were clear and focused as she took in the injury, then told Kith to stop being a crybaby.

Chase rubbed his forehead, pushing around the solid layer of blood, sweat, and dirt accumulating there. Truth be told, he didn't mind it. The dirt helped camouflage who he was. *What* he was. As if his willowy, graceful, too-thin body wasn't enough of a reminder, the swarthy complexion of his skin helped anybody to recall. Darkborn. Universally mistrusted, thought to be villains and ne'er-do-wells, all because of a huge falling-out between the Lightborn and Darkborn years and years ago. At least his slightly below average height, pleasant but not beautiful looks, and short-cropped brown hair helped him blend in just about anywhere. Only, that was not going to help anybody if they didn't make it out.

The balcony more than twenty feet above was clearly not sturdy. Cilia, weighing at least thirty pounds less than Kith, might theoretically be able to make it up if they hooked another part of the crumbling stone balcony, but considering it was already half-broken, he doubted it. That meant they'd need something else to help them along.

Chase sighed. It wasn't how he'd wanted to approach it. Even so, he shut up and got to it.

[You have walked the Steps and reached the third Tier. Through the Light deck, that grants you the right to choose three new cards.]

Where Chase came from, the Waves, anybody with a card was a power, somebody lifted up from the common mass of everybody else, gifted with strength and abilities that made them better, stronger and more important. Even so, it was a well-known fact that the cards of the first Tier were nowhere near as powerful as those later on. First-Tier cards could kill a man. Fifth-Tier cards could level a neighborhood. Or so they said.

Chase quickly blazed through half the information arriving straight into his head. Then he focused on one card which he'd almost passed, before taking in the description yet again. He let out a relieved sigh.

[Steps of Brilliance
Rare, Light rogue
Tier one
Active, instant
This card grants you the option of creating three palm-sized platforms wherever you may choose. These platforms are visible *and* tangible only to yourself, unless faced up against an adversary with much higher Mental Power than yours. The platforms only last for a short duration, but you may constantly create up to three platforms.
"I saw him, once. His was not the power of flight. No, it was a lot more unnatural. He moved like he did not belong in this world." A bystander, about the Acrobat of Virn.]

At first, he'd nearly dismissed the card, thinking of it only as a way to optimize movement in combat. At a closer look, he realized he'd be able to place those platforms wherever he chose, on the ground or in the air. So, not only was the card rare, but it also granted him exactly what he needed. It would still be a stretch, but he'd practiced climbing walls the day before. This would just be an expansion on it.

Chase felt the card solidifying inside him, shuddering from the sensation of magic settling and becoming an intrinsic part of who he was. With a growl, he focused on summoning the card to the forefront of his right arm and activated it. In front of him, three glowing platforms came alive, like a glowing tiny staircase leading straight onto the opening above. He picked up speed, ran faster, jumped...and missed the third platform by an inch, slamming hard into the wall.

It took three more attempts and twice that time to explain that, no, he hadn't gone insane. Then Chase successfully launched through the air, taking three long steps on the glowing platforms before pushing off from the wall and launching into the air...and onto the half-broken stone balcony.

After that, it was just a matter of locating a solid recess in the floor that would hold the grappling hook, and they took turns climbing up. Liam pretty much pulled Cilia up to join them, even as the magical seals below finally broke down, letting in the defenders.

In the following days, Chase would have trouble describing their subsequent flight through the twisting corridors of the cathedral. It was chaotic, messy, and constantly loud. Everywhere, people were screaming, crying for help, for information on what was happening, for their gods to aid them.

They didn't stop for anything. Any defenders they met, they knocked down or pushed back. Yet, the Lightborn were all congregated on the lower levels, trying to trap their crew, and they kept moving. Once, Kith's arm lit up in a bright glow, and he summoned a massive, ugly monstrosity to block a corridor where a group of guards appeared from out of nowhere. The noise of his summon being hacked apart faded quickly as they sprinted away.

Eventually, they found themselves on the roof of the massive ceiling, looking down upon the city below. Fortunately, any guards up here had long since moved into the towering edifice below. Isarn spread over large stretches of land, from the taller upper city with its carefully planned and maintained noble residences and streets, over the teeming lower city and its chaotic buildings, straight down to Lake Isarn and the ugly hodgepodge of rafts floating on the Waves far beyond. It was enough to make one feel nostalgic...if one weren't fleeing for one's life.

A few quick glances confirmed the situation. A smaller crowd congregated around the main entrance of the church below, yet the rear of the church was blessedly silent. Even if it felt like forever since they'd entered the place, it was still early morning, and the city had not entirely awoken. They placed the grappling hook securely on the balustrade, before descending the building one by one and fading out into Isarn to disappear.

CHAPTER 2

"The nomenclature of the geography of Ordei is oft biased or downright hurtful. In letting the aspected leaders name their own lands and cities, we come across some horribly misleading naming conventions. Liberty Fields? Where is the liberty? The Temple of the Savior? Who did he ever save? Elemental naming conventions might be dull, but at least they are accurate. Visit the Elemental towers and see for yourself." This rolls over into an explanation of why the Savior—the High Priest who brought low the Church of Darkness—might as well have been named the Butcher. This is page 1. I...think I'm going to enjoy this history tome. (Pages 1-2.)

"When you said you had a plan that would give us everything we'd always wanted...was this what you had in mind?" Kith's words were innocent enough. The all-telling glance at their surroundings were anything but.

"Yes, Kith," Chase answered scornfully. "Back on the Waves, when I lay awake at night, dreaming of better days, this was what I always wanted. Becoming a caarnath herder." He glanced ahead of them, where the lumbering shapes of caarnaths blocked every sight. The bitter tang of the heavy reptilians was ever-present, even out on the verdant plains. The rumbling groans of their calls drowned out any other sound nearby.

Kith held up an admonishing finger. "Ah ah. *Assistant* caarnath herders. None of us are talented enough to become proper caarnath herders, mate."

Chase rolled his eyes. Kith wasn't wrong, obviously. They weren't going to learn how to herd the huge beasts, and they damn well weren't going to do a real attempt either. "Listen, man. It was this or march by ourselves. And with the attention we've got on us, I don't think any of us really wanted to try that."

Kith grinned, a shit-eating grin showing off the vibrant colors of his eyes brimming with joy. It was almost enough to drown out how he was entirely caked with the result of walking for almost a full day under the hot sun, within the eternal clouds of dust and worse in the teeming group of beasts. "I'm good, man. After our fun in the armies of Light? This is pure relaxation! I think you might find that other members of our group disagree, though." He gestured with his head at something behind them.

Chase followed his gaze and tamped down a grin of his own. A dozen feet behind them, Sera and then Cilia followed.

Cilia had her head deep inside one of her tomes. She had her Heart card engaged, ignoring the rest of the world, allowing her to walk and read at the same time.

Sera…was also trying to forget about the world. Her rough woolen robes surrounded her, and she had a light scarf wrapped around her head, hiding her golden curls. She was wrapped up enough that she would be able to blend in anywhere in their current surroundings. The bright-blue eyes behind the scarf shot daggers, making no secret of just how much she was enjoying herself.

"Yeah. Starting your life on the Heights and then stooping this low? It's one spine-shattering drop!" Chase admitted. "She's…taking it well, though."

"I can *hear* you, you know?" Sera snapped. "And I am *not* taking this well. By any means. We need to do something, or I will kill somebody. My *underwear* smells like manure!"

Chase fought down a burst of laughter. "I think you're doing great." That wasn't even that much of a lie. Considering everything that had happened to the erstwhile noble daughter, she was holding up pretty damn well. The Darkborn looked at his own skin, caked in a layer of dirt and worse. At least he didn't have to be too afraid that people were going to point to him as a Darkborn. Everybody had the same skin color in this mess. He looked back to Kith and shrugged. "You know this wasn't the plan. If it weren't for what Cilia managed to learn, we wouldn't be here either. So, I'd spend my time blaming her."

"Who's blaming anybody?" Kith grinned. "I'm having the time of my life here. Merely watching the princess is a never-ending source of fun."

"I can *still* hear you!" Sera snarled.

"Oh, I know."

Chase laughed out loud. He couldn't help it. He shook his head, considering their situation. It wasn't like they'd planned for this. Their situation had slowly transformed into one where their current position—actually *paying* to be allowed to tag alongside a bunch of Lightborn herders and help with a herd of caarnaths in their hundreds—was preferrable to the alternative.

He blamed Cilia. Blamed her for being so damn attentive and clever.

They'd stood there, in the center of the power of Lightborn in Isarn, victorious and powerful, having just taken down a damn inquisitor. Not only that, but Chase had immediately discovered that he was able to not only gain a handful of Light cards from the Deck of Light on display in the cathedral, but he'd also been able to take the entire damn deck for himself. Meaning, he'd be able to share out Light cards to *anybody* in the future, not just their tight group. If that wasn't enough to make a man slightly drunk with power, he didn't know what qualified.

Only Cilia had kept her head attached and her eyes on the task. While they were reveling in the fact that they gained their cards, she'd had the wherewithal to wake up the passed-out high priest and ask him a handful of questions. Very pointed questions, triggered by her reading and re-reading of a journal by the deceased former holder of the Deck of Darkness, Arnault.

The High Priest of Isarn had not held back. Believing that his life was on the line, he'd answered any question Cilia asked, spilling things that were definitely not for commoners to know. He confirmed the position of inquisitors in the Church of the Circle. Not too much of a shocker, really, what with the corpse of the inquisitor lying in a pool of its own blood a dozen feet away from him. The specifics, however, were.

He verified that, not only were the inquisitors very much an active, autonomous part of the church as a whole, they were also a surprisingly powerful group, for not having their powers defined to the public. It was the Twenty-fourth Schism, or whatever. Chase didn't really care about the specifics. But, at a certain point, the church had decided, in its wisdom, that the continuous existence of the inquisitors was too much to grasp for the feeble minds of the commonalty. Hence, they'd enhanced their powers, and made their existence a poorly hidden secret. Made them the hidden dagger in the white glove of the armies of Light.

They hadn't stayed long in the city. Just long enough to purchase provisions and ensure they wouldn't die from thirst or hunger. Then they bribed a guard known for being on the take to look the other way while they slipped out the southern gate.

If only that had been all they had to deal with, Chase would've considered himself a lucky traitor to the Light. But no. Not only were those damn inquisitors a powerful force in the lands of Light, working semi-independently from the rest of the church, but they were also bestowed powers to match. Their group could attest to those powers, having barely managed to best a single inquisitor in combat. Only, their weapons, as they called their combat-trained inquisitors, were the straightforward ones. Their seekers, however? They were the dangerous ones. Inquisitors with the knowledge to move both among commoners and the higher-ups of society, with few limiters to their power. As to their actual *powers*? Those were even worse. The seekers were as varied as the persons themselves, coming from different walks of life, as were their cards. Yet, they all had one thing in common. One thing, known to high priests. Inquisitors retained their original purpose, to seek out any dangers to the

Light. As such, they were all granted one specific card. One purpose. A replacement to their Heart card—something Chase didn't even know was possible—granting them a passive power to spot those with Dark cards.

It was supposedly a tiered power, one that adjusted itself to the power of the person wielding a Dark card and the inquisitor. A Tier-one Dark wielder of cards would be a spark in the dark, only to be spotted from right up close by a high-Tier inquisitor, while a Tier-five Dark wielder would look like a bonfire to any inquisitor.

That tiny piece of knowledge torched the entire plan their group had for the future. How would they be able to build a future for themselves anywhere in the lands of Light, knowing that any inquisitor passing by might be able to spot the existence of their Dark cards from afar and bring the wrath of the Church of the Circle down upon them?

Sure, they'd be able to put down roots anywhere, even outside of any towns, and with the Deck of Darkness, Chase could create a Wellspring that would start protecting them, spewing Dark monsters to defend them from any enemies...and announce their presence to the world better than any town crier. Not really an option. They needed anonymity.

Chase leaned closer to Kith and spoke lower. "Do you think she's all right? Seriously?"

Kith grimaced, looking into the distance. "I...no. Of course, she isn't. We've plucked her from the Heights, and now she's down in the muck. Also, we're about to leave the lands of Light, possibly forever. Nobody in their right mind would take that easily. But we're doing what we can to help, aren't we?"

Chase shrugged. Were they? There wasn't really that much they *could* do, the way he saw things. The stronger they got, the easier it would be for any inquisitor to spot them in the lands of Light. That meant leaving. And unless they wanted to live in the wilderness forever, there were only three possible destinations: The wilds of the Furyborn. The lands of Liberty. Or Earth's Ward, the center of Elemental power.

When it came to the Furyborn, those were simply out of the question. Within the lands of Light, they were known as mindless hordes, famous only for fighting and pillaging. Chase took every bit of propaganda coming from Lightborn with a grain of salt. Even so, he had to admit that the thought of approaching their lands was...not an inviting one. They'd had Furyborn Guardians trying to kill them before. Light or Dark cards notwithstanding, he couldn't picture a situation where they'd be met with anything but violence.

As to the lands of Liberty? That one was even worse. Where the Furyborn were known for, from time to time, producing armies that would come roaring down upon the Lightborn countryside to murder and pillage, Liberators were an unknown threat. They guarded their borders with a passion, and any army sent their way simply disappeared. Over the years, the Lightborn had decided to stop throwing away their cards and stopped sending forces their way. The borders of Liberty never expanded, so it seemed like the Liberators were fine with that arrangement. Approaching them, though? It sounded like a one-way slide down into the Pits.

That left Earth's Ward, the home of the Elemental nation. The Elementals were not officially at war with the Lightborn. The two powers had managed an uneasy non-aggression pact of sorts for decades now, one that let the Elementals rule as they wanted in their own, limited area and granted them freedom of passage outside their borders. Elementals were not allowed to own land or operate businesses outside their own borders, though. As such, the borders were entirely set in stone.

That didn't bother Chase and the rest. Sure, the Elemental lands might be limited in scope. However, an area where Lightborn were only allowed to visit, not to stay? It sounded like just the thing. They just needed to make their way there and earn the right to settle down somewhere around the Elemental towers, however they'd have to swing that. Hence, the reason to tag along with the Lightborn herders. Although he was sure there would be Lightborn, and maybe even inquisitors, looking for them right now, they probably wouldn't be looking for a runaway noble within the stench of manure.

Chase looked at his own skin as he walked. The darkness of his skin was nothing new. If anything, the dust of the travels and the disturbed soil, churned up by the hundreds of clawed feet, made them lighter to the eye. The cards on his arms, meanwhile, *were* new. The simple look of the brilliant, sparkling borders around his newly won Light cards never failed to astound him. It just looked *wrong*. Fancy, but wrong.

Still, he couldn't deny the utility of what he'd gotten. His Tier-two card was straightforward and lovely.

[**Race of Life**
Uncommon, Light rogue
Tier two
Active, medium duration
This card, once tapped, grants you a small boost to Agility. It can be used several times a day, making it perfect for those who often need to work in bursts.

Medium cooldown
"Some people say that life is a marathon, not a sprint. Some people are wrong. Life, the way I see it, is a marathon of sprints. And we should plan accordingly."]

Compared to his Dark Tier-two card, Nights of Criffhaven, which granted a boost at a maximum of +15, the boost was not impressive. Even so, it worked instantly, gave a +4 boost, and would be improved to a +9 with Sera's own buff on top. In short, it worked perfectly, for when he needed an instant buff and didn't have the luxury of stringing out a conflict.

He'd had the chance to use his Tier-one card, Steps of Brilliance, a lot in the meantime. At first, he'd felt bad, knowing that he picked it just to escape. But it turned out it was more than just a nice gimmick. Sure, it was a movement card, pure and simple. One that worked only for himself. Kith gave him so much crap for choosing a card that couldn't even be seen by anybody else. Yet, it was everything Chase ever wanted in a movement power. It would allow him to run into the air, fend off a fall if he dropped off heights, climb walls that were too tall for him. In short, it granted him the power to perform movements that would otherwise be entirely impossible.

It wasn't perfect. At the moment, he wasn't quite at the level of Mental Power where he'd be able to use it constantly on the fly, let alone in combat. However, if he were running away? He'd be able to escape pursuit with this—leap walls or use it to move from roof to roof, even if the distance was far. At rare, the cooldown allowed him to *keep* producing the platforms, three at a time. Only somebody with their own *good* movement power would be able to follow. In time, he might improve his Mental Power to where he'd be able to consistently use it in battle. He pictured being able to turn unnaturally fast, even using platforms to ricochet items off. After all, it wasn't just him, but also items thrown by him that they worked for. First came training, though.

As for training... Chase couldn't help but smile when he thought of his final, Tier-three card. It was probably his favorite of the lot. Even if he found a place where he'd be able to permanently swap over to his favorite cards irrespective of their aspect, he'd likely have this one active most of the time. It was that good.

[Spoils of the Undeserving
Rare, Light rogue
Tier three
Permanent, passive

In this life, all good comes to those who earn it. Some people, though, are able to adjust the tendrils of fate, carve off more for themselves than what they actually deserve. With this card, the wielder will improve their attributes through training at a triple pace compared to others.
"You can tell me, man. What potions are you on? I want some."]

If there was one thing he had found to be true over the past couple of months, it was this: his upbringing had seriously stymied his potential power. With the cards and the windfalls he'd earned from killing Arnault and Inquisitor Callas, as well as gaining the Decks of Darkness and Light on top of that, he'd gone a damn long way to make up for lost time. However, if he'd had a better base level in his attributes beforehand, he'd have been better off by an order of magnitudes.

He would never get back his lost youth or his hand, of course. But he might make up for the shortcomings with this card. Pits, he'd already decided he was going to train hard to get his attributes, especially Mental Power, to a more acceptable level. This card would cut the time needed down to a third. Likely less, if he got it to Epic or Legendary.

He checked over his attributes.

Personal Info:
Name: Chase
Title: Dark/Light rogue
Step: 17 (Tier 3)

Strength: 11
Agility: 18 (+8 Tier bonus) = 26
Toughness: 13
Mental Power: 11
Potential: 25

Chase was still going with his original approach. He spent nearly all his attribute points in Potential. With that, and his high Agility and his Dark cards granting him the ability to steal attributes from others (and on rare occasions, keep said attributes permanently), he did just fine. In time, his training card should be able to raise him to untold heights.

In front of Chase, the dust clouds were slowly settling. He couldn't keep a wide grin from building on his face as he turned toward the others. "Looks like we're settling down for the evening. It's almost time for the *real* work to start!"

His outburst was met with groans.

CHAPTER 3

"Do you yearn for power? Book learning? The best edu-cation available on Ordei? Come to the Elemental towers. Do you desire peace? Stay away." This is weird. Not sure I'm get-ting the point. It feels like an in-joke. I do truly look forward to seeing their library. (Page 4.)

Kith was a force of nature. That felt like a uncomforta-ble parallel. Furyborn in general were seen as close to nature, and, with their rage and tempers, often portrayed as being little better than beasts. That was horrid prejudice. Even so, with Kith's new cards, Chase couldn't see him any other way. Especially mid-combat.

Kith moved aggressively. He always had. His much-worn hand axes slammed down at Liam, left and right hand moving independently of each other. However, there was more to it right now. He seemed taller than usual, more alive, as if glowing with an inner light. His attacks hit harder, and he moved faster.

Liam was left huddling behind his shield, moving and striking defensively. He shouted at the top of his lungs, "I hate that new summon!"

The Lightborn was, beyond a doubt, the most handsome of their group. Even Sera admitted as much. The easy smile and short-cropped blond hair *just* wavy enough to ruffle would have made him a pest, if it weren't for his natural affability. Well. When he wasn't attacking you.

Kith stumbled mid-attack, his pace off for a moment. From within his body, a bright shape continued for a half-step, emerging from his body as a separate, sparkling entity. When it did, Kith's movement grew perceptibly slower, less agile.

Liam punished him right away, moving on the attack. His mace thundered down, striking at Kith's left leg. His left arm flashed and his entire body moved forward at an increased pace, unstoppable like a juggernaut.

Chase grinned from the sidelines. It was one of Liam's two new cards.

[Waterfall of Light
Uncommon, Light fighter
Tier one
Active, instant

There are those fighters who advocate for technique, know-how, and weapon control to save the day. They tend to ignore one detail: with enough power, everything else falls at the wayside. Tapping this card causes your next attack to gain Trample. The attack will be very difficult to deflect or block, and has a medium chance to stun the enemy or knock them prone.
Short cooldown
"Rise, good sir. I was merely delivering a point. Get up...please."
The chevalier earns his exile.]

Kith had no way of defending against the force of the attack. He moved with it, trying to pull his leg out of the way. Even so, the mace stroke would not be denied and flung his leg back with implacable power. He hit the ground with an undignified squawk and rolled away to escape Liam's follow-up attack. As he did, the blinding force inside him burst forth and exploded right in Liam's face.

Chase cursed, looking away as the world turned into spots in front of his eyes. Within a few seconds, his vision cleared. It would be worse for Liam, he knew. He'd been on the receiving end of that particular card of Kith's as well. It was insidious. Kith was fortunate enough to receive the card at Rare.

[Divine Mentor
Rare, Light summoner
Tier one
Active, medium duration
This summon brings forth a divine entity from the heavens. Internalized, the being will aid the summoner, increasing all their attributes and improving their movement speed. It can also be expended, guiding the entity to a chosen position before making it burst in a blinding light.
Long cooldown
"Behold, oh mortal. I am you. Only better, bereft of this fragile shell of yours. Follow my guidance, if you can."]

Liam reeled back, entirely blinded. He was completely open to any counterattacks.

Meanwhile, Kith reached out and brought forth his second summoned creature. He had made some serious choices with his new cards. He knew now that his approach to being a summoner, with his shadow summons for distracting and scouting on top of his Tainted Earth for slowing enemies down while draining them of Toughness, was good but flawed. It worked perfectly when he was able to keep his distance and gradually wear them down. For truly strong enemies, though, it wouldn't do.

The Divine Mentor had been Kith's first Light card, entirely meant to gain him a surprising edge in combat. The other card was also an admission to this possible weakness, and a way to, eventually, even the scales.

It was a simple summon. As Kith had expressed it, a "summon and release" skill he could use and then forget about, with minimal control required. Although he'd picked it while they were fleeing, to hold back Lightborn guards, he was satisfied with it, even in hindsight.

[Crescendo of Might
Rare, Light summoner
Tier two
Active, short duration
Most summons are brought into the world with the desire to keep them present and active for as long as possible, given that they are the tools with which the summoner interacts with Ordei. This summon is the exact opposite. It comes with a time limit and the express desire to create as much damage as possible while it can.
Medium cooldown
"I am reading its mind right now. 'Rend, tear, kill!' Are you sure this is a being of Light?"]

The summon, when brought into existence, was nothing that Chase would have pictured as a being of Light. It came into being as a bulky, nearly shapeless, humanoid primate with large, fleshy limbs. It was simple in nature too, unable to do anything but attack straight on. What made it truly effective was the way it was instantly overcharged with a shimmering force of increasing light that caused it to grow uncontrollably, both physically and in power, right up until it overloaded its physical shell and simply fell apart. Its limbs would bloat and change. Its size and bulk inflate. Its attacks did Light damage, too.

Both these new cards could do a lot to shore up the weaknesses of Kith's Dark cards. Because he had been the one to land the final blow on the inquisitor in the Sanctum, he had gained a full four Steps, nearly getting him to the next Tier. Kith had divided the four attribute points according to his planned approach as a melee summoner, adding one to Strength and one to Agility. However, he did make one grudging admittance to the necessity of increased control over his summons, adding two points to Mental Power.

Personal Info:
Name: Kith

Title: Dark/Light summoner
Step: 14 (Tier 2)
Strength: 16
Agility: 16
Toughness: 13
Mental Power: 12
Potential: 11 (+6 Tier bonus) = 17

Kith leapt back up, swinging at the stumbling form of the blinded Liam. He had him exactly where he wanted him. Next to him, the shambling form of the Crescendo flanked the fighter.

Except, a shimmering wave formed over Liam's body. When it died away, he stood tall, unaffected by the blinding effects of the summon blowing up. He sidestepped, putting Kith between him and the lumbering shape of Kith's own summon. His shield held against Kith's strong attacks, and his truncheon rose and fell once, twice.

Kith fell with a cry, holding a hand up in surrender. "My shoulder. My gods-cursed shoulder! That's such an unfair card! I had you!"

Liam twirled the truncheon like it was a tiny baton. Then he flexed his left bicep, showing off his final new card for the onlookers.

[Cleansing Fire
Uncommon, Light fighter
Tier two
Active, instant
When activated, this card sends a wave of purifying power through the body of the wielder. It cleanses the body of most diseases and hostile effects, while also granting the wielder a weak healing effect.
Medium cooldown
"Who's ready for the next round? I can keep this up forever."]
He really could. Liam had gained a single Step from the fight with the inquisitor, landing him at the twelfth Step.

Personal Info:
Name: Liam
Title: Dark/Light fighter
Step: 12 (Tier 2)
Strength: 14 (+6 Tier bonus) = 20
Agility: 12
Toughness: 21
Mental Power: 10

Potential: 10

His Mental Power and Potential were right at the level of normal people, and Agility not far ahead. Yet, he could go toe to toe with anybody.

"You actually did have him. Except, you made two errors. Can you tell me which?" Sera's calm voice came from the sidelines, where she and Chase sat, deep in their mental exercises. Well, she had been deep in her mental exercise.

Chase enjoyed the entertainment too much.

Kith slowly climbed to his feet, holding his shoulder with a grimace. "Well, for one, I underestimated how damn *fast* he can use that cleansing card of his!"

The Lightborn healer nodded with a slight smile. "Instant means instant."

Kith grimaced. "As for the second...are you really going to make me say it?"

"Are you going to ask for healing in a second?" she shot back.

He rolled his eyes. The colors within were flecked with all hues, showing quite clearly that he was acting it up. "Okay then, oh exalted teacher. It is like you said right back near the start. Even with the two added points, I need more Mental Power. I lost control of my Divine Mentor, and had to blind Liam to earn me a reprieve. On top of that, I didn't fully use Crescendo of Might."

She smiled and got up. "Well done for getting straight to the point. That Divine Mentor card is incredibly versatile, but only if you master the art of keeping it in flux with your own body. Its blinding effect is good, but hardly overwhelming, especially when your opponent has the ability to cancel it out. Also, your other card does become powerful, but starts out clumsy and relatively weak."

Kith nodded, eyes downcast. "I know. I'll get there. Do you mind...?"

"Not in the least." Sera smiled. Gone was the frustration from the day's march, the strained expression from knowing that they were on the run, in a precarious position. A light flashed from her, enveloping Kith.

When it had passed, he slowly pressed his rib, and a wide smile built on his face. "Okay. I admit it. There is something to be said for straightforward. That new card of yours is damn useful, mate."

"I do enjoy it. I will admit to that. On the whole, it is not as powerful as my Dark cards. However, this is more along the lines of what I always imagined I would earn growing up." Sera smiled, holding a hand to her left forearm.

Chase knew the image was as wholesome as the card itself. It showed a middle-aged man lit up from within by a warm glow, a beatific expression on his lined face.

[Warmth of the Circle
Rare, Light healer
Tier one
Active, instant
This healing card is not the most powerful of all heals, granting a medium effect heal. However, it has an exceedingly fast effect and leaves the recipient with a small boost to Toughness that has a medium duration.
Medium cooldown
"This sensation. There is a joy here, a lingering trace of something divine. I thank you, Priestess, for this gift."]

Chase smiled at her. "I get it. And honestly? Having that card, ready to switch around makes you a lot more powerful. Especially given that the boost will be additionally increased if you have your Dark buff equipped. Somebody going from being wounded to being fully healed with an added nine to Toughness, mid-combat? That's a winner! And with that other new card on top of that? You can decide upon your approach based on what we're facing and adjust from there."

If anything, Sera's smile grew wider. "I know. If we're looking at a drawn-out battle, my Dark cards will be strongest, no discussion. Yet, sometimes, we will need an instant boost, or the power of an instant heal. My new cards will be great for that."

[Spark of Divinity
Uncommon, Light healer
Tier two
Passive, long duration
Sometimes, it is less about the power of the boost than the adaptability, being able to apply what you want and where. Tapping this card allows you to select an attribute. You can then select to either apply it to a single person for a medium increase to said attribute or your entire group for a small increase. Also, for the full duration of the boost, you may change your selection.

"Ah hah hah, Lord Agravon. You have grown stronger since last we met. Allow me a second to adjust. It would not do for me to fall behind."]

Sera had also gained a single Step in that final fight in the Sanctum. Sera's approach to walking the Steps was a tad different from the others. As a noble, she had been brought up with a long range of strict tutors and instructors, who helped her gain an impressive base set of attributes, even before she got her very first card. This had allowed her to focus her every gained attribute point afterward on Mental Power, making her increasingly powerful as a healer.

Personal Info:
Name: Serafine
Title: Dark/Light healer
Step: 11 (Tier 2)
Strength: 12
Agility: 15
Toughness: 14
Mental Power: 26 (+6) = 32
Potential: 12

It had taken a long while for the group to make it outside of Isarn and reach a place where they felt safe enough to sit down and discuss card choices, with the herders at a safe distance. When they finally did, Chase was impressed by how they came together, with the eye on the cohesion of the group, instead of selecting powers with only their own desires in mind. Hence, all their choices had been made, not only to make their own builds more balanced but to introduce additional versatility and adaptability to the group as a whole. That, and of course, the power of letting them all masquerade as regular Light card wielders in order for them to settle down and create a new life elsewhere.

In case they were attacked by beasts, or some Light soldiers actually tracked them down, they agreed, all bets were off. They'd switch to whichever combination of cards would be best for the conflict. Fortunately, whatever powers decided how cards worked in the first place was gracious enough that you were able to switch cards fast. The first swap you made took only a few seconds to take effect. Thereafter, however, there was a grace period of about an hour before you were able to rearrange them again. Meaning, you'd better make the right choice the first time around, or better yet, travel with a selection of cards equipped that would work well for nearly anything.

Cilia might have been outed as the single exception to that rule. Yet, they all agreed that her choice was not only understandable, but the best possible choice under the circumstances.

Her first card had been extremely unsurprising.

[**Manipulate Light**
Common, Light crafter
Tier one
Permanent Passive
This card opens the gates, allowing you to manipulate the Light aspect within you and, eventually, add them to your crafts in myriad ways. Manipulating your aspect will drain your stamina. *"Some people hack and slash to spread Light into this world. Not us. We, my dear, create."* World-famous Light artist Everam Witteras.]

Tier two was where she gained the most interesting card.

[**Apex of Growth**
Uncommon, Light crafter
Tier two
Permanent, passive
There are few ultimate truths as a crafter. One of the rare exceptions is this: Aspects do not blend well. This card ameliorates some of the natural imbalances existing between the different aspects, making it easier to craft items merging powers from different aspects. Any difficulties from crafting items with conflicting abilities or powers still remain.
"Take the cold control of Liberty. Add a splash of unbridled Fury. Mix in the pure decadence of Darkness. Oh, my friends. This sinful concoction will be unforgettable."]

Cilia had vacillated over the choice for a long time, but finally went for it. Her reasoning, which they ultimately all agreed with, was that the card in itself, for anybody who recognized the image, didn't give anything away but the fact that she had access to more than one aspect. And the potential payoff of eventually being able to create items that held bonuses from both Light and Dark, maybe even Elemental aspects? Buyers would be lining up to throw gold at her.

Her attributes had improved markedly, as had those of everybody else in their group. Where most of the others distributed their attributes over several different ones, Cilia focused on a single one, Mental Power. She aimed to stay in the back and focus on crafting, with her aversion to direct combat being quite clear.

Personal Info:
Name: Cilia
Title: Dark/Light crafter
Step: 11 (Tier 2)
Strength: 10
Agility: 14
Toughness: 11
    Mental Power: 22 (+6 Tier bonus) = 28
    Potential: 11

Still, Cilia was working hard to improve her physical attributes to the point where she wouldn't slow the others down.

Chase got up, stretching after sitting unmoving in his meditating position for a while. "You mind if I take over the beatdown of Liam, now that you've softened him?"

Kith winced. "By all means. If anything, I've just proved to myself that my time is better spent trying to chase the next increase to Mental Power. That big brute is becoming ridiculous to deal with. Whoever figured that he needed the power to heal himself on top of his unfair Strength and Toughness needs a stern talking-to. Possibly a kidney shot."

Chase shrugged. "Oh, it's not that bad. You just need to avoid getting hit. He strikes like a gaborn. Powerful, but easy to avoid."

Liam cracked his neck and twirled his truncheon. "Comparing me to a stinking beast? You do recall that you can't steal my attributes as long as you stick to your Light cards? I just need to catch you."

"Yeah. *Just.* I'm not a lady to swoon from your ridiculous good looks. You'll have to put in some actual effort here," Chase taunted.

"You'll need to make him pant. And *sweat*," Kith added helpfully from the sidelines.

Chase and Liam shared a glance.

Liam rumbled, "You had to go and make it weird. Can't we just beat each other up like normal adults?"

His sparring partner nodded. "Yeah. Ignore him. He should focus on sitting still for a long, long time and thinking really hard, like he loves!"

A groan from the sidelines punctuated their interchange before they sprang at each other, weapons flashing out.

This had been what their evenings had transformed into over the course of the past couple of days. Hard practice, mental and physical, tons of teasing, and not too much thinking about the day of tomorrow. Sera had also taken to teaching Chase how to read and write, because she found the alternative offensive.

Why didn't they spend more time planning their approach? Because everything was speculation at this point. They knew a couple of facts about the Elemental towers, some of it derived from talking to the caarnath herders in charge:

- Everybody was allowed to approach Earth's Ward, the center of the Elemental nation, regardless of race and cards. Even Liberty. The Elementals valued learning and trade above all else.

- *Not* everybody was allowed to settle or create businesses in the place.

- Even fewer were allowed entry to the Elemental towers, where you could join their classes and earn your cards. They were well-known for having the best classes known to man, but the access was limited, for some reason.

The specifics were not widely shared. Or, at least, none of the herders they'd joined knew the specifics. So, they accepted that they'd not be able to learn what to do before they arrived, and focused on improving what they *could* in the meantime. They got to know their new powers, using them in pairs and groups and otherwise eking out any attribute increases they could as they traveled.

Chase had already gained one point to Strength and had a sensation that Mental Power wasn't far away for him. The new card that boosted training results for him definitely helped, but the fact that they all pulled together, completely dedicated to improving all of them, made for a huge difference. Cilia had gained a point to Toughness, as had Kith, and even Sera, with her outrageous starter attributes, had managed to gain a point to Agility from the constant training.

It also helped distract Chase from the final updates he'd gotten when he absorbed the Deck of Light from the sanctuary in Isarn, along with its myriad implications.

[You have bonded with a Deck of Light. From now on, through you, anybody may share in the gifts of Light. In addition, any Wellspring you create will be strengthened, carrying attributes and granting bonuses born of both Dark and Light.]

There had been another, longer, message afterward.

[You have continued working to restore the balance. Absorbing additional decks from other aspects and adding them to the wielders of the Deck of Darkness further tips the scale in the right direction. As a reward, the first ten card wielders of Darkness are granted an additional bonus to their Title based on their class. You have received +2 to Agility from the rogue class. The wielders of cards from the secondary Deck of Darkness have received a +1 boost.

From the secondary Deck absorbed, Light, you have received a boost to your health. Detrimental effects to your attributes and mentality last only half as long, and you are much less likely to fall ill.]

Apart from the bonus being amazing for their entire group, Chase really wanted to ignore the implications of what this meant. And yet, he really, really couldn't. There was no doubt by now that the Deck of Darkness wanted to grow. It wanted to add further decks to the world. There was a clear desire for Chase to do whatever it would take to absorb other decks and boost the wielders of the Deck of Darkness. In short, the deck rewarded conflict...and it would likely bring them into even worse conflict with the forces of Light and the inquisitors, should he start to listen to its clarion call. Nope. That was not for him. He would take whatever gifts it gave freely, use the deck for the benefits of him and his people, and avoid getting into whatever trouble it tried to pull him into.

In time, when they knew the general climate of the Elemental lands, they might be able to use the deck more actively. Pits, if they could get some new card wielders, add some more Dark cards to the world from the safety of the Elemental lands? He'd be all for that. It would allow them to grow, while they could stay out of reach of any inquisitors. But that was way off. For now, they would stay under the guise of a freshly knit-together group of Light card wielders and figure out what the deal was.

He just hoped that whatever Gunnha and the other card wielders who'd earned Dark cards back in Isarn were up to, they wouldn't be hit too hard by the aftermath of their escape. He'd love to watch their faces as they gained a boost to their attributes out of nowhere, though.

CHAPTER 4

"I am not a proper historian. I am biased, opinionated,
jump to conclusions, ignore facts that do not agree with me,
and am not properly critical of my own sources. The main thing
that differentiates me from my peers? I am upfront about it." I
thought this was going to be a dull tome of history. Instead, it's
promising to become my favorite guilty pleasure. I think Chase
has noticed me smiling. It's unbecoming. (Page 2.)

Over the past few days, the terrain had been subtly
rising. Now, as they passed through an opening in a
tall set of earthen ramparts that spanned into the distance, the
Elemental lands spread out before them, beyond the dust clouds
of the caarnath herd. The small group stood still for a while in
silent contemplation as the animals slowly trudged away from
them.

"It's...kind of underwhelming," Kith eventually ventured.
"I mean, not the defenses behind us. They looked properly dangerous and likely able to keep back a few Lightborn armies. Oh,
and the soldiers were impressive too, even if they did like
searching Liam just a bit too much. He enjoyed it, no doubt, but
there's a limit, right?"

Cilia released a shuddering breath, ignoring most of his
blathering. "It's the center of learning for the known world.
Where everybody goes for the best teachers, the highest quality
goods...and you call it *underwhelming?*"

He shrugged. "I'd expected...dunno. Less fields?"

The vista before them had an abundance of farmland. For
miles upon miles, the land was divided into tidy squares of fields,
orchards, and other crops. Workers were busy for as far as the
eye could see. Every square was edged by straight, tidy blue
lines of water, a few feet wide, and sometimes, as if without
rhyme and reason, further encompassed by weird constructions
or surrounded by walls.

Chase scratched his nose. "Sorry, Cil, but I need to agree
with the uncultured brute here. Those are fields. Not exactly
vaunted halls of learning and whatnot. We had fields at home."

The tiny crafter closed her eyes and took a deep breath.
"Help me here, Sera, before I start yelling."

Sera was looking at their surroundings with something
approaching awe. "I'd love to." She turned to Chase and Kith.
"You are excused for thinking that. And Chase is entirely right
in his comment."

Chase grinned, turning toward Cilia.

Sera interrupted whatever he was going to say. "You *are* uncultured brutes." She pointed at the farmland stretching out across the lowlands ahead for miles upon miles before the land started rising again, leading up toward the huge, distant mountain half-lost on the horizon. "Those can accurately be described as 'just fields' in the same way that our little group can be described as 'slightly annoying' to the forces of Light. First off, the entirety of this area has been artificially landscaped to allow the water to spread out to every single part that needs it. I could spend a lot of time going on about just how impressive that feat is, but it would be lost on you."

She pointed from one ringed-in walled area to the next. "Then, we have the defensiveness. Look at that. Just *look*. Every single area is defended according to its importance. That field of wheat? No wall. Earthfruits over there? Small walls. Then you have other areas, with tall walls as *well* as guards. Those will be Elemental-infused crops or even rarer growths." She flung up her hands. "That is without going into details about the security systems, traps, and Elemental spells they will have in place. There is a reason that the forces of Light have a tenuous peace with the Elementals. They might not have a tenth of the lands other races have, but they make the most of it." The twinkle in Sera's eyes belied her admonishing demeanor. "Besides, if you are just looking for physically imposing, you will just have to look again in half a day or so."

Late that day, the truth of Sera's words became clear, as the center of the Elemental lands came into view above them in the evening sun.

Chase winced at his own lack of eloquence, but it couldn't be denied. The Elemental towers *towered* above them, beyond the city of Earth's Ward. The herders explained that it would still be another day before they reached Earth's Ward. Craning back his neck to take in the height of the towers, that seemed downright impossible.

Earth's Ward by itself wasn't that impressive. It was a huge city, no discussion there. Had to be ten times bigger than Isarn, maybe even twenty. A hundred thousand people and more. The circular construction of the city was ringed on all sides by massive walls that were quite an accomplishment. It was, however, of little consequence compared to the towers themselves.

Where Earth's Ward surrounded the base of the mountain, the Elemental towers *were* the mountain. In tall, unnatural shapes, the myriad towers expanded from the mountain, ringing all sides of the towering peaks. Their size alone was impressive, yet the magic involved was even more breathtaking, given that the elements in question were so clearly a part of the construction. Some towers were neutral, while others clearly were attuned to one element or another. The earthen towers were bulky, dirt-colored and blockish, almost blending in with the mountainside. Air towers were tall, needle-like peaks with daunting bridges between them. Water was constructed *within* a series of massive waterfalls, making the myriad pools and arches of the liquid part of the construction. Finally, the fire towers stood tall and proud, the dark red shimmering with heat as if the walls themselves were covered with fire.

Kith's voice was hoarse. "I take it back. Can I take it back? Liberty release me, that's impressive! I'm glad I lived to see this."

Sera's voice was no less impressed. "Light blind me. I have read about it. Only, seeing it in person? It is so much more! Can you imagine how many Elemental crafters must have worked together to create this? There must be thousands of people living within each tower!"

"Tens of thousands," Cilia added. "But we had better pick up the slack. Otherwise, we won't be able to find the time for training tonight. Something tells me that we're going to regret it, if we don't cram in as much activity as we can out here."

Nobody disagreed with that.

The following day, early in the afternoon, the lead herder bid them farewell near a large number of animal pens. It was an unemotional affair. Neither party had gelled with the other, and theirs had only been an association of convenience. Now that they'd all arrived at Earth's Ward unmolested, nobody wanted to prolong things more than was absolutely necessary.

On their way across the Elemental lands, they'd passed several small guard groups patrolling beyond the battlements. Those guards were, it seemed like, mostly there for show. With the Elemental lands bordering both the lands of Light and the Liberty nation, roaming Guardians out for the blood of other nations were a fact of life. Yet, the small groups would in no way be able to handle larger groups of Guardians, let alone any invading armies. Mostly, it looked like they were there to scout or look impressive. Between the Colored Ramparts and Earth's Ward, there were fewer guards. Chase would bet that they were only there as scouts or to ensure that nobody got any stupid ideas about raiding the large fields. Though, who would take that chance with the might of battlements behind them and the huge towers in front, Chase couldn't fathom.

The noise on all sides was impressive. They were currently still outside Earth's Ward proper, but they could finally get a decent concept of how the city was constructed. They'd already gotten the idea that the city surrounded the entirety of the huge base of the mountain, making it large enough to sprawl for miles upon end. What hadn't become clear before now was the way the city had been constructed to protect against anybody considering an assault. The outer part of the city on the *outside* of the city wall, where they were right now, was entirely open and looked like one big, sprawling marketplace. People of all nations and races mixed with myriad species of animals; merchants hawked all sorts of wares, from weapons to political favors, and everybody seemed to be shouting at the top of their lungs. And the smells! Sour sweat, interesting spices, meats and sweets of all sorts mingled in the air, promising anything you could ever want. In short, apart from Sera, their merry band felt right at home.

Back in Isarn, Elementals were a rare vision. They did arrive from time to time, mostly singular travelers or groups of traders. It wasn't enough that Chase had gained a full understanding of the specifics of the race. Truth be told, he'd believed that Elementals as a whole were cut of the same cloth, with smaller variations. Walking among hundreds of examples of their kind, he now learned that nothing could be further from the truth.

The physical differences between the different aspects of the Elemental races were staggering. Where air-aspected Elementals were tall, bright-skinned, and willowy, almost like a blend between Lightborn and Darkborn, earth-aspected Elementals were squat and solid, with a dark, earthy coloration to their skin. Fire-aspected Elementals, meanwhile, stood out from far away, with glaring, red-orange hair, bright skin, and freckles...and, it appeared, a flair for the dramatic. Chase decided the water-aspected people had lost whatever racial competition they participated in, their single defining point being a sickly, unhealthy pallor to the skin that made them look like they were constantly sweating, as if from a bad fever.

Liam was ecstatic. He spent more time spinning around than actually walking, praising the myriad diverse examples of female beauty around them with his eyes and his voice. Right until Cilia threatened to whip him.

One notable detail about their surroundings was that everything out here seemed to be temporary. There were carts aplenty, with wooden stalls, tarps, tents, fences and animal pens everywhere—but nothing that couldn't be dismantled in an afternoon. Also, there seemed to be no planning to the roads or constructions. It was a chaotic mess...fertile soil for any pickpockets. As far as they could see, this continued all the way around the outside of the wall.

The wall. That was the one overwhelming structure in Earth's Ward. It lay like a razor-straight line separating chaos from order, the outside from the inside, right from wrong. Okay, that was likely just Chase's natural inclinations trying to over-simplify the situation. Still, it was impossible not to notice the wall, what it signified, and what it *might* mean on top of that.

It was created of some sort of earth-like material, but had a glazed look, as if it had somehow been treated. That wasn't what really made it stand out, though. No, it was the scope of it, and the shape. The first twenty feet, it went straight up into the air. Then, it curved inward for the next handful of feet, before arching up and out, actually stretching out to become near hor-izontal on top somewhere between thirty-five and forty feet in the air. It looked vaguely like the shape of a huge question mark. If a question mark had large groups of Elemental Guardians and soldiers patrolling on top, looking down upon the outer city. Be-hind and on the wall, what looked like siege towers rose up even higher, dotting the wall every few hundred feet. Gleaming metal from the soldiers and even siege weaponry promised death and dismemberment to anybody who might try anything. If you weren't invited into Earth's Ward proper, you weren't *getting* in.

Liam gestured around them. "How are we supposed to find our way here? This is almost as chaotic as the Lower Market on a feast day. Where do we even go from here? Barahn back there—the lead herder—knew where to buy and sell all sorts of stuff, but he didn't know much beyond that."

Cilia snorted. "Liam, you surprise me. You are so good with people, but sometimes, you fail to realize the simplest of things." She pointed at the people passing by on all sides. "Just look at everybody. Elementals. Furyborn. Lightborn. Darkborn. Pits, there are even a few Liberators. But what *aren't* we see-ing?"

Chase furrowed his brow. "Erm. I don't know?"

She rolled her eyes. "Buildings, Liam. There are no actual buildings here. Whatever this is, it isn't even the city. Now, let's find an entrance, see where we get into Earth's Ward proper."

It took a couple of minutes and a couple of questions be-fore they were guided in an easterly direction. They stopped to pay for a quick meal, before continuing on their path with a large wooden skewer with grilled meat and vegetables.

"Light fend. I hope the locals don't always enjoy this level of spices on their food." Liam blew on his skewer. "Where are we going again?"

Chase grinned. "To you, salt is spicy, mate. You could do with a bit of toughening. As to our goal... I'm not too sure. The last one just said we were right on time and we'd see it, what-ever that means."

Liam, who was the tallest of their group, stopped and gawked at the gathering in front of them. "I think we're about to figure it out."

They halted and stared at the scene in front of them. Farther back, they saw the wall, and the first obvious gate into the wall they'd seen so far. It wasn't like the gate back in Isarn, which was almost permanently open except for the rare occasion when an extraordinarily large monster group made it past the Border. This was the other kind of gate. The kind that said: "You're out there for a reason, and you're damn well not coming in unless we say so." The visuals included spikes, portcullises, threatening openings in the wall above the gate, and an overabundance of Elemental soldiers hanging around.

The incredible part was that the gate itself wasn't what held people's attention. No, they were all looking at the stage.

Right next to the gate itself, a large stage was set up. It lay beneath the shade of the overhanging wall, sheltering it from any squalls, and it was the closest thing to a permanent fixture in the outer city of Earth's Ward they'd seen so far. The stage was adorned with several flagpoles sporting the four-fold imagery of the Elemental coat of arms. The flags flapped proudly in the slight breeze, providing a natural backdrop to the display of opulent showmanship taking place on the stage itself.

The stage was huge. At least a hundred feet wide and thirty feet deep, it sported a long table, at which sat a half-dozen officiously dressed Elementals. A long line of persons stretched from within the crowd, reaching up onto the stage. Before the stage itself, a crowd of several thousand people was gathered, watching with rapt attention. The weird setup was made to look more normal in comparison to the speaker, however.

He was an Elemental. In fact, he was the most *Elemental* Elemental Chase had ever seen. Like somebody had taken the image of an Elemental, writ it large and then decided to double down. The tall man sported a shock of wild, flame-red hair and an even wilder beard. He wore an elaborate robe that blended red, black, and gold with arcane symbols in a way that would make the most garish of street entertainers raise an eyebrow in disdain. The fire-aspected Elemental clearly knew what effect his clothes had and didn't care in the least. He strode across the stage in front of the long line of people and the tall table, looking out upon the large crowd in front of him. His robe billowed out behind him with a flash that couldn't entirely be explained by just his clothes, and his voice rang out over the crowd.

It was loud. Louder than should be physically possible. His voice reached the farthest edges of the crowd. "Are these truly all? Have the Elemental towers lost their attraction to you, good people of Ordei? The wonders of Earth's Ward?" Theatrically, he held a hand up to his breastbone. With a stage whisper, he said, "Let me remind you. Not only do we guarantee the fairness of the lottery, but we lay it out for you, as clearly as possible, allowing you to see and feel for yourself. *This. Is. True.* Everywhere in the world, the odds are biased against those of poor upbringings, tilting the scales to favor those of one race or another. Here? We accept anybody, and give you even odds. Only the capricious nature of luck itself is allowed to define who will earn three months' access to Earth's Ward."

He waited, then added, voice slowly climbing in intensity until it boomed into a full-on shout, "*Three months.* Need I remind you what you have in there? Full access to our libraries. An option—nay, the *right* to apply to become a recruit in the Elemental towers." The Elemental raised a finger, purring. "That's correct! If you win the lottery, only your aptitude defines whether you can earn your way into the Elemental towers, where, need I remind you, any recruit will be granted an Elemental card straightaway, and fully-fledged Protectors will earn a full set of cards! All of this could be yours, just for the cost of one silver flame. *Is this not fair?*"

A roar from the crowd answered him.

Beaming, the Elemental waved at the long line. "You have half an hour still. Then the lottery begins."

Chase looked at the weird man. Then he looked at the line of people quickly moving toward the tables, and turned to the rest of the group. "Who's got the money? I'm joining the lottery."

Sera raised an eyebrow. She looked pointedly at the number of people ahead of him. "Really? You believe that your odds are good at winning?"

"*Please*," he answered scornfully. "No. Pits no. I just need to know how it works."

The line moved quickly and consistently. It seemed like whatever system they had in place had long since been tempered into perfection. Chase struck up a conversation with the richly clad Lightborn ahead of him. "First time?"

The woman shook her head, looking anxiously at the many people still ahead of them in the line. "I...think we should make it before the cutoff time. Sorry. No. Not my first time here. Seventh. There are less people here today, though. We should have good odds." She flashed a quick smile at him, then looked ahead.

Chase smiled. "I wish you all the best. It's my first time, though. How many people do they grant access?"

"Luck to you too, stranger." She chuckled. "As long as I get in, of course. They pick ten winners a day. It's a fixed number."

Chase frowned at the Furyborn who was pushing up against him in the line. He checked his purse, relieved to see that the man was just eager to get ahead. He turned back around. "Ten is a decent number. Have you seen any other Lightborn win?"

She beamed. "Three yesterday. That's how I know it's not rigged. It's completely random. There were even two Liberators who won three days back. One of these days, I'm going to win...and when I do, I get to walk Earth's Ward and make all the contacts I need to gain some *permanent* trade agreements. It'll earn itself back with dividends."

Chase nodded and smiled, keeping up the chat as the line edged its way closer and eventually up on the stage itself. All the while, the colorful Elemental on stage used his bountiful charisma to attract a constant traffic of newcomers to the line. The mood everywhere seemed relaxed and optimistic, and he spotted no conflicts in or around the line. These people clearly believed they had a chance of winning.

They made it to the long table, and the merchant in front of Chase gave a sigh of relief. "Just in time. You can hear the speaker's amping up the rhetoric for a final blast."

Along the table, on the other side, were six different persons, all Elementals, seated in comfortable-looking chairs, but with less colorful clothing than the fire-aspected Elemental attracting people to the lottery. An officious-looking low-set man with a paunch and the dirt-colored skin of an earth-aspected Elemental waved Chase forward. "First-timer or returnee?" he asked briskly.

"Em. First-timer."

A brisk nod was his only answer.

He paid the attendance fee of a single silver ryzark, also called a flame, which was the Elemental equivalent of three silver emehdi, plus a few coppers for the exchange fee.

The man packed away the money with practiced efficiency. "All right. Can you write?"

"Not a whole lot."

A hint of annoyance flashed on the man's face, like his day just got a bit more tiring. "But you can recognize your own name, yes?"

"I can." Chase had seen it enough times it wasn't an issue. He wanted to come back with a sarcastic answer but tamped down the desire.

"Good. Here, I will write your name and race on this scrap of parchment. You will then carry this parchment to one of our scribes right next to me." He pointed to the next official behind the table. "Where they will inscribe your name onto a token. You will be allowed to check the veracity of the writing and ask any bystander to verify the correctness of it for yourself. After that, you will toss it into the vault for yourself." He pointed at a large container set on a wheeled contraption past the far end of the table. "Any questions?"

"Eh… Yeah. When do we get the result?"

"Approximately twenty minutes from now. Depends on the *eloquence* of the announcer." From his tone, he'd about had it with the colorful speaker.

Chase couldn't rightly blame him. If he had to listen to the ebullient man day after day, he'd be mentally exhausted as well. He just nodded, though, and focused on carefully watching every part of the process.

The process was deceptively simple. The official got his name, glanced at a stone glowing green next to him and checked a short piece of parchment filled with writing. He wrote "Chase—no last name—Darkborn male" on a piece of parchment. He gave the thick, engraved piece of parchment to Chase, who carried it onward to one of the three waiting scribes. The tired-looking scribe took the parchment without looking up, grabbed a block of carved wood with the other hand, and squinted at it. Within seconds, a tiny column of smoke arose from the block of wood, and the content on the piece of parchment was *burned* into the hard wood. With a tired nod, the fire-aspected man presented the block to Chase for approval, and he was allowed to carry it to the vault.

The vault was a see-through square glass container, adorned with arcane symbols on all sides. It was affixed to a wheeled getup that had a handle with a steel rod going all the way through the container. Right now, a fist-sized opening on the container was open, and an elegant, tall air-aspected Elemental woman with a form-fitting sequin-adorned dress waved him forward with a smile to put his block of wood inside the container.

Moments later, he was down with the others, looking at the proceedings on stage. About a quarter hour later, the process continued to the next part. The announcer, with colorful, merry language, proceeded to tease out the announcements with painful slowness. Finally, however, he allowed the pretty presenter to turn the handle on the contraption to let the several hundred wooden blocks churn around inside the container, mixing it up properly before she fished out ten wooden blocks and read the names aloud in front of the crowd, to groans of disappointment and screams of excitement from the winners.

Chase watched the final part of the process like a hawk, not looking away for a second. When it was finally over, he turned to the others.

Sera raised an eyebrow. "Worth it? You didn't win!"

He chuckled. "Of course I didn't. It was never about winning. It was all about figuring out how it works so we can cheat our way in!"

CHAPTER 5

"Outside of Earth's Ward, the dichotomy of race is oft confused and two-tongued. Lightborn will insist that your race has no bearing on your personality and go straight to shunning Darkborn. Here? We face our differences and embrace them. Anything else is folly." No. Embracing stereotypes is folly. This is trash. (Page 16.)

Sera was the only one who was surprised by Chase's statement. The others had taken it as a matter of fact.

Cilia mused, "There were several hundred blocks in that crate. I would estimate four hundred. With ten winners a day, even adding all our names on a daily basis is not viable. It would take us...several months, at least, to win entrance for all of us in the regular way. The last person needing to win would have horrible odds."

Sera nodded. "Also, the cost would become more than we could bear. More than a gold lyka a day for all of us. We would be out of money in a week."

"Less," Cilia said.

Kith pointed toward the stage. "We couldn't get a good look from here. How closely does that lass look at you when you put in that block?"

Chase shrugged. "She was pretty attentive. I could maybe toss in an extra or two, if we were able to create some convincing fakes. Still, they may have counters in place. I wouldn't give good odds of my managing to do it several times over, and it doesn't change our chances that much."

Kith shrugged. "But can't we just add more? Wait, scratch that."

Chase chuckled. "Yeah. If they were to pull more than one instance of the same name, we probably wouldn't like the consequences. I doubt they're lenient on cheaters."

Liam furrowed his brows. "This is getting complicated. What do we do?"

Nobody spoke up straightaway. Finally, Chase cleared his throat. "I think we need to learn more. Find a place to stay, then ask questions and find out more about the process?"

"Drink and make friends? I can do that!" Liam's face lit up.

Cilia rolled her eyes. "Don't overdo it. We're on a budget. That inquisitor and the high priest had deep pockets, but our funds are not endless. Still, yes. That sounds like the wisest approach. We find a place, then split up to learn more. Tomorrow, we sit down and make a proper plan that doesn't hinge on knee-jerk reactions and intuitive leaps."

"Thank you for being the voice of reason, Cilia. Besides, I am sure we will be able to find a way to enter that does not revolve around petty crime." Sera smiled.

"Nothing petty about work," Kith grumbled. "It ain't much, but it's dishonest."

They did as advocated, finding a place that rented horribly overpriced tents. Then, they split up in pairs and, with the evening fast approaching, went out to learn more about Earth's Ward.

The day after, they met up at noon for food and a talk. They'd found a place that served pekat—a local dish of mixed rice, vegetables, and caarnath meat in a sweet and savory yellow sauce. The group bought a bowl each, then sat around one of the dozen campfires maintained for that exact purpose.

Sera eyed her dish with distaste. She put it before her and folded her hands. "I would like to be the first to share my findings." Seeing nobody disagreeing, she continued. "I have to admit that I dislike the idea that we would have to cheat to enter. Hence, I have spent less time trying to find out ways to cheat the system, but rather figuring out whether we *should* cheat. There should be a way to legally and rightfully gain access to Earth's Ward." With a frustrated huff, she glared at her feet. "Only, I have yet to find it. Elementals are *very* persnickety about access rights, and they do not allow anybody to enter unless they are born here or have won access. It seems they are particular about Earth's Ward being for Elementals. That being said, I believe that, were we to spend some time, we would find a legal way to earn the coin needed to handle this properly."

Kith sneered. "Come on, princess. You want us to hang out on the outside until we somehow earn enough to make it? You don't even believe that yourself. Even if we don't look at how long that would take, you know where that would leave us. Out here. Among the inquisitors. You can do better than that."

She didn't respond, but the blush half-hidden behind her curls answered for her.

Liam, having shoveled the contents of his bowl into his mouth in record time, wiped his mouth with the back of his hand. "That hit the spot. Mind if I take yours?"

Sera willingly surrendered the bowl.

Cilia spoke up next. "First off, I invested in a tome. A history tome that should help me learn more about Earth's Ward and the Elemental towers." She patted a hefty book in her lap. "Next, I decided to look into some of the things that had me wondering. For instance, how come they let anybody join the lottery. I figured that it was weird how they would let just anybody earn access to their vaunted kingdom, regardless of race and origin." She paused for emphasis.

Before she could continue, Kith spoke up over his food. "They don't."

The mixed-race crafter raised her eyebrows. "Well, I want to know how you figured that out. *I* learned that through a good deal of conversations with outsider merchants here outside the city. They keep a keen eye on who is allowed in. In short, if you're a merchant or the like, anybody with real power, you're not likely to win. Sure, they make a good show of letting anybody participate and so on, but it's a badly kept secret that they don't. Not really. I'm not sure how they do it, though."

Still chewing, Kith said, "I am."

"Well, if you're so damn clever, how about you let the rest of us in on the secret?" she snapped.

"Would love to." Kith put his bowl aside for a moment and stood up. He indicated their group with open arms. "While all of you have likely been busy, working hard to penetrate the secrets in Earth's Ward, I took a different approach. Something simpler, yet insidiously effective."

"Cilia! Kith is being punchable again. Can we punch him?" Sera complained.

"Seriously," Chase urged. "Please! Get to the point, or Liam's going to be your fixed sparring partner for the next *year!*"

Kith grinned and pointed to his eyes. "My secret? I used my peepers." Reveling in the chorus of groans, he rolled his shoulders. "Yesterday, when the lottery was on. You should all have seen it for yourself, really. There were guards watching, from the crowd. Not uniformed ones, just cloaked bystanders. Guards nonetheless. Ones with cards."

"Oh," Chase said, crestfallen. "I *did* miss that."

"They were pros. But definitely guards. There to keep an eye on things, make sure everything was nice and peaceful. They didn't intervene, though."

Cilia cursed. Then she furrowed her brow. "That still doesn't explain their methods, just that they have guards in place in case somebody acts up."

"There was a list." Chase remembered. "When I said my name. They checked my name against the list."

"Oh." She blinked. "That civil? So, anybody important enough to merit being blacklisted will be sent away once they tell the scribes their names and they realize they're on the no-entry list."

"What's stopping them from lying about their names, though?" Kith mused. "That's what I'd do. Just give a fake name...then, when I'd earned my cards, I'd laugh my ass off."

"It's the stones," Chase said. "The ones next to the scribes. They've clearly been infused with some magic. They glow bright green when people give off their names. What are you willing to bet, it'll change color if people lie about that?"

Kith scowled. "There goes that idea. Yeah. That'd work. Wait. We can craft that, Cil? Something to detect lies?"

"With five years of practice, perhaps," Cilia responded. "And unlimited gold to buy materials."

Sera frowned. "I cannot help but wonder. In Isarn, my peers talked about gaining Elemental cards like it was simply a matter of paying a fixed cost, and you would receive them. That seems incongruous with what you are saying here. Lightborn nobility would fit the exact criteria for who the Elementals should not want to allow entry."

"That does seem weird," Chase allowed.

For a while, they subsided into companionable silence.

With a satisfied sigh, Liam finished Sera's bowl and stretched. He burped, then nodded companionably at Sera. "It's because of the corruption, of course."

"Corruption?"

"Yeah. Whoever's corrupt, selling entry to the city on the sly." Liam nodded. "The rates are probably extortionate, but the nobles wouldn't care about that, would they?"

Kith pointed at him. "It does sound like something that could crop up. You guessing, or is this real?"

The big Lightborn shrugged and leaned down to poke the bonfire between them with a piece of lumber. "Bit of both? I mean, I've heard people talk about it like it's fact, but they don't share anything beyond that, even if they're really drunk. Way I see it, that means they don't know who's in charge or what's really going on. Also, likely, whoever's in charge of it doesn't like people talking."

Sera looked dejected. "There is no winning this, is there? If we do things by the number, we will not have the money to earn access, and it will take us forever. If we do not, we are bound to get in trouble with either the authorities, or whoever is ostensibly running that scheme."

Chase grinned. "Spoken like a true believer in authority." He leaned forward, lowering his voice. "Thing is, Sera, this is just like back on the Waves. You could hardly spit for schemes, jobs, and possibly messing with somebody else's plans. The trick, as always, is to not get caught. Apart from that, if there is a single thing we should take from Liam's point? It's this: There is a system for cheating our way in. We just need to figure it out, and then we can use it for ourselves. Once we're in, we're in."

Two days later, they were no closer to figuring out how everything worked. They'd reconvened near the lottery and were currently spectating, trying to find anything incriminating.

"Three ales. One chilled lemonade. And one horrible fermented caarnath milk monstrosity." Chase shared the drinks and sat down near the others, at the far end of the square where they could oversee everything. The enthusiastic fire-aspected Elemental was back on the stage, encouraging everybody to join the lottery.

"Hey. I like the milk," Kith said. "It's memorable. Same as when Liam smooched with that Elemental. Memorable."

"I told you already," Liam grumbled. "*She* set that drink on fire. Not me."

Cilia interrupted them. "If you morons are done rambling, could you focus?" She nodded at the venue ahead of them. There were more people than average today and the mood was that of a feast day back in Isarn. In fact, every evening, when the results of the lottery were out, resulted in a large celebration, with any winners being the center of attention. "I agree with Kith, by the way. Once you know they are there, spotting the guards working for Earth's Ward isn't that hard." She nodded ahead of her, to a water-aspected Elemental who stood with her back against the wall, hard eyes fixed on the crowd.

"True. They are not being that covert about it. But then again, I suppose that suits their purposes. If it is an openly kept secret that certain people might as well not bother joining the lottery and there are guards ready to handle any troublemakers..." Sera shrugged. "I still fail to see any evidence that Liam's theory is correct and somebody is cheating."

The tall Lightborn downed half his mug and let out a satisfied sigh. "That really only proves I'm right. Their scheme wouldn't last long if it was easy to spot."

Sera cocked her head. "That is a very confusing theory, but okay. Run me through it. If you were to try to cheat the system—what would you do?"

Chase scratched his chin thoughtfully. "Well. Let's look at it from one end to the other. First, we have the scribes, who check that any contestants aren't on the forbidden lists, and jot down the details. They look like a professional bunch, but all told, it'd be hard to fake anything regarding their task, because the contestants all confirm what they write down. That doesn't entirely discount the idea that there could be illusions or mental cards at use with them, but...the odds are bad, especially given that the next ones, the fire-aspected mages who sear the names into the blocks, take over from them."

"Are we just going to ignore the hidden agents themselves? With them hiding in the crowds, aren't they in the perfect position to influence something?" Cilia asked.

"Eh. Not really? Sure, they could possibly influence the people joining the lottery...but I can't see how they'd influence the process itself, with them being down in the crowd." Chase shrugged and cleared his throat. "Moving on. Those mages. They sear the name of the contestant into the blocks, have the contestants confirm that it's looking correct, and then hand the wooden blocks back to the contestants. If they're part of whatever gig they've got running here, they'll have to do it in a way that either has the contestants themselves in on it, or cheats the contestants' senses too."

"It feels like you skipped a few steps for me here. What am I missing?" Sera asked.

"Well, look at the stage. Once people have paid and joined the lottery, they're allowed to jump back down to wait and see who wins. That means, theoretically, if they could convince the mages to put in the wrong names, regardless of what the scribes wrote down, that's where the wrong winners could come and earn their access. They might not even realize that they'd been cheated at all. Only...I'm sure there's some sort of control afterward, where they check the blocks against the parchment scraps, something like that. That way, they will be able to keep check on their employees."

"This is giving me a headache," Sera complained.

"Hang on. We're nearly there, princess. Because that's basically it. Once they've tossed the blocks into that vault of theirs, the Elemental can basically do whatever they feel like. They could have marked blocks for that woman to pick, all sorts of fancy tricks to make sure they choose the exact winners they want to...except, from the rumors out there, that's not happening either. The winners truly look to *be* random, as long as people aren't blacklisted by the Elemental lands. And the moment you're picked to win? You win. With all the onlookers here, once they read a name aloud, the winners go straight into the city. There's no taking it back."

"What is the conclusion, then? Where is the weak link?" Sera asked.

Chase grimaced. He took a deep pull at his ale, glaring at the stage. "There isn't any. Not from what I can see. The system isn't flawless, but I can't see a way to easily cheat it. Not as it stands, and definitely not without a lot of effort and powers. They would have to...hrm."

"You have an idea?" Cilia asked.

"Yeah. Or at least a way we can prove who might be doing it. Sera. Would you mind trying your luck with the lottery for me?"

Half an hour later, the Elemental presenter was whipping the crowd into a frenzy as the announcements of the winners drew closer.

Serafine Valerian pushed her way back to their group, curls bouncing merrily around her flushed face. She hurried over to them and spoke up right away. "I might have something. How did you know?"

"Know what?" Liam had wandered off and returned with a small bowl filled with kitberries drenched in honey.

"Two things," Chase said. "First was that you're not on any of their lists—"

"*What?*" Sera snapped. "That was a test?"

He raised his hands apologetically. "Not a test...I just couldn't see my way around it. Sorry. Not like you could lie about your name, was it? Besides, I was almost sure. You're not important enough, and they're clearly working *against* the Lightborn, not with them. We needed you to act as natural as possible, and thinking about that wouldn't have been good for your nerves."

Sera flushed even darker, this time with anger. "I... You... You had better tell me something like that another time." She turned to Liam, putting her back to Chase. "What we wanted to know was if anybody up there was doing something surreptitious. Anybody who might seem suspicious. Do you remember my Heart card?"

Liam nodded with his mouth full. "Information," he managed through his chewing.

"Exactly. I get to see information about people I touch, depending on their Mental Power pinned against mine. Steps. Active effects and cards, if I am lucky. Sometimes even attributes. But I can *always* read their class. What this rude lowlife here figured was that there might be something to be learned there. Some hidden detail that might give away anybody trying to cheat the system."

"And I was right!" Chase celebrated. "Who was it?"

"One of the scribes. I will be honest. I did not get much from him. His Mental Power must be impressive, to block out that much of my card. But I got three things. His Step, which was sixteen—a Tier three in a menial position like this is impressive—his active cards and effects, which registered as none right this moment, and his class, which came out as Elemental/Light caster. *Somebody* is moonlighting for the other side."

***

The mood in the large, well-lit chamber was somber, as befit the situation. Marble tiles extended, covered in exquisite carvings. The clear skies allowed the sunlight to enter through the stained-glass windows, creating a swimming, blurred reflection of the depicted scene on the white-tile floor.

The spokesman spared the illuminated scene little notice. He had reflected upon the image so many times it was a part of him. Of them all. The just retaliation and bringing low of the archbishop of Darkness, for all his crimes.

It looked like he was alone in the chamber. Yet, somebody like him was never alone. Slight movement at key places betrayed hidden guards in recessed alcoves. He ignored the grandness of the scene, the quiet magnificence, and touched the Light Wellspring at the core of the capital city of Stradeburg.

"Do you have anything to add to your report?" He kept his voice level and professional, for all his inner turmoil.

"No, Esteemed Father. Judging from everything, the thieves are long gone, and the deck with them." The disembodied voice coming from the other Wellspring was anything but professional. Obsequious, unsteady, and with a hefty dose of fear.

As well it should be.

"Thank you, High Priest de Merion. I would hear from the rest of you. What would you suggest?" He knew what had to happen, of course. Even so, he preferred to sound the others out, to learn about them. How they thought...*whether* they thought.

"We need to bring in a regiment, scourge Isarn, and put any criminals to the question. That will roust the thieves, bring them scurrying out like the cockroaches they are." The disembodied, haughty voice came from Priest Hortus. Full of divine justice, fire, and enough repressed violence that he should have been a Furyborn. A tool, and a useful one, as long as one did not burn their hands on the handle.

"Isarn is a frontier city. Half the city's population, including the nobility, will have criminal elements. You would burn the entire city and have the remaining populace up in rebellion in a week. Besides which, the thieves will be long gone by now, so there will be no payoff." The sly, sardonic voice came from High Priest Desahl. One to watch. If he did not misstep, he would rise through the ranks. "What I want to know is where the Deck of Darkness came from in the first place. How did we not notice it?

Was Isarn infiltrated or was this a lightning strike to steal a deck and grow stronger?"

"We don't know," De Merion complained. "As I've already explained, the first report of anything strange came from our army being defeated by demonic enemies. Then, a stray report of a noble daughter being subsumed by Dark but wanting to repent. We sent forces to quell them and thought we'd stomped out anything, but the attack, the theft, came out of the blue."

You could practically hear him sweating. As well he should. One wrong, uninformed decision after the other, allowing the forces of Darkness to publicly show their strength again and again. Then the theft, and the murder.

The archbishop decided to add a touch of pressure, show who was in charge. "High Priest Desahl. Insults and recrimination are not useful. We need to plot a course. What would you suggest?"

The response was swift. "I would mostly ignore Isarn, Esteemed Father. Punishing High Priest de Merion would do little good. We will need him in the years to come to rebuild Isarn, root out any rogue elements and make sure that Isarn becomes a boon to the lands of Light, not a drain. Besides, scouring the populace would put us at odds with the nobility. The nobles may be idiots, but we need them to believe that they are the ones running the empire."

The archbishop nodded to himself. At least there, they were in agreement.

"We should send a token force to Isarn to help him right the ship. Then, we should focus our energy on finding out where the attackers came from and where they went. That is my suggestion."

"Any other suggestions?" the archbishop asked.

The responses were as could be expected. Variations of what had already been said; priests and high priests quick to leap in and support, curry favor, join whichever way the winds were blowing. A choice few decided to get in some quick jibes and barbs.

The archbishop noted those for what they were. Mosquitos, trying to attach themselves to the largest vessel. The few to be watched were either vague in their support or abstained from commenting entirely. He did notice with frustration how at least a third of them were quick to support or add to Desahl's ideas.

Finally, he spoke up. "Thank you all. First, allow me to say how heartening it is to hear everybody come together. When the topic is as important as it is today, we cannot waste our time on infighting and petty disagreements." A slap on the wrist to the few impertinent socialites among them should bring them to heel. "Next. Desahl is mostly right in his assessment."

"Thank you, Esteemed Father."

For the first time, the archbishop smiled. He could *hear* the uncertainty in Desahl's voice at his use of the word *mostly*. "The Deck of Darkness, after all these years, has risen to the surface. Our old enemy is back. Whether it is a concerted attack or a lightning strike to gain a deck before they try to hide again, we cannot know. What we *do* know is that we cannot in good conscience ignore it. High Priest Desahl suggests we send a larger force to attempt to find answers about where they came from. I will allow that, though I believe it unlikely to bring true answers." He would let High Priest Desahl waste his political capital there and look foolish when the forces returned without results. "The important part here is that we need to find where they went. Send out messages to all inquisitors, inform them about what has happened. Seekers and hunters should be out there on Ordei, looking for the culprits. Every tiny hamlet, every large city...we need them searching. Our weapons should be ready to move to the attack at any sign."

"And Isarn?" De Merion's voice trembled.

The archbishop frowned. He really was a pitiful man. No wonder he had been assigned to a frontier city. "Ah, yes. We will send a token force of priests to aid in quelling rumors and bring the populace back into place, a low-Tier inquisitor to investigate if any Dark wielders should, against all odds, have stayed in the city. Also, your replacement will be along shortly."

"My...replacement?"

The archbishop allowed himself a tiny smile. "Yes. These are trying times. Our old enemy is back. And although High Priest Desahl might be willing to ignore somebody colluding with the enemy, I will not." He steeled his voice, quashing the broken protesting outburst from de Merion. "You gave information to the enemy. We are at *war*. What you have done is nothing less than treason. Soldiers will take you to your cell immediately and your cards will be rescinded, High Priest de Merion. You will be thoroughly questioned. If we find your transgressions are redeemable, you may eventually redeem yourself as an indebted. For now, step down, and await punishment. Does anybody have any comments?"

The sound of silence was overwhelming. Nobody dared to say anything. Not even Desahl. He was clever enough to know he'd misstepped. The mere word *treason* was one that couldn't be cleaned off, should it first be associated with your name.

With a brilliant smile, the archbishop gave them all the blessing of the Light and stepped away from the Wellspring. In truth, the development was fortuitous. They would finally be able to capture the Deck of Darkness and absorb its powers. Once that was done, their Wellspring would grow in power to where the church would be unassailable. Then they could dissolve the pesky nobility, and he would reign absolute.

CHAPTER 6

"Denizens of the towers tout the Elemental lands as something out of the ordinary. A paradise, bereft of crime. That is obviously ludicrous. Wherever people exist, crime follows. However, with us living in the closed system that we do, any element is tightly knit with the rest of society. What criminals exist on our lands know damn well not to rock the boat." This could be problematic...and it could be a boon. So, crime is acceptable as long as we don't overdo it and step on the wrong toes? This means that we need to know what's going on before we start any real work. (Page 8.)

Boredom. Chase was back to boredom again. Usually, living a life of crime was touted as being a thrilling and scary experience. The people who told those tales weren't wrong...but they clearly had no idea how much time and effort went into everything leading up to that thrill.

It would likely be less boring if he knew what he was looking for. This was a whim. It could very well be a dead end. The only thing they knew for certain was that, at some point, one of the scribes had somehow entered a church in the lands of Light and been allowed to earn a set of Light cards on top of his existing Elemental caster cards.

This wasn't an absolute affirmation of his guilt. The Elementals, on the whole, were a closed society, and with their aversity to outside influences...there could very well be something there. Only, their target was being annoyingly nondescript and...scribe-like. He just sat there on the stage, looked like he hated the world and everybody in it, spoke in short, terse sentences, and performed his duties. They had spent more than two hours today waiting to see if anything happened, and there were at least two more hours until the lottery. It wasn't looking like anything was going to happen today. Perhaps they were dead wrong? The rumor that the lottery was rigged might be just that—a rumor. Chase was familiar with how the mood of the people could be turned against authority, to the point where it would skew any clear thinking.

Kith lay on his back on the ground next to him, eyes closed. "Why is this bastard so damn boring?" he complained. "He's like a summon, just sitting there, emotionless, doing his job. Nobody's that boring, are they?"

Chase chuckled. "Don't know about that. Remember Mavina?"

The Furyborn laughed out loud. "Gods. How could I forget? Her favorite activity was watching people paint walls. Said there was something wholesome and fulfilling about seeing the old and dirty being covered over little by little. Personally, I think it was the fumes—" He sat up with a jolt. His eyes were still closed, but he was hyper focused, frozen in his posture. "Got you, bastard!"

Chase did not bound to his feet. He didn't yell in surprise, point or make any overt movements. He did don a burgeoning, hopeful smile. "Did you catch them?"

Kith's sclera were awash with dark, satisfied colors. "Oh yes. They finally messed up."

In the evening, they'd managed to bring everybody together again around the bonfires near their tents. During the day, while Chase and Kith were stuck keeping an eye on the lottery, the rest of the crew had dispersed throughout the outer city: Liam to fish for useful rumors, Sera keeping Cilia company as they trawled the markets, looking for useful materials for crafting.

Cilia was presenting her findings. "Earth's Ward is something entirely different from Isarn. Unfortunate, for us. There are so many carded crafters here—Light ones too. At this stage, there is no way that I would be able to craft something at their level. They have searing daggers, leather bracelets with shield effects, potions with boosting effects of every kind. Anything you would want to buy, you can."

Sera nodded. "They are not just Light and Elemental crafters, either. I saw a Liberator, claiming that he was selling a bracelet that could protect you from any mental effects Tier four or below. That sounds insane."

Cilia smiled fondly at the other girl. "Exactly. I realized that I wouldn't be able to match their quality, not without a lot of time and effort. Hence, I decided to go with the Waves approach."

"The Waves approach? What's that? Steal what you can and never pay?" Chase asked.

Kith snorted. "Or 'It's not food poisoning if you can still crawl.'"

Liam laughed out loud. "I'm not dirty if the Waves smell worse 'n I do."

"Oooh, wait." Chase slapped his forehead. "Make it crappy, but cheap?"

Cilia snickered, pointing at Chase. "Just so." She straightened and held her hands out toward the dwindling heat from the bonfire. With a shudder, she gestured out at the growing darkness around them. "The majority of the people here have arrived for one of two reasons. Either they're here for the lottery, trying to enter the city proper...or for business. And those who are here for business intend to make a profit." She looked at the others expectantly before frowning. "Sometimes, you're too slow. It means, they'll have to recuperate travel costs, pay for their employees, hiring caarnaths, all sorts of stuff. Us? We don't need that much. We just want to make enough that we can stick around to find out what we need."

Liam scratched his chin thoughtfully. "So, you plan to be making quick and easy stuff for cheap?"

"Exactly. With simple Light effects. Wristbands, likely. Time-limited light to shine your way around at night in your tent or on the street. Blinding light in case of an assault. Stuff like that, with a limited duration. Enough that it will make me stand out from the unaspected crafters, but make it cheap, and crappy enough that I'm not real competition to the *real* leatherworkers."

"I like it." Chase nodded approvingly. "And since you're a perfectionist, your quality is going to be way higher than what you think yourself. There'll be plenty of return customers. But we do have good news on our side."

"Have you found something?" Sera asked.

"We found *someone*." Kith grinned. "It was one of the scribes. The exact one you pointed out, princess. I spent excruciating *hours,* draining my powers for the effort of helping our team. I toiled—"

Liam reached out and slapped him on the back of the head. "Less grandstanding. More telling."

"Ow." Kith rubbed his head. "Okay, okay. We agreed that me using my shadow card would probably be safe, since I would be able to hide it inside the shadow of the overarching wall above. I mean, what would the odds be of an inquisitor coming by and catching me in the act?"

"Don't jinx it," Cilia admonished. "What did you see?"

"A flash. He wore heavy robes to hide it, but it was clear as day, when you knew what to look for. He used a card just a moment after talking to a Lightborn. It was the *only* time he used a card that day, too. And nobody here should be surprised that the Lightborn on the other side of the table was one of the ten to win the lottery." Kith grinned triumphantly.

Liam smiled. "So, I was right. And you have more to tell, or you wouldn't be so impressed with yourself!"

"I am insulted, good sir!" Kith held a hand to his breastbone in mock offense. "Insulted that you know me so well." He laughed. "Obviously, I knew I was operating on limited time, so I took in anything about that Lightborn and any others in line at that time. There was no doubt. The Lightborn was the guy." He grimaced. "The only issue was that I couldn't see what his trick was. Nothing changed that I could spot. No real powers at work. No illusions, shields, no…" He waved his hand around, like fluttering birds. "Wooden blocks magically flying into the vault." Kith leaned forward; eyes gleaming vividly in the flames from the bonfire. "But I think I know how to spot them now. That Lightborn? He wore boring robes, dull and nondescript, to the point where you'd forget about him in a second—with one exception. A brooch with a simple sunburst, right over his heart."

Liam leaned back, brushing his big hands together. "You believe that is how they recognize their customers? That would make sense, if the scribe doesn't know who he's supposed to allow entry beforehand. So…what's the plan? Do we all go up there, wearing brooches?"

Chase shook his head. "Too obvious. We don't want to alert whoever's running the scam that we're on to them. No. First, we figure out exactly how the scam works, *then* we plot the rest out." He pointed at Sera. "Of course, with you on board, we're in the perfect position to figuring that out. We just need to wait for the next sunburst to get up there."

In the end, it took another two days of dull, uneventful surveillance before anything further happened. Cilia started in on her crafting and was soon proved right in her guess. The locals were definitely in the market for low-priced, low-quality goods with simple, but useful Light effects imbued. Nobody seemed to care that the quality of her leatherworking was nowhere near the level of the other craftsmen around. Well, except for the other crafters, who treated her with obvious disdain, both for being a mixed-race wielding Light cards, and for shoddy craftsmanship. The money didn't care about any of that, of course.

Now, however, they were back near the bonfire, and Sera beamed with joy. Earlier that day, they had spotted another Lightborn—this one a woman—and Sera followed right behind her in the line for the lottery. Once she was back, she aimed straight for the markets of the outer city, promising answers in the evening.

"Don't leave us hanging, princess. We've been patient," Kith said.

Sera raised an eyebrow. "By all rights, I should be drawing this out and tease you…but I do not have it in me. Yes. You were entirely right. And I know what card the scribe is using.

This time, I saw the flash too. A moment after the Lightborn had moved past, he activated his card."

Kith beamed at her. "With you right in the position to use your Heart card and see which active cards he had. Clever."

"Just so. I had to speak to a number of Lightborn casters in the markets before I could confirm what it was. Layers of Light. It is not a commonly known card, but neither is it extremely rare. It allows a wielder to create convincing illusions. They will not hold up to physical touch or anything. Yet, visually, unless your Mental Power is through the roof, you will be unable to pierce them. The reason why it is not commonly used is that the illusions are relatively small. So, you would not be able to hide a person, but you might hide a dagger or disguise it as something else."

Liam frowned. "Wait a minute. I don't get it. The scribe gets the name of the person. The *real* name or a fake one? Then he writes it down and uses the illusion to hide it. How does that help, when the next caster writes it down? This is too confusing! Can't you find somebody for me to hit?"

Kith snorted. "The Lightborn couldn't really use a fake name—that gem would show off a different color. There are two parts to the trick. First is that he writes down a different name than what the Lightborn actually says. That doesn't trigger the gem. Then she carries the parchment to the inscriber, who *also* writes down a fake name, hands the block back to the Lightborn..."

Liam slapped his forehead. "And *then* he uses his illusion. *After* the caster has inscribed the block. That way, the illusion will hold until the Lightborn has won the lottery...and once it fades away afterward, there will be no evidence that anybody's cheated. Is that it?"

"Exactly. Well, almost," Kith said. "Can you guess what's missing?"

"No, he can't, mate. You've got issues," Chase said. "The missing link is that, with that illusion, the winner still has to *win!*"

"That presenter is in on it? I knew it! He seemed too over the top to be trustworthy!" Liam said.

Chase snorted. "Sorry, man. Not him. It's the girl."

"What? But she looked so...trustworthy." Liam twisted in his seat.

Chase, Cilia, and Kith all laughed.

Chase leaned forward with a smirk. "I think the word you're looking for is 'hot.' Also, once again, this explains so much about the women you've been entangled with." He snickered to himself before continuing. "But yeah. He creates an illusion that holds the *real* name of the person who's supposed to win. Also, he adds a small detail at the end. A shiny, gleaming mote of light. Hard to notice from the distance, unless you know what you're looking for. But for the person picking out the wooden blocks? It's easy."

They sat in companionable silence for a while. Cilia was the one to bring up what they were thinking. "Good. Now we know what the trick is. How do we abuse it?"

CHAPTER 7

"The powers of the world are disparate, with vastly differing qualities. The Lightborn shine, pun intended, with their vast numbers and recruitment pools. The Furyborn impress with their bloodlust and sheer defiance of death. The armies of Liberty must be vast, to keep as tight a stranglehold over their lands as they do. Yet, matched against each other, nobody can provide as powerful a force as an Elemental soldier. Because we provide them with the knowledge and learning to grow before we risk their lives on the battlefield." They keep talking about all this learning. I just want us all to be able to access it.
(Page 12.)

"I can't believe that worked." Liam stared with wide eyes at the city gates that were slowly opening before them.

"It's taking a huge chance, really. Five in one day, and two of us Lightborn? That's likely not normal." Chase slapped him on the back. "We're counting on them being caught off guard, too slow to catch us. Still, the first part did go off flawlessly. As long as we can get off the streets and hide in a moment, we'll be fine. Won't be the first time we've had to go to ground and hide. Besides, we agreed. It was this, or work up to something elaborate, and there'd always be the risk of getting spotted in the process."

Sera kept looking behind them nervously. "I still cannot believe that she did not call for security. She looked like she was about to wet herself, when *five* persons had tokens marked for being chosen."

Chase grinned widely and spun himself around, as Earth's Ward opened in front of him. "I gave the pretty lass a nice, big smile too, and a wink, just to let her know that we knew. They might go tattling to their superiors. Still, there's a risk to anything. If we tried to extort them beforehand, they would have the chance to rat us out and prepare a reaction. From the looks of things, she did *not* take well to surprises."

They walked close together, all bedecked in their cloaks with the hoods up, to make it harder for any onlookers to recognize them. The five other fortunates who had won access to the city in the lottery walked apart from their crew, and looked both intimidated and cowed by their surroundings.

The huge earth-aspected Elemental city guard who walked in front of them halted in front of their group. He looked at them with cold, hard eyes. "You have won the lottery. Congratulations. That earns you the right to enter our grand city and stay there for up to three months. You may stand tall, as you join our proud capitol. But not too tall. Please respect our citizens, as well as our laws. We are fair, but firm, when it comes to dealing with any sort of disruptions, and anything but misdemeanors *will* result in your trial being cut short."

Chase was impressed. The man must have said that line over and over again, yet he managed to still look intimidating and not in the least bit bored.

The guard indicated the city behind him. "For now, our city is yours. Treat it well, and it will be kind to you in return. Try anything funny, and I will be there to take care of you."

He suspected the man had been chosen simply for the way he managed to look disapproving, even with his face set in neutral folds. From within a pocket, he extracted a handful of simple necklaces, glowing with a subtle green glow. "These are your access passes. You will be required to wear them at all times." He waited until they'd dispersed the necklaces and put them on. "Once your time in the city is up, the color of the necklace will change to yellow. After that, you have forty-eight hours to leave the city. After that, it changes to red. You do *not* want to get caught in here with a red necklace—or without one."

The earth-aspected Elemental's gaze didn't soften one bit. He looked emotionless enough that, just for a second, Chase entertained the idea that he might be a summon instead of a real person.

"I am aware that there are many questions from any newcomers. We understand that. We recommend that you all stay at the Elemental Services Inn. It is run by our academy and is familiar with the questions most asked by new visitors to our fair city. Apart from that, we realize that the joy in getting to know Earth's Ward is just that—the discovery. So, we recommend you do that. As for anybody so enthralled with our fair city that they want to stay, we recommend that you visit the towers. This is where you apply to become a real citizen." Having fired off that long speech, it seemed the Elemental's tolerance for social interaction was cut short. He turned on his heels and stalked away.

One of the winners made to follow him, until he realized that that was it. They were cut loose.

For a moment, they were completely at a loss of what to do, glancing at one another. With a smirk, Chase took the lead. "That was damn underwhelming. Nice of him to at least tell us where *not* to spend the night."

Sera frowned. "But he said—"

"I know what he said. Saying something is run by an official organ is basically the same as saying it's run at thrice the price, with half the service."

Sera blinked, looking like she didn't know whether to be offended or not. "But...we want what he was explaining, do we not? Learning how the city works seems like the only logical choice before we decide our approach."

The group laughed. Even Cilia hid a smile behind her hand.

Liam took pity on her. "You're completely right. Only...who do you believe is going to give us real answers about the city? An inn that's *run* by those in charge?"

"Well, they would know what they were talking about, obviously. Oh..." She trailed off. "But they would also be biased."

"Spot on." Chase smiled. "You don't want to tick off the people who pay your wages by telling everybody what the world is *really* like, do you? Let's all go for a walk. We can find somebody who can tell us the *actual* truth about the city."

The street kid wasn't dirty. Dirty was a stage he'd passed ages ago. Now, he'd come out the other side where dirt was the basis, and you only kept building on it. His actual race was a question mark. He didn't have the ears of a Liberator, and lacked the colorful sclera of a Furyborn. Apart from that, he could've been any race. With all the dirt caked in his hair, he might even be a fire-aspected Elemental. He also wasn't holding back, at all. "Thing is, you're here to be milked, yeah? Stupid foreigners with too much gold and too little sense. Way too impressed with your own importance, you'll say yes to anything, without thinking it through. Then, when you leave, you'll realize that the pet gaborn you bought was lame and you've been cheated...only, you won't have any way to get back into the city."

"What? How dare you?" Sera sputtered. She turned to the others, then gawked as she saw them nodding along.

"He dares, because we asked him to. Also, it makes absolute sense. That's what we'd do, if we could get away with it." Chase peered at the look of affront on her face. "Oh, come on now. Look at it this way. You've got a bunch of ignorant marks entering *your* place. They are obnoxious and stupid and think they know everything. Also, in three months, they're going to be gone forever. Is there really anything wrong with earning a bit of extra money from their stupidity?"

"Yes! Of course there is. These are innocent people," she protested.

"Okay. Coming to an agreement here may take a while. Please continue—Scab, was it? So, we should definitely be wary of anybody with business propositions that seem too good to be true. What else? How's crime?"

The kid, brilliantly named Scab from the horribly decorative pattern of scabs under his dirt-matted hair, shrugged. "Not too bad. Not many die. Mostly it's just the drink. Somebody gets drunk, does something stupid and gets what's coming to them. Wake up without money, undressed except for a layer of bruises."

"Ah." Kith nodded. "I'm betting the city guard doesn't look too much into that?"

"Protectors," Scab said. "There's no city guard here. All from the towers. Same difference, though. They only take an interest if something really bad's gone down. Nobody wants that."

Chase frowned. "What does that mean exactly? Is there any organization among the criminals? Or are they part of the military?" Seeing the street kid look to all sides, he smirked. "Listen, Scab. We aren't judging. We just don't want to get mixed up in something without knowing it." He held a silver piece between two fingers and fished another one out of a pant pocket. The boy snatched for the silver, but Chase pulled his hand back. "Knowledge first. Then money."

"No. No corruption in the military. Sometimes, some hot-shot tries, but it always turns out bad. They're real harsh about stuff like that. Beheading harsh." The hardened youngster shrugged with the practiced cynicism of the homeless. "Still. Serves 'em right. They should just know their limits. Long as you don't overstep, the military don't care. Steal a bit? No problem, long as you don't get caught. Climb a window and nick some jewelry? Nobody'll care. Sell bad whiff or get a Protector killed? You're in a world of trouble."

Kith smiled at Sera. "See? This is the kind of info we need. Knowing just how far you can go without stepping in it is worth gold." He looked at Scab. "Well. Silver, at least. Nobody cares about all the dry stuff, like how many people live here, numbers and stuff."

Sera looked put-upon, but Scab just nodded. "I know that too. More'n a hundred thousand. It's the biggest Elemental city in the world. Hah. The only *real* Elemental city. Best city in the world, too."

Kith snorted. "Sure, kid. How about outsiders making a living here and staying in the city?"

The boy had a finger halfway up his nostril. "Not happening. Not unless you're going to join the Protectors, I guess. Look around, man. Don't see a lot of non-Elementals, do you?"

"But...the guy holding the lottery said—" Sera started.

Scab interrupted her, flicking a booger from his finger. "Psht. *That* guy? Everybody knows about him. He'll say anything to make people buy a ticket. Usually, they're not complete lies. He'll just make it sound like he's saying something other than what he is."

"So, what *is* the real truth? Outsiders can't own businesses or buildings in the city? What about the line about full access to the knowledge and joining the Elemental towers?"

"You can join up all you want. But that's only for those who're strong enough. Also, if you join, you're stuck fighting for your life or joining the armies outside. Who wants that? As for all those dusty books? Sure. There's a big library in the city, and a larger one near the towers if you care to stand in line for ages to get a pass. But nobody wants to waste their time with *that*!"

"I think you'll find you're mistaken about that," Chase said, with a glance at the affront on Cilia's face. "But okay. We hear what you're saying. That means there's nobody who will give us a chance to prove ourselves and earn a place in the city unless...what? Unless we go and join the army?"

"That's exactly it. Join the army and go out into the world, or join the Protectors and defend the towers. Nobody wants filthy outsiders here. I mean, except for maybe the windies. They'd take anybody in."

"I'm going to regret asking. I already know. The windies? Wind-aspected Elementals?"

The boy nodded emphatically. "Those. Bunch of scaredy-cats, who'd rather float along with the breeze, even if it leads to the Lightborn invading us all, than stand up to 'em like proper Elementals." He slammed his fist on his chest in a gesture of defiance. It might have seemed more impressive if he wasn't as scrawny as Chase had been, back when he was a kid.

"That's good to know. So, not everybody's against the Lightborn?" Sera asked mildly.

"'Course not," Scab said scornfully. "People are people. They'll think and say a million different things. But there are a few factions. Flamies want to see the world burn, of course. Solid earthers, like me, know the clever thing is to defend. We've got the best defenders in the world, you know. Wavies...are confusing. Even to themselves. Splash every which way, savvy? But it's mostly just the windies who're dumb enough that they think the proper solution is to open our gates to our enemies."

"Okay. That's...useful for later. Most likely." Chase pondered. "For now, there's just one more thing we'll want from you, then you've earned your coin. Take us to a place to stay. Cheap, and where we won't attract attention."

"I can do that. Just don't try to run away, eh? I have connections, you know?"

The defiance of the tiny kid was laughable, but Chase held his composure. You didn't have much on the street. There was no need to mess with a person's pride.

They walked through Earth's Ward, gawking at the marvels. Chase had thought that the upper district in Isarn was classy, what with their regular patrols, noble mansions, and servants underfoot everywhere. Here...was something entirely different. Earth's Ward was built in a circle around the pinnacles housing the Elemental towers. It was a huge sprawling city, with limited space, yet no seeming limit to the population. There were people *everywhere.* Quite the opposite of the city outside the walls, it was mostly Elementals in here. Chase noted a general trend going toward people dressing in the colors of their race. Earth-aspected Elementals dressed in drab, solid clothing; water-aspected in cool, serene blue and white; wind-attuned in flowing neutral robes; and fire-aspected in garish fiery colors.

Oh, and Scab was right. There was a thriving criminal underbelly to the society. During the half hour they'd walked so far, Chase had watched one guardsman, Protector or whatever he was, taking bribes, two pickpockets, and what he suspected was somebody being lured into an alley for a mugging. It made him feel right at home.

It was sorely needed, too. Because where the questionable lawfulness of Earth's Ward felt wholly familiar, the architecture was anything but. Sure, it made sense for a city that had liberal access to people with earth powers. Yet, watching it in practice was something entirely different, and the explanations from the kid made things even more outlandish.

Physics in here weren't what Chase and the others were used to. Architecture wasn't a question of having bricks made or stone carved. Rather, it was a question of contracting an earth-aspected caster and telling him which shape of building you desired. Then you'd pay based upon a number of things—mostly the dimensions and the quality of the creation you wanted. Then the caster would go straight ahead and manipulate the existing soil to create whichever dwelling you desired. If you wanted something really big, you'd need added soil brought in from the outside—but that was it. And the city reflected it. Where Isarn was mostly limited to squarish constructions—brick, stone, and mud being the main elements—here, the buildings were whichever form the owner desired. They saw silo-like constructions, circular, yurt-like things, wavey buildings, even constructions that messed with the eye, dimensions that looked slightly off.

"The real issue here's space, of course. You know we can't expand, right? 'Course you do. You look a bit brighter than the usual outsiders we get. Anyway, space is limited, so most folk with money still can't ever get room to create their own building. They take over whichever old hovel they can buy, then they pay to have it remade." Scab walked in front of them, obviously quite self-satisfied with being in charge of explaining how the world worked.

"What about rich pricks, then?" Kith ignored the barbed look from Sera. "They've got to have something to put 'em apart from normal poor folk, right?"

"Sure they do. You can see one right back...there."

Kith squinted at the three-story building. "Not seeing it. Just a tower, isn't it? Tall, for sure, and well-made, but it looks duller than most of the other buildings here."

"Sure it does." Scab grinned. "But look at the surface."

"It's...kinda shiny?"

"That's it exactly. If you've got just an earthie, you'll need to repair it every so often. And you won't want to build beyond two stories, because it'll fall apart under the pressure. But this? You can see it's made with a combination of an earthie and a flamie. If they know what they're doing, they can work together and create a...glazier—"

"A glacé, I believe," Sera added.

"Whatever. It makes the building tougher. You can toss a stone at it real hard, and it'll just fall down. Means you can build your buildings taller...and height makes you stand out here in the city."

"Ah. So, the quality by itself makes it stand out, but the height of the building proves beyond a doubt that they've paid for quality work?" Sera nodded approvingly.

"Yep." Scab spat. "'Course, sometimes, they cut corners and try to build something tall with just a strong earthie. Always fun to watch those fall apart in an Elemental storm."

Liam had been walking by himself at the back of the group with a huge flatbread filled with meat, just gawking at the city. Now he spoke up for the first time in a while in a, for him, small voice. "Elemental...storm?"

The kid grew even taller. "Oh, you don't know about those? You're gonna owe me a bonus!"

"Could you finish with the buildings first, please? I rather enjoyed your explanation," Sera asked.

The boy sneered, then screwed up his face. "You're okay, for an outsider. Not much more to say, though. You want to show the world you're a rich prick, you build your house with more'n one aspect. Build tall. Build fancy." He waved his hand at the city beyond, where, true enough, towers stabbed into the heights at intervals, with wildly differing shapes and levels. The tallest must have been three times the height of the cathedral in Isarn, yet the width of a needle, compared to their height.

"If you've got money, you hire an earth caster. If you're truly loaded, you combine that with a flamie for the *glace* thing, wind for some fancy illusions or water for some water-repelling thing or some of those mind-bending things they can make." Scab lifted his head back and looked at the peaks towering above them. For the first time since they'd met him, he held a look that carried something other than scorn. National pride. Awe, even. "And if you've got all four? That's when you can create the stuff that legends are made of." He looked wistfully at the Elemental towers farther beyond, dwarfing the impressive edifices of the city.

"That... I'm not even going to go into which *mind stuff* you're talking about," Kith ventured. "But okay, that makes sense. So, if somebody wanted to make sure their target had money, it would just be a question of finding the tallest tower down here?"

"Kith!" Sera scolded.

"What? Just trying to understand the local customs," he said innocently.

"Shut up," Cilia interrupted in a voice that brooked no argument. "Don't look. We're being followed."

Sera's head immediately turned.

Chase intervened in a flash, grabbing her shoulder and pulling her back. He let go of her, pointed at a tower in the distance. "Do *not* look. Seriously, we need to practice this!"

Chastised, she blushed. "Sorry."

Cilia put an arm over Kith's shoulder amiably, then spoke in a low voice. "There's at least two. Might be more. One's following us in the crowd, a couple dozen feet back. The other's hanging back farther. They look dangerous. No uniforms."

"Okay. What do we do?" Liam shrugged his shoulders, getting a feel for his shield and weapons.

"First, we ask the expert," Chase said. "Scab. There's two people following us. You're about to earn an extra bonus, if you can tell us who they are."

Scab beamed and skipped ahead of them in joy, just like a regular kid. No street kid had ever skipped like that in their life, though. When he was a dozen feet ahead of them, he turned and gestured at their surroundings. "Just look at it. Earth's Ward is so impressive! It's almost sad that wonderful people like you won't be allowed to stay!"

He stayed there, smiling, until they caught up with him. As he turned, his face fell. "That looks like bad business. Hard people. How'd you get mixed with them?"

"We...don't even know who they are?" Kith shrugged.

The kid groaned. "Of course you don't. Damn outsiders! Well, they look pissed off. Give me my money. I'm not sticking around."

Chase protested. "Not until you tell us where we're going. Part of the deal was for you to tell us a good place to hide out in safety."

"Not happening if you're bringing violence down on 'em. That's bad business, it is!"

Chase smirked. "Come now, kid. This isn't a problem. Tell us where we're going, then we'll pay you, and lose these two. Then we'll continue in peace and quiet to wherever we're going. I'm sure you're getting a kickback for bringing business to the establishment too."

Scab vacillated just for a moment. Then he rattled off lengthy instructions for finding a flophouse in a less well-off district on the far side of the towers. "Now, pay up."

Chase nodded and swiftly led his hand slide into the kid's dirty pocket, dumping four silver coins. "Okay. Take care, Scab. We'll make sure to mention your name to them when we get there."

The boy was already jogging off into the crowd. He turned around and grinned at them. "I'd worry about not getting caught first. Good luck."

CHAPTER 8

"Many newcomers define the state of the Elemental towers as one of torpor. That could not be further from the truth and just proves their shortsightedness. There are so many currents running underneath the surface, that outsiders inevitably miss it as stagnation. The truth is that the political state of the Elemental towers is in a constant fluctuation of political might and debate." Not sure about this one. If nothing really changes, does it even count as something happening? I might call it torpor myself. (Page 15.)

"**W**e are *so* screwed," Liam said. "I've heard an Elemental mention the real criminals in the city. And it wasn't the nice kind of mention. He was *afraid* of them. I think these are the Elemental versions of Makem's crew. You know, the crew that used to be all summoning those—"

"I remember. Unfortunately. There's no reason to panic. We can all agree we're not going to fight here, right? We have no interest in picking a fight with some of the top army guys around here. So, we just need to get away. Besides, I've been bored for a while anyway. I really need to stretch my legs." Chase grinned. "How about you guys take off, and I do what I do best?"

Kith prodded Chase's stump. "You mean get caught and take the fall for all of us?"

Chase stared at him open-mouthed. "*Low* blow, man. Low blow! What I mean is, I'm the best at running away on a busy street. This..." He waved at the packed streets of Earth's Ward. "Definitely qualifies."

Cilia gave a deep, suffering sigh. "Okay. But *please* be careful. Let's make sure that you have a chance of survival first."

They spent a minute quickly coming up with a plan. Following that, Chase activated his Race of Life card, feeling his Agility grow, further boosted by Sera's Blessing of the Night—at least while she was still in range.

Next, Sera activated Spark of Divinity, boosting his Toughness enough to grant him some added staying power.

He rolled his shoulders, feeling energized, limber and ready to go.

After that, Cilia handed over an armband that could blind anybody close enough when activated, and cautiously pointed the two followers out to Chase, making sure he'd be able to recognize them.

Kith hissed, "I think they're moving closer. They might have become suspicious."

Chase nodded, continuing to roll his shoulders. "Okay then. Best of luck. See you all at the flophouse. Oh, and if they catch me?" He blew a kiss at them. "I'm ratting out Kith first."

He laughed. "We love you too. Go time?"

"Go!"

A dark light flashed once, twice on Kith's right arm. Then, his shadow summons appeared in the distance, coming to life right on top of the followers and drowning their vision. Except for Chase, they sprinted into the crowd, moving for a passage that went perpendicular to the main road they were strolling along.

Chase didn't move. He jumped up and down on the spot, feeling that oh so familiar sensation of exhilaration drumming into his veins. That knowledge that, any moment now, he was going to be running for his life. One second. Two. The followers were still embroiled in the person-shaped shadows that seemed to follow them, whichever way they went, and ruin their vision. Then, they seemed to burst into action and the shadows fell behind as the pursuers leapt out from the cover of the shadow summons.

He still didn't leave. He stood in the center of the thoroughfare, letting the crowd spill around him. He waited, as their gazes searched and finally fixed onto him, fury spreading on their faces. With a slow, measured movement, he held up his hand, asking them to wait. Carefully, Chase started digging around inside his coat pocket. He put on a surprised expression as he searched his pocket, then, with a wide grin on his face, he extracted his hand, raised it...and gave them the finger. Then he turned on his heel and ran.

The streets of Earth's Ward passed by as a blur, as did the people. Everything was so uncommon to Chase, yet so familiar. Clothes were different, as were monuments and buildings. Even so, the feeling of the crowd was the same. The early evening had the feeling of weekend festivities, with a large crowd out and about, with more than a few starting to get drunk and rowdy. Chase dipped in between a group of middle-aged craftsmen drinking out front of a streetside tavern, making sure to jostle a few of them as he passed. The crafters, predictably, froze up and started shouting and shaking their fists at him, making it harder for his pursuit to keep up.

Only, the pursuers, whoever and *whatever* they were, were damn fast, and they knew their stuff. This wasn't like the city guard back in Isarn. These people were clearly physically fit, and they knew the city, making use of shortcuts in between monuments and buildings to catch up to him. Race of Life was the first card Chase had activated, to grant himself an Agility boost and raise his speed. Now, he was stressing over whether he should have swapped to his growing Agility boost, Nights of Criffhaven, instead. Because he was not getting any farther away from them. In fact, they were slowly closing on him, somehow.

It would have been easier if it wasn't for the fact that both of them were carded. The first pursuer was attention-drawing. Every step he took, he left brief sparks where he ran, clearly from some fire-aspected card boosting his movement. The other was clearly a windie, like the kid had said, looking as if he ran on *top* of a pillow of air. Between the two, they spread out to either side of the street, ready to react whenever he'd try to make a break for it.

Chase had no doubt that, whenever they'd catch up to him, they would have some nasty surprises on top of their movement skills. Everything indicated that this wasn't the first time they'd tried to catch some poor sucker. Well, at least this time, Chase would be able to show them the difference between some poor Elemental punk who'd never been elsewhere and an Isarn kid, who was used to dodging city guards, nosy nobles, *and* Lightborn Guardians.

Chase was slightly winded, knowing full well he wouldn't have the Toughness to keep up with the others for too long. That wasn't the point, though. He didn't need to outlast them, just escape. He sped up as he approached a large open space, realizing that it might do the trick. It was a market. A small, specialized one, for sure, but a market nonetheless. There were three different paved roads leading from the open space, all of them slightly less crowded. It looked like it had sort of been birthed into being around a large open two-story tavern, with tons of offshoots, tarps, and added carts joining in the confusion around the central edifice. The courtyard itself was near circular, with homes lining the edges of the place. The tavern and add-ons had annexed the place to the point where the people walking around only had a scant few feet at the edge, and the center itself was entirely taken over by revelry.

If he wanted any chance at making it through the crowd without slowing down, he'd be forced to veer to either side of the tavern. Otherwise, the press of people was simply too tight for him to sprint through without getting pummeled to oblivion. Behind him, the pursuit split out to either side, having anticipated this issue. Chase decided to not play along with their approach. Instead, he raced straight for the central tavern. There was a large open grill with a long table holding a huge ice tray, containing all sorts of meat cuts. It looked like you could pick your choice cut and have it spiced and grilled to your liking straightaway.

That wasn't as pertinent to Chase right now as the fact that the long table ended next to a couple of large, stacked crates, placed right next to the tavern itself. Only a divide of about ten feet separated the top of the crates from the wall of the tavern. Anybody with enough speed, Agility, and stupidity would be able to jump onto the table, then step up onto the crates and leap face-first into the wall of the tavern itself.

He sped up and pushed himself past a heavyset fire-aspected Elemental drooling over the meat on display. Then he leapt onto the table, almost slipping with the slick sensation of the meat and ice underfoot. He managed to keep his speed and balance through momentum and sheer tenacity. Then he leapt onto the crate, breathed a quick prayer, and activated his Steps of Brilliance. In front of him, three gleaming hand-sized platforms appeared, one after the other, leading up into the air. Like climbing stairs at speed, he raced the three steps, then hurled himself up and into the air.

Chase's heart was thumping so loud, it almost burst inside his chest. Beneath him, something sizzling slammed into the wall of the tavern. A card from one of the thugs who realized what he was doing? No time to ponder. He sailed into the air and cleared the edge of the tavern roof by practically a foot.

He almost slipped right then and there. The roof felt like hardened clay, rough and easy to move on. Yet, it had clearly never been cleaned and was slick with dirt, run-off, and decades of birds' droppings. Chase managed to slam himself forward, instead of back, and scaled the rest of the incline hunched over with his hand trailing the roof for comfort.

Once he hit the peak of the roof, he quickly gained his bearings. The roof led down to the same situation on the other side: a large, open market, filled with wine and food merchants, as well as a crowd of people. He glanced back over the top of the roof at his pursuit on the far side, watching with joy how one of the two was just staring open-mouthed at him in astonishment, while the other one made his way through the crowd, hoping to reach Chase on the other side. He gave them both a jaunty wave, then he slid down the far side, considered his situation, and after a single moment of hesitation, slipped into an open window on the roof and into the tavern.

It was one eternal nugget of truth that Chase had learned after more than his share of being chased. If people followed you and saw you disappear out of view, there was one logical conclusion. If they knew where an avenue led to, the human thing was to continue searching in that direction. The thought that somebody might simply stop and hide or try to blend in with a crowd simply did not occur to most people.

To Chase, it was the only thing that made sense. He could either chance the streets, that the pursuers clearly knew better than himself, or he could dip into the very conveniently opened window *right* there and hide out.

Luck was with him today. On all counts. Whoever his pursuers were, they failed to search for him inside the nice, busy tavern. Chase spent a brief while catching his breath in a room filled with drying laundry, then he turned his cloak inside out, exposing the light brown underside instead of the darker upper side he'd used so far. He also took off his hat and tucked it into his shirt. A minute later, he listened for noise near the door, then slid outside and made his way into the common room.

Two minutes later, Chase sat near the bar, talking to a *very* nice gentleman about the advantages of using water-aspected crafter powers in the creation of wine. Regardless of how little he understood of the techniques in question, he'd rarely enjoyed a discussion quite so much.

The flophouse was just that. A cheap place where you could pay for a cot and a horrible, yet filling, meal. In the morning, you'd get a large bowl of gruel. In the evening, you got the same, sometimes accompanied by a haunch of salted meat, provenance unknown. The place was rundown, dusty, with no inch of privacy whatsoever, and there'd be no doubt that any item left unguarded here would be gone minutes later. To Chase, it immediately felt like home. Not the least because the others were all gathered at the end of the large sleeping chamber, deep in discussion, when he sauntered in.

Liam got up and gave him a huge hug. The big Lightborn beamed with joy. Then his face scrunched up. "Sweat, I understand. But you reek of *wine?* How exactly did you get away from them?"

Chase smirked. "Ah, you know. Escaping from hostile card wielders is thirsty work. I had to take a pit stop halfway." He waggled his eyebrows, then grew more serious. "You made it here without too much attention?"

Cilia lowered her voice. "It was no issue. We took one of the first side streets we found, then split up to ensure that there would be no way to recognize us all. We also changed our looks slightly along the way."

"What about Kith?"

Kith spoke up. "What *about* Kith?"

Chase shrugged. "It's a new city. You needed to find something from a simple description. Who helped you, if you split up?"

"*One* time. One time, I got lost in Isarn. And I was drunk, I might add."

"Answer the man." Liam nudged.

"Cilia hung back so I could follow her from a distance," Kith growled. "You absolute bastards."

When the laughter died down, nobody started talking.

Finally, Sera took the lead. "Correct me if I am wrong, but it would appear that our original goal—finding a permanent home—will be tougher to complete than we initially envisioned?"

Chase snorted. "Yeah. If they're not letting people stay here without having been in the army or joining the Protectors first? That's a problem, for sure."

Sera nodded. "However, if there is one thing I have learned from staying with you, it is that nothing is quite as straightforward as you would immediately envision. Hence, I suggest that we get a good night's sleep, and tomorrow we go out there and try to find out whichever loopholes we can use to make a place for ourselves regardless of that fact."

Chase smiled, then laughed outright. "No discussion. I'm proud of you! Here I was about to go through the whole gamut of depression and annoyance before I'd come to the same conclusion that took you thirty seconds."

"And a drunken binge or two, most likely," Kith added.

"That too," Chase agreed amiably. "Sera's right, though. There are no rules without exceptions. Tomorrow, we take a bit of time to figure out how to go through the city without getting made by the people following us. Then, we just need to figure out how to make this city our bitch."

"I agree," Sera said. "Without the unnecessary vernacular."

"One question," the broad Lightborn warrior rumbled. "The people who followed us. Of course we avoid them. As long as we have some decent disguises, that should be no issue. Do we need to find out who they are?"

Cilia snorted. "No need. They are obviously the ones who ran whatever sting we appropriated when we rigged the lottery. They were obviously going to figure out who we were and ruin our day. But asking around, in a city we don't know, is a recipe for disaster. We just do the logical thing: lay low, let the attention die down, dress like the locals. Three months from now, they'll have forgotten all about us."

Kith said, "Yeah. No discussion. Criminals are notorious for having short attention spans." He winked at Cilia. "Just look at us."

Sera cut through the low laughter. "Does this mean...we actually made it? As long as we are not discovered and find a way to stay here, we are safe? We can actually relax?"

Chase laid his hand on her shoulder. "Yeah, princess. The flight is off. There won't be any inquisitors trying to take you down in here. Let down your hair and be yourself! We're about to find out how to make this glorious, colorful, lovely place of wonders our home!"

CHAPTER 9

"People are so gods-cursed naive when it comes to defense. They always believe that the strengths of the Elemental lands lie in our walls and soldiers. Please. If it were like that, anybody with a really tall ladder would be able to make it past. Also, is anybody really stupid enough to believe that our forces could stand up to the numberless armies of Light? No, our strength is manyfold. Our crafters, toiling endlessly to improve our defenses and make the most of our limited lands. Our armies, constantly struggling in search of strength. And finally, our wordslingers, embroiled in a never-ending struggle for concessions and peace." Wordslingers? That's a new one. I hope I will learn more about those. (Page 18.)

Chase woke up by degrees. The first was an in-between state, a kind of not-quite-awake experience, where he realized that it was still night, yet some part of him insisted that the time for sleep was over. Next came a smooth development where his crust-filled eyes shot all around him, looking for a hint of what had managed to nudge him into awareness. That part was ingrained into him. A never-ending checklist that ran whenever you awakened, and, to a certain degree, also while you were asleep. That was life on the Waves for you. Movement? None. No flickering lights or shadows indicating movement either. Smells? Nothing, except for the accumulated stink of twenty-plus people stuffed into a too-small room. Sweat, alcohol, and flatulence. Nothing out of the ordinary. Noise? No noise. None.

He allowed his eyes to close again and steadied his breathing, lying still as if he'd fallen back asleep again. He let his hand slide ever so slowly under his hard pillow. He grasped the hilt of the dagger he stowed there, while stretching his foot out to prod Kith in the bunk behind his.

"That's quite enough of that. Leave the weapon. You should all wake up now." A cold, muffled voice filled the silence.

Chase sat up slowly, letting his hand drop from the backup weapon. Around him, the others slowly awoke. Cilia prodded Liam several times before he came to.

Sera was clearly befuddled. "What is going on? Why—"

"Somebody's got the drop on us," Chase said. "We let our guard down. They're carded, and they've got people waiting outside. They aren't planning to attack straightaway."

A dark chuckle filled the room. "Now, that *is* an interesting conclusion. Presumptuous, even. Why would you think that I'm not planning to attack?"

Chase finally spotted the person. Or rather, where the person was.

They sat on a rickety chair in the center of the crowded room. Beyond the dark, dusty smoothness of the voice, there was nothing to indicate anything about them, not even the gender. The shape on the chair was covered in a translucent layer of...*waves* was the only word he could come up with to properly describe it. A moving, living tapestry of dark-grey waves constantly rotating inches above the shape of the person beneath, obscuring the clothes, the face, anything that might be used to identify the person. The only thing that stood out was how the waves seemed to billow from the shoulder of the person, like an ethereal cloak.

Chase cleared his throat. "First off. Thank you for confirming that you've got people outside—"

A whizzing sound ended in a *thwock* as a throwing dagger embedded itself in the bunk right between Chase's legs. "Answer my question."

Hoarsely, Chase said, "You've managed to get everybody else in the room out, while we slept. No way we slept through that naturally. That means you've got cards, and if you wanted to, you could have taken half of us out already."

The laughter coming from the figure sounded slightly unhinged. A flash came from a point at their back, and they disappeared. In a foggy flash of movement, they appeared and reappeared five times before fading back into a sitting position. "Half of you? Please."

In a choir of exclamations, they flung themselves back. Every single one of them sported a tiny cut somewhere. Chase gasped. So goddamn fast! Also, that card flashed on the right leg! That meant at least Tier four! He fought to keep his voice steady. "Point taken. So. Unknown, cloaked figure. What can we do for you? We haven't been in the city for long, so we aren't stocked up on refreshments."

In a voice suddenly wholly bereft of amusement, the figure spat, "You can tell me how you managed to cheat your way into *my* city!"

Chase's mind whirled. *How in the Pits?* They'd made it in flawlessly, without stirring up any trouble. *How had they been made?*

Before he came up with a smart retort, Cilia spoke up. "We didn't come up with anything. We're newcomers here. We abused a system that was already in place." She turned her head to the others. "Doesn't matter how they know. We got caught.

The only way that would happen is if they were already paying attention." She sat up on her bed and turned back to the cloaked figure. "Am I right? You already suspected that something was wrong?"

"Yes. We just didn't know *how* the system was broken." The figure leaned forward; its gaze nearly physical as it pinned them down. "You are going to tell me exactly how you broke the system, and who helped you. If you do that to my satisfaction, I will toss you out of the city unharmed. If not...you will come to regret your choice."

"Counteroffer." Chase felt almost light-headed. He knew, beyond a doubt, that they were in real, tangible danger. He also very much suspected that the figure in front of him would be able to take him out without any struggles. However, he didn't sense any tangible malevolence from the person in their midst. It was more a sensation of somebody using everything they could to milk them of everything they had. "We're here, because we're looking for a home. As in somewhere where we want to stay for the rest of our lives. Nothing illegal, nothing hidden. We want to make this place our own. That's why we cheated our way in. If we'd been able to do that legally, we would. But here's our offer. We're not powerless. We're all either Tier two or three. We even have a Tier-two crafter among us. We can be *good* to Earth's Ward. Just let us stay. We'll go above and beyond. We'll do any job you want. Tell you anything you'd like. Please, just don't throw somebody out who could be of real benefit to your home!"

The figure leaned back in the chair. For a moment, it seemed appalled. Then it burst into laughter. Unrestrained bursts of laughter, making the person double over in the chair.

Chase couldn't help but think that there was something feminine in there. Even with everything hidden and the voice clearly muffled to hide what they were, the way they held a hand in front of their mouth when they laughed. The poise, the careful posture. Yeah. He was nearly certain it was a woman.

Regardless of gender, there was no warmth in their voice when they stopped laughing. "You have some nerve. You come to my home, break the laws, and then you have the gall to try to argue that you should be allowed to *stay*, on top of everything? I'll let you in on a little secret. *You have no power here.* You will do exactly as I say, or die. That is exactly how far I'm willing to bend."

"Okay. We will talk," Cilia said, with a stern glance at Chase. "There is no need for bodily harm and we will cooperate."

"I know you will." The frost in the shadowy figure's voice could have chilled a drink.

Chase's mind whirled. *Was this it?* Would they just give away what they'd figured out and let themselves get tossed right back out the gate where they came from? Back to hiding from the inquisitors, fearing that they could get spotted anywhere they moved? *Pits no.* This was a *chance.* This person had the power to grant them exactly what they wanted. Refuge. A permanent place to stay. Citizenship. He just didn't know how he could twist the situation to their advantage.

"Oh. Of course we'll cooperate. I'm just a bit surprised. Usually, you expect somebody powerful to also be clever." Chase had a split second to see the incredulous look on Sera's face. Then the air blurred before him, and his world dissolved in pain. Something hit him hard enough to tip him over on the bed. A wave of pain and nausea threatened to overwhelm him as his world tilted, until he realized that the shadowy person sat astride him. With her dagger embedded deep in his neck, near the clavicle.

Her face was inches away. It was still nothing but a wash of movement, of blue-grey forces swirling around in front of a blank slate. Her breath smelled of mint and something ephemeral. Her voice came out cold and emotionless. "When I pull this dagger back out, I can do one of two things. I can do it cleanly. You may suffer a bit of permanent damage, but should be able to heal it, if your friends there stanch the bleeding quickly. I can also choose to twist the dagger, and watch you bleed out right under me. Which result you get will depend entirely on your next words."

Chase grimaced and bit his lip to not cry out from the excruciating pain. "We...will tell you everything." His words came out in fits and starts. "Except, that will only give you the grunts. The people who did the work. You won't find out who's behind the scheme. Because the people who ran the sting, I promise you, don't know anything about the big picture."

She leaned down on him even harder. "How would you know that?"

With every bit of challenge in him, he gave her a shit-eating grin, only mildly ruined by the sweat running down his face. "Quite simply, and with respect, Sir or Madam...it's how I'd set it up myself." He cried as the pain in his shoulder intensified and blossomed into a burst of fiery suffering.

Then, the figure was back in her chair, leaving only a swirling afterimage in front of his retina. "I am listening."

The room lit up, as Sera used her Light healing power, and the flesh in his shoulder started to knit itself together.

Chase spoke up again, in between breaks to breathe. "We are, as you have probably already guessed, slightly more used to the...shall we say *less* legal sides of society. We are also, given that we've just entered your city for the first time ever, blank slates. We don't have any associations or past histories here that can end up tainting what we do. Meaning, we're in the perfect position to investigate things for you and figure out who is behind this scheme."

"Why would you assume that I cannot do this by myself?"

He had her now. She was genuinely listening, practically asking to be convinced. His mind worked on overdrive. "Because of what you aren't."

The smirk in her voice was clear now. "So, you do know who I am? Who I work for?"

"No. But it's quite obvious. We've been told that organized crime in Earth's Ward is...shall we say, limited. If they overreach, they get discouraged." He paused, but she didn't disagree. "If you were able to scare everyone else in this room out of here without any complaints? That means, you work for either the higher-Tier criminals or the people in charge. The clandestine side of the Elemental powers. With the way you talk, you're clearly not a criminal. On top of that...that disguise of yours, effective as it must be, clearly has its limits. Everybody who talks to you will know who you work for. And I'm guessing whoever you are in real life, isn't in a position to do a ton of digging for herself either." He shrugged and instantly regretted it as pain flooded into his shoulder. "Light burn me, that was stupid. Anyway, we're outsiders, clearly with no ties to the city, with Light cards. We can make the connections, ask the questions that you cannot. Nobody'll suspect *us* of working with those in power."

For a while, she sat there, gaze aimed straight at him.

He knew she was looking at him, could *feel* it, but couldn't see her eyes. The sensation was extremely disconcerting, like a colony of ants traipsing around under his clothes. Yet, he didn't dare twitch, and just looked back at her. He noticed a weird detail about her. He couldn't see her face, obviously, but her head jerked around in the tiniest increments, in birdlike motions, like she was constantly staying alert, moving to catch any danger around her.

"Okay. You have a point. You are wrong here and there, but there is one thing you said that I agree with. I do believe that I can use you." Her dagger, still liberally covered in Chase's blood, tapped softly against the edge of the chair seat between her legs as she pondered. "This is what is going to happen. You are going to tell me everything you know. I will investigate your claims. Then, and only then, will we consider whether we will be working together. Until then—" She threw a handful of bronze arm rings on the floor in front of them. "You will all put these on. They will ensure that I know exactly where you are."

Cilia cleared her throat. "There is one thing I would recommend." Her voice was calm, collected.

The cloaked woman's was not. "I am running out of patience here."

Cilia nodded, acknowledging the fact. "Once we've told you who was corrupt, please don't take them in and interrogate them. That would give the game away. Look into their personages, rummage through their stuff, change things up so they can't continue letting people in...whatever you need to do. But if their bosses, whoever they are, know that they've been caught, it's going to make things a lot harder for us. It will be harder for us to catch the masterminds behind things."

A low sound came from her throat, but she relented. "That depends entirely on what you're about to tell me. Tell me everything, and don't leave out *anything*."

They did just what she said. In a shifting, leaping mess of explanations, they explained exactly what they'd done to figure out how the scribe and the female presenter were cheating the system. They made no bones about the fact that it was a commonly known secret both in the outer city and back among the nobility of Isarn that access could be bought. Finally, after her insistence, they explained how they had used Sera's Heart card to figure out who among the employees might be cheating.

The camouflaged person was silent for a while after that, sitting still besides those tiny head movements. Finally, she nodded. "Acceptable. I am obviously going to need to confirm all of this. But it corresponds to what I expected to find."

"Expected?" Kith burst out. "So, you already suspected that somebody was cheating on the scales?"

"Of course we did. We are not blind. There had been indicators for a while. Hints that not everything was truly random. Our process has always been hands-off with the employees of the lottery, in order to ensure that everybody knows that we are honest about it being random."

"Except for your agents sorting out any undesirables they recognize who try to enter the lottery, of course."

"Except that," she grudgingly admitted. "However, the rumors getting back to us were too persistent to ignore, as were the numbers. It was becoming clear that something had changed."

Chase prodded his neck. It still hurt like the Pits. "So...what do we do now? Do we start laying the groundwork for finding the underground here in the city while you investigate?"

The figure got up and wiped off the dagger on a cot next to her. She sheathed it before shaking her head. "No. Tomorrow, we have initiation tests. You are going to move to the Elemental towers and apply to join the recruits."

They exchanged glances, unsure just what was going on.

Finally, Sera spoke up. "Is that not counterintuitive to what you want us to do? Applying for the towers, if we complete the first test, would send us into a route that leads to us being locked away from Earth's Ward, and away from the culprits—is that not right?"

This time, the figure was clearly enjoying herself. "That's entirely incorrect."

"It is?" Sera spread her hands helplessly.

"We have been looking into this for a while. Whoever is orchestrating everything is not likely to be found in the seedy underbelly of the city. Too many important people are involved. Rather, they are likely to be part of the towers. Hence, you will enroll in the towers, and you will take part in the day-to-day business there, ostensibly to earn your place in the Elemental Protectors. Instead, what you will be doing is using your time and effort to unearth whoever is trying to undermine the security of the Elemental lands. If you manage that, then we may be able to do something to ensure that you may stay in or around the city and not get tossed out for being criminals."

The woman's voice was suddenly dangerous. Intent. "I need you to understand one thing. You are all refugees here. Less than visitors. You are temporarily granted a reprieve. *You have not earned your clemency.* If you fail us, fail to do what you claim you can? You will be expelled. If you try to mess with us? You will never be found."

There was little to be said to that.

CHAPTER 10

"This is what we do. We cherish and improve every class in the academy. Without summoners, we have only our own bodies to take the brunt of any assault. Without healers, who would patch us up? All classes are created equal. As such, the academy welcomes and encourages people of all races and classes to join." Hmm. The book started out as self-aware. This sounds more like propaganda. (Page 20.)

"Remind me again why we're doing this?" Kith glared at the gate and waiting crowd ahead of them. It was a diverse crowd, formed of mixed races, yet with Elementals outnumbering the rest. Oh, and the Elementals were already shooting dirty glances at the rest, because of course they were.

The backdrop was overwhelming enough that it was hard to keep from staring. They, along with everybody else who intended to join this month's intake of recruits for the Elemental towers, had been directed to the Gates of Elements, the towering, domineering edifices which were the only break in the seamless, daunting construction that was the final defensive wall surrounding the mountain, keeping the slopes of the mountain, the Elemental towers, and the impressive compound around the towers walled off from the rest of Earth's Ward. Above them, the huge towers rose, half-hidden in the clouds, surrounded by half-seen shapes monstrous and humanoid both.

Cilia ignored the scenery in the same way that she avoided the glances—just like she had for her entire life—and stared at him as if he'd grown a third ear. "Because we need to? Because I don't want to die? Because the scary Tier-five woman said to shut up and do as we were told? Because the vaunted Library of Earth's Ward is right here on the compound and I need to visit it!" The last sentence, she said with a longing glance at the impressive library building looming on the other side of the Gates of Elements, just out of reach.

Kith rolled his eyes and waved at the vista of them. "Not that. *This.* If we're supposed to somehow infiltrate the damn towers, why don't they supply us with an edge, with a way in? If half of us fail the test, odds are, the rest of us will have a damn hard time finding them."

"Plenty of reasons come to mind," Cilia said coldly. "Maybe she wanted us to prove our worth. Maybe, like Chase said, she isn't in a position to make any overt moves in her regular employment. Also, maybe she just didn't like us very much."

"Or all of the above." Liam chuckled. "So, whenever people out in the outer city talk about the tests, they don't share what happens. Why is that, you think?"

"Honestly?" Sera said. "I believe they simply do not know. Again, I know only a few Lightborn nobles who have gained Elemental cards. One of them spoke of his time in the towers with disdain, like it was of little consequence. Whether that was because it was easy, or because of him being a *thoroughly* disagreeable person, I could not say."

Chase laughed. "My money's on *they don't know* as well. If the security measures back there are any hint, they're not letting anybody in here who doesn't plan to actually go through with joining. And those who do join are likely going to be above gossiping in the outer city."

A noise interrupted their chatter. It was a slowly building boom of drums, a crescendo of noise starting low and ramping up in power, to the point where everybody could feel the slow rhythm in their chests. The pace increased as well, going from a ponderous boom to a steady booming march. With a final tooth-loosening roll, the drums silenced. A person stepped forward.

It was a stately-looking woman, bedecked in a flowing, tasseled dress of a color that made Chase think of storm clouds, going from a stark white over sky blue to a dark, dirty grey. The fact that she walked barefoot didn't diminish from her presence. Every inch of this wind-aspected Elemental screamed control and power. The tassels moved around her, making the entirety of her dress seem like a living sky. Her long, white hair moved around her, as if she walked in the middle of a storm. Beneath the tassels, her skin showed hints of cards. Too many cards. Arms. Stomach. Legs. Even the pit of her throat showed a glimmering card.

Chase cursed and murmured, "Tier six? At least Tier six! Fury shred me!"

"Shh," Sera admonished.

The setting in front of the crowd changed. A loud murmuring arose, then died to a sudden, awestruck silence as the woman stepped up on an elaborate, gold-plated lectern placed on a tiered wooden stage. She looked down upon all the assembled people below, her stern face judging, assessing. When she spoke, her voice was low, but clearly audible to everybody, as if she sat but a couple of feet away from each of those assembled on the grounds. "I am High Elementalist Tatiana Skysworn. On behalf of the Elemental lands, I thank you. Each of those assembled here. We are in your debt. Look around."

Everybody shared confused glances with the people around them. Nothing there but other confused people, mostly young and unscarred.

Her voice continued. "We, the Elementals, are a logical unlikelihood. An existence that should not be possible. We are cut off from the world, kept from moving freely, from expanding naturally, from strengthening our numbers. Yet, even so, we fight off and even grow our strength. With every year, we, as a whole, become stronger, more well-founded, harder to remove from this, our home. Why, you ask?" A warm smile appeared on her face. "Because of people like you."

She pointed toward the distance. "The Lightborn take the opposite approach. They conquer the wide world, challenging anybody out there for possession of every square foot. The Furyborn are at their throats constantly, only they keep on the move, roaming and adapting, yet still fighting for space. The Liberators managed to lock down large swathes of land early on and challenge anybody for it as if they were their heartlands. We? We do not have that luxury. Instead, we opt for quality. We equip and teach our people better than anybody else out there. We do not accept just anybody. Because we are challenged when it comes to space and numbers, we take *only* the best. The best...like you!"

She leaned forward on the lectern, focused. "Look around. These people around you? They are the picture of dedication. Of sacrifice! Anybody here today is ready to give up at least seven years of their lives—that is two years of intense training, and at minimum five years of service—in defense of the Elemental lands. Possibly even their lives and limbs. *That* is dedication! *That* is valor! What matter which race they are? Anybody here has already accepted that sacrifice, made their peace with what this could cost them."

Kith made a noise in the back of his throat. "I...didn't accept anything. No sacrifices for me, please! Could you please point me toward the exit? And *seven years?*"

Chase shushed him. "Like we'd go that far, man. We need to act the role, though."

The woman continued, unperturbed. "If we are to stand up to the powers out there, we cannot make do with weak soldiers. This means that each of us here has the chance and privilege to be molded and taught, until we finally emerge as gems, as the shining examples of Elemental powerhouses that protect our borders and keep us safe at night. As you all know, that means that we cannot accept just anybody. We need those with the brightest minds, the strongest arms. Yet, we are not unfair. For those who have not had the chance, we will temper you. We will *help* you grow. Anybody who does not meet the towering standards we require will be allowed to join the Elemental armies instead, to help you improve your strength and earn experience. You may retry the exam at a later date, or quit if you have learned that it was too much."

Liam shook his head and spoke, way too loud. "This is insane. This is just like Isarn. They send out people to die in their armies if we don't meet the standards?"

A nasal voice intruded from the side. "What of it, *Lightborn?*" The speaker was a fire-aspected Elemental. Flowing red-blond hair crowned a tall, lithe man. He was willow-thin and handsome, carrying an inborn grace that was only ruined by the sneer on his face. "You should have spent a little less time being impressed by the supremacy of your own race and more time reading what you're going into. And the Elemental armies are nothing like the grinders of the Lightborn. We care about our people surviving and thriving. Not throwing away our own because we have too many unwanted people in our backwater cities."

"Stow it, Sticks. Somebody's trying to listen here," Chase spat.

The tall man held a hand to his chest bone, as if shocked that anybody would speak to him like that. He never responded, however. Tatiana Skysworn started to speak again, and he turned back to her, fervent awe clear on his mien.

"The requirements for making it to the top are high. You know that. You have seen our defenders, standing tall wherever they walk. Yet, most people do not know just how arduous the task is. The process for reaching the top and becoming a fully-fledged member of our guard takes two full years. Two years with constant tests, physical and mental, where you need to prove that you are among the best. Only then will you be able to earn your cards and join the vaunted ranks and fight for the protection of our home. Today, we have around three hundred volunteers here. Only a hundred and twenty will join the classes. Of those, only about twenty will be granted acceptance into their ranks, becoming the shields, mages, and crafters that toil to keep us all safe."

Sera nodded decisively. "Good. That is what we need to do, then. We simply all need to become Protectors."

"Simply?" A choked noise came from the Elemental. He looked like he was about to explode.

The High Elementalist outpaced him. "You have all heard the stories. Defending our borders is a dangerous task, with constant attrition. Yet, we also deliver the best. High-quality equipment. The best of educators. Every theoretical and practical application we can help to improve the situation of our home.

Hence, only the best of the best will be accepted among their rank. In a moment, our staff will guide you to be tested. Please follow their directions to the letter."

A group of people approached from the gate.

The fire-aspected Elemental next to them decided this was enough time to lay some truths on them. "It's clear that none of you have any clue what you have gotten yourselves mixed up with. So, I'll just give you this tip. It's too late for you to back down, of course. But our kind don't just throw away soldiers like where you come from. Surviving a tour as a recruit for you isn't entirely impossible, regardless of how clueless you are. So, do the tour, and then *go back home.* Because the Protector training is even more dangerous than the tour—especially for somebody as inept as you lot." Having gotten that off his chest, the agile Elemental turned his back and walked away, red-blond curls leaving a bright halo around his face.

Liam scrunched up his face. "Am I the only one who got the feeling he actually thought he was doing us a favor?"

"Nope," Chase said. "New rules. We need to be accepted into the school, obviously. That's the most important. Second most is stealing the spot from that uppity bastard!"

The throng of people were marshalled through the gate. They entered the tunnel leading through the towering gate in silent contemplation, all of them gawking as if they'd never seen architecture before. Plenty of reasons for that, too.

The art was impressive. Divided into four sections, each section of the gate was carved or sculpted into an homage to an element. Colorful and vivid, the different sections portrayed both scenery and creatures. Animals and otherworldly creatures, embroiled in an ocean of its element. A phoenix cried to the heavens next to a flame-covered abomination, and dozens of other creatures, all rising out of a sea of fire. There were a hundred more creations, all looking lifelike enough that Chase believed he could learn about the creatures just by observing the art. It wasn't just the art, though.

Nestled among the creatures were openings. Sometimes, they were disguised as mouths—tiny, threatening holes, in a pack of spike-covered fish, clearly ready to bestow some kind of death or other. Others were larger—vertical slashes that might bring down anything from a huge blade to a portcullis. One opening, as tall as a man, near the roof of the ceiling, was portrayed on the fire section as the center of a living, pulsating portal of fire. Chase shuddered to think what that might bring. The defenses weren't everything either, though.

The sheer size was what really brought things home. The tunnel through the wall was at least eighty foot long, and the roof of the tunnel loomed sixty feet above them. At a glance, the damn tunnel would be able to fit the entire city guard of Isarn, at once. And the wall loomed even higher above the tunnel. Chase was no architect, but he knew there was no way they would be able to erect something as mountainous as this with simple labor.

Once they had passed the gate tunnel, they were ushered to the side and divided into a long line. Above them, the heights of the towers soared. Around them, a massive courtyard held the entrance to the towers, the library, and a huge range of other edifices. Chase didn't have the time to take it all in, before he found himself in a line, leading toward a long table, with six serious-looking administrators seated.

"This looks familiar," Kith said. "They're really into scribes, aren't they?" An Elemental ahead of him in the line shushed him, and Kith quieted down.

Chase frowned at the setting. They really did take everything seriously, especially if it was just a question of the scribes taking notes about them or something like that. The line moved quickly and efficiently. This was clearly something they'd done tons of times before. The further they progressed in the line, the more the setting confused him. Everybody who went through the process with the scribes was then pointed to stand in the large open courtyard beyond, arranged into a neat line, which kept expanding to either side.

It wasn't a peaceful experience, which was what *really* confused him. People took the division weirdly. Some were clearly happy by their position in the line, while others seemed upset. One tall Liberator sobbed, as he walked to the very end of the line.

"Name, class, and Tier?" a strict Elemental woman with a professional mien, the sallow, glistening looks of being water-aspected, and a bob of short, tight, black curls asked him.

"Chase, no surname. Rogue. Three," he responded.

A curt nod was his only response. "Are you carded? Which aspect?"

"Yeah. Light." He nodded. They'd decided beforehand that they'd need to keep the Dark cards a secret. He just hoped they didn't have any truthstones like the one they'd used to verify names in the lottery, or he'd be screwed.

"Thank you. Move on please." She passed the scrap of parchment she'd written on to the next scribe in line.

The eager-looking youngster with the wild mane and sky-flecked eyes of a wind aspect was less officious than the woman before. "Hi...Chase. This is very important and you need to be brutally honest, understand? Also, being an outsider, we will check your name with the lottery, so there is no use lying here."

"I get you, man. Just ask. I have no reason to lie about my name," Chase said with a crooked smile. Inside, he chuckled at the many other things he had reasons to lie about.

"Are you or your family in any sort of conflict with the Elemental lands?"

Chase snorted. "Nah. I mean...do people even apply if they are?"

"You would be surprised," the young Elemental said. "Are there any other issues, personal, business, legal, or other-wise, which might interfere with you taking on the mantle of a Guardian or as a soldier in the Elemental Army?"

Chase shook his head. "Nothing I can think of." *As long as the inquisitors stay outside this place, I'll be just fine.*

The young man's hand moved flawlessly over the parch-ment, the quill adding a couple of lines of tight, economical writ-ing. "Do you undertake any crafts that may be of value to our forces?"

Chase shook his head. "Mmh. Maybe? I used to be a run-ner. Messages and otherwise. That count?"

"That could be useful. Thank you." He jotted down an-other line, then handed the parchment to Chase and pointed to the side with his thumb. "Since you're not a crafter, you can skip the next one."

Chase thanked him and walked past a weary-looking Fu-ryborn woman with huge, muscular arms. She must have been a smith, he decided.

Next came another Elemental. The uniformed man was earth-aspected, and everything about him looked solid, to a de-gree where he seemed more like a summoned golem than an actual human being. He had a short, no-nonsense dark-brown haircut to go with an oft-broken nose. The countless scars and wounds on his hands looked more like they were painted on, and he had a blockiness, a solidity to him that told Chase this was not a person he'd want to try on in a duel.

The Elemental accepted the piece of parchment and read it. He put it aside with a grunt, then let his gaze roam over Chase. "Darkborn, eh? You a criminal?"

Chase considered the best approach. Should he lie? Try to avoid the question? *No.* As blunt as the man was, honest and straightforward was likely the best response. "Used to be." He rolled up his left sleeve, exposing the stump where they'd cut off his hand. "Then I got caught, more than five years ago. Now, I'm trying to find a better path."

Another grunt. "That'll limit your usefulness in combat."

He nodded. Seemed like the man was fishing, trying to make Chase defend his usefulness. Except, of course, it made him less useful. Chase knew very well how much his lack of a hand limited his capabilities.

"Says here you're a runner. Any good at it?"

"Used to be good. With the cards I have now, I'm great," Chase said with conviction. With his improved attributes, his buffs, and his new Light platforms, he'd bet on himself against any other runners nine times out of ten.

"How about combat? Fought anything?"

"Yes. Beasts and Guardians, a near-dozen times. Men as well, out in the Wastes." And a few inquisitors. That...likely wasn't a selling point.

The warrior's eyebrow rose the tiniest bit. "Anybody carded?"

"Yes."

He grunted again, jotted something down on the parchment. "How are you at fighting? Think you could take me in a duel?"

Chase snorted, then blinked as the warrior kept staring at him. "Wait. That was a real question?" Chase's eyes zipped over the muscular man, the scars from a hundred lethal encounters, the no-nonsense attitude and lidded eyes. He noted the vague outline of cards on each arm. At least Tier two then. "Pits no. I don't do duels in the first place. Playing by the rules when you're lighter and weaker than your opponent doesn't seem too wise. I might be able to take you in an ambush. But I wouldn't give myself good odds. You look like somebody who's hard to surprise."

The man observed him for a moment later, then nodded and slid the parchment forward. "Move on then."

The next official was another Elemental, and a fire-aspected one. This one dressed himself less flamboyantly, adorned in a simple light-grey robe. Together with his neatly trimmed red-blond beard, it gave him the appearance of a kindly grandfather. He read the parchment. "Welcome, child. I just have a few simple questions."

Chase instinctively distrusted him. Somebody who looked that trustworthy had to have some agenda. He adopted a pleasant expression and nodded amiably.

"A former criminal?" the man asked. "We make no judgment here, of course. I would guess that this means your schooling is limited?"

He nodded. "True. I know a lot, but not school learning."

"Reading? Writing?"

"I've started learning, but not fully."

He huffed. "On a scale from one to five, where would you put your knowledge of the world? One is the lowest."

Chase grimaced. "Two."

"How about knowledge of history?"

"One."

"Laws and rules?"

Chase sighed. This wasn't going well.

A minute later, the man let him go. The final parts hadn't been too bad, because Chase believed that he did have a decent grasp on cards and crafts in general. With Cilia nearby and having worked for Gunnha, he'd had to deal with all sorts. Too bad his head hadn't been able to contain all the boring stuff.

The final administrator, a middle-aged water-aspected Elemental with a tight expression, had just one comment for him. "Please place your hand on this plate and outline your attributes."

Chase did as he was asked.

Midway through, the official held up her hand, cursing. She extracted a stone from the back of the wooden plate, held it up to the light and tossed it nonchalantly into a bin next to her. She extracted a new stone from the carefully secured purse at her side.

No. Not a stone. A Dark-cursed agate. That was insane! They actually used gems to make sure they didn't lie about their attributes. No wonder they didn't use it for every single question they asked, or they'd have to go through fortunes.

Strength: 11

Agility: 18 (+8 Tier bonus) = 26

Toughness: 13

Mental Power: 11

Potential: 25

When he was done, he took a moment to marvel at how far he'd come. Just a few months ago, he'd sported an average of about eleven in all his attributes. Now, he'd passed an average of seventeen. It made for a world of difference, in every aspect of his life. The slightly improved Toughness meant he could run, fight, and move for a lot longer without getting winded. His Mental Power made his decisions come a tad quicker and with less hesitation, and the activations of his cards easier and faster. His Potential ensured that any future cards he won were likely to be at least Uncommon, possibly even Rare or better. His Strength and Mental Power especially still needed some work, but Strength remained the one attribute that he felt he could safely neglect, just a bit.

The Elemental official ahead of him didn't react in any obvious manner. She just nodded and continued. "Tier three? Show me your cards."

He did as ordered, then proceeded to show her his arms, stomach, and empty right leg, confirming to her that he was exactly Tier three.

She tapped her lower lip for a moment, then extracted a scroll in a large scroll case on her left. Running down the text, she nodded to herself. "Please confirm the titles and rarities of your cards in order."

"Steps of Brilliance, Rare. Race of Life, Uncommon. Spoils of the Undeserving, Rare."

She nodded in confirmation of each one. "Steps of Brilliance at rare, was it? We only have details for the Uncommon version. Please tell me the details of the card, with the exact wording."

Chase focused on the knowledge nestled safely at the back of his head and repeated the wording of the card.

The official nodded. "Good. Best of luck." She handed the piece of parchment back to him with a tight smile.

For a moment, Chase didn't know where to go. Then he noticed the single person still standing between him and the growing line of people. The High Elementalist. With a shrug, he grabbed the parchment and walked to her, holding up the document. As he neared her, his eyes shot up in surprise. The seeming movement of her dress and hair wasn't just an effect. There was an actual ongoing zone of rapidly moving air surrounding her. It almost ripped the document out of his hands.

The woman's eyes barely seemed to gloss over the contents of the document. Instead, it seemed as if her eyes bored into him, seeing straight through him. Finally, her arm shot out, and she indicated a spot to her left, a third from the far end of the line.

Chase walked to the indicated spot. Then the shoe finally dropped and he lambasted himself for being so slow. They were ranking them. Of course. Anybody at the other end of the line was already doomed to get kicked back out or go into the army, while those on his end were...well, they might have a decent chance of making it into the towers. That very much would depend on how powerful and useful the rest of the applicants were. Also...that might mean that he would get in, but some of the others wouldn't. That'd depend entirely on how they ranked their usefulness, their attributes, and cards on the whole.

He wondered for a short while why they would do it like this. It seemed unnecessarily cruel. They could just wait and deliberate on the results instead of having people go through this ordeal. Except...okay, he got it. If people could go back to the city and spread the information about the questions, it would make it much easier for others to prepare and give them the information they needed to make it in. This way, people would go straight into the Elemental towers or the army, and the secret would stay here. Also, he guessed, it did send a couple of pretty important messages. One, that they didn't really care about you, but they cared a *lot* about strength. If somebody else could do the job better than you? They'd get in. Also, that they really, really cared about their applicants if they had a Tier six like the High Elementalist making the final decisions on their rankings.

Chase's nerves were entirely shot as he watched his own crew divided after him.

Sera took up a place right near the end of the line. The good end. To be expected, really. Talented healers were rare to begin with, and with her impressive attributes to boot, she'd be a safe win for any force.

Liam also made it pretty far up the line. His combination of Strength, massive Toughness, and cards that enabled him to take a beating were a safe bet anywhere.

Kith...didn't. Clearly, they weren't too impressed by a summoner with a deficit in Mental Power. Despite that, he must have managed to say something to make them consider him, because he made it past the halfway mark. Barely.

Cilia was a surprise. Chase was afraid that her lack of crafting experience would make an issue of her prospects. Only, it would seem that they valued combat experience and good attributes over actual crafting knowledge—that, or they had a dearth of good crafters—because she was placed even farther up the line than Chase.

Slowly, the lines progressed and Chase watched people having their fates decided for them. He kept counting, over and over again. Kith was close to the cutoff line, but fortunately, the back of the line seemed to have some of the weaker prospects, and he was slowly moved across to where he'd possibly be accepted into the towers.

People, in general, took the decisions well. Those who applied must know, better than they did, at least, what their decision entailed the moment they entered the application process. There was some grumbling from people who watched themselves displaced farther down the line, where they could see that they weren't going to make it into the towers.

One Elemental started shouting, how he was better and stronger than somebody who'd made it in last time. His tantrum didn't last long, and he was forcibly carried away. After that, people stopped complaining.

At long last, the final applicant was processed and, half-sulking, pointed to the bad end of the line.

The High Elementalist turned toward them. Raising her hands, the stack of parchments she'd received from the applicants joined together in a fluttering dance around her. "We appreciate you all. You, the assembled races of Ordei, have stood up before us today and shown your willingness to lay down your lives for the benefit of the Elemental lands. The towers will respond in kind." She turned toward the far end, with the people who had been tested, but found too weak, too unskilled or unfit to make it into the towers. "To those of you who do not, after this test, currently have the strength we need to defend our home, I say this. Do not be discouraged. Take this lesson to heart, but do not let it wear you down. In the year to come, you will be tested; you will be hardened, and you will prove your worth. Of those who try to apply a second time, more than every second person makes it past the cut."

A murmur of appreciation arose among those bound for the army. Chase noticed that she didn't mention just how many had died before then.

"As a gesture of goodwill, to help you make it back to us, I give you this. Every single person who is bound for conflict after today will be awarded with an enchanted piece of armor."

A roar arose among the crowd—even those who knew they'd made the cut. Something like that might mean the difference between life and death.

Chase reconsidered his stance. If they were willing to put that kind of money into their recruits...they might be less fatalistic toward the applicants than the Lightborn.

"A final word. A lot of you have kept a count and believe you have made it in. That, however, is not how it works here. One thing you will learn quickly among the towers is that we place a lot of importance on practicality. Hence, one thing is what you might be able to handle in theory. Now? You get to prove it."

The confusion was physical. From the tables behind the High Elementalist, the six people who Chase had thought were scribes or administrators arose. The first one—the water-aspected Elemental with the curls—stepped forward and spoke up with a voice almost too low to hear. "I am Aminda Shallowstream. All prospective casters, please follow me."

Damn. Chase finally got it. The bastards. They weren't in the clear yet. They were actually going to make them prove they had what they claimed.

CHAPTER 11

"There is something eminently wondrous about the towers. Not just their looks, their sturdiness, magnificence, or towering heights. No, the fact that, despite all their vaunted greatness, they care about results above all. Words are cheap. Delivering on them, less so." That *is* an impressive claim. Among the Lightborn, everything was about connections and political favors. Time will tell if this is just another exaggeration. (Page 23.)

"This is our penultimate test. It is quite simple. Judging from the last couple of examples, I believe that most of you are looking forward to something that requires less thinking for you to complete." The unnamed woman—a middle-aged water-aspected Elemental, who looked and acted as though she'd just bitten into a rancid sausage—had been the final administrator. According to an awed recruit, she was also the highest-ranked rogue teacher among the towers. "Rogues are used for many different aspects in the field. As messengers, scouts, assassins, or as combatants with less focus on direct approaches. One thing that holds true for every single one of these is that you will need speed, agility, and control of your body. That is what we test here. You simply need to enter this building and make it to the other side, without the use of any cards."

Chase sighed in relief. He really didn't mind that. So far, they'd been through a bunch of different tests, each of them more grueling than the last.

They'd done physical tests until they couldn't stand upright anymore, testing their endurance, running style...even taken it so far as to put them unarmed up against an experienced soldier inside a marked-off area. The marks from that one still hurt. He'd managed to avoid the soldier for a while, but couldn't take him down.

For another test, they'd been forced to memorize messages, been given a limited time to recall as much about a scene as possible, then asked to retell the details and more. He praised the Dark for Sera's mental training there. Several of her exercises were pretty close to that experience, and he'd done fairly well there, he believed.

For hours, they'd moved back and forth between physical and mental tests, pushing Chase on areas where he sometimes didn't even know what the Pits was going on. What on Ordei would they learn from him trying to speak with four summoners and then pairing them with their summons? It made no sense.

Running and dodging? That was different. That was like coming home.

Chase was the fifth person to enter the building. It was a simple wooden door, yet there was nothing to be spotted from the outside, and no sounds escaped the building.

He entered the door at a sprint. Whatever they might have hidden for him in here, it shouldn't be able to tax his stamina to the point where it'd be an issue. In short, overwhelming speed was his friend.

Inside, he was met with a choice. A short hallway split into three. Chase approached them fast, turning left without stopping to slow down. If there was one thing he'd learned running away from the city guard and other pursuers in Isarn, it was that a questionable choice at speed often beat making a slow choice. And the woman had asked for speed.

A movement from above caught his attention. He doubled down and sped up. Something slammed into the ground behind him with a loud thud.

Chase's nostrils flared as he tamped down hard on a burst of panicked nerves. It was like that, was it? Traps and obstacles to slow him down or knock him out? They weren't going to catch *him* out! He kept his vision expanded on the entire hallway, unfocused, to keep him more attentive to movement.

Another turn, another left. This one turned into a dead end just five feet past the corner, with a large trap door slamming open at the first touch of his leading foot. Darkness hid what lay underneath. Chase managed to set off into a half-jump with his back foot, slam into the wall at the end of the doorway, and use it to clumsily jump back to the other side of the gaping hole.

With a muted curse, he stumbled back into his run, taking the next left. Those bastards wouldn't get him!

Nearly a minute later, he sprinted out the open door at the opposite end of the building, gasping for air and skidding to a sliding halt on the well-polished cobblestones of the courtyard. They really had pulled out all the stops. Blades swinging out from half-hidden recesses, darts flying from suspicious holes in the walls, floorboards breaking away to try to trap the foot—he really wanted to have a chat with whoever designed the damn place. The wide, wooden-mace-wielding fighter guarding the final doorway was a nice touch, too—if you were a sadist. Chase made it past with a shoulder hurting from a glancing blow.

Chase had an inkling who might be the designer. At the very least, he thought he caught a tiny smile playing at the edge of the middle-aged rogue's mouth when she saw him emerge.

She glanced at a glass contraption which had water slowly dripping through a curved tube. Then she nodded. "Eighty-two seconds. Could be worse." Making a shooing gesture with her hands, she added, "Move along now. The next one will arrive soon."

There was just a single test following this. A perception test, asking the rogues to figure out who among a teeming crowd of soldiers milling about was a pickpocket. Most people were able to spot at least one of the three pickpockets moving about the crowd. Only Chase and a water-aspected Elemental girl, who looked like she'd come straight from the slums, spotted the rogue instructor pocketing items from the applicants as well.

All the prospective students were left to themselves for fifteen minutes in the courtyard where they'd first gathered to answer questions, while the rogue teacher and her assistants went off to deliberate. The applicants stood mostly to themselves, the rare few who knew each other clustering together, while several complained about certain aspects of some of the tests.

Finally, they started to shout out names. At first, they believed they were the ones who'd made it, reacting with cries of relief. Only, it turned out everybody was called, one by one, and ordered to enter a short tent at the end of the courtyard. This time, Chase was one of the last ones to be called, and his heart pounded wildly. He entered the tent, blinking as he realized the sound from the crowd outside was cut off entirely.

Inside, the rogue instructor sat in a comfortable chair. She had no documents, no notes. Her hands were cradled as her eyes bored into his, then scanned around and behind him for threats. "Chase. No last name. Decent attributes, especially for a Darkborn with no prospects. Good movement skills and rapid reaction. Good perception. Acceptable cards, especially training-wise. *Absolutely atrocious* learning and knowledge base. Also, clearly handicapped with the lack of a hand. Why should the towers welcome you?"

Chase blinked at the harsh words. Then he had an epiphany and nearly chuckled. "Honestly? Because I think you've already made up your mind. This is likely to see how I react to stress. In short, though? You should welcome me, because my lack of learning and knowledge isn't due to laziness on my part, but because I've always been poor. That, I can catch up. Also, I don't lack *all* knowledge. I know how to read people—and that is harder to teach than how to read letters."

She frowned up at him. The prim features of the middle-aged woman tightened even further. The water aspect of her lineage made her skin glisten like she'd been sitting in the sun. "That is extremely presumptuous of you, young man. And you didn't even comment upon your handicap."

"I disagree. It's not presumptuous. Not if I'm right." Chase beamed, heart pounding harder than after the physical tests. With a shrug, he continued. "As to my handicap? It really is only a handicap if you pigeonhole me into specific functions that I wouldn't work well for, like a ranged attacker. For everything else, I've lived like this long enough to know my limitations—and in certain situations, it can even be an advantage. Because nobody ever expects a *cripple* to be able to fight."

The two stared at each other for a while, neither lowering their gaze. Finally, the upper lip of the Elemental quirked up slightly. "I expect you to match that wit with effort, young man."

"I look forward to it."

Chase was led away from her tent, to join up with everybody else who'd been allowed in. It felt like a huge weight had lifted off his chest. He'd done it! Whatever else happened, even if the other four failed to get in, he'd be able to join the Elemental school and would be able to, possibly, complete his task and earn the reward. Not just that; he *knew* that now that he was in, he'd be able to find connections, create openings for himself and his crew. He'd be able to work people, figure out shortcuts, and find a way for them all to be able to stay here.

The cloudy weather of the day had dissipated somewhat and the sun peeked down upon him. Chase halted in his stride as he saw the Elemental towers from up close in all their majesty.

It wasn't just the magnitude of the constructions. Nor was it the shapes or the materials involved. It was more the sheer impossibility of the combination. Down where Chase walked, the plateau surrounding the mountain formed a tight circle, a ring around the towers themselves, crammed full with buildings and people walking to and fro. There were carts with produce rushing in and out of the gate, and soldiers training and marching about. All told, it gave the impression of a place that never stood still. The towers themselves were different.

The central parts of the towers must once have been the mountain itself. It was still mostly mountain-shaped, in general, as in having a general cone shape, and growing thinner toward the top, miles up. That was the only comparison he really could make with a real mountain. Any material visible from outside was clearly magical in nature. From a couple hundred feet away, he spotted no obvious seams, no places where blocks were put together—just one wide, unnaturally smooth surface. It looked like a large cone-shaped tower, studded with arrow slits on the first handful of floors, only with dimensions that belied physics. It must have been at least a mile tall. And that was just the central shape.

Even with that unlikely feat of engineering and magic, the towers themselves put the central part to shame. That street kid had said that the towers were what happened when you got experienced crafters from each aspect to work together. The towers... and miracles, clearly.

The western side was dominated by the water aspect, and it seemed almost a living organism rather than something crafted. Sprouting from a gargantuan bulb-like construction near the base of the mountain, which, to Chase, looked disturbingly like a living, beating heart, the water-aspected constructions stretched upward, as if yearning for the warmth of the sun. Some were wide and squat, like gigantic tuber vegetables. Others were spindly and thin, intertwined around central constructions like vines stretching around a tree, toward the sky. As if in defiance of natural order, a constant blanket of roiling clouds moved around the western side, only allowing for occasional glimpses of the constructions. True to the name, yet, again, defying normal precepts, streams of water fell down the sides of the mountain alongside the constructions, sometimes falling down the towers themselves, sometimes following carved streams around or *through* the massive buildings.

One didn't have to guess as to where the water-aspected side of the towers bordered upon the northern earth-aspected part. The line where the two met were writ in green, as an abundance of greenery divided the two styles. At first glance, it looked overwhelming and uncontrolled. Yet, upon further inspection, it was clear that all growths were held to that thin stretch of border, kept carefully in check. The earth-aspected zone of the towers were, Chase decided, the ugliest parts—only, that didn't make them any less impressive. Where the water-aspected parts looked natural and flowing, as if grown or carved from the water streams, the earthen towers were clearly man-made, squarish, and harsh against the backdrop of the tall mountain. Everything about those towers shouted defiance, power, and solidity. When Chase had first seen the earthen embankment surrounding Soil, he'd been impressed. Yet, that felt like a child's construction, compared to the militant, stoic towers of the earth-aspected side of the Elemental towers. They were the constructions clinging the tightest to the slopes of the mountain, giving off a feeling that if you wanted to challenge their solidity, you'd have to take down the entire mountain.

Along the east came the fire-aspected part of the towers. With the earth-aspected side stoutly emanating defiance in the face of any attackers, the fire-aspected towers shouted the largest, daring to take on *anybody*—challengers, beasts and human alike...natural or supernatural forces. The fire side was crafted in blackened, red and orange materials. They sported a creation of battlements and whirling, moving materials that covered their entire side of the mountain, carving the natural craggy development of the peaks into one mind-boggling, flowing, domineering visual aspect. The entire side of the edifice shimmered, as if covered in a heat haze. The structure looked for the world like an implausibly large flame licking up toward the heavens. Apparently not ones for subtlety, both sides of the fire-aspected divide were limned by slow-flowing streams of living fire.

After the glaring display of power, Chase almost suffered visual whiplash from taking in the air-aspected side of the tower. Where earth was ready for any attackers, and fire shouted at anybody, even *gods* to come against them, the air-aspected side seemed to defy gravity itself. The buildings were thin, white and beautifully fragile-looking, clearly too spindly to reach as high as they did—yet even so, they persevered. Needles reached into the sky in artistic clusters of thin towers. Some were solitary, reaching hundreds and hundreds of feet into the air with no support. Others were artfully arranged in clusters, painting geometric symbols, eye-pleasing images...in one place, even the clear-cut image of a large gem rose. Stretching between the thin towers were unnaturally narrow, uncovered walkways, connecting the air-aspected buildings in an artful network. Chase's hand started sweating at the mere thought of walking out on one of those walkways, a thousand feet, a mile, above the abyss below.

At the peak of the mountain, a single construction reigned—a huge, towering dome. Without any of the overt signs of the Elemental aspects, it observed the rest, like a kingly crown upon the brow of a benevolent dictator. It covered the entire top, the circular dome capping the mountain itself. Where every other building on the mountain had a stylized look according to their aspect, this tower was entirely translucent, with a slight gleam of magic making it shine in the intermittent sunrays.

Not everything was entirely divided. Some aspects were universal. For instance, smaller blockish towers, ostensibly for defense, clearly showing the earth-aspected style, were distributed all over the mountain. From some of the larger towers, the spindly, whimsical walkways so rich on the air-aspected side connected earth, fire, and water alike. And carefully cultivated water streams did adorn the outsides of the mountain everywhere, though nowhere as dominant as on the water side.

Somebody bumped into Chase and cursed at him. With a mental effort, Chase brought his gaze down to the crowd waiting for them and started to walk again. At least he wasn't the only one looking like a country bumpkin, gawking at the sight. Meanwhile, it was damn easy to take in the locals, who marched on, focused on the gathering ahead. In small groups, other acceptees joined the crowd, having aced their respective tests.

In ones and twos, loud shouts arose as people joyfully spotted friends and companions among the waiting groups, or started shouting for news of those they couldn't see. Chase was no exception. He sprang forward with a cry of relief as he spotted both Cilia and Sera chatting at the edge of the groups.

"You made it! I'm so damn proud of you!" In relief, the thief leapt on the two, enfolding both girls in a hug.

Sera froze entirely, then relaxed with an impish grin.

Cilia, meanwhile, suffered the hug for a handful of seconds before disentangling herself. "Enough already." Less harshly, she continued, "How were your tests? Have you seen any of the others?"

"Haven't seen them. I'll have to admit, I expected the tests to be harder. Especially with, y'know." He waggled his stump back and forth. "Anyway, you should have seen some of the competition. There was this water-aspected rogue, dressed out in the most expensive garb. She was so nervous she dropped her daggers, twice. Amateur hour. How about yours?"

Sera shrugged. "I found it manageable. They had a lot of questions regarding knowledge—more than I expected for a healer class. Anatomy, alchemy, herbs, disease, and such. In Isarn, if you have a healer card that is just slightly acceptable, you will be accepted into the ranks regardless of how little you know. Here, it would seem, they have higher standards."

Cilia frowned. "I don't know. It was weird. I never really felt any pressure like they were going to let me go. Even with me being a questionable crafter at best. From their questions, it felt more like they wanted to reassure themselves I was ready to learn."

"Huh. That *is* weird," Chase said. "How about their tests, then? They had me run through traps and pitfalls."

"Nothing of that kind. They had a couple questions about my combat experience and seemed positively surprised that I'd actually *seen* action. The only tests were to see me try to craft something. Which, well, that went okay."

Chase snorted. "You're a Step-eleven crafter with combat experience who's almost entirely focused on Mental Power and who's wasted few points on extraneous attributes. I think they'd take you even if you were—wait! There's Liam!"

The tall Lightborn walked toward them, alongside a smaller group of people. The rest of the group spouted small wounds and scuffs, one earth-aspected teen limping markedly. Liam was chatting animatedly with the teen, who seemed awkward about the situation. Soon, he disentangled himself from the rest of the group with a cheery wave and made it over to the others. "Well, that was fun."

"Fun," Cilia said emotionlessly. "You've just edged out the most promising contenders for one of the most prestigious learning facilities of the world and you call it fun. *It was nothing of the sort.*" Her eyes shot daggers at the broad man.

"Aw, lighten up, Cil. It was all good fun. They were good sports about it. Some of them were damn good too. I'll be feeling a few of those strikes in the morning." He laughed. "Where's Kith hiding?" He blinked, looking around the crowd.

Chase looked at the ground. "We're still waiting for him. Some of that group over there were among the summoners, I'm certain. But I don't know. He *was* right near the losing side of the line when we started."

"What? No! There's no way he's not making it. That wouldn't be right. We need to stick together!" Liam rumbled. "Look, I'm going to go talk to those others, see what's going on."

With a sigh of relief, Sera interrupted him, pointing. "There is no need. There he is."

Kith walked at the forefront of three other summoner prospects, following another servant. Where the other groups arriving were mostly overjoyed by having been accepted, Kith's group looked anything but. The other summoners glared daggers at Kith's back. Each of them was bruised and bloodied, clearly having been put through their paces. Kith, shorter and smaller than any of the rest, stood tall. He sported a massive black eye; a tear on his arm bled freely, dripping blood onto the grounds. Yet, he walked with a triumphant gaze in his eyes, oozing satisfaction.

Liam enfolded him in a massive hug.

Kith hissed in pain, but returned the hug, patting him on the back. "There we go, big guy." He disengaged himself from the tall man and looked at the others in relief. "We all made it? That's a damn miracle."

Chase laughed. "We were starting to get worried about you, man. Way to slack off and save your entrance for last."

Kith snorted. "They were not impressed with my alternate approach to summoning. I'm guessing, with all their walls, they're fans of the theory where you stand safely in the distance and let your summons roam below."

Sera looked to the three others walking past them. "It certainly looks like you convinced them, though." She moved in close to him, and her card flashed.

With a nauseating movement of flesh, the wound in his arm oozed closed and the swelling in the eye reduced to where he could see out of the eye again.

"I took a hands-on approach. I dared the teacher to put me up against any other applicant here. Some of those poor bastards are going to be feeling their defeat in the morning."

One of the passing summoners turned around. He was a scrawny kid, maybe around sixteen years old. His earth-aspected Elemental looks, along with some of the baby fat still on his face, made him look like a painting that hadn't dried properly. "Laugh all you like, you nutjob. You'll die first time you're past the wall, while the rest of us look down on you."

"That would be more convincing if I hadn't just beat the snot out of you, whelp. Now, shush. The big hats are about to speak." Kith grinned at the poor youngster.

The High Elementalist Tatiana Skysworn was back in front of their, now reduced, numbers. This time, her voice was equally ceremonial, but contained a hint of joy. "I am thrilled to see all of you here. My fellow teachers tell me that they are impressed by the overall level of competence among you. Not only that, a large number of those who failed to pass our requirements have joined with the armies to grow in strength and make it next year. Let their dedication be a guiding light to us all."

She beamed out at all of them, before raising both hands. "I realize today has been hard for you. For today, however, you are done. All you need to do is follow my associates, and you will be fed and introduced to your home for the next two years." The ceremonial tinge to her voice dropped off, and her voice grew warm and fond. "The year to come is not going to be easy. There will be trials to overcome, and nobody here is guaranteed graduating or being offered a place among the Protectors. Yet, you have all done amazing today. Let me say this with all my heart. *Welcome to the Elemental towers.*"

CHAPTER 12

*"What they all tend to forget, each and every outsider,
is this. We require much from our Protectors, because we need
to. We cannot bring the numbers to bear that the Lightborn do.
We do not hold the advantageous terrain that Liberty does.
Hence, each of us needs to be better and stronger than the
best of the others."* Heh. Again with the elitism. I cannot wait
to see how that actually stacks up against reality. If it's just
half as hard as he claims, we're going to be worked to the
bone. (Page 15.)

The group quickly realized several things as they were led into the towers proper. The first detail was hammered home after just the second style change and turn of the large corridors. This place was going to be *incredibly* difficult to navigate. It looked like it had been created one room at a time, through a collaboration of people with wildly differing tastes and no consensus on what the end result should be like. They were led through hallway after hallway, past locked doors, towering statues, and elaborate paintings. Everywhere, people hurried around, officious-looking administrators brushing shoulders with dust-covered workers. So far, there was no logic, no rhyme or reason they could see. The only real conclusion was that they weren't going to be seeing a lot of sun in the towers. Most of their walking was in rune-lit corridors, with no sign they were actually on a mountain.

The mess hall looked like anything *but* a mess hall. Towering arches covered the ceiling high above, and the dark grey of the distant walls were covered with elaborate mosaics on the windows that led to the outside. Chase decided that, were the leaders of the Church of the Circle to see this place, they'd want to steal it for a cathedral immediately. The place had a religious look to it, like the low stage at the far end of the room should be used for sermons and not for the collection of dirty crockery, while the heavy wooden furniture really should be replaced with stone benches and a few hundred fanatic believers to sell the look.

To Chase, the experience was near-religious anyway. The food was simply divine. Outside of his few meals at the Moonlit Moat in Isarn, Chase had never been allowed to try anything as good or as plentiful as what they were fed in the towers. From the look of things, however, this was simply a matter of fact to the residents, who seemed less interested in devouring the wondrous spread than anything else.

Everywhere around them, chatting students sat in an informal atmosphere. All the new inductees had been placed at two long wooden tables at the center of the room, like colorful animals for the remaining students to gawk at. And gawk they did. They all felt the attention, as the surrounding students openly watched and loudly commented on the newcomers and how liable they were to get thrown out in the first month, how spindly and weak they looked.

Still, Chase didn't mind. He could see the hazing for what it was. A ritual, performed every time new students were admitted, showcasing the superiority of those who'd already spent months on the inside. He had to admit that the difference between the older students and themselves was marked. Not only were the existing students, on the whole, in excellent shape, sporting impressive physiques, they also *looked* experienced, with sharp, focused gazes that made Chase think of Inquisitor Callas...hunters looking for prey. He was impressed by what he saw and, despite the less than advantageous situation they found themselves in, looked forward to experiencing the schooling that left these students looking as formidable as they did.

"Darkborn scum."

The voice came from behind Chase. He turned his head to see what he was dealing with, before feeling his chair kicked out from under him. Chase stumbled back, his stump striking the floor, keeping him from a complete wipe-out. Instinctually, his hand flew to his belt, and he sprang to his feet, dagger in hand.

"See? That's the kind of people they let in here! The lowest of the low, curs so untrained they're prepared to bite at the hand that feeds them at the least provocation." The speaker, talking loud enough for anybody to hear, was an Elemental, slicked-back dark hair and oily features clearly showing off his water-aspected characteristics. Behind him, four other Elementals trailed, including the fire-aspected Elemental who had insulted them in the crowd outside. All looked at him with disdain.

Chase looked his water-aspected attacker up and down, quickly evaluating him. Tall. Muscled and athletic. Poised, with a readiness that clearly portrayed him as combat-trained. Cardless, though. Chase knew beyond a doubt that he could take him down, especially if he used cards. Only, he could see the attention of the crowd was on him, and the mood did not look positive. At the far end of the room, a woman in a teacher's uniform looked on without intervening. Yeah. A fight would likely not end well for him. "What's your problem, prick?" he asked.

"My problem?" The man scoffed, looking at his followers. "I'll tell you my problem. This moment today was going to be the proud entrance of me and my kid sister into the towers. Only, I am the only one here. She's walking back to our parents, head hung low in shame as she contemplates how to break the news that a goddamn *mongrel* made it in instead of her. And here you all sit, sullying the place that proper people should be sitting in."

Chase could see where this was going. He couldn't see any way to keep it from heading to a bad place, though, only minimize the collateral damage. He shrugged. "Sorry to hear that, mate. It's nothing I did on purpose... But of course, you knew that. Still, attacking me over your sister's failure? How does that make sense? Your superiors made the rules. Only the best get in, right? My friends and I are here because we were better than her, plain and simple. So, either go blame those in power, or go suck a turnip. Whatever you decide, *go away.*"

His voice pitched higher. "Typical outsider speak. You come here, take up space and resources from real people, increase our risks, and act all high and mighty. Only, you're not going to stay around. Why do I know this?" He put his head real close to Chase's, letting him observe the thin layer of moisture on his skin. The scent of cleanness, of nature was mixed with an underlying hint of spice Chase didn't recognize. "Because your kind never does. You flunk out, desert from the towers, or just straight up *die*. Incompetents and cowards all. You can say whatever you want. But if you're trying to convince me that you're going to stick around, that you can do better than a family who's defended the towers for eight generations? I'm not buying it."

Chase reeled. How could he possibly rebut that? It was a baseless accusation, yet he didn't have any proper arguments that would back his side. "Well, I'm not selling anything. We're here because we want to make a home for ourselves—a *real* home—here in the Elemental lands. We'll pay the cost too. If you don't believe that? Not my Lights-cursed problem. The only real problem here is that I'm trying to eat in peace, and your smell is making the cream curdle. So, would you mind doing like your sister and get out of here?"

The Elemental colored in rage. His fingers inched toward a dagger on his belt. With a snarl, he edged his hand away. "I am going to get you for that! Just you wait and see." He turned and stalked away, his flunkies following on his heels.

Chase grimaced, putting his chair back and sitting down with a sigh. "Well, that went well."

From a bit farther down the table, another rookie Elemental burst into raucous laughter. "Making an enemy of Ernest

Chalico on your first day? If that's your definition of *well*, don't invite me to your team, darkie."

The rest of the meal went by blessedly uninterrupted. After a while, they got to enjoying the food again, comparing the different sorts of tests they'd been put through. It was becoming clear to them that the towers stressed certain approaches and strengths. Speed and agility for rogues. Strength and hardiness for warriors. Overall healing capabilities, card-based or otherwise for healers. Attributes and sheer mental concentration capabilities for crafters. Also, apparently, the ability to send off summons to die in place of the summoners. The Elementals at their table didn't bother talking to them. Chase's poor reception had clearly not gone unnoticed, and the other aspirants stonewalled them. Even Liam had no luck engaging them in conversation.

When they finished eating, the High Elementalist arrived at the front of the mess. Silence spread in seconds as they realized who was waiting for them to wake up.

"Soon, you will look back to this first day, and recall it with fond remembrance. We are entirely aware that it will be one of the hardest, most stressful, and experience-packed days of your lives. Yet, that is what we expect of our Protectors. Hardiness. Perseverance. Mental fortitude. I am thrilled to be able to tell you the good news now. The only remaining test of the day is the one most of you have been waiting for your entire lives. You are about to receive your first card."

The table erupted in cheers and excited chatter.

She looked down on them with a bemused expression. A gentle gesture created a funnel of air that pushed down the long table, catching their collective attention again. "At this point, I find it necessary to outline exactly what this means. Rumors are many, as are the customs of other nations." Her smile was kind, but hard. She gently touched her right arm. "We will unlock your access to your first card alone, regardless which Step you are on. Nothing more. If you make it into the Protectors, we will unlock the full suite. Those few of you still not on your fifth Step and able to earn your first card will do so during the first two months of your training. This way, we will be able to judge you on as level a playing field as possible. We want to know who will be the best fit for the towers in the long run, not just now.

"For practical reasons, let me say this, just once. We do not decide the aspect of the card choices you are offered. Even after years and years of study, we do not have a definite answer for that. Elementals of a certain aspect are more likely to gain cards of that aspect, but it is not a given. Apart from that, however, it seems to be mostly a question of your innermost personal convictions. Some are offered cards from several different aspects, while others only get to choose from one aspect. Once you have chosen? There will be no retrying. Even if you have your cards removed and earn them again, you will gain the same primary card. So, choose wisely."

Apart from the helpful information, Chase could see the issues with the recruitment straightaway. Of course, those who had other cards already, or those who'd walked further along the Steps would be more powerful. That meant, if they gave free access to all the cards, like the Lightborn did, that'd ensure that those further along the Tiers were more likely to become Protectors, even if the lower-Tier choices might outgrow them in time. This choice did a bit to even out that advantage, but didn't remove it entirely. Obviously, he wasn't going to complain, considering it meant that he and his companions had a decent step up on the competition, already having cards beyond the first Tier.

"These cards, you must know, *are not yours to keep*." Her voice was strict now, unbending. "In the first years, we allowed everybody who'd earned the privilege of competing to keep their cards. That, unfortunately, opened the gates to a lot of unwanted attention—people who got their cards and then quit the training, enjoying the unearned power they'd received. No. Those of you who flush out before time will have your Elemental cards removed. I am aware it is not the same way it is done in other lands, but this is the Elemental way."

Chase grimaced. He hadn't seen *that* coming. He'd figured at the very least they'd be able to leave the towers stronger than when they entered. Ah, well. That just meant they had to hang in there. Also, she said that everybody was going to hit the fifth Step during training, so at least that meant they'd be gaining Ænima, and grow somewhat stronger, even if their group was already well beyond the first Tier. Also, with his training card, he'd definitely be earning additional attributes.

"Access to the towers is always open, though. Anybody will be able to join up and try out for the training at a later date. Now, follow me. Even if you do not make it into the Protectors, this will be a moment worth telling your future children."

She started for the exit, and the students followed individually or in small groups, abuzz with excitement. Chase and the others were no different. Discounting what might eventually happen months from now, today they were growing stronger. They talked about possibilities while they walked...strategies, ideas for what they were going to receive.

Within the first ten minutes, the chatter had died down due to the constant climbing. Wherever they were going, it was only up. One staircase after the other, they rose higher and higher in the air. From the occasional window, arrow slit, or ventilation access, they could see the ground below growing increasingly distant.

The minutes ticked by, and some of the students stopped talking entirely, focusing their energy on the climb, panting with the effort. Chase and the others were decently off, compared to the average, though Cilia's cheeks were flush with more than just excitement. Still, they climbed.

Now, they moved past security checkpoints. Armed guards, rune-clad casters, summoners and their exotic summons stood prepared at fortified positions or roamed the halls, alert and dangerous. Glowing magical inscriptions covered the walls on occasion—for decoration or for defensive purposes, nobody knew.

Their surroundings changed so often it left them overwhelmed, unable to mentally keep up. Still, they climbed. Once, they had to pause, as they were led to cross one of the spindly bridges on the air-aspected side of the towers. Regardless of the fact that the bridge was covered in some sort of protective shell, guarding them from the wind which had to be howling at hurricane speeds at this height, one student—a thick-set, earth-aspected Elemental—was overcome with vertigo and had to be helped across with closed eyes.

That gave Chase the chance to really take in the surroundings. They were maybe two-thirds up now, and in between clouds, he managed to catch glimpses of the dome above. It likely had a majestic name, at least if there was any justice in the world. Where the outer additions to the towers were dedicated to the separate aspects covering each side, the upper third of the mountain was different. It was created as a cohesive whole, every aspect included in every creation, every building, each stretch of ground. The equidistant, needle-thin towers that jutted into the sky all around the central dome all sported harsh-looking earth-aspected stations, where creatures or people watched from the inside. The towers gleamed with magical shields, and carried large, glowing ballista-like installations, oozing with threat as they pointed down on the lands far below.

It was a war, of beauty clashing with functionality and the ever-present presence of force, ready to be thrown against enemies. Sometimes, the massive constructions were beautiful enough it left Chase breathless. At other times, they were bare bones, focused on violence and violence alone, like when they were led single-file through a thin tunnel entrance and then through a rough dome brimming with Protectors, a killing ground shaped only with defense in mind.

Yet, the dome outshone it all. Above every surrounding tower, the perfect half circle dominated the skies. Every inch was covered in magical script, runes, or installations, to the point where it was hard to even look at. It shone, with magic, with light, with sheer power.

Several security checkpoints later, they climbed a large, wide spiral staircase surrounding the peak of the mountain like a deity-sized viper aiming to squeeze the life out of the snow-covered slopes. Finally, they arrived at the wide bridge leading to the top of the entire construction. The very top of the towers, high enough to challenge the heavens. A single group of Protectors stood there, the image of professionalism. They bowed, making way for the High Elementalist to walk past.

Bedazzled and half-blinded from the ever-present magic that was thick enough in the air it was almost tangible, they followed along, slack-jawed and wide-eyed. Finally, they were allowed to see it. The center of power. The core of the towers.

From the outside, the dome looked impressive. From inside, it was outright impossible. Towering walls shot hundreds of feet into the air before curving inward and meeting in a seamless junction at the top. Every part of the walls and roof was covered with vivid colors, every inch sporting a retelling of some sort. Chase saw battles, diplomatic occasions, cards being wielded in hundreds of different ways, all around the recurring image of building, improving, and defending this very dome.

Cilia made a noise low in her throat. She looked at the walls with longing, like she wanted nothing else than to dedicate her life to studying everything in here.

Kith jabbed her with an elbow, breaking her out of her reverie. She glared at him, right until she noticed that the High Elementalist was waiting for them.

The interior of the dome was sparse. A central setting of five equally large throne-like chairs were set around a huge, circular table in the center. Somehow, that felt right. The burdens of years and years of history and magic pushing down on where the current decision-makers in the towers gathered to steer the Elementals in the right direction. Divided throughout the room were tall constructions. Large marble plinths rose into the air at even intervals, making the interior of the dome almost look like a petrified forest. At the top of each plinth were...decks. Held aloft by a four-fold Elemental force, each of the decks slowly rotated through the air over each plinth.

Chase gawked at them. There were so many! At least twenty-five. What did that mean? Chase was in the rare position of having obtained an original deck himself. He received another, secondary deck when he granted cards to ten wielders, and would get a third at a hundred wielders. When would the next come then? A thousand? Then ten thousand? But that progression couldn't continue, or the Elementals would need...okay, he didn't even have the math for that. A lot. They'd need a lot more citizens than what they actually had to earn the decks they had floating around right now.

With his attention all over the place, Chase missed the details of what was said. However, soon, the voice of the High Elementalist interrupted his distraction.

"This is the heart of our power. Behold and take it in, in all its splendor. This is what we fight to defend. The power at the core of Earth's Ward and the Elemental towers. Soon, they will also be a part of you, helping you grow stronger." Behind her, a plinth slowly receded, fading into the floor with no discernible mechanism guiding the descent.

With a beatific smile, the powerful Elemental grasped the deck reverentially and placed it on a pillow. She stood, expectant, her head bowed. "Whatever else may happen, you can say this. You have seen the heart of our might. Tomorrow, the decks will be back behind their defensive magic. Today, they are here, for you to earn a taste of what you might gain. Line up. Be patient. One by one, come and touch the deck. As we share our strength with the towers, let the towers share its strength with you."

The jostling was kept to a minimum. It seemed like most of the students were at least somewhat awestruck by the atmosphere of the situation and their surroundings. Right in that moment, they stood in the place where every single Protector since the creation of the towers had received their cards. Especially to the Elementals, that had them somber. The outsiders were less affected, but the mood and the setting kept them respectful.

One by one, the students were led to approach the High Elementalist, touch the deck, and choose their upgrade, upon which, they were carefully guided by a Protector to move back near the entrance to wait until the entire ceremony had concluded.

Chase and the others were among the middle of the pack. They were able to take in the situation from the outside, for once, with no pressure or rush to conclude. No Lightborn hunting them this very minute.

Some of the students finished their selections in seconds, walking away from the deck with a businesslike look, as though they'd known exactly what they'd be getting. Chase would bet those were the crafters. Others spent full minutes as they considered the choices. Eventually, the line ahead of Chase disappeared, and he was able to step forward, only slightly queasy at the prospect of increasing his powers.

He was "only" getting another Tier-one card. He already knew that, compared to the Dark and Light Tier-one cards he already held, it'd have to be insanely powerful to compete. The attribute boosts he would gain over time from his Sticky Fingers cards was enough to justify the legendary rank of the card, and his Steps of Brilliance card granted him impressive, gravity-defying movement skills. What could the Elements offer to match that?

The first notification had nothing at all to do with his card choices. He managed to suppress the need to giggle.

[You have located an Elemental Deck. As the holder of a Deck of Darkness, you have the option to accept cards from it or bond with the deck, absorbing it. Which do you choose?]

Wouldn't that *be interesting?* For the briefest of moments, some devil-may-care side of him considered absorbing it, just to see what would happen. Of course, he'd never get out of there alive, which removed part of the fun.

[You have decided not to bond with the Elemental Deck. Your Wellspring is unchanged. However, adding Elemental power to your arsenal improves your Title. In addition to the regular increased Agility from your Title, you receive +1 to each Attribute.]

Chase welcomed the notice with joy. It was yet another advantage their group would have, this one over *anybody* who didn't have cards of other colors! Enough of this, they'd be certain to rise to the top with little effort.

Finally, the cards were available, and Chase absorbed himself in the pros and cons of the different choices. This time, his Potential was hard at work. There was not a single Common card; two were Uncommon and a full *three* were Rare. Three of the cards were air-aspected, with the other two being fire and water. That...sounded about right to Chase. Speed and evasion for the majority, a bit of a temper, and a bit of a pathological need to avoid trouble? That might not be at all how things worked, but it seemed likely to him. No defensive, stoic earth-aspected cards for him. Heh. No surprise there.

He ignored the two Uncommon cards straightaway. Burst of Speed was exactly like his Light card, granting him a temporary increase to Agility. The fire card...might have some effect as a utility card, given that it would imbue any attack he made with fire damage for a short while, allowing him to actually set things on fire. Only...with the rest of his skillset in mind, it being designed around *avoiding* the worst direct confrontations, added damage was not his first choice. Especially considering some of the other possible choices.

[**No Easy Catch**
Rare, Elemental rogue
Tier one
Active, medium duration
The life of a rogue is often problematic. At some point or other, people tend to try to catch you, and never for positive interactions. This card makes your life easier, granting you a covering of magical residue, slippery to anybody but yourself. Any attempts at grabbing you, and even attacks that are not entirely head-on, will have a tendency to simply slide away. As the card increases in rarity, the effect becomes more pronounced.
"This ain't no catch and release program, scoundrel. Stand still, Fury rend you!"]

This card was...truly the wet dream of past him back in Isarn. This card would allow him to basically ensure that he'd never get caught. Today, it had slightly less appeal, unfortunately, since anybody coming after him was likely to want to kill him, eat him or both. Sure, it could still be useful. Just...less so, unless he spent his precious future upgrades to ensure it reached a higher rarity later on.

The next air-aspected card felt more like a winner.

[**Permanent Headwind**
Rare, Elemental rogue
Tier one
Permanent, passive
This card can be activated at any time and has no cooldown. When activated, centralized funnels of air will spawn, creating a constant headwind against any enemies. The funnels will move with the enemies and become more concentrated, the fewer enemies present.
"Oh, come now, Ramirez. This is but a friendly bout. We have barely touched blades. Why are you panting so? Have you become...winded?"]

Disregarding the horrible wordplay near the end, the card really *was* cool. It would be an excellent effect that could help Chase if he was up against several smaller enemies, like those blasted gleam skippers, and would likely also be a strong deterrent if he were up against a single person.

Yet, judging from the wording, it didn't sound like it would be overly effective if he faced several opponents at the same time, or a single large enemy. Also...it was Tier one. If he had to use this for a fight, he'd be giving up the mobility of Steps of Brilliance or the draining and boosting effect of Sticky Fingers. It...just didn't seem like it would be something that he would choose often. Especially with the last card he could choose.

[Squall Sling
Rare, Elemental rogue
Tier one
Active, instant
This card allows you to create a localized brief burst of concentrated air from your hand. This will allow you to add increased impetus to thrown items, deflect incoming strikes, or even change your direction mid-air.
Very short cooldown
"Out-throw Kargar the Giant? Kargar laugh! Kargar... HOW YOU DO THAT?"]

This was a solution to a problem he'd considered several times now. Chase knew that he'd never be the perfect ranged damage dealer...or even a *good* one. He wasn't strong enough to use throwing weapons properly, and his missing hand discounted the use of most ranged weapons. Yet, he'd seen time and time again, where he could've made a difference with some sort of ranged damage. This, combined with either a sling, some sort of ranged weapons like daggers, or some of Cilia's crafted items? Yeah, he could see that working just fine. With a lot of practice.

He made his choice of Squall Sling and was guided away with a wide grin on his face. Moments later, he was joined by Cilia, who'd made her selection in seconds. Easy, considering there were but two options available to her: water and fire. She'd gotten the increase in attributes from her Title too.

[Manipulate Fire
Common, Elemental crafter
Tier one
Permanent, passive
This card lights your inner furnace, allowing you to manipulate the fire aspect within you and, eventually, add them to your crafts in myriad ways. Manipulating your aspect will drain your stamina.
"Feel that? That rage, that wonderful heat. 'Tis yours, with but a thought. Feel it warm your soul."]

The others arrived in short succession and showed off their choices.

Liam's was simply wonderful. It had to be, to compete with his health-sharing One Heart, Opened card and his Waterfall of Light card that granted him the ability to run straight over enemies. And it was. It really was. Unsurprisingly, Liam's options had been all earth, except a single fire. He'd gone with earth too.

[**Become the Clay**
Uncommon, Elemental fighter
Tier one
Active, short duration
For a short while after activation, the outermost layer of your skin is converted into magically thickened wet clay. The clay will make it much harder for any attacks to pierce and may cause weapons to get stuck. The layer is heavy and may make it harder for you to move if you do not have the Strength to handle the weight.
Medium cooldown
"Give that back, you stupid, filthy weapon thief." A master duelist is defeated.]

Strength...was not an issue for Liam. Besides, it went *very* well with his Tier-two Dark card. Not only would that combination allow Liam a chance to avoid a lot of damage but it would also allow him and the Draining Ward to outlast just about anybody and drain their Agility at the same time.

Sera had opted for a different course. At this point, with her healing power secured via her Light Tier-one card and Dark granting her the attribute-boosting and anti-Light debuffing effect, she went for something else. A choice that Chase did not see coming.

[**Tongues of Pride**
Uncommon, Elemental healer
Tier one
Active, long duration
Once tapped, this card grants two effects. A weak fiery layer comes into being, adding itself to your weapon, as well as any allies' weapons in range. You will have weak fire damage added to your attacks. Finally, it carries a minor cleanse ability, continually working against any lower-Tier poison or debuffs used on allies.
"You ask me to bring the heat? Really? That is ironic." A Plague Knight falters.]

In itself, it was an excellent addition to their arsenal. Nothing purely overwhelming, but a definite strength boost against any enemies weak against magical damage—and from the wording, the fire damage would definitely grow as the card increased in rarity. The real surprise to Chase was that Sera was even offered fire cards—but according to her, she was offered two fire, three water. In that light, Chase could see it. Entirely evasive, right up until it was needed. Then, she didn't back down.

Kith, to nobody's surprise, went with something unconventional. His Tier-one cards so far were anything but the regular summoner approach, of course. The Dark Tier-one summon was an excellent tool for spying and blinding enemies, and the Light one allowed him to grow in strength and...well, blind his enemies. His new card was special, though, even for him.

[**Apian God**
Rare, Elemental summoner
Tier one
Active, medium duration
The queens are commonly recognized as the highest ranking in a beehive. However, with the use of this card, you summon something else: an apian god, controlling hundreds of tiny air-aspected summons. They are not as large as regular bees, but still cause tiny amounts of stinging air damage.
In addition to this, depending on the Mental Power of the summoner, nearby regular flying insects may recognize the natural hierarchy of the apian god and join in the attack.
"I. Summon you. Into. Beeing!" The Court summoner finally snaps.]

"Why is it that every time *I* pick a card, you all feel the need to criticize it?" Kith flung up his hands. "Cil changed her entire damn *class* and you didn't complain half as hard!"

"Feel free to take that question and really think about it, Kith," Cilia shot back. "Tier three, with so many cards to pick from...and you still don't have a single normal summon that can cause damage...except for that Crescendo of Might creature, which falls *apart* when it's done!"

Kith didn't relent in the least. "You saw those bastards. The only kind of summoner they wanted to accept was the weak, blubbering kind who needs to hide behind his mates while his friends do all the fighting. You want me to be like them? Forget it. This card, though, can help me win against any of those losers. If their attention is shot, I can beat them."

Behind them, a whipcord-lean Elemental glared daggers at Kith.

Kith didn't back down, merely glared back, pointing at the Elemental. "Yeah. Like that guy. You guys really think I'll make it in here without them calling me out all the damn time? I needed something that would help me put other summoners on the defensive."

Cilia raised an admonishing finger. Then she paused. "That's a decent point. It may not be the best choice for your balance overall, but it might do wonders in your specific situation. Also, I suppose it would be good if we are facing other people."

They talked quietly for a while longer, but their hearts really weren't in it. They could see others looking around with glazed-over eyes, all the action and new input of the day slowly getting to them.

Ten minutes later, the final student stumbled away from the deck with tears of joy streaming from his eyes.

The High Elementalist raised her hands. "Today, my friends, marks the most important day in your lives. You have been accepted as a part of the towers. Part of our tribe. Honor this. Respect it. And pay it back. You will find that we will return the respect in kind. Now, I know this has been a long day. Administrator Throckton will take care of you and lead you to your homes for the foreseeable future."

CHAPTER 13

"Words are easy. Especially, when it comes to promises. Yet, we deliver on our promises. Especially here. In the armies of Light, amid the Furyborn? You will never advance without proper backing and money. Here? If you are strong and talented enough, we pay for you." See, that's what a girl likes to hear. (Page 21.)

They didn't have to wait long. A bored-looking official addressed them. "Follow me," he droned, as if there were a thousand other things he'd rather be doing. Once they were all outside the dome and the massive doors slid closed behind them, he stopped. "In a moment, I will lead you to your rooms. Before you ask. No. We do not differentiate. Your rooms have been randomly assigned and no amount of complaining on your end will change things. Tomorrow, we will come to you in the morning and lead you back to the mess hall. Every morning for the first week, you will be guided from the mess hall to the classrooms. After that, it will be your own responsibility to show up to your classes on time. Any tardiness will subtract from your ranking for the next Culling. Any lack of respect, disturbance of the peace, or ill-conceived prank will subtract from your ranking."

The official let his gaze slide over the large group, letting it show clearly that he was *not* impressed. "We get typically between five hundred and a thousand of your kind in here each year. Only a couple of hundred make it to graduation. The rest flunk out, are injured or killed during training, or are banned from the towers for eternity. Do try to become part of the exception. As for any fancy magically crafted equipment, weaponry, and such? You are allowed to keep it in your rooms, but the towers will not be responsible for it if it is lost. You will be allowed to use some equipment or weapons in the towers, but only where it is previously cleared by your instructors. Otherwise, the only use your fancy equipment will see is on excursions into the city and for impressing the other empty-headed recruits."

Without another word, he turned around and marched off, letting the stunned students follow him in baffled amazement. That was a far cry from the warm, official welcome from the High Elementalist.

Half an hour later, the group sat clustered in Liam's room. After a lengthy walk through the bewildering labyrinth that was the towers and a speedy and chaotic distribution of the rooms, they'd been granted a key, a strict admonishment that they'd pay for any replacements, and were summarily left alone. The official had claimed the distribution of rooms was random, and Chase believed it. There was no rhyme or reason to the selection or the contents of their rooms. They'd gotten rooms close to one another, though, with Liam's, Chase's, and Sera's being next door.

Kith got a dark broom closet of a room with a bed and a tiny table—with a massive bookshelf taking up half the room, for some reason. Sera received an ascetic, brick-layered room, which mostly reminded them of a cell, but with a large outside balcony overlooking Earth's Ward below. Chase's room next door was a flowing, living collection of warped stone, looking like a cave above a waterfall, replete with an actual stream of water trickling through the corner of the room and a large, heavy window allowing him to get in some air. It smelled like nature, life, and wet soil. Cilia's was the most resplendent, small and cozy, yet with ornate, carved wood planking covering every inch of every surface, even the floors.

"This is the weirdest place," Chase mused, as he bounced up and down on the bed in Liam's room. "Look at this. Every room has the same granite-hard bed, one chair, and small bedside table. Apart from that, it's a crapshoot. I mean, you could fit Kith's room four times over in here."

"Rub it in, will ya?" Kith grumbled.

"I think I prefer my room." Cilia looked through the large, empty closet in the huge, wide brick-walled room. "This is a lot larger, but it has the personality of a workshop. Everything's scuffed and spent. It does allow all of us to be here without having to smell each other's armpits, though."

"I do agree with Chase here," Sera said. "It looks like no architectural planning was involved in preparing these rooms—like no professionals were involved. Perhaps the rooms were created before they knew that they were going to turn part of the towers into an academy. It *is* interesting to see that the lower layers have not been adapted into the different Elemental aspects, like the higher ones have."

Chase nodded. "Yeah. It feels more like whoever used to live in these rooms was left to do what they wanted with their own space. Some haven't done anything, while others, like the owner of my room, have gone nuts adapting it to their own style." He sighed and sat down on the bed, putting his back against the wall and rubbing his eyes. "We'd better focus on another sort of planning, though. What the Pits are we even *doing* in here?"

Liam sat down carefully next to him, leaned back, and closed his eyes. "You can say that again. Things have moved so fast, my head hasn't really had the chance to wrap itself around our situation."

Kith snorted. He sat with his chair facing backward. "I'll sum it up for you. We're screwed. We just wanted to find a place to stay where we wouldn't have to look over our shoulders for inquisitors all the damn time. Now, we're enrolled in the most dangerous academy in the world, where we'll be hard-pressed to even keep up, everybody hates us, and even if we are able to eventually graduate, we'll have to fight monsters for five damn years. If we wanted to die, we could've just joined the Lightborn armies! I mean, without being an indebted."

Cilia added drily, "You forgot that cloaked stranger."

Kith flung his hands into the air. "I wasn't done. But yeah. We also have to figure out a conspiracy for some damn secretive clandestine agent of sorts, who'll likely get us all killed in the process or backstab us even if we *do* succeed. Oh, and we're not allowed to use our good weapons or anything that Cil crafts for us inside the towers. That about sum it up?"

"Everything is going to sound bad, when you put it like that!" Chase smirked. "Okay, yeah, it's not the best situation we've ever been in...but it damn well isn't the worst either. And regardless of what happens, we're going to make it. Because we're in this together, and we'll see it through together. You hear?"

Kith frowned but relented. "Yeah, yeah. I hear."

Sera, face composed, got up and looked at the three on the bed. "I believe," she started, "that I would like to challenge you all. Before we start planning anything."

Chase blinked. "This sounds like it's going to be interesting. Go ahead!"

She took a deep breath. "Okay. We can likely agree that we have been victims of circumstance more than anything else."

"What's that mean?" Kith asked.

"Means that we've been flung together by circumstances that weren't of our own doing, you dolt," Cilia admonished.

"Thank you. Yes," Sera said. "It has not, for my part, been an entirely unenjoyable experience, although you have forced me to reevaluate some of my preconceptions. Now, however, I believe it is your turn." She indicated Chase. "You said, right from the start, that your intention was to gain powers and then find a place where you would be able to put down roots, build your own life."

Chase nodded.

"In that case," she continued, "I believe that you are mistaken for looking at this like a bad outcome. Yes, the situation is rather convoluted, especially with the involvement of that secret police. Even so, consider it this way: We are all, right at this point, in a position most Elementals would kill for. We are about to receive an education that will help us use our Lightborn powers to the utmost, and possibly even earn us a full suite of Elemental cards. Add to that, that it would propel us to the social pinnacle of Elemental society... How is that not exactly what we want?" She held up a single finger, stalling any complaints.

"Yes, I realize that there are dangers involved. Of course there are. But these are not the Lightborn armies. They are going to train us, provide us with the best possible education, and, I expect, equipment for any real fights. So, we should all take a moment to consider whether this is worth it. Do we want to risk our lives for this, to build a life in peace? Or do we take the consequence, flee the damn place and try to find some tiny village in the Lightborn lands where we can possibly live in peace?" She looked at each of them in turn, challenging. "Whichever choice, we should definitely stop complaining and get to deciding!"

For a while, nobody said anything.

Then Kith howled with laughter. "Damn, woman! You don't pull your punches, do you? So, you think we're a bunch of babies who should grow up?"

Sera looked confused. "That's not what—"

"I completely agree!" Kith said.

"This seems to have taken a turn somewhere, and I'm not sure what's happening." Liam looked from one to the other.

Chase smiled ruefully at Sera. "We're being called out. And a good thing, too. It's easy to lose sight of whether you're right to complain or you're just complaining because that's what you always do. There's a real question in there, too. We've mostly been floating, working without really looking at the long-term consequences of what we're doing. Do we actually want to try this? Do we want to risk the danger? Do we want to settle down in the Elemental lands?"

"Do we want to stop stealing and cheating people?" Sera pressed.

"Whoa now." Kith laughed. "Those are very different questions."

"They really aren't," Cilia said. "We've talked a bit about it before. If we're going to stay in any place for good, we'll have to consider how we're going to make it. And if we stay in Earth's

Ward, where crime is tightly controlled? Our old professions might not make it in the long run."

Chase held up a hand. "Okay. There's definitely a point there. But that discussion, I say, we shelve for the moment. Finding out exactly which professions we want to choose for the rest of our lives is getting *wildly* ahead of ourselves. Decision time. Do we want to get the Pits out of this place, go to ground somewhere else? Or do we take our chances, try to see if we can make Earth's Ward our home?"

Liam grinned. "I vote we stay. Their fighters were not half bad."

Cilia scoffed. "The best teachers in Ordei. *Library!* Of course, we should stay."

Chase said, "I'm ready to take a chance on the Elementals. Some of them seem pretty prejudiced, but they've also got so much magic here. So much power everywhere. And if there's any truth to all their claims, it'll be ours for the taking. This could be the place where we actually make a proper home for ourselves. Not just a refuge."

"You all know what I think." Sera smiled. "Not only do I think this is an excellent chance, I also think it could be the boon of a lifetime. Which Lightborn would ever try to come to find us in here?"

They all looked at Kith. He scowled at them, then burst into a brilliant laughter. "All right, count me in. Besides, if this goes sideways, we can always fill our arms with loot and run!"

They shared a laugh.

Once the noise died down, Kith asked, "We're prospective Elementals then. But…what's the next move? Even if we're all agreed on that, we've still got those criminals we need to find and I've no clue where to start!"

Chase nodded. "That's a good point. We're used to Isarn, to a well-known city where we know all the people, the tricks and the rules. Right now, we're completely in the blank. In short—we need knowledge!" He pointed at each of them in turn. "Kith needs to spot the cheaters and backdoor dealers. Cilia will need to bury her head in several boring tomes. Liam has to make a lot of friends. Sera should find some fellow Lightborn snobs and hobnob it over the lousy behavior of all us lowly peons."

"Hey!" Sera protested.

He ignored her. "Once we've managed that? We'll be able to sit down. Then I can come up with a harebrained scheme for Cilia to pull apart."

"In other words, business as usual?" Sera asked.

"Sure. With the exception that we're starting further from behind than what we're used to." He shrugged.

Sera mulled that over before nodding in agreement. "I like it. Yes, we are deep in it. We will have plenty to do just to keep up with the rest in the academy, let alone trying to uncover whoever is behind the scam. But we are anything but weaponless—and if there is one thing we have learned, it is that we can go toe-to-toe with the strongest and come out on top. In short, I think we should go to bed now and get prepared for what tomorrow will bring us. Because we will be ready to meet it head-on!"

* * *

"They did what? Explain yourself!"

The words rang out into the long, empty room. The unstrung bows, crossbows, and other ranged weapons all arrayed on the long table at one side, in addition to the inert targets sized up at different distances, were enough to disclose the point of the room. It carried the smell of oiled leather, steel, and a distant hint of the sweat of hard work. Of course, the two persons currently in the middle of an argument were familiar enough with the towers that they knew their way around the place very well. After all, they'd chosen this place so they wouldn't chance upon any random strangers.

"Ma'am. You should know by now what I do and do not do. I deliver the information to you, for *very* decent renumeration," the smaller person said, reproach front and center in his voice. His voice was civil, yet there was steel there. "I encourage you to recall, I am a middleman. I am *not* your employee, like some of those students you have at your beck and call. I am not responsible for what has happened. I am not responsible for how they managed to find the weak link in your system and will accept neither blame, nor recrimination." Clearing his throat, he bowed his head slightly and continued in a more formal tone. "I will, however, take whatever orders and questions you have and bring them, directly and undiluted, to those who can carry them out."

The nostrils of the slightly taller person flared. She exhaled a shuddering breath. "I apologize. That was below me. It's only out of the blue. Last month, everything was running according to schedule. Now, you tell me that not only has somebody managed to subvert the security breach we've been abusing, but they have also enrolled right here at the towers?"

"Just so."

"What are the odds that the two are unrelated?"

"Very poor, I would assume, ma'am."

The Elemental cleared her throat. "As if that wasn't enough, those responsible for our security decided to try to catch one of them, failed, and made a public spectacle of themselves?"

"Exactly, ma'am. Given that these are associates chosen for less than full disclosure, they were...not the most competent out there. They do not know enough to give anything important away, I would estimate." With a frown, the smaller man fingered the edge of a throwing dagger on a table. "If you prefer, of course, we could replace them and ensure they do not give anything away."

She sighed. "A waste of effort. You cannot expect the world from hired help like them." She held up the unfurled piece of parchment once again, then crumbled it into a fist. "Say I agree with your assessment that neither the timing, nor the ensuing enrollment in the towers is a coincidence. A more difficult question, then: two Lightborn, a Furyborn, a mongrel, and a fire-scoured *Darkborn*. All carded, and strong enough to pass the initial exams. Which of the powers is able to bring together such a motley crew, and why?"

The smaller man looked thoughtful. "I surmise, that most powers, should they want to, would be able to. As to the reasoning? That one is more difficult, and I do so hate speculation. Yet, I will say that I doubt that it's a coincidence."

The woman snorted. "You've got that right. Well, whoever decided to try to intervene is shortly going to find out that they misstepped and done so badly. These are *my* towers, and I'm not going to accept any bungling idiot trying to mess with me, when we're so close to success."

"Orders, ma'am?"

"Yes. Orders. First off, we're going to continue running the operations at the gates."

"Ma'am? Whoever knows will likely realize that anybody being admitted by your interference is on purpose."

"Sure." She shrugged. "They should not, however, be able to unravel our system. There's a reason we made it autonomous. Stopping now would just alert them that we know *they* know. So, we keep it going. On top of that? We capture one of theirs, interrogate them, and find out what their plans are. That Darkborn is a rogue. They have crowd training on the second week. Secure him and let me know."

"Understood. And the others?"

A moment of hesitation. "I will handle that. Our applicants in the towers will keep an eye on them. We will not move on them until we know more." She grabbed an item from one of the tables and faced the smaller man. "Throughout our entire work, you have been a professional accomplice. The next few months are the linchpin of our entire action." She slammed the throwing dagger point-first into the hard wood table. The point of the dagger seared the wood, allowing a tight coil of smoke to rise into the air. "You need to make it *completely* obvious to your underlings that professionalism is the least that we expect for the final stretch. Anybody who acts outside of their orders will be *dealt with*."

The smaller man didn't back off. He merely nodded. "Understood. You will receive a message using the normal channels once we're ready to move on the Darkborn."

CHAPTER 14

"Furyborn? Insane berserkers out to get you. Liberty? Isolationist ghosts. Darkborn? Erased from the surface of the earth. Elementals? Huddling behind their shields, focusing everything on defense. This is everything you would know if you were to follow the teachings of the Lightborn. I thank the cards that I was brought up in Earth's Ward, where we have the education to learn the actual state of Ordei." This is exactly what I've always said. I can't wait for the classes to start! (Page 45.)

"*Keep your goddamn traps shut!*" the stout Elemental bellowed at the assembled crowd. Her face was a painting of fury, her earth-aspected low-set musculature an image reminiscent of a volcano mid-eruption.

Any hint at good-spirited discussions from the recruits assembled to read up on their schedule died in an instant.

Her hissed voice didn't detract from the volcano imagery as she started to walk back and forth in front of the large crowd. "I was going to enjoy a silent morning in bed with an entirely well-deserved hangover. Instead, Instructor Withers decided to go and fall ill, despite having more than twenty in Toughness. *Very* convenient timing, if you ask me. But since I'm a dependable, well-adjusted, and conscientious teacher, I, Instructor Boneridge, am here, when he's lounging about, deep asleep."

Chase met Sera's eyes. Her eyebrows were raised comically high. They didn't need to speak to get the meaning across. This *was a teacher? What the Pits were they about to get mixed up in?*

Right in front of Chase, a young fire-aspected Elemental whispered to a beautiful Furyborn next to him. "Boneridge is a legend! She's defended the towers for years and years. My brother—"

The woman shouted, spittle flying from her lips. "*YOU!* Yes, you right there! Pasty-faced, lard-assed fire-boy."

The youth pointed at himself, confusion clear on his face. "M-me?"

"Who else just decided to speak to that gorgeous lass, even if I told you all not to? What's your name?"

"Z-zarthiel Lifebringer, Ms. Professor." The kid looked like he wanted nothing more than to sink into the ground.

"Lifebringer? How pretentious. You should've been a Lightborn. Now, Zarthiel. Two things. First, that girl is entirely uninterested and *way* out of your league. Second, you've earned yourself your first decrease in ranking. Likely the first of many." She ignored his shocked look, turning toward the rest of the crowd. "I will say this once. This is not going to be fun. It's not going to be easy. You'll be learning to kill, to survive in less-than-optimal situations, and challenge yourself to rise above what you thought was possible. And a lot of you are going to fail. In fact, in two months, we will be cutting one in three from your group. I will personally be responsible for a lot of those."

Stunned silence reigned supreme.

With fire in her eyes, the professor turned her back on them. She took her right hand and scooped into the wall next to her. From out of the wall, she pulled an earth-colored protrusion that grew as she pulled it through her hands, extending into a foot-and-a-half-long flat stick. She slammed the stick into the blackboards behind her with a resounding slap that made half the class jump.

"This!" she said, voice down to the initial intense half-whisper. "Is a list of the courses that you will be taking, depending on your class. No. You do not get to swap classes or choose something you'd rather like. Once you've made it past the first Culling without quitting, getting yourself killed, or getting tossed out? Then, you get to choose a few classes for yourself. Until then? You're chaff. Now, you have thirty seconds to memorize your classes before we leave for your first one."

Chase was suddenly struggling against all the other students to find what he needed. He spotted one of the rogues who'd completed the tests with him yesterday gawking at a specific blackboard and grabbed Sera's shoulder. "Please read that one aloud to me."

She scoffed. "We *need* to teach you how to read properly. Your classes are World Lore, Monster Lore, Combat Training, Orientation and Movement, and Applied Practice. Today will be the same for everybody, though. World Lore for all classes, and then Combat Training for all classes. All following days, we'll be divided, depending on our classes. You had better—"

"*That's it!* Moving on now. Today, we're starting you rookies off softly with World Lore and a bit of introduction. This afternoon? You're mine."

The instructor's words arrived with such a level of mean-spirited satisfaction that Chase couldn't help but wince. Then, he was too busy to do anything but race to keep up with her hastily disappearing back.

They didn't stay on the ground levels. They were led up and up through the towers, moving from types of construction and style that differed enough it felt like they were racing through an account of the entire Elemental construction history. One moment, they huffed up spiral iron staircases through a narrow grey-brick tower that looked like it had been constructed as cheap and fast as possible, and the next, they ascended a set of white marble staircase that would've looked right at home in the richest Lightborn mansion in Isarn. They weren't allowed the time to take it in, though. Normally, Chase wouldn't mind. Sightseeing was for people who had a surplus of time and money to waste. However, the marvels around them had him wishing that they'd pulled anybody but the belligerent instructor to guide them.

Once, he caught a glimpse of a platform, open to the world outside, with what looked like an entire jungle, right there through the doorway. In another spot, a window in the cast-iron door portrayed a flaming inferno on the other side. On these lower levels, the tower seemed to be made a little at a time, in the style of the craftsman in question and without consideration of the overall direction.

Chase allowed himself to marvel at the sights. Yet, he spent as much time and mental surplus as he could trying to mark the route they were taking. After ten minutes, he felt certain they were taking a roundabout route to wherever they were going. From the myriad direction changes, the infrequent glances at the sun's position in the sky through the windows, and the way they were both climbing stairs up *and* down, Chase decided something was going on. He didn't bother trying to come up with the why—the instructor was clearly mean-spirited enough that she didn't need a reason. He just kept focused on the path, to ensure he wouldn't get entirely lost.

After a full half hour's racing to keep up with the rapidly moving instructor, the large group was finally led to their goal. They arrived through a dark mud tunnel, lit only by intermittent sconces. At this point, it was easy to tell who was working with severe training or attribute deficits. Some students were flagging, breathing hard and sweating, while others were chugging along with no issues. The entire back of the group was taken up by a near-dozen students who were barely keeping up with the hindmost of the other students. They were mostly crafter prospects, but there were also other classes in there.

For a crafter, Cilia was doing very well. On average for the assembled students, she was starting to look a little worse for wear. Even Chase was starting to flag a bit, but kept focused, taking deep breaths and trying to pace himself. The rest of their group were having no issues, their Toughness attributes being impressive enough that the fast pace barely had them winded.

When they finally broke into the amphitheater, it came as a complete surprise. One moment, they walked through the dark, nondescript hallway. The next, they fumbled into the base of a huge tiered open area carved halfway into the side of the mountain. Blinking with the sudden appearance of the sun, they stood befuddled at the sight. It was not artistic, nor detailed work. The creations here were rough, the stonework simple. However, the sheer scale of it was daunting. At the bottom of the tiered area, a large stage with five speaker's plinths were arrayed, while, behind them, above and on either side of the entrance tunnel, tiers and tiers of semi-circular stone benches allowed for easy overview over the podium below. Near the back of the podium, seven tall poles carried latched-up bolts of cloth that looked like flags, ready to lower.

Liam whistled softly. "Pits. This'll hold a thousand people, easy. Thousands, even."

Cilia shook her head softly. "Darkness hide me. You think that's impressive? Feel the wind? No, you don't. *It's not open to the outside.*"

It took a moment for it to sink in for Chase. Then, he saw it, and felt it. At this point, they would have to be at least a third of the way up the side of the mountain. The winds would be noticeable and loud. But they weren't. In fact, it felt like they were still inside one of the myriad towers. He squinted and spotted a slight sheen a hundred feet out, a semi-translucent shimmer between them and the elements. A magical shield of sorts. But of that size, and permanent?

Where the others gawked, Sera kept her eyes on the task. "Move. Let's find a place to sit down. We're not messing with that instructor."

Chase glanced down to see the instructor standing off to the side of the podium, with a mean smile playing on her face. He nodded to himself and followed Sera rapidly, sitting down on one of the foremost layers of benches, rather than one of the more anonymous ones farther up he would have preferred.

Just a few seconds after they'd sat down, Instructor Boneridge barked out, "Because of your Dark-smothered lack of stamina, we are late. In the towers, we do not care for tardiness. Tardy students not only ruin the flow of the education, they also waste the time of anybody else present. The last five people to sit down are going to be rewarded with a reduced ranking."

That triggered an avalanche of students rushing for the nearest benches, falling over one another to avoid being the last ones there. Meanwhile, the instructor observed, mean-spirited smirk glued in place. The final five students had their names noted.

After that, another speaker took her turn. She was a strict-looking water-aspected Elemental. Her tightly drawn ponytail made her look like a bookish chaperone, while her elegant silver-stitched dark ceremonial robes granted her a certain gravitas.

"I am Professor Brookwatch. This is World Lore, and you have been designated the Red Tortoise class. Remember it. World Lore is the short description of this class as well as an extremely lackluster definition of what we are going to pound into your heads here." Her crisp, slightly bored voice rang out easily across the amphitheater, arriving just like she was standing next to them. "Every year, I try to have the name of the class changed. Every year, I am voted down, out of an absolutely illogical deference to history and a reverence to decorum I fail to understand." The short, mousey woman looked challengingly at the crowd above her. "What would I call it, then? *Death to Ignorance!* That, young fools, is my task." Her sneer looked entirely out of place on her bland features. "The other teachers and instructors here have easier tasks—apologies, Instructor Boneridge."

The muscular woman snorted and barked, "Not an insult if it's the truth, is it?"

"Just so. They have to beat your physique into something matching our tall requirements, teach you how to manage cards and group cohesion, teach you new skills and worse. It is all manageable, however. Why? Because they have to teach you something new. These are all new lands for you to traverse, levels of expertise you did not hold before. Hence, you will be more willing to take to their teachings. My task, meanwhile, is all the more difficult, because I have to defeat *what's already there!*" She shouted those last words. "That's right! You stroll in here, carrying so many misconceptions and twisted facts in your young heads. Add to that the hormones of youth and the toil of your schedules in the tower, and my odds of getting through to you might be minuscule. Only..." She smiled a tight smile. "I consistently do it. Year and again, I throw knowledge at you, slamming my way through the fortresses of ignorance that you have built around yourself, tear down the battlements of misconceptions you have created in your head. Why do I do this, you ask? Because a weapon without a mind can be turned against its wielder as readily as the enemy."

Chase felt almost winded at the harassment. He opened his mouth to ask something of the others, then thought better of it. He ended up staring in amazement at Cilia, who didn't look as taken aback as he was. In fact, she looked straight at the professor, something akin to love in her gaze.

The professor didn't cease her onslaught. "You are going to think me unfair, biased, and often oppressive. You will, in your quiet mind and with your friends, accuse me of not caring about your emotions, of being judgmental and unreasonable. You will be only partly right. Because I do not care about you or your judgment. Yet, I am not biased. It will only seem that way, because I will be trying to destroy the misconceptions about the world you have carefully constructed over the scant few years of your life. *You.* What is the purpose of the Protectors?" She pointed to a broad-shouldered fire-aspected Elemental, one of the latest to arrive.

It took the stunned Elemental awhile to react. With a deep bass, he answered, with more certainty than Chase would have been able to. "To defend Earth's Ward against the Lightborn and everybody else."

"*Thank* you!" The professor bowed respectfully.

The Elemental preened, grinning to his friends.

She continued. "Thank you for so eloquently proving my point about just how Lights-blinded *indoctrinated* you all are. Fight against the Lightborn? You see the Lightborn armies at our gates? No, you don't. *Because they're not there!* The closest Lightborn are right out there, outside the outer walls of Earth's Ward, providing us with livestock and materials our whole damn society needs to survive and thrive, while other Lightborn are right there on the pews with you, listening to me rant."

Now, there was complete silence among her audience.

Cilia, eyes shining and wide, turned to Chase and mouthed *"I love her!"*

"These are my tasks then. To defeat the ignorance instilled in you by those who should know better. To teach you the real situation, so that, if you eventually rise to become Protectors, you will know how to act in the right way, so that you *can* defend us when needed. More than that, however, you need to know why and when you need to step up." With a serious tone, she added, after a long moment of silence, "Finally, I will mark those of you that I believe do *not* hold the intelligence needed to manage the responsibility bestowed upon future Elemental Protectors."

She walked the amphitheater, looking up at the students sitting quietly, each with their attention entirely fixed on her. Nobody dared look away or say anything. Finally, she ended her scrutiny and nodded to herself. "Today? Today, we start smaller. Because you need to understand exactly how our system works. The towers are tough and demanding. Yet, they are also fair. And for you to have a chance at improving your lot and earning a place amid the Protectors, you need to understand exactly how our system works."

She strode around the podium and untied the bolts of cloth hanging on them, one by one. The bolts unfurled, rolling down to expose seven different lists. They were empty, yet, as she passed them, a tiny flash of light from a bracelet on her arm showed the activation of a magical effect. Letters and numbers flowed to appear on the banners in large, glowing, multicolored lines.

Chase had learned the basics of numbers, even if proper reading still evaded him. Hence, he recognized that the hundred and twenty numbers in total, divided onto the seven different banners, had to correspond to the students. He also recognized the titles as pertaining to class names. "What do the banners say?" he whispered to Sera.

Professor Brookwatch answered the question for them. "Throughout the entire admittance test, you were assessed and ranked according to our requirements. Here, you can see your current ranking, along with your *overall* ranking among the entire hundred and twenty applicants."

Chase tried to spot the recognizable curls of his own name. Finally, he spotted it on a banner titled "Rogues" and cursed inwardly as he recognized the position on the list. His overall ranking wasn't horrible, sixty-eight of the total, but there were apparently some really promising students among the rogues, considering he was third from the bottom on that list. Kith was even worse off, being placed at a very unflattering seventy-eighth position and the bottom place of all summoners. Sera was the highest at fourteen, with Liam following up at twenty-two and Cilia at twenty-six.

"One thing I rarely have to explain to new students, yet I still do it every time—attrition among the Elemental Protectors is high. The position is as dangerous as it is prestigious. Each year, we have a number of unfortunate deaths and debilitating injuries, on top of the regular retiring from the guard to enjoy the permanent benefits obtained from this. This means that we need to have a constant influx of new Protectors of each class. Yet, we are not going to dispense with the high requirements we have. This is the visual depiction of your class right now. It will be placed in the mess hall for all to observe and updated on an ongoing basis. Hence, you will always know where you stand and how close you are to getting kicked out without any benefits but the learning you have managed to secure." She was silent for a while, before continuing. "Only one in six here is going to become an Elemental Protector. One in six. The education for the prospective Protector is intensive, tough, and undisputedly expensive. Hence, we are not going to pay for a full year's education for all of you. The first cut is in two months. By then, this class will be reduced to eighty."

A susurrus broke out among the students.

With an unamused smile, the professor nodded. "That is exactly right. At this very moment, one in three of you stand to get kicked out in the first Culling, unless you change your situation."

Chase considered the comment. He raised his hand.

After a moment, the professor noticed him and nodded. "I expect I can guess your question, but yes?"

Hoarsely, Chase asked, "Questions, really, Professor. How do we change our position, exactly how is our ranking decided, and how are the students cut? Simply the forty lowest ranking?"

The water-aspected professor raised an assessing eyebrow. "Preparing already. You will need that to improve." She held up one finger to them all. "Positioning. It is decided by one factor and one factor alone. Competence! Every single teacher you have will keep a current ranking of the students in their class. The rankings will be public. No secrets. *Death to Ignorance!*" she shouted suddenly. "It is like I said. You will need to learn how to master *all* your topics, not just a single one. Elemental Protectors may learn specialist functions, but they need competence in all classes to make it." She paused, letting it sink in, before continuing. "And your ranks will be *constantly* in motion, depending on whether your teachers are satisfied with your performance or not. Ask insightful questions or perform well in training? Your ranking improves. The opposite is true as well."

With another flash, the numbers on the rogue banner changed subtly. Now, Chase had a glowing sixty-seven next to his name instead of sixty-eight. From across the amphitheater, a Furyborn girl who might have been the former number sixty-seven glowered at him.

Brookwatch didn't deign to notice. "Your ranks in the respective classes determine your overall ranking among the fellows of your respective class. Eventually, your ranking among your peers will determine whether you leave in disappointment or stay to join our vaunted ranks.

"As to *how* those who are cut? That is slightly more involved." She made a hand gesture, and several glowing lines appeared on the lists. "Attrition among the Protectors is high. I have already mentioned that. Even so, it is nowhere near evenly distributed among the classes. Crafters are more likely to die in the early years of their service, while they find their feet. Later on, with a fully crafted and customized satchel of tricks and equipment, they are safer. In the same vein, healers, ranged, and summoners tend to see fewer deaths, comparatively speaking. As such, there will be a smaller need for new numbers of their kind, compared to fighters and rogues. Taking fighters as an example? Please take a look at the banner."

They did as ordered. Chase noted that, comparatively, they were not the very highest of the numbers, with just a single fighter ranking in the top ten and the majority of them ranking in the mid to bottom Tier of every rank. There were also two lines under the fourth and the eleventh of the fighters.

[Red Tortoise class – Fighter ranking

Fighter Ranking	Name	Overall Ranking
1	Caldren B.	9
2	Liam (No last name)	22
3	Genevere M.	33
4	Jonathan de T.	49
5	Lissen T. S.	58
6	Mattem (No last name)	66
7	Ruth S.	79
8	Terbent V.	83
9	Pellen of W.	91
10	Alicia C.	98
11	Bartholomew Z.	102
12	Arcangelo (No last name)	118

"This is, on the whole, a rather poor showing among the fighters, with nearly half of you in the lower third of the total ranking," the professor said with little heat in her voice. "You should try to prove me wrong on that count in the months to come. Now, this upper cut-off shows that we have currently capped the minimum requirement of fighters that the towers need of this class at four—meaning that, whatever else happens, when the dust settles at the end of the training and cullings, the four highest-ranking fighters among you will be inducted into the Elemental Protectors. Anybody below will be gone."

That caused a ruckus. On a bench a few tiers higher from Chase, a Furyborn raised his hand. When the professor allowed him to speak, he snarled challengingly, "Isn't that unfair, though? That means that you won't get the best students overall, and it will be harder for other classes to make it in, all because fighters tend to die off easier than the rest of us, right?"

The professor chuckled. "Your name?"

The Furyborn blinked. "Hargren, ma'am."

"Well, Hargren. You are entirely right. However, you are also shortsighted. *Nothing* about this process is supposed to be fair for you. It is all about what the towers need. In this case, it needs a slightly larger portion of the best fighters and rogues than the remainder of classes because more of them die or are crippled than the other classes." With a nod to him, she turned to the rest of the crowd, while, on a banner in the background, Hargren's name ticked a number down.

The Furyborn looked like he was about to blow up. For the rest of the crowd, the general look was one of horrified realization. Not only would they have to do well enough to avoid hitting the cutoff in their respective classes for *every* single time during the year that their numbers would be culled but it would also be a matter of constant and continuous challenge, with those doing well pushing those who did less well further and further down.

"What about the bottom line of the rankings, then?" an earth-aspected Elemental with a high-pitched voice asked.

"Ah. That is for all of you to avoid getting complacent, and to increase competition. Regardless of ranking and class, we *will* cut the lowest-ranking person in every single category during each cull. We do not tolerate slackers."

CHAPTER 15

*"One reason to join the Towers? Our vaunted Library.
Any who join our ranks is not just encouraged to partake in its
collected wisdom, but expected to. We demand brilliance."* I
am showing Kith this. That, and a stick might help him improve. Page 34.

"They're insane. Okay, I'm done for. Can I leave now?" Kith groaned.

Their heads were pounding with the knowledge that had been forced into them over the past three hours, and they were suffering from massive information overload. They had been spared any further changes to their ranking, though a handful of other students had seen theirs improve or worsen during the class. Now, they were on their way back to the mess hall for dinner, with other students walking behind and ahead of them, alone or in groups.

"I get you, brother. It seems like you've been hit by the worst of everything," Liam commiserated, slapping Kith on the back. "Seems like too few summoners get themselves killed, since they only plan for two summoners to graduate to full Protectors, where it's four fighters and four rogues."

"Three crafters and three healers too," Sera added with a wince.

"Yeah. Competition is also a lot nastier with the summoners, it looks like. The lowest-ranked among you guys was, what, seventy or something?" Liam asked.

"Sixty-nine. And the one after that was in the early fifties," Kith said sullenly. "With me dead last at a hundred and sixteen."

Chase cracked his neck. "I get it. It's a shitty start. But let's relax with the predictions of doom here, mate. The only reason you started with such a crappy ranking is that they haven't seen you properly in action and don't love your build. Once you can show them your worth, you'll be climbing the ranks in leaps and bounds. That goes for all of us. None of this is going to be easy—especially with that other mission we have. But as long as we work together, we'll have what a lot of the others don't have—family, that we can draw upon."

Kith frowned, then nodded. "All right. I'll stop sulking. What do you think about the rest of her class?"

"It was amazing!" Cilia said dreamily. "Challenging our preconceptions. Trying to widen our horizons, not only geographically but politically. And not once did she discriminate based on origins or races."

Kith snorted. "Yeah. It was all based on how big a brain you had. No wonder you like her."

Cilia glared him down. "I cannot believe how wrong some of the general preconceptions in the world about Elementals and their empire are. No wonder the author of this tome is so snippy when it comes to outsiders in general—when the way we all perceive the Elementals doesn't correspond to their actual situation."

"I didn't really get that part," Liam admitted. "She was saying that the Elementals aren't really under siege, only they are? And then she turned it into something like they were sitting around discussing everything like old friends with the Lightborn...except the Elemental Protectors still die on the border every so often?"

"It *is* complicated," Sera admitted. "You are aware of the geographical situation of Earth's Ward, are you not?"

The big guy shrugged as they walked. "I guess. The Lightborn surround most of their lands, except for the parts that border against Liberty...right? Sending their summoned Guardian beasts against each other, fighting all the damn time."

"Geographically, that is right. Politically and practically, less so," Sera said, animatedly gesturing. "See, the Lightborn and the Furyborn used to fight, for a long time. Only after both sides lost a large number of card wielders did they figure out that it had become a continuous battle, with neither of the sides winning. The Lightborn might press the Elementals back to Earth's Ward and they even breached the outer walls once; yet, the power of the towers themselves was too overwhelming, too entrenched and well-founded. As for the Elementals? They held their own extremely well. Yet, the few times they tried to spread out from the tightly controlled confines of their defensive walls, the Lightborn were able to dominate them with numbers and positioning."

"Dude. We *just* left from a lecture on this," Kith marveled. "I was bored too, but how could you not have caught all of this?"

Liam shrugged. "Did you not see that Darkborn girl like three rows up on the far right? I swear, she was glancing at me all the time!"

"The...one with the burn scars? She looked *scary!* Man, what's the matter with you?"

His eyes blazed. "A man likes what a man likes."

"A man should learn how to pay attention to Sera when she's doing you a favor," Cilia snapped. "Seriously. We *just* talked about how we'll need to step up to make it!"

"Sorry," Liam murmured. "I'll do better."

Sera watched the exchange as they walked, half exasperated, half entertained. "So. The Lightborn and Elementals were at a stalemate. Not only that, but Liberty had just enabled their defense."

"Oooh. That rolling fog bank everywhere around their lands?" Kith said.

"Exactly. From time to time, Liberty attackers emerged, or Liberty Guardians. The Elementals fended those off as well. Yet, when they tried to send forces *into* the cloud, they disappeared. Forever."

"That sounds complicated." Liam scrunched up his brow.

"Complicated indeed," Sera admitted. "Which is why the Lightborn and Elementals entered into negotiations and eventually ceased hostilities."

"But...they're still surrounded here?"

"Complicated, remember?" Sera said, with a smile. "This was about four decades ago. Since then, the negotiations have warmed up considerably. Now, there is a lot of active trade ongoing between the two nations, and the Lightborn even allow entire Elemental forces to pass through their borders from time to time—"

"Under strict supervision," Cilia murmured.

"Under supervision, obviously, yes. Even so, they are allowed to pass to fight against the unaspected in certain areas and then return home to Earth's Ward."

Liam groaned. "This is why I'd rather look at a beautiful girl. That makes *no* sense. They're still up in arms at the borders. But they're letting whole armies through?"

"Think about it like this," Sera said. "Nothing in the general situation has truly changed. If the Lightborn were to let the Elementals expand their territories, with their current level of expertise, training, and consolidation of power, they might eventually be able to overpower the Lightborn empire. However, what does it cost the Lightborn to let a few Elemental armies go whet their teeth on unaspected, or maybe even Furyborn, in return for a few trade concessions or having a few important Lightborn be granted access to the towers? Nothing, really, as long as they can keep them in check and make sure they do not run off to establish an Elemental Wellspring somewhere."

"But they still send their Guardians at each other to kill?" Liam asked.

"Exactly. Yet, you need to realize that this is not a bad thing. To the Elementals, this is what helps them train their forces and walk the Steps, seeing as how they are generally unable to access the rest of the world. And to the Lightborn, the threat is negligible, because they let the Elemental Guardians spill out over a huge area and grind them down, and they get to try different strategies in practice."

Chase mused over the situation. "It seems like a pretty uneasy stalemate. How come nobody's tried to backstab the others?"

Sera's laugh rang out over the hallway, making a stern-faced robed Elemental glare at her. "Oh, they have. Both sides have made attempts. Only, with each failure, they have ended up looking less competent. By now, the factions on either side vying for peaceful solutions outweigh the martial proponents."

"My tome said something about that as well," Cilia added. "That the Lightborn have a ton of different factions, with plenty of infighting, but the more powerful factions are tired of the large expenditures on the attempts to break the Elemental defense. Meanwhile, the Elementals are, with a few exceptions, divided into factions alongside their aspects. The fire-aspected are for war, ever and always. Earth enjoy life as it stands today, slowly expanding a solid, impenetrable fortress that cannot be chipped away at."

"Sounds like the way to go," Liam mused.

"Pfft. Sounds boring, rather." Kith scoffed.

"The water-aspected are likely the most agreeable on the subject. They are also the ones most geared on negotiations. They have carved out any number of concessions and improvements to the general agreement between the two nations over the past decades. In my opinion, they are the ones who might eventually end up brokering an end to this eternal stalemate."

"Wait a minute," said Kith. "I just remembered. Back in Isarn, word on the street was that the Elementals were under pressure. That we'd get them to join the folds any day now?"

Sera grimaced. "Propaganda. I am sorry. Behind the scenes, a lot of the nobility were frustrated with the actual lack of progress. Some had started to advocate openly for not pouring any more money into the conflict and focus on trade and, like the Elementals, using it as a training area."

"Guys. I'm sorry, but I think we should get a move on, maybe save this for later," Chase said. "Remember how Instructor Boneridge rushed us up here? I wouldn't be surprised if they actually judge us on how fast we get back down—and worse if we get lost or something."

Ahead of their group, a surprised squawk sounded. A lithe Lightborn man turned around. His white face blazed red with embarrassment. "Sorry. Sorry. I didn't mean to listen in, but...well, I was. And now, I realize I don't want to get pushed even further down the ranking for being late." With a quick wave, he took off at a brisk pace.

Sera gawked at his retreating back. "I honestly believe we should follow his example. I could see that instructor coming up with something like that. She did seem extraordinarily belligerent. I am nearly done with my explanation, too."

Liam exhaled in relief. "Good. I mean, thank you. Just the air-aspected Elementals left then? What's with them?"

She schooled her features into stillness. "Oh, they are very changeable. Some days, they believe one thing, the next another. They are less unified than the other factions."

Chase looked at her, deadpan. "You're saying the windies are...flighty?" He rubbed his forehead. "You should be ashamed of yourself."

A titter escaped her.

This time around, there were no consequences for those arriving latest back to the mess hall. Apparently, the instructor had just taken a long, winding path to mess with them, or out of spite. They managed to get a full meal in, almost without interruptions. Ernest, the young man who had gone off on Chase for taking his sister's spot, came around again to deliver a few scathing remarks, but when they didn't rise to his provocations, he left, leaving them to enjoy the warm, excellent meal in peace.

When Instructor Boneridge arrived to bring the students with her, two students still hadn't made it back. Chase knew where they were likely to be—the path back down had been both confounding and long. They were likely trying to make their way back to them this very moment. The tough instructor adjusted the bracelet on her arm, penalizing the ranking of the two offenders, and off they went again.

Because the next class was Combat Training, Chase expected them to be whisked down to the huge training area in front of the tower itself. Hence, he was surprised to see the instructor veering off for higher slopes of the towers again, in a westerly direction.

This time, with the students aware that slacking, tardiness, smart-assery, or basically *anything* could be punished with little warning, everybody was keeping time with the instructor, hurrying along right at her heels. The same went for their group, of course.

Chase noticed that the earth-aspected instructor no longer looked as piqued as she had in the morning. In fact, she looked downright happy, though the cruel tilt to her lips as she walked in silence led him to severe misgivings about the training to come. Also, about whether he should have had seconds.

Their route this time was equally circuitous. Chase, again not as hard-pressed as some of the poor crafter classes, came up with a theory as they passed a series of long, similar rooms that looked suspiciously like offices, standing out amid the magic and wonders of the towers. "Guys." He huffed. "Keep your attention up, and try to remember your surroundings at all times. I think it will come in handy later."

"Why?" Kith complained. "You know how I am with directions!"

"Just do it," he hissed, and they returned to their jog.

The area they arrived to was, like the amphitheater, open to the sky outside. It was also huge. These, however, were the only similarities between the two places.

Where the amphitheater was tall, open, and clearly built to impress, this place was wide, unassuming, and built to be used. It was a dirt-covered arena, large enough that it would take several minutes to enter the hallway back to the towers on the far side. It was open and undisturbed in places, while others were cluttered with equipment or people. Alongside the large, oval area lay several wooden buildings at equal distances that made Chase think of vendors back in Isarn, with a single person seated at a desk and spacious room in the back. At the far end, an even larger brick building was sealed off, giving no hint as to what it hid. There was no magic shield sheltering them from the outside here. The winds howled past them at high speed, even with the weather being pretty good; the sun peeked out between a thin spread of clouds. Two-thirds of the way across the area, a person walked backward, hands stretched out. Where he walked, a chest-high earthen wall rose, building an elaborate formation.

Chase spotted a large group setting up what looked like archery targets. As he stared, at first, he didn't notice the instructor turning around to observe them. Once he did, his pulse quickened. Earlier, when her smile had seemed cruel, he'd been disturbed. Now, looking at the devilish grin she wore, he was downright afraid.

"Welcome to my domain," Instructor Boneridge said. "This is where you are going to spend more than one full day a week for the next two months."

She looked so demented at that point, Chase truly wanted to just run away. Except, he had been through worse. They had *all* been through worse. And he was definitely not going to show fear in front of a full-fledged sadist like this one.

She sneered, gesturing at the area around them. "The water lilies—water-aspected Elementals, for you ignorants—are mostly useless. They prefer talking over acting, prefer planning over doing, and entirely lack the ability to face an enemy head-on. Damn cowards," she spat, seemingly enjoying the affronted look on the faces on some of the water-aspected Elementals among them.

"But there's one thing they do well. Administration. One of those ink-stained losers sat down and figured out exactly why people leave the towers within the first two months. Because not all are removed at the Culling." She shrugged and continued, purring, enjoying the monologuing. "About half, seventeen of forty, are cut at the Culling. Those recruits do their best. Their best just isn't good enough. Just like I expect to see from most of you. Then there's another handful who manage to earn direct expulsion. Those are typically the cheaters, the liars, and the thieves. Those who look at the competition and decide they need to use underhanded tricks to compete." Her hands tightened into fists the size of loaves. "I dare any of you to try that venue with me. Us instructors get a bit of...leeway, if we catch somebody in the act."

She raised an eyebrow before continuing. "There're the accidents, too. These are the early days, but we still get 'em. Some are clumsy. Some are plain unlucky. Whatever the reason, we lose some hands, legs, or lives, typically a handful of those as well." She snorted and pointed at Chase. "Most people tend to give up after that, cripple—not all are as stubborn as you look to be. Moving on, finally, the rest of 'em are the quitters. Those who figure out what our demands are, academically and physically, and just can't take it, giving up before time. That little water lily of ours who crunched the numbers? She figured out that the single main reason for losers quitting before the first Culling? Was me!"

Voice hoarse with naked emotion, she moved closer to them, looking from one to the next, eyes searching and piercing. "Over the next two months, I am going to torment you. I am going to push you through the wringer, push you past what you believed your body would be able to handle, again and again. Every time you surpass what you thought you'd be able to take, be it pain, challenges, or sheer adversity? I am going to reward you with something even worse. My current record stands at making nineteen out of forty quit within the first two months. I aim to break that record."

"Why?" a thin, reedy voice asked. The speaker was a stick-thin Darkborn with thin limbs, heavy burn scars along her neck, and long, charcoal-dark hair gathered into a ponytail. Her scowling face challenged the instructor. "That is a real question. You are supposed to help us train and become the best we can be. How does breaking us down manage anything but chase away those who could've been great?"

The instructor faced the Darkborn. "Emilia, aren't you?" Her predatory grin widened at the responding nod. "I get why you're asking. You crafters are prime targets. You're *weak!*" She barked the word loudly enough that a young man next to Chase jumped. "Physically. You also suffer from the notion that you don't need to learn how to fight properly, that you just need to learn how to craft and then that's it. That would all be well and good if we wanted good card wielders in the towers." She stood up ramrod straight now, looking like a mountain made of muscle and soil.

"We don't want good wielders. *We want the best.* Life as an Elemental Protector isn't easy. There will be pressure on all sides. Physical danger. Attempts at bribery, mental and social manipulation. We need somebody who can handle everything and hold their own in complicated situations. And we, I am very pleased to tell you, are not going to hold back. We will be *thorough.*"

The instructor's voice sounded like the experience was almost sexual to her. She faced the poor Darkborn again, who held her ground almost without flinching. In a low voice, she said, "Does that scare you, Emilia? Do you want to quit now?"

The young woman took a deep breath, then stood up straighter. "Scare me? Yes. Quit? Never!"

The smile on Instructor Boneridge's face widened to where it seemed like it was going to unhinge her jaw. "Good," she purred. "Also, good question. I reward candor." She touched her armband, which lit up.

In the distance, Chase was certain Emilia's ranking rose on the banner.

"*Now!*" she snapped, turning to the rest of the group. "Tell me what you think we're going to be doing over the next couple of months?"

A couple of people voiced their thoughts. Weapons training. Training to work in groups. Assessing their skills to divide them into smaller groups for more specialized combat training.

Chase's mind raced, going over what she had said so far. He spoke up. "You'll be tempering us."

The instructor raised a finger at that, halting any other comments, as she marched over to face him. "That is an interesting word choice. Elaborate."

Chase considered the situation. It really wasn't that removed from where they'd found themselves among the indebted. Sure, there was a world of difference between the general level of competence, strength, and bodily health between the sorry bastards who were forced to be bait, and the healthy, well-fed, well-trained specimens here among the students. Only, the same principles still applied.

He nodded. "The way I see it, you won't be bothering with a ton of individual training at this point. Why put us into groups and train us at...dagger throwing or whatnot, if it turns out that we can't stand up to the level of hard work you're going to require from us? Also, it's like you said. You want the best. That means having people with the highest attributes. You're going to put us through the paces, test our pain tolerance and our work effort, and increase our attributes as much as you possibly can before the first Culling. That way, once you start to specialize and group up people, you know that we aren't going to fall apart from a hard poke or some honest work."

The instructor tapped her lip. She snorted. "Look at that cripple. Such a clever mind. I guess you'd *have* to be smart with those skinny arms of yours." She walked right up in his face and let her index finger slide down Chase's chin. It was calloused and rough and applied just enough pressure that Chase could feel the strength behind it. With a heady voice, she continued, "Oh, I am going to *temper* you."

With a brisk whirl, she turned away, shouting at everybody. "I am going to temper you *all!* I will put you through the crucible. Find out who among you are bad steel. Some will break. But those who make it out the other side will be the stronger for it! *Now, line up!*"

CHAPTER 16

"The key to the strength of the Elemental Protectors is simple: knowledge. Other nations may spend additional effort grooming a few select groups. Earth's Ward collects all available knowledge, disseminates it, and distributes it to perfect our Protectors. We take everything we know to build the perfect distribution of cards and then multiply that exponentially by matching them with other card wielders whose powers will enhance those even higher. That, and a lot of grueling, hard work, of course." I really look forward to seeing that knowledge, eventually. So far, it's all been the physical torture. Not a fan. (Page 51.)

The instructor was true to her word. Over the following three hours, their group was introduced to a grueling training, seemingly designed to take them right to the edge of their physical capability, holding them there on the brink for long enough they thought they'd break, then moving on to do the exact same thing with other muscle groups.

They quickly realized the point of the booths. They were the caretakers, handling all the different equipment needed to break the recruits, or the casters with earth affinity who broke up and redistributed the terrain to fit their needs. There were small items, like weights and blunted weapons, and larger set-ups, like rope-and-pole arrangements; half the training area could even be transformed into a specialized training environment with fake walls and soil rearrangement powers.

The first day, though, they barely used equipment. The instructor walked among them, shouting demands and pushing them to the limit. One second, she'd be circling their group as they sprinted from one edge of the lined-off area to the next at her mark; the next, she'd be all over one poor fire-aspected Elemental who looked like he hadn't been giving it his all.

They cycled through exercises and muscle groups, leaving people battered and on the verge of breakdown. Then, the instructor made them get up and start all over again. Minutes turned to hours at a glacial speed, leaving them all dripping sweat, eyeing the sun to estimate when the torture would stop.

Chase pushed himself as hard as he possibly could, knowing that his Spoils of the Undeserving card would pay him back for every drop of sweat, allowing him to grow his attributes faster than normal. Still, it was hard to discount the draining effect of having every section of the body thoroughly abused, then starting all over again.

He entered into a world of his own, the only distraction being Ernest "accidentally" tripping him.

Finally, the instructor called a halt and told them all to gather at one of the buildings they hadn't visited yet. Limping, wheezing, and cursing, they followed along. The gleam in her eye made Chase uneasy. The much-scuffed wooden surface of the counter was barely to be seen beneath the piles and piles of weapons. Sharp-edged, real weapons. "This is one of my favorite moments," Instructor Boneridge said. "When I get to finally test you properly for the first time and see what you're made of. Right!" She clapped her hands together. "Everybody. Pick the weapon that best suits you, then step back."

A wind-aspected Elemental balked at that. "But... I have no weapon training. What do I do?"

"What would you do if you were attacked in an alley today?" the instructor challenged. "Do the best with what you can! I am not here to coddle you. I'm here to test you. That means seeing what I have to work with, when your back is against the wall."

They massed up to the servant in the building, picking the weapon they thought best complemented them. There were no limits, and the selections were vast and eclectic. One massive earth-aspected Elemental made away with a ball-and-chain flail with three heads. A Lightborn picked a spear that was at least ten feet tall, making him look like a dwarf. Liam picked his favorite getup: a simple, spiked mace and a large shield to go with it. Kith went with two heavy machetes that were a decent match to his regular hand axes. Chase picked a short sword, giving him a tiny bit more range than he usually had from his trusty dagger. Cilia went with an iron-headed quarterstaff. Sera, after some deliberation, went with two sword breakers.

They were led off to the center of the open area. A section had been cordoned off with cloth wrapped from poles, creating a large, rectangular space where you couldn't see what was happening.

The instructor guided them to the center of the area, then pointed at the flap hiding the entrance to the space beyond. "I said I would lead you through the crucible. This is the first real test. Not all our forces are out there simply killing Lightborn or Liberty Guardians to grow stronger and defend our borders. Some of them have...more specialized tasks. One of our best teams have managed to catch a number of Lightborn monsters and bring them back here. Now, we are going to pit you against them and see what you're made of. You can use any cards you

145

have, Heart cards or otherwise. We *always* lose somebody at this stage. I have no issue with this. Better to see what you're made of now, than wasting our resources on you for a long while."

"But we're already done in," one Furyborn student said, at the edge of tears. "If I'd known there would be real fighting, I wouldn't have pushed myself so hard."

"That's the Dark-scourged point, you weakling!" Spittle flew from her lips as she shouted. She settled down slightly, as her arm stabbed out in the direction of the bottom of the mountain. "But you always have the coward's way out. Quit. Quit and leave the towers stronger, for having excised your weakness! Or stay. Just know that, for that, I will be choosing one of the stronger monsters for you alone." Her eyes gleamed dangerously.

Beyond them in the massive sectioned-off enclosure, a loud growl erupted, drowning out all attempts at whispered conversation.

Chase squinted in suspicion. Everything about this reeked. The way the instructor spoke. The whole setup. Only...he'd play along for now.

The offending student was the first to go in. Boneridge followed him in, and moments later, growls filled the air. At one point, a loud, pain-filled scream ripped through the air. Then it grew silent again.

The instructor walked back out, chuckling. "I saw that one coming from far away. Now, who's next? I'll pick...you!" She pointed at a student at random.

One by one, the students were led in through the flap, followed by sounds of battle. The sounds differed wildly. Sometimes, there were growls; sometimes, chirps or weird clicks. Quite often, there were cries of pain. They never got to see what happened. The students, after entering, were led away elsewhere and, according to the instructor, they would reveal the tally of how many students they lost. Outside, they whispered and talked—some defiant, others clearly afraid.

A fire-aspected Elemental, who had been one of the hangers-on with Ernest, marched up, scowling at their group. "I look forward to seeing you all drop out, filth." He glared at Chase. "But you, especially. You really shouldn't have come here and wasted our space. I hope you get killed and eaten in there!"

Liam looked at him in confusion. "Yesterday, you were talking about how damn benevolent your forces are, how they help us grow. Do you really feel like they're helping?"

The lithe man opened his mouth, then shut it and stalked away with a scornful look at them and a hissed curse.

Liam entered first. His cries were defiant and bellowing, right up until they ended, cut off abruptly. Kith was the next of their group, and there were a few loud chuckles, at his ongoing cursing, audible even through the material.

Suddenly, it clicked for Chase. He sidled over to Sera, who stood, clutching the sword breakers hard enough to make the veins stand out on her forearms. The instructor had just ducked in with another student, and he whispered, "Don't worry."

"How should I not worry?" she whispered. "This is what I am the worst at. My cards can barely help me here. I might freeze in there, and it can get me killed or worse."

Chase spotted movement near the flap and whispered quickly. "It's not real. Just do your best."

As luck would have it, Chase was the next one picked. He beamed an encouraging smile at Sera, who met his gaze with mixed confusion and deep thought. Cilia also met his gaze, but she was entirely composed. Chase suspected she'd figured it out as well.

Instructor Boneridge led him through the first flap into a small, introductory passage. He took it all in. The soil below them was still the hard-packed surface of the training area, making for good footing. The air reeked of nervous sweat and blood, but little else. The fresh air from the mountain carried away anything else. From what seemed like a few feet away, on the other side of the next flap, wheezing growls rose up to welcome Chase. The instructor faced him, looking straight at him with lidded eyes. "This is your last chance to bow out. No shame in admitting this isn't for you. You'll be judged harder than most others, and I cannot afford to make things easier for you, so this is *not* a favorable setup."

Chase smiled calmly. "No thank you, Instructor Boneridge. Any other rules I should be made aware of?"

She shook her head. "As long as you do not hit anybody outside the tent with any of your effects, you are free to do whatever you need to survive, use all your cards. Are you ready?"

He gave her a curt nod, tamping down the smile that wanted to make its way onto his face. If he started using *all* his cards, she'd likely sing a different tune.

She opened the next flap and turned to him. "If I believe you're about to die, I will step in. Only, it will count as you quitting. Go ahead! Surprise us all! Show us that you have what it takes!" With those words, she stepped back, allowing him a glance at what was facing him.

It was huge. He didn't know the beast, but it was clearly like they had intimated: a Lightborn animal. The stark-white, catlike beast stood tall, its neck at around his chest height, and it was at least eight feet long, rippling with tight muscle. The paws held finger-long, razor-sharp claws. Also…there was something wrong with its neck. Something glimmered there, a hint of magic, like something ready to shoot out at him at any given moment.

The animal was currently tied down, chained by its hind leg to a block of iron at the center of the cordoned-off area. The arena, for lack of a better word, was around fifty by fifty feet. A large area—only, looking at the size of the damn thing facing him, Chase knew it would feel way too small before long.

From behind him, the instructor called out, "We're unleashing it in five seconds. Good luck."

Chase held on tight to his short sword, taking deep breaths. He really, *really* hoped he was right about this thing being a setup.

The chain slid open with a silent *clack*. The huge, white feline erupted from a standing halt into a thunderous charge with the speed of a blockaded waterfall being unleashed.

Chase cursed and moved into action. He activated his Race of Life card, feeling his Agility increase slightly. Facing the big beast head-on, he decided this wasn't the time for a lengthy, drawn-out fight like those he was used to. Not when he didn't have access to his attribute-draining cards and being up against that combination of size and speed. No, he needed to go big and use everything at his disposal straightaway. He sprinted straight at the beast, all his pent-up nervousness and energy unleashed into the dead run, as if they were at a race to see who'd get to the center first.

The distance between them faded away in seconds, like the memories of Cilia's lessons excised by too much grain alcohol. Twenty feet. Ten. Teeth and claws created a living, glittering tapestry of death rushing to enfold Chase in its embrace.

Chase activated his Steps of Brilliance card, throwing every platform at his disposal out straight ahead and up, like a tiny, three-stepped, glowing staircase available and visible only to himself. He took the steps at a sprint—one, two, three—then flung himself out head-first with the short sword carving through the air ahead of him.

The feline, still charging, had an almost human look of shock to its face, as Chase stepped into the open air, rising above its charge. Trying to forestall its onslaught, its hind legs clawed against the ground, hindquarters skidding comically against the dirt. Meanwhile, its mouth snapped up to try to catch the elusive morsel.

Chase brought the sword down hard on its head. The sharp edge of the blade carved into its forehead, opening a nasty cut all the way down to its mouth. Blood spilled everywhere. With a cry of triumph, he sailed on, airborne. Then, surprisingly, the weapon pulled him downward. The tip of the sword had caught unexpectedly on something alongside the beast's head. Chase held on desperately to the hilt as his body flopped downward. Air was expelled from his lungs with a *whoof*, as his body bounced off the back of the beast and onto the dirt of the arena behind it.

Ignoring the pain and disorientation from the impact, he immediately flung himself to his feet, legs scrabbling for purchase against the ground before he was even entirely sure which way was up.

The beast, bleeding freely and with one eye entirely obscured by the flowing blood, was already charging back at him. It didn't look hurt, though—more furious than anything.

He snarled right back at it, weaving left, before sprinting at the beast, veering toward the injured side of its head.

Mid-battle was always a muddled-up jumble of emotions, instincts, and thoughts. Chase had found, that the more his Mental Power increased, the less his emotions ruled, and the clearer and faster his thoughts came. On top of that, he became faster at processing his instincts, deciding when they were right on the money, and when they were mired with his emotions, with fear, wishful thinking, or a desire for violence to run the show. When he was fully charged, having drained the attributes of his enemies, sporting twice his regular Mental Power, he felt like his intuition and thoughts walked in lockstep, presenting him with an almost supernatural ability to decide and process his decisions. With his Mental Power down at its current base of twelve, however, things were not that simple. He could only hope that his intuition didn't guide him off course.

He was six feet from the monster, veering left to keep the feline off-balance and aiming to hit it with another slice to the head before retreating, instead of an all-out attack like the last. The only warning he got was a brief flash from the monster's neck region, as it swiftly turned, presenting its side to him.

Chase managed to turn his head away and nearly closed his eyes in time as he slid to a halt. It just wasn't enough. From behind the neck, a torrential gust of wind exploded, slamming him off-balance and blinding him in one massive, centralized expanse of air. From between a swimming gaze and large, colored spots in his vision, Chase felt, more than saw, the huge beast bearing down on him, savage glee in its eyes.

Chase was out of luck. He was half-blind, out of momentum, and nearly out of tricks. He could swap his Spoils of the Undeserving card for his Dark Free of Perdition card. That would allow him to, if he beat the Mental Power of the big beasty, exchange his Toughness with the animal's. Only, that would expose his secret. He had to hope that he was right in his guesses.

With a furious yell, he sprang into motion. Unsteadily, he ran straight for the beast, just like last time. He didn't build up the same speed, though. It was bearing down on him too fast.

Mid-stride, he activated Steps of Brilliance again. This time, instead of trying to leap *over* the beast, he placed the steps in a half-corkscrew, veering left. His first step had him turning left, trusting in his ability as he stepped on thin air. The second step gave him the sensation of falling, as his body became increasingly parallel to the ground. The final step saw him completely vertical as the tight turn allowed him the footing to make an unnaturally tight turn in the air. With the full weight of his foot on the third step, he propelled himself off the step in a steep dive, flinging himself sideways and away, out of the reach and into the blind spot of its bleeding eye.

It wasn't fast enough. Its paw struck him out of the air. Hitting his ankle, it upset his motion, flinging him into an uncontrolled, spreadeagled spin. Chase hit the ground hard, landing on his shoulder and bouncing twice. His sword careened away in an unseen direction. He tried to ignore the pain and fight himself to his feet, only his body didn't react as fast as he needed it to. Between the pain, the spots in his vision, and the sailing, churning change in his eyesight, he was starting to lose control over his senses.

Fighting down the desire to vomit, Chase's vision solidified slightly into the disturbing image of the beast's head growing larger. Only now did he realize just how large its head was. It could comfortably crush his own head in a single bite.

Out of time and out of breath, Chase trusted in his suspicion and did the only thing he could think of that he'd be able to do in time. Panting, ignoring the pain, he raised his hand...and gave the charging beast a one-finger salute.

CHAPTER 17

"There are so many threats to our society, I can barely name them all. However, the Elemental towers do what we must, all aspects working together in a common front. Fire burns any attackers. Earth builds, preparing and solidifying our defenses. Water adapts, changes and merges into whatever needs to be done. Air...is there too, I suppose." I do enjoy how his prejudices are very front and center. He doesn't hide how much he looks down on the air-aspected Elementals. Time will tell whether I end up thinking the same. (Page 53.)

The beast was ugly up close. *Really* ugly. Its breath was not as bad as Chase had pictured, though. In fact, it didn't reek at all.

From one second to the next, it blinked out of existence.

Chase's head slumped down on the hard-packed earth of the ground. He'd been right.

A slow clapping emerged from nearby and grew louder.

Chase sat back up, watching Instructor Boneridge stride closer to him, the sardonic smile that seemed second nature to her plastered on her face.

She stopped clapping and placed her fists at her sides. "So, you figured it out then, cripple? What was it that tipped you off?"

Wavering slightly, he got back to his feet. He nodded. "A few things. Mostly your performance out there." He indicated with his head where the rest of the students were waiting for their turn. "It seemed...well, like a performance. And, having seen a few con men in my time...I apologize, but that's not where your talents lie. Also, the things just didn't match up. Have us risk our lives to prove our commitment? Sure. But putting us in a place where support is just out of reach? The towers pride themselves on doing things the clever way, and I just didn't see it."

Chase laughed nervously, pointing at the Elemental and the Lightborn sitting along the edge of the arena. "What was it then? A summoning card? Or some sort of advanced mental manipulation?"

"Summon. Avani there has the gift to repeatedly summon lifelike versions of any beast she's encountered." The instructor smirked. "And Chiver can strengthen those beasts, and manage a few distracting effects, like that air effect that hit you. They're a good combination." The convivial tone was so far from the harsh, challenging tone she'd taken with her students. It turned more businesslike as she clapped. "Now, we're running out of time and I have fifteen more students to run through the grinder. You saw through the ruse but failed to beat the beastie. How would you rate your fight?"

Chase frowned. He did not see *that* coming. "I'd say...passable, but not excellent. That beast was a bad matchup for me, yet I almost got it. I decided that it was big and fast enough I would need to put it down fast. If you pitted me against it again, though, I reckon I'd be able to take it, now that I know what to look for. I believe I'd try to aim for its extremities instead, cripple it, bleed it slowly. With a good hit on a leg, I'd be able to wear it down."

"How about the way you handled the blast?" There was genuine interest in her voice.

He grimaced. "Not excellent. There was a visual warning on its neck, so I should have been more alert. Of course, in most situations, I'd have more of an idea what I'd be coming up against, but...yeah. I could've tackled that better."

Instructor Boneridge's eyes bored right through him. "You're saying all the right things to make my old trainer's heart all soppy." Her voice grew harder, less amiable. "Only, I don't judge people by their words alone, but also by their actions. And there were many, many things in this short fight that we need to improve on. Your footwork was atrocious. That movement skill of yours could have been employed to vastly better results. Also, have you ever even *wielded* a short sword before? That crash landing was horrible." She shook her head. "There may be potential here, and you seem to have the head for it. But there will be a *lot* of work for you in the future if you need to reach a level where I proclaim you ready for the Protectors."

Chase leapt to his feet, ignoring the bruises shouting about the injustice of him moving again. He brushed his hands off. "I look forward to it." He winked at the hard-faced older woman. "I got a new card, not long ago. Triples the attribute improvements from any training. So, I look forward to future training sessions."

"Is. That. Right?"

The look of expectant glee in her eyes made Chase realize he'd made a mistake. She looked like she was already knee-deep in planning atrocities for him.

"I'll...just make my way out then?" he said, uneasily walking over to pick his sword up, ready to leave the tent. From there, a servant took the sword and led him to the exit on the far side.

Liam and Kith were waiting for him there, when he came out. They quickly compared results. Neither of the two had figured out that it was all a ruse beforehand. Still, they'd managed decent showings.

Liam had faced a shell-covered abomination that sent congealed spikes at him from its mouth. It was tough, yet surprisingly agile. However, its damage output wasn't too overwhelming. With his shield, careful maneuvering, and his self-healing Cleansing Fire card, he managed to top himself up, using his Waterfall of Light to knock the beast to its shell, and break through the resistant shell while it was off-kilter. They'd cut the fight short, when they realized he'd likely wear it down in time.

Kith had surprised them. His opponents had been a pair of agile, poison-spitting, six-legged critters with the ability to summon short-lived magical shields around themselves. An awful match for summoners, who'd have to handle multiple fast opponents, while dodging or protecting from the dangerous poison attacks.

He had not played according to their game plan. Within a second of the match starting, he'd used his Crescendo of Might card, letting it loose on one enemy, while he charged straight at the other. Then he'd used his Divine Mentor card, internalizing it to boost his own powers. The combination of his own, already decent, combat prowess, and the boost from the Divine Mentor, had the critter reeling back in seconds. When he eventually expended the summons with a flash, blinding and stunning the enemy, that critter became an easy target.

Alone against his Crescendo of Might summon, the other beast might have persevered. The lumbering summons was big and strong, growing all the time, but it was also slowly falling apart. The critter was fast enough that it evaded most attacks too. Right up until Kith arrived. Together, they tore the other beast apart in short succession.

Cilia and Sera arrived shortly after they were done trading stories.

Sera beamed with satisfaction. The warning from Chase had been enough that she'd avoided getting too caught up inside her own head. She hadn't won, but with her heal and her Spark of Divinity boosting her Agility, she'd weathered or avoided the attacks of her many-limbed opponent for a full two minutes. Afterward, she'd stoically argued that as a win, since she was never planning to take down any enemies alone.

Cilia didn't do so well. She had seen through the ruse even before Chase said anything. The lack of logic in the explanations and the incongruencies in the choices made her realize they were being set up. However, she was still suffering from a major physical attribute deficit compared to the others. She had fought to the best of her ability, only, like she had already admitted to herself, that wasn't very impressive. The large, tough humanoid-shaped earth summon that pummeled her to the ground was stronger and tougher than anything she could handle, and her Agility or skill wasn't to the level where she'd be able to outmaneuver the beast. At least she'd avoided complete embarrassment, and afterward, once the adrenaline died off, she'd been able to list off a long and coherent list of the reasons why this was obviously a setup.

Once they were all there, they returned to the mess hall. Some of the others of the ridiculously named Red Tortoise class had clearly been there for longer, and everybody, it looked like, were either licking their wounds or gossiping about their own matchups. Quite a few people sported impressive bruises and injuries. Chase had to admit to himself that, despite it all being a ruse, of sorts, meant to determine who among them had the wits to figure things out or the fortitude to risk it all for a place among the Protectors, it had been a dangerous game.

After they'd feasted on a meal of curried rice and prawns which had *no* right being this fresh as far inland as they were, Cilia leaned back with a contemplative look. "A hundred and sixteen."

"Are we counting how many people are sending Chase here the evil eye? Because I made it out to be eighty-nine." Kith grinned.

Chase rolled his eyes and pointed at the banner showing off their overall ranking. The lowest-ranking person on the list now registered as number one hundred and sixteen. "That's four people missing? Damn. Seems like at least part of what Boneridge said was right. They were going to cut a good number of people away today. Oh. Wait a moment—be right back." He got up and walked to the end of the table where another person had just sat down. "Hey. Emilia, was it?"

The Darkborn crafter lifted her head from where she'd been resting on the table, groaning. She was seated at the far end of the table, across from just a single water-aspected Elemental. She blinked in confusion, then squinted. "Yeah. Emilia. What do you want?"

Chase shrugged. "Honestly? Just to see how you were doing. It's not often I see fellow Darkborn, especially in Earth's Ward. Good on you for standing up to the instructor. I found out too late that they were just testing us, or I'd have said something."

She scoffed. "Yeah. That would have been useful."

Now that she raised her head, Chase could see that the entire left side of the face was going to end up one big bruise. He could also see why Liam thought she looked attractive. Burn scars notwithstanding, she had a statuesque look to her, and her dark skin, along with her fine features and agile, willowy stature, gave her an aloof air, of somebody just outside your reach.

She studied him for a second, then shook her head. "Listen. Whatever your name is."

"Chase."

"What*ever* your name is. Normally, I wouldn't mind talking to you, or that lovely tall blond guy you're hanging out with. Except, word has gotten around. *People* don't like you. Associating with you is going to make life harder for a prospective Protector." She gave an infinitesimally small nod at a table nearby, sporting Ernest Chalico and a few of his followers. "So, no offense, but life here as a Darkborn is already tough enough as it stands. I don't need any further complications. If you don't mind?" She made a shooing gesture with her hands. Her eyes held something else. Something softer and sad. An apology.

"All right, then," Chase said, loudly, nodding back at her. "You don't have to be a *bitch* about it." He winked and walked away. Inside, however, he was fuming. That prick was becoming an annoyance. At some point, he might have to strike back at him. For that to happen, he had to learn more about him, to know where his weak spots were. As Chase sat down, to the merciless teasing of his group at him being shot down, he cursed. As if he didn't have enough going on already. He didn't care about this petty crap. Only, he'd have to do something about it if he wanted to handle his other responsibilities.

It was already early evening. After the meal, they didn't plan. They talked about it, even agreed that, now that they'd been admitted, they were going to sit down and plot how to find out whoever was selling entrance to Earth's Ward. Only, as they pulled themselves up from the hardwood chairs of the mess hall, their bodies quite simply told them to shove it. The bruises were starting to come to the fore, with raised skin and pretty colors, and limbs started to lock up from sitting still too long. In the end, they simply decided that they needed the rest more than they needed anything else and walked stiffly and painfully back to their rooms.

Chase leapt out of bed, hand grabbing for the dagger underneath his covers. He scrambled for it, finding nothing, while his brain was catching up to what was going on. What was wrong? Noise? Nothing. Visually? Nothing. Smell? Tea. Why did it smell like tea? He didn't even like tea. Where *was* that damn dagger?

A dark chuckle arrived from the far end of his room.

Something slowly eased into view, like a hand being removed from in front of his eyes, only it had been there the entire time. The effect was rather disconcerting, as Chase's room slowly rearranged itself. They were still the same natural, earth-colored, flowing lines of his cave-like room, only, now, a vague, cloaked shape stood right inside his door, face covered in waves of roiling mist. In her hand, she held what had ostensibly woken Chase up. A steaming cup of tea, smelling of ginger and mint.

"That was entertaining." The voice was exactly like Chase recalled it. Nondescript, androgynous, close to bereft of emotion. "I did not come here to be entertained, though. I came to remind you of something." Chase's dagger whipped from her other hand and stuck into his bedpost, vibrating. "You are here to do a job. Not to socialize. Not to make friends. Not even to make it in and become a Protector. You're here to find whoever has been infecting our society, selling entrance into Earth's Ward to the highest bidders."

Chase gulped. He remembered that the person in front of him didn't appear to have much of a sense of acceptance of his insouciance. Then, he reconsidered. She had decided to give them a chance. That meant, whatever else, she was going to have to learn to deal with him as he was. "Thank you," he said earnestly, flinging his legs around to place them on the floor, smiling with the sensation of the well-worn wooden floor.

"For what?" she asked.

"For the congratulations. I expect you're here to congratulate us for all making it into the towers, beating the odds, and also passing the first real test? No?"

"This is not a joke," she hissed.

"Oh, you're damn right it isn't," Chase snapped. "So, stop treating it like one!"

In a blink of movement, she was right before Chase again, a hidden blade raised against his throat.

This time, he didn't back down. "Listen, lady." He felt her tense up at the word. *Score! He knew it!* "I don't know who you are or what you do in your day-to-day job. But this? Cheating others and getting our grubby hands on things and information that we really shouldn't have? That's been *our* day-to-day job for years. Yet, if we're going to do that job? You need to give us the chance to do it. And that means socializing. It means making friends, and at least *appearing* to do our best to make it into the damn Protectors. If we don't? Nobody's going to believe our cover for a second."

"Listen. I am the one calling the shots here. Unless—"

"Unless you want us to fail, you need to back up. Otherwise, you might as well get to stabbing. Also, I hope you packed a lot of rags to wipe up my blood. I'm a bleeder."

The dagger moved blindingly fast. It nicked Chase's neck ever so slightly, causing a droplet of blood to trickle out. Then the blade was gone again, hidden who-knew-where. "Acceptable. But you need to recognize who's in charge."

"You are. There's no disputing that. Even if you couldn't sneak in and kill all of us in our beds, you'd likely be able to cause all sorts of trouble for us in here. But honestly, if you really want to ensure our success? Help us! We need information. Who's in charge of distributing the cards here? How does that work in practice? Who, apart from you, are in on the secrets? Where are the Wellsprings and how are they guarded? Also, who the Pits is Ernest Chalico?"

"Chalico?" For the first time, the figure looked properly surprised. "Why would you even know that name? They aren't at your level, politically, socially, or otherwise."

Chase shrugged. "Well, seems like Ernest has it in for me. Apparently, me and my people making it in to the towers displaced his sister. Also, I think he's just pretty damn racist to begin with."

She sighed and held a hand to her face.

The visual was rather disturbing, as the tips of her fingers disappeared *into* the shadows swirling on her face. "That is...black luck. However, you will just have to work around it. Under no circumstance should you do anything to antagonize him further. The Chalicos are one of the largest trading families in Earth's Ward. The High Elementalist two generations ago was a Chalico, and their extended family prides itself on delivering a consistently large number of Elemental Protectors."

Chase winced. "Well, that not antagonizing him further part is a bit too late, I think. I appreciate the information, though. What about the cards, then? Those are questions that might be suspicious to ask of regular people, and we likely need the information if we are to narrow down who might be responsible."

She looked at him for a long time. Well, most likely, she did. Her body was tilted in his direction and her silence seemed to be contemplative rather than overtly hostile. After a while, she raised her cup of tea. The uppermost part of the cup disappeared. She said, voice low and distinct, "Let me be entirely clear. This is not going to be a regular thing. I am not going to pop in and socialize with you. Neither will I allow you to call on me whenever it suits you. But your request is fair. I will explain what you need to know. Also, I will leave you with one option to get in touch with me, should you need to. One. Only use it when you have found what you need to."

Chase nodded. "Thank you. Seriously. We might not exactly see face-to-face on this relationship—no pun intended—but I think that we could end up in a place that'll be good, both for Earth's Ward and for our little group."

"That remains to be seen." Her fingers drummed noiselessly on the edge of her cloak. "I...am deciding where exactly to start. The level of information you will need depends on exactly how clueless you are."

Chase snorted. "We really should've had Cilia here for this. I'm pretty damn clueless, with some surprising gaps in my ignorance."

"One of those being Wellsprings, it would appear. Not everybody knows about those." She was silent, for a good long while, until she nodded, once. "Yes. That is where we should start. Wellsprings. The origins of all cards. You are aware, then, that a Wellspring is something you establish, causing Guardians to start appearing and making their way into the world to defend your deck? The Wellspring also has other functions, but those aren't relevant to you right now. What is relevant, but is *not* common knowledge, is the growth function of decks. As a nation grows, both in quantity and quality of card wielders, more and more decks will arrive, at certain thresholds. These decks will simply appear near the original decks, and each of them, though lesser in strength than the original deck, will grant the wielder who grabs them the power to bestow cards themselves, or to create their own Wellspring. Also, the more decks or Wellsprings a nation possesses, the stronger it is, and the more benefits and possibilities the original Wellspring will hold."

Chase decided he'd better not act *too* knowledgeable about them. It wasn't like just anybody would be able to become the wielder of a deck. "Oh. So that's why the forces of Light are so widespread and strong? They have so many wielders, decks, and Wellsprings that they've grown extremely strong?"

"To a lesser degree, that is true. They have an obscene number of wielders spread throughout the lands of Light. This means that they hold many more decks compared to us."

"How come Earth's Ward hasn't been overrun, then, if they're that much stronger than you? Also, why doesn't the towers award cards to any Elemental in and around Earth's Ward? If more decks is better, I mean. You'd think it would be better for every single grown-up to have access to their cards."

"Why do you think?"

"Well, the teachers do go on about the quality of the Elemental Protector being much higher than the average Lightborn soldier—so, I'd wager that there's some elitism in there. Though, given that they could just let everybody have cards and *still* train the elite, I don't really see that as being true. How are the decks guarded? Are they afraid that people will run off and sell the decks to the Lightborn?"

She was silent for a while. Eventually, a minuscule shake of her head came as the singular reaction. "You know, if you and your crew manage to find our spy, you might actually end up becoming a boon to the Protectors, or even the Cloaks – our secret defenders. Your mind is suited for it." Her finger stabbed at the ceiling, aimed at the far pinnacle of the peaks. "The decks are very well-guarded and only brought out every second month, for the arrival of the new initiates and our graduation ceremonies. We have the highest-Tier Elementalists present too, both for ceremonial and protection purposes. No need for you to worry about that part. However, the direction your thoughts take is commendable. They do not let cards out into the general populace, because we cannot afford to have the *information* contained in our decks become general knowledge. If the Lightborn knew everything about our cards, our strengths and weaknesses, they would be able to break our defenses. I believe that is what our infiltrators are working on."

"Ooh." Chase's mind raced, as he considered the implications. "They keep the information a secret. And the teachers and upper-Tier Elementalists make it all about national pride as well, so those who make it in can lord it over others. That way, people are even *less* likely to give up the secrets in their cards to outsiders. Diabolical!"

"That is *not* at all what they intend!"

Chase blinked. "What? I was impressed! Also...how do you know what they think? Unless...of course. You're one of the inner circle, aren't you? One of those in the know. Of course you are. If those Cloaks you mentioned are a secret spy group, you'd have to have a decently high position to be kept informed."

"What? That's ridiculous. Also, not at all the point. The entire reason for not sharing cards is that we will limit the knowledge about Elemental cards making it past our borders and to our enemies. If the occasional card becomes known, so be it. However, if they manage to build up entire dossiers and map out our classes properly, they will be able to build effective counter strategies to everything we have."

Chase slapped his forehead. He remembered how he'd thought it was weird that the administrator at the initial test asked him to spell out the details of his training card. "Just like you guys do. I *thought* it was weird that you guys even let other races into the towers. But you do it so you can keep a knowledge advantage against the other races, don't you? That is why you record all card details of anybody entering the Protectors."

A curt nod. "Yes. That is a secret, but not a large one. Part of our strategy is to be as prepared as possible, allowing our smaller numbers to be outweighed by our strength and knowledge surplus."

Chase nodded. "Okay. I get it. Thank you for sharing. Now we don't have to spend a lot of time looking into the wrong ideas. We can focus more on knowledge, of those who seem to ask too many questions."

"Just don't become too focused on one specific avenue. I wouldn't want you to miss something obvious."

"I appreciate the sentiment. But over not dying during training, avoiding getting kicked out in the Culling, and actually finding somebody who'll lower themselves to talk to the Dark-born runt...it's kinda low on my list."

CHAPTER 18

"Liberty attacked in strength. Once, in the early years. They swarmed our lands, with higher-tiered wielders in numbers never seen before or after, cards we have never even heard of before. That day, our earth-aspected saved us. Those dull, defensive bores, with their quiet training and unrelenting preparation. They died in droves, holding them back, unleashing traps and defenses they had built up for years. Yet, they succeeded. When Liberty pulled back, we stood triumphant, the walls of the towers unbreached. And our earth-aspected have kept preparing ever since." That is a pretty scary thought. An entire group that's done nothing but prepare traps and defenses for eventual attacks for, what, years? Decades? I wouldn't want to be the attacker there. (Page 62.)

"**W**hat do you think we're going to learn today?" Kith asked. "I hope it'll be more useful than last time. I mean, it was a bit over the top, all that *the Towers are what matter. You are just a tiny ant.*"

They had arrived early to the next World Knowledge class and chose a remote section of the amphitheater to sit down in. Amid heavy bouts of yawning, Chase filled them in on what the Cloak, if that was what she was, had told him at night. Then, their conversation veered toward the World Knowledge class itself.

"I thought it was extremely interesting," Sera countered. "An entire system built around the needs of the Towers? Put up against the power feuds among the nobility of the Lightborn and the Church of the Light, I can see the strength of this."

"Yeah. Same here, sister. At least, here, there's a point to things." An unfamiliar voice intruded on their conversation.

They turned their heads to see the stranger. He was a young Lightborn, one they'd seen in training but not spoken to, trailed by two others, a wiry Lightborn teenager and a twenty-something Furyborn woman with a mess of beaded braids.

"Jonathan. Jonathan de Torran," he said, with a huge, white smile. The Lightborn was large, clearly a physical class, with an athletic build that spoke of both power and control. "I'm a fighter, but of course, you already know that." He grinned at Liam.

"A strong one, too." Liam purposefully turned his head toward the central part of the foremost bench, where Ernest was holding court, surrounded by friends and followers. "Are you strong enough, though?" Liam segued, not unkindly. "Haven't you heard? Associating with the likes of us means messing with the Chalicos."

Jonathan laughed, a warm, amiable sound. "Cha-li-cos," he intoned. "Even the *name* sounds fancy. Now, I don't know about you guys, but last time I checked, I was Lightborn, not an Elemental. What one cocky, self-important little runt thinks doesn't really mean much to me. What *I* want to know is how you managed to tick him off."

"Not me. This guy here." Liam nudged Chase.

Chase shrugged. "We joined together, the five of us. Apparently, us making it in managed to knock his precious sister below the cutoff line. That, plus me being a Darkborn and existing seems to be an issue for him."

"Pay. Up!" the Lightborn teenager said happily, nudging Jonathan.

Reluctantly, Jonathan relented, counting a couple of silver out into the waiting palm. "Damn. I felt sure that somebody as conceited as that guy would be petty enough to simply choose a target without any reason at all."

The teen winked at them. He was a thin youth with arms that seemed like corded rope. It looked unnatural on somebody who likely wasn't even eighteen. "Name's Rowan. I bet that you being a Darkborn was definitely part of it."

"Tam. I didn't bet," the Furyborn behind them said, then subsided into the calm silence that seemed to be her go-to mood.

Chase frowned. "So, you're not worried about him and his influential family?"

Jonathan scoffed. "Please. He can worry about mine in turn." Rowan joined him in laughing. "To be entirely honest, that was the reason we came over here in the first place."

"Because...your family is super important?" Kith asked with a raised eyebrow.

The large Lightborn snorted a laugh. "No. Gods, no. Or, well, yes."

Rowan hid his face behind his hand. "I can't believe your parents are setting you up to be the heir. Do they *know* that you're like this?"

Jonathan scowled at him. "You're really not helping!" He rolled his eyes and continued. "No. What I mean is...there seems to be a bit of a bias against outsiders here in the towers. Given that we don't care about any of that, and just want to make it into the Protectors? We thought that you guys might not be bad to hang around. You seem to have a clue what you're doing in the different classes at least."

Rowan grinned. "And what he's *not* saying is that we've taken a good, hard look at the competition, and decided that you guys might actually have a *real* shot at making it in. Seems like the kind of people we want to be around, train and study with."

Chase looked at the others. None of them looked directly opposed to the idea. Cilia looked wary, but that was her standard expression when it came to new people. This might be just the windfall they needed. With a large part of the students already set against them, having access to somebody other than their own group would vastly increase what they could figure out. "Sounds good to me. We could definitely do with some new faces to look at."

"Yeah. It's worse for us, who have to look at your ugly mug," Kith quipped.

Chase raised his stump. "Hey. Guess which finger I'm holding up."

Once the laughter died down, Chase asked, "What's your story then? How did you three get to know one another?"

They spent the time leading up to the class swapping stories with the trio.

It turned out that Jonathan came from a relatively important family, back in the capital Lightborn city of Stradeburg, though he was a fourth son. That lent him the leniency to help decide what to make of himself. Instead of opting to join the forces of Light, like so many others, he chose to take a chance and try to earn Elemental cards for himself. If he succeeded, the five years spent as a Protector would pay their way back threefold, with his stock in the family increasing along with his personal power once he returned. Also, he reckoned that, considering he was only at the very beginning of the second Tier, he'd be safer in the towers compared to the questionable grind of the Lightborn armies.

Rowan was a childhood friend of Jonathan's and a ranged class. From the start, his family had encouraged him to shmooze up to the taller aristocrat, who had better prospects than their own much less influential craftsman family. Somehow, in spite of this, the two struck up a real friendship, and when Jonathan presented his idea to join the Protectors, Rowan was right there with him. Against heavy odds, they both managed to make it through the lottery. Rowan won his access first, and they had but a few days to spare before his access ran out, when Jonathan won as well. In their words, it had been costly but would be worth it.

Tam was a late addition, having only made their acquaintance a bit before they started on their way to the towers. The taciturn Furyborn didn't talk much but admitted that she simply

163

preferred not being alone and was already planning to join the Protectors. She was a Tier-three healer, and, judging from the scars covering her arms, she seemed to make up for her lack of book learning with personal experience. Her cards weren't ringed with the regular bright frame of the Light deck, but a thorny, bristling mess of a frame that showed Fury cards. Actual Fury cards.

All told, though, the trio weren't that different from their own group. They were young, in excellent shape, and determined to make it past the competition and into the Protectors. They also seemed good-natured and accommodating. Best of all, they opened up the closed access to others, and to knowledge about the towers. If some started to disregard Ernest and his followers, surely others would follow.

The class started before they could really get to know one another. However, the three decided to stay, sitting near them instead of returning to their own seats a couple of benches farther down.

"I am glad to see you back with us," Professor Brookwatch started. "Also, good to see that we have started weeding out the chaff. I make it…four people missing after your first training?" A few muttered complaints made the water-aspected teacher break out into an uncharacteristically wicked smile. "What? They were your friends and compatriots? I thought that I had made it quite clear to you last time. *The towers do not care about you.* We care about doing the best for the Elemental lands. And anybody weak enough to break before the promise of pain would never have made it into the ranks regardless."

The stern-looking professor passed her hands through her perpetually wet-looking hair and folded them before her. "Last time, that was the topic of our discussion. Why the towers do what we do and how that affects you in the greater whole. Today, we are going to talk about your possible role in the Protectors and what that actually means." She held both hands up wardingly. "Mind you, there is no discussing the numbers. Take a good, hard look around you. Less than one in five of those who are present are going to become part of the Protectors. Those are facts. For that reason, you need to leave your sentimentality at the door. Any family, friends, lovers, or similar here? Hope the best for them, but wasting your time applying factions or outside relations in here? Just don't. We are going to pick the best, regardless of who you are and who you know."

"But if you want the best for the towers, shouldn't you ban Lightborn?"

The voice raised in self-righteous condescension was one Chase knew. Ernest.

"Oh, this will be interesting." The professor rubbed her hands together with an expression of glee. "Pray tell, Mr. Chalico. Why would the towers cut themselves off from expanding our cards beyond Elemental ones and limiting our possible recruiting force by a huge degree?"

Chase chuckled. He could see Ernest's rank dropping by the second.

To his credit, the Elemental didn't back down. "Elementals all want what is good for the towers. Outsiders, especially the Lightborn, want what is good for *them*. In the long run, they care the least about Earth's Ward."

"Sure, Mr. Chalico. Just like you only care about the greater good, and not at all about the prestige of yourself and your family."

This time, laughter arose all around the amphitheater.

Ernest smiled, though it seemed like it cost him. "Of course. I am just a human. Yet, there is no debating that Elementals are going to care more about the future of Earth's Ward than outsiders." With a sneer, he added, "Besides, we've all heard about what happens to the Lightborn who make it into the Protectors. They desert, or they 'die.' Is that the kind of Protector we want? Is that the kind of help that the towers need?"

A murmur swept through the gathered students. One that showed that Ernest had made a real point.

The professor shook her head. However, it seemed like even she didn't have a direct contradiction to his words. "That kind of loose talk is not what the Protectors need. You should focus on your own progression, or you will find yourself falling behind and kicked out at the next Culling. Now. Moving on." She faced the rest of them. "Last time, we talked about the misconceptions about the Protectors. One common misunderstanding is how we fight that fight. Like you so eloquently defined it, Mr. Chalico, *we're defending Earth's Ward against the Lightborn.*" She shook her head, then continued. "We *are* the shield between Earth's Ward and the world. But that doesn't always mean fighting. Somebody, sum up the current state between the Elementals and Lightborn. One sentence."

The Darkborn Chase had tried approaching, Emilia, raised her hand. "The...longest, most violent stalemate in history?"

Laughter broke out everywhere. Professor Brookwatch shushed them. "That is *very* precise." She pointed out at the open sky behind her. "You can see the border from here on a clear day. That border, along with all our defensive works, traps, and the Protectors are what defends Earth's Ward from the rest of the world. The Elemental empire used to be huge. Now, and for the past forty-odd years, we have resided in this one place, pressed back to this one remaining stronghold. The *might* of the Protectors is the reason the Lightborn haven't defeated us yet. Only, *there is no outright war.* Because of our consistent victories, we have beaten them back enough times that they do not dare come at us. For every time we manage to beat back the Lightborn and Liberty Guardians flung at us, we grow stronger and better equipped to maintaining a *permanent* defense against them."

"But...they're still attacking us?" one of Ernest's hangers-on complained.

"This. This is exactly what we need to fight. *Death to ignorance!*" she hissed, in a tone that made no secret of the fact that that person was going to drop in rank. "You believe that they are really, truly attacking us? The Guardians of Light pressing us on the border are not a real attack. They are, in fact, right at the lower limits of what we need in order to keep our Protectors sharp. Hear me on this. *The worst the Lightborn could do would be to stop their Guardians from attacking us.* Do you not get it? We are carefully negotiating with the Lightborn, each and every year, in negotiations as hard-fought as any out there on the border, and we want *more* Guardians to test us. Because any Ænima we can reap from them means stronger Protectors and a better defense for us. In time, we will even win back the right to expand our lands once again."

"But...if they're not the enemy, then what is?" the poor Elemental persisted, confused.

"Everybody. Anybody." Reveling in the confusion of the Elemental, Professor Brookwatch spoke up. "For our next class, you are all required to read the first eight chapters of *History of Earth's Ward*. That should clear up any confusion. For the interim, I will boil it down to the following: We do not currently expect any all-out attacks on Earth's Ward. We are, however, preparing for anybody to launch an all-or-nothing strike against us, so that, in case it actually happens, we are not overrun." She held up a hand, waiting until everybody was hanging on her next word. "I am going to deliver a lot of knowledge to you, and expect you to pay attention to every iota of it. I will ensure that anybody who doesn't will receive a corresponding rank in my class. Even for those of you who seem determined to get yourself cut in the first Culling, I want you to take this with you, ensure that you take it to heart and teach everybody to know the actual purpose of the Protectors."

She walked back to the massive blackboard behind her and gestured. As she spoke, the words appeared behind her, written large enough to be easily visible from the upper benches.

Chase patiently spelled his way through the first to realize they were the same as the words she said, enunciating each word with care.

"Diplomat. Sword. Shield. Sacrifice. Scout. Runner. Bait." Her words rang out, as passionate as she had earlier been condescending. "Each of these titles, and more, may be required of a Protector on any given day. Should you beat the odds and end up among the chosen few, I want this to resonate within you, to become part of you. The roles of the Protectors are many and varied. And we need you to not only learn these roles, but learn when to apply each and any one of them to any given situation." Her voice hardened. "Right now, we are not there. In fact, we are so far from that situation, that we can't even see it on the horizon. Today, we are going to teach you the basics required to ensure that you know the bare minimum about the world and our place within it."

The class devolved into a detailed presentation about the Elementals and their place in the world. It skimmed over a good deal of the general history, focusing more on the situation as it stood today. A good part of it was well-known, at least to those from outside Earth's Ward, such as the state of the Lightborn empire, the fact that it was carved up into a ton of smaller city-states, with clear and obvious trouble cooperating, and what bearing that had on the state in Earth's Ward. Other details were less well-known, such as the fact that the last known true attack of Liberty soldiers on *any* known area on Ordei was a strong charge on Earth's Ward, eight years back. That attack had been supremely costly for the Elementals in resources, but less so in lives, because the attack was spotted early on, allowing the Protectors to retreat to a safe distance and set off an inhuman number of defensive measures. After that, the Liberty offensives were almost clinically measurable, with steady Guardian excursions, but no soldier presences.

At the tail end of the class, the professor sprang a test on them, granting them limited time to answer a dozen detailed questions revolving around the day's lecture. Sera and Cilia both aced them. Liam had forgotten some of the details. Kith believed that he did all right, considering he'd actually struggled to pay attention to everything.

Chase...messed up. They got summoned one by one, and had limited time to read the questions before having to give their answers directly to the teacher. His reading prowess was questionable and some of the longer words stymied him. He ended up missing a handful of the later questions. When they walked out, Chase's ranking dropped instantly. He was entirely certain he needed to speed up his reading lessons or he'd fail the class entirely. That also gave him a burning desire to do better in his next class, to make up for the bad result in this one.

CHAPTER 19

"Earth's Ward is an amazing place. Wonderfully planned...every part of its erection plotted to maximize utility, ease of access, and the optimal delegation of lands. Of course, that was back in the day. It was not prepared for the deluge of refugees who ended up living here, screwing up all plans, building horrible malformities left and right." That explains so much. If the city was actually planned properly, but has since then exploded? It would account for the...questionable style choices on top of the generally well-planned causeways and lines of the city. (Page 32.)

After the lecture, they'd hurried back to the mess hall before they parted ways, each of them going in different directions. This afternoon was the first time that they were going to have separate lectures, derived solely from their respective classes. Chase was both wary and thrilled at the prospect. Thrilled, because he wanted the chance to show what he was able to do—that he wasn't defined by his lack of a hand, regardless of any snipes by that gormless runt of an Elemental. Wary, because they didn't give any information away, and, so far, in the towers, they seemed somewhat set in their ways about how the different classes *should* behave.

Kith was off for Summoning Theory. Cilia, for Elemental Theory, which she expected to be something else than what the title implied. Sera was bound for Healer Training classes, which seemed rather self-explanatory, and Liam was off for Body Training, which sounded rather like what they were already being subjected to from Instructor Boneridge.

Chase's class was called Orientation and Movement, which was obscure enough that he couldn't tell what it was supposed to be. Based on the tests, he expected it to be similar to when they had to spot the pickpockets in the crowd. That, it turned out, was true, but far from the full picture.

Where the others were led to different parts of the towers, Chase and his fellow rogues—sixteen in total, with just a few being ones he recognized—were led first down into the courtyards in front of the towers and then farther into Earth's Ward proper by a domineering air-aspected Elemental. He was a tall, middle-aged man with a razor-thin beard. His neat, wavy, dark-brown hair and handsome features would make any female Waves worker giggle and call out suggestively, while the ropy muscle, from which his entire body seemed to be comprised of, would make any bruiser think twice about him being an easy mark.

They also learned that the man, Instructor Highstream, also had a shifty temper and a *very* noticeable voice. The rasping, slightly squeaky voice thundered out over the smaller market square, quietly bustling in the warmth of the early afternoon, making heads turn their way. The Elemental didn't seem to notice or care, leaping up to the edge of a fanciful fountain showing Elementals of all four aspects working together to build...something. "Rogues die!" he shouted, balancing precariously on the edge, pausing and nodding to himself at their shocked expressions. "That is no secret. Rogues are, by definition, known for having skillsets and powers that help us *avoid* conflict. When thrown into a situation that insists on conflict? We die. Today, I am going to start guiding you onto a path that can, hopefully, help you avoid that fate."

He paused, and a buzz of conversations erupted among their groups.

Without raising his voice, he interrupted them. "Chief among the lessons I am going to impart on you is this one. *Stay observant.* Rogues in the Protectors have the most varied positions of all classes. We can be lead scouts, distractions for the fighters, roaming attackers, and even assassins working alone, depending on aptitude, attributes, and the situation. However, the sole thing that stands out among those rogues who consistently survive is our ability to persistently observe and parse situations quickly and efficiently." His hand snapped out, and he pointed at Chase and a water-aspected Elemental teenager Chase recognized from the initial acceptance test. "You and you. Step forward. You two were the most observant in the pickpocket test. Why is that?"

The teenager spoke up first, hands behind her back like she was presenting in front of a classroom. "I have had extensive classes since childhood. Memorization techniques, perception tests, a lot of different ways to ensure that I take in every detail of a—"

"YOU!" Instructor Highstream barked at a pair behind her who were exchanging whispered words. "I tell you that the key to survival as a rogue is observation and attention, and you immediately distract yourselves? I would kick you from this group if I was allowed. *You just made yourselves rank last.*" With the virulent outburst finished, he turned back to the water teen and nodded. "Please proceed."

Halting and stumbling from the show of rage, she tried to find her place. "I-I...I've been taught well. For that reason, Mental Power is also one of my highest attributes. This aids my concentration, perception, and swift ability to react to situations."

The instructor nodded, one eyebrow raised. "But not, it seems, the ability to adapt to shock. Work on that." He turned his head to Chase. "You?"

"I've worked a lot of crowds. There's tricks, like she says," Chase nodded at the teen, "to spotting things that stand out, if you know what you need to look out for. Also, reading the crowd wrong can result in bad results." He raised his stump and shrugged. "You only get so many chances."

"Hah!" The instructor barked a laugh. He leapt down from the edge and walked closer to the group. "I'm glad we got one of you." He turned to the others. "See? This is somebody who's learned to survive by themselves, instead of through the means of expensive tutors and fancy memorization techniques." He looked Chase up and down. "So, you were...a thief?"

Chase shrugged. "When I needed to be, among other things."

"Good." The instructor beamed. "I'm not going to ask you all to learn from this young man. That would be ridiculous. He has clearly not had the schooling that most of you had. He will be working from behind, when it comes to knowledge, techniques, and likely, monetary considerations. Also, his Mental Power is one of the lowest in the class. But." He raised an admonishing finger. "Somebody like him is proof that you can flourish where you'd otherwise wilt, *if you know your environment.*" He rubbed his hands together, seeming to enjoy himself immensely. "Oh. Thief boy. If you were to choose between all the experience you own and a high Mental Power, what would you choose?"

Chase scratched his neck. "Both? Heh. Honestly, the question is kind of cheating. I mean, take me out of a crowd, and a lot of what I've learned is worth little. Mental Power is worth more there. But in most situations in a city, I'd count on myself. Although there can always be surprises."

The instructor danced from one leg to the other, now looking to be back in a brilliant mood. "Take this to mind. Tricks that help you stay alert, awake, and attentive are all good. Having a high Mental Power is excellent too. Knowledge about your environs? Even better. All those, combined with the physical attributes to move and act swiftly and efficiently, however, is how a rogue thrives and survives persistently. If you're slow? Exercise. If you don't have a decent Mental Power? Train. Train until your eyes bleed and your mind hurts. If your Agility and Mental Power are high, learn! Learn about your surroundings, about the dangers, the monsters, human and otherwise, the gangs, the nobility, the important traders—*everything*."

"The...traders? Sir? Are you implying that the traders here in Earth's Ward are a threat?" a well-groomed and dressed rogue in his mid-twenties asked, disbelief obvious in his eyes. His garish red-and-orange clothes were partly see-through, tastefully showing off his status as a Duo, as well as his impeccable biceps.

Instructor Highstream stared, wide-eyed at the fire-aspected man. He walked back, silently, to sit at the edge of the fountain, dipped a hand into the water, and splashed some on his face. Then he howled with laughter. For a full minute, he just laughed, while the well-dressed man grew progressively redder in the face. Finally, the instructor composed himself and wiped his eyes. "Whoo. That was good. Thank you *so* much for that."

He leapt to his feet, light as a bird, rubbing his hands. "You two." His finger shot out at the pair who had been whispering earlier. "Good news. You just got bumped up from your bottom ranking." The finger moved back to the well-dressed man. "You. Are you *fucking* kidding me? Have you ever spilled a fruit drink on the scion of a wealthy trader? No, you haven't. Because you're still here, not carting dung for farmers. In Earth's Ward, traders are among the most powerful families, *with all that entails*. They have riches, connections, and power. They can ruin your reputation, your trade, and your future, without even talking to you. And you...need to expand your horizon. If you walk into the world with this kind of limited worldview, you aren't long for this class, let alone life as a rogue."

He clapped loudly, making a few of the other rogues jump. "I am getting sidetracked, though. What we are going to do in this class is learn by doing. I am going to throw you into the deep end. Then I will give you some pointers on where you need to improve and what you need to work on. For some, like our dark-skinned thief here, one answer is obvious—improving his Mental Power. For others, the answer may lead you in vastly different directions. Some will need to train their movement. Others will need to do some serious work in a crowd. Others again must find their answers in a book. Altogether, that will help you become the best possible rogue, and help you survive where you otherwise would not."

"Mr. Highstream?" a rat-faced fire-aspected Elemental asked. "In the other classes, it seemed like these first two months before the first Culling would be kept to general training? That they wanted to limit the expenses they'd use on us before removing the worst of us. Why is it different here?"

The instructor tapped his chin, piercing eyes boring into the smaller youth. He tapped on his armband. "That is...a decent question."

The Elemental visibly deflated with relief.

"The short answer? It's not different. We're not throwing any money at you, expensive tutors, or specialized education. However, given that training a well-versed rogue means having knowledge and abilities in *many* areas? I find it better to get you started on the most lacking parts immediately. Mind you, you are going to be doing all the work yourselves. Not nudging you in the right direction from the start would simply be a waste."

Chase noticed a wave of relief among the group. He silently agreed. He understood the theory behind what the towers did. Their tests were far from perfect. There would always be some people getting through the eye of the needle who then proceeded to show that they didn't have what it took to be part of the Protectors long-term. Getting rid of the worst of those would make for a much more cost-efficient approach. It still rankled, making it in and not being allowed to *learn*. At least here, they'd be able to start on improving where it would be most efficient for their own good. Even if Chase suspected that there would be a *lot* of Mental Power-increasing exercises for him in his near future.

The instructor walked around them, putting his back between them and the huge circular expanse that was Earth's Ward. He pointed with his thumb behind himself. "See the three-pronged tower back there? The ostentatious, glimmering one with the fire illusions around it? The first five of you who make it there are going to gain increases in rank." He held up a hand, forestalling the rogues who jolted like they wanted to take off that very second. "But...between here and there, I've placed at least five persons with red hats. When you arrive, you are going to tell me as much as you can about these persons, and the degree of accuracy will be part of your final ranking."

Chase's mind raced. That was devious! The tower was likely about two miles away. A decent run, but nothing insanely taxing on his Toughness. With his Agility and Steps of Brilliance card, he'd probably be able to outpace most of his competitors. But if he sped up and took the fastest route possible, he would likely miss some of the marks and details.

The instructor didn't give them much time to think about it. "We're off in three. Two. One. *Go!*" Instructor Highstream activated a card and...vanished.

Chase shot forward, passing by a handful of his fellow rogues who froze at the instructor's disappearance.

One person, one of the two Elementals who'd been scolded for not paying attention, raced ahead of them all, at a pace not likely to be sustainable. Only, he increased in speed again, and yet again.

Chase didn't need to spot the flash to know he'd used a movement-based card of some sort. He didn't try keeping up with the man either, as he swiftly disappeared into the crowd ahead. He could just hope that the man was unable to properly spot all the marks with that kind of speed.

One other rogue outpaced him, sprinting fast enough that he wouldn't be able to keep up. However, from the strained look on her face, Chase doubted she'd be able to keep the pace for the full two miles.

Chase quickly fell into one of his old rhythms. Not the "fleeing from pursuit" rhythm. That one was full-on speed and trouble, discarding caution for the need to get away as fast as possible. No, this one was "job finished, now to switch areas, so we aren't recognized." It was a decently fast pace but sustainable, and based on Agility and making yourself small enough that you'd slide through the crowd, not smash through them.

The first two marks were less than a hundred feet into the run. In the center of the street, a fire-aspected Elemental strode along in a form-fitting red dress and matching hat. Her curves, flaming red hair, and remarkable looks almost made him ignore the short sword on her hip. It *also* almost made you miss the nondescript cobbler sitting in his stall along the side of the avenue, with his unremarkable, tight-fitting red cap. Grinning, Chase took in the man's looks, including the, for a cobbler, surprisingly fancy shirt, and turned his attention back onto running and spotting anything red.

He settled into his pace. It felt familiar, like coming home. He moved through the crowd with ease, feeling comfortable in a way he hadn't in ages. If there was one thing he knew, it was moving through a crowd and keeping an eye open. He also realized just how much he had grown, attribute-wise. He kept a pace which, for him back in Isarn, would've been a full sprint. Now, it felt like a comfortable jog, and he could even increase the pace a little without flagging. With a thought, he activated his Race of Life card and felt even lighter.

The city stretched out ahead of him. The route, this time, was fairly obvious. There was just one main avenue that led straight to where they were going, one of four roads that encircled the entire city. It had a ton of side streets—some large cobbled connecting streets...others little better than alleys, only fit for relieving yourself or getting mugged. With the large tower in sight along the curve of the ring street, detours were only likely to lead to delays and missing some of the marks.

A few signs of chaos showed the progress of the two rogues ahead of him. One tall Lightborn sprawled on the ground, cursing long and loud at somebody ahead of him, while a scree of spilled produce showed where one of the two in the lead had likely become overzealous in their race.

Chase used his Steps of Brilliance judiciously. For the most part, he kept to the ground, bobbing and weaving to make the least fuss. Once, he used it to leap over a cart turning mid-lane and blocking half the street. Another time, he used two platforms at chest height to bounce off of them and twist left of a drunken merchant instead of bowling him over. Most often, he just used a single platform, swiftly erected to give him additional purchase, allowing him to turn with otherwise impossible precision.

One mark presented herself in a second-story window: earth-aspected Elemental with a woolen red cap half-hidden behind wafting curtains and an oversized fan. Another was a worker, strolling down the side of the street behind a caarnath-pulled cart filled with manure.

Chase didn't con himself into believing that he'd located each and every mark. Pits, there might even be *more* than the five Mr. Highstream had named. But he purposefully kept alert and kept at it, gaze roaming back and forth, well-honed senses trying to make out those attempting to hide from him. If he was able to come in at third place, but give a well-rounded description of at least five marks? That should hopefully put him in a decent position for a good starting rank in this class, counter-acting the bad results from his lack of scholarly skills.

He was not ready for the spell appearing right in his face.

CHAPTER 20

"We have so many wonders in this city. Wonders of cunning, architecture, knowledge, magic, or martial efforts. Whichever your predilection, Earth's Ward and the Elemental towers has got you covered. The lottery is ever increasing in cost, yet the applicants still line up, and for good reason. We have something for everybody." And there we have the self-importance again. It annoys me that it's not entirely unwarranted. Earth's Ward really *is* impressive. (Page 26.)

The vision appeared in front of Chase's eyes like a flash. Then it stayed there, floating in the air, hovering like a butterfly as he sprinted along. It was pretty...a kaleidoscopic, ever-moving creation of colors and magic. He barely noticed how he slowed down and veered off course to follow the thing. He was captivated by just how impressive the thing was, how it felt like it was right at the edge of his comprehension. If only he was able to take it in a bit better, he'd understand what was happening.

Chase's thoughts were slow. Detached. Like he was watching from far away. Meanwhile, his body acted by itself, following the glowing apparition. He walked down a side street, then farther into an alley. The alley was dark and cramped, houses cluttered closely together, allowing for blind angles and spots everywhere. Deep within him, something screamed and was buried, again, beneath the marvel of what he was following.

He ducked into an open door and walked softly up the scoffed earthen stairs, first one, then another floor. Whatever this building was, it was *not* part of the omnipresent Elemental intent to outdo one's neighbor. This place was dirty and crude, seemingly constructed in a hurry and forgotten about afterward. Yet, Chase couldn't bear to waste time thinking about it. Not when he was just about to solve what was attracting him so about that magical visage in front of him. He almost had it.

A sudden sound disrupted his concentration. It was the slamming of a door behind him. Chase shook his head, then paid it no heed. He was *busy*, dammit.

"Hey. Watch that, idiot. Loud noises and too much movement can break the effect of the card."

The sound was inconsequential. Unimportant, compared to the single, overarching importance of understanding the *meaning* of this wonderful thing. Parts of the words tickled Chase's mind, though, before he wrinkled his nose and moved closer to the apparition. It was now wafting gently back and forth in front of a wall. A sturdy, earthen wall that beautifully offset the kaleidoscopic dance of the tiny miracle.

A snort. "I've seen you use that a dozen times. The only time it was close to breaking was with that bookish fob. Look at this loser. Does he look bookish to you?"

"I know. It's Mental Power that defines how much of a hold I have over 'em. That doesn't change the fact. Don't go ruining my control, you blasted moron. If you absolutely *have* to waltz around, help get the chair ready instead. Then, we'll get started on the questions. Funny. Doesn't look like this guy's a pro, does it?"

It moved now. The tiny ball of ever-changing wonders soared across the wall, past a sturdy window and into the room, to the center, where a single chair sat, sunk down into the earthen floor by means Chase couldn't perceive. Leather straps extended along the armrests, holding some implication that Chase couldn't really fathom right now. A person stood right behind, fiddling with the ties on the straps. Another held a hand firmly on his left arm, guiding him along. The screams inside his head were back now, and louder. They were so annoying. If only he could make them—

"Come on now. He's like that fat blob of money we caught last week. Totally gone. It's gonna take us twenty minutes just to get him out of the trance." A pair of hands came together in a loud slap, right above Chase's head.

"Stop it, I said. You'll—"

For the briefest of moments, Chase was back to himself. Just a split second, nowhere near enough that he could really think about anything. Yet, that deeply buried, screaming part of him reacted before he could stop and focus on what he was doing. He rearranged one card on his body, swapping Spoils of the Undeserving for its Tier-three Dark equivalent, Free of Perdition. Then he activated it, choosing the person behind the chair for a target.

Chase's mind started to fade again, sinking back into the warm and fuzzy comfort of watching the colorful apparition. Then, the card kicked in and his mind became fresher, more awake. Within seconds, much too slowly, Chase realized what the hell was going on. He was being magically subdued and about to be trapped into a chair. Definitely with no good intentions. With his Mental Power brought up to the same level as the caster, though, he was able to push the attraction away, ignore the pull—at least for this short, fleeting instant.

He jerked away in a hard, pulling moment. The hand on his arm slid down over the elbow, then clamped down hard.

Chase taught the man a valuable lesson: it's hard to grab onto a sweaty arm, when there is no hand to arrest the grasping hand from sliding farther down.

For a brief, glorious second, Chase stood back, free, staring at his would-be captors.

They were Elementals—one water, one earth—and both looked to be the rougher sort. They were also completely taken aback by the card not working.

Chase could still feel it pulling. Trying to lull him into the warmth of its oblivion.

"You—" the earth-aspected one, who'd clapped in front of him, started.

Chase didn't wait to hear what came next. The door to the room was on the far side of the two. They were both carded, with at least two cards apiece visible on their bare arms, and wore cudgels on their belt. The situation was about the worst possible for Chase, who would not be able to physically stand up to the strong pair. Right now, he *really* wished he'd picked No Easy Catch. Having a card that could turn him into a greased pig seemed like a wise choice right this moment. He could switch to Squall Sling...push one of them back, perhaps.

He went for the painful option. Wincing in advance from what it was going to cost him, he flung himself straight at the small, sturdy window forming the only possible escape from the room.

The latch keeping the window ajar was poorly made. That was likely the only reason that Chase survived. From behind, a freezing pulse struck his legs, threatening to lock them in place. Yet, his dive was already initiated. As he slammed, arm-first, into the window, the latch broke first, then half the window did, as the wooden frame shot outward. Chase suddenly found himself frozen, bleeding, and, more importantly, airborne, with nothing between him and the ground, maybe thirty feet below.

Mid-air, the last few weeks' intensive training in using his Steps of Brilliance card paid off. Hurting and confused, with his arm badly battered and his head still foggy from the card used on him, Chase nonetheless managed to produce three small platforms in the general path of his downward trajectory. He flailed wildly, catching one with a half-frozen leg, righting himself slightly, before catching the other with his hand, and stopping his descent for just a second before the step faded away into nothing. Right away, he used the power again, this time managing to craft a more controlled set of steps. The first one, he hit with his ass, blessedly stopping most of his downward momentum and allowing him to hit the next two at the same time with his feet, halting the fall entirely. From then on, the downward path was almost leisurely, if you discounted the ice missile whizzing past his ears from above, and the colorful creation still trying to catch his attention.

Chase hit the ground awkwardly, nearly stumbling before managing to make his legs cooperate. He burst into a lurching run, away from this place and toward safety.

CHAPTER 21

"There is no prejudice in the towers. We accept anyone equally, regardless of race, origin, or political association. As long as you work toward the betterment of our society and are willing to put in the work, there is a place for you here." Regardless of the obvious lie, that really isn't as impressive as he tries to make it sound. "As long as you're willing to give up seven years of your life and risk your life for us, you're welcome here." (Page 18.)

Chase didn't know what to expect when he finally made it to the tower and the waiting Instructor Highstream. Most likely a bottom place in the ranking, unless his detailed descriptions of the red-hat-wearing marks were enough to keep him from that questionable honor. Possibly being called out for bragging about all his street experience and then getting himself nearly captured and whatnot, on their very first public outing. Or just being called a liar. He did not see the actual result coming.

"Repeat that, boy. Somebody tried to capture you? They were not just trying to rob you?" The instructor's attention was fully fixed on him, looking like one of those damn bright wolves ready for the pounce.

"No. Definitely not. One of them had a card that trapped my mind and made me veer off path and toward where they were waiting. The other was a water-aspected Elemental with freezing powers to lock me down. They could have caved my skull in the very moment I arrived. Instead, they were about to tie me to a chair and talked about questioning me." Chase shrugged. On the remaining run, his mind had churned, trying to come up with exactly what to say. He decided to play it as close to the truth as he could, without giving away what he suspected. "If they hadn't made a stupid mistake, I'd never have gotten away."

Instructor Highstream's eyes glanced to his arm, still dripping blood. They hardened. "I believe you. Another student said they saw you slowing down and veering off along the route for no good reason. I will ask you more questions on the move. Can you keep up? We are going to get some feet on the ground, and then we will try to catch them."

Chase blinked. That almost sounded...concerned? Nah. It had to be his imagination. "I've had worse. I bet they're long gone, though. They looked like your average bruisers. People who knew what they were doing...all business, but not too imaginative."

The wiry Elemental huffed. Then he barked a brief instruction for the remaining students to run back to the towers, before setting off with Chase in tow. As they ran, he alternated between asking Chase detailed questions and unleashing short, high-pitched signals on a tin whistle. Within minutes, whistles answered on and off all around them. Once, he thought he saw the swirling colors of a magical cloak looking at him from the distance. He shook his head and continued.

They found the room deserted, just as expected. There was no sign the pair had ever been there, except for the chair still sunken into the floor. The instructor took in the room, then unleashed a long stream of different signals on the whistle. Then, with a remarkably soft expression, he turned back to Chase. "Sorry. They're long gone. But don't you worry. Earth's Ward is large, but we know our city. Our Protectors will find them."

Chase was feeling kind of light-headed. He blinked, as he realized it was the Mental Power that left him again. Funny...it also kept off part of the pain? Mental Power really was amazing. He shrugged. "Otherwise, that's what the Cloaks are for, right?" he said. Then he froze, realizing his mistake right away.

The instructor narrowed his gaze on the Darkborn. "You really *are* informed. Not many learn about the Cloaks for a long, long time. But sure. This could be a job for them, if our Protectors fail to reel them in. Your description was detailed enough that they have a decent chance of spotting them out in the open."

Chase took a deep breath, trying to fend off the haziness. "Speaking of descriptions. I know I came in last. But I think I got decent descriptions of the marks. I...may have missed a few on the last stretch. Can I—"

Instructor Highstream's surprised guffaw interrupted his line of thought. The wiry man shook his head. He gestured at the door. "Never mind me. Let's get out of this place. You can explain what you spotted along the way."

Getting back to the towers took a while. They had to stop and bandage Chase's arm, because one of the cuts was deeper than it had appeared and wouldn't stop bleeding. Along the way, the instructor questioned Chase again and again, with more, increasingly inquisitive and detailed questions, about the thugs who attacked him. What had the distracting ability looked like? Did he spot any of their cards? If he were to guess at their everyday occupations, what would they be?

Chase answered to the best of his ability. Eventually, she also started asking about the marks he'd spotted along the way. Upon returning to the towers, he was led to the infirmary. Ignoring Chase's protests that Sera would be able to handle things just fine, Highstream dragged him right past a long line of waiting patients and into a healer's room. A brief discussion later, and a warm sensation spread throughout his body, pushing away the pain and discomfort as a niggling sliver of glass slid out of his arm and dropped onto the floor. That wasn't all, though. The healer insisted on a lengthy range of investigations and questioning to ascertain whether the mind-affecting card still held any sort of influence on him. It turned out that not only were such cards not common, they were actually illegal for anybody but city officials in extremely specific positions.

It was late in the evening when he was finally allowed to return to his chambers. He sighed happily at the sight of his door. He wanted nothing more than to fall into his bed and sleep the night away.

The anxious group exclaiming the moment he opened the door made him forget sleep as a fever dream. His crew were all there, talking to the point where he couldn't understand a thing.

Chase shot a longing glance at the bed. Then he sighed, shoulders sinking, and he shuffled forward. "At least let me sit down. I'll tell you what happened."

It turned out that the situation had been the talk of the towers for the entire evening. The other rogues returned to the premises, each sharing a wilder story than the previous one. It didn't help that the towers had turned out a large number of Protectors within the hour who ventured into the city to find those culpable.

"Also, you went from middle of the pack to number one in the Orientation and Movement class ranking. What the Pits happened?" Kith half shouted.

Chase made Kith move off his bed to let him plop down with a weary sigh. Then, with his small chamber crowded by the extra four people, he recounted the entire happening, including what he'd been able to learn about the attackers. He was pleasantly surprised to learn that the instructor's careful questioning had let him piece together more about them than he'd managed on his own. Not only had the pair likely been career criminals, they'd also been surprisingly unprofessional about the whole thing.

He finished his retelling. "I don't know. If they were back in Isarn, a pair like these would've been chewed up and spat out. Picture the Church of the Circle learning that somebody was stupid enough to lure somebody with an official position into a trap in plain sight, during the day?"

Kith snorted. "Or somebody on the Waves hearing about it. Makil's Reavers would end them, simply for the heat they'd bring down on everybody."

"Focus," Cilia scolded. "This teaches us a lot of things. Some of them, we should have expected. Such as the fact that our pursuit isn't letting up just because we made it into the towers. This is clearly related to the pair who trailed us when we first entered Earth's Ward."

Chase shrugged uncomfortably. "There's also the tiny detail that they were going to kill me. The way they were talking about the questioning and their plans? It didn't speak to letting me go."

"Yeah." Kith nodded. "Also, another point to them being happy amateurs. If you want answers, you don't let a mark guess that you're going to bury him afterward."

"They might have relied on that card of theirs coaxing answers from him. It sounded like it messed with his mind enough it could have made him talk," Sera pointed out.

"True," Chase said. "It all leads up to one ugly conclusion, though." He fought down the exhaustion looming over him, looked over his friends in turn. "We are going to need to step up our actions to find out who they are."

Sera said, "But we know so little about...everything here."

"True. Yet, look at what we do know. We know that somebody is trying to get to us. We know that they aren't afraid to act during the day, and care little about consequences. We *also* know that they are able to learn about our schedules, hence, they can plot their attacks for whenever it suits them best," Chase said.

Sera frowned. "That also confirms that they have help inside the towers. We already guessed, but this seals it."

"Just so. That by itself might not be the worst." Chase grimaced. "But let's face it. We are out of our element here. Not just the school and all the Lights-cursed reading or the damn racist Elementals. The entire damn society. We don't know what's what. And we're not going to learn how everything works in time. We have less than two months before the first Culling. We can't assume that we're all going to make it through. We all have our weak spots. If one of us fails? They're left to themselves out in Earth's Ward, easy pickings for anybody who wants to go after us. In short? We only have two months. We can't wait until we have the lay of the land and understand who's who to start making our moves. We need to act, and we need to act *now*."

The cramped room filled with silence. Then Cilia started cursing. Long and hard.

After a while, Liam asked, "Are you all right?"

"All right? Of course I'm not all right. My one reason for existing is keeping Chase in line and curtailing his insane plans. Now, we're in a position where we don't have the luxury of learning what we need in order to survive. We're doomed! Doomed!"

"I'm...not that bad, am I?" Chase asked.

Liam snorted. "Remember when you wanted to rob the Reavers? Your words, I believe, were 'They're so powerful. Nobody will believe we were stupid enough to try.'"

Cilia joined in with her head in her hands. "Or when he decided a Tier three with a clearly magical armor was an excellent mark, because that fancy armor would be too heavy to run in?"

"I was twelve! I'm...feeling very attacked right now," Chase said.

With a tight laugh, Cilia said, "Okay. So, we agree. We need to act and we are low on time. However, that doesn't mean that we get to act without forethought. It just means we may have to take some chances that I would not approve of otherwise. Now, it's not like I haven't been thinking about how to go about this. How about I line up what I've got so far, and you tell me what you think?"

Without waiting for their approval, she launched into a description. "First off, let us start with the actual goal we were given. We need to expose who was behind the scheme that allowed people to cheat the lottery and enter Earth's Ward unbidden. That, by itself, might seem doable. Yet, given the latest developments, we suspect that they're not doing it just for the money."

"We do?" Liam asked, baffled.

"Yes, we do, Liam." She shook her head. "Just entering Earth's Ward in and by itself sounds like an excellent plan for anybody trying to make trade connections, see the sights, visit the library." She gave an almost heady sigh at the mention of the library. "Yet, now that we know there are ties here to the towers? That speaks of a bigger plot. Something tied to entry into the Protectors itself. Following that, we have our defenses. We will, I am certain, have other situations shortly, where some of us are exposed, going into the town or perhaps even outside of Earth's Ward itself. We need to learn about this, have emergency plans in place to ensure that we're prepared and aren't caught off guard like Chase was. Finally, we have the Culling. Even if we are running on limited time here, we cannot lose sight of that goal. Even with everything else going on, our ultimate chance at staying in the city would be to join the Protectors. Missing out on that would be a choice not taken lightly."

Chase nodded. "Agreed. And I'll say, if one of us is forced to drop out, we should make a pact to all drop out. We are not leaving anybody by themselves in Earth's Ward, ready to be picked off at our hunters' leisure." He looked around at all of them, smiling to see them nodding in agreement. "That's a great summary, Cil. I have a few thoughts on some of it—but I'm guessing you already have something planned out to get us started?"

"Of course I do. Starting with the end goal. The Culling. Keeping that in mind all the time is not so much a choice as a necessity. It will allow us to grow stronger, enable us to defend ourselves and make us blend in better. That means we need to train as hard as anybody else—on top of our other issues."

"To think I thought you low-life scum when first I met you," Sera mused. "You are truly more disciplined than most soldiers I have known, not to mention the nobility."

Kith groaned. "Not by choice, princess. Give me a chance! I'll be low-life scum!"

Cilia slapped him on the shoulder. "*I know,*" she spoke up over Kith, "that you are already giving it your all in training and in the classes. Where we will truly be able to get a step up on the competition is in between classes. These are mostly singular applicants, who have to rely on a friend or two, or temporary agreements to have somebody else to perform critique, aid them and help lift each other up. We, however, are able to group up on a daily basis and help train one another where we are weak. I have been able to ascertain that access to the combat training area is open to all, at all hours. Equipment is only distributed during classes or with special passes the teachers give out. Be that as it may, we can, and should, spend at least an hour each day on additional training."

"You're right," Chase said. "We should also add in at least an hour a day of mental exercises—at least for Kith and me. We're going to need it."

Kith grimaced but didn't complain.

With a frown, Chase added, "Reading, too. It is going to cost me if I don't learn faster."

Cilia started writing down pointers on a piece of parchment. "This is already relatively time-consuming, especially for Chase—but I agree. Moving backward through our goals, we have our preparation for any other ambushes. That one is mainly on me. I will spend less time on mental exercises, and more on crafting or theorizing the crafting of items that can, hopefully, help us survive any ugly surprises. Preferably, something explosive."

Sera added, "I will help there as well. As long as we work together, my boosts will improve your crafts. Also, I can use the time productively to study our situation and the Towers. I sat with Tam—that Furyborn healer—during classes this afternoon, and she is surprisingly knowledgeable on the towers and our situation. I believe that her input, along with some actual literature, can help uncloud our situation and possibly even pinpoint our schedule. This way, we could predict any risky outings in advance."

"In addition to this, we should take precautions when moving about outside the towers—if possible, always stay in the company of others, reducing the likelihood of any attacks," Cilia prompted. The pointed ears of the tiny woman twitched noticeably as she bent over her parchment, scribbling furiously. "The final part, I admit, is presenting me with some difficulties." She laid the tome on her knees and gazed intently at the others over it. "How do we find out who's behind the scheme and expose them?"

They all avoided her gaze.

Chase cracked his knuckles. "There's no perfect answer here, I think. Not for now. You said it yourself, Cil. We know too little and are way out of our depths. Only, it's not going to stay that way. So, I think we take a crack at this in our own way. Liam, you talk to people—those who're willing to talk to us, anyway. Learn about people, about those with weird connections and reputations, figure out who might be able to arrange something like this. Cil, you and Sera are going to spend time in the library anyway. You should try to figure out who might *want* to do something like this and why. Kith, you're with me."

"I am?" Kith asked. "What are we doing?"

"While Liam's busy figuring out the 'who' of things, and the girls are trying to figure out the 'why'? We're being the bastards, trying to come up with the *how*. If they're pulling the threads from within the towers, there must be some clandestine meetings, messages being run back and forth. That Cloak said that they haven't figured out any connection so far. Even so, there's got to be some communication, even though it's likely one-sided. Once we get the chance to sit down and figure out how they might be handling the scam from up high, we can work out how we're going to bust them. How does that sound to everybody?"

Murmurs of agreement ran around the room.

Liam cleared his throat. "There was one thing. Something I think we should all try to figure out." He smiled warmly as they all looked at him. "Rumors, you know? When something is well-known enough that it becomes a common rumor, there's often something to it. We've heard, a bunch of times now, that

Lightborn and others are getting into the Protectors, only to desert or die."

Chase blinked. "You think there's some sort of connection? Lightborn being allowed access, getting their cards, and then running off to safety?"

"Maybe even faking their own deaths!" Kith added. The Furyborn's eyes flashed in the dimly lit room. "That would be damn clever."

"It would also speak to a level of involvement that is on a larger scale than what we can handle. And given the incompetence—apologies, Chase—of those trying to catch us, I do not see it as likely. Still, you are right. It's something we should keep in mind," Sera said. "Like everything else we do, this is something we should keep working on, share our progress daily. Before we know it, we will see patterns emerge and figure out for ourselves what we should do."

Chase snapped his fingers. "The bracelets!" He raised his hand, revealing the tracking bracelet that the Cloak had given them. "I felt half convinced I actually spotted the Cloak in a crowd when we were running back to where they trapped me, but then I forgot about it again."

Sera tapped her lower lip. "That could make sense. Perhaps. We are not aware exactly *what* these bracelets transmit. However, if they share more than your location—"

"Even *if* it's just the location, I suddenly deviated from my path." He grimaced. "But yeah, that's a stretch. She'd have to know my schedule *and* the exact path and what I was up to at that exact time." With a dismissive gesture, he continued. "That's not my point, anyway. My point is, we should have access to that information. It would let us watch out for each other a lot better."

They agreed they would try to confront the Cloak about that the next time she approached them. Slowly, the talk turned more relaxed, and they shared what they had been spending the afternoon on.

Body Training, what Liam had been engaged in, was not a continuation of their regular combat training. Rather, it was a practical class meant to integrate and perfect optimal combat practices, get the fighters used to all the tiny movements that they needed to have down as second nature for when they made it into combat. "My Light-scourged feet! We spent an entire class just looking at the way we *stand* and moving in all directions. They must've made me topple over a hundred times! And many of these damn Elementals seem to have been taking classes in this for years."

Sera gave him a commiserating glance. "Sorry. That *is* a core exercise in regular melee training. Only with proper footing will you be able to move properly and avoid getting yourself killed. So my old trainer used to say, at least. And while it has cost you a couple of spots in the ranking, you will be able to regain them, once you learn." She cleared her throat before continuing. "Healer Training is exactly what you would expect. And more. We were all brought into the infirmary and made to participate in the official rotation, help with any healing necessary. No cards, nothing combat related. I believe they might have low standards for their beginner healers in general, if this is the level they start at." She brightened up. "The good part is that they let us in on *everything*. That includes regular sickness, training exercises, and even the Protectors returning injured from patrols. I saw wounds today I had never experienced before. Also, they let us into the morgue to study interesting corpses. Knowing how muscles, veins, and tissue works makes my healing so much more efficient. My ranking remains acceptable."

Kith rolled his eyes. "Second place is *acceptable?*" He laughed and shuddered. "You know, the way you're all fired up about corpses brings me back to the Waves, and not in a nice, fuzzy way. For me, Summoning Theory was...fair. It also showed *exactly* how weak I am when it comes to the summoning itself, and just how focused they are on doing things *the right way.*" He snorted. "Like there's only one right way. I will admit, though, the mental techniques for summoning properly are going to help in the long run—placing them correctly, doing it faster, summoning them mid-attack...stuff like that. It's also one place where me and my Mental Power are horribly lacking." He bared his teeth. "We spent the entire class going over theories, practicing mental summoning techniques and mental improvement techniques...clear your head, ignore distractions and the like. They wouldn't even let us summon anything! The next time, we're going to spend the entire time doing the exact same thing, except we're going to be moving to avoid enemy fire and spells. I...might kill somebody."

Cilia nodded matter-of-factly. "Please ensure that it's one of your competitors then. It would improve your chances." She didn't let her amusement show. "You *will* keep at it. This is what needs to happen, and you already knew this was one of your weaker sides. Rote learning, mental exercises, and repetition is exactly what you need. Your ranking remains horrible, but you have what it takes and you *will* give it your all!"

"Yes, Mum," he grumbled.

"What was that?"

"Nothing."

"That's what I thought." The officious woman ignored the chuckles from around her. "Elemental Theory is *exactly* what I have craved for so long. You remember what I told you about the sensation of the different Elements? Elemental Theory delves into that and defines, through decades of experimentation, exactly which attributes and effects you can efficiently apply through different forms of crafting." She wrinkled her nose. "To be expected, there is a heavy emphasis on the Elemental aspects of crafting. As you can imagine, they have notes on carded Lightborn going through the process in the towers as well. Once I take it all in, I will know exactly what I can most easily and efficiently craft, what I should barely be able to create, and what is beyond me." She beamed. "The next crafter class we have is Elemental Crafting. Meaning, we will most certainly be able to learn how to best put our theories into practice there." She blinked, and gave a quick, tight smile. "I am ranked fifth in the class now. They seem to enjoy a methodical approach to things."

Chase finished. He'd already told them about the details of the day's task, letting him jump straight to the conclusion. "I liked the instructor. He seemed a bit unhinged, but his ideas? He was all about movement and perception, about figuring out where our weakest areas were and then having us work on that. It won't be too specialized, but it should round out some of my weaker sides. Also, and this is just guessing, but I think it'll be about having us learn different ways of helping a group of Protectors that's not just fighting. Scouting, keeping watch, estimating threats...stuff like that."

"Hey. That's *my* job," Kith complained. Then he scrunched up his face. "Wait. If you take over, I get more sleep. Forget I said anything."

Laughing, they rounded off the conversation and Chase threw them out of his room. His body was weary with the aftermath of the magical healing, and if the schedule was maintained, the following day would bring Combat Training. He *needed* rest for that.

CHAPTER 22

"Watching the Protectors approach a monster flood is a lesson in efficiency and power. Nowhere is the power of Earth's Ward as evident as in the tight groups of well-versed wielders moving out in strength to handle anything thrown at them." A monster...flood? That sounds wild. My thoughts go back to Arnault's hordes. Very unpleasant. (Page 52.)

Combat Training was every bit as grueling as the last time. Instructor Boneridge seemed to take particular pleasure in tormenting those few students who were still suffering the aftermath of the last training session two days earlier. She walked among them like a general in the midst of her army, shouting orders and insults with equal aplomb. "You! Water lass with the dreadful hair. Don't hold back. Throw that rock like it insulted your mother. And you. Fury with the extra chins. Yeah, you. Speed *up*, Light scourge you, or you'll never lose that extra bit of blubber slowing you down."

Chase gave it his all. He'd long since switched back to Spoils of the Undeserving as he knew he'd never get as excellent a chance at improving his attributes as in these torturous sessions. Although the instructor felt like a demon, she also took care to correct (and berate) anybody who tried carrying something too heavy or wielded the long, weighted poles with less than proper technique. He did try to encourage Cilia whenever he had the chance. Out of their entire group, she was the one who struggled the hardest. Kith was also not having an easy time of it, with his relatively poor Toughness, but he went at the work with a bullheaded, furious doggedness like he was trying to kill the equipment.

Something had changed, though, and Chase wasn't sure what it was. The work was as hard as ever, and the environment was the same as last time. In fact, he appreciated one thing being ever so slightly familiar. It felt like he might actually, at some point, find his place and flourish even in this competitive environment. *Oh. Competition. That was it.* He wrapped up the current exercise, a sprinting exercise topped with ropes meaning to trip you up, and breathed for a moment, while his eyes roamed the wide-open practice area.

The taunts had faded. The nasty looks, the stinging elbows and feet trying to hook him off his balance whenever the instructor looked away. Well, the looks were still there. However, it had been more than a day since old Ernest had come up with anything worse than a scathing look. Perhaps, with Chase ranking first in the Orientation and Movement classes, they'd finally realized that he wasn't a slacker. Or maybe it was because Ernest had arrived late to training and had to focus on not dropping in rank.

Chase set his shoulders and flung himself into the next sprint. Or, perhaps, they were simply too busy trying to not die from the strain of Boneridge bleeding them of their last drop of energy. He once again shut out everything else and dedicated himself fully to the practice. They could do whatever they wanted. Once he was done, he'd be at a level of fitness where even the fighters wouldn't be able to touch him! Chase didn't realize, entirely consumed with concentration, but he was grinning through the strain.

Two-thirds through the practice, a loud howling noise erupted. From...above the training area? The applicants stopped what they were doing and looked around in confusion. The noise seemed to emerge from within the towers.

Kith halted a sprint next to Chase, panting, and pointing. "Look."

On the far end of the training area, students were streaming away from their exercises in practiced efficiency, lining up at the booths and receiving equipment.

"Break!" Instructor Boneridge's hoarse voice cut through the chatter. "Gather up, everybody."

They hurried over to form up around her.

She looked like the noise was a personal affront to her. "Of course, it had to be during *my* sessions. But don't worry. I will be less lenient two days from now. I will *not* see you slacking." A few affronted gasps made her show her teeth. "This? It's the outbreak alarm. It warns of an impending monster flood. Often as not, they're false alarms, raised by rookies. When they're not, they are general alerts, telling our Protectors they need to move out in force, and the more advanced students," she pointed at the students at the far end of the area, "get the chance to get some much-needed practical experience mopping up after the real fighters." Raising an eyebrow, her hardened demeanor cracked into a grin. "As for you? You get to cower in your rooms like the scared little chicklets that you are. Now *move*. Back to your rooms, at a run!"

They were corralled back to their rooms at an orderly pace, with the instructor keeping watch over them all, ensuring that nobody ran off. After berating them all that they should spend their unexpected spare time on training, she checked off a list, one by one, as each student was led into their rooms, and they were informed to lock the doors behind them.

Chase took the advice to heart. With the guidance from his Orientation and Movement classes and the very real example of how a higher Mental Power could save his damn life, he settled into some of the mental exercises that Sera had taught them.

Time faded away, as he tried to pour himself into the exercises. At first, they had ticked him off on a constant basis, nearly as bad as they had Kith. Chase was *not* used to sitting still for long stretches of time and absolutely loathed inactivity. The forced stillness of some of the meditative poses were anathema to him. As he slowly learned how to lean into them, he found that the stillness actually did him some good, applying a level of enforced calmness that helped hone his hyperactive mind and focus on what was important.

Today, however, he had trouble finding that center of detachedness that helped with the mental improvement of the meditation exercises. At first, he thought it was because he was still mentally wired from the physical exercises. After a while, he realized the reason was deeper founded. There were simply too many topics weighing on his mind, trying to distract him. The pressure of trying to excel in the classes. The mental load of learning to read, to constantly improve. Finding the culprit. Nearly damn *dying*. It was no wonder he had trouble finding the peace to center himself.

Good thing that Sera had taught them a handful of different exercises. Some were mental puzzles, which still challenged Chase. Pitting your own mind *against* yourself in imagined games still felt entirely unnatural to him, though Sera insisted it would come in time. Instead, he launched into another series of exercises, a set of breathing and stretching exercises that she'd introduced more as a lead-up to the actual exercises. The purpose of these were to clear the mind, combined with physical movement and mental focus to chase away distractions.

Chase felt the effect straightaway. The stretches gave his muscles, still warm from the practice, a nice, tight burn, while his breathing settled and he kept his gaze and attention on proper posture. His mind still tried to run away from him, focusing on the mental vision of the chair with the leather straps, on the dust bunnies under his bed as he lay on his stomach, trying to reach his ankles. On— "What in the ever-expanding Pits?"

He halted his exercise and reached under the bed. What was *that?* A heavy, dark bundle was tucked under the bed, as far as it could go. The only reason he spotted it was that he was on his stomach, arse-up, with his head on the floor. He reached in and pulled it out. It clunked.

The bundle of dark cloth was nondescript, looked like nothing more than a rolled-up blanket. He unfurled it carefully, then sat back on his heels as he looked at it. "Fire burn me."

It was a short sword. Not just any sword, though. If he'd seen this for sale in Isarn, he would instantly know this was a red-hot item being fenced. Everything about it screamed *expensive*. Chase was far from an expert. Yet the metal looked well-polished, the hilt held fancy filigree patterns that he'd bet were actual silver, and—he put his nose closer to the metal and nodded to himself—there was a warmth to it, a heat stored *within* the blade that felt like it was begging to be unleashed. This...was a damn expensive blade. How did it come to be here, under his bed?

Immediately, alarm bells went off. Not an actual alarm this time, but an internal alarm. There was *no* way this was a coincidence. It had, for sure, not been here when he moved in. Something shady was going on. But...he couldn't leave the room with the sword. There was a servant posted outside to ensure they stayed put during the alarm and didn't try to run off and make trouble. He'd be spotted immediately.

Chase wrapped up the bundle again, then considered his options. Whatever else, he could say one thing for sure. He wasn't supposed to have that sword, and getting caught with it would mean no end of trouble for him. He opened his large window, considering the drop outside. There was no place to hide it here either. He could dump it, of course...only, the towers sloped underneath him, and below him lay the extended area surrounding the towers. People would *probably* notice swords falling out of the sky. The nearest balcony was Sera's, and that was twenty feet away. No way he could manage that without a run-up.

Loud, clanking footsteps sounded from behind him in the hallway.

Chase's heart sank. Of course. There it was. The trap, closing around him.

Somebody knocked on his door and an authoritative voice bellowed, "Student Chase. In the name of the towers, open this door this instant!"

His mind raced. He hefted the bundle with the strong wind pushing hard against him, reconsidering the throw. "Just a second. I'm naked," he yelled. Then he cursed whoever had set this up and grit his teeth. Pits, no. He wasn't getting hit in a sting as simplistic as this. He put his foot up on the windowsill, and leapt.

Chase didn't bother thinking about consequences. That wasn't his thing. He had Cilia for that. There was a yawning depth beneath him and a howling wind trying to tug him down and *he had no time for any of that crap.* There was just the distance ahead of him, and Sera's balcony. Steps of Brilliance flashed. He almost missed the first platform. Only half his foot fit on the glowing platform, and he teetered sideways. Fighting down panic, he placed the next platform ahead of him, but at an angle, allowing him to counter the direction. The final platform had him back on track, and he leapt with all he had, clearing the edge of the small balcony with almost a foot to spare.

He flung open the balcony door, glorying in the fact that it wasn't locked. A second later, his brain almost shut down at the sight of a topless, *very* confused Sera with wet curls plastered around her face, looking up at him from above a water basin. "No time for panic! Kill me later. Hide this!" he snapped and slid the bundle across the floor. Then he closed the door again and leapt out into the gaping pit of open air trying to pull him to his death.

Trying to nail the landing on the first platform, he looked down. The pull in his stomach made him almost hurl, yet he summoned every scrap of mental fortitude and fixed his gaze on the single point of safety in his known world: his open window. One more platform, fixed in place just in time; then the final one, at an angle, to allow him to push off and hit the open window at an angle. The window itself was not fastened and was in the process of slamming shut. Chase barely managed to put a hand ahead of himself and nudge it away, keeping it from closing his entrance, before tumbling back into his room at an uncontrolled roll.

"Or we will break down the door this instant!" The voice from the door sounded furious.

"Yeah, yeah. I'm there now," he shouted, scrambling to his feet and closing the window behind him. He paused only to tug his shirt askew, not needing much after the strong wind outside the tower, before reaching the door and unlocking it.

He was slammed aside by a trio of armed Protectors, who stormed into his room and started tearing everything apart.

Chase's heart thundered in his chest. He *had* been set up. He focused on playing the act of the affronted student, asking what they were doing, cursing them for rummaging through his few belongings. Inside, however, he was cold. Set. *Ernest.* It had to have been him. He'd even arrived late to training. The Protectors eventually left his room, with a mumbled comment about "being honor-bound to uphold strict security measures." Chase slammed the door shut behind them, then sank to the ground, covered in sweat, as he listened at the door, hoping beyond hope that they weren't going to continue in an all-out search.

It didn't sound like it, though. There was a harsh exchange of words just within ear's reach of Chase's room, but he couldn't hear what was going on. Judging from the direction, it definitely wasn't from any of his crew's rooms. Moments later, the footsteps thundered off into the distance.

"I *cannot* believe that he would stoop to do something like this! Even if he hates you, this is...is *criminal!*" Sera's face was twisted in a grimace of fury.

They were back in Liam's large room, hanging out after lunch. The monster flood had turned out to be a false alarm, and Protectors were still returning, including, it seemed, some of the teachers. The afternoon lessons were postponed for the time being, though they hadn't been locked in this time. Chase didn't mind Sera's fury for the moment. She'd forgotten about how he found her in the room. That suited him just fine. He loitered on the other side of the room, lounging against the wall.

Kith occupied half the bed. He scowled. "It being criminal was kind of the point, princess. If it was only frowned upon, it wouldn't get Chase kicked from the towers, would it?"

Liam harrumphed from his place on the single hard-backed chair. "Even so. This was...excessive. I heard the news from Jonathan. Apparently, somebody stole that short sword from one of the booths up at the training areas. It's magical equipment for the actual Protectors training. And, get this, one of Ernest's flunkies was the one who reported you!"

"Well, that seals it! He is going *down!*" Kith barked.

"Patience," Cilia snapped from her cross-legged pose on the bed. "Liam. Are we certain he is the one? Or is this just a rumor?"

Liam grimaced. "Jonathan said it was a badly kept secret, and the Protectors went straight to confront the guy after searching you."

She slammed a hand down on the tome in her lap. "So. Nothing but Jonathan's word then. Have we learned nothing about not jumping to conclusions? Remember Efrem?"

Chase shuddered. "Please. I've been trying to forget Efrem."

Sera, looking from one to the other, confused, asked, "Who is Efrem?"

Reluctantly, Chase got up from leaning on the wall. "Efrem was...a lesson." He nodded at Cilia, whose finger was running through a section of the tome again. "I think we mentioned it before. Some bastard, back on the Waves, in the early years, stole our tarps and our food during the night. It was winter, and it was an ugly one. Cilia got sick. Bad sick. She barely pulled through, and what we did to make it through the winter..." He snarled. "Anyway. When we woke up and realized the tarps—our only defense against the weather—was gone, we obviously went looking to get them back. We found nothing, though. Word on the Waves was that one small-timer hadn't been seen for quite some time. So, we figured, of course, that he was hiding out with his loot." Chase's lip twisted.

"What happened?"

"Well, we found him. He...wasn't the thief. He'd been ill. Violently so. We burst onto his raft, into his tent, and it was just *everywhere*."

Liam closed his eyes. "I still say that you're overreacting. It was nasty, sure, but it was just vomit and...stuff."

"Yeah, well, you didn't get it in your *hair!*" Chase countered.

"The point is," Cilia pronounced carefully, "that these two *should* have learned by now that jumping to conclusions is a bad idea."

"It'll leave you smeared in vomit and worse," Chase grumbled. He flung up his hand. "Okay. Yes. We'll figure out whether it's actually true. But as long as it is...that means the ceasefire's over, right?"

Cilia nodded, a fire lit in her eyes. "Oh yes. Whoever did this is going *down*."

"One question," Sera said. "The sword? For now, it is hidden in my closet. What do we do about it? We cannot very well deliver it back, can we?"

"We could," Chase said. "I mean, we could just dump it, late at night, in a corridor somewhere. That should take care of that." He perked up. "Heh. I don't know if it was the stress or the concentration, but this gained me an increase to Mental Power. Anyway, I don't think we should get rid of it. First, there's the risk that we'd be spotted. That would be just as bad as me getting made in the first place. Even worse, really. Second, I honestly don't mind the idea of having a real weapon for backup. Whatever is going to happen in the next two months, at some point, we might end up in trouble. Having something other than training weapons to rely on could mean the difference between life and death for us." He cracked his neck. "Sure, there's a risk that they find it, but compared to ending up needing a real weapon and falling short? I vote we keep it."

"Me too," Kith added. "We can find a way to hide it better too. Besides, if they kick us out, that sword will go a long way to paying for food."

"Kith!" Sera scolded.

"What?"

CHAPTER 23

"Ah, but no one ever talks about the Cloaks. Why, you may ask? Superstition, mostly. Some of it misguided, other heartfelt and patriotic. That, and a healthy dose of fear. What else would you think about a cadre of faceless, strong wielders, sworn only to the towers, living by their own code? Can you really count upon them to always do right? Of course you can. Clandestine, they may be. But do not think for a second that these martial fearmongers would dare operate outside the purview of the High Elementalists." Yeah. Secret police, who only, possibly, answer to the highest instances of authority in the entire land. Such a wonder that people are anxious about voicing their thoughts on the topic. (Page 73.)

Two hours later than expected, Chase was led with the other rogues down to the courtyard at the foot of the towers. Some of the others looked uneasy at what had happened, and Chase caught more than a few suspicious glances sent his way. Of course. Whatever else happened, the rumor mill would do what it did. Most seemed to take it in stride, though, and the fire-aspected Elemental with the pinched face strolled along without a care in the world.

"Hey. Darkie," a voice shot his way.

With a sneer, Chase turned around, to see the rat-faced youth—it was his high cheekbones and large teeth that gave him that pinched look—meeting his gaze with open curiosity. "Name's Chase. What?"

Grinning, the youth tilted his head. "Chase. Yeah, that's fitting. Hey, so did you steal that sword or what?"

Chase took a deep breath and sneered. "Yes. Of course I did. Because my family and I made it into an academy that could secure us a place for life...but I figured it made more sense to risk it all and steal a shiny sword instead."

The young man's face transformed when he laughed. His face still looked pinched, but his mirth broke through. "That's a decent point, there." He sauntered over and held out his hand. "Name's Galvon. For the record, I figured it was weird, you being singled out as the target. I think, this time, I'll go with my intuition over the opinion of the damn Chalicos."

Chase squinted at him. "You're not afraid to face the wrath of the mighty Ernest?" He barely repressed a grin at the scandalized look on the face of several of the onlookers.

Galvon shrugged. "My dad's done well enough for himself. He can stand up against one spoiled brat. Even if he can buy half of Earth's Ward. But...I don't blame any of the others. The Chalicos *do* have a long reach." Behind him, another Elemental nodded, before realizing what he was doing and stopping, looking around to see whether anybody noticed.

Chase stared darkly at the ground as they walked past a group of stinking, mud-covered advanced-class students returning from outside. "I'm not entirely as nice as that. I am not above blaming somebody. Especially whoever decided to turn me in to the Protectors. That was a sucker punch, and if I figure out who's behind it, I'm not going to sit idle and take it!"

"That's fair. Holding a grudge against you, reasonable or otherwise, is one thing. Trying to trap you? That goes against what we're supposed to become. And while we're rogues, there's rogues and there's *rogues*, you hear me?"

Chase smiled at that. "I hear you. So, you have any idea what Applied Practice is supposed to be about?"

The two chatted as they walked, and the short walk turned a lot more comfortable. To Chase, it felt like progress. Like people were finally starting to get around to seeing that he was just like all the others. He also noticed a few of the other rogues eyeing Galvon with confusion, doubt, and...curiosity. Of course, Chase didn't fully buy Galvon's story. There was likely more to it. Perhaps a desire to tie himself to somebody who might look like a rising star at the moment. Perhaps just a grudge against Ernest. He could definitely get behind that. Regardless, he'd take the outstretched hand if it brought him a better position, and be wary of any daggers held behind their backs.

Eventually, they reached the courtyard beneath the towers. The servant bringing them along left them to their own devices in the center of the open, paved circuit. The sixteen rogue prospects stood, blinking at the scenery around them, as nothing happened. Servants, soldiers, and students milled about in every direction, all engaged with their tiny bubbles of life. For a moment, Chase was filled with longing, with the desire to have a life like theirs. Where he had clearly defined responsibilities, knew exactly what he was supposed to do at all times and there were no mysterious threats in the shadows, no overhanging deadlines with ugly consequences lurking on the horizon. Then again, it sounded damn boring.

"Is this a joke?" The well-dressed fire-aspected Elemental from the day before was even more ostentatiously dressed today, with a sleeveless orange and black vest with a high collar that looked like flames licking up his neck. "I have trained for the Protectors my entire life, expecting perfection. Not being left to wait like some common *servant*."

Chase frowned, addressing Galvon. "I thought you didn't have nobles in Earth's Ward."

"We don't," the smaller rogue responded. "Why?"

Chase didn't bother to lower his voice. He'd seen the hints of distaste in a few of the other rogues. "Well, it looks like somebody forgot to tell that to this guy. He'd be right at home with the snooty nobility of the Lightborn."

"How *dare* you?" the Elemental scoffed.

"I dare, because you're being annoyingly dense." Chase smirked at him. "There's two options here. Either we're being tested somehow, or the instructor being late is tied to the monster attack they just suffered. Either way, your bitching about having to wait a few minutes gives you nothing except a surefire way to drop in rankings, because nobody likes a complainer. In fact, I'm doing you a favor here. If you want to get kicked out? By all means, continue. Bitch to your heart's delight, and act as if the damn towers were created to serve you. It'll lead you right to being culled."

The man blushed a color to match the orange of his vest but didn't say anything.

Moments later, one of the two rogues who had been scolded for interrupting the day before shouted, "Hey. There's something here." He knelt to a spot a dozen feet away from the group and picked up a tiny piece of parchment that had been held down by a small rock. "Congratulations. Your ranking improves slightly," he read aloud. "Hey, nice!" Then, he read the next sentences silently. With a nasty grin, he curled up the piece of parchment and tossed it into the air, opening his mouth to catch it.

A brief, powerful gust of wind pushed the curled-up parchment askew. A small shape barreled him over, before catching the now-crumbled-up piece of parchment in the air. The attacker was a girl, but one who clearly didn't conform to the local customs of long, flowing dresses and finery.

At first, Chase suspected she was earth-aspected, but at another look at her long, flowing limbs, he realized she was air-aspected. She was just dirty, and her rough burlap clothes looked like something he'd have worn on the Waves.

With a shout of triumph and a filthy gesture at the downed rogue who was fighting his way back to his feet, she handed the parchment over to Galvon, who was closest to her. "What's it say? I can't read." She shrugged unabashedly.

Galvon unfurled the piece of parchment; then, frowning, turned it to the other side as if trying to find the point. *"Find me! That's all it says."*

Chase laughed. "A test it is." He started looking around, while others discussed what it meant. He ignored them. The courtyard milled with people at any hour of the day and this was no exception. What did he have to start with? For one, the schedule had stated their teacher to be Instructor Swansong. He wasn't familiar enough with Elemental naming but would guess that to be either a water or air-aspected Elemental. Not enough of a certainty to rule out any of the other, though. What else? Anybody twenty and younger were out, of course. Also, anybody who was clearly walking in groups in a direction which would take them away from the courtyard were out. Any cards he could recognize should likely be rogue's cards too. That left...at least a few dozen possibilities.

Workers were coming and going at all times, and the courtyard was where people loaded and unloaded goods from the city to be distributed into the towers proper. Chase sidled closer, taking in any of the workers or the tower servants currently at work. Three wagons and carts were being unloaded, with eight outside workers covered in sweat, along with a handful of tower servants. One of them looked suspiciously at him, as he moved closer to them. The crates at his feet held what looked like something Cilia would start slobbering all over, crystals and whatnot that she would be able to use in her crafting.

No. These weren't it. All workers, except for two, had short sleeves and no cards. The remaining two were too young to be a teacher, Chase decided. As for the tower servants...three were already finishing their tasks, loading the items into crates, stacking them onto trolleys which they were about to wheel into the tower. This would effectively remove them from the possibilities. Apart from them, one was a young girl, and the final one, a stocky man in an apron who was scolding a worker with a clipboard in hand, Chase had seen before in the same place.

His gaze turned to the rest of the courtyard. The other rogues had split up. A handful were still at the center of the open area, deep in discussion. The rest had opted for different approaches, a few looking like they had plans; others just ambled aimlessly about. Could he be going about this wrong? The instructor, for all he knew, had an invisibility card and was standing and observing them right now. Only, there'd be no way for him to spot that. On top of that, Instructor Highstream had talked a lot about rogues having to rely heavily on their perception and judgment calls.

Chase felt how the mental exercises he had initially hated were now starting to help him, in myriad ways. He'd always been able to take in a lot of details in a crowd. Only, now, with the added practice in ignoring distractions and focusing on certain sensations and mental aspects, he felt...better. Even more in tune with his surroundings. He found himself spending less and less time weighing and discarding each possibility, until his options boiled down to a few. He broke into a slow run, watching the possible marks as he went.

One, he saved for later. The cooper's assistant might be a possibility, but her gaze was far-off and confused, like she wasn't all there. Also, the stout, strong woman was fire aspected. Another, a hard-boiled Furyborn fletcher hard at work, he discounted, when she brushed sweat off her brow, revealing a crafter's card on her arm very similar to the Manipulate Light and Manipulate Dark cards Cilia had. That left...

Chase approached the woman working the bellows at the open-air smith lining the courtyard. She was an Elemental, water-aspected...only, it was barely discernible beneath the layers of dirt and sweat on her body. That, and her impressive physique, made her look more earth aspected. Her shoulder-length hair was held in a tight ponytail, and her sleeves hid any cards on her arms. For a moment, Chase's senses worked in overdrive, taking in everything about her. The irregularity of her breathing, that either had her tired or unused to the work. Her gaze, focused on the bellows, though a normal worker might look up to see why anybody was approaching her. Also...he smiled. "Instructor Swansong?"

The woman paused her work, indicating for another worker nearby to help. "'Scuse me?" she asked, hoarsely.

He bowed, ignoring the tiny twinge of doubt that he might be wrong. He finally recognized her from the initial tests. It was the unnamed rogue instructor who'd grilled him. "I believe we're ready for our class to begin."

She met his eyes, confused...then the confusion was chased away, like the stench of the Waves by a strong morning breeze, and replaced by a direct, bright look. "Well done. Which part made you suspect me?"

Not "What gave me away?" or "What did I do wrong?" Whatever hints she gave off here were on purpose, it would seem. He nodded at the bellows. "Warm clothes on a warm day for a sweaty task. You didn't even pull up your sleeves. Also, you were out of breath, with a task that you have to be able to keep up for a long time. And eventually, I recognized you, though whatever tricks you're using to disguise your facial features are amazing. Wouldn't have seen it was you if I wasn't already suspicious. The real hint? Those shoes."

Her shoes were sensible. Well-worn and used. They were also well-crafted caarnath skin. They would cost way more than a simple worker should be able to afford, even if they paid workers in the towers well above the average.

She nodded. "That will do. You could also have noted the smith being a family venture with all three others clearly related, or me wearing an expensive earring." She wiped the dirt off her brow with a cloth, then dropped it in a bucket and nodded to the smith. "Appreciate the assistance, Mr. Darkbloom."

Within a minute, they were gathered at the center of the courtyard. Instructor Swansong had cleaned off her face and arms, exchanged her filthy shirt for a nondescript white woolen shirt and unleashed her hair from her ponytail. The water-aspected Elemental looked...entirely nondescript. Like any number of people they'd pass by and forget about. Her demeanor was calm and collected as she faced them, looking them over coolly.

Eventually, she spoke. Her voice was as detached as her gaze. "Rogues die." She waited, observing them. "You've heard that before. Instructor Highstream insists on always including this tiny nugget of questionable wisdom in his lectures."

"You disagree then?" Galvon asked.

Her gaze swiveled to fix on him.

Quickly, he added the honorific. "Instructor Swansong. What I mean is, the numbers tend to agree with him. That's what Professor Brookwatch says, too. Fighters and rogues die the most."

Her lip twitched in an almost-smile. "So we do." Her voice rose in strength, spilling over with an intensity that seemed very unlike the calm, nondescript demeanor of the thirty-something woman before them. "But let me tell you what actually kills rogues. Bad habits kill rogues. A refusal to learn, to adapt, kills rogues. Finally and foremost, the denial to face reality is what kills rogues."

"Which reality would that be?" the haughty fire-aspected Elemental asked.

"That we're soft," she breathed. "Put in the same situation, of all the classes, we are the least likely to survive, bar perhaps the crafters—and they're a special case. We're soft, we tend to rely on movement, perception, and agility, and do not have the armor, summons, or defensive cards to help us survive that other classes do. Put in melee situations that go south? We're the first to croak."

Chase narrowed his eyes. "Instructor Highstream, it would seem, urged us to lean into perception, knowledge, and

Agility. To learn enough that we'd be able to control a battlefield or situation. Do you disagree with that approach?"

There it was again, that tiny twitch of her head. Her thumbs locked beneath her belt. Something about her movements made Chase think he'd seen her before.

She spoke agreeably enough. "Disagree? No. Instructor Highstream does what he does well, which is making sure that you are the most likely to survive combat, teaching you to find the approach that works for you. Meanwhile, I am here to teach you ways to avoid combat entirely."

"But...we're supposed to become Protectors. The entire purpose is for us to fight!" The disheveled earth-aspected girl looked confused by the statement.

"Is it now?" She didn't hide her disdain. "Picture that you are Protectors. You come upon a group of Lightborn, way out in the designated combat area. One is dressed as a merchant, but the others are ready for combat. Or you are caught by a bad squall during a scouting mission and find yourself beset by Liberty Guardians right on the verge of the Liberty border. Alternatively, you are outside Earth's Ward, shopping, in your Protector uniform, when a Furyborn group of fighters starts shouting about Elemental cheaters. In which of these cases is it best to fight, rather than finding an alternative solution?"

The girl blinked. "None of them?"

The instructor shook her head. "I will not deduct from your ranking for this. Not today. However, note, that, following today, I expect you to think harder about your answers, think about the lessons our other teachers have already tried to impart upon you instead of spouting what you think I want to hear. *You aren't here just to fight.* Quite often, the answer is diplomacy. Or running away, calling for backup or lying...any number of things, that all depend on the details of the situation in question. *That's* what I'm going to teach you here. Applied Practice revolves around taking the numerous lessons received throughout your other classes and getting them to stick, teaching you the myriad alternatives we have to avoid combat entirely—or at least ensure they're turned to your advantage. *Rogues die first in combat.* That is reality. What we need to ensure, then, is that we only enter combat when it is to our advantage, and that we use our powers to eke out every advantage we possibly can, to ensure that the Protectors win, combat or not."

The instructor leaned back, waiting. A frown built on her face as she observed them. "A few of you seem to have gotten the point. For the rest of you." She nodded at the haughty guy with his flame-collared vest. "Your demeanor-adapting card would be a blessing in any diplomatic situation." Her gaze continued to the dirty wind-aspected girl. "Your ability to improve or ruin footing will allow you to outrun almost anybody, even with those short legs." Her eyes fixed on Chase. "Your platform ability will let you avoid pursuit and use avenues that are otherwise unavailable or problematic." She addressed the bulk of their group. "Each of you here, bar two persons, has cards that will aid you in non-combat situations. And, wouldn't you know it? The towers need those powers too! Because having rogues who can adapt as runners, as distractions, as scouts, trappers, and diplomats? *That* is how Earth's Ward survives."

Chase had trouble fighting down his grin and found that he didn't even want to try. This felt like a class made *just* for him. Teaching them how to improvise, to adapt, to turn bad situations on their head? *He needed that!* His crew needed that. If he learned this, and learned it properly, he would be able to help his family weather anything, adapt to whatever the cruel world might fling at them!

CHAPTER 24

"The secrets. Ah, but the secrets. 'Tis but an acknowl-edgment of the facts. The towers abound with secrets. The far-ther up you go, the more amazing the constructions, the se-crets, the knowledge. Anybody worth knowing is aware of this. Part of the reward for becoming an important part of the tow-ers is unlocking access to the secrets we keep. For my part, I believe this is exactly how it should be." Smug. So fire-blasted smug. I would hate him for that. Only, if I were in on the se-crets, I'd be the exact same. Now I need in! (Page 13.)

Instructor Swansong didn't move much. She had a still-ness to her that seemed calculated, studied. Like a predator observing the world beneath her, ready to pounce. That tiny almost-smile of hers and the small, almost impercepti-ble movements of her head as she watched everything around her only helped reinforce the sensation. She was the predator. Everybody else was prey. Her thumbs in her belt, she almost smiled, then announced, "How am I to do that then? Teach you all to survive, to adapt, to think on your feet? Am I to take each of you, hone your individual strengths and ensure you shine to the best of your ability? *Of course not.* This is one topic where I agree with every one of my peers. There are too many applicants for the Protectors, and too many join for the wrong reasons, with the wrong qualifications or the wrong attitudes. If it were up to me, I would cull half of you this very second, because I believe you are a waste of my time and I'm capable enough to decide which of you will not make it."

Did her eyes linger on Chase for a second when she said that?

"Alas, I am not allowed to do that. So, I will do what I *am* allowed to do. I will toss you all into unfamiliar situations, force you to think on your feet, reward those who adapt and overcome, and punish those who fail to adjust. I will let you de-cide your own fate." The last words were delivered with a level of glee that Chase felt to the depths of his soul.

Stepping back and flinging a hand out at the towers above them, she smiled brightly. "Starting. Right. Now. This is a test that every single rogue to ever attend my classes has gone through. At the end of this, there will be bruises, bruised egos, and the occasional death by some who attempt...unwise methods. The test is simple. Get as far up into the towers as you possibly can."

"That sounds suspiciously simple." Galvon frowned.

"Good. You are starting to think." She bared her teeth at them in a carnivorous grin. "Every servant, every Protector inside the tower has been informed of your likeness and instructed to halt you in your progress. If you subside peacefully, they will also be peaceful. If you try to evade them, they are allowed to become slightly more forceful in their endeavors."

The guy who had attempted to eat the parchment earlier asked, "Are we allowed to fight back?"

The instructor sighed. "I am *going* to assume that you meant using measured amounts of force when trying to avoid them. Because the alternative would be too blasted embarrassing for me to consider. Yes. You are allowed to use a degree of force when and if they try to apprehend you. However, if you cause exaggerated or, Liberty fend, permanent harm on any defenders in the tower, I have been bestowed with the authority to cull you immediately. *Is that understood?*"

They fell over themselves confirming to the instructor that, yes, of course they understood.

Once again, she watched them as if she were deciding who to eat first. She purred the next words. "Once we start, you have five minutes' head start. Then, I give the signal, and the defenders will be allowed to apprehend you. Now, this is the best chance you will ever get to impress me on your own. So, go out there, and come up with something ingenious. Something surprising. Show me why you are worth the trouble of the towers coddling you and throwing money, fame, and cards after you! Questions!"

"Are there any other opponents, apart from the defenders?" the earth-aspected street kid asked.

"Good question. Yes. Once you reach a certain height, the tower itself will have defenses and traps. On the lower levels, they will not be dangerous. Higher up?" She chuckled.

"Can we use our own items and equipment for this?" the snobby Elemental asked, focused.

"Anything on you, yes. It will count as being properly prepared."

"Are you part of the game?" Galvon asked.

She shook her head. "No. Apparently, that would be an unfair advantage over you. Anything else?"

Chase's mind worked on overtime. Simply running would be an option. It would, however, also be moronic. For one, two of the others had already proved they were faster than him. It would also make him stand out. He *could* use his Steps of Brilliance to try climbing from the outside. Only...yeah, no. That would be the best way to become one of those rare casualties. The towers were bound to have outside defenses farther up as well. That left... "Are we being watched right now? And will anybody follow our progress, visually or in person, for the first five minutes?"

The half-smile appeared for another split second. "Nobody's watching. The moment you step into the towers, though, they may watch. Yet, they will not follow or interfere until the five minutes have passed."

A few other questions rang out, which the instructor answered in good mood. Then, she clapped her hands together in a resounding clash. "*Good.* I hope you are prepared to shine. We start the five minutes *now!*"

Their small group exploded. Half the rogues started to run immediately. Most ran for the main entrance to the towers, while two veered off, clearly trying a less traveled route. Of the remaining, a pair started discussing loudly, while the street kid loped toward the smith. Of the remaining two, Galvon was wildly rearranging his clothes, turning his shirt inside out and taking out a cap from somewhere, while the haughty fire-aspected Elemental chugged first one, then another vividly colored flask.

Chase couldn't quite fight down the stupid grin that kept emerging on his face, as he jogged over to where the remaining workers were still re-distributing items from the carts and into crates that were then loaded onto trolleys. Some of the crates were small. Others... He stepped up with a grin. "Hello there. Now, I don't know about you, but I happen to be of the opinion that manual labor is *intensely* underpaid around these parts."

An eternity later, the lid of his crate he'd hidden inside was pried open, and a smugly grinning elderly Protector looked down upon him. "Gotcha." Behind him, the servant looked at Chase with a sheepish smile and walked off with a wave, flipping the silver coin he'd just earned.

Chase half fell out of the crate, as his legs refused to work under him, cramping up something fierce. "Don't worry. I'm not running anywhere. No need to slap me silly."

The elderly Protector guffawed. "I'm too old and slow for that, regardless. I'd just use my card." He bared his biceps, showing a card depicting a storm cloud. "Lightning, y'see? I'd have you dancing a jolly tap dance on the floor here."

Massaging his legs, he responded, "No worries on that count. I've only peed myself in public once. Don't need a do-over." He tried to look over the shoulder of the Protector. "Hey, how far up did I get?"

The Protector shrugged. "Seventeenth floor. Not half bad, especially for somebody as recognizable as you. How ever did you manage that?"

Chase grinned in relief. "Whew. That's above the training ground, at least. As for how, I just had a chat with the workers. They know this game. They know that anything goes, so them helping me in exchange for a bit of coin is harmless. They stuffed me into a crate and went on with their work, like nothing had changed." He massaged his calf, which was threatening to jump ship and leave his leg entirely. "I tried talking them into carrying me all the way up to the High Elementalist, but apparently that was out of the question, even for a game."

The old man snorted. "Probably for the best. There's security up there you don't want to face."

"Oh. Well, that's a relief then. How far up did the others get?"

"No clue. I did hear some kerfuffle down from the kitchen. I'm betting somebody tried to swap clothes with some kitchen workers. They always do." The old man guffawed again, then slapped Chase on the shoulder.

His hand felt like sheer granite. Chase congratulated himself on deciding not to run and relaxed. He'd done the best he could. Now, to see how he'd done.

He was led down to the courtyard again, to be met with a sorry sight. Half the rogues were bruised or bloodied, with disheveled or torn clothes. Two were outright missing.

Galvon waved him over. He had his arm in a sling and his clothes were singed. "Hey! How did you do?"

"Seventeenth floor, apparently. How about you? How're you feeling?"

The smaller youth laughed, then winced. "Regretful, mostly. I figured that I'd use my sparks to create diversions." He rolled up his sleeve, showing a card. It sported a crowd staring at burgeoning fires in a house while a robed figure slinked away in the background. "That's what I've got. Limited fire control, but with a nice, long range. I can create flames and control their heat. I thought I'd be able to create some nice, convincing heatless distractions, then sneak past while they were busy handling those." He shrugged, embarrassed. "Control isn't my strong suit. I managed to build it a bit too hot. The Protectors really didn't like that."

"Oof." Chase commiserated. "How about the others? Anybody come up with a surprise?"

"Well, you haven't explained how you managed yet." He laughed. "Gemma did well."

The short-haired earth-aspected Elemental grinned back at Galvon. "It was easy. I stole a bag of roots, put 'em on my back, then marched for the stores. Got caught on the eighth level, when I tried to grab a kitchen uniform, though."

"The Protector who caught me said somebody always tries that." Chase nodded.

Gemma grinned, a secret, triumphant grin. "I'm not sure if I was the next highest after you then. But I did a whole lot better than Mallard there." She nodded at the guy who'd tried to screw them over with the parchment earlier. "He managed to get himself caught within seconds of the signal."

The young man blushed. "I miscalculated. I opted for pure speed, believing I could catch them unprepared, if only I got far enough. Turned out, they were evenly stationed. Everywhere. Speed wasn't an option."

"He tripped over his own feet." Gemma laughed.

"I did *not!*" Mallard protested.

The two bickered, while Chase looked around. At least it looked like nobody had been badly hurt. One Furyborn sported two black eyes and was messing around with an *impressively* broken nose. From the looks of his knuckles, he'd given as good as he got, though. But two people were still missing, though. One of the persons who'd stayed in the courtyard, bickering, and...that haughty guy.

The bickering guy came first. A shout rang out from *within* the courtyard, and minutes later, two Protectors came forward, pushing the man ahead of them. Apparently, he'd decided that, because there was no time limit on the test, he'd hide out here where there was no security and make his move later on.

That left only the haughty fire-aspected Elemental who'd chugged down two potions at the beginning of the game. They waited for nearly half an hour, growing increasingly more bored, until he finally returned, as flawlessly dressed as before, not a hair out of place. Accompanied by Instructor Swansong.

The instructor didn't waste any time. She stopped in the center of their lopsided group and spoke up without preamble. "Congratulations. You managed to avoid getting anybody killed. That clears the lowest bar we have. Unfortunately, that is the only praise I have for most of you." Her finger shot out to point at Mallard. "Five seconds? That is the second-fastest capture *ever*." It continued to Galvon. "And you. You have caused damage worth hundreds of ryzark. *If* you manage to graduate, which I sincerely doubt, that will be detracted from your pay." She continued, berating one at a time. After a while, she started pointing out the good things they'd done too. "You." She indicated

Gemma. "Well done on abusing the fact that nobody looks closer at servants, especially if they're dirty and plain-looking. You should have changed tacks once you reached the stores, however, and gone for stealth or another method of subterfuge. You were already past the heavily guarded areas."

She moved on, singling out Chase. "You? Bribing the servants? Good choice. Of course, it wouldn't have worked outside the scope of the game."

One Liberty rogue who usually never said anything shouted, "But that's cheating!"

Instructor Swansong shook her head. Her eyes moved from one to the other, in tiny, birdlike movements. "Like I said earlier. I will not punish you for stupidity on the first day. Yet, from here on out, I will not take it easy on you. I explained the rules, allowed you to ask any questions. The onus was on you to ensure you understood the parameters of the test." She nodded to herself, then moved on. "The winner here is Tandor. He drank a potion to temporarily alter his features. After that, he used his card to talk one of the simpler Protectors into swapping clothes. Then, he moved farther and farther up the levels under the guise of being a roaming Protector."

She patted the haughty Elemental's shoulder. "His social work was exquisite. He applied his card to good effect and moved like a Protector, had his reasonings in order. He was only caught because he didn't know that the upper levels have passwords." She paused, then delivered the final words. "On the twenty-sixth floor. Please take note of this. That is where the private residence of higher-ranked Elementalists start. If he was an enemy, he could do some real damage." She put her thumbs in her belt again, then finished. "There are glimmers of promise in your small group. Continue like this, and surprise me, next time. I do not hold great hopes for you in general. Even so, I do so like being positively surprised. Dismissed."

Chase stood there as the instructor strode away, as taken aback as the others by the abrupt dismissal. He mulled over the implications from the lesson, the possibilities, and the warm sensation that this was a class that seemed tailor-made for him. For him, and, truly, for creating Protectors who would be exceptional at other things than just straight-up fighting. Runners. Diplomats. Scouts... Spies. *Crap.*

He launched into a sudden run, not caring about the surprised calls of the others. All the time, he berated himself. *How come he hadn't seen it?* The mannerisms were there. Those minuscule movements of her head. The manner of speaking. The logic as well.

He caught up to her before they reached the ornate main gates of the towers. Heart thundering in his chest, more with the impulse than the run, he looked around him to confirm that there wasn't anybody nearby. "It's you," he simply said.

The unremarkable-looking woman raised an eyebrow, as if confused. Despite this, her body was stock-still. Ready to act. "Me?"

"You're..." Chase hesitated, then mouthed "The Cloak" without saying the words out loud. In a low tone, he barreled on. "Obviously, I couldn't see it was you. But you stand in the same way. Move your head in the same manner. It makes so much sense too. Applied Practice. How many of your recruits come from your class?"

She hissed. Literally hissed, like a kettle coming off the boil. She moved forward with a speed that belied her earlier calm and grabbed him by his neck.

Her hand, so normal, so dismissible, felt like a vise to Chase, inescapable and solid. The pulse in his neck thundered against her hand, where it clenched him tight.

"Not. Another. Word," she said. For two seconds, five, she just looked him in the eyes. Then she lowered her head, grimacing in distaste. "We will talk about this. Do *not* ever mention this in public. I will find you. And your small friends."

That sounded more like a threat than a promise. Chase felt certain that he'd made a horrible mistake in blurting out his realization.

CHAPTER 25

"There is something to be said for the Light's approach. Spread your fields far and wide, and exceptional plants will be revealed occasionally. Ah, but how many promising plants could have grown to greater heights, had they not been snuffed needlessly by weeds along the way? We Elementals pick our plants carefully, and help them flourish." I like how he says that like it's not by necessity, due to the lack of space for actual growth. Even so, being one of those "promising plants"? I can't say I don't like that thought. (Page 36.)

They were back in the amphitheater, with Kith already looking at the stage with growing fear of another long-winded lecture. Chase, meanwhile, was starting to like Professor Brookwatch. For all the information she expected them to take in, he'd yet to find her logic totally off. She seemed to know what she was talking about.

Their crew, amid the evening's mental and physical practice, had discussed the revelation that Instructor Swansong was the heretofore unnamed Cloak. Unfortunately, they decided, it didn't change anything. The only thing it really did was give them a chance to find her, in case of emergencies. Any thoughts at using the knowledge for something unsavory were easily quelled, since she held all the advantages here.

The classes of the others the day before had been of varying satisfaction. Liam had endured another Body Training lesson, dropping another place in the ranks. Fighters, before the first Culling, had the fewest different classes. He suffered stoically, insisting there was a *little* progress at least, indicating a rare increase to Mental Power as proof.

Sera had lessons in Plant Knowledge. According to her, it was to be an amalgamation of learning about plants and crafting ingredients focused on healing and disease prevention, and a few poisons. For the first time ever, she was not at the forefront of the class. Despite this, the hours and hours of walking with Cilia through the wilderness, searching for useful plants helped her somewhat. The rest, she judged, was mostly a matter of memorization and logic.

Kith was, for once, animated about his class. Summoning Practice was, according to him, centered on just that. Practicing the theory they'd learned in their earlier classes. Calling their summons in the exact spot they wanted, making them obey their commands exactly as ordered, crisply and efficiently. "I'm still crap. I'm third last in that class, and you don't want to see the two last ones. They're lost causes. Still, what they're teaching in this class is actually *useful*! When I'm done catching up to the others there, and add my combat prowess on top? They won't know what hit them! Two months to the Culling? I'll start climbing the ranks in two weeks!"

Cilia was anxious about hers. "I was right in my earlier guess. They took us to a training area on the northern side, which is like the martial training area, only for crafters. Elemental Crafting is just that. Taking the theories we learned about the Elements and practicing how to incorporate them into our crafts. Only...everybody here has been learning and perfecting a craft since childhood. I am the only one who is not entirely specialized. I am *far* behind. Only my Mental Power being higher than most others and the fact that most of the remaining crafters have only had cards for a short while gives me a head start. Once they catch up? I'm in trouble."

Chase didn't see it that way. Cilia was way ahead of the others, both attribute-wise and theoretically. She had a...feeling for the Elements that was impressive. Also, her knowledge and understanding left her ranked in the upper third in World Knowledge and Elemental Theory. Besides, she had Light cards to play around with, where most of the others only had an Elemental crafting card.

Chase himself was doing a lot worse in World Knowledge, ranking third last. He just hoped he could improve his reading and catch up. Fortunately, his good results in Applied Practice and Orientation saw him safe for the moment, and his Combat Training wasn't horrible.

Sera...did amazing. Unsurprisingly with her upbringing, she looked to leave the rest of them in the lurch. She ranked eighth in World Knowledge, dead first in Healer Training, and just above the average in Plant Knowledge. Her only real issue was Combat Training. However, *all* healers except for one brutish air-aspected Elemental flagged in that class.

Liam and Kith were the real issues.

Liam was in the low ends of the middle in World Knowledge. He knew his letters, but had trouble processing, when the teachers added too much knowledge or theory. Combat Training saw him well-placed, comfortably in the upper third. Competition was increasing among the fighters, though, and with him at the low ends of Body Training, his position among the fighters was precarious.

Kith was even worse. He complained at the levels of knowledge they had to take in for World Knowledge, struggled with Summoning Theory, and hadn't gotten properly started with Summoning Practice. The only thing saving him from ranking dead last among the summoners was his good position in Combat Training.

There was one saving grace. Their attributes had started to see results from the training. Liam earned a point to Agility on top of the Mental Power. Cilia saw one to both Strength *and* Toughness. Kith earned himself a point to Mental Power, which gave him some much-needed impetus. Chase thanked the stars for his new card. One point to Strength, one to Toughness, *and* one to Mental Power. There was no doubt the speed at which he was improving would stall at some point, but for now, a few months of furious training could give him the chance to get ahead of the pack.

"We've got our final new class this afternoon, right?" Jonathan yawned. The trio—Jonathan, Tam, and Rowan—had joined them again for the World Knowledge class. "Anybody know what it's about?"

Liam smiled amiably. He liked the Lightborn and his easy-going personality. "Monster Knowledge. You know as much as we do. If I were to guess, I'd say that we're going to learn knowledge. About monsters."

"Har har." Jonathan rolled his eyes. "Truth be told, I don't mind that. That can actually be useful. Not like this class. What is the political climate between Liberty and Fury? *What do I care?*"

"You will care if you find yourself caught in the open between groups of both," Sera admonished. "Now, hush. Professor Brookwatch is here."

The professor was, in fact, there. She stepped out onto the stage, a small figure with an impressive presence, and started to talk.

Immediately, the crowd quieted.

Her voice was still magically transported to reach every part of the amphitheater. However, it was less ebullient today, more subdued. "I have been here for a long time. My entire adult life. First among the Protectors, and then, here, as a teacher. I have seen many of you pass through, learn, grow, and invariably, die. Sometimes, it can be hard for me to remember that my task here is not just to guide you in the right direction or inform you what the towers need of you. No, part of my task is also to encourage you to *want* to grow. To show you exactly how much you have to fight for and show you what the towers can do for *you*."

Suddenly, she had their full attention. This was a full 180 degrees from their earlier talks about them being there for the towers' sake and not the other way around.

Her first words were straightforward. "The first thing we do for you? That one's simple. Cards. Everybody here realized how much the access to cards would change their lives. For most of you, that was likely a huge part of the reason you joined up in the first place."

Smiles and chuckles spread across the stone benches. Chase shared a wry smile with Sera. If they hadn't been forced into it? Sure, that would have been a logical trail of thought.

"That is as it should be. Cards *are* a life-changing experience. Yet, we have already gone into why we don't share them with just anybody. Keep up the good work, eke past the competition? Those cards will be yours to keep. For some, they will just be a warm memory, of course, or the impetus to guide you to push yourself to make it back here to try to complete the Protector training at a later point in your life." She delivered the words perfunctorily, without warmth, like she didn't really believe them.

"The next thing we provide you with? Equally simplistic and also something you already know. Training. The best of training, equipment, and access to knowledge. Stick with it, and you will learn more, grow faster, improve yourself and become better and stronger than anywhere else in the world. That includes access to crafting equipment and materials that are expensive, hard to find, and sometimes even illegal. The towers provide."

Chase thought the whole experience felt a bit off. She sounded like she was reading lines off a script. The moment she continued speaking, however, he forgot all about it again.

"Before I delve into the details about what specifically we can provide for the students who make it past the first Culling, there are two other things you need to know. The *main* reason you should be thanking the Elements you made it in, and focusing your every pinch of energy into making it into the Protectors, is this. *We provide the opportunity to walk the Steps.*"

She pointed behind her at the lands below. "Look at where we are. If you leave the Elemental lands, you can choose your path. As an individual Elemental, you're allowed to travel the lands of Light freely. You may not be *welcome* everywhere, but you can. You can also waltz into the wilds, face off against the Guardians of the different aspects as you so choose, unfettered by any of the myriad rules and regulations of this place. So, why is it worth it, staying here, suffering the hardships and challenges to stay in the top of your classes? Simple. Because, out there, you die. You may survive a lone roaming Furyborn Guardian, a couple of unaspected beasts roaming about wildly. You might learn how to navigate the bandits calling the wilds home. But sooner or later, death *will* find you. A pack of blitz tunnelers will find you in your sleep. A roaming throng of thresher claws will overwhelm you."

Chase and Kith shared a shuddering glance at the memory.

The professor continued, unperturbed. "Why? Because there are no systems in place to aid you! Oh, sure, there are alternatives to the towers. Some illegal settlements work hard to enable hunting for those willing to risk their lives. The forces of Light grant another option, of servitude in return for unflinching obeisance. Joining the Furyborn and completing their ritualistic rites of passage, yet another. But in no place will you find a single system of defense that so effortlessly and efficiently allows you to take on Guardians from other aspects and survive as in the towers."

Chase thought about this and couldn't see anything off about the statement. Sure, if you were part of the Church of the Circle, or some important Lightborn nobleman, you could find some shortcuts. Enough coin could likely see you find possibilities that might rival the towers, at least for a while. But even the armies of Light were just roaming, reacting to whatever erupted and moved about out there. Here? They worked hard to keep everybody alive. Those who made it past the eye of the needle and into the Protectors, at least.

The instructor waited for the excited chatter to die down. Now, she sported a small smile, like somebody with a secret she'd been waiting to share. "There is one final detail that you should know. Not something we grant you directly, but something that is bestowed upon you inadvertently, that will follow you for the remainder of your life. You may have heard hints about this, but it is not something that is widespread knowledge. In the towers—"

"If she says 'in the towers' one more time, I'm going to punch myself in the head," Kith grumbled.

"We have tracked information nearly since the start. This allows us to know for a fact some of the many advantages that walking the Steps bestows upon a person, beyond the simple rewards of Titles."

Exclamations of puzzlement arose around them. Chase's gaze searched Cilia's, but she merely shrugged at him.

The professor continued. "One detail is commonly known. Aging. When you walk the Steps and gain your cards, you stop aging at the same rate as non-wielders. The exact numbers are, of course, subject to debate. However, the result is indisputable. Wielders age slower than the uncarded. If you are Tier one, you will likely add five to ten years to your age. Twenty to forty at Tier three, while we have known a few Tier fives to live as long as a hundred and fifty."

The Darkborn girl Chase had tried to approach asked, "But that's depending on Toughness, isn't it?"

The professor made a cutting gesture. "No. That is a common misconception. Slower aging is not dependent on your attribute allocation. Think of all the famously long-lived legends. The Dancer of Astarte. Landsing of Titans. Even the Eternal Carver. All of these are famously known as having passed Tier six. Every single one of these passed the hundred and fifty-year mark. Yet, none of them invested heavily into Toughness." She looked up at the crowd to see whether her point got across.

Nodding, she continued. "Other side effects? Your health improves. You are less likely to fall ill. Common sicknesses have less of an impact on you. Some claim that it is the increased energy of your aspect flowing through you that aids combating sickness in your body. Regardless of the reason, the result is indisputable." Holding up a finger, she added, "Again, this is without further Toughness. Investing into Toughness will increase this effect to the point where some have noted an effect even against poisons." She cleared her throat and frowned. "This is veering off course. Allow me to demonstrate my point with an example."

The elderly professor walked forward on the stage. Today, she wore a practical pants suit, with a light, colored shawl. She held up a hand, as if to call for silence. Then, from a standing motion, she dipped down and launched straight into a backward somersault.

In a long, flowing motion, she tucked her legs in and nailed the landing, at all times in perfect control. She continued speaking, not out of breath in the least. "Scholars in the towers—"

From next to Chase came a thud and a curse from Kith.

"—have given it different names. The core increase. Magical saturation. Effect appropriation. Some called it the god-like effect, but that is rightfully seen as sacrilegious. Whatever the name, the effect is indisputable. The higher you rise in the Tiers, the more your body improves toward an ultimate state. Think of that, my young ones. What we offer here is not merely the chance at old age, but the chance at near-immortality, with a physique, equilibrium, and resilience that will keep you spry and moving, even in the winter years of your life. Yet, this is for those who succeed, who stay in the ranks of the Protectors, who fend off attackers and absorb their Ænima for years to come. To the victors, the spoils. Nowhere is this as clear and present as in Earth's Ward. And we do not begrudge our Protectors what they gain."

Everywhere, chatter erupted. Chase stared wide-eyed at Sera, who looked back at him, equally surprised. Higher-Tier wielders were usually in good shape. However, everybody expected that was because people spent their attribute points to improve their life. Knowing that you'd be able to spend every single attribute point in the attributes that mattered to your cards, and your physique would still keep up? That was *insane*.

The professor spent the entire lecture talking about what the towers did for the Protector who made it through the eye of the needle. You could visibly *see* the difference from the start to the end of the lecture. Students sat up straighter, were more attentive. There was a fire in their eyes that hadn't been there before. As well there should be. People in the city, the teachers...Pits, even Cilia's braggadocious tome, all kept speaking about how the towers gave the best to their chosen. Yet, they hadn't gotten details. Not before now. And what details!

The teaching they were so proud of was but one thing. But it was not to be discounted. Once you made it into the Protectors, they created individually tailored training regimens, built specifically for you, your fighting style, chosen weapons and prowess—and adjusted them to fit your given cards optimally. This was just the start, too. They arranged for running assignments and constant testing to find other wielders that amplified your style in order to find the perfect squad for you—following which, they created specialized training and card theorizing *for your entire group*. You wouldn't have to come up with efficient theories yourselves. No, you would have trained professionals dedicating time for this, building on the notes from decades of intensive training and actual combat.

Training was just one thing. Equipment was another, and a big one. There was a reason that, despite the relatively limited mortality rate of crafters compared to other classes, they continuously brought in new crafters with each new class. Protectors were equipped with tailor-made equipment, again, crafted to suit their fighting style and their part in a squad. If you were a stealth-type ranged with a card that allowed for range shots? Your bow would reflect this, and you would have arrows with magical effects. If you were a close combat specialist focusing on Strength? You would have the best, heaviest armor available, enchanted for your protection. Not only that, but they would keep everything maintained, at no cost to the Protector. *And* everybody would be equipped with an expansive suit of crafted items to assist them and prepare them for a wide range of situations. Potions to enhance attributes and senses. Items to reduce or improve light, mobility, shield from damage, *cause* damage...any possible thing. As long as it was part of your wielder skillset, was not prohibitively expensive, and made sense for your squad, you would have it. For free. And when you finally left the Protectors, with a sizable pension, you would be allowed to keep all your regular gear.

Crafters, one might think, were in a worse position here. They were still on the rotation, fighting outside Guardians. How else would they walk the Steps and improve as crafters? Only, they had few or no cards to help them adjust the power difference between them and combat-oriented wielders. Except, the towers worked on a merit system for crafters. Everything they created was graded and granted points. The points they assembled allowed them to either keep their own creations or trade against crafted items from other crafters. This meant that the most industrious crafters were powerhouses, walking arsenals, outfitted with the best of the best in potions, poisons, and equipment. Not only that, crafters who retired from the towers were pretty much guaranteed a comfy job with nice pay for the rest of their lives, should they so choose.

Retirement was quite the selling point, for everybody. Anybody retiring from the Protectors was left with a sizable pension. Nothing lavish, but enough to live a decent life. They were still expected to give a hand, should an emergency arise within Earth's Ward, but, strictly speaking, nothing held them to it.

Chase felt quite light-headed at that revelation. Earth's Ward had decades of the current system in place. The city itself was brimming with veterans, wielders with impressive physiques, the experience of countless battles and nothing to do in their day. He and his crew had actually considered putting down in the city and *robbing people for a living?* They'd dodged an arrow there.

Every single time a class ended, there'd be a wave of talk and laughter erupting, as the students relaxed from the pressure of keeping up and presenting the best face to the professor. This time, however, the huge, open area virtually exploded in waves of chatter and excited shouts.

Liam was no different. He looked at the others with a gleam in his eyes. "You hear that? Not only are they setting us up for life, we're getting full armor and equipment too!"

Cilia was as wide-eyed as anybody else. "I was expecting to craft my own items. Being able to trade for anything they can create, in the entire towers? That's insane!"

Chase grinned and threw an arm over Sera's shoulder. "I know this wasn't the original plan. But I think we may have lucked out here. For what they're offering? I say going on the straight and narrow is worth it!"

Kith beamed. "Yeah. We just need to crush the opposition and make sure we earn the spots. What was that next class again? We'll need to show them all that we're better than all these other losers!"

CHAPTER 26

"There are things I will only allude to. Secrets you will only learn once you earn access to the upper echelons of the towers. Believe me this. It is worth it. The way they approach training alone. All you prospective Protectors will see. Oh, you will see." Sure. More hints at just how great the Towers are. I'm starting to suspect this tome was commissioned by the damn Protectors. (Page 61.)

The next class was called Monster Knowledge, and that tidbit of information cooled Kith's enthusiasm instantly. "Really? We just left one hours-long lecture, and after a quick snack we're supposed to move straight into another one?"

They walked the halls again. By now, they were getting used to the confusing, winding hallways of the towers. Even the constant traversing of stairways failed to wind them by now and the knowledge that they had to climb or drop a dozen floors between classes was lamented more for the time involved than the physical exertion.

Cilia scolded him. Her index finger shook threateningly at him as they walked. "Kith, you are about to get on my last nerve. You are going to stop complaining, and you will do it now!"

He blinked at the smaller woman, ducking. "I was just—"

"Well, don't," she snapped. "You said it yourself. We'll need to dominate the others. That doesn't change, just because the class might be one that's not perfect for you. So, get your butt moving and get ready to look awake and interested!"

Sera cleared her throat. "Am I the only one who is surprised by the setting?"

Chase nearly stumbled over a step on the wide marble stairs they were climbing. "I hadn't thought about it, but yeah, it *is* weird. If we're just supposed to learn theory about beasts, what are we doing back on the training grounds?"

"Today, you are being inducted into a secret." Instructor Boneridge seemed oddly happy about that fact.

This, in turn, had most of the students anxious about what was about to happen, because her happiness seemed to be proportional with the physical pain and stress that the students were going to suffer.

They were currently in another part of the training area than what they usually frequented. Today, there were no training instruments, no elaborate obstacle courses set up. Just the instructor, a large area of hard-packed dirt, and a dozen head-high earthen partitions set up equidistant in a half circle lining the outside edge of the reserved area, with a servant standing at each one. One of the servants, confusingly, sent Chase a pitying glance.

Instructor Boneridge ignored the partitions, barking a question at the students. "Does anybody here know how any other factions handle their Guardians? What do they do with them after they are summoned?"

For once, Kith was the one to answer. "Well, the Lightborn, at least where I'm from, didn't do much of anything with 'em. They unleash the Guardians of Light onto the streets of the city. Then, the monsters wander the streets, slowly grow more solid and tangible until they're sent to play defense at the Border. If the Furyborn and unaspected Guardians take 'em down, that's where they end their existence. Otherwise, if they grow enough in numbers on the Border, they're sent to harass the Furyborn or others, maybe cull the numbers of unaspected Guardians roaming about...possibly even come as far as here."

"A frontier city, then?" At his affirmative, she nodded. "The closer to the more active war zones of the Lightborn, the less interaction the nobility in charge of the Wellsprings tend to have with their Guardians. They just view them as expendable troops, fodder to force the enemies into defensive positions. In bigger cities, farther from the front lines, they have additional uses. They use them for parades, line them up for morale purposes, sometimes even for corporal punishment. Watching a criminal torn to pieces by a blitzer lion is said to be very effective to teach other criminals how to behave. However, there still is generally little direct control of them. The Furyborn have a very different viewpoint on Guardians. They view them as spirit protectors, creations to be venerated before unleashing them to serve their own purposes." A cruel smile played on her lips. "Here, we have a different outlook again. We don't have unlimited numbers of Guardians. Hence, we tend to treat them very differently. Like a resource. Something to be treasured, but ultimately spent, as wisely as possible."

Sera gave a small gasp. Excitedly, she raised her hand. "You use them here, to teach us about monster physiology in practice?"

The stocky instructor chortled. "Oh, that's just part of it." She gestured and, behind her, a massive roar rang out, causing students to jump and reach for weapons—weapons they weren't carrying.

A huge monster barreled out of an opening in one of the dozen earth partitions: a massive, blocky earthen monstrosity vaguely shaped as a salamander with six segmented legs and a wide, dirt-colored head sporting too many teeth to count. It measured at least twenty feet from head to tail and stood as tall as the largest student. The hardened earth practically exploded where its shoulder impacted.

The students scattered. Light flashed from several places in the courtyard, as at least a handful of students activated cards. Spell-like effects struck the beast, or covered the students with wards of all sorts.

Chase nearly activated his own Agility boost. A hand on his shoulder stopped him. Sera's knowing, controlled smile made him calm down a bit, and he kept himself still, with a major effort.

The beast froze, wide jaws dripping slobber onto the soil. Instructor Boneridge laughed—loud, boisterous guffaws.

The students froze. They knew they were the butts of a joke, but nobody spoke up.

Finally, Instructor Boneridge subsided. "Aah. I never tire of that reaction." She shook her head, then faced the students. "We aren't the Light. We don't have endless elbow room and can afford to just use our Guardians to go out and die. We need to think about how we best spend our resources." She pointed at Sera. "You think right. But you think too small. We use our Guardians as a way of instructing students of beast physiology and ways to best handle those. That is the merest part of it, though. Why would we ship our Guardians off merrily and waste them on killing Lightborn, Liberty, and unaspected Guardians? That merely wastes Ænima that we could use here. No. They are our training partners, our teachers, and part of our growth."

With a small voice, Galvon asked, pointing at the huge earthen salamander, "I'm fighting…that?"

The instructor was all teeth. "You bet. Not for a while still. You're still weak and puny. But eventually, we will have you face off against something the size of this lovely creature here." She patted the flank of the monstrous form. "Eventually, she will give her life and her Ænima to a skilled student here, and she will end up becoming part of you in the future. Both as a valuable lesson and as part of your life force, granting you a Step or two in the process. *This* is how the towers handle things. We let you earn your wings and start walking the Steps in here. That way, once you get out there…" She pointed at the open air and the lands beyond Earth's Ward, miles away and hundreds of feet below. "You have an inkling what to do."

The instructor nodded up at the beast. "Is it safe? Of course not. This is training. Accidents happen, especially controlling large, dangerous creatures such as these. Is it safer than going out there and facing the Lightborn, Liberty, and unaspected beasts head-on?" Her intense stare turned into a smirk. "Well, you'll get to see that for yourself."

Slowly, understanding dawned among the students. All around their numbers, relieved chuckles and chatter arose, as they realized they'd have the chance to gain some experience against different kinds of monsters, before they'd have to face the real kind.

The instructor motioned them all forward. "Now, stop acting like babies straight out of the nursery. Move on up and take a look at Germina here. Then, I want to hear your opinion. If you're faced off against a beast like this, how are you going to handle it? Which cards, and which strategies are you going to use? Also, which magical abilities would you expect from a beast like this?"

They spent the next twenty minutes debating how to successfully fight a beast like the one in front of them. Tam actually knew the animal race the Elemental Guardian was based off, a needle-toothed behemoth, and was able to tell what she knew about it. Apparently, the thin, spike-like teeth were hollow and contained a paralyzing agent. Also, it was surprisingly agile, especially with twisting and turning. Its forward speed was nothing to speak of, though. Everybody agreed facing it head-on was akin to suicide, and most focused on some sort of attrition-based strategy, or overpowering damage to the head.

Then, Boneridge revealed beasts in the other partitions. They were all Guardians, grouped up by their race. Some small, spindly and grouped up. Others large and bulky. A few were even fliers. All of them were clearly Elemental in nature, favoring one element or other. With a rapid-fire list of commands, she allowed the students to fetch weapons, then distributed each of them to a partition, facing them off against one type of beast or another.

Chase and the other rogues faced a pack of canine beasts. A smaller group, these were thin, almost emaciated beasts. They were, however, clearly water-aspected, liquid dripping constantly from their open jaws as well as soaking the ground underneath their shapes. They moved in fits and starts that made Chase seem slow. The group that had been selected to confront them were, with few exceptions, rogues or, at a guess, ranged. The general body type was wiry and small, and they tended toward lighter weapons, with a good deal of bows and throwing weapons in the mix.

The instructor went to another group first. Then she turned her back on that group and allowed the servant to take over. Behind her, a crafter clearly panicked, as an insect-like Guardian was set loose upon him.

Instructor Boneridge ignored the screams behind her, instead performing a theatrical wave at the dogs in the partition ahead of them. "These are wave hounds. They usually attack in packs of six to nine beasts. Because you're rookies, and because I'm in a good mood, you will be allowed to face off against a single one at first. Who's first?"

Chase considered the situation. There was a much larger risk of getting his ass handed to him, being first, but it would also allow him to stand out among the crowd, if he didn't mess up horribly. He raised his hand.

She nodded, smiling a wicked smile. "Interesting. Let's see how the cripple fares." She gestured at the partition. "Get in there."

Chase frowned. There was nothing keeping the Guardians inside the walled-off earthen area. In fact, the canines looked as though they wanted nothing more than the chance to be unleashed upon the fresh meat outside the partition. Only, they kept to one side of the partition, and now, all dogs except one were pulling back toward the side. He looked at the servant, who was observing the partition with a look of focus plastered on his face. The servant carried an elaborate stone armband. *Ah.* Without further delay, Chase hefted the long dagger he'd chosen and walked into the opening in the rough earthen wall.

The instant he hit the ground on the other side, the instructor barked, "Go!"

The canine blinked once, twice. Then its eyes settled on Chase, and it barreled straight toward him.

Chase had been prepared for this. He activated his Race of Life card and dodged with all the boosted Agility available to him. The animal still nearly got him, jaws snapping shut mere inches from Chase's retreating sleeve. He sprinted as fast as possible away from the dog, then realized it was right at his heels.

Activating Steps of Brilliance, he took three impossibly steep steps, air turning solid in mid-air, allowing him to turn ninety degrees without skidding, without wasting a single inch of momentum. Mid-step, he glanced back and realized three things.

One, this beast was faster than him, even with the boost from his card. That was a nasty surprise. He'd gotten used to being the fastest person around. This dog was undeniably faster. It had almost caught up to him when he turned.

Two, even though this was training, it was also *real*. Those fangs under the small, inhuman eyes were dripping with saliva in the anticipation of biting down on his jugular. If he messed up bad enough, no healer would be able to save him.

Three, he was in trouble. The hard-packed earth where the dog had sprinted looked like a huge snail had crawled over it, leaving a thin, greasy layer of residue. He had no clue what it did, but it likely wasn't good for his odds if he stepped in it. The saliva might be poisonous too.

The conclusion was simple. He'd have to finish the battle, and he'd have to do it fast. Effectively. Conclusively. Drawing out the battle would ensure that the greasy-looking substance would cover more and more of the arena, turning it near-impossible for him to move around.

Sprinting again, he came up with a plan. Okay, if Cilia were to describe it, she'd use different words. Harsher words. Curse a lot, probably. The truth was, that, he was outclassed here, and surprise would be the only thing to get him through. His feet churned up dirt like Liam caught by a jealous husband. One second, two, and he was barreling ahead like somebody was behind him, aching to take his other hand. His grip on the long dagger grew tighter, almost feverish, and he leapt.

Life as a thief taught him a lot of things, many of them unsavory and questionable. Always keeping an eye out for exits. Knowing where he was in the city and keeping in mind nearby bolt-holes and shortcuts. Which guards could be bribed. To Chase, one of the lessons he'd taken the closest to heart was that of mobility. If there was an obstacle in the way, he'd be able to scramble over it. If there was a tiny hole in a crowd, that hole would fit Chase, no discussion. Whichever panicked motion and ridiculous maneuver existed, Chase had certainly tried it in his life-long list of clashes with pursuit of different kinds.

He flung himself forward, feet-first. Flying parallel to the ground, he looked certain to hit badly and hurt himself. Instead, his feet landed on the two platforms he'd prepared for himself. He dipped, braced himself, and then unleashed his built-up momentum. Like a leaping viper uncoiling from his hiding place, he exploded in a leap, in the opposite direction that he'd been running a second before.

The wave hound was alert, bloodthirsty, and fast. It was not clever. Its brain was focused on the hunt, ready to catch up to him farther ahead. The physical impossibility of him stopping mid-air and then reversing direction in seconds completely tricked the hound. Mid-bound, its tongue lapped comically outside its mouth, gaze fixed farther ahead.

Its beady eyes moved as if struggling against a freeze card, veering ever so slowly toward Chase barreling straight at its chasing form. A flash of light was the sun hitting the out-stretched dagger held ahead of its prey, suddenly moving to the attack.

Chase hit hard. He didn't have the skill to be certain of landing a finishing blow, so he didn't try. What he did have was more weight than the hound—and a well-maintained weapon. Hound and man collided at speed. Chase was set for the clash. The hound was not.

Magical or not, the lighter beast didn't take the collision well.

Chase led with the knife's edge, felt it bite into the hound's front leg. Then his shoulder and the rest of his body struck, and he heard a cracking noise, even as his world went tumbling end over end.

He came to a painful rest on *top* of the hound. With a cry and a desperate heave, he pushed himself off the body of the beast using his stump and the fist clenching his dagger. He nearly gagged from the hot air of the hound's fetid breath as it snapped after him. He rolled off and bounded away in a grace-less scramble. Fighting to his feet, he kept running, shooting a glance over his shoulder to see the pursuit. A brazen grin emerged on his face as he watched the hound slowly getting back up without putting weight on the bleeding leg.

Triumphantly, Chase clenched his hand, raising his dagger to go on the offensive. At that exact moment, he figured out precisely what the effect of the liquid covering the beast did, as the slimy substance slid through his fingers...and caused his dagger to slip through his grip and onto the ground.

The next thirty seconds were anything but graceful. Chase kept evading the now badly injured beast, wiping his hand furiously against his clothes. Thankfully, the hound was much slower with its damaged leg. His Steps of Brilliance helped him step over the slime-covered patches of soil the beast had passed. He'd been fortunate in avoiding getting any under his shoes. Fi-nally, he was able to pick his dagger back up and turn on the offensive—and with that, the fight was decided. A short while later, the beast sank to the ground, bleeding, and did not rise. Chase stood over its pierced body, panting.

"Congratulations, sir. Would you mind leaving the prem-ises and let us clean up for the next round?" the servant with the stone armband asked politely.

Chase jumped with shock, then nodded and shook his head as he left the cordoned-off area. He regretted his decision to go first now. Not because it had gone badly. Not really. He figured being able to win would be seen as decently impressive, especially given the attributes of the beast. However, the fight had made one thing perfectly clear to him. The towers didn't mind casualties. Sure, that servant was almost certainly in control of the beast. He was also, most likely, able to stop any attack at a moment's thought. Still, that wouldn't help Chase if he had his throat torn out. Those teeth had been...yeah. This was learning by doing, taken to the absolute extreme.

"That was a *blast*!" A hyped-up high-pitched voice sounded from behind him. Galvon emerged, grinning. "How the Pits did you make that move when you attacked? It looked like you decided to take a leap off the air itself!"

"It's my card," Chase said with a shaky smile. Behind him, the hound was being dragged off the field, and another one commanded to pace forward. Chase felt a moment's pity for the Guardians. Sure, they were summoned creatures, little more than magic made flesh. Even so, being summoned for the simple purpose of being killed? It felt dirty. He shook his head and activated his Steps of Brilliance, taking a few steps off the ground. "Little more than a gimmick, but you can see how it can be useful."

Galvon's eyes grew wide. "Useful indeed." He hinted with his head at the hounds. "Any tips?"

Chase considered his response. Galvon was a competitor. Chase really should be focusing on improving his own lot, not helping others. Except... "You saw most of it. That slime is really something. Greasy and slippery. If you step in it, you're done. Also, the beast is faster than a Darkborn caught peeking in a nun's changing room. Strike first and strike hard!"

Galvon nodded, eyes widening. "Appreciated."

The next hours flew by. After the first moment of panicked combat, Chase was reduced to an observational position, taking it in as every other person in his group got a chance to face off against the wave hounds. He also reveled in the fact that the Ænima from the wave hound actually earned him his eighteenth Step. He put his free point in Potential. After that, he simply watched. He'd never before gotten the chance to see so many people using their cards in combat from a safe position. Slowly, as the matches progressed, he came to a few conclusions.

One, he was, attribute-wise and Steps-wise, above the average of the students. Only one other student sported three cards, and quite a few of them only had one. On top of that, Chase was most definitely the consistently fastest of the lot. Well, except for the snobbish Tandor with his speed-increasing card.

Two, his skill set was by far and large one of the most passive of the lot. Most of the others had at least one hard-hitting, strike-first-ask-questions-later skill. Galvon, for instance, used a card to make his fists burst into actual fire. Then he took down his hound with a single, well-aimed strike to the throat. The variations were bountiful, but they all seemed to have at least one card aimed at allowing them to cause some serious damage. The only other exception to that rule was the Liberty rogue, Camille. Instead, she had a single orb floating around her body, which didn't do anything obvious, until the hound chomped down on her arm, causing the orb to disappear and the jaws to spring back up as if they'd struck an invisible barrier.

Third, and most importantly, a lot of the students were not used to fighting. At all. The third matchup sported a tall, strong archer holding a bow taller than himself. The Furyborn ranged summoned an arrow that sparkled, blazing, drumming with power to the point where it could be *sensed* outside of the fighting area. He missed. Well, not entirely. The arrow, aimed at the hound's head, struck the beast in the chin and carved a damaging, bloody furrow down the side of its face. The Guardian was thrown to the ground, but soon regained its pace and resumed its charge at the archer. The archer froze. Face carved into a rictus of fear, his next arrow dropped from senseless fingers, and he stared helplessly at the advancing beast. Thankfully, the servant noticed and called off the match at the last moment, deeming it a loss. The loss of control was the first, but by no means the last. Some, like the haughty Tandor, put on a good face and eked out hard-fought wins. But mostly, the rogues and ranged managed to end their fights swiftly or not at all. If their first, hard-hitting card, shot, or effect failed, they were left to scramble and, often as not, panicked. Two were carted off with nasty wounds to see nearby healers. One of them did not return.

Between fights, Chase took to glancing at the other matchups around the area. He started to see a theme going in the different groupings. The Guardians they were facing up against had to be selected to present challenges to the specific classes.

The fast, agile hounds in his spot were clearly picked out to cause trouble to fast-moving people like rogues and ranged.

The fighters of the lot (as well as a few brawny healers and a single buff rogue) were faced with what looked like an oversized, chitin-armored praying mantis. The beast was ponderous and slow, but the scythe-shaped forearms of the beast had a wide range and were strong and punishing.

Summoners and casters were presented with small groups of winged, fist-sized pests that moved erratically, yet caused comparatively little damage.

Finally, the crafters and healers seemed to get the easiest opponents, comparatively speaking, at least. Crafters faced a cat-faced flying beast the size of a human. They were agile in the air, yet clumsy and awkward if the crafters managed to strike them down to the ground, their long claws as much a hindrance as a help.

Healers were up against a toad. A single damn toad. Knee-tall and ugly, they looked like a joke, only, they spat wads of caustic slime and their jumps took them far, helping them evade the often defensively oriented healers.

He missed Liam's fight. At least Liam was still standing, and what he saw from the rest of his crew was encouraging. Cilia, wielding a steel-shod quarterstaff, downed her aerial opponent and proceeded to whack it into oblivion. Sera was awkward, and her swings were anything but precise. However, she moved faster than usual, clearly having used her Spark of Divinity to boost her Agility, and ignored or healed what damage the toad got in, before she pinned the agile Guardian and finished it with her sword breakers.

Kith...was a sight to behold. He summoned the Crescendo of Might being, sending it charging madly against the small, flying pests. Then he used his Divine Mentor to boost his own attributes and speed and went on the offensive. He ignored any single attack by the flying beasts, except where it allowed him to get a strike in against them, punishing them with fast strikes of his twin machetes. Just like against the gleam skippers, he made the small beasts pay. He ended up bleeding from a dozen superficial cuts but took down all of the pests except one that inadvertently fled Kith's strikes, right into the path of his flailing, clumsy summon.

Once the fights concluded, Instructor Boneridge had them all gather next to the large salamander-like beast. Both Sera and Liam earned themselves a Step from the fight. Both kept to their strategies, Liam adding the point to Toughness and Sera to Mental Power.

The large group that got together now didn't much resemble the cocky students who had assembled just a few hours earlier. Anybody who needed it had been healed. With rare few exceptions—mostly the ranged who'd managed to kill their opponent before it got close—they were looking much the worse for wear. They were covered in dirt, blood, or worse. Their clothes were cut and torn. Also, several of them had a faraway, haunted look in their eyes.

The instructor beamed at them, like she'd won a prize.

Right then and there, Chase decided that whatever else happened, he needed to show her up. Wise or not, she was simply taking too much enjoyment from this!

CHAPTER 27

"There is one thing we do wrong, I believe. Those who fail at becoming Protectors? They are told to try again, to aim for the top. However, some quite clearly will never make the top. I believe that we should be better at utilizing the resource that is the 'nearly-good-enough.' What could we do if all the crafters who wanted to become part of the Protectors but failed were associated with us? The casters? There is a lot of potential here, and I believe we are squandering it." That is...surprisingly insightful. I also agree. They are tossing a huge number of their applicants to the wayside, where they could have formed part of their defenses to some extent. Wasteful. (Page 68.)

"**T**his. *This* is what I like to see." The instructor beamed. "You there." She strode over to a crafter with a fancy embroidered vest, the sleeve torn half off, and a haunted look in her eyes. Facing the crafter head-on, she gloated. "This moment is my favorite leading up to the first Culling. This moment, where all pretenses are done away with, the veil is torn from your eyes and you finally face what it *means* to be a Protector." She walked even closer into the young woman's personal space, ignoring her forlorn look, and looked down into her eyes from just a few inches away.

The training area was dead silent as she purred her next words. "*This* is being a Protector. Putting your life on the line. At every hour, being ready to risk your life, for the defense of Earth's Ward. Sometimes, you're lucky and understand what you face, get the chance to formulate a plan. At other times, you don't, and have to make do as best you can. *This* is the moment where you learn if you're hard enough for that." Her voice was sensual, almost erotic, as she faced the crestfallen crafter. "Look deep, doll. Because I am only getting started."

Boneridge turned away from the crafter, who started to cry, with long, shuddering sobs. She faced the remaining students, her mien suddenly hard, confrontational. "That goes for all of you. If today has scared you? Good! Use that to learn about yourself. Are you hard enough to use that to improve, to grow? Then do it! Otherwise, *quit!* Spare us all a lot of wasted effort and leave these sacred premises now. Because you are wasting our time!" That final sentence, she shouted, spittle flying from her lips. "Some of you, I admit, much to my surprise, might have what it takes. But most of you have been coddled, protected, told you are the best, the strongest. I am here to tell you how that is a lie. How you are nothing compared to the legends of old. With time, you may grow into it. You might grow a pair, grow strong, and earn a spot among the legends of Earth's Ward. But today is not that day."

She smirked, challenging them, one by one. "Of course, I could be wrong. You have faced off against some of the weakest monsters that our Protectors face on a daily basis. Do any of you have what it takes to face a *real* beast?" She gestured at the huge salamander-shaped monstrosity behind her, sneering at the students.

Chase saw in a flash how this was supposed to go. They would, of course, admit that they were too weak to face off against something as huge and powerful as this. Then, she would have fun mocking them for a while, probably making a few of them quit out of sheer shame and a sense of weakness. After that, she could start showing just how they could stop being weak, if they gave it their all, and eventually, they would follow her advice and those who passed the Culling would earn a tad of respect. His gaze was drawn to the crafter, who'd stopped sobbing out loud and just stared into the distance, gaze lost and endlessly sad.

He looked at Kith, who scowled back at him. Then at Sera, watching the shame and frustration burn in her gaze. Liam, stoic and dependable. Cilia... Cilia might never forgive him.

Boneridge snorted. "I thought as much. Not a single backbone—"

"We can do it." Chase stepped forward.

"What?" The instructor frowned.

"I said we can do it." He shot a glance behind him.

One by one, the others—his friends, his damn *family*—stepped up, hefting their weapons, even if Cilia's gaze promised retribution.

"Did I say you could use a full team?" The earth-aspected powerhouse actually sounded confused.

He faced Instructor Boneridge. "You're not going to suggest that you'd send your precious Protectors to face off against something like that one-on-one, just to prove how tough they are? I thought the towers were all about pragmatism?" He pointed his long dagger at the huge beast. "So, how about we take a stab at this thing?"

She squinted suspiciously at him. "Do you have a death wish, cripple?"

"Nah. But I have a thing against those in power who take it out on those who are smaller than themselves."

She blinked, then her face changed. She laughed uproariously. "By all means, then. Never let it be said that I don't allow my students the chance to get themselves crushed."

Instructor Boneridge took a detour to talk to some of the servants in the place. They clearly weren't prepared for this scenario. However, within a couple of minutes, the space had been cleared, and one of the partitions had been expanded to accommodate the size of the behemoth and their group. It was now a sixty-by-sixty-foot square area that would allow them a ton of space to run around in, with tall earthen ramparts on the top, where the rest of the class could see what they were doing. It seemed way too small for the huge beast.

Speaking of the rest of the class, they clearly thought the five were insane. Galvon told Chase as much. Jonathan, Tam, and Rowan simply wished them luck. Ernest loudly exclaimed that he hoped they would all die. There was one surprise. The Darkborn girl, Emilia, walked over to wish them the best, for everybody to see. Her gaze flicked back to the put-upon crafter who was now staring at their group with something approaching awe in her expression.

Cilia was, unsurprisingly, not happy. "Are you planning to get us all killed?"

"Of course I'm not. But what was I supposed to do? Just stand there and watch her run roughshod over all of us?"

"Yes!" she said emphatically. "What's it to us? If she gets a handful of our competition tossed out, because they realize they're not made for this, that's all the better."

Snarling, Chase pointed at her. "Yeah. Well. Damn." He deflated. "You're right. Okay? I couldn't take any more of her being such a tyrant. Should we call it off, take the loss? I really do think we've got a chance at beating this thing. It's big, but so was the damn gaborn."

Cilia looked him straight in the eyes for a dozen long seconds. Then she shook her head. "No. We'll take it down. Getting beat would probably be better than backing down at this point, as long as we make a good showing of ourselves." Cilia glanced at the rows upon rows of long, needle-thin teeth. "Besides, I'm drooling at the thought of just how much Ænima I'm going to get from that thing!"

They spent a short while going over the strategy and changing to the proper cards. For this one, they were going to go with a standard setup, one they rarely ever had the chance to use.

Liam, with his mace and shield setup, would be the best placed to keep the beast occupied, and he was the only one with a card to counteract the poison of the animal, Cleansing Fire.

233

That, along with Become the Clay helping him take any hits and stray needles, should help him hold his own.

Meanwhile, Sera would be entirely on healing and buffing detail, while Cilia and her small bag of tricks should help distract the enemy.

Chase and Kith would be working entirely on doing damage, attacking the beast from the back. Chase knew he would mostly be able to help set up Kith and Kith's massive, strong summon for the real finishers, since his own Strength was no real answer to the thick chitinous armor of the huge salamander, but he didn't mind. Playing distraction was one of his prime skills. Well, Kith was better, but for this, he and his machetes would be in charge of dismantling. Squall Sling, his actual sling, and a large pouch of iron pellets would help him in that regard.

The combat area was silent as they faced off against the beast. Their entire class gathered on the ramparts, looking down upon them with equal parts awe, ridicule, and fear.

From what Chase could tell, it wasn't just their class, either. A bunch of people in servant's clothing, and other recruits he didn't recognize from other classes, made the numbers of the onlookers swell as they kept trickling in.

Chase checked his own weapons again. He kept the long dagger ready in its sheath, but fully intended to stay just out of reach of the beast to use his sling, an annoying mosquito to keep the behemoth frustrated and chasing him.

Liam already had his truncheon and shield ready, rolling his neck to limber up.

Kith was waving his machetes up and down, trying to get the onlookers to cheer.

Cilia concentrated, her hand gliding over her many pouches. She wiped her hands incessantly over her clothes, holding the steel-capped quarterstaff with one hand.

Sera decided to eschew weapons this time, choosing only a large shield. She knew her task.

Instructor Boneridge took the ruckus in stride. She stood, posture relaxed, with one hand on the front leg of the behemoth. Eventually, she shouted, "Silence!" As the noise slowly died down, she pointed at their group. "This...is folly. This small group insists that they should be allowed to prove themselves, show how they are good enough to take on something that experienced Protectors can have trouble with. Well, we shall let them. This is not your father's band of personal guards. These are the Protectors. We do not coddle our recruits. If they overextend, that is on them. If they need to lose half their number to learn a lesson, so be it." She walked briskly away from the large monster, standing against the earthen rampart. "Attack!"

The behemoth lumbered forward. Its long, prehensile body made a slithering motion as it moved, reminiscent of a snake moving across earth.

Chase exploded into motion. He sensed the various buffs on him, boosting his Agility. His own Race of Life bonus added to Sera's Spark of Divinity, landing him at a total of thirty-three Agility. He felt lithe and limber, fast, in control of his every movement, as he ran across the hard soil and to the left, while Kith took the other side.

The beast, perhaps observing that Kith was the slower of the two, started to move in that direction. Its forward motion wasn't too fast, somewhere between a jog and a sprint for a human. Even so, in the square arena, it would be all too easy to become trapped in a corner.

Chase dropped an iron pellet into his sling and started to whirl. He released, letting Squall Sling empower the shot with a focused burst of air. The half-inch pellet whizzed through the air and hit the beast in the face, right above its massive set of jaws.

The behemoth froze for a moment, just as a small line of blood drizzled down its horrid face. Then it ruffled its neck in a roiling motion and bore down on Chase.

Chase didn't see it coming right away. The ruffling of its neck sent a shower of droplets spraying everywhere in the vicinity. He had to act quickly and activated Squall Sling again in a wide burst of air to fend off any drops aimed his way. Only then did he see the huge beast racing his way like a redonite bull with a grudge, and raced to avoid it.

The behemoth pursued him, veering lightning quick to follow his sideways sprint, but fell behind as he started to sprint straightaway. So that part was true. Quick to turn, less quick in a head-on race.

A shout from behind came from Liam. "Watch out for the drops. They give a tiny debuff to Toughness. You can run on the ones on the ground. Just don't roll in it, or get sprayed." A flash indicated him activating his Cleansing Fire to get the bit of poison out of his system.

Calmly, Sera added her own shout. "I'm switching to Tongues of Pride. We'll need the continuous cleanse, and with the beast being water-aspected, the fire damage will help."

Chase grimaced. That meant they wouldn't have the best heal available. Still, she was right. No way were they going to be able to keep avoiding that poison. The behemoth, falling behind, was still following him. Apparently, it was rather dogged in its approach.

Then Kith arrived. With a shout, he leapt and came down swinging hard, focusing on bringing down a single machete as forcefully as possible.

The behemoth's tail wasn't long. Only about four to five feet of the entire twenty-foot length. It was hefty, though, and looked like it could pack a punch if it managed to hit somebody.

Kith apparently decided to try to resolve that threat straightaway. His heavy blade slammed down on the center of the tail, making a burst of blood explode up as the machete carved deep into the flesh. Where the blade impacted, the blood hissed from the fire damage caused by Sera's buff.

The behemoth reacted immediately. With astounding speed, it turned on itself, veering a hundred and eighty degrees in a single second, snapping at its attacker.

Kith squawked and flung himself away, leaving the machete buried hilt-deep in the wide tail and running as fast as he could to distance himself.

The beast, right behind him, slowly fell behind. However, Kith was swiftly approaching one of the ramparts. On top of the ramparts, onlookers nervously backed away.

"Close your eyes!" Cilia's shout rang out, and they hurried to oblige. A split second later, a burst of bright light erupted right before the beast, as she tossed one of her crafted blinding bracelets.

The beast screeched, clawing at its eyes as the pain left it momentarily blinded. Its neck frills ruffled again and a defensive burst of droplets filled the air around it.

Kith, who was running away, and Liam, who was closing to aid him, were both caught by the outer fringes of the cloud. They both sagged at the debilitating effect.

Only, Sera's Tongues of Pride was already hard at work. Small tongues of healing flame licked across their bodies and puffs of vapor showed the damaging poison evaporating.

Liam closed upon the hindquarters of the still-blinded lizard. He hefted his truncheon and let it fall hard down on where the machete was still embedded in the tail. The crunching sound was followed by a pained hiss, and Liam pulled back immediately, shield raised in preparation of a swift counterattack.

The large jaws of the behemoth snapped out—once, twice...wildly and inaccurately. The last bite blindly clanged down on Liam's shield, but the head bounced away, striking his clay-covered shoulders and rebounding. Behind it, the tail flopped, only tethered to the rest of the body by a thin strip of flesh.

The attack exposed the reason for the name "needle-toothed." As Liam retreated, focused and sharp, his left shoulder and neck sported a half-dozen long teeth embedded in the heavy layer of magical clay covering him. It didn't look like the poison had any effect on him as he moved back, ready to react.

Now, Kith's first summon joined the fray. The summon from his Crescendo of Might card stayed behind them all, growing and evolving. Kith seemed to save that one for until it had grown in strength and could provide a real difference in the fight. The same was not the case for the Apian God card.

At first, it was just a barely visible blur in the air around the behemoth's face. Then the blur grew and started to give off an audible buzz. They were flying insects. Dozens of them, hundreds. Small ones, sized somewhere between mosquitos and bees, barely annoying as a single presence, but biting, stinging. Distracting.

Chase used the opportunity and released a sling shot that hit the pained, distracted beast right at the edge of one of its large eyes. He suppressed a grin to see the tiny burst of fire near the impact. He'd forgotten that Sera's buff even worked on ranged weapons. Immediately, the eye closed, and a liquid somewhere between blood and something else seeped out from between the eyelids. "I'll try to blind the other eye," he shouted. "You keep it distracted. Hit and run from behind. Don't get pinned down."

They had it outmatched. It wasn't fast enough to catch any one of them, and as long as they could keep it reacting and distracted, they'd be able to slowly bleed it to death.

In response, the behemoth started to shake.

They all backed away quickly, prepared for the spray of poison to erupt from it. Only, this time, it was something different.

Their group had gone up against a good number of different Guardians so far. They'd fended off Guardians of Dark fleeing from where Arnault was killed, fought Guardians of Light and Furyborn Guardians on their way back to Isarn, and even hunted a few. They knew that Guardians weren't regular beasts, that they could take on magic and internalize it from the aspects they represented, use it for dangerous effects.

They had never seen anything like this.

As the behemoth shook, it slowly turned glossy, as if it converted into a living thing of moving, whirling liquid. A thin layer of glistening water covered the behemoth, starting from the head and moving back over its entire body, until it finished the conversion, looking like it had been turned into an actual Elemental beast, comprised purely of water. Then it hissed, water receding to show the massive sets of teeth lurking behind the layer of water—and went on the offensive.

Kith was first to react. From behind Liam, he sent his monstrous Crescendo of Might summon tumbling forward to meet the behemoth. The hulking beast had grown into a shapeless form twice as tall as himself. Its limbs were large and club-like, and it threw itself onto the glistening, watery beast.

The goliaths met in a giant spray of liquid. The taller summon landed on top of the giant lizard, which twisted and contorted itself to chomp down on one of the creature's arms.

"We need to hurt it, while it's down," Chase shouted. Following his own advice, he shot once, twice, trying to hit the other eye. He struck first the massive chin, then the edge of the other eye. Except, it seemed as if the liquid acted like a physical shield, robbing most of the momentum and damage.

Kith and Liam went to work on the beast's hind legs, trying to ruin its mobility. Like lumberjacks trying for a performance bonus, their arms rose and fell as they did their utmost to destroy the behemoth. Only, the watery shield dulled their attacks, and they were unable to get through fully. Even the fire damage from Sera's buff only penetrated briefly, until the liquid rushed in to fill up the shield once again.

The Apian God was undone as well. The insects were caught in the viscous liquid and were left to slowly drown, unable to fly away.

From underneath the larger summon, the huge lizard twisted and struggled against the unwieldy creature. Its teeth bore down again and again, ripping into the shapeless body. One huge arm looked nearly ready to tear away.

Chase cursed. He looked at Kith and Liam, who were still struggling, but failing to make any headway. They simply didn't have the kind of damage it would take to make it through the shield. Grimacing, he looked to the side of the arena, searching for Instructor Boneridge. This was going to hurt their rankings horribly, yet he couldn't see how they could conceivably beat the behemoth. He opened his mouth, ready to concede defeat.

Instructor Boneridge lay on her side on the ground. Her eyes were wide open, and it looked like she was twitching.

Chase panted. It felt as though something pushed down on his ribs, making it harder for him to breathe. With an effort, he grabbed hold of himself. He'd had his share of close calls before. He called out at the top of his lungs to the onlookers. "Instructor Boneridge is unconscious. Somebody do something."

Somebody did do something. They panicked. Loud and hard. Realizing that the instructor was unconscious, and the beast was effectively off its leash, half the onlookers exploded into some sort of action. Some screamed, others ran away. Some yelled for help, while others again started using their cards.

The entire arena became a chaotic kaleidoscope of sound, light, and movement. Chase realized that they were soon about to become the center of a veritable bombardment of cards used by fear-stricken recruits. He made a snap decision and shouted over the noise. "Last resort! Right now!"

It was the code word they'd agreed on. How they would know that everything had gone to crap and they would need to use *any* available means to survive, including the use of the Dark cards.

Liam stepped up first. A flash on his left arm indicated that he used his Tier-two card. "I'll hold it. Do what you need to do."

Chase knew what that meant. Liam had activated Draining Ward. That would increase his defense and drain the beast's Agility if it struck Liam. He was taking it straight-on. Suicide.

Sera didn't change anything. With Liam moving away from Cleansing Fire, she needed to keep up the Tongues of Pride to stave off the poisons from its teeth.

Stuck without a recourse, Chase considered his approach. The huge thing wasn't too fast for them. They could deal with that. They simply had to make it through that damn layer of water. And they had to do it fast, before they were killed by the damn thing, or a stray effect. Grimacing, he made the change. He felt as his Spoils of the Undeserving card warped, changed into something else, something darker and *hungry*. The second after that, he activated Free of Perdition and targeted the behemoth's Toughness.

The Crescendo of Might summon was fading now, slowly being torn apart and turning into sparkling vapor.

Chase's approach was a gamble. If it didn't work, they would have to flee, and trust to servants and nearby Protectors to take on the rampaging beast. He felt the solidity of his body rapidly improve, like he'd be able to sprint for hours, take a thousand punches and stay standing. His Toughness increased to fifty-three. Good. That wasn't the real test, though.

The watery layer flickered and nearly evaporated from the beast.

Chase laughed in relief. It paid off. The damn thing didn't have the Mental Power to stand against the second part of the Free of Perdition card, and it had now exchanged its own Toughness score with Chase's. A Toughness of eighteen was nothing to sneeze at...if you were a human. For a huge beast, it was a massive downgrade. "Attack! You can damage it now, I hope!" he yelled. Following his own advice, he whirled the sling and shot an iron pellet straight at its face.

The layer of water repelled his fiery shot. Only, for a moment, it flowed, dimming from a fist-sized part of the rest of the body.

The others reacted on that immediately. All except Liam, who remained huddled in front of the beast, ready to take on its attack.

Chase kept flinging the pellets. Kith started to attack its hindquarters with a vengeance.

The beast ignored them all, bearing down on Liam with its jaw wide open, like it intended to swallow him whole.

Over Liam's shoulder, a dark, oblong shape flew through the air. It was Cilia's quarterstaff, aimed straight at the open maw of the behemoth.

The behemoth reacted instinctively. Seeing something flash at its mouth, its sinuous neck twisted and it veered to catch the attacker. It bit down...and caught the staff in its mouth. For a second, it froze, comically, with its mouth wide open as it tried to chomp down on the offending stick and failed. The quarterstaff was stuck, lodged between the hind part of the upper jaw and the lower set of its front teeth. The behemoth shook its head wildly, bucking to dislodge the thing.

Then the next thing sailed through the air from Cilia. It was a small, see-through object that flew straight, ricochetted off the tongue, and hit the back of its throat.

The fire potion exploded inside the behemoth's mouth.

It wasn't a huge explosion. Yet it struck right where the watery shield didn't reach. The fire, antithetical to the beast's own element, caused it to bellow in pain...and slam its jaws closed.

With its erstwhile Toughness of above fifty, the staff would surely have been a splintered mess. Now, the liquid spilled to the ground, and the behemoth showed a brief moment of absolute confusion on its bestial face, as the tip of the steel-capped staff burst through its forehead. It didn't die fast. It didn't die easy. But it died nonetheless.

CHAPTER 28

"Every decade in Earth's Ward has one. Sometimes more. Heroes to go on to earn the ever-living adoration of the entire population for their accomplishments in the Protectors. The Bulwark of Water. Jill, the Eye. Cranesh, the Living Brush. Avalanche. Bobellus, the Constructor. May they forever live in our consciousness." Funny that he doesn't mention how many died along the way. Hero worship is all well and good, but I do not intend to lay my life down for it. This place is dangerous. (Page 71.)

"**W**hat happened earlier was a travesty. It was so far from what the towers stand for that it...it makes no sense! I have no words."

For having no words, he sure spoke a lot. Chase wasn't sure who exactly he was. He was some official in a higher administrative function or other. He was also the fourth person they'd spoken to after the behemoth went nuts. They'd been corralled away from the arena swiftly, parted from their fellow students. Then, they'd been forced to sit through one investigation after another, moved from one room to the next.

The first one was almost hostile in tone, with the overseeing servant of the training area asking pointed questions. Did they do anything? Why did Instructor Boneridge suddenly fall over? Why were they even fighting such a powerful Guardian, when they were just scrubs?

The next investigation, three floors higher on the mountain, this one in an actual room, not just in the middle of a hallway, was different. Slightly panicked, as if they hadn't gotten around to understanding what had taken place. The questions were different too. "Did you notice anything weird? Did you see any flashes, anybody activating cards as the instructor fainted?" There was still an undercurrent of suspicion, though. How had they defeated such a powerful beast as that?

They did what they'd always done when faced with undue attention and suspicion: stick to ignorance. It was easier to profess ignorance than it was to come up with any big lies on the fly. At least the officials kept them together, didn't split them up to really grill them, check for inconsistencies in their explanations. On top of that, the first investigator hadn't thought to check their cards...although they'd long switched back from their Dark cards. Eventually, the Elementals called for a healer to check for any lingering effects after the fight.

That allowed them to discuss an official explanation they'd be able to stick to. Yes, they'd taken their chances against the beast, even though they had underestimated its strength and fiery prowess. No, they didn't truly know how they'd overcome it. In the midst of the chaos, there'd been a lot of cards activated. Likely, some among the crowd had used their cards on the behemoth and helped weaken it.

The third official was by far the kindest. He placed them in a large room that outdid their brief stint in the Tender Loin, allowed them to sink into the warm, plush wingback chairs, and arranged for a meal, even better than what they were used to in the mess hall. Then, he gave them the chance to relax and calm down. Sera tried to start a conversation about the fight, once, but the others waved her off. There was no telling whether they were still being suspected, if people were listening in. After about an hour, where the official walked in three times to ensure they were all right and didn't suffer any lingering effects from the battle, they were slowly getting tired of nothing happened. Then the fourth person arrived and started to apologize. It had been twenty minutes, and it felt like he was coming full circle, starting over with his first apologies.

After a lull in the conversation, Sera cleared her throat. "It is okay. Really. We are very understanding of the fact that this was unexpected, unwarranted, and unacceptable. For now, we would honestly just like an explanation. A proper one, I mean. What happened, and what is going to happen to us?"

The official, a water-aspected Elemental, looked out of his depths. His face was pale and carried a layer of liquid that was more than just the regular sheen of the water aspect. "Look. I'll level with you. I don't know *anything*. I'm nobody important."

This contrasted with the card Chase spotted with a haunting blue glow under his right pants leg, meaning he was at Tier four. Also, he might seem nervous, but the sword at his belt was well-maintained and steady.

The man continued. "I was just told to keep you safe and out of trouble. If there's anything I can do for you—food, drink, the like—you just say the word. Otherwise...I really need to keep you here until the higher-ups finish their investigations."

Higher-ups? Chase blinked. They were using a Tier *four* as a kid handler, while higher-ups looked into things? That meant they had to really be going all out.

An hour later, they finally got a sign of just how seriously the towers took everything. High Elementalist Tatiana Skysworn strode into the room, dismissing the minder with a nod. The man looked eminently grateful to be allowed to leave.

The High Elementalist looked even more impressive in person. Chase could *sense* the constant motion of air from the other side of the large room. On top of that, there was a sensation that he'd never felt before, like pressure mixed with the scent of ozone and...power. Chase didn't know how best to define it. Sera scrambled to her feet, bowing deeply. With a delay, the others followed, with varying degrees of sincerity.

Tatiana Skysworn looked at the assembled group for a while, before finally allowing herself a small smile. "Look at you. You're nothing like what I was told. I was expecting a group of hardened killers."

Kith shrugged, then said, "We're...sorry?"

She laughed. Her laughter sounded heartfelt. The voice was also different when she was alone as opposed to speaking to a crowd. Less officious or theatrical. More pleasant. Deep, with a nice warmth to it. "Don't be. I am here to clear up any confusion and tell you what we believe has happened and decide what's going to happen from here on out." She strode across the room and pulled up a chair of her own. She didn't even strain as she lifted the ornate wingback chair and placed it before their half circle.

"That sounds good," Chase tried. "This last fellow was nice, but he seemed a touch nervous, and...not used to taking care of people, I think?"

She laughed again. "That's Corren for you. Best at ease in a group of monsters." Her gaze turned serious as she looked at them in turn. "Today, somebody tried to murder you."

Kith snorted. "We kinda gathered that."

The High Elementalist shook her head. The pressure of her gaze caused even Kith to turn serious for a while. "You don't understand. Somebody tried to kill you. In the towers. Under the eyes of one of our most experienced instructors. We promote healthy competition. We even tolerate a certain degree of hazing, because we *need* hardiness in the Protectors. We cannot afford people among us who succumb to social pressure. But this? This is attempted murder. It will *not* go unpunished." The steel in her eyes made no secret of her resolve. "What we know is this: Somebody used a card or a magical item on Instructor Boneridge. This caused her to pass out at the very moment where she would be expected to call off the behemoth and have you forfeit the match. As such, the beast continued its rampage and tried its very best to slay you." One finely arched eyebrow rose. "Any disagreement so far?"

They looked at one another, then shook their heads.

Liam frowned. "Couldn't it be poison? No. The timing was too precise for that. Forget I said anything."

She chuckled. "Exactly. We are investigating everything that has led up to this point. We are, of course, aware of the misguided rivalry of Mr. Chalico. He is, at this moment, placed in another room, and having his own discussion with officials in the tower. That," she added, drily, "will be a much less cordial discussion than the one we are currently having. His compatriots are having similar, concurrent experiences." She frowned. "Judging from what we have learned so far, we do not expect to be able to place the blame at the feet of Mr. Chalico."

"What a surprise." Chase snorted. "His family's got a fortune and connections. Of course they won't do that."

"Do not," the High Elementalist said, with a raised finger, "mistake thoroughness for weakness. I do not tolerate corruption in *my* towers. If there is any proof, Mr. Chalico or his friends will be summarily executed, and nobody in the town would dare speak up against me. That does not seem to be the case, however. And we do *not* judge people based on accusations."

Chase opened his mouth, then thought better of it. "I'm...sorry. I'm used to the justice of Lightborn cities."

The High Elementalist inclined her head, acknowledging the point. "We do attempt to keep it different here. Still, that leaves us with a handful of issues, mostly centering around your group. I have been informed by a *cloaked* acquaintance about the real reason for your joining up, and the explanation for how come you were able to join as a group." She frowned. "While I am not a fan of the methods she has taken, I understand that you intend to honor the agreements of the Protectors, should you earn your keep?"

Chase's jaw dropped. Then he almost slapped himself. She was the highest-ranking leader of the damn place. If she didn't have connections in the secret police, who would?

Cilia was the first to adjust to their new world image. "I take it that your frankness means we are free to talk here?"

Ms. Skysworn said, "Within reason. You can never be entirely sure. I would not give any details you would prefer hidden."

Cilia nodded. "In that case, yes. Joining the Protectors would give us exactly what we need. Powers, money, and, above all, a place to call home."

The regal woman leaned back in her chair. She held a finger up, and a curl of her hair twirled around her finger, as if propelled by a stray current of air. "Acceptable. Here is what I surmise. We are likely not going to find the perpetrator. Obviously, Mr. Chalico, even if he was culpable, would not admit to any wrongdoing, and I doubt we will find any proof either way. There are simply too many who could be responsible. This does leave your group exposed and open to another attack. We could place guards on your rooms, yet, in the long run, anybody with the inclination and recklessness to arrange an attack like today will be able to do so again."

"No guards." Chase waved off the suggestion immediately. "It'll make us stand out. Besides, if we're supposed to do what our mutual friend wanted us to? We'll need to be able to move around without added attention. Any guards would make us seem too important. If you *do* want to help, having your friend aid us more directly would be a major boon. More knowledge. Possibly help to get into places where we otherwise couldn't."

"I will see what I can do. My influence over her is not absolute, you understand." The High Elementalist drummed her fingers on the edge of her chair. "I will not interfere with your training or your ranking. As much as it would make sense to make sure you pass, a thumb on the scale would be visible to those who know what to look for." She paused, then smiled, a friendly, direct smile that warmed up the room. "Besides, I doubt it will be necessary. From what your instructors intimate, you are of the rare sort who actually try to focus on your flaws and work to correct them, without having to be prompted. Even Instructor Boneridge praised you."

That took them aback. The instructor had not uttered a single word of praise so far, for anybody.

Cilia asked, "She...she did?"

The High Elementalist's smile was brilliant. "Yes. She was rather miffed at the thought that somebody tried to get to you through her. Her exact words were, I believe, *Those morons had the guts to face off against a behemoth. Nobody gets to break them but me!* High praise, coming from her."

Kith massaged his brow. "I'm pretty sure that woman doesn't know what praise looks like. So, that means we go back on our merry way, get back to the training and everything? Nothing changes, except the other students will know somebody's after us?"

"Pretty much," she agreed. "Most of them will assume the Chalicos kept up their misguided hatred against you, which, of course, could very well be the truth. Even so, you will not be sent back entirely empty-handed. Since this was obviously a breach in tower security, it would not be amiss to present you all with a complimentary gift—as an official apology, you understand. Meanwhile, I will expect you to continue on your agreed task with our acquaintance. Anything you find that you turn over to her will make its way to me."

Chase did understand. They weren't going to, in any way, *officially* support or aid them. But they would go out of the way to give them items that could help them. "In that case, we look forward to seeing what official gifts look like here at the center of the world."

* * *

The young man was nervous. This in itself was nothing new to him. Most days, here, he was nervous. He was out of his element, literally. He did not have family nearby who he could count on, and yet had a responsibility on which their fate rested, and ultimately, perhaps even the world. Today was worse than usual. He was about to meet his contact for the first time. The solid stone of the windowsill did nothing but betray his nerves from the clammy feel of the sweat on his hands. He took deep breaths to calm himself and observed the lands below. This blasted place. The Light would scourge it of its heresy.

"Do not turn around."

The voice was adult, measured, and...recognizable. *Her?* He did not turn around. His mind raced, though. He'd known it could be someone with whom they interacted daily, but this was a shock. The questions piled up inside his mind, but he kept them bottled up.

"You consistently fail to bring me anything useful," the voice continued, disapprovingly.

"I have done everything that was asked of me." He disliked his own voice like this. It was thin. Defensive. Wheedling. Not at all how he saw himself. He hardened his tone. "They keep to themselves and share their own council. If I wanted to get really close to them...it would seem weird. Be suspicious. Besides, *you* are the one messing up, not me. That is exactly what I have written in my reports as well."

"You did what?"

The incredulity in her voice was astounding. Good. He hadn't expected to actually put her off-kilter. But he needed to. Light, how he hated this position, caught between two forces, both strong enough to annihilate him utterly. "I reported it. No embellishments. No lies. Simply what you did, with my thoughts on how intelligent it was. Especially given that it failed."

She scoffed.

The sound of her voice was closer now, but he hadn't heard her move.

"I did what anybody would have done. I saw a chance to eliminate them all at once."

"And *failed*." He hated that his voice quavered. He snarled. "We don't have all the time in the world. This is out of the way, but somebody could still come along and see us together. Neither of us wants that. Now, I am supposed to pass a message back to you, from both our masters. No more half-baked attempts. We do not *need* to handle them. The plans will progress on schedule."

"They aren't my *masters*." She hissed the words. "And they don't know what I do. I have listeners around this place. Not many, and they need to be very cautious. Yet, in the chaos of the aftermath of my attack...my *failed* attack...they caught parts of the conversation between their group and the High Elementalist." Her voice was intense now, direct. *"They talked about the Cloaks.* Do you understand what this means? If they aren't already onto us, they *will* be."

For just a second, he dreamed that he was home. Away from all these damn demands, with servants tending his every need. Bunching his hands into fists, he rested his weight on the windowsill and took a deep breath. "Stop!" he barked. "Am I supposed to be the student here or is it you? Panic will bring us *nothing.*" He turned around now, looked her straight in the eyes.

Her nostrils flared in rage. "You—"

"I already recognized you," he shot out, drowning out the pounding of his heart. "You need to work on modulating your voice if you want to remain unknown. Also, get some damn disguises. Those are your regular clothes." Indeed, they were. The multihued garb of the teachers of the towers were recognizable from afar.

She shook her head, affronted. "Getting recognized in a disguise would be even worse. There are plenty of teachers walking the halls at all times."

"Be that as it may. You need to stop getting distracted. I don't know much about your vaunted Cloaks." He saw her open her mouth and cut her off with a slashing gesture. "I also don't care. Our plan proceeds as it should. We will be in place, in time. What you need to do is ensure that nobody interrupts that."

"And how do you suggest I do that?" she demanded. "The deal was that I grant you access, help you in, and that you would take care of the rest."

His lip quirked up in a sarcastic smile. "You say that like I'm in charge. In this, I'm as much a servant as you. Before you say you're not, what do you think would happen if *our* masters expose your secret?"

"It would be even worse for you, being an outsider," she hissed.

He laughed, a mirthless sound. "Somehow I doubt either of us would enjoy the experience. The point stands. You need to cooperate, or this might still fail."

She sighed. "Okay. What do you need me to do?"

"That...is a work in progress. I will inform our masters that the Cloaks are involved. Then, we need to plan. But, all told, their group being here, working for the Cloaks is a *good* thing. It means that the Cloaks don't know what's going on, yet. It means that they are attempting a different tack at figuring out what is going on. We can use that. Use it to feed them false information, send them in the wrong direction." He observed her standing there with her head bowed. Like this, she looked nothing like she usually did. Really, she looked *weak.* Like all her kind. Good thing they were going to be ruined.

Her gaze shot up to face his. "No. You may be right. I am too far involved in this to back out now. But you listen to me when I say this. *Do not try to match the Cloaks in a game of wits.* They're the ones who are responsible for the towers still standing after all this time. You have your opinions, of course. But I want you to send this to your Lights-cursed masters. Either act like nothing is going on—or take them out. Permanently."

He smirked. She wasn't entirely without fire then. Even if that wasn't her aspect. "You do realize that if we move against them, like you did, we'll have to make some overt moves—and that will include you?"

She nodded, hesitantly. "I may not like it. But I will do what it takes."

CHAPTER 29

"Systems. This is what separates the Elemental training procedures from the other races. The Lightborn have trainers that match ours in skills. The Furyborn most definitely have some who have ours beat in sheer strength. Liberty...heh. Dark knows what they have. Yet, we have systems in place that ensure that all our training is optimized. At times, I do wonder if we have gone too far. If we are quelling new thinkers and innovation." Kith would have opinions on this. Best not show it to him. Unless he annoys me. (Page 68.)

After the attack on their lives, something gave. At first, it was barely noticeable. Small nods in the hallway in the morning on the way to the mess hall. A sudden decrease in the taunts, prods, or elbows thrown their way.

"Is it me, or did that ranger just flirt with me?" Liam asked through a mouthful of his thick soup. They were seated at their usual spot, at the end of one of the long benches in the mess hall.

Kith shuddered. "I can't believe you can *eat* that. Soup for breakfast. Besides, it's got the consistency of caarnath droppings!"

Liam smiled around another healthy mouthful. "I like it. It's warm and tasty. And the lumps are bacon. What's not to like?"

"You know, I think she actually did." Sera ignored them both. "I believe I know why."

"Does it have anything to do with that?" Chase pointed at a large blackboard at the far end of the huge area.

"It has *everything* to do with that." Their group were now all ranked in the top ten of the Combat Training class. Even Cilia and Sera. Even if the High Elementalist said she wasn't going to influence their ranking, *something* had changed, and they were now, one and all, ranked higher even than most of the fighters in their class. Liam ranked dead first, with Chase at third. "We see it in the nobility all the time. As long as a family is down on their luck, they are the target of scorn, gossip, filthy pranks."

"Pranks?" Kith gaped. "You're telling me the Light-blessed, holier-than-me, highborn nobility of Isarn spend their time playing stupid *pranks* on each other?"

Sera rolled her eyes. "Please. The only thing most of them hold holy is the prospect of stabbing each other in the back for gains. Pranks are but another method for raising yourself up at the expense of somebody else."

"I think we're veering off topic," Liam said. "So, she *was* flirting with me?"

Chase snorted. "Yes, dammit, Liam. She was flirting with you. You're ranked first in Combat Training right now. We're all in a much better position than we were before. On top of that, I'm pretty sure Ernest was told in no uncertain terms what would happen if he were to move against us. This means that we're no longer the perfect target."

Liam pushed his plate away. "I wasn't asking for politics. I just wanted to be sure she was flirting. She's a bit stony-faced, so it can be easy to miscalculate. See you guys in class." He winked and walked to the girl's table.

Cilia, gaping, looked at his retreating back. She huffed. "Sometimes, I think he's too simple for this world."

Kith shook his head. "Sometimes, I think he's everything I want to be."

From above them, a warm voice rang out. "Hey, make room. Some of us want to know exactly what the Pits you did to kill that beast! I thought you were going to die for sure, and Tam was betting against you."

"I was not!" the taciturn healer said vehemently.

Chase laughed. "Well, we believed we were dead too. Sit down, and we'll tell you all about it. In return, you can tell us all the gossip about Ernest. What's the word?"

The word was out, and the word was good. Chase and the others were no longer unwanted, easy targets for cheap social points. Instead, they were being hailed as too powerful to mess with. At first, they couldn't believe it. Yet, as they attended classes and training, it became clearer and clearer. The attitude toward them had flipped. No longer were they being ostracized and scorned. Instead, when they talked, people *listened.*

It was a disconcerting experience, especially for somebody like Kith with his unconventional power set. However, he found that a few of the others were starting to come around, and some of the summoners had started to take Combat Training a lot more seriously, trying their hand at other pursuits than ranged combat.

Liam finally got through to some of the other recruits and got them to open up. He reported that, once he started chatting with them, they were no longer as hateful as they'd appeared. In fact, they generally seemed like normal, young people, with little to hold them together, apart from the struggle they all shared—the desire to join the Protectors. Apart from spending time with Liam, their groups still tended to stick to their own, even if they did open up some.

Classes and training persisted in the same theme that they had started. By now, the first cracks were showing, and the difference in aptitude *and* attitude of the students became clear. As the following weeks flew by, rankings changed in the different classes on a constant basis, sometimes in ways that seemed unfair. Even so, over time, the changes solidified into general trends, where you started seeing evidence of who would make it past the first Culling and who wouldn't. For some, it became a wake-up call, the impetus to realize they'd need to work harder, grow stronger, to make it past the first massive cut. For others, it was a devastating discovery, as they realized that the competition was harder, the level of competence higher than they'd hoped and thought. A few quit along the way, having realized there was no chance of them making it past the cut. At this point, there were only a hundred and five students remaining in the vaunted Red Tortoise class.

Their classes continued in the same vein they'd started. This didn't mean that there was nothing new to learn. World Knowledge consistently challenged their view on the world in general, as well as the ingrained idea they had of the way of the world.

For instance, regardless how reclusive they were, Liberty did actually send bi-yearly trading caravans to all other factions. They brought some coveted foodstuffs and delicacies that grew nowhere outside of the lands of Liberty. Also, they carried rather specialized crafted goods for sale, with a focus on highly effective magical shields, personal as well as larger ones, growing as big as to protect entire wagons.

The same applied to Fury. Where they, in Isarn, were presented as raging, battle-crazed maniacs, it turned out they had a highly developed tribal society, along with an elaborate process that did allow occasional visitors from the outside. They also sold very well-trained hunting pets and the best leather goods and crafted hunting arrows on Ordei.

Knowledge of the world wasn't all they learned, though. There was also the question of etiquette between factions, knowledge about valuation, trading, produce, crafting, diplomacy and politics—anything a Protector likely to meet anything from roaming beasts over Guardians to trading caravans might need. Chase finally managed to crack the code on reading, and even if he still read at a tenth of Cilia's pace, at least it rarely provided him horrible problems in class anymore. Kith and Liam were also slowly improving, though they still had their issues.

Combat Training remained a positive for them. Their rankings did lower some, and Liam was reduced to second, then third place in the class. Even so, it looked like his spot was starting to solidify. They continued giving it their all, concentrating on figuring out their weak spots and working together after-hours to improve, and it paid off. Even Cilia, who thoroughly disliked the violence, improved to the point where she consistently ranked first among the crafters.

Focus remained almost exclusively on physical attributes, with a few bouts of dueling interspersed. For now, there was little focus on group tactics—or tactics of any kind. Instructor Boneridge seemed stubbornly persistent in building up their musculature before tackling anything else.

Monster Knowledge became a net positive for them as well. The first class had been more of a shocker, trying to open their eyes to the dangers of monsters. The following lectures were a mix of lore about monster physiology and information about the kinds of magical gifts beasts could have, with practical examples to seal in the information. Only rarely did they have monster fights, and then usually to punctuate a lesson. Their practical experience against wild beasts and Guardians gave them a leg up on their opponents. Adding the perspectives of Cilia, who started practically *living* in the library, they had the theoretical parts covered too.

Liam finally started to improve in Body Training. Repetition along with his stubbornness proved the key to finally climbing the ranks. He was nowhere near the top, and their instructor always had a few choice words for his poor technique, but he was getting there. He admitted that he could tell the difference in sparring as well, proper techniques and footwork helping him achieve better effects using less Strength and stamina.

Sera thrived. In Healer Training, World Knowledge, and, eventually, Plant Knowledge, she excelled. Her prior training had placed her in a position to start out ahead, and swiftly take in those parts that she didn't know. She consistently placed top three in all classes. When she stated that she knew she would be able to stay there, nobody doubted her. On top of that, she took to using her Heart card compulsively. She used it on anybody she met, to learn as much as possible about them or their classes. Anybody with Light cards, be they Protectors or recruits, made it to a list of people to watch.

Cilia enjoyed her classes as well. Especially Elemental Theory. She had already achieved a decent intuitive understanding of the aspects she could achieve beforehand. Now, however, she aimed for comprehensive understanding and greedily drank up the information that was served. At times, she complained at the fact that most of it was aimed at Elementals as well as their understanding, but...it made sense. Those were the vast majority of their students, hence where they got their information from. Cilia remained extremely impressed by how the Elementals kept and sorted through *all* their crafting students and applied the information from them and their creations. Her own knowledge about the fire aspect exploded, and the others often caught her lost in introspection at the thoughts of what she could and would craft. The single explosive fire thing she'd managed to craft as a prototype for the fight against the behemoth became the starting point for more fiery crafts.

Elemental Crafting still challenged her. Where she had started out dead last in her class, she worked hard enough to have at least climbed two ranks and was above the cutoff line. Her creations were improving, but...still limited. She learned, to her dismay, that the chosen element had a lot to do with how they interacted with different materials. Leatherworking and fire were a notoriously bad match for rookies.

Still, she started to crack the code on certain creations. For instance, she learned that Light was relatively good for shielding from Elemental attacks, and managed to create a pair of basic magic shielding bracers for both Kith and Chase to wear. This should allow them to deflect a couple of Elemental attacks without fear of damage. However, she was far from satisfied with these sojourns crafting armor. The creations were still not permanent, lasting about a month, the craftsmanship was questionable and the armor value dismissible. Mostly, she focused on utility. She avoided using her Manipulate Darkness card, for fear of what it could reveal, even if they still had a small bag of stakes that created globes of darkness. Light still allowed her to create a few amazing things. She managed a few sharply defined leather patches: tightly sown, with an arcane pattern stitched on the front and two flailing straps of leather dangling from the back. If you pulled the strips hard, it would create a massive, delayed, blinding effect on the front.

She also started really working out her Manipulate Fire card. She perfected a tight and efficient creation which she called fire droplets: Little, hardened, tightly sown pellets of leather which, when impacting with a target, would unleash a small, centralized burst of caustic fire. More importantly, she also learned how to create a bag that would keep the fire droplets inactive until she took them out.

Kith was also, finally, moving up the ranks. His improved Mental Power had reached the point where he could keep his Divine Mentor card internalized regardless of how wild his exertions were. That made him an absolute terror to fight against. On top of that, his control of his Crescendo of Might summons improved a lot. In the beginnings of any clashes, it was still mostly lumbering and useless, but if they allowed it to survive, it grew fast and nigh-unstoppable. On top of that, his Apian God card garnered a lot of well-earned hate from the other summoners, providing stinging, annoying distractions for anybody he was up against. He was still not doing too well in the knowledge classes, but he was improving, slowly, as his growing Mental Power helped him keep focus.

Chase loved the Orientation and Movement classes. They suited his mindset extremely well and taught him how to constantly be alert and pay attention to his surroundings. Their focus was everywhere and nowhere, sometimes spending the day going over tells on human behavior, and at other times learning memorization techniques. It was never consistent, always interesting. Chase figured, as long as he paid attention, he could become an extremely decent scout, should he decide to go that way. And it would make him an even better thief, no discussion. He was never going to be the fastest in the class, but he consistently placed in the top three, taking first now and again.

Still, it was nothing compared to the joy that was Applied Practice. It was like they'd taken everything he knew about being a curious, manipulative bastard who tried to take in everything happening around him all the time and condensed it into a single, excruciatingly demanding class. He often left the class feeling like he'd been put through a wringer, mentally and physically. Applied Practice didn't just teach who to watch but *how* to watch, and always, always challenged their creativity and their skill at thinking up solutions on the fly.

Before they knew it, six weeks had passed since they joined up, and they were staring down at the first Culling, only two weeks away. Their rankings at this point were a joy to look at, compared to the borderline catastrophic situations they'd been looking at in the early days.

Overall ranking:
Sera: 12/105
Liam: 22/105
Chase: 27/105
Cilia: 37/105
Kith: 52/105

It wasn't perfect. Apart from Sera, they still had areas to work on if they intended to aim for entrance to the Protectors. Because they spent so much time focusing on improving, at this point they *knew* what their specific issues were and were learning what they needed to do. For some, like Cilia, it was mostly a matter of practice. For others, like Kith, it was both a matter of knowledge and attributes.

Even so, at this point, Chase was no longer worried about the first Culling. They'd pass with flying colors, unless something catastrophic happened. Especially considering the gift that the High Elementalist had given them, ostensibly as an apology for what they'd suffered. They were potions. Crafted potions, clearly marked, glowing with warmth, colored light and life. Also, magic. The potions temporarily boosted every single attribute there was by an unknown amount, and there were five wooden crates, each carrying a full set of potions. Chase knew that she had said she wasn't going to interfere with their rankings or studies. Still, with these, they would be able to boost their attributes, focusing on whichever was needed for any especially grueling tests. With judicious use and swapping around what was needed, Chase would bet anything he had that they'd be able to make it through the first couple of Cullings with no issues.

The rigorous training had one other, entirely expected result. Their attribute gains skyrocketed as they applied themselves both physically and mentally.

Liam earned a point to Agility and Mental Power each, and even an extra point to his already prodigious Strength.

Personal Info:
Name: Liam
Title: Dark/Elemental/Light fighter
Step: 12 (Tier 2)
Strength: 15 (+7 Tier bonus) = 22
Agility: 14 (+1 Tier bonus) = 15
Toughness: 22 (+1 Tier bonus) = 23
Mental Power: 12 (+1 Tier bonus) = 13
Potential: 10 (+1 Tier bonus) = 11

At this point, his Agility was high enough that he rivaled what Chase's Agility used to be, back on the Waves. On top of his impressive Strength and Toughness, his ability to out-position and fend off other fighters solidified.

Kith gained a point to Agility and Toughness each, and an extra *two* to Mental Power, focused as he was on improving his summoning control.

Personal Info:
Name: Kith
Title: Dark/Elemental/Light summoner
Step: 14 (Tier 2)

Strength: 16 (+1 Tier bonus) = 17
Agility: 17 (+1 Tier bonus) = 18
Toughness: 14 (+1 Tier bonus) = 15
Mental Power: 15 (+1 Tier bonus) = 16
Potential: 11 (+7 Tier bonus) = 18

Cilia, spurred on by her increased Steps in their recent fight, ran with her choices, focusing on how to apply herself in combat in ways that would involve her potentially using her crafted items without putting herself in direct danger. In practice, that meant a sharp focus on evasion and the staying power to keep going, which netted her two points to Agility and one to Toughness.

Personal Info:
Name: Cilia
Title: Dark/Elemental/Light crafter
Step: 13 (Tier 2)
Strength: 11 (+1 Tier bonus) = 12
Agility: 16 (+1 Tier bonus) = 17
Toughness: 14 (+1 Tier bonus) = 15
Mental Power: 24 (+7 Tier bonus) = 31
Potential: 11 (+1 Tier bonus) = 12

Sera went with an all-round approach to training. She wanted to be able to defend herself if need be, and didn't shy from the challenge. She also found that the approaches of the instructors in the towers were different enough that her gains were less impeded by her earlier training than she had feared. She managed a point to Strength, Agility, and Toughness each.

Personal Info:
Name: Serafine
Title: Dark/Elemental/Light healer
Step: 11 (Tier 2)
Strength: 13 (+1 Tier bonus) = 14
Agility: 16 (+1 Tier bonus) = 17
Toughness: 15 (+1 Tier bonus) = 16
Mental Power: 27 (+7 Tier bonus) = 34
Potential: 12 (+1 Tier bonus) = 13

Sera was still staying ahead of Cilia, especially when it came to Strength, but the smaller woman was competitive, and the two, both focused on Mental Power, egged each other on, competing to see who could improve the most.

Chase, meanwhile, made full use of his Spoils of the Undeserving card. His attributes skyrocketed, to the point where he could hardly recognize himself from the whipcord-lean, malnourished youth who'd scraped by back on the Waves. His body was becoming hard, packed muscle, reacting to his every move instantly, and his mind was focused and *sharp*. In the six weeks, he managed to improve a full *eight* points, including a single point to his already impressive Agility. If this kept up, he would soon be able to arm wrestle the fighters and win!

Personal Info:
Name: Chase
Title: Dark/Elemental/Light rogue
Step: 18 (Tier 3)
Strength: 15 (+1 Tier bonus) = 16
Agility: 19 (+9 Tier bonus) = 28
Toughness: 17 (+1 Tier bonus) = 18
Mental Power: 15 (+1 Tier bonus) = 16
Potential: 26 (+1 Tier bonus) = 27

As to their actual task of luring out whoever was selling access to the towers? They worked on it on the side. With the constant classes and eternal training, it was hard to find the time to leave the premises and learn more. Especially considering that a lot of it was also dependent on other students—students who, as often as not, worked every bit as hard as they did.

Liam managed, inch by inch, to warm the relationships with several other students. It was a matter of persistence, of constant interactions, friendly greetings, remembering names, and keeping up a good mood.

Just watching it from afar made Chase tired. But it worked. There was no denying that.

Over the weeks, Liam became friendly with a lot of their competitors. It wasn't like he suddenly became a fixed part of their lives. He merely managed to show them that he was good company, an unending font of good-natured jokes and a shoulder to lean on. Not everybody opened up, obviously. The clique around Ernest Chalico remained stalwartly opposed to their group, even though they were a lot diminished. On top of that, the very nature of the admittance into the towers ensured that the students were, by and large, individuals, focused on their own advancement above anything else. Still, humans were flock animals and craved company. Liam made no demands, just offered friendship, no strings attached—so a lot of them responded.

Shortly, their information started to improve. Only, what they got out of it was anything but useful. Nobody knew who might be behind the attack or the raid on Chase's crew. Oh, there were accusations and theories aplenty. Yet, they were mostly fueled by idle speculation, generally gossip-mongering or personal dislike of whomever the finger pointed at. Even more frustrating, the single solid lead they had, that the stolen sword and raid on Chase's room came from one of Chalico's hangers-on, turned out to be a fluke, a repeated piece of unfounded gossip. Liam concluded that the next step would be to start befriending some of the residents of the Towers, then the educators.

Chase and Kith went exploring. The towers seemed intimidatingly large. Yet, Chase was building up a minimal idea of how they were structured and divided. They were certain that, as they passed the Culling, they'd be slowly introduced to new areas, new possibilities and openings. That was way too slow for them. As such, they decided to treat it like a job, act as if the towers were a place they wanted to rob and try to figure out the flaws and openings to see what that would bring them.

This opened a cascade of rules, regulations, and invisible limitations. The lower floors of the towers themselves, they found, weren't off-limits. Not at all. Any student could access the training areas at all times, for instance. The same went for the mess hall, the bathrooms, showers, general areas, studying areas, and workshops. This latter detail surprised Chase. He knew that there were workshops and crafting stations for most everything, but the fact that they were open and available at all hours was a surprise. The reasoning, a bored cleaner explained, was that the towers knew students were more likely to push themselves if they could craft anything at any hours. To his regret, though, this didn't open the stores for them to filch crafting materials.

Ignoring the vast numbers of available possibilities on the lower floors, they found that there were a lot of limitations in place. Tons of rooms and complete areas were sealed off, guarded, or locked entirely. Some were simple locks, while others were magical in nature or intricate to the point where even Kith and his talented fingers would be unable to gain entrance. The reasoning varied. Some places, like the wooden buildings in the training area, were sealed off after-hours, securing the weapons and training materials. Other rooms were simply closed with no explanation, or were for the exclusive use of staff, teachers, or similar.

At this point, Kith's lack of a sense of direction actually proved a boon. He consistently got lost and had to ask for directions. When he inevitably entered rooms that were supposed to be off-limits, his natural confusion helped defuse any issues. And the scope of the towers slowly grew more tangible. At least to Chase.

The lower floors of the towers were mostly for the use of the staff. The mess hall and the general workshops were also placed low, due to the quantities of material that were moving in and out of the towers on a daily basis. On top of that, there were also staff rooms aplenty, restrooms, prep rooms for Protectors about to move on patrol, and all sorts of practical rooms. There were not, on these floors, any actual limitations or protections, Elemental-wise. That changed around the tenth floor—which, incidentally, was also where security started to appear. Anybody moving up the floors would find the hallways leading to centralized areas with helpful staff ready to guide you in the right direction and, firmly, but politely, steer you back down if you had no legitimate excuse for being there.

That, of course, led to the next phase of their process. Discovering the limits of the security. The pair took great pains in not overextending their discovery. Still, they wanted to learn exactly how things were arranged. Chase's principal test in Applied Practice had shown that security got progressively stronger the more you ascended. Only, was it possible to beat it here at the lower levels? Could you gain access to areas and rooms you weren't supposed to? How would anybody even have gone about stealing a sword from the damn booths?

Quickly, they found that security on the lower third of the towers was depressively bad. Anybody with a note that seemed legitimate would be allowed entry, and there was no security beyond that to speak of. On top of that, any Tier twos were admitted without question. That led to the pair taking in the first floors where the different aspects had consistently created a space to match their Elements. The fire-aspected sections were bright and dark in turn, with brilliant gem-like stones creating a sensation of living flames inside the walls. Air-aspected halls were tall and towering, with large windows showing access to the outside. The first of the spindly air-aspected towers on their side sprouted from their side. Water presented tall, cavernous areas filled with plants and clean water areas. Even to Chase, a city boy through and through, the clean smell of life was a balm to his soul. Earth was more oppressive than expected. They held defensive stations and were also the only ones who actually had security checkpoints on these lower floors. Only a quick lie by Kith saved them from being discovered during their trespassing.

The useful lessons from their discovery sessions were extremely limited. They figured out that security was one-way only. Anybody moving from the upper levels down could do whatever they pleased on the lower floors, while the reverse was anything but true. Meaning, if their suspect was somebody with their rightful place on the upper floors, they weren't limited in their movement at all, and could roam the lower floors at their leisure.

Floor security around the dorm rooms of the students was equally shoddy. The roaming guard patrol was limited to nights only, and, as explained by a chatty kitchen worker, was mostly a matter of keeping boys and girls separate and avoiding too many scandals and unplanned pregnancies. Chase had no doubt he'd be able to sneak out if need be.

Regarding the weapons, that was a bit trickier. The people staffing the vendor-like buildings were all carded and looked vigilant and alert. Of course, Chase knew that people were never as alert as after a crime had been committed, given that the boss would be looking for any slackers. There was also some sort of system in place, where any items lent out were noted and had to be approved by either a teacher present at the area or in writing. That latter permission, of course, opened up a whole possible venue of abuse that Chase had to clamp down *hard* on his desire to make use of. The gossip clearly talked about the sword having been *stolen*, physically. That implied straight up snatching it. Something not easily done with the items strapped down, far out of reach inside the buildings. That would take somebody with some fancy manipulation cards...or somebody with connections and accomplices. Like Ernest.

Cilia and Sera went with a different approach. They turned to the famous library for knowledge and tried to see whether the accumulated wisdom of the entire Elemental nation might provide them with some answers. In what seemed to Chase a fool's errand, they pored through endless tomes filled with knowledge, meetings, decisions, politics, and...all sorts of things that could bore a whole country to pieces. Most tomes had to stay inside the library, with a good part of them being unavailable to students, some even to full Protectors.

At first, the research did nothing, except help the pair improve in the World Knowledge classes with obscure snippets of information. Later on, however, the two got increasingly focused on some aspect or other, sacrificing sleep for the purpose of staying up late and studying. They refused to tell what was going on, insisting that they wanted to be certain before they started going in a particular direction.

One evening, about an hour before curfew, Chase and Kith sat with Liam in his room, discussing whether there was anything they needed to focus on for the final two weeks before the first Culling. Liam argued that Kith needed to find alternative applications of his summons, so everything wasn't based around his direct combat. Kith was not particularly receptive. Chase sat cross-legged, meditating, listening to their friendly bickering with one ear and considering whether it was worth the effort to join the discussion, when the door slammed open.

Sera strode in, eyes gleaming. Cilia followed right behind her, with a maniacal and very unfamiliar grin on her face. She shut the door behind her hard enough that Chase almost missed Sera's proclamation. Almost.

"We know what's happening!"

***

The archbishop was furious. He, the most powerful person in the lands of Light, possibly all of Ordei, had almost been outplayed. It had taken a stray comment in a report to reveal what was happening, and it could have unraveled their long-term plans.

He slammed a hand down on the Wellspring and spoke without preamble. "We are moving up the schedule."

The protestations were, as expected, numerous and strong. He fended them off with a single phrase. "We are on the verge of being discovered. We still do not know who they work for, but there is a group currently on the edge of discovering everything."

That made them shut up for a blessed moment.

He continued. "Right now, our choices are between abandoning everything, pulling out our forces and cutting our losses, and enacting the plan early. Does anybody have reservations? *Real* reservations, not just petty fears or concerns that can be overcome."

For a moment, nobody dared answer. Then a voice arrived. High Priest Desahl. *Of course.*

"We are behind you. Entirely. We will not let small things like logistics come in our way. However, as you well know, our Church's situation is currently precarious. They are already crying for reducing our influence in their affairs. If we do not succeed...the results will be immense."

The archbishop grimaced but nodded to himself. He knew very well what was said behind those words. *"If you fail, you're taking the fall."* One final time, he touched the Wellspring and let his words flow to his subordinates, letting them sense his resolve. "For the Light, everything, brothers. This will let us finally win that which we need to spread the Light everywhere."

CHAPTER 30

"In the towers, we rely on trust. Yet, that does not mean we are naïve. It means that we give people the chance to prove themselves, consistently. Working for the common good and betterment of all of Earth's Ward will grant you a level of trust. Being more dedicated will earn you more. This way, we ensure that only those who truly work in the interest of our people are raised up the highest." No. In this case, I believe the word truly is naivety. How about somebody who works against them, but is willing to put in the work and time? Or somebody who...changed their allegiance? Of course, that's where the Cloaks come in, but still... (Page 41.)

"You did what?" The words were cold, hissed. Instructor Swansong did not look amused at their insistence that their group should be allowed a brief meeting in the early evening. "You are aware that the presence of your group inconveniences my other work."

"We know. We'll make up something, if anybody sees us, but...it's necessary," Chase said confidently. "Cilia and Sera figured out what they're working toward. This is bigger than just finding a few dirty administrators."

The Cloak looked very different in her official raiment as a teacher. The multicolored, flowing tassels were only dyed at the ends, a sign Chase was coming to learn meant she was not high in the hierarchy of the towers. Even so, the robe made her look dangerous, entirely different from her earlier nondescript clothing and demeanor. It went well with the style of her official personal workspace, a cramped room filled with paraphernalia and books seeming to cover every possible topic from agriculture to folklore. The room and setup in tandem reinforced her authority as she demanded, from the seat of her high-back, uncomfortable-looking wooden chair. "All right. Show me."

Sera rushed forward. She laid out three rolled-up pieces of parchment on the already overflowing surface of the wooden desk placed in the center of the small room. "This was the work of several weeks. We started out with the assumption that we knew nothing at all about the organization, placement, and responsibilities within the towers. That way we would not be prejudiced and jump to conclusions."

"Sound approach," the instructor said in a level tone. "What did you find?"

"At first, nothing." Cilia grimaced. "In fact, less than nothing. We figured out that you can't just find the responsibilities of all people employed at the Towers, which makes sense, given that it'd be a major security risk."

"Also for several other reasons. I am not hearing any conclusions, however," Instructor Swansong said briskly. Her tone sounded like she was warming up to their thought process, though.

"Well, this limited our approach somewhat. We initially undertook the task, intending to narrow down who inside the towers had the wherewithal and connections needed to be our culprit," Sera said. "Yet, without access to those lists, we needed to take a different tack. We started down the path of elimination instead, attempting to figure out methods that could help us given all the information we did *not* have."

Cilia jumped in, more animated than usual for her. "Of course, this left us with an abundance of information, yet none of it actionable. We spent almost a week compiling lists of what we could theoretically use the freely available information for." She unfurled the first piece of parchment.

Instructor Swansong skimmed the tight script. "Number of people in the towers. Number of people in the Protectors. Number of...how do you think you'd be able to pinpoint the number of *servants* in the towers without access to actual employment lists?"

Sera blinked, then perked up. "Oh, that one was rather simple. We located a copy of a standard employment contract for non-carded servants. It lays out the right to a new uniform every other year. Given that these aren't created in the towers and we have access to lists outlining—"

"*Please.* Can we move on with this?" Kith groaned. "We're not supposed to be here, remember?"

Sera blushed.

Instructor Swansong cleared her throat. "Yes. We had better. Now, I assume that the last entry is the important one?"

"Third to last *and* the last entries are the important ones, actually. It took us awhile before we figured out what we'd be able to use it for," Cilia said.

"*Numbers and race of those accepted into the Protectors,*" the instructor read aloud. "And *deaths and race of those accepted into the Protectors.*" She tapped her lip. "We do have official entrance lists, though they are redacted, to prevent recognition. Deaths, I can see too. The actual lists with the details of those who die are guarded from the public, of course, yet we do disclose the numbers of deaths and dates. Where did you get the races?"

263

"They bring in different priests for the different ceremonies, when non-Elementals die. Priests, coming from Earth's Ward, whose arrival is noted, and freely available," Cilia said.

The instructor looked like she was just about to crack a smile. Instead, she gave a grudging nod. "So you can see which races are killed. And...who enters. What did that tell you?"

"At first, nothing," Sera admitted. She unfurled the second piece of parchment, which was nothing but rows and rows of numbers. "Actually, you will find the races are tacked on afterward. We did not focus on that, until we found the deserter lists." She held up a hand to Kith, forestalling his complaints. "We are *right* there. The deserter lists are nothing but wanted posters, holding paintings or descriptions of Protectors found missing or presumed deserted. Cilia noted a tendency among them, which led us to look further into it."

She presented the final document with a triumphant flourish, pointing at the tight script. "Thirty years ago, a total of two hundred and thirty-six Protectors graduated. Twelve of these were Lightborn. A hundred and six Protectors died or deserted the same year, among them, four Lightborn." She moved her finger farther down the parchment. "Last year, two hundred and fifty-eight Protectors graduated. Forty-one of these were Lightborn." To a backdrop of utter silence, she finished. "The same year, of the hundred and fifty-six dead or deserted, a full thirty-six were Lightborn."

Any inclination that Instructor Swansong might actually smile was entirely gone, scrubbed from the existence of Ordei. "Do you realize...of course you do." Her voice was breathless and hoarse. "Have you been able to verify the numbers elsewhere?"

Cilia shook her head. "No. As you can see, our sources are only what we've been able to scrounge up ourselves."

The instructor combed her hand through her hair and huffed. "I'm amazed what you've managed with so little. I will double-check your findings myself. Then, we will make a decision from there."

"Hold up. What am I missing here? You were making a lot of sense, then suddenly you all got serious." Liam looked at them all, confused. "What?"

Kith sighed. "I get such bad scores in World Knowledge because it's so damn dull. You...we really need to work on you, brother. What they're saying is that we stumbled onto something that's *way* bigger than we expected. Whoever's arranging for people to gain entrance to the city illegally aren't just letting people into the city. They're also arranging for them to be admitted into the Protectors and then they help them desert, and possibly fake their own deaths." He punched his own palm repeatedly, then turned to the others. "Did I miss anything?"

Sera nodded, wide-eyed. "You missed where this is almost certainly an undertaking of the nobility or somebody equally important. Nobody should be able to arrange something of this magnitude, and involving so many Lightborn, without involving somebody high up in the nobility."

Instructor Swansong growled under her breath. "Now you are leaping to conclusions. You will stop that immediately." She blinked and huffed. "I am going to use my own sources to verify that your numbers are right. Then I will personally take this to the High Elementalist and ensure that appropriate steps are taken."

Liam scrunched up his face. "Does this mean that we're done? Did we complete our task? Go team!"

The instructor looked at him like he was something she'd stepped in on the street. "Have you found the persons culpable for letting people into Earth's Ward? No, you haven't. So you haven't completed your task." Her face softened. "But...if this is actually right, you have done us a great service. The coming weeks and months are going to be...interesting."

Sera nodded. "If this is something orchestrated, or at least sanctioned by the Lightborn nobility, what does that mean? Ignoring whoever is arranging it in the first place, how many have been through the program? How much information has been smuggled out?"

"Indeed. Who among the students *right now* were introduced by underhanded means? And what about the Protectors themselves? Can we even trust any of the Lightborn who remain among the Protectors?" The instructor shook her head. "If this is right, it promises an upheaval the likes of which has never been seen in the Towers, and repercussions for years to come." She drummed on the scuffed, much-used wood of her table. "For now, I need you to continue as if nothing has happened. Continue doing exactly what you're doing. That includes searching for whoever's responsible."

"But wouldn't that place us in further danger?" Chase asked.

"Of course it would. However, if anybody is keeping an eye on you, changing your behavior might do the very same." The instructor rose and held out her hands, palms up. "There is no safe path at this point. We cannot vouchsafe your safety. But I can personally guarantee that if you are right about this and we manage to save the towers from a possible security breach of this size? You have a home. Forever."

Back in Liam's room a while later, nobody seemed keen to speak first. They each stayed silent, looking contemplative, morose, or otherwise marinating in their own mental soups. Cilia sat on the bed with her arms folded around her legs, with Sera right next to her.

Eventually, Chase broke the silence. "We have a home, then?"

Cilia said, "*If—*"

"Yeah, yeah. If you're actually right," Chase interrupted. "Do you actually think this is just happenstance or bad numbers? Because I don't."

Sera shook her head. "Me neither. This is real. This is happening. We have gotten caught up in something much larger than we could imagine."

"Agreed. So, in order to steer this in a direction that'll let us move on. First off. *This is us.* I'll admit that we weren't prepared for working in Earth's Ward. Not without knowing the powers and everything. That backfired beautifully. Sera's approach? That was just as bad. Working within the rules just makes us easy targets for anybody who doesn't care about the rules. This, however? This, we can do. Working within the rules whenever it suits us, learning the ropes, and bending the rules whenever we need to. As long as we keep alert and test the limits to know what we can get away with? This will do well for our general approach from here on out. And hopefully, ensure we don't get backstabbed by whoever's behind this scheme. Does that work for everybody?"

There was a general consensus of muttered agreements. Sera didn't look entirely convinced by the necessity of breaking the rules, and Kith looked similarly miffed at having to work within the confines and rules of the towers. Nobody disagreed.

Chase smiled. "Brilliant. That leads us to the second part. Now that we know our approach, and have an idea what the near future is going to bring, we need to figure where we're going with that. How do we go about it? Just go through the paces and act like we're continuing the same routines, except without stirring up any trouble? Do we actually try to find whoever's behind it?"

Kith, sitting on a chair leaned back precariously far, let it tip forward to clatter on the floor. He pointed at Chase with two fingers. "Answering that question is easy. My answer's the same as that to any question back on the Waves. How do I make sure this profits me the most?"

Chase narrowed his eyes. "Well. How *do* we make sure this profits us?"

"Me," Kith said, then chuckled. "The way I see it is like this. We've still got the big bad figure in the shadows out there, roaming about, right? If our friendly neighborhood Cloak has done her job right, he has no clue that he's even being watched. Now, if we manage to find him—"

"Or her," Sera added.

"Or her. Sure," Kith agreed. "We're going to earn a nice fat reward, for certain. But is it much more impressive than what we'd get with what we've already managed? I rather doubt it."

"You're voting for caution, then?" Cilia nodded approvingly.

"No. And yes. We're taking it on faith that the Cloaks know what they're doing. The same Cloaks who failed in figuring out how this was going on under their noses all this time. If we stop keeping our eyes and ears open, that'll leave us blind to daggers in the dark. So, I vote that we go out there, still try to figure out what's going on...only we tone it down a bit and focus on defense. It doesn't matter that you know what your enemy's wearing, if he manages to set your raft on fire in the dead of night."

Cilia screwed up her eyes. "That might be the worst mixed metaphor I've ever heard. Stop that." She frowned, then nodded. "Nevertheless, I agree. The possible reward for us finding the culprit just isn't worth us risking our necks. However, going fully defensive may leave us open to clandestine attacks. In short, our first focus will be on making it past the first Culling. Kith, you need to focus more on World Knowledge, and I *will* test you on it."

Kith groaned.

She continued. "I need to work harder in Combat Training. My ranking is dropping faster than I had hoped. My...issues with combat still remain. Yet, with some further points to Agility or Toughness, I believe I might be able to handle things better. Liam. You need to keep up your Body Training *and* World Knowledge. You are improving so well, but you do tend to coast when you've reached a decent level."

"Sorry." Liam bowed his head.

"Don't be sorry. Just be better," Cilia scolded. "As long as we keep on as we are doing, we *will* do fine. Next, we need to work on our defense. We'll need to figure out some way to ensure that we aren't stabbed in the backs. Liam, try to rope other students into watching out on behalf of us, alerting us if they see something off. The rest of us keep our eyes open. What else? Should we craft some real defenses for our rooms?"

Kith snorted. "Yeah. Because a servant setting off a trap is going to go over *so* well."

"What he said. Also, we need to stay even more focused on not breaking our cover," Chase offered. "As long as we survive for as long as is needed for the higher-ups to check that our suspicions are correct? We're golden. But if our cover's blown beforehand, they might have to kick us out, if nothing else, to keep the illusion that they don't know what's going on."

Kith grunted and scratched his neck. "That means only using our Dark cards if we're about to get splattered and not trapping our rooms. What else?"

"Yes, Kith," Cilia said, exasperation oozing from her. "It also means not talking too openly about them, in case somebody overhears."

"All right, Mom," he said, not the least bit apologetic. "I mean it, though. What else? Do we stop investigating every last thing?"

"No," Liam said. "You heard what Swansong said. We need to keep on the way we've been and not act suspicious. Maybe just cut down on the activities that could get us kicked from the towers."

"Awww. But those are the most fun." Kith tittered. "Seriously, though. That's the way to go. Just make sure we don't get our asses booted from here, and otherwise, we keep it up. If that means we stumble on something good, go team!"

"In practice," Chase mused. "That means that you girls keep up in the library. Liam keeps making friends everywhere...and Kith and I should probably tone down our attempts at breaking security on the towers. A serious misstep there could get us in real trouble."

"What do you intend to do then?" Sera asked. "If you are not going to keep that up? Join Liam in his endeavor to make friends?"

"Hmm. No. I don't think so. Rather, I think I'd like to try to make some enemies. See what shakes out."

CHAPTER 31

"Mentally, we are closer to the Furyborn civilization than the Lightborn. Yet, they live in squalor in mud huts. How does that make sense, you argue? Because the Lightborn are only ever run top-down. We know that, in order to run optimally, we have to make sure that our family works best. Just like the tribes of the Furyborn." Oh, nice. Elitism *and* condescension. Not really feeling the family vibe here, to be honest. (Page 61.)

"You want to know what the Protectors are actually like? Pay attention! There will be time for questions later."

They were back in the training area with Instructor Boneridge. The squat combat trainer looked to have a fire in her eyes today, and Chase made sure that he was attentive and didn't raise her ire.

At this point, they'd gotten used to most of the idiosyncrasies of the different teachers. Brookwatch, for instance, didn't mind chatter, as long as she felt the students still paid attention. Swansong wouldn't call out anybody who failed to pay attention; she took it out on them in the rankings instead. (And one Elemental rogue Chase didn't know well, despite warnings and proof to the contrary, kept insisting that couldn't be what had him at the second-lowest ranking.) Instructor Highstream required full attention at all times, even when he sprang deliberate distractions on them. Boneridge, despite her bluster, wasn't the strictest of the lot. As long as they didn't speak too loudly and disrupt classes, they'd be allowed a bit of leeway.

Right at this instant, there were no distractions. A great deal of barely audible chatter, however. Because they finally got to see the Protectors in action. At this moment, a quintet of well-armed, armored, and equipped persons strode across the packed dirt of the training area toward Instructor Boneridge. They were a varied lot. One tall, dreadlock-wearing Furyborn carried a heavy bow that was taller than herself. A water-aspected Elemental wore gold-rimmed spectacles and a fine silver-trimmed vest-and-pants attire that seemed incongruous with anybody tasked to fight. Another Elemental, her fire aspect disclosed from across the other side of the area with the visible fiery haze around her, carried a two-handed club on her shoulder that looked more like a monolith than an actual weapon. Beside her, a chainmail-wearing, earth-aspected Elemental looked as gritty and spent as his battered tower shield. The fifth, a Lightborn with twin daggers strapped on his hips, seemed to fade in and out of visibility. Every single one of these Protectors had at least two cards, and Chase spotted a glint on the Lightborn rogue's leg indicating he was at least a Tier four. This was *real* power.

"Red Tortoise class. I want you all to take in the splendor that is our current bronze team." A susurrus ran through the crowd. "That's right. This is the current year's third-ranked team of *all* Protectors throughout the towers. They are fourth in kills. Third in accurate monster sightings and *second* in crisis aversion. This—" Instructor Boneridge proudly gestured with her arm, "is why the towers remain undefeated."

Chase looked them over. By themselves, they didn't look too impressive. Well, that fire-aspected one looked like death incarnate. And the Furyborn looked like she'd be able to put an arrow through Chase's head at a mile's distance. The guy with the chainmail, however, looked tired more than anything. At a glance, they were all between twenty and thirty years old, with the chainmail guy possibly at forty. One thing they had in common? They were fully equipped. Every part of their attire looked carefully selected, and the holsters and belts—carried even by the officious-looking Elemental with the spectacles—were worn with use and filled with items. What really impressed Chase was the way they walked. The self-assuredness, the way their gazes weighed, assessed, discarded. Even as the group lined up in front of the class, most of them had their eyes constantly roaming, alert for anything.

"Hold your questions, for now. What you are about to see should grant you enough fodder for questions afterward." The instructor turned to the Protectors and directed them to a spot at the far end of the training area. It was a replica of what the students had seen back when they had been divided into groups and made to fight monsters one by one.

The team moved cautiously, the chainmail-wielder and the guy with the vest placing themselves at the back of the group, with the three others fanning out in front, rogue on the left, fire-aspected mace-wielder front and center, and the archer to the right.

"Are you ready?" The hoarse voice of Instructor Boneridge was audible from her spot hundreds of feet back. She turned toward the students. "We have the best scouts. Those with visual improvements, stealth cards, even a few cards that I am not allowed to tell you about...*yet*." The final word lingered, tantalizing in its offer to let you in on the secrets. "Even so, our border is a dangerous place. Often, Protectors have little warning and need to adjust on the fly. Today, you get to see what that looks like in practice." She turned back to the vista in front of her, raised her voice and shouted, in a deafening voice, "Release!"

The five enclosures facing the front of the Protectors started spilling monsters. It was almost too fast for Chase to register. There was a trio of man-sized, bipedal, lumbering, shell-covered brutes. A flittering group, too many to count, of flying beasts, like winged rats made of teeth and claws. A near-dozen of smaller, agile fox-sized shapes rushing across the ground in stops and starts, fading in and out of view. A group of raccoon-like creatures that started carving small furrows into the soil of the arena and flinging it at the Protectors. Finally, at the back, one large wolf-shaped beast stretched, fire rippling across its back.

The students erupted in shocked shouts and talk. This was insane. They'd mostly been forced to handle one monster apiece, sometimes smaller groups. The Protectors took on...what? Fifty monsters? And they were all so different.

The Protectors sprang to action. With a bellowed shout, the tall fire-aspected fighter was surrounded by plumes of flame and grew at least a foot in size. Her stone mace stayed the same, yet suddenly it didn't seem nearly as oversized in her huge hands. The archer was a blur, her hands already working as fast as Chase could see, red-tinged arrows leaving her bow, then multiplying as they raced for the enemies. The Lightborn rogue was ready, blades held up as he matched the cautious advance of the fighter on his right. And from the back, the shield carrier flashed several times in quick succession as his cards activated, shooting beams straight for the three front-most Protectors, while the guy with the vest observed with his spectacles lowered, like he was bored.

Before the Protectors even clashed with any of the monsters, the archer wreaked havoc. The arrows fell as a hailstorm among the flying monsters and the smaller, raccoon-like creatures, taking out more than half their numbers in a single barrage.

The monsters, obviously, weren't satisfied with just taking the damage and soldiering on. The flying beasts started evasive maneuvers, circling and moving higher to make it more difficult for the archer to hit. The raccoons started to target the archer as well. The soil they flung clearly took on some icy aspect, pelting the area around her with a speed and impact that couldn't be explained by their small paws.

That was when the value of the vest-wearing Elemental came to light. A tall, man-sized blue shield came into being in front of the archer, attacks falling to the ground as they struck the shield. She took it in step, accepting the shelter like she'd been waiting for it, and barely slowing her attack as she stepped out from the shield to release, then back in safety to nock the next arrow. The man with the vest remained unaffected.

The fire-aspected fighter either got bored, or decided it was her time. With a shout and a flash, she hefted her oversized pillar of a mace and charged. The look was ridiculous. Even with her increased size, both the wolf creature and the three bipedal monsters outsized her. Yet, she ignored it all, charging straight for the dead center of the onrushing wave of monsters. Ten feet. Five. Right before she hit, a card flashed on her, and her first, massive swing was followed by a veritable wave of fire, that charred and flung back the smaller monsters. Then, she took the fight to the taller monsters, and did not back away a single step. The damage she did was dramatic. A few of the smaller, half-hidden creatures were killed by the impact of the flame wave. Yet, their numbers were impressive, and the attack did little to the three bipedal monsters who lumbered forward to face off with her. By herself, she would've been overwhelmed in seconds. Instead, she trusted in her team—and the team stepped up.

On her left, the rogue raced into action. Where the fighter was a force of nature, a battering ram, the Lightborn rogue was a scalpel. Sprinting from enemy to enemy, the rogue never stayed in place for more than one second, lashing out in a single attack before fading away to continue with the next monster. Every slash of his blade carried an Elemental charge. One held fire, and the other ice, burning or slowing the enemies, and his steps seemed to carry him farther than should be possible.

On the right side, the archer changed her tack. Now, instead of the multiple indiscriminate arrow storms, her ranged attacks became slower, deliberate and damaging. Each of them aimed at a target surrounding the fighter, drilling *into* the armor of their targets when they hit. Constantly switching, she targeted each of the three bipedal monsters in succession, aiming for joints, necks, heads.

The lead fighter stood tall and did not back down. Fire and force followed her attacks, buffeting and damaging anybody stupid enough to go claw-to-toe with her. With the assists on both sides, as well as carefully chosen buffs and shields from behind, it seemed like nobody was able to stand against them.

Yet, as the wave of monsters clashed with them, they couldn't hold back all the monsters. There were simply too many. From above, and in between the three Protectors, monsters rushed past, aiming for the two, seemingly less martially capable members of their group.

The shield-carrying healer activated a card and stepped forward, placing himself ten feet in front of the vest-wearing Elemental. Around his shield, a force field appeared. Every single monster that roamed close enough to hit the barrier was either jolted or flung back forcibly from the field.

A few monsters adjusted quickly, trying to spill around the field, to attack from behind or take on the final member of the team.

With a nonchalant, dismissive gesture, he started to lob small glass orbs at the trespassers. Wherever they hit, the orbs burst into one effect or other. One was stunned. Another burst into fire. One bat-like flier was enfolded by a web-like substance and crashed hard. Despite their busyness, both the hindmost Protectors kept aware of the battle at the front, summoning shields or beams to aid their comrades as needed. The man with the vest pointed at select monsters in turn, who were subsequently hit by a translucent force that didn't do anything obvious.

The three bipedal creatures fell. It was not really a competition. The force behind the mace was monstrous, crushing bones and breaking skulls alike. Meanwhile, the archer kept taking potshots at weaker enemies and haranguing the stronger ones. The raccoon-like creatures were, at this point, largely gone. Their attacks barely fazed the fighter, and it didn't look like they'd hit the archer or the rogue once.

Now, the fire-covered wolf stepped forward to face the fighter. Languidly, with movement that reminded Chase more of a snake than a wolf, it idled forward. It stood a head and a half taller than the fighter. As it bared its teeth down at her, the fire running over its back expanded, growing into an inferno that shot out ten feet in each direction.

The fighter calmly took a potion from her belt pouch and drank it down. Ignoring the flames, she waited patiently in a ready position, with her mace resting on the ground, ready to be swung.

For a moment, the battlefield looked like it coalesced into one final, ultimate duel between the two giants. Except, of course, the remaining creatures didn't allow for anything that easy. Whoever steered the beasts knew about the fire from the wolf-like creature and directed all remaining monsters to swarm the rest of the group. In a mixed wave of claws, wings, teeth, and Elemental attacks, the surviving monsters charged.

The rogue activated a card and disappeared. When he reappeared, it was at the rear of the oncoming monster wave, and he cheerfully struck at the backs of the numerous enemies. The archer, meanwhile, activated a card herself and then...stood still. The single arrow on the string pulsated, brighter and brighter, while the monsters rushed in. When they were less than a dozen feet ahead, she unleashed the arrow and immediately ducked behind the shield.

The explosion slammed out at everything in front of her, flinging back anything on the edges of the damaging force. Cold as ice, the Furyborn popped back out from behind the shield and took potshots at the beasts downed by the explosion.

Behind the frontal trio, only a trickle of monsters approached. Mostly the few remaining winged creatures, as well as some of the illusion-covered, foxlike creatures. The force field and the vest-carrier's orbs held them in check, killing and stunning them in turn. Three of the foxes managed to creep past the force shield and evade the orbs of the man in the vest, ready to attack his side...but fell to the ground, stunned, right before they hit him.

At the front, the battle had turned into a spectacle. A show of agility and languid grace versus primal strength. The wolf, even with its massive size, slid from the fighter's attacks, while the skill, technique, and impressive footwork of the Elemental fighter blunted and stopped any claw attack or snapping of jaws. For a moment, they looked evenly matched. Then an arrow sank into the neck of the beast. The archer, having finished off all monsters around her, took the chance to do damage. The fighter's next swooping mace attack struck fiery flesh, as the wounded beast was too slow to pull back.

After that, it was a matter of mopping up. There were no powerful creatures remaining capable of standing against the fighter, and the rogue and archer took down beasts one at the time, with precise, magic-boosted attacks. The two at the back, having fended off the remnants, returned to boosting and shielding where necessary. Yet, their assistance was really not needed at this point.

A couple of minutes later, the five walked to face the throng of awed students. They were met with a large wave of heartfelt applause, led by the Elementals. This might be the first time they had seen their local heroes in the flesh.

Instructor Boneridge didn't look entirely as happy, for some reason. She held back, however, letting the students lavish their adoration on the team in front of them.

Chase had to admit, the five Protectors didn't look like somebody who'd just been fighting for their lives. Like they'd done a bit of carousing, perhaps, but there was no blood, no torn armor or wounds.

The instructor stepped forward, holding up a hand. "Many thanks to our defenders! Before you believe that you will be able to handle something like this, remember—these are trained Protectors, who have fought and worked together for years on end, who have spilled blood with and for each other. They have been trained to the best our educators permit and outfitted with the most expensive, tailored equipment sets we could come up with. This is the pinnacle of our accomplishments. This is what you aspire to." She gave a grudging smile. "But you may get there in time. Now, do any of you have any questions for them?"

The training area exploded with shouts.

"Which card was that explosive arrow?"

"Was that a real inferno wolf?"

"Why did you spread out like that?"

Shaking her head, the instructor held up a hand again. The buzz eventually died down. "I'll allow this, since it's likely the first time you've seen them in action. Yet, *think*. Make your questions count. Use them to figure out something important. If you come up with too many stupid questions, I'll let them leave immediately."

There was a brief moment of silence. Then Gemma, the earth-aspected rogue, spoke up. "Two of five out of you don't have any weapons. How come?"

The man resting his arms on the tower shield glanced at Boneridge, who nodded. "If you make it past the first Culling, you'll undergo a wide series of tests. You will find out which combination of weapons you operate best with. Then, you will be further tested with that in group settings. For instance—"

"Enough details, Mr. Ruderine. That will come in good order," Instructor Boneridge interrupted.

"Okay. Sure." He collected himself. "Anyway, we found out that I work best as what's called a full-defensive. My cards lend themselves well to fending off enemies indeterminably, while helping the others. It's a risky business, of course, and hard to walk the Steps doing it, though I have some...never mind that." He shot another glance at Instructor Boneridge. "Kartan here is what we call utility. He has the perception and the state of mind needed to keep an eye out for anything and adjust accordingly. Given the types of formations we operate with, he or I are actually the most likely to survive in an overwhelming monster attack."

"What about your communication?" Galvon shouted. "You barely even spoke during the fight. Do you have any secret communication cards?"

The fighter, leaning on her massive slab of a mace, snorted. "If we had, d'ya think we'd give it away?" She shook her head, as laughter rained down over the unfortunate rogue. "Nah. Practice. Lots of practice. Lots of combat. Lots of tense situations. We speak when we need to." The side of her mouth quirked up. "Kartan, also when he doesn't need to."

The vest-clad gentleman rolled his eyes at her.

Slowly, the students warmed up to their task. They asked questions on tactics, on monster attacks in general, good group composition, and more. The team took turns responding, showing that, whatever their strengths were, they'd definitely been drilled and trained enough that they knew what they were talking about. Also, they had seen a *lot* of action. They downplayed it, but their experience shone through.

Cilia brought up a question of her own. "You clearly had some combinations of cards and tactics. The way you created that shield for her to hide behind, in between shots. That card— I'm guessing a debuff of some sort?—you used on the larger beasts facing the fighter. The way you used your force shield to trap monsters between your frontliners and yourself for him to bombard with orbs. Is that something you taught yourself or something learned?"

The healer shook his head with a harsh smile. "The towers need you to work, and they need you to work hard. You don't get gifted anything here for free. But, the good news here is that it's there for the taking for those who put in the hours, lass. Trainers and..." He shot another glance at Instructor Boneridge. "Other personnel keep an eye out for us. They note any especially effective combinations of cards and equipment. There are thousands of cards in each aspect. Yet, there are more common power sets that get used a lot. And the towers never throw away knowledge. So, if you manage to make it in, and get a good group going, you'll be able to peruse the library to find out which combinations are there for you to use. Maybe you'll even come up with some sort of prize-winning combinations yourself." He winked.

"That's *more* than enough, Mr. Ruderine," the instructor scolded. "Okay, I think that is enough for today. We are going to take two hours of reaction training, and I am going to come down like Jessabel's mace here on anybody who's not giving it their all!"

A collective chorus of groans arose, as the Protectors started to walk back to the towers.

Chase decided to take the chance and rushed after the instructor. "Instructor Boneridge. Could I have a word?"

The woman didn't stop, but slowed down slightly. Her demeanor seemed anything but jolly, however. "You have until we reach the store. What do you want?"

Chase thought quickly. *How could he phrase this?* "I wanted to ask. I didn't think it was something I should just burst out with, but...did the bronze team actually defend successfully?"

Now, Instructor Boneridge did stop. She turned about and faced him down. "Better think about what you're about to say, boy. You've done acceptably in my classes, for a rogue, but I will *not* hesitate in dropping you to the bottom of the ranks."

He gulped. "Those foxes. They made it all the way to that Kartan guy unimpeded, then they suddenly fell to the ground, stunned. There were no orbs flung, no cards flashing that I could see. If you tell me that it was some card, I'll believe that...but it didn't look like it. I..." He gesticulated, searching for the words. "Just want to know if I saw what I think I saw."

The instructor cursed softly. Her fingers clenched into fists. She expelled her breath in a huff. "Yes. You did see correctly. One of the handlers made a judgment call, and a correct one at that. Kartan...has been overworked, lately, and he reacted too slowly. Their attacks could have killed him or hurt him badly."

Chase considered the implications. He grimaced. Knowing that it had to be said, he asked, "Was it all staged?"

Instructor Boneridge did something Chase did *not* expect. She chortled. Shaking her head, her eyes gleamed with mirth. "Give my compliments to your instructors. Both to Highstream for teaching you to spot it in the first place, and Swansong for teaching you to be enough of a suspicious bastard to come to that conclusion. No. It was not staged. None of it was staged, and the team was not informed of what they were going to face beforehand."

"But—"

She interrupted him, mirth fading from her face. "*However.* The bronze team is a crucial part of the defense of our towers, and Kartan is important for their continued survival. Should we have taken the chance and hoped that Kartan survived the attack, simply for the monster attack to be more genuine, more real? If they were a lesser team, if we had more defenders, I might have. But we do not have those numbers." She reached out and grasped Chase's shoulder. "Do I care about our heroes *looking* like heroes? Not in the least. If I had the chance, the numbers, I'd let somebody like Kartan get attacked instead of messing with the integrity of the drill. But I simply don't. Everything we do here is for the survival of the towers. *Everything.* In this case, that means cheating a bit to make one of our top teams look undefeatable. Do you understand that?"

Chase nodded awkwardly. "I understand."

"Good. Now, get back to the others, and I don't want to hear that you've been running your mouth."

Chase jogged back to the others while the instructor strode on to fetch equipment from the store. His thoughts raced. He believed her words. Every bit of it. Yet, what did that say about the state of the towers that they didn't have enough surplus Protectors? That they weren't willing to face the possible loss of one caster, even a top-Tier one? Was it a good thing? Bad? Had they attached themselves to a sinking ship?

CHAPTER 32

"Really, the odds of the towers still standing in the face of the surrounding powers are beyond horrible. Some attribute it to providence. Others, to some special ingrained quality in the Elemental race. I most certainly disagree. It is a matter of consistent, well-planned hard work. And the work is not yet done." I think I will show this to the others. They may become inspired. Except for Kith. There's just no getting through that thick skull. (Page 11.)

Cilia

"Today, we are doing something different. Hopefully inspiring." The words of the air-aspected Elemental were hopeful, edging up in tone near the end, as if to elicit a positive response. His head bobbed like it was about to fall off his skeletal frame, and the wispy, white mustache—the only hair on his head—pointed toward the ceiling in a second, even more ingratiating smile than his actual one.

Cilia didn't get her hopes up. Their Elemental Theory teacher, Instructor Godewin, had the personality of a sodden doormat and the stage presence to match. She had no doubt that he knew what he was talking about, but somehow, each interaction with the man left you with a desire to be somewhere else. It was a good thing that the vast majority of the knowledge they needed to absorb in the classes could be found in the library, or she'd be ranking a lot lower. Sometimes, she envied Serafine, who'd been brought up with a string of questionable teachers and an education that taught her to ignore unlikeable persons. She would have done a lot better at acting like she actually liked the bloated old frog.

"Last week, you took note of the materials you need to craft your dream creation. I told you to be realistic and stick within a certain budget. Don't think I didn't notice you describing an entire palace you wanted to craft, Ajia, you silly girl." Instructor Godewin gave a chuckle that turned into a cough when nobody else laughed.

If the edges of Cilia's mouth twitched, it wasn't upward. The old ass might seem affable to the point of obsequiousness, but he didn't mess about with the ranking. Anybody who didn't follow instructions or pay attention would only know his displeasure when they dropped in rank.

"Today, we are going to move into the markets outside Earth's Ward and talk to different merchants."

Cilia perked up. Well, that was new. Until now, they'd stuck entirely to theory in this class, with little pertaining to how they'd actually match the theory to practice. She didn't mind that much, because Crafting Practice went so heavy on the other part, she got plenty of practice. Sometimes, however, she wanted for some link, some chance to take the theories she'd learned from her classes and test them without having to try crafting it outright. Today might be the day.

"Are we going to buy our materials?" The voice was a high-pitched squeal that *grated* on Cilia's nerves. Tammy Winterfeast. Elemental, pretty, and oh-so-rich. Also, aiming straight to be culled, and seemingly oblivious about it.

"No, Tammy. While I certainly appreciated the brilliance of your suggested jewelry collection, that is unfortunately not something the towers are likely to sponsor." He almost seemed like he *was* sad that she wouldn't get to craft the elaborate jewelry she had planned and talked incessantly about. "If you do make it into the Protectors, dear Tammy, you will sometimes need high-quality materials—materials that aren't readily available in the towers. Some can be requisitioned through the towers. Others, you will have to pick out and barter for yourself. Today, you will get to talk to different traders, hear their pitches and learn how to discern quality from trade talk in your chosen profession."

At that, Cilia *did* perk up. Until then, she'd been faking studious interest as best she could. She raised her hand. "Sir, if we find something we would like to buy, are we allowed to spend our own money? For personal projects, I mean."

The professor tapped his lip, messing up his questionable facial hair. Then he nodded. "Yes. That would be allowed. You know that we encourage you spending your free time to advance your own skills. I will give you...fifteen minutes to leave for your rooms and pick up any spending money you want to bring."

An hour and a half later, they'd picked up whatever cash they wanted, waited five minutes for Tammy, who was definitely keeping her last-ranked position, and walked the entire way through the towers, into the city proper, and past the security checkpoint into the sprawling tent camps outside of Earth's Ward.

Cilia looked around, taking in the chaotic, sprawling atmosphere, the noise of hundreds of people of different races haggling, arguing, and fighting, and the scent of unwashed people mingling with the stench of herd animals lingering in the background. It felt like home.

"I am going to give you a general introduction to the rules of conduct out here in the markets. After that, you will be allowed to leave by yourself for the rest of the class. That means we will meet here in an hour and a half. Anybody not here will have to find their own way back to the towers."

Cilia grimaced. They would definitely also see a nasty drop to their ranking, if they managed that.

"Your task today is to figure out what it would cost to create your personal project. That includes haggling over the price, of course. Some of you may find that this is very unusual, and I entirely sympathize." Somehow, he managed to make that sound both over the top *and* condescending at the same time. "However, this will test you on two very important qualities that we need for crafters in the towers. Knowing your materials, including their prices. And applying critical thinking to your own projects, including the materials you use."

Cilia was already moving, though Instructor Godewin kept talking, expanding with general information about the markets surrounding them. This was going to be painful. She would need to talk to some of the others for this. She was going to need security, for sure. And security, in this case, would only come in numbers. She couldn't be certain, of course, but she had strong suspicions that whoever had tried to question Chase would still be keeping an eye out for them. That meant walking around alone in the chaotic mess that was the markets outside Earth's Ward was the last thing she should be doing! Chase and the others rarely understood the sacrifices she made for them.

"Hello, Tammy. How would you like to have some company for this exercise?"

The fire-aspected Elemental girl's voice rose in pitch. "Wait. You're... Salia, right? You don't talk to anybody!" Her gaze fixed on Cilia, fiery curls bobbing around her annoyingly gorgeous face.

Cilia grimaced. "Cilia. And no. I am not a people person."

"That's *so* weird! People are the best. That's half the fun of crafting! Being in a room with others and chatting while your fingers do all the work! I mean, that's how I know what's going on in the city and who's who!"

Cilia's eyes twitched. She was already regretting this. However, despite her many, many flaws, Tammy was actually nice. And due to her rich family, she constantly kept people around her. It would be the best protection Cilia could find for the duration of the class. "That isn't really me. And that's kind of the problem. I know enough about haggling—"

"We've noticed. Somebody's aiming for that top spot in the ranking, eh?" Renee Coroden. Another Elemental, earth-aspected and a seamstress-in-training. She did *not* share Tammy's affable personality.

Cilia shrugged. She was not going to be dragged into whatever popularity games they had going on here. "I care more about learning things well. And while I know my haggling and am starting to learn about the different materials, I don't really know this place."

The sour-mouthed Renee sneered. "I don't think—"

Tammy spoke up, cutting over whatever Renee was going to say. "Of course you can join us. I know *all* about this place. My parents have dragged me with them hundreds of times, buying fabrics and iron and whatnot. This will be fun!"

Fun. Somebody clearly never needed money to survive here. Still, Cilia smiled and didn't say anything else. She needed the company for the class, and, besides, it probably wouldn't hurt to get to know some of the others a bit better. She might be able to learn something.

Fifteen minutes later, Cilia had learned that she would likely be better off going solo, at least for her mental well-being. Apart from Cilia, three girls and one guy were circling around Tammy in a never-ending social dance that might have been entertaining in its subtleness, were it not for Tammy being entirely oblivious to it. The incessant chatter was making Cilia dumber by the minute. So far, "haggling" had been reduced to checking out a few exclusive cloth merchants for new purchases and yammering on about important people in Earth's Ward.

Currently, they were in one of the pricier sections of the markets, where rich citizens and those with more elaborate needs went for their purchases. It was also where Elemental vendors congregated, with outsiders being relegated to secondary status, with a few rare exceptions.

"I think I recall there being a smith in this direction, right next to a leather salesman," Cilia tried. "Tammy, you need infused metals for your project, right? We could check that out, and I could hear about the leather components I need."

"Aw. But there was this idea I had. I could use carved bone! Have you heard about that? Some crafters can infuse bone with liquid silver and get this..."

Cilia stopped dead in the street, listening to a voice that rang out over the din. A familiar voice.

"It *worked*, moron. Not my fault you didn't drink it in the first twelve hours like I told you to."

"What's the matter, Cilly? Why did you stop? We can go there, if you really want to. I'll *insist* that we go to see my dad's friend first. She has this mannequin that's been..."

With a mental effort, Cilia tuned out Tammy's voice and ignored the infantilization of her name. It *was* him. She shook her head and turned back to the group. They were all staring at her. She made a rash decision, lambasting herself for it. This was something *Chase* would do. Still. "Oh, that is really nice of you, Tammy. I just remembered there was one shop I needed to see, but it's probably two miles away. I'll have to hurry to make it back in time."

"Are you sure? We can keep you company. Godie doesn't mind if we show up a bit late."

The grimaces on the others around her showed just how wrong that was.

Cilia smiled and lied through her teeth. "No, I wouldn't want to inconvenience you. It was lovely to chat with you all, though. You enjoy the shopping."

They took forever to move out of sight. Finally, however, the path was clear, and Cilia re-emerged from the tent she'd been hiding behind.

She strode with confident steps into the large, much-mended tent oozing mint-scented smoke that the voice had originated from. She took in the spacious interior, the carefully arranged channels leading any toxic smoke up through vents in the roof, the large tables carrying stretches of apparatus, and the slack-jawed Elemental in the center of everything staring right at her. With a curt smile, she nodded. "Hello, Nordon."

After the initial shock and worry that she was there to bring security down on him, Cilia managed to calm down the stressed-out water-aspected alchemist they'd met in Soil before it was overrun by Lightborn troops.

He eventually mixed and drank a concoction of his own making, before pouring himself another one.

"Is it a calming potion?" Cilia asked.

He shook his head and wiped his mouth. "No. Well, yes. It's moonshine. Brewed on local cinna berries. It's quite rough but not entirely horrible. Just like this surprise of yours." He guffawed and took another sip. "Seriously, I thought you kids had kicked it. You seemed too fresh-faced to make it on your own."

Cilia said, "I'm not sorry to disappoint you. We honestly didn't expect you to make it either."

"Oh, *please*. Like it's the first time the Lightborn have come down hard on illegal outposts. I pay scouts to report to me and left with most of my inventory, hours before they attacked." He grimaced, circling the glass in front of his nose as he sniffed. "I'm going to miss the setup, though. Also, my favorite alembic cracked in the hurry."

"Do you know what happened, then? Afterward, I mean?"

He shrugged. "What always happens. They killed everybody who moved, picked up anything worth keeping, and then burned what was left of Soil. Then they got distracted by the next shiny thing. As for me, I decided to seek my entertainment elsewhere for a while. Since I'd built up a decent stock of hard-to-come-by ingredients and potions, I decided a tiny trip to Earth's Ward would be worth it." He smiled beatifically at her. "And here I am. You sure you're not here to rat me out?"

Cilia rolled her eyes. "Please. We're in the same boat. If I were to find some Lightborn official I could turn you in to, I might as well put the shackles on my own hands." She hesitated before taking a chance. "Any news about Isarn?"

Nordon snorted. "You could say that. Apparently, somebody stirred a hornet's nest down there. They went and attacked the..." He froze. "No!" He slapped his thigh and stared at Cilia. "That was you! I know the Lightborn armies have been circulating descriptions of the devil worshippers trying to take down the Lightborn empire! You!" He cracked into a sputtering laughter before eventually resurfacing, gasping for air. "I have to say, they got a few things wrong. You are portrayed as fully Darkborn. And neither are you as physically intimidating as they said you to be."

Cilia grimaced and decided she might as well give up a few details. "Well, we didn't expect it to go over silently. Honestly, though, it was just a move that went wrong. We wanted to sneak in and pick up cards for ourselves. That's all."

He held a hand forward, resting right before her sleeve. "May I?"

She nodded.

He lifted the sleeve of her tunic, revealing her Manipulate Light card, nodding to himself. "Well, you succeeded. You also disrupted the power balance of the entire Lights-cursed region when you stole that deck. They had to get another deck transported in, at no small cost to the city, to reestablish their hold over the south. The nobility even deposed the ruler of Isarn."

Cilia exhaled softly. They'd known that stealing the deck and killing the inquisitor would have consequences. However, they hadn't been in a position to learn exactly what those consequences might be. In a small voice, she asked, "Did anything else happen in the city? Is it peaceful?"

Nordon squinted at her. "What *else* have you been up to? Oh, wait, you were from the Waves. Yeah, the poor tend to suffer when the rich quarrel. From the old news I've heard, the rest of the city's pretty much unchanged. They had a few weeks of enforced curfew, but that's all. There *is* an inquisitor arriving, or so it's rumored."

Cilia tried to not show just how relieved that made her. It didn't sound like Gunnha and the other holders of Dark cards in Isarn had been exposed, yet. Also, considering they were all low-Tier, it would be hard for the inquisitor to spot them. The longer that went by without any troubles, the better they'd be able to quietly share Dark cards into the trusted members of Isarn's populace. It wasn't a good situation by any means, but not something that should blow up straightaway.

Hopefully, at some point, Gunnha and the others would be able to reveal their cards and just...exist normally. It was a long way away for anybody else, though, and not at all on the table here in Earth's Ward. They were already being looked at askance for having Light cards. The result of them showing that they had Dark cards would not end well. She smiled, suddenly thoughtful, at the bartender/alchemist. "Well, now that we're up to speed on each other's comings and goings...what can you tell me about the news here in Earth's Ward?"

"Now, listen here, missy. You might be telling some interesting tales. That don't mean that old Nordon is suddenly going to survive on giving everything away for free."

She stared him down. "Not even if I can trade with news from the towers?"

He slapped his thigh again. "Darkness take my eyes, but you kids do live interesting lives. Okay. You go first."

When Cilia finally left the tent, she had to race to make it to the meeting place. She didn't mind, though, even though she imagined enemies lurking everywhere, and had one hand in her bag, ready to use one of her trinkets. She would never hear the end of it from the others, having gone off by herself after giving them such a hard time. Still, the risk and the time spent had been worth it. Not only had she learned a lot, she also got the crafty alchemist to spill a few mental exercises for improving her own crafting processes. Back in Soil, he'd asked an extortionate fee for teaching her how to craft. Now that she had already learned how to craft, he agreed to a much more reasonable price, because it would just improve her efficiency slightly.

CHAPTER 33

"Would we rather be at peace? Proper, lasting peace with a geographically secure situation, where we're able to expand at will? See, that's an interesting question. Because, although everybody is busy telling you that they're trying to make peace last...our system revolves around conflict. Good luck finding somebody who'll give you their honest opinion on the subject." That was surprisingly candid. Worthy of praise. (Page 62.)

"**N**ow we have to look over our shoulder for Nordon sending inquisitors after us, too?" Kith groaned.

Chase shot a glance around the near-empty amphitheater. Rowan, Tam, and Jonathan hadn't arrived yet, leaving them free to speak as they wanted. "Keep it down, will ya?" he hissed. "Besides, if Nordon were to try betraying us, he'd be in trouble himself—because we'd turn on him right away."

"Which you had best believe I told him," Cilia added in no uncertain terms.

"Thank you." Chase nodded. "Besides, the Lightborn would likely be able to make a lot of trouble for us here. But if they were to try, we could damn well do the same to them. The towers might take us in, if we told them what we'd done, and what we've learned about Arnault."

"Or they might use us for political capital," Cilia added. "Let's not test it."

"Good plan. So...did you learn anything else useful from him? Anything about the Lightborn here in the towers?"

Cilia huffed and scratched her neck. "No. He confirmed that he'd heard about the potential loophole that could get people into Earth's Ward, but, according to him, it would just be a waste of money, because the real deals were made out there."

"So no conspiracies. No Lightborn armies lurking nearby. That's slightly uplifting." Chase smiled.

Kith mused. "Hey. You guys ever think that we should try to do what we did in Isarn?"

"Nearly crash the present power structure?" Chase asked.

"No, I—"

"Be poor enough that a cold spell almost killed me?" Cilia asked.

"Have your family try to kill, betray, *and* disown you in a handful of days?" Sera added.

"Race naked through the Lower Market on a dare?" Liam joined in gleefully.

"I hate you all. No, dammit. Share the cards in Earth's Ward! There aren't any inquisitors here, and even if there were, they wouldn't have any pull. Besides, most Elementals hate Lightborn. Not Darkborn."

Chase scoffed. "Tell that to Ernest. But no. Just...no. Even though it'd be cool to make them more normal and commonplace, and I *really* want to see what happens to the Dark deck when we get a hundred wielders, the last thing we need right now is more attention."

Their conversation slowly died down as more students trickled in, sitting nearby.

Finally, Professor Brookwatch arrived and started talking right away. "Today, we are going to talk about diplomacy."

Kith slid noticeably farther down on the stone bench until Cilia pinched his ear.

"Many of you," the stern-faced teacher said, "believe that our chosen diplomacy means prostrating ourselves before others, letting them walk all over us, because their nations are stronger than ours." She looked up at the dozens of students clinging to her every word and said, with clear emphasis, "You could not be more wrong."

A few catcalls rang out among the crowd, and a bunch of students applauded. One audacious student yelled, "You tell 'em, teach."

Professor Brookwatch's demeanor didn't change in the least. "As for those of you who believe that diplomacy means standing tall in the face of those who approach our lands and showing them who's boss?" More cheers. "You are even more wrong."

A confused silence spread over the amphitheater.

She let her gaze slide over her audience, taking in the reactions, sometimes nodding to herself. A full minute later, she continued. "The most important task of the Protectors, and the one that will fall to you, should you manage to make the final Culling, is deciding when to stand tall, when to prostrate yourself, and when to attack."

That didn't lessen the confusion. Chase met Kith's eyes. The Furyborn just shrugged.

"Thirty-two years ago, a minor team of Protectors halted a group of Lightborn claiming to be travelling nobility. They were not. In fact, they were the spearhead of an attack, meant to strike first and open a breach in our defenses. Eighteen years ago, a Furyborn came stumbling, bleeding, pursued by an entire trio of inquisitors. Six months ago, a minor noble from Stradeburg claimed the present Protector team didn't have the rights to search his coach and insisted on continuing on his way, undisturbed." She paused for a moment. "Every single one of these situations could, with the wrong kind of reaction, lead to huge and undesirable consequences for the Towers. What would the right choice have been in these situations?" She waited for their reactions.

Tandor raised his hand. The well-dressed rogue had a self-satisfied smile on his lips.

She acknowledged him, and he started talking. "In the first situation, I think—"

"That's quite enough, thank you, Mr. Emberspore." She sneered in disgust. "The only right answer at this point is *I don't know!* You, despite your upbringing, have not received the training, the legal knowledge, or the tools to come up with a proper answer. You... *I am already slashing your ranking, Tandor Emberspore. Lower that hand, or you will hit the bottom.*"

Tandor's hand lowered. He looked ready to kill somebody.

Professor Brookwatch continued, unperturbed. "A lot of people have an image of Earth's Ward being this isolated core of civilization in a roiling mass of monsters and Lightborn or Liberty attackers. That *has* been the case a few times, historically speaking. In general, that is far from how the situation is these days. The real issue is that you never know what you are going to face on any given day. Do you see a few unaspected beasts struggling in, already wounded from facing other monsters, ripe for the harvesting of Ænima? Is one of the Liberty outbreaks slightly earlier than expected? Do we have foreigners bringing in illegal trading goods, trying to hide the fact? These are just a few of the many, many possible situations Protectors will have to deal with on a constant basis. The trick is learning what to do, when you need to call in help, and when you need to delegate."

One of the fighters, the biggest, wildest Furyborn Chase had ever seen, with a massive bird's nest for hair, called out, "Do we all have to handle that stuff? Some of us are best suited for bashing monster skulls in."

Laughter arose over the congregated students. Even the professor cracked a smile. "Oh no. We realize that not everybody is best suited for diplomacy. In fact, for those of you who pass the first couple of Cullings, some of you will be encouraged to take additional or specialized lessons in diplomacy. Some are best suited to focus on the more knowledge-aspected part of things, court manners, insignia, lore, knowing what to expect, while others lean more toward person-to-person management.

Others, again," she drily added, "are encouraged to learn to keep their traps shut."

Laughter arose again, louder than expected. They were not used to Professor Brookwatch cracking jokes.

She continued. "I am not joking. As they progress and improve, we highly encourage people to specialize in addition to their classes and take on further responsibilities. Some of that means coming to peace with where your talents do *not* lie."

"That mean we don't need to learn this stuff?" the Furyborn fighter tried again.

The professor shook her head and tapped her bracelet. Behind her, his ranking took a hit. "The first comment was relevant, Mr. Asaid. Now, you are veering onto the path of stupidity. You might not need to specialize in diplomacy. However, Protectors do not accept ignorance, willful or otherwise. You are going to need to learn the basics of the world we live in, as well as your place within it, if you intend to walk the path of the Protector. Also, anybody who does not master any of these additional talents will be judged the harsher in their other areas of expertise. Now, I realize that this is not something we're going to be able to teach you in a single lesson."

Relieved murmurs arose.

Right up until the professor raised a finger. "Of course, that does not mean we aren't going to get a good head start on the many lessons to come today."

It was as promised. So far, in the World Knowledge class, they'd spent most of the time trying to explain the situation the Towers and Earth's Ward were set in, compared to the rest of the world. Now, the professor did her utmost to paint the correct picture of the day-to-day existence of the Protectors. A picture that got increasingly complex as the lesson droned on. It appeared that Protectors would have to wear many hats. Guardians. Diplomats. Lorekeepers and socialites, well-versed in legalities as well as convoluted situations between countries. On top of that, they would also be expected to know when to handle situations themselves, and when to call for backup.

Once Chase got over the overwhelming idea of having to learn everything in the world, he started appreciating the intricacy of the task. He divided the possible tasks of Protectors into smaller bites, carving them up and seeing how they would fit his team. Suddenly, the prospect didn't seem so overwhelming.

Liam would be the perfect face for the group when talking to any new arrivals nearing the Elemental lands. He'd be able to set newcomers at ease and make them relaxed and ready for any deeper inquiries.

Chase imagined he'd be decently suited for the more demanding intricacies of diplomacy, where they had to question suspicious newcomers, grill anybody who seemed reticent to cooperate, and in general figure out who was hiding something, why they were nervous, or sniff out any secrets.

Obviously, if things veered off into tangents that required a more learned diplomatic approach, or a touch of knowledge about how to behave among nobility—or, to be fair, just to behave in general—he'd pass them onto Sera. She'd be able to navigate those murky waters where he'd be in danger of drowning.

On top of that, he didn't even need to turn his head to see Cilia's excitement at the prospect of having to memorize thousands of tidbits of knowledge that would overload the minds of the rest of their crew. She would be the mastermind, keeping all the legal and general knowledge tight and ready in that pointy-eared head of hers.

Kith... Yeah. Kith would be the perfect backup and scout while they all did this. From a distance, preferably.

Once he came to the realization that they were already supremely set for dividing these tasks among them, the lecture became less daunting, and he paid more attention, listening carefully, trying to pinpoint the parts of the task that would suit him the best. Chase barely even noticed how he'd mentally adjusted to the future of being a lawkeeper instead of a lawbreaker.

***

"We've got them!" His young voice was higher pitched than usual, imbued with a frenetic energy that immediately caused her dislike.

The Elemental snapped, "I have made this abundantly clear to you. There is no *we*. We do not work together. In fact, I am pretty fire-scorched certain that I explicitly told you to stay the Pits away from me unless you had specific orders from your higher ranks about the final steps of our plan."

He made to say something, but she didn't care for it and barreled onward, ignoring his affronted look. "I *also* told you that any meeting like this adds to the chance that we are discovered. Which part of that did you not understand? I am going to contact your puppet masters and tell them to pull your Dark-cursed strings tight and not let go. Do you hear me? Or do I need to get you kicked out? I could."

He reeled for a moment. Then, to her amazement, he rallied and shot back, "That is my exact point. I have orders for the next step."

"I notice that you didn't say the final step."

He sneered. "Really? We've been over this. You're going to do what they ordered, and you're going to do it *tonight*. However, even if you don't like being at their beck and call, I believe that you're going to enjoy this one." He handed her a piece of parchment.

She read it, took three deep breaths to keep her hands from shaking, then read it again. "Do they know what they are risking with this?"

He shrugged. "You know as much as I do. But think about it. Whatever they might have figured out about us at this point, whatever they're plotting...it all comes to nothing, if you cut off the head."

She shook her head. "It's foolish. We are *this* close to the final steps of our plan. Two months and thirteen days!"

"*It won't matter, if they find out about you first!* Don't you get it? It says so right there. They've been reporting directly to her, as late as yesterday. Not only that, one of our sources overheard a bit of their conversation. It wasn't much, so we can't be sure—but they know about the Lightborn padding the ranks. We are moving up the timeline." He rolled his eyes, sneering at her.

Inside her mind, the rage boiled, telling her just how easily she could crush his boy-like, puffed-up airs, if she so chose.

He continued. "Either way, you're talking out your ass. You're at their beck and call and this needs to happen. If you want *any* chance at your precious towers surviving what's to come, you'll do your part. Your part is just going to be a bit more...direct than we anticipated."

She hung her head. "But how? You know who we're dealing with here. The head of the Cloaks? They're infamous for being able to disappear into thin air. Do we even know it's her? I would never have suspected her. It's...too obvious."

"Don't you worry about the ifs. If they say it's her, it's her. Regarding the hows, I got separate instructions. You do the deed, tonight—we'll make sure your back is free."

CHAPTER 34

*"It's in times of strife that people and organizations re-
ally prove their worth. Thus, the towers have proved themselves able to stand up to the world, time and again. We may
bicker and moan, disagree over the tiniest of things. However,
when push comes to shove, we have each other's backs."* I rather like that sentiment. Not sure it'll hold up in practice...but
if it does, that's another indication that this is a good place to
stay. (Page 91.)

Chase awoke to the sounds of shouts and armored
boots from the corridor. Still befuddled with sleep, he
looked at the window, only to see utter darkness without a hint
of dawn.

He stumbled to the door, still in his undergarments, and
stuck out his head. There, he saw other students opening their
doors, as bewildered as he was. One red-faced hall guard
pointed from door to door and yelled, "Stay in your rooms. That's
an order! We're under attack!"

Chase closed the door again, keeping it open a crack on
the off chance he'd hear anything useful. His heart pounded.
What was this? A monster attack? No. There were no howling
sirens, like they'd used for the monster attack. *Something in the
towers, then. Something closer.* He prepared for the worst and
hurried to strap on what weapons and defensive items he had,
ready to burst into action should any sounds of battle spread his
way, regardless of what that guard said. He knew that, although
most of the students were likely huddling in fear in their rooms,
the others would be preparing just like he was, ready to fight.

Minutes ticked by. The activity continued, with booted
feet racing both ways through the halls outside, along with the
occasional shouted command. Anybody trying to leave their
room, regardless of reason, was forcibly turned back. The
minutes turned into hours. At some point, somebody noticed
Chase's door was ajar and closed it, hard.

Chase tried to keep himself from falling asleep again,
though his exhaustion warred with the tension. Finally, after
several hours—Chase didn't know how long—his door was flung
open. Outside, a guard waited, grim-faced, while another guard
paced farther down the hallway, flinging open door after door.

"Line up! Shut up. We're going to the Supplication."

The students fell into line, confused voices crying out,
asking what was going on.

There was no response, apart from the repeated order. The students found themselves corralled along with one guard ahead and one in the back, like a long line of sheep.

As they progressed farther down the towers, they encountered other lines of students like theirs, looking equally confused. Protectors accompanied them, servants as well. In short succession, they learned that *everybody* was marching for the chapel. The entirety of the towers was being emptied. Whatever had happened had everything turned upside down.

The Supplication, they'd learned during their World Knowledge classes, was the central spot in the courtyard before the towers. It was dominated by the tall, four-Elemental fountain, magically crafted to have all four Elements swirling in a constant, living kaleidoscope of colors within. The huge monument was a callback to the historical moment where the first High Elementalist had supplicated to her people to make a stand against their enemies in this very spot.

Today, there were no visible enemies. However, the High Elementalist was there, head bowed. And thousands upon thousands of people were gathered all around them, while more kept streaming into the courtyard.

Chase and the others were led to a spot several hundred feet from the central fountain. The guards stayed with them, as more and more people funneled in. Some arrived in something approaching order, while a great many simply barreled forward, aiming to get closer and find out what in the Pits was going on.

One thing he found reassuring was that there were no *overt* signs of any attacks. No burning towers, no ash-covered or bloodied Protectors. Whatever had happened must have been limited in scope.

At long last, the incoming masses quieted down somewhat. High Elementalist Tatiana Skysworn raised her head. In a grave voice, that rang out over the entire courtyard, she intoned, "My friends. We have been attacked."

All eyes were glued to her, people jostling to see better.

"Earlier tonight, Applied Practice Instructor Swansong was attacked in her office, and killed."

Shouts of surprise and dismay rang out across the crowd. Chase's gaze shot to meet those of his friends. They showed the same shock, confusion, and fright he was sure was echoed in his own eyes. *They'd killed her! The head of the Cloaks! How? What?*

"How do we know this is an attack on the towers and not something personal?" the High Elementalist continued. "Instructor Swansong was very talented. She clearly fought to defend herself, and did a lot of damage in the process. Yet, while we had other officials working nearby, no sound was heard from the adjacent offices or the hallway. This must have taken either a number of trained attackers, powerful crafted artifacts, or a combination."

Her voice rose in power, and she looked straight out at the crowd. For a moment, Chase felt certain her eyes rested square on his. "Knowing that we are under attack is nothing new. Over the years, we have seen every sort of attack there is. Trained assassins. Monster waves. Even unaspected beasts corralled our way. *There is nothing new to this.* How does this affect you all, then?" She paused. "For the vast majority of you, it doesn't. The fact that our enemies will stop at nothing to undermine our strength, even stooping so low as to wickedly assassinate a kindly and beloved teacher, is no surprise. That they got away with it merely shows that they have funneled more resources into it than many similar attempts. However, for those responsible for keeping us safe and for whittling out the secret attackers, you know what this means. There will be no rest, until we know that we are, once again, protected and safe from those who would do us harm. We will take this horrid assault and use it to emerge, once again, stronger and safer."

A muted cry rose out from several people among the crowd.

The High Elementalist held up a hand, asking for silence. She paused, the air rising above her, making the tassels of her dress whirl about her in a furious pattern. "Some of you may ask yourselves why I even inform you of this. I cannot promise that we will find those responsible and hold them accountable. I cannot ensure that I will be able to find the exact method that they used to perpetrate this nefarious attack."

Mutters welled up among the students surrounding Chase.

She didn't seem to notice. Instead, she continued, voice growing louder again, with the whirling wind behind her somehow adding to the volume. "I can, of course, promise you that we will do the utmost in our power to find those culpable. To keep you safe. I can promise that Protectors will be heavy on the ground in the days to come; visible at the edge of your vision. Yet, that is not enough. It would be so much easier, to just keep quiet, hide the misdeed while we worked covertly."

Chase very much doubted that. News, such as a bloody, violent attack, had a way of getting out, regardless of any restrictions or regulations.

"I tell you," the High Elementalist shouted, wind now visible as a twister surrounding the hard-to-see woman and growing ever taller. "Because that is the Elemental way. We do not hide our coveted secrets from our brethren, afraid that they sap our strengths. We do not shy from ugly truths, hoping that they will go away by themselves. We stand, side by side, and face what is to come. Together. Brother alongside sister. Earth. Solid, dependable, ready to defend. Water. Adaptable. Quick, ready to react. Air. Fast. Ephemeral. Ready to move. Finally, fire. Blazing. Strong. Ready to *strike*." She punctuated the final word with a blast of air that could be felt even from a hundred feet away.

Calmer, with her head bowed, she spoke on. "Finally, we tell you everything, because Instructor Swansong is worth telling the truth for. She dedicated her life to ensuring that the towers would be better equipped to handle anything the world might throw at it. She deserves nothing less than the respect afforded her through the full disclosure of the truth about the lengths her enemies—*our* enemies—would go to, to ensure that she is silenced."

The somber woman grew quiet, and the hush spread around her. She stood with her head bowed in contemplation, in respect. When she finally spoke, her voice was hoarse, emotional. "I ask of *you*. People of the Towers. Are you going to be afraid? Are you going to slink along the walls out of fear of what may come? Or are you going to honor the life of Instructor Swansong and *stand tall in the face of whatever may come*?"

The roar that answered her deafened Chase for a moment. He barely noticed, though, because he was screaming along with the rest of them. His might not be the same experience as that of the others. Even so, the sentiment behind it was the same, as was the reaction. Whatever they knew, whatever they did...those bastards were not going to stand between Chase and his family earning a safe place for themselves.

Back in their room, afterward, they had but a short time to eat breakfast and then get to the Monster Knowledge class. Chase burst right into talking about what was on all their minds. "I know. We need to agree what we do next. But first. I found this in my pocket after the speech." He pulled out a crisply folded piece of parchment and handed it to Sera.

She looked at the parchment and then read it aloud. "We all suspect who did this. No proof. I received a proper debrief. We are looking into the numbers right now. Wait for further information. If you have any information, turn it in to Clerk Hortensia Willowby." She turned the parchment over and over. "No signature. There is no doubt who it is from, however. Is there?"

"'Course not." Chase scoffed. "The High Elementalist. The question is just...do we leave it at this? If they're confident enough to move against Swansong...who's to say we aren't next in line?"

"That isn't all, either," Kith added drily. "We've already talked about how the Cloaks may have been slacking in locating any hidden enemies. Now, they just had their head cut off. How efficient do you all think they're going to be at finding them now?"

Sera blinked. "I mean, we *are* talking about an entire organization. Surely, the loss of a single person cannot cripple them." She sounded anything but certain.

Kith sneered. "Do we even *know* they're an entire organization? For all we know, they cooked it up as a way to intimidate the foreigners." He rolled his eyes and continued. "Okay, I don't even believe that myself. Way too much effort for little payoff. Still, my point stands. We don't know that they're able to deliver what we need."

Cilia had been pacing back and forth with her hands behind her back. Now, she stopped and turned toward Kith. "I believe there is a suggestion in there somewhere. We need to get moving. Say it out loud. What do you propose we do?"

For once, Kith wasn't snarky. "You said it yourself. We need to get moving. Caution was all well and good when we expected the Cloaks to find out everything. Now, we need to act. Those in charge have no issue taking the time to wait for results...but they're not the ones who're next in line to be attacked. We are. I say we kick it up a notch."

"In defiance of what the High Elementalist wants?" Sera asked, shocked.

"That...doesn't necessarily have to be the case," Chase mused. "You know she gave us the means to contact her, right? Well, here's what I'm thinking. We get in touch with her, we tell her the situation as we see it...then we provide her with an alternative."

"What exactly should that alternative be?" Sera asked.

"Bait," Chase said, with no doubt. "We already *are* bait, waiting for the big mean fishies to come gobble us up. There's no discussing it. We might as well use it to our advantage. If we figure out when our mysterious enemy might try to jump us, then try to turn the trap on *them* instead, with some help from above? That should help solve things. It's not like it's going to cost the higher-ups a lot."

"Yeah. That's what I'm talking about, mate," Kith agreed. Then he furrowed his brow. "What kind of help, though? I mean, how do we turn a trap we aren't even entirely sure is there?"

Chase tsked. "Kith, my dear, simple friend. When you are faced with a difficult question that requires learning, wits, and patience, what do you tell yourself?"

Kith blinked. "I should ask Cil to do it?"

"Exactly!" Chase burst out laughing at the affronted look on Cilia's face. "Now, I know you may think that Kith is a horrible person—"

"*Somebody* is, that's for sure," Sera grumbled.

"But he's got a point. What we need to do here is exactly what you and Sera do best. Figure out what we need to pinpoint who might move against us and when. For instance, I'm thinking we'll need a full schedule of our classes, to see when any of us might be exposed to surprise attacks. But apart from that? I'm stumped what knowledge we should ask for. I can come up with some *items* that could help, but..."

"All right. All right. I get it. And we'll handle it," Cilia said. "Won't we, Sera?"

Serafine nodded. "Once we have finished the Monster Knowledge class today, we will. With the right information, we will be able to turn this situation around. After that, we should finally be able to get to the bottom of this. If, before then, the Cloaks manage to handle things, that is simply serendipity. However, I agree that we should not wait around and rely on faith."

Liam nodded and smiled. "I don't know what singing has to do with things, but I completely agree. I'm itching to get this out in the open."

They all turned to look at Liam.

Eventually, Sera said, "I know I will regret this. Singing?"

The big man shrugged. "Yeah. Seren-what's-his-face? That's singing to some broad on a balcony, isn't it?"

Sera blinked. Without another word, she turned around and opened the door. "I quit!"

"But...this isn't a job?" Kith called.

"Quit!"

CHAPTER 35

"Ordei is a world of rivalry. Of borders and pitched forces. They say it was different, once upon a time. Myth or no? Nobody will be able to tell. Yet, I believe the Elemental approach is as close as we can possibly get. We do accept anybody as they are, as long as they work for the good of the towers." Right. And as long as they don't stand out and they give up seven years of their lives. If that's the best attempt at bringing the people of Ordei together, it's not that impressive. (Page 71.)

"We all know what happened earlier with Instructor Swansong. It is a shock, no discussion. However, that too should be a teaching moment to you. The world of the Towers is one of sudden loss, of death and violence. If you doubt that you can get used to that? By all means, quit! It might be the first traumatic experience for you here, but it sure isn't going to be the last. Either we take you poor sheltered kittens and turn you into proper predators, or we toss you back to your pampered lives."

Instructor Boneridge was smiling. That in itself was always suspicious. She was also bobbing on her feet and rubbing her hands, making Chase truly leery of what was to come next.

The Elemental didn't try to honor the fallen instructor. Rather, she flung the murder in their faces, trying to see whether she could elicit any reactions. One Elemental had already called her out on her lack of decorum, only to be subjected to such ridicule that he stomped off in a huff. He still hadn't returned.

Now, the instructor moved on to another topic. "There will be many situations here, where you will face crossroads you are not keen on, but will have to handle the consequences regardless. For instance, you are going to hate some people here in the towers. This is not up for discussion. It's a simple fact of life. You are all adults, or at least getting there. Even so, you have been raised with certain prejudices, be that against races, religions, habits, card choices—there are many possibilities. Inside the towers, you will meet, and be forced to work with, all sorts. You will learn to handle that, in a professional way, or you will be culled. It's that simple."

Behind her was a walled-off area with large rectangular constructions of raised earth, and small adjoining tunnels of soil leading from one to the next. The first area was a hundred feet by three hundred. The next was a tiny square, little bigger than their old raft on the Waves. The final one was the largest of the lot. Maybe the size of the entire Church of the Circle back in Isarn.

The instructor continued. "Like I mentioned more than a month ago, I adjust my exercises according to you sorry lot. I pinpoint the spots where you are weak and train you until you pass muster. Even so, there are certain repeat exercises and happenings for each new batch of recruits. This one is one of my favorites. I have banded up with certain other teachers and put together some dossiers on you, your likes and dislikes." Beaming, she waved at the large group of students assembled in the training area. "We have tried to put together pairings that are the absolute worst for you. Personality-wise, race-wise, class-wise—we've tried to ensure that today is going to be as horrible for you as absolutely possible. And, of course, we will put you through a series of exercises to see how well you work together."

Chase groaned. He was not the only one. All across the open area, people looked crestfallen or apprehensive. Chase, for once, didn't even need to wonder. With his rivalry with Ernest being as well-known as it was, he already knew who he'd be teamed up with.

The instructor didn't ignore them. In fact, she seemed to thrive on it. "This is your chance to *learn*. To realize that the towers is not for you. You can go back to your comfortable homes, take what you've learned here and apply it to a world that's a lot softer than what we offer here. Or, you can try to get over your hang-ups. Grow up. Learn that, perhaps, just perhaps, there are things in the world that are more important than your prejudices. If you don't, obviously, you will get to see your ranking tank." She started to read the pairings aloud.

Even before their names came up, Ernest Chalico approached Chase. He'd realized where the wind was blowing as well, and idled closer. The water-aspected Elemental oozed reticence. Everything, from the sneer on his lips to the way his hand clenched on his gold-embroidered leather belt, told Chase about how much the young man disliked him.

When the instructor mentioned their names, they already faced each other. Chase was searching for words that could see him through the exercise without the two turning to pummel each other...but failed. The weeks of constant harassing, jibes at his expense, on top of the things Chase suspected him of...it was just too much. So, he stood there and looked into his eyes, hatred staring back at him.

The instructor, now grinning widely, let her voice carry into the dozens of awkward silences across the area, as bad pairings found each other. "There will be three exercises, one after the other. You will not be awarded the chance to see what they entail. However, the final one *will* be a fight. You will have five minutes to discuss beforehand. Go!"

Eventually, the taller man spoke, chin raised. "Chase. What kind of name even is that? How you spent your youth as a criminal, I expect?"

Chase spat, "That's exactly it. Not all of us had a wealthy family backing us. I lived *alone* on the street, with just my wits and my feet to help me survive. So, I stole, I lied, and I was chased. Yes. I also lost my first friend to a merchant's beating when I was five. Would you like to make fun of that too?"

The slick Elemental blanched. He opened his mouth, but no sound came out. With a huff, he shook his head. "Look. I am never going to like you—"

"Have no doubt, it's mutual," Chase interrupted.

"But I care more about making it into the Protectors than anything else. What do you say? Truce?" From the look on his face, it cost him to say that much.

Chase snorted. "So, you can belittle me and sabotage me whenever you feel like it, but the moment things could be inconvenient for *your* career, I'm supposed to just play along? You know what? I think my ranking can take the beating and still have me survive the Culling. How about yours?" That was the benefit of having the rankings constantly updated and made public. Anybody could see how everybody else was doing. To be honest, Ernest wasn't doing *bad*. He was clearly schooled and had done decently for himself in the World Knowledge class, as well as the two caster-centric classes. But he was only middle of the pack in Combat Training and Monster Knowledge.

"You would be so petty as to..." the caster sputtered, then caught himself, possibly even spotting the hypocrisy of trying to talk about pettiness. He closed his eyes and took two deep breaths. "I was not the one who attacked you," he blurted. "Neither was I the one who tried to get you caught in whoever stole that sword."

Chase smirked. He relished this. The sensation of having power over Ernest felt intoxicating. "That's easy to say at this point, isn't it? Are you being entirely earnest, Ernest?"

The caster bristled. He pulled a hand angrily through his slicked-back hair, then huffed. "Forget I said anything. This isn't worth it." He started to turn his back.

Chase narrowed his eyes, then called out, "Ernest. Wait."

The Elemental turned back around, dislike clear in his posture.

Considering his position, Chase came to an unfortunate conclusion. "Okay. Let me be completely honest with you, mate. I don't like you. I don't like your entitlement, your haughty attitude, or the fact that you've had it so easy. Also, I'm not getting around the fact that I'm horribly biased against anybody with money. Even so, I'm in the same position as you. I care more about succeeding in the towers than any damn vendetta with you. So, I'm willing to put it out there and go for a temporary truce, if you are."

Ernest gave a curt nod. "No reason we should learn to like each other. We just need to work together for a brief while."

"Exactly. So, with that in mind, we should talk."

"You're right." The regal young man tapped his lip. "Since this is meant to stress the fact that we need to cooperate with people we dislike, I expect us to be faced with some sort of trust exercise, possibly a physical test that will be near-impossible to handle solo, and then of course the fight in the end. What do you think? Beasts or Protectors?"

Chase picked up his jaw and cleared his throat. "That sounds...very logical. I think you're entirely right." It *would* be like the frustrating instructor to force them to work together or fail as one. "As for the fight, I'm thinking beasts. It *is* Monster Knowledge, after all." Now, Chase finally saw the *real* pitfall. If they were to succeed in the class, they'd likely be pushed to the limit. And in order to succeed... "I'm a rogue."

Ernest blinked, befuddled. "I...know that, of course."

"Oh, shut up," he shot without any real vehemence. "That's not what I'm saying. I'm a Tier-three rogue. I focus on mobility and evasion, with little damage-dealing efficiency. I have Light cards, and the single Elemental one, of course. My Light cards allow me limited movement on air for quick periods of time, a medium burst of Agility and a training advantage that I won't be able to use here. My Elemental card will allow me added mobility, and a bit of deterrence, mostly against smaller enemies." He snorted. "Oh, and my Heart card is totally useless in most circumstances, since it only allows me to fade into the background a bit. Useful in crowds. Useless against a frothing monster."

Ernest blinked. "You..." He trailed off at the unexpected openness from Chase. Then he nodded to himself and harrumphed. "I am a Tier-two caster. I only have the single Elemental card. I focus on outright damage, but with a side of versatility. My card allows me to create water and convert it into propelled blades of ice. However, I have been working on adding options, making the blades blunt to use as defense, to make enemies stumble and similar." He hesitated only for a split second before finishing. "My Heart card allows me to amend my hearing for a limited time. Not to increase it, but move the area I can listen to for a while. It allows me to scout ahead, but no farther than around a hundred feet."

Chase fought to keep his face straight. *Crap.* Did that mean that Ernest had been listening in when he was dismissive of his sister during the trials? He could slap himself. *Of course it did.* No doubt, that was where part of his unreasonable hatred came from. Likely, he was also just something of a dick, but hearing an outsider bad-mouth your family right when they were tossed to the curb? Yeah, that had to suck! Hoarsely, he hurried to say something. "That has to be useful to keep up with gossip."

Ernest rolled his eyes. "I have better things to do with my time...but yes."

Chase rolled his neck. "All right. Appreciate the vote of confidence. We can make this work. The way I see it, I'm on de-coy duty then, while you do the damage? That should work for most scenarios. I'm pretty good at ticking off others and keeping them mad."

Ernest snorted a laugh, then held a hand over his mouth, as if surprised at the reaction. Drily, he responded, "You are at that. I'm better at sniping and moving on."

"We still talking about combat?" Chase asked with a raised eyebrow and crooked smile.

His old nemesis was saved from answering, when Instructor Boneridge marshalled them to the booths to choose their weapons. Chase picked his usual long dagger and a holster holding three throwing daggers that he strapped onto his left arm. Ernest picked no weapons, only a light, circular buckler he strapped onto his left forearm. Then, they were led onward to gather before the opening. Knowing her temper, the pairs swiftly closed up in ranks to listen to her instructions.

It was clear to see that these were anything but optimal pairings. Hateful glares were common, but awkward glances at friends, eyerolls, and wringing of hands was just as common. Chase spotted Kith sneering at his partner, another summoner. In the background, he saw Sera whispering to a standoffish Furyborn he recognized as a caster.

"We are sending you through in pairs with a minute and a half between you. The rules are as follows: Those who complete the tests are ranked based on their completion time. If, at any point, the pair behind you catches up to you? You fail. If you're too hurt to continue? You fail. If you fall? You fail. Anybody who fails will be ranked accordingly alongside their fellow failures."

Chase grimaced. Then he turned to Ernest. "That means the safe choice is to go after completing first and foremost, and ranking high after that."

Ernest sneered, sniffing disdainfully. "I have never been one for the safe choices. I mean to *win.*"

Despite himself, Chase found a grin building on his face. He nodded.

"Apollo and Gertrude Redwing. Step up!" the instructor bellowed. Behind her, the earthen wall of the closed-off tunnel leading into the first area slid away into the ground like a mudslide, leaving a bright, ominous opening.

Apollo moved forward. He was the lead fighter, and number one on the overall ranking. Wielding a spear and shield combination, with a heavy chainmail coif and helmet, long, steel-lined leather gauntlets, and steel-ridged boots, the fire-aspected Elemental was a sight to behold. His companion...less so. The other Elemental was a crafter. That was all Chase knew. She also looked like she was about to faint, and shook hard enough that it was visible from afar.

"I hope you have agreed upon your chosen strategies. Because from now on, any second wasted on discussion will be one that the pair behind you is catching up on you."

The instructor looked as smug as that priest of the Circle who loved to preach in the Lower Market, telling the poor why they deserved to live worse lives than the upper crust. Chase wished the same fate on her as that damn priest had suffered. Served him right.

"Get moving in three. Two. One. *Now!*" Instructor Boneridge raised her arm, and the pair ducked into the first tunnel and disappeared from sight.

For a while, there was silence. Then, everybody realized that it would be a minute and a half until the next pair was allowed entry, and whispered conversations rose up among the students.

"We will be...about...twentieth or so." Ernest nodded. "That gives us about half an hour, before we are allowed in."

Chase frowned. Then he got it. "Ah. You think we're entering based on ranking of the highest-ranked of us. Makes sense. Let's spend the time to talk about our cards. What do your blades work like? Do you need to throw them straight? And do you throw them with your muscles or the card itself?"

They spent the time discussing their powers and limitations. Every minute and a half, one of the pairs was summoned to enter. Kith and the other summoner went in as the fifth group, due to the other summoner being high-ranked. It looked like they'd reached a *very* uneasy equilibrium.

It turned out that Ernest's powers had a bit more versatility to them than Chase expected. Earnest had learned how to shape the water into ice, and magically propelled the resulting blades forward, with very little cooldown between attacks. The card suited the attributes he'd always relied on, which were Mental Power, Agility, and Toughness, in that order. His high Mental Power also meant he was very keen at shaping them and had a wide range: from ultra-hardened, sharp ice, to blunt missiles, or even to a blinding stream of sludge.

Chase, in return, extolled the specifics of his cards and his attributes, obviously leaving out his Dark cards. Neither of them said their exact attributes—they weren't at that point yet—but they eventually agreed that Chase should start with Steps of Brilliance active, since he already had that chosen, and only shift to Squall Sling if it made sense.

Eventually, their time was up, and they encroached upon the low tunnel leading into the unknown with only slight glances at each other. When the instructor shouted, they loped off into the tunnel, ready to take on anything.

CHAPTER 36

"The gifts of the Elementals are beyond measure. However, I will never understand a person who decides to dedicate themselves to but a single element in their cards. After all, just like you see in our society, our strength lies not in specialization, but in the combination of all the Elements." Not sure I actually agree here. I'd say that the strength of the towers lies in the combination of deeply specialized people. If everybody went for versatility in their own powers, we would likely come out weaker. (Page 82.)

They ran through the tunnel at an easy jog. The tunnel curved and then opened into a large, wide area. The place was open to the air, and the first twenty feet was simple soil, as were the last twenty feet. In between was...a pit. It could hardly be described otherwise. A several hundred feet long and hundred feet wide pit. It wasn't deeper than eight feet, but that didn't matter. The pit was filled with a muddy substance that looked like tar, and would most definitely halt anybody unlucky enough to drop.

"If you fall, you fail," Chase snarled. "Meaning, we need to make it across those."

"Those" were the only obvious paths across the pit: two narrow walkways running from one side of the pit to the other. In actuality, "walkway" was a bit of an exaggeration. They looked like narrow boards, no more than eight to ten inches wide, held up by long metal poles hammered into the ground below, and they ran side by side with maybe two feet of open air in between the walkways.

Waltzing across the boards would be no issue for Chase. None whatsoever. At Tier three, with an Agility of thirty-two with Race of Life active, he felt certain he'd be able to walk across with closed eyes, if need be. The real issue was human. Interspersed along the sides of the pits were four tall platforms, each holding a person. The foremost of them, clearly a caster, summoned a ball of earth into being in his palm and started to toss it up and down. His other hand gave a jaunty wave at the pair. Behind him, the other Elements were represented.

Time was ticking. Chase narrowed his eyes. If he wanted to, this could be the easiest challenge for him ever. He would be able to *sprint* across the divide, secure in the knowledge he had

Steps of Brilliance waiting for him in case of any missteps. Ernest...that was another story. The caster was *not* defensively minded and would have a hard time handling the attacks and staying on the platforms at the same time. He grimaced, looking sideways at the man who was taking in the situation in silence. If he wanted to, he could leave him behind easily and hope he'd be able to handle the next challenges by himself. In spite of his desire to do *just* that, he found himself talking, fast. "Change of plans. Here's what we're going to do."

Seconds later, after a quick switch to Squall Sling, they stepped forward, side by side, and started to run. It must have looked rather comical. An unlikely pair like those two. One dark. One bright. One poor and badly dressed. One rich and wearing the fanciest of finery. Stepping forward and building into a run as one, while both held their arms out to the other, Ernest's right hand grasping tight onto Chase's left forearm.

They ran onto the boards like they were the finely paved streets of Earth's Ward, accelerating instead of slowing down. Chase found that the boards were more solid than he'd feared, with only a little give in them. With his high Agility and Ernest's Agility not trailing too far behind, they had little trouble keeping their balance, especially with each other to adjust if they over-balanced.

Then the first enemy started to attack. A rock-hard lump of earth raced at Chase's midriff—fast, but not inhumanly fast. With a grunt, Chase managed to deflect the missile with his long dagger. He set down his foot without missing a stride. The next earthen missile was already building in the caster's palm, soon racing for Ernest's head.

Ernest deflected the clod with the buckler without break-ing stride, without even breathing hard. They raced on, boards thundering beneath their feet, and he spoke up evenly. "Watch out. The next one will start in a second."

Chase realized the danger. On their left, the Elemental on the next platform was building up a bolt of fire, sending a grim smile at the two runners as he did. That meant that they would be in the range of at *least* two attackers at the same time, would have to defend from missiles of different Elements from either side, and still keep their footing. "Keep on. Take the hit if need be. It's more important that we don't stop."

The fire-aspected Elemental proved a problem to Chase. Ernest effortlessly blocked the first attack with his buckler. The second one, however, aimed straight at Chase's leg, and he had to jump to avoid it. Chase kept his balance, but couldn't avoid pulling Ernest slightly toward him.

Squall Sling activated at Chase's very thought. He'd practiced a *lot* with it over the past six weeks, both for movement and attack purposes. In a split second, the force of the card pushed the pair back onto their path, as if nothing had happened in the first place. They picked up the pace. Chase wasn't aware, but he had a grin on his face.

The next twenty seconds were a blur. The missiles differed a *lot*—in weight, impact, and form—and it turned out that three of the Elementals were in range at the same time. Chase engaged his Agility and used his Squall Sling card to the utmost and kept them on track. Ernest, in return, got one lucky shot off and nailed the final caster, an air-aspected Elemental, tossing him off his platform. Hence, the final part of the balancing act was unchallenged, and the Elementals stopped attacking as soon as they set foot on the far side.

"Well done." Ernest let go of Chase's forearm. With a grudging nod, his nostrils flared and he looked at the next tunnel. "Let's move on!"

Without a further word, Chase loped ahead. He believed they were doing well, speed-wise, for the first test. Anybody who wanted to fight their way forward would likely have to move more cautiously across the boards...but they couldn't be sure.

The next tunnel opened before them, leading them into...a confusing scenario. They skidded to a halt inside a small area, filled with but a single thing: a square table, holding a bored-looking administrator with a sheaf of papers, quill, and ink. The man, sporting a hairline that was nearly receding into the neck of his tunic, looked at them over the rim of his glasses. "You will need to answer three questions correctly to move on. Name one of the ruling figures of Stradeburg as well as his responsibility."

Chase gaped. He looked to Ernest, who looked equally out of his depths. Quickly, he tried, "Can we get a new question?"

"Very well. Name three instances where outbreaks from Liberty have *not* resulted in battle."

Chase cursed.

Ernest grunted, before looking at Chase and saying, "Another question, please."

Within the next half minute, the duo realized that this was *not* their strong suit. Chase was late to the world of learning, and Ernest was only middle of the pack in World Knowledge. However, they soon understood the name of the game. The questions revolved around information that Protectors would be required to know...meaning, they weren't going to be able to cheat their way past this—but they weren't clueless, either. They skipped quickly past questions that had them stumped.

Ernest got one first, naming three illegal substances from the Furyborn lands that were not allowed in Earth's Ward. Then, Chase managed a simple question revolving around the Church of the Circle, after which they had four bad questions that almost had them desperate, before they stumbled over each other telling the answer to the next one.

"That was not a win," Chase growled, as they ran for the next tunnel.

"It really wasn't," Ernest agreed.

It probably wasn't as bad as it felt. There had been maybe fifteen questions total. Still, that meant somebody who answered all first three questions right could win nearly a damn *minute* on them.

When they stepped into the last area, Chase was ready to race ahead with a grin on his face. It was an obstacle course. The area was packed with hazards, and the ground broken and challenging. Spears were placed into the soil, jutting out. Spikes formed everywhere, with the ground lopsided, caved in and pockmarked in turn. Every sort of possible ankle-twisting danger was present. Chase would be able to *dance* his way past this, and sing a ditty as he did so.

Ernest grabbed his arm. "Quiet."

"What?" Chase looked at him, confused. The place, despite its broken setup, was open and uninhabited...oh. Damn. It was *too* open. Too easy. He held a hand over his mouth, signaling his silence.

Ernest nodded. Then a flash near his heart showed him engaging his Heart card, and he closed his eyes in concentration. Seconds later, his eyes opened again. "Fury scourge those stealthy cheaters!"

"Surprises?"

"Something. Several somethings. Don't know what. Skittering, scratching things. They're buried in the soil, about halfway to the other side."

Chase nodded. "Okay. Time to enact my first plan then." He waggled his eyebrows. "Run ahead and let you deal with those." He paused for timing. *"Kidding!"* Holding up his hand, he asked, "Original plan, then? I'm the distraction, you're damage? I move, you kill; we mow them up, and move for the win."

Ernest shook his head in exasperation. "Yeah. Let's go."

Chase nodded. He took off, enjoying the sensation from the added +4 to Agility from Race of Life that made his pace smoother, faster. He burst into a run, leaping over the broken wreckage of the ground.

They emerged as one. If Ernest hadn't made him aware of the enemies lurking in ambush for them, he might have been taken entirely by surprise. Instead, spotting the beast was easy. It dug itself out from within the earth, a rare level stretch of ground replaced in seconds by a thing of claws and chitin leaping up.

Chase met it with a stab to the neck. The long dagger pierced right through the thin chitin and it slid back into the hole.

Several ear-tearing screeches overwhelmed the momentary sensation of grim exultation. Seconds later, Chase was fighting for his life.

Their enemies were spindly. The earth-colored insects were fast, agile, and seemed to be made out of thin insectile legs, teeth, and claws, with little to spare for an actual body. They were skittering, leaping pests, and there were seven remaining of them.

For just a second, right at the start, Chase pondered how easy it would be for Ernest to stab him in the back. Just hold back, or mistime an ice blade to hit Chase instead. Then he was back to fighting for survival. With a shout, he sprang at the nearest nightmare-inducing stick figure and stabbed out at its thorax. Then, the Pits opened, and it seemed the entire world was trying to kill him.

For one second—several, really—it was all he could do to survive, to avoid the maelstrom of incoming claws. Chase sprinted and leapt for all he was worth, focusing his every bit of energy on not getting stabbed and avoiding getting himself killed on the devilishly tricky terrain. Then a frosty blade tore into the single beast behind him and the exit, and his back was free. Suddenly Chase had the surplus time to realize a couple of things, as he pulled back toward the exit, defending from the six remaining attackers, giving Ernest the chance to take them down, one by one.

First, Ernest was *not* going to backstab him. Whatever else he might say about the bastard, he apparently had honor. Second, although the critters were fast and outnumbered them, they were also small. They likely didn't weigh any more than thirty pounds at the most—Chase had managed to punt one of them ten feet at the start. Third, they really weren't *that* fast. If they'd been singular animals, and not beasts held in tow, controlled by a single person, Chase would've been able to play around with them. Even as it was, with all of them trying as one to pin him in, they kind of felt...slow. The thrill from the streets back in Isarn raced through his body, telling him to push it up a notch, to show them how outmatched they were.

The person in control apparently came to the same conclusion. As one, the beasts turned and skittered toward Ernest instead. Chase fought the desire to leave him and skip toward the exit in success. But no. Ernest had played it fair, and so would he. He dropped his long dagger and plucked every throwing dagger he had from their sheath, sending them against the leading beasts, propelled even faster by tapping Squall Sling; targeted bursts of air flung the small daggers with the speed of a championship thrower. His aim wasn't perfect, but two of the three connected, tearing right through the small creatures. With a grin, he picked up the long dagger again and loped after the hindmost beasts.

Twenty seconds later, Chase put his leg on an insect's body and pulled out the long dagger with a grunt. It had partly stuck on something inside the beast. As he pulled it back out, the thing deflated and lay still. Chase's gaze met with Ernest's in an adrenaline-crazed grin. The two had finished the remaining beasts in a frenzied flurry, Ernest proving surprisingly adept at using an oversized version of his magically summoned blades in close combat.

The water-aspected caster was wide-eyed and disheveled. His slicked-back hair stood out in every direction, and he panted hard. His finger rose slowly, and he pointed past Chase. "Race you for the exit?"

Ten seconds later, Chase tore through the tunnel. He looked back at the grinning caster sprinting right after him, then saw the ground behind them swallow the corpses of the dead beasts, even as a large, bipedal beast lumbered from a newly formed side opening in the wall, turning in preparation for the next duo to arrive. Shaking his head, Chase continued running, then changed his mind and fell back to run next to Ernest.

The tunnel veered, and another administrator met them. "Ernest Chalico and Chase...just Chase. Four minutes, forty-two seconds. Well done. Please wait for the conclusion with the others."

Chase held out his fist for Ernest to bump. The Elemental looked slightly confused, then grasped his forearm in a warrior's grip. He laughed and adjusted, grasping Ernest's forearm as they faced each other's gaze. Beyond them, the other contenders stood, mostly dispersed into their usual cliques.

Ernest nodded to Chase and, noticing a friend, started to move toward him.

With a split-second decision, Chase called out, "Listen. I know me and my friends are the reason your sister didn't get in. Also...I might, in the heat of the moment, have made some disparaging comments about her. Sorry about that. But I don't have anything against you. I mean, you're annoying, stubborn, easy to rile up, and don't back down…but that's pretty much like looking into a mirror for me. So, if you want to extend that truce? I can work with that."

The Elemental ran a hand through his hair, mostly managing to get his hair back into place. He looked from Chase to his friend. Something unspoken ran between them, and he gave a short, tight smile. "Truce." The smile turned into a smirk. "Though your name is still stupid."

"Too earnest, Ernest," Chase shot back.

At irregular periods over the next three-quarters of an hour, the remaining students came in. Some entered in pairs, triumphantly; some solitary. Chase's crew did decently, overall. Liam's partner was a nervous wreck, but managed to summon the power to help, at least a bit, even though Liam had literally had to carry him across the first pit. Kith managed to finish alone, with his partner refusing to even contemplate working together and getting himself tossed into the first pit. Sera and the Furyborn caster had been torn up something bad by their last opponent, an aggressive, wolverine-like beast, but managed to drag it down, eventually. Cilia had done what Cilia did best. Her partner, an air-aspected fighter, was opinionated, headstrong, and disliked outsiders…but she tore him down with words and made him cooperate. They took one look at the large beast facing them in the last challenge and, eventually, managed to outrun it for the exit.

Finally, Instructor Boneridge arrived as the last one through. She carried an unconscious rogue, that Liberty girl, Camille, dumping her unceremoniously at her feet. Without preamble, her hoarse voice rang out. "There was a fourth rule."

Everybody froze straightaway.

"Of course there was. You think we tell you everything? You're fresh-faced little turds, who know nothing. There are many things, each day, that we use to judge you, most of which we are never going to tell you about. This one, however, I am going to drag out and rub in your faces, because you should have guessed it." She looked uncommonly furious right now, beyond even her regular belligerence. "I told you. Right at the start. *We need you to get over your dislikes and petty rivalries!* Yet, half of you only listened to the *rules* I gave you and continued to not care a whit about the Light-cursed *point!* Anybody here who tried to mend fences, to get over their inborn prejudices and actually work together with their forced pairing is going to receive a better ranking, regardless of their result—*especially* if they scored lower because they tried. Like this girl, who fell trying to help the caster who *insists* on treating her like a lesser person because of her race." She prodded the unconscious, bleeding

Camille. Then she spat, "For those of you who still haven't gotten the point? The gloves are off. Try to challenge me on this and see what happens." With that thunderous rebuke, the instructor turned on her heel and marched off, leaving the downed rogue lying on the ground.

Chase met the gaze of the others. "That was...something."

Cilia nodded. Without even looking at him, she said, "One word about that time of the month, Kith, and I *will* end you."

Sera added cautiously, "You think...you know, I think I'll just go heal that girl."

CHAPTER 37

"To sum up, my friends...in the towers, we are making history. Building something lasting, that should not be possible. I encourage all to join us, to work to construct a bigger and better world, despite the odds. Together, you and the Elementals as a whole can flourish." A bit flowery, in the end, but...okay. He got to me. I'm in. We can do this. (Page 101.)

For the next couple of days, they resumed their regular rhythm.

Sera and Cilia finished the list of what they believed they needed to crack the code and find whoever was behind everything. The others added their own input and ideas, resulting in a rather large list. However, they decided that it was worth it, that the chance of actually *receiving* the information they'd need to get to the bottom of everything would justify the effort involved. Full schedules. Historical lists of rankings, teachers, and students. Full lists of current and past Protectors, as well as their races. Lists of monster outbreaks, deaths, costs...*so* many lists.

Chase delivered their request to the administrator that the High Elementalist had specified. He was rather nervous about that whole thing. If anybody was able to pierce what they were up to, they'd be more exposed than ever. Even so, they all agreed it was worth the risk.

They worked as hard as ever. These days had added Combat Training and Monster Knowledge classes, meaning additional time with Instructor Boneridge. They expected it was due to Swansong's murder. Whatever the reason, it wasn't exactly quality time. The instructor seemed to be in a foul mood after the latest exercise, constantly forcing them into new groupings, quite often uncomfortable, uneven, or challenging ones. She also, as threatened, came down harder than ever on anybody trying to continue with old rivalries or prejudices. The result was a charged, uneasy atmosphere in what had earlier been tough, but ultimately enjoyable, classes.

There were still tangible results, though. Even if the new and changing groupings pushed them hard, they also faced Elemental Guardians more often than ever. The Ænima from the defeated beasts was impressive, and, quite often, victories were punctuated by one student or other joyfully celebrating another Step they'd earned.

Liam managed to earn another Step, making it to thirteenth, and Sera made it to fourteenth. None of them had reached the next Tier yet, though it was looking closer than ever for Kith, who'd been at the fourteenth Step for a while.

On top of that, Chase managed another point to Strength through the training. He was now at seventeen and was starting to rival some of the lowest-ranked fighters among the students in sheer physical power. He realized just what a full two years of training like this could do to him and resolved to not let up in his efforts. Sera managed a rare point to Agility, and Cilia also got another to Agility. Kith, through serious dedication, managed to nudge his Mental Power yet another point higher, reaching seventeen.

Just two days after requesting the information, they got a response. The response was overwhelming and made an already hard schedule even harder. In the middle of the night, a group of servants silently appeared. Crates upon crates of books and rolled-up parchment were rolled into Chase's already cramped room, before the servants left again, just as silently. Once they were gone, he stared at a room that was only barely recognizable between the stacks.

Sera and Cilia dove right in whenever they had any spare time. Hours in, they realized just how big a task it was. The information wasn't easily sorted, and just getting an idea of what they were dealing with was tough. They roped everybody into helping, asking for help to categorize what they had, and appointed specific details for them to find in certain stacks.

In between the bone-breaking training sessions, challenging team building, and increasingly hard monster fights in Monster Knowledge, they were pushed to the limit.

With just eight days to the Culling, they were gathered in Chase's room and ready to give up.

"Argh. Can't we just move back to the Waves? Being poor beats having to look through inventories," Kith complained from his throne on top of a crate of dusty tomes. "Look at this. Seriously. We're not going to learn anything useful here! I now know how many carren beans the towers consume on a yearly basis. My brain doesn't *need* that! In fact, I reject that knowledge. Grrrrn." He clawed at his head theatrically.

Sera scoffed. "It would do you well to learn something else other than how to beat or cheat people."

"Why? I can get by *just* fine as a Protector, just beating people! It's like...two-thirds of the job description!"

Cilia, who had been busily organizing documents on all sides of herself on the bed, with her in the middle, like some sort of organizational Mental Power exercise, blinked owlishly. "See,

Kith? This is the reason why I often use my Heart card in these settings. You know very well that you are wrong. In fact, at least a third of our classes are dedicated to educating you on just how wrong you are, yet you *insist* on spewing nonsense like that." She held up a document. "Just to show how wrong you are. I now know why the combat practice has been increased the past week."

That caught their attention. "Do go on, Cil. How did you manage that?" Liam rumbled.

"Well, one of these piles—atrocious sorting, by the way: if I manage to catch whichever clerk is responsible, I am going to trounce him—holds the schedule plans for the new students in the previous thirty years. A lot of the details change over time. For instance, did you know that Applied Practice is a new class, Chase? Just five years old."

"*Please* don't draw it out, Cil. I'll be a good boy," Kith complained.

Cilia's dark eyes sparkled with evil intent. "*Yet!* The one thing that holds true for at least the final ten years is that, at some point leading up to the first Culling, one day in the last couple weeks is dedicated to an outing. Border Patrol, they call it. *And,* cross-referencing the post-ordeal conclusions over there," she pointed at another stack, "I have found out another detail. It's a team outing. I'm not sure exactly what will be happening, but we'll be going along with the actual Protectors. Hence, the need to ensure we're ready for action."

Kith slammed his crate. "Light take my eyes, that *is* cool. Well done. It doesn't change much...but at least we know why Instructor Boneridge is cranky. She knows we need to up it, or we'll get ourselves eaten."

"Speeeaking of which," Liam said, eyes open in sudden realization. "Wouldn't that be a perfect chance to take us out?"

After a moment's stunned silence, they all started speaking at once.

Sera spoke over the others. "Cilia. Can you see how many were on the teams?"

"Yes. Four to six. Apparently, choosing a good team is part of what you're judged on. There are a few additional details, but apparently, it's an ongoing event happening over several days, to ensure that we're faced with real-life situations. We'll be attached to an actual Protector detail and will be put to assisting them...mopping up remnants of monster attacks, sorting through carts for contraband, that kind of thing." Cilia tapped the parchment in front of her. "Also, deaths and injuries happen. Every time."

"Damn," Chase said. "We *know* that whoever's out to get us knows the schedule. We also suspect that they're in contact with the Lightborn. What are the odds that they're going to ignore this chance to get to us all?"

"I know I would, if the roles were reversed. At least, as long as I'd be able to hide my involvement." Kith shrugged.

"This...is perfect!" Chase said enthusiastically. He got up and started to pace. Only after a while did he notice the rest staring at him. "What? It is! This is the best chance ever to turn the tables on them and find out who's after us. We've got the time we need to prepare, the gifts we got from the High Elementalist to boost us, and the forewarning to have an idea what we're going into. Now, we simply need to figure out a way to turn this trap on its maker."

"If there is one," Liam murmured. "This sounds pretty far-fetched to me."

Sera reached over and patted his shoulder. "That is because you do not have a single sneaky bone in your body."

"Hey. Just because I prefer heavy stealth doesn't mean I'm not stealthy," the big man complained.

"Heavy stealth?" Sera asked, confused.

"Yeah. If nobody's conscious to see me, that means I'm being   stealthy."

They eventually agreed that this might be the best chance they'd get to draw their enemies out in the open, and focused first on how to predict and turn any given traps, then on how to figure out who was behind it all.

Eventually, it all came down to orders. They realized that orders worked extremely differently than with the Lightborn. Inside the towers, the chains of command were a lot shorter and less formalized. They lived in a situation where every single day could bring with it an overwhelming monster attack. Hence, they relied to a much larger degree on verbal orders and trust than the Lightborn, who were sticklers for written orders, stamps, and verification. They knew that any of a hundred different points of entry might realize something was ongoing, whether diplomatic, trade-based, or martial, and they had a highly developed verbal system for spreading information inside the towers to where it needed to go.

On the downside, this meant that it was much easier to obfuscate the origins of any given order, given that it would be extremely easy to simply lie or mislead. On the upside, however, they now knew what to look for, meaning they should be able to either track any verbal order back to its origin, or at least spot where it started to deviate. Once they had that, they'd be able to either investigate themselves or alert the High Elementalist to who they needed to look into.

Outside the towers, things were different. It took them quite a bit of time to figure out how that worked, until Liam finally found a Protector who didn't mind explaining it. In short, although there were a lot of different carded Elementals employed who watched over the surrounding lands from the towers, they didn't have anybody who was able to communicate with the Protectors on patrol. As such, they'd devised a light-based system, with a bunch of differently colored codes that were easily discernable from afar. Any group would be designated with a color code and have a list of codes that they knew how to react to. The people who sent those codes? They *were* monitored, given the importance of their messages.

At first, Sera nearly fainted with joy at the prospect of them having to learn an entirely new language, if a simplistic one. Kith countered that they didn't have to learn exactly what all codes meant. They just had to spot and memorize any code that was sent from the towers in order. Then, they could verify afterward. This took the wind out of Sera's sails, but she bowed to the more pragmatic approach. It wasn't like they didn't have other things to learn.

A few days later, the outing was announced, along with the message that their behavior during the outing would have a big impact on their ranking in the different classes. As such, they were all encouraged to form the best possible teams and practice religiously. It would be a three-day event, starting four days before the Culling, meaning that immediately following the event, they would know who had failed and who could move forward to the next step of becoming Protectors. It would be a staged event, with teams taking off in turns.

They confirmed their own five-man team right away. Instructor Boneridge didn't comment—and nobody was really surprised. The fact that they were close was well-known, and with how much they'd worked together, it would have been weirder if they hadn't teamed up.

Of course, even with the event, the teachers weren't going easy on them. They packed a busy schedule of physical exercise for those who weren't away for the event—and those who *returned* were immediately put into their own teams and not allowed to fraternize with the rest of the students until the event had concluded.

Time raced, especially for Chase and his friends, who were spending any moment not dedicated to training on figuring out other details that might help them.

They did locate confirmation of their former speculations, coming closer to an actual year where the changes had started taking effects. Unfortunately, that arrived simultaneously with a massive attack from Liberty and a subsequent large number of fresh recruits, new teachers, and changes in management. In short, it was harder to tell exactly which new administrator, teacher, or higher-up Protector might be the one or ones responsible.

They also located *one* other detail.

For once, only Sera and Chase were studying the stacks of information. Liam was out making friends, Kith had recused himself for the day to work on his Mental Power, and Cilia had decided that she wanted to try creating something special that might help them during the event. Hence, just the two were sitting on either end of Chase's bed, deep in concentration on their own separate islands of parchment, dust, and disjointed tidbits of knowledge.

Chase yawned and put down the tome he'd been perusing. He rubbed his eyes, which only made the itching worse. "I don't know what's worse—the dusty information *in* these huge works or the dust itself. Both together make me want to go to sleep *so* bad."

Sera laughed. "I quite like the smell of books." She grimaced. "That is a good thing too. Otherwise, my upbringing would have been even less enjoyable."

Chase wrinkled his nose. He knew that, even if her parents had been noble, her youth hadn't exactly been wonderful, with her being raised as a potential price cow to eventually be sold to the highest bidding suitor. He gave a fake laugh and tried to sidetrack her. "Oh, please. Don't try to tell me there isn't at least *one* teacher you loathed!"

The barb had the desired effect. She chuckled. "Oh, there was. My family was reduced somewhat in power and riches as I grew up. You know they gave me over to Reddick to educate. But when I was younger, it was one parade of private teachers after the other. One tutor spent *one* afternoon with me. Then he gave his initial assessment to my parents. I saved the card." She bit her lips and looked up. "Bright mind. Intolerable attitude. Beyond my limits as a student. Possibly beyond the limits of anybody." She laughed, the sound deep and throaty. "All because I challenged him on the actual reasons for inheritance among Lightborn nobility always being primogenital and did not back down."

"What sort of genitals now?" Chase winked. "Just kidding. That is an *amazing* grade card, though. You could show that to prospective suitors as an introduction. Go...screw me! "

"Go screw me?" Sera asked, one eyebrow raised.

Chase held up a hand, while he sorted through the tomes in front of him. Then, he opened three different ones, leafed through them one by one until he reached the pages he wanted. He pumped his fist. "Yes! I'm a genius!"

Sera smirked. "I am going to need proof before I agree to that!"

He turned the tomes around and nodded down at them. "Go ahead, then. See if you can spot it." He beamed a challenging smile at her.

"Challenge accepted." Focusing on the books below her, she mused aloud, "These are...ranking lists, divided by the different classes, over the years. In and by themselves not horribly useful." Sera blinked. "We already went over these, did we not? Decided that there were no clear deviations..."

He nodded and grinned a devilish grin.

She moved her attention to another tome. "This, then, is the list of deaths and desertion reports? And this one would be the list of...Cullings and promotions to full Protector? There is a pattern there. Only, I am not seeing it." Sera tapped the ranking lists. "These were the initials for the teachers, right? Did we go over it to see if any of the teachers treated the Lightborn any different than other races? We did, right?"

Chase rolled his eyes. "Oh, you did. You also tried to teach everybody about a lot of things I decided to forget straightaway. Something about applied static."

"Applied statistics. The knowledge of using numbers *properly*. It is useful in more places than one would imagine. And there is no need to repeat that *horrible* joke you made. How would you even get that many kittens?" She shook her head as if clearing it of distractions. "I am still not seeing it. These rankings are from seven years ago. Yet, there are no obvious deviations that I can spot."

"That's because we only looked at the *numbers*." Chase leaned forward and shuffled a few pages back. "Think about it, applied to the real world. We have somebody here in the towers who's either helping people cheat on their tests or actively puffing up their rankings. When do you think they would do that?"

Sera's eyes opened wide. "Darkness hide from my gaze! Of course. If they were actively cheating and planning for somebody to either fake their death or desert, they might not cheat the entire time. Only when it was needed to pass a test or to raise their ranking to what is needed."

"Exactly!" Chase grinned triumphantly. "We don't need to look for classes where Lightborn have higher rankings consistently. We need to look for where the rankings are higher leading up to Cullings and the final tests. Like right *here*." He pointed at two pages, where the rankings from one week to the next indicated a leap in the rankings for three students. "Three students. Three Lightborn. Moving from the middle of the class rankings to a passing rank later on." Chase's finger rose in the air, and with a flourish, he deposited it straight on another tome. "And there's the proof. Three Lightborn, deserted, with a few months in between."

She looked at the page. Her curls fell in front of her eyes, as she observed the page, deep in thought. "You do realize this is not proof? You would need substantial evidence to prove that this was on purpose. Even if you did find that, you would not know what or who caused the changes. Only that something was not legit."

"Yeah. That's true." Chase grimaced. "But it's better than nothing, isn't it?"

"Are you kidding me? This is a major breakthrough! Now, we merely need to do the work. Pass me that list of deaths. I will start making notations of the dates of deaths and desertions, and you can keep looking for patterns in the rankings. Soon, we will be able to see exactly where they have cheated the system and which instructors. Following that, we might be able to find the pattern to see who is cheating *right now*."

Chase blinked. "Liberty release me. You're right. We might even spot it from the daily rankings in the mess hall. What are we going to do about it if we're right?"

"We are right. I have no doubt. I can sense it. I believe, if we have the proof in hand, we should simply turn it in to the High Elementalist. They will be able to take over any question-ing from there. Besides, once we have the pattern, the rest should unravel, and grant us—I mean, the towers—the tools to defend from this approach in the future."

Chase looked at her flushed face and felt a spark of ex-citement. "Pits, princess. You can almost make books sound in-teresting."

"Books *are* exhilarating, peasant," she said in a snobbish tone. With an infectious grin, she added. "Sometimes, you just need the right situation and approach to realize it."

"And the company." He smiled.

"Well,   that   goes   without   saying."

CHAPTER 38

"Have you ever met a Protector? A real Protector, experienced, hardened from years of service to the towers? Once you do, you will learn two things. First, the towers trains the best, the strongest, most resilient of people. Second, there is a cost to it. For all that I love my home, and approve of what they are doing to keep us all safe, I have paid it, so that my son must not. The hereditary families are made of special stuff." Special. Right. Indoctrination is alive and kicking, it seems. (Page 45.)

Their few spare hours faded away into nothing, as they were all introduced to Chase's theory and helped search for incriminating evidence. The numbers slowly added up, as they started to compile the information into something useful.

There was no further information disclosed about the final training event. The intensity of the training reached a fevered pitch, however, where they often found it hard to summon the energy for anything at all.

The evening before the test started, the ones who were to have their test on the first day were let off early by Instructor Boneridge and told in no uncertain terms that they were to rest. The same applied for the following days, with the only change being that the people returning from the tests were separated from the rest, for training, meals...anything. They weren't even allowed to fraternize with the others, likely regarding the risk that they were going to give the other students unfair advantages in their own tests.

Finally, it was time for Chase and his crew. They gathered in Liam's room, ostensibly resting in preparation for the following day's schedule. In actuality, they were back at the books.

Kith, as always, was not afraid to share his enthusiasm for the project. "Kill me!" he groaned.

"Shut up and get to work," Cilia commanded. "We still have these older lists to go through."

"Nope," Liam said. "Did those yesterday. Even followed orders and looked for what you said I should. Nothing to be found. It's like we suspected. Around ten years ago. That was when the change came."

Cilia paused, admonishing finger raised at Kith. "Then…what else do we need? Kith *will* help."

"Nothing." Sera stood in the center of the room, hands behind her back the way she always did when she presented anything for the teachers. "I had Chase focus on a few final details yesterday, and I sacrificed a few hours of sleep tonight to be sure we didn't miss anything. We have pinpointed where they are cheating the system."

For once, there were no comments. The rest sat attentively, wide-eyed.

"As you have probably noticed by now, they do not swap teachers. Hence, we cannot know for certain whether the classes or the teachers themselves are suspects. What we know for certain is that there are three classes that are involved, and they are all general classes—that is, classes that start the year and run for the entirety of the Protector training. World Knowledge, Combat Training, and Monster Knowledge. We have clear and concise evidence that these classes have seen a preponderance of cases where rankings for Lightborn have gone up right in time for Cullings or the final tests."

"How did we miss that the first time around? Shouldn't there be larger numbers of Lightborn passing in these classes than the other ones?" Cilia looked affronted by the whole thing.

"That is the clever part. There is a slightly higher average of Lightborn passing the Cullings and finally graduating in these classes compared to the others. However, that is hidden inside another fact."

Chase, lounging on the bed with one leg over the edge of the bed, laughed. "Sera was actually the one who figured out that part. Again, just goes to show that she has the kind of sneaky, devious mindset of your not-so-common criminal."

"Oh, stop, you."

"Could you stop your weird flirting and get on with it?" Kith stretched on the hard stone floor, trying to alleviate a nasty punch to the thigh from earlier in the day.

Chase snorted and sat up, eyes sparkling with mirth. "Picture this. Somebody's trying to cheat. They obviously want to get away with it, on as large a scale as possible—only, they can't flaunt it. If they were to just put Lightborn in the top five of every class where they could cheat, that'd be discovered fast. Except, they're clever. They know that everybody's not going to be able to make it through the entire curriculum and become Protectors. So, they have a limit. It's not entirely fixed in stone, but right around the ten-rank mark. Whenever anybody's able to keep within about a five to ten ranks average of what they need in order to pass? They cheat. Regardless how they do it, they adjust the ranking and make sure they have enough to make it past the threshold. Who wants to guess what happens if they're below that?" Chase waggled his eyebrows.

Kith slapped his thigh hard enough that it echoed through the room. "They die! Fury plow my narrow fields—"

"Kith!" Sera admonished.

"Oh, come on, princess. It's not like you haven't heard worse from me." He chuckled. "That is *devious*. It's a full-blown system. If the people who cheated to get into the program in the first place can keep up by themselves in the classes, they don't even have to do anything. If they're just below the limits they'll need, the cheaters will ensure that they reach what's needed. And if they're too close to dropping out, they make sure that they 'die' and still get to keep the one card they've gotten access to."

Chase tapped his nose. "That's exactly it. Now, I'm not a noble, but even I have to admit that's a good deal. Join the Protectors. If you're good enough...or close enough that we can fake it...you'll end up with a full hand of Elemental cards. If you're not good enough, you're still getting one Elemental card."

"What is the end goal?" Sera mused. "I know whoever arranges for this to happen will receive a lot of money. But is that really the end goal? Or is it something more sinister?"

Kith blew a raspberry. "Like we care. Now, we can deliver this and lean back to watch the higher-ups take care of everything. If that doesn't earn us an honorary membership to the Protectors, I don't know what will."

Sera shook her head. "First off, I believe you underestimate the towers' adherence to their principles. Second, you ignore the larger scope."

"'Course I do. It's gotten me to where I am so far." He grinned, warm colors swirling in his sclera. He paused his stretching, blinking, and added in a musing tone, "Of course, where I am is likely about to get me ambushed. Okay, hit us with the larger scope."

"If this is just a minor scheme—one dedicated to granting chosen nobles access to powers otherwise inaccessible, and possibly destabilizing the towers somewhat along the way? Everything is fine. However, what if there is more to it? What if the Lightborn still here among the Protectors have remained, not because they are unaffiliated with this scheme, but because they *are*?"

"Oh." Liam had been performing minor limbering up exercises with the armsmaster's mace. Now, he sat down on his bed and almost brained himself with it as he put his head in his hands. "Oh," he repeated. "That would be bad news. That would mean that there are scores of hostile Lightborn still in and around the towers."

Chase nodded, wide-eyed. "That's not all, either. What about all the former Lightborn Protectors who passed their five years' service and are still in Earth's Ward? Is this an invasion?"

"Exactly." The curly-haired healer pointed out, "We cannot know at this point. The blessing is that we do not *need* to know. This is one headache we can safely pass on to those in charge. But, we need to do so tonight. They should know that we may be in danger. I speculated earlier that they would not care for our safety, compared to their rules. The scope of this...things may have changed. Regardless, I feel we should inform them, before we go out and put ourselves in danger. Whatever happens, they should know, so they will be able to adjust. We might have to take some risks to find who is culpable."

Chase's nostrils flared. He rose from the bed and faced Sera. Slowly, he raised his hand...and then he flicked her nose.

"Ow!"

Looking firmly at Sera with his face way too close to hers, Chase's arm shot out at the others. "We're not fans of rules and laws. We'll abide by them, when they suit us. We just have a few rules ourselves. What is *the* rule on heroics?"

"No heroics," the others droned monotonously.

"That's damn right. No heroics. Heroics get people killed. People with brains run away to win another day. Just a few days ago, we figured that tomorrow would be the chance to find out who was behind everything. Only, now, we have what we need. Meaning, there's no need for unnecessary risks. We do what you say...tell the High Elementalist what's going on and that we're likely to get attacked tomorrow and to please, for the sake of all the damn Elements, make sure that doesn't happen. On top of that, of course, we take whatever steps we need to ensure safety for ourselves, because bureaucracy always gets some things wrong."

For a brief moment, Chase looked taller than he was. His voice rang with command. "Sera. You're in charge of making sure that we can present everything to the High Elementalist in a clear and concise form that she can understand and react to *today*. Copy or transcribe whatever you need. Rope in Liam if you need to—he has a legible hand. Wrap it up in whatever diplomatic flowery speech you need to and make sure the danger is clear."

He looked at each of them in turn. "Liam. Help Sera. Apart from that, make any final preparations we need for our equipment. Sharpen and pack everything that's needed.

"Kith." Chase looked at the Furyborn who lounged on the floor, with a feral glint in his eyes. "Get some sleep right now. Sorry, but you're not sleeping tonight. We need your shadows tonight, peeking through the walls and out into the hallway, to warn us if anybody does try anything inside the towers."

"Sleep? Now that you got me so fired up?" Kith cursed under his breath all the while, but walked out of the room, slamming the door behind him.

"Meanwhile, I'll be thinking of any trick they could pull against us, or any combination we can put together to protect us tomorrow. We've already practiced a lot, but I'm thinking there will be more. Especially with the latest few brilliant additions you've made for us, Cilia."

The smaller crafter looked at him, deadpan. "You left me for last. You're thinking I'll object to your plan?"

"Pits, no. I *know* you'll object to it. That's your part, as always. Make this crap work. Take this hot mess of ideas and tidbits and make sure I don't get us all killed."

Cilia glared at him, sneering.

"No pressure?"

She flung a boot at his head.

In a frenzy of hard work, they came together to prepare for the following day. Most of their preparations had long since been finalized, meaning that the remainder basically came down to last-minute ideas and additions. Cilia and Chase put their heads together, discussing applications of potions and crafted items, combined with their different cards, while Sera monopolized Liam, making him copy out essential passages and numbers from the larger tomes. Chase's idea of just ripping the pages from the books was met with a glare from Sera and a cuff around the neck from Cilia.

Soon, they wound down, and Chase ran off, with an hour to spare before the curfew. He made his way to the administrator in charge and found her diligently looking through a tome that looked dusty enough to make him weep. A minute with her ensured Chase that she took the message seriously and would make certain the High Elementalist would receive it the same day. She would not, however, guarantee that she was going to actually review it on the same day. "The leader of Earth's Ward has many responsibilities, and I cannot decide for her which is the most important. But I will impart on her your exact words. Less the cursing."

Chase decided that was the best they were going to get, returned to the others and told them where that left them. Then, he went to bed in the knowledge that he'd need the rest if he were to make sure his entire family made it safely through the test.

Of course, this translated to him lying in bed, tossing and turning while his brain refused to shut off. After a while, he got up again and paced back and forth, annoyed by how it kept firing. *Why was it acting the way it was?*

Back in Isarn, they'd always been at risk. That was a certainty. Life on the Waves was in a constant flux, with no fixed rule sets, protectors, or authority figures. At any point, you might get jumped. One of the gangs might decide that you were becoming too uppity, somebody would take offense by something you'd done, or the attacker might simply decide that you were too weak, a nice, soft target. Even so, it wasn't *personal* as such. It was just the way things went.

This? It wasn't personal either. But it was operating on an entirely different level. They were being perceived as a threat, not because they were growing stronger, or because they were encroaching on somebody's territory, or something *tangible.* This was all shapes in the fog, unseen threats looming just out of sight, possibly wielding massive powers and looking at you like a piece on a board that stood in the way for them. It was utterly insane. Chase was not meant for this kind of thinking!

Somewhere around midnight, a light knock sounded on his door. Chase leapt straight for the door. *Was it Kith? Was something happening?*

Outside, Sera stood. Her bright curls were tousled and matted on one side, as if she'd been lying down. She didn't face his gaze.

Chase looked to either side of her. Then he exhaled. There was no emergency. No attack.

"Can I come in?" she asked.

He stepped back and let her in. With a soft prod, he closed the door behind her. Then he sat down on the bed and waited for her to join him.

She didn't. Instead, she kept standing, looking disheveled and rather out of it. After a short while, she spoke. "I couldn't sleep. I...was listening outside your door, and I could hear you walking around in here."

Chase raised an eyebrow. "Serafine Valerian. Breaking curfew. What a disgrace."

She smirked. "The hall guard was at the other end of the hallway. And Serafine Valerian has done much worse than this." She trailed off. With a much smaller voice, she continued, looking at the floor. "If I have to be honest, Serafine Valerian was a coddled little brat. I am having trouble, acclimatizing to something like this. Knowing that I will be going out tomorrow, knowing full well that I might be ambushed and die? My nerves are *shot.* How do you do it?"

Chase reached out and grabbed her hand. With a lop-sided grin, he said, "Did you notice *me* sleeping, princess?" Shaking his head, he barreled on. "Death was more common than I'd have liked, growing up on the Waves. You become sort of inured to its presence at some point. That's likely why conflict and violence come easier to us rabble. Death may come to any-body. Our kind more often than not. Yet, it's not something you can avoid forever—so what's a little risk?"

"Why do you do that?" Sera knelt before him with her hand still in his, head tilted slightly in a questioning look. Her voice was measured. "Denigrate yourself? I have only known your tiny family for, what? A few months now? It feels like more. Yet, I know beyond a doubt that you are all stronger, warmer, more caring and thoughtful than any noble I can think of."

He rubbed his thumb over her palm. The difference from when he'd first met her was impressive. She had never been a pampered beauty, too good to do her own work. Yet, she *had* been sheltered, before. Her hand showed the difference. Myriad fresh, small scars and bruises from dueling, calluses from the constant weapon practice. "We know who we are, and who we care about, Sera. The world may look down upon us. What should we care? The only thing that matters—the *only* thing—is what the family thinks. So, sure, we play it off to the world at large, exaggerate our flaws, prove and play off their prejudices. Part of it *is* true. We may be common as muck. Lower than that, even. Yet, to the people who matter, we are worth more than all the titles and wealth on Ordei."

Suddenly, Sera seemed to realize how she was kneeling. She cleared her throat and moved to sit next to him instead, curls spilling forward to obscure the blush on her cheeks.

Chase continued. "How do we get used to it? Well, that part I don't much like. Because it looks like, if you stick with us, you're going to find out for yourself. You get accustomed to the violence, the uncertainty, all of it, learn to react instead of think-ing. I'd rather that none of us had to learn it for ourselves, but here we are. I *can* say that I think you're a quick enough study in, well, whatever you put your head to, that you'll get there."

"I'm not going anywhere." Her words came instantly, with not a shadow of a doubt.

"Good. Because we're not planning on letting you go. Be-sides, if we teach you how to survive in bad company, I was hop-ing you could give me a hand with the high-brow stuff...because all this intrigue crap is *killing* me. I'll take a nice, heated feud with Cornball Nick every damn day. Before you ask, yes, that's his name."

She chortled. Then she looked away, anywhere but at Chase. Finally, she cleared her throat. "Earlier today, when Kith said we were flirting. You know I didn't mean to, right? If I did, it was probably just something subconscious. I..."

Chase smiled at her, looking at her face behind the curtain of bright corkscrews of her locks, until she finally met his gaze. "That's a shame," he said softly. "I *absolutely* meant to flirt with you. Have been for a while, but it's not exactly my strongest suit. I'll back off if you want me to, obviously, but I'm not letting any misunderstandings get in the way. I think you're exactly what nobles *should* be like. You're—"

He didn't get any further. Her lips met his in a rush of flushed skin, shining eyes, and a brilliance to match the sun.

Eventually, they slept.

CHAPTER 39

*"The society of the Elementals can be hard to under-
stand from the outside. Earth's Ward, with its indolence and focus on enjoyment and cheap thrills, clashes hard with the hard-
boiled structure of the towers. Yet, we have one, so we may enjoy the other."* This, I really like. If only we'd gotten more of a
chance to actually enjoy Earth's Ward ourselves. (Page 15.)

"Listen up. You've all been equipped and outfitted.
You look like the sorriest sacks of shit I've ever had
the misfortune to lay my eyes on, and the only thing that can
cure this much ugly is a good fire storm."

The Protector was getting warmed up now. Chase could
tell from the slight hint of color in the cheeks of the ruddy, low-
slung brawler. The earth-aspected Elemental, who, but for his
magical breastplate, looked more like one of the seedy killers
back on the Waves than an actual Protector, had taken them
through the paces this morning. He'd criticized their looks, their
state of preparedness, their equipment and mothers. Then, he'd
graciously allowed those who *didn't* bring full sets of equipment
and weaponry with them from the outside, to add to their own
equipment from the towers' stores, before berating them some
more.

The tower grounds were abuzz with activity. Workers and
Protectors ran everywhere, and carts and runners entered and
left the place in a continuous stream. In the courtyard, constructions arose in preparation for the next batch of recruits who
would arrive to be tested on the following day.

The Protector attending them ignored it all. "What's going to happen today is this. You are going to go out there, each
of your so-called teams of toddlers attached to a *real* team. You
are going to get a taste of what the actual work of the Protectors
is like. Then, you're going to be bored to frigging tears for hours
on end, because most of our work *is* hopelessly boring. But
you're going to focus and you're going to do your best to stay
alert, because otherwise you're going to be failed directly. One
or two of your teams may see some hint of what the actual work
of a Protector is like, though it's not likely that we see any hostile
Guardians. When and if that happens? You'd better hope you remember what they taught you up there." He pointed up to the
towers. "Because we'll be standing back and taking notes. Protector Erram. Did I forget anything?"

The robe-wearing Furyborn next to him who'd spent the time picking her nose sneered. "I liked your speech yesterday better. *I have a hangover. Stay quiet and follow, maggots.*" With a braying laughter, she turned on her heels and strode away for the stables.

The animals weren't scary. In fact, they were as far from scary as could possibly be. For some reason, that struck Chase as wrong. The steeds that brought the Protectors out to defend the towers should be intimidating, shouldn't they? Instead, they were low-slung, insectile beasts with an uncannily long and wide hairy body. To Chase, they looked like what would happen if you inflated a centipede to a hundred times its size and crossed it with a coarse, hairy rug. Then you gave the abomination saddles.

Regardless, once he strapped into the well-worn, comfortable saddle, he realized that it wasn't half bad. The long, many-legged beasts had a gait that slightly jerked him about, yet was surprisingly steady and fast to boot. They could carry at least a dozen per beast, but the beast Chase and his crew rode on only held ten: the four-man team going with them, an animal handler lounging near the head of the beast, and themselves.

By now, they had all been back out in Earth's Ward for certain exercises, field trips, or simply for them to see former Protectors who had settled into regular careers after the service. Still, they had never been there as today, going out to actually do the work of Protectors, stand between the Elementals and the world as a whole.

At first, it was barely noticeable. A wide-eyed glance here. A tiny dip of the head there. Yet, when Chase started to notice it, it became increasingly obvious. Protectors were honored. Not just respected or admired. There was hero worship here, that was for sure, but the sensations were different. There was warmth, a sensation of being accepted, an *embrace.*

An old woman carrying a basket with vegetables nearly as large as herself beamed a toothless smile at him. A town guard, reeling from alcohol, nevertheless managed a sloppy salute and growled, "Fire 'em up!" A grizzled old enchanter looked up past the piece he was investigating in his roadside stall and shouted, "Show them the Pits, youngster."

Everywhere they moved, they were adored; they were accepted and treated as heroes. Chase knew crowds. He knew people, and when people faked. This was *real*. The people of Earth's Ward genuinely adored their Protectors.

Oh, there were darker sensations there as well. Waves of resentment, of envy. Sometimes even hate. Yet, in the sea of support, it drowned and became irrelevant, as they were carried through the city and toward the outer gates.

The team they had been assigned barely looked at the people surrounding them. Still, they felt it too. There was a grace to them, a mutual respect, and wherever their gazes rested on the citizens, they nodded and greeted as courteously as could be expected.

In front of him, a Liberty male with a short, curved bow placed on his lap turned around. He emanated danger. His bald head gleamed in the sun above pointy ears, his sharp eyes attentive even at ease. Everything about him was immaculate, every inch from the gleaming bald pate to the finely trimmed beard portraying somebody in control. His voice came forth as a warm rumble. "Hope you're enjoying the attention, kids. Now, we go to earn it."

Chase mulled it over. There was something there. Something rare and unknown for him. Something he couldn't quite touch. Back in Isarn, other people had always been there. A few were friendly, even somebody Chase respected. Most were a bland, faceless mass—potential, above all. Potential risks, potential marks, potential inadvertent helpers in a headlong flight. Not truly people. More a resource.

Yet here...there was more. There was an understanding between Protectors and the people. It wasn't all one-sided. The respect and adoration were real. Yet, there was respect going the other way, too. Protectors—at least the good ones—*cared*. They cared about protecting the city, about maintaining the equilibrium—and they weren't afraid to pay the ultimate price. Chase had to admit that the sensation rankled at him. Mostly, because he'd never had anything like that. Only...if they made the towers their home, he felt that he eventually might. Another sensation in the pit of his stomach questioned whether they were going to make it that far. The High Elementalist had not gotten back to them. *What did that mean? Had she read their report? Did she disagree? Had she arranged for protection somehow?* The questions gnawed at him, and he tried to push them down, failing often as not.

They left Earth's Ward behind and rode out into the surroundings, taking the northern path. When they arrived, their eyes were glued to Earth's Ward and the towers at its center, the impressive architecture and promises of power drawing the gaze away from the lands leading up to the walls. In the meantime, they'd learned a lot about their surroundings and knew what to look for—and everything suddenly looked a lot more impressive than when they'd arrived.

The miles upon miles of agricultural lands were multi-hued, and busy. The myriad huge fields were sown with diverse crops and attended to by massive teams of workers. Yet, they were clearly not the result of agriculture alone. The earth itself had been adjusted, creating perfectly level ground and magically enriched to grow more fertile, and supported by an intricate arrangement of irrigation channels. Among the large teams of workers, others walked, imposing figures who were dressed richer, carried themselves with the assurance of veterans. There were Elemental mages, retired Protectors, whose control had been adjusted to benefit the city in other ways. There were crafters, adjusting large totem-like poles jutting from the ground or attending to huge, ritual-like glowing circles inscribed on the ground itself. Yet, where, upon their entry, it had all looked chaotic and overwhelming, now they started to see the system in it, how everything flowed and worked together.

Cilia pointed out a few constructions that stood out among the many agriculturally aligned creations. Liberally mixed among the fields stood small, square earthen constructions reminiscent of the ones adorning the towers. Large tubes pointed away from the city at regular intervals, glowing lightly with arcane symbols that Cilia explained constituted large-scale weapons that drew magic from the surroundings and channeling them into the tubes, to be released upon any enemies who made it this far. Also, every second mile or so, a tall guard tower jutted into the sky, with alert non-carded soldiers keeping a watch on their surroundings, looking for messages from the towers, intruders, or anything out of the ordinary. Specific magical crops were walled off and well-guarded.

As they moved farther out, the scope of the constructions became clear. There was no space wasted, little break between the fields and the martial defenses. On top of that, Chase knew, some space would be planted with traps, known to the defenders and the workers, but not visible to the untrained eye of an invader.

Traffic was busy, even though it was still early in the day: foot traffic, trader carts, and, once, a large herd of wald-cattle, the massive, rat-shaped beasts famous for the tenderness of their meat.

Finally, they reached the Colored Ramparts. Chase was hit by the same sense of awe he had when they arrived from the other direction, except, now that he knew what he was looking at, it was even more spectacular.

The multicolored, flamboyant construction was beyond impressive. Twenty feet tall and twice that in width; closed, to prevent fliers from entering; magically fortified, with only small openings for defenders to use for firing at any inbound enemies. Those were just the well-known details of its construction. Their classes had imparted plenty of additional information. For instance, not all sections of the wall were defended at all times.

Most were empty, to be occupied and held in times of trouble—monster waves and enemy armies. Yet, those that were occupied were separated, allowing soldiers to secede from a section of the wall and retreat to the next ones, without allowing the enemies to pass *through* the wall. Tunnels were heavily trapped and even rigged for collapse or worse, in case the enemy penetrated sections of the defense.

They didn't stop at the Ramparts, though. Instead, they were waved through the open gates, and moved forward, soon veering off on one of the many side paths. Now, they started to see the occasional Protector team, waving or nodding as they passed. On top of that, traffic died down to a minimum the farther they went.

"Why don't all Protectors defend the Ramparts?" Kith asked. It was the first time anybody had spoken for a long time, and the loud question caught everybody's attention.

The Protector ahead of Chase smirked. "I'm sure you've heard the answer to that in your World Knowledge classes."

Kith snorted. "Sure. The Protector needs to be a lot of things. A defender, a diplomat, a courtesan, and a cobbler. I just don't see why we can't do all that *behind* the nice, safe walls."

The bald Liberty archer grunted something that might be a laugh. "I'm sure Professor Brookwatch just *loves* you. There're two answers to that, son. First one is that, if we were to hole up in the Ramparts, all nice and comfy, it'd be too easy to take us down. Sure, they're defensive and all...but if our enemies could walk right up to us without getting spotted or softened up beforehand, some high-Tier cards could do some nasty damage on the Ramparts and those inside. That, or they could just tunnel through, fly over...plenty of options. We need people out front to spot what's happening and react properly. Second answer's a little grim, but you look like you can handle it."

He frowned at Kith. "Think about what'd happen if we were all holed up inside the walls. Me, I have my bow. I'd be soaking up Ænima like nobody's business. But what about one-hand there? Or your big guy? They'd have to wait until the enemies broke through to the inside, and I don't have to tell you that doesn't happen too often." The ranged shrugged. "We'd end up with some seriously under-strength classes. How long would the Elemental lands survive, if we didn't have anybody capable of taking a hit, or healing those who're hurt?"

Sera spoke up. "Besides, there would be no chance for the teams to earn as much experience fighting together inside the walls. The towers depend on the cooperation of their teams for their strength, so sacrificing the chance for practicing your teamwork would be a losing proposition."

"You've got it, blondie," the man said. "That's why we're even taking rookies like you out. You need to earn the Ænima. If you don't, you'll be letting down the towers. And a couple'a deaths are well worth that cost." Having delivered that message, he turned back around and let the others share glances in silence.

More than an hour and a half after the departure from the towers, they arrived at their destination: a nondescript meeting of three well-worn paths, apparently in the middle of nothing and nowhere. A few miles behind them, the Kaleidoscopic Ramparts waited, a comforting presence, while, ahead of them, the far edge of the Elemental lands was not clearly delineated.

The Protector team leapt off their transport beast and shared a few words with the handler. Then, once the rest of them were off, massaging behinds unused to this form of movement, the beast laboriously turned in a wide circle and trotted at a placid pace back toward the city again.

The ranged stretched his back, taking in the vista, before turning back to them with a wicked grin. "Who is ready to risk their lives, then?"

CHAPTER 40

The bond between Protectors...it is inviolable, tougher than steel. This family of risk-takers, gathered in a common goal, willing to make the ultimate sacrifice to defend that which they believe in. Yet, there is one bond stronger—that between a Protector team. Risking your life together on a weekly basis? You cannot break that bond. I'd agree...if it weren't for all the evidence to the contrary we just delivered to the High Elementalist. It makes for a less convincing argument. (Page 94.)

"I don't envy the poor bastards who have to teach you lazy slugs back in the towers." Another of the Protectors turned out to be the spokesman for the lot, though clearly not because of his diplomacy. The tall, air-aspected Elemental looked like a tanner who accidentally decided to cure his own hide. He was nearly orange with sunburn, and his skin looked leathery and like it was pulled tight against his bony skeleton. They couldn't tell his class from the looks alone—he wore regular chainmail over boiled leather, yet carried a steel-capped quarterstaff. "Some of you may be all right. Still, there are way too many slackers among the lot. Personally, I think they should have this event right at the start of the year, check your resolve right away." His cadaverous grin was more hideous than infectious. "Apparently, they prefer that less of you die, though. Guess we need to accommodate them."

The man waved with his arms to the wide-open steppes beyond. "This here impressive ground is officially called the arse-end of nowhere. The Pits are we doing out here, then? Well, you'll get the chance to prove how you handle boredom. And if we're lucky, you get some blood on those fancy recruit uniforms of yours. That brings us to my favorite part of this 'ere game. Because in a moment me and my friends are going...to take a nap. We'll be leaving you to handle everything."

Chase blinked. *Was this the trap?* He reached for his sheath, ready for anything.

The Protector spotted his movement and laughed uproariously. "Fire-touched newbie. You see any enemies?" He shook his head. "Time to apply everything you've learned, idiots. Our section today is a rarely used approach to the city. A few roads converge around here, from a few northern Lightborn cities and the occasional batch of Liberty tradesmen. If we get attackers, they might be Liberty, Lightborn, or unaspected Guardians, or a fun mix. Any questions?"

Chase took a deep breath. It seemed like this was just a regular part of the test.

Cilia stepped up. "We can handle ourselves. What is your task in this event?"

The sickly-looking man smirked. "Like I said. A nap. Well-deserved, I might add." He chortled. "We're also keeping an eye on you rookies, of course. If you make any horrible mistakes, we step in. If you're about to get yourself killed through ignorance, we step in. Also, if there's a challenge that somebody like you isn't supposed to be able to handle. Mostly, we make it in time. But life here on the edge is an uncertain one. So, I recommend you take this as seriously as if we weren't there to begin with."

Chase found his tongue. "At which point is asking you questions acceptable?"

"Let's call that part of the test. If we need to go to you, you'll see it reflected in your rankings. If you come to us and ask a dumb question? Same thing. Clever questions reflect well on you." The man stretched and pointed at a patch of grass some hundred feet back. "Now, that spot right there looks nice and comfy. Don't get yourselves killed. Or if you do, don't wake me up. I'm cranky when I wake. We're going back twelve hours from now."

"I'm guessing this isn't an ambush?" Kith asked.

They stood in a group ahead of the Protectors, letting their eyes roam over the terrain beyond. Liam positioned himself to have a clear view of everything, not letting the Protectors out of his sight. He was the highest ranked among them, and they decided that it would be worth it to ensure that the Protectors didn't jump them undetected.

"Is it the lack of blood that gave it away?" Cilia snapped. She shook her head. "Sorry. The lack of a response from the High Elementalist has me cranky."

Kith waved it away. "Never mind. We never did find any hints what the test was, did we?"

Chase responded. "No. Only the fact that it was real enough that some recruits do die. I'm thinking this can't be all, though. Just putting us out here at random won't ensure that we're tested. Whatever we are going to meet, we will see coming from miles ahead, and the odds of things coming our way instead of to any of the other Protectors—or recruits, I suppose—on the horizon, aren't really that high." He tapped his lip. "Except, of course, if they cheat, somehow."

With conviction, Sera said, "Regardless, our recourse remains the same. Act as we have been taught. Keep our eyes open in *any* direction. Act as if our lives are on the line—because they are. I wouldn't want us to have wasted all those nice gifts from the High Elementalist."

They'd consumed most of them. It seemed like the right choice, when they learned the potions lasted for up to a full day. There was this one event between them and safety, and holding back seemed like a horrible idea—especially when they were expecting an ambush. They poured down the costly potions like they were cheap ale, only keeping those in reserve that they thought would be an absolute waste, like giving Cilia a Strength potion. One by one, they lined up their attributes, so they could see where they were at.

> Personal Info:
> Name: Cilia
> Title: Dark/Elemental/Light crafter
> Step: 13 (Tier 2)
> Strength: 12 (+1 Tier bonus) = 13
> Agility: 17 (+1 Tier bonus) (+5) = 23
> Toughness: 14 (+1 Tier bonus) (+5) = 20
> Mental Power: 24 (+7 Tier bonus) = 31
> Potential: 11 (+1 Tier bonus) = 12

Cilia, in her training, had managed to earn another point to Strength. This, on top of her decent Agility and Toughness, had her at a point where she'd be able to stave off or outmaneuver some of the weaker fighters, at least if they didn't use their cards. With the potions whirling through her system, she was fast and tough enough that she'd be able to outpace even some rogues.

> Personal Info:
> Name: Serafine
> Title: Dark/Elemental/Light healer
> Step: 11 (Tier 2)
> Strength: 14 (+1 Tier bonus) (+5) = 20
> Agility: 17 (+1 Tier bonus) (+5) = 23
> Toughness: 15 (+1 Tier bonus) (+5) = 21
> Mental Power: 27 (+7 Tier bonus) (+5) = 39
> Potential: 12 (+1 Tier bonus) = 13

Sera, as well, had managed to earn another point to Strength. This, on top of downing all potions she had, had the healer near to bursting from the energy roaming around inside her. Although she was still no fonder of physical combat than when they'd met her, she was growing accustomed to it. At this point, she was becoming more than adept at using sword breakers for disarming enemies, and her Mental Power made her split-second decisions sharper, faster, more efficient.

Personal Info:
Name: Liam
Title: Dark/Elemental/Light fighter
Step: 13 (Tier 2)
Strength: 15 (+7 Tier bonus) (+5) = 27
Agility: 14 (+1 Tier bonus) (+5) = 20
Toughness: 23 (+1 Tier bonus) (+5) = 29
Mental Power: 13 (+1 Tier bonus) = 14
Potential: 10 (+1 Tier bonus) = 11

Liam, in a show of companionship, had taken to joining Kith in his ever-present quest to better his Mental Power, and had earned another point for himself. Apart from that, he was growing into an absolute physical powerhouse. There were just a handful of other fighters among their class who outmatched him, attribute-wise, at this point, and at this rate he would be in the top three within the month.

Personal Info:
Name: Kith
Title: Dark/Elemental/Light summoner
Step: 14 (Tier 2)
Strength: 16 (+1 Tier bonus) (+5) = 22
Agility: 17 (+1 Tier bonus) (+5) = 23
Toughness: 14 (+1 Tier bonus) (+5) = 20
Mental Power: 17 (+1 Tier bonus) (+5) = 23
Potential: 11 (+7 Tier bonus) = 18

Although Kith's attributes seemed to be on the lower end of their group, that was for a simple reason. He was the only one who needed every single attribute, even if it had taken him some time to come around to accepting the necessity of improving his Mental Power. His dogged persistence, however, earned him yet another point to Mental Power, and he was catching up on the competition in the summoner ranks. Also, he insisted that he could *feel* the third Tier, just in reach.

Personal Info:
Name: Chase
Title: Dark/Elemental/Light rogue
Step: 18 (Tier 3)
Strength: 16 (+1 Tier bonus) (+5) = 22
Agility: 20 (+9 Tier bonus) (+5) = 34
Toughness: 17 (+1 Tier bonus) (+5) = 23
Mental Power: 15 (+1 Tier bonus) (+5) = 21
Potential: 26 (+1 Tier bonus) = 27

Chase had earned himself another point to Agility. Although he was constantly grateful for his card boosting training results, he hadn't quite realized just how grateful he ought to be. His increases had been meteoric, and Kith, who had always been his physical superior, had been left in the lurch. He could clearly visualize how he would eventually be able to outrace even Liam's prodigious Strength, as long as they kept up their training. In fact, this might just be the single best way for him to keep his family safe.

Safe in the knowledge that they were as strong and ready as they were going to get, they settled into an easy silence, as they kept an eye on the horizon and the few people visible from far away. Shortly, time started passing by, with only a few chats to break the silence. Only a few persons seemed to be moving in their direction while others seemed to be walking or riding for other checkpoints.

"I wonder how many Protectors there really are. We never did learn that, did we?" Liam mused.

"Two thousand, five hundred, give or take," Sera said. At the shocked silence, she shrugged. "What? This is simple math. We are between ten and twelve miles out from the towers. There is maybe 0.8 miles from us to the next group in the circle and typically five persons in a group. That makes for maybe forty to forty-five groups. Allowing for rotations, other postings—"

Liam snorted. "We know you're smart. No reason to make stuff up because you were lucky enough to find the answer in a document somewhere."

"What?" Her mouth gaped open, too shocked to even come up with a proper response.

"Yeah." Kith put a hand on her shoulder. "It's all right. But I do like knowing that you're petty enough to lie about something as simple as this."

Despite their hazing, they stayed focused and applied some of the many teachings they'd learned in the different classes. Combat training taught them to stagger their activity, ensuring that, when they had a twelve-hour shift like this one, unless needed, they'd have one person resting at all times in order for everybody to get a chance to rest. In this case, the resting person just happened to keep an eye on the group of Protectors relaxing behind them.

The hours passed more slowly than they had any right to. Watching the groups and persons move on the plains ahead of them in glacial tempo showed them that patience would be an absolute necessity in this position. Obviously, they'd been placed way out on the outskirts for this test, showing that the point wasn't to check their capability to deal with the people swarming to Earth's Ward.

Eventually, a few people did show up. The first was a dirt-covered family of Lightborn, walking the route. They were poor and had few possessions besides the packs on their backs and the baby in a sling. According to their explanations, they were going to Earth's Ward to find work with a family caravan arriving from the south. Once the family answered the standard questions, they were allowed to continue on their way.

The next to arrive, hours later, was a large cart, pulled by six persons of different races. According to the group, they were from the same area and decided to band together for safer travels. Their plan was to go to the market outside Earth's Ward and sell various crafted materials, and return with seeds and other needed purchases for their village. The items backed up their explanation, but Chase noticed one of their group acting nervous. After a brief chat with the others, they decided to search the man and his belongings, and found a bag of dried herbs tied within a fake bottom in his backpack.

They took the bag to the Protectors, who collectively bowled over in laughter. "That's frostburn. Not the first time and not the last. It's for smoking, and the Church of the Circle don't like it." He shouted at the top of his lungs, *"It's legal here, you dimwits!"* Turning back to Chase, he rolled his eyes. "Send 'em on their way, and give the moron a clap around the earhole. Good eyes, kid."

After that experience, they were faced with a whole lot of waiting around and doing nothing. They stayed alert for several hours, eating in shifts, taking breaks and using the exercises they'd been taught to ensure they kept an eye on anything that might be suspicious.

Around the halfway mark, Sera stood tall. "Attention," she barked, her voice uncommonly demanding. "A few hundred feet out, behind and to the right of the mile marker. What do you see?"

They leapt to their feet, suddenly fully awake and aware.

"Something moving. Like a heat haze, only localized. It's got to be magic," Cilia assessed.

"Or a card," Chase added. "This could be a cloaking effect." He squinted and tried to get a hold of the dimensions involved. It was like looking at the water and trying to divulge something from the ripples. "Looks like several somethings. Has to be either monsters or a group effect."

Kith glanced over his shoulder to where the Protectors were still lounging, apparently oblivious to what was coming. "Do we alert them or handle it ourselves?"

"Both," Cilia said. "Protocol says we must always be alert to our surroundings and report any observations." She turned around and yelled to the Protectors, "Reporting a sighting. Unsure if monsters or card wielders." Turning back around, she asked tersely, "How do we figure out—"

"Way ahead of you." Chase grinned. His sling was a blur already, fully in motion. He released the leather at the precise point of the arc, engaged his Squall Sling to double the speed, and watched the smooth rock hurtle through the air, straight at the center of one of the incoming blurred areas.

One second, there was nothing there but a blur, a vaguely fuzzy area where you could see the ground underneath as well as the space behind it. The next, a large canine with a blockish, weirdly angular shape, reared back, howling from where the rock struck it on the hindquarters. The other shapes remained cloaked.

"Guardians. Lightborn, I think. I'm counting five," Cilia shouted.

From behind them, a piercing whistle rang out from the Protector group, three short and one long blows. They were getting to their feet, preparing weapons and loosening limbs. Yet, they did not move in, staying back to watch what the group would do. In the far distance, the whistle signal was repeated. Moments later, a series of flashes, from way back up on the towers, responded.

Chase took one look at the beast, as it resumed its effortless lope toward their group, now with a slight limp. "All right. We can do this. Liam, out front. Kith, summons up...face them up front with Liam. Sera, buff us and assist. Cil, help me reveal them and make sure we don't have any more incoming."

"Fire droplets?" Cilia asked.

"Fire droplets. A couple for a test, more if need be."

They were her latest creation, the eventual perfection of the experimental item she'd tossed at the behemoth. Small, tightly compressed beads made out of soft leather. The tightly stitched and compressed pellets looked like nothing extraordinary, except she'd woven fire into every single one of them. Any hard impacts made the things unfurl and release the fire for a small explosion and lingering fire damage. They were dangerous to handle and be around—and she was very proud of them.

Chase and Cilia worked in tandem, iron pellets and fire droplets flying out to greet the heretofore unrevealed canines. Knowing what kind of shapes they were dealing with helped immensely—as did the boost to Agility that arrived to buff all of them, as Sera activated her Spark of Divinity card. In quick succession, four additional beasts were revealed. One came to groggily, its head having been rocked back by one of Chase's pellets, boosted by Squall Sling. Another growled and whined, from where the fire damage of a fire droplet caught on its fur, making small waves of flame rush over its neck and blockish shoulders.

"The final one's staying too far back," Cilia snapped. "I'll keep an eye on it."

"Good," Chase answered. Raising his voice, he ordered, "Go all out from the start. We want to reduce their numbers quickly if we can. Keep alert for any surprises. I'm on ranged. Let's see if I can't do some real damage."

At this point, the five beasts that had been forced out of their camouflage were well and truly angry. They loped toward them with massive snarls, sharp teeth contorted in furious grimaces. However, the attacks had them arriving displaced, with a bit of distance between the foremost three, and the final two— the one which had been struck in the head, and the one that was still on fire.

This left their front line squaring off with the canines on a one-to-one basis. Liam was front and center, beating his truncheon on his large shield to draw their attention. Behind him and to the right, Kith waited, hand axes gripped tightly with a ghastly glow to him from having the Divine Mentor summoned to guide his movements and aid his attributes. His eyes slowly came into focus, as his other summoned card activated on Liam's right side. The hideous summons from the Crescendo of Might card immediately started to grow, fleshy protuberances emerging even as it began to fall forward toward the enemies.

The collision between the two groups, when it happened, was anything but the controlled clashes they were used to from their Combat Training classes. One moment, the large hounds leapt forward, eerily silent, each of the three hounds sizing their separate enemy up. The next, they veered off and all converged on Liam, barking and snarling at him, before their ugly fangs snapped out to rend tendons and drag him to the ground.

Liam wasn't having any of it. He calmly retreated, shield held in place close to the ground, truncheon rising and falling at a rapid pace. "Armor!" he called out, voice strained. "The bulk on their fronts is armor. Hard to break."

Kith hesitated for a split second, then he and his summons charged in tandem, moving in on the canines from either side of Liam.

The summoned creature didn't play fair. It didn't attack properly, didn't strike and return. Instead, it slowly fell forward and smothered one of the canines below it. Its five—no, six— flabby, sausage limbs all hit, kicked, and punished the canine, even as the ugly thing kept growing in size.

Kith guided his axes down with a certainty and inevitability that belied his smaller frame. He had spent a lot of time practicing using the weapons independently of each other. Now, it paid off, as the weapons descended toward the midriff and hindquarters of a bestial hound at the same time.

With a dexterous lunge, the beast managed to turn the front of its body, interposing its squarish shoulder instead of its ribs. However, to do that, the hind legs were firmly placed on the ground.

Kith's right axe bounced off harmlessly. The left axe blade, meanwhile, carved deep into the hind leg, nearly severing it. "Hind legs are unprotected!" he shouted triumphantly.

The beast tried attacking him, but the leg couldn't carry the weight and it fell.

His axes were already flying again, twin trajectories moving toward different parts of his enemy.

Next to him, Liam stopped retreating. A flash enveloped him and suddenly he rushed forward, forces of Light following in his wake like a towering, brilliant wave. Where the mace descended, the hound rose to meet it, taking the hit on the neck as its teeth snapped for Liam's face. Except, this time, the momentum of his attack continued, regardless of its defenses, as the powers of the card unleashed. Like a tidal wave, the forces pounded the beast to the ground, flipping it over.

Liam followed up, heavy truncheon rising and falling like a tolling bell of doom. The cracking, crunching sounds that followed his attacks were ugly, wet, and final.

The two remaining hounds had started out practically at the heels of the first. However, Chase kept up his ranged onslaught on them both, and they took a couple of good hits, halting and slowing the beasts. Chase's attacks weren't enough to truly damage them, though a lucky strike might pop out an eye or break a leg. The canines were still fast, though, and bore down on the already engaged front liners.

Sera rushed past Kith, who was still dismantling his enemy.

Chase felt the fleeting rush as Agility faded from his body, and Sera changed the buff to Strength.

In the face of the two remaining canines, Sera looked very small. One bloodied, the other covered in still-smoldering fur, they looked like something out of a horror tale. Yet, her sword breakers did not waver for a second. She faced the dogs stoutly, wicked blades ready to pounce on any attacker.

The axe arrived first. One second, the two dogs were converging on Sera from either side. The next, one of Kith's hand axes flew end over end to impact the back of the leftmost canine. It struck hilt first, yet the force was enough that they heard an audible crack.

Sera didn't waste her opening. From either side, the sword breakers struck at the remaining beast. Blood flew, as one blade tore into its ugly face, yet was stopped by the hardened bulk of their armor. With her teeth tightly clenched, she nonetheless let her other attack fly unrelentingly, and the second sword breaker pierced the beast's hind leg twice in quick succession.

Then Liam arrived. He'd ended his first hound and struck the one Kith's axe hit with the unstoppable force of a cart rolling down a hill. His shield slammed sideways into its head, and the truncheon whistled through the air even before it hit the ground.

Kith rushed to catch up—but there was no need. Next to Liam, Sera was dismantling her own latecomer. The Crescendo of Might summons was still fighting with its own bestial enemy, yet the movement from underneath it had nearly stilled, as the summons grew ever larger and stronger.

Chase spoke up cautiously. "Well done. I—"

A whooshing sound interrupted him. From off to the side, a canine shape appeared, keening with fury over the flames rushing across its furry body.

"Caught you!" Cilia announced with satisfaction. "He was trying to sneak around while we were distracted."

Together now, they took down the remaining hound with no issue whatsoever. Fast though it may be, it was no match for their growing attributes, the martial skills, and teamwork that had been beaten into them over the past weeks. Triumphantly, they stood, panting with the exertion and the adrenaline, looking in all directions around them to see whether that was it. Finally, they focused on one thing: the team of Protectors bearing down on them.

CHAPTER 41

"Have there been setbacks over time? Of course there have. Betrayals, overwhelming odds, unknown enemies, skills, or cards. Yet, the one thing Elementals always agree on is that we learn. Learn and adapt, improve for the next time." I approve of the sentiment, of course. Yet, it's funny that they still believe the lie of the Lightborns about the Darkborn. Somebody should tell them. Not me, though. (Page 79.)

They were tense. Ready to act, to defend themselves. Right up until the emaciated Protector started talking.

"That wasn't horrible." He pointed to Cilia. "You there. Good on you for keeping an eye on the surroundings and spotting the last one. Blur hounds are notorious ambush predators. They'll try to weather your attacks, get you off-balance, nip at your feet and back until you're down and at their mercy—and there's often one or more trying to hit you from the back." He looked sternly down at the shorter woman. "However, your gaze kept wandering back to us. We told you we weren't going to be saving you today. Don't let yourself get distracted. That can get you killed."

Chase wanted to applaud the tiny crafter. All of this, and still she'd managed to keep an eye on the Protectors, in case they were going to spring an ambush on them? Impressive!

The air-aspected Protector moved on. "Blondie. Well done on spotting them in the first place. Enemies like these are rare, but not too rare, if you catch my point. Protectors who want to see retirement better keep their eyes open. Also, well done on stepping up to tighten the flanks when needed. Not all healers are ready for that.

"Rogue." The man turned to Chase. "You didn't do much. But you helped reveal them, distracted them, and directed people well. Also, your weapons aren't the best for armored enemies in any case. Best get some enchanted ammunition for that sling, so you can do some real damage.

"Tall guy." He smiled at Liam. "You can stand between me and monsters any day. Decent form. *Good* power.

"You." He bore down on Kith, who was wiping down his axes. "Your approach was reckless and headstrong, and the summoning teachers would roll their eyes at the way you put yourself in harm's way. But your summons tied one enemy down while you handled one yourself. Can't argue with results." He shrugged. "Just one thing for you to learn. If you're gonna make a habit of throwing your weapons away, you'll need to have them balanced for throwing, and get some practice in."

"And have spares," a summoner in a dirty robe strewn with arcane symbols behind him drawled.

"Always have spares." The Protector nodded, while two other Protectors in the background mouthed along with the refrain. He held up a finger, then seemed to think better of it. "Nah. Actually, that was it. Don't worry about the carcasses. We'll summon for some crafters to pick them apart, take anything that's useful. Now, you lot, back to work. You got lucky and were hit with some actual action on your first outing. That's some much-needed Ænima and experience for you. Thank us later. I need to go catch up on my beauty sleep."

The summoner behind him nearly choked on his laughter.

The rest of the shift faded away slowly, as they fought to stay alert, ready for anything in case they were going to get jumped. Except nothing happened. They had a handful of solitary travelers, workers seeking labor, and one fortune seeker who'd heard about the lottery and meant to try his luck to get in. Chase considered telling him it was rigged, but chickened out at the thought of explaining exactly how he knew about that.

They took turns eating, resting, and recuperating, never letting their guard down. Yet, nothing transpired. Finally, a dot in the distance turned into their ride home. The many-legged beast was a welcome sight, and they felt the stress and the exhaustion of the day's encounters.

The moment they were finally back in the saddle, strapped in, Chase allowed himself a sigh of relief. Perhaps the High Elementalist had indeed arranged for protection? Or perhaps they'd simply overreacted and nobody was going to try to jump them. It *would* be very obvious so soon after the death of Instructor Swansong.

Soon, the smooth pace of the beast was trying its utmost to rock him to sleep. He didn't succumb, though. He'd allow himself to relax when he was back in his room and had heard from the High Elementalist—and not a moment before.

Even so, he wasn't the first one to notice something had happened a mile or so down the road. One of the Protectors did, a few seats up on their transportation beast. The Protector rose into a half-standing position and held up his hand.

A low, murmured conversation arose, and within seconds, the beast slowed and stopped.

Their too-thin caretaker jumped off and turned to them. His lined face looked frustrated. "Listen. We've got a bit of a situation here. There's a cart broken down out there." He pointed in the direction away from Earth's Ward, off the beaten paths. "It happens sometimes. Some joker thinks he can take a shortcut and leaves the roads. Then, the cart breaks, his produce goes bad, he loses his livelihood..." He trailed off. "It's a whole thing. Anyway, protocol says we need to investigate. That means a delay for us. You kids stay here with the handler." His ugly face lit into a sarcastic grin. "You'll get to see how real professionals handle themselves. Sit back and enjoy."

The Protectors leapt off the beast and spread out in an easy, much-practiced pattern, before moving forward. The moment they were out of earshot, Chase unbuckled himself and slid off the animal.

The handler called back at him. "Oi. Thought 'e said you're to sit still?"

"Yeah. We're sticking around. Just stretching," he answered. Then, with badly concealed panic, he turned to the rest and gestured for them to get down and join him.

Kith took his time. Yawning widely, he slowly slid off the side of the beast. "What? You seriously can't think—"

"I can and I do. Get down and get ready," he whispered. "This is the perfect time for it. We're tired, our protection's gone, and we're unprepared. *Arm up.*"

They caught the urgency in his voice and readied themselves. Spreading out on either side of the beast so anybody hoping to jump them couldn't hide behind its massive bulk, they prepared themselves as best they could without giving the game away. Fortunately, it had been long enough since their last battle that everything was off cooldown.

Sera engaged Spark of Divinity, adding some extra Toughness to their mix. Kith used Divine Mentor, using it to bolster his attributes and movement speed. Chase engaged his Race of Life, granting himself an extra touch of Agility.

Then they waited. In increasing tension, they observed their surroundings, looking out for everybody and anybody who might seek to do them wrong. In the background, the Protectors moved closer and closer to the ruined cart.

A drop of sweat ran down Chase's spine. They were ready. They'd be able to handle anything—or simply run away. They were but a few miles from the Ramparts. There, they'd be able to hole up against anything. Only, if that were the case, why was he so tense? Maybe it was *because* there was nothing to be seen. The uncertainty of it. It messed with his mind. They'd been so close, and now they were back to wondering again. *Could there be other camouflaged creatures out there? Or perhaps they could be tunneling through the earth.* They'd heard about those. His eyes roamed over the surroundings, looking in all cardinal directions.

He should have looked up.

The cry came in the last possible second. It was Kith, leaning against the round back of their transport animal, relaxing, who slacked from his duty. It was horrible form. Yet, it might have saved their lives.

Chase saw the Furyborn jolt. Then, he screamed, a shocked, torn cry, and knelt near the bulk of the transport animal, even as he pawed at his scabbards for his weapons. *"Fliers!"*

The group reacted with impressive speed. They flung themselves to the ground, moved away, dodged.

It was not fast enough. One moment, Liam was there, right next to them. The next, he simply *disappeared,* thrown sideways from some impact.

Chase nearly caved under the panic. What could they do? *What could they do?* The ingrained training from the past months came back to him then, and he shouted hoarsely, at the top of his lungs. *"Last resort! We go dark!"*

Everything was chaos around them. Chase felt himself buffeted and then he was falling as well. It was the transport beast, screeching with pain and shock, which took off, ignoring the handler's panicked cries. He'd been lucky it was just its flank that pushed him, rather than one of the massive legs.

Chase hit the ground, barely managing to tuck his shoulder under himself, and rolled several times. It still hurt, and he had the breath knocked out of him. He struggled to get to his feet and spotted his dagger, dropped a few feet away. He scrambled for the weapon, even as he saw Cilia out of the corner of his eye, raising something to the sky.

Oh crap, he thought. He leapt onto the dagger, barely finding it with his fingers.

Then the world went dark.

It was part one of a new tactic. If they were ever entirely shocked and needed to reset the board, they would *go dark.* Cilia would use one of her Dark stakes, with them at the center, smothering them in a blanket of shadows and hiding them from attackers for a few seconds. Chase, still on the ground, closed his eyes, screwing them up tight, knowing what was next.

Even behind his eyelids, the light was painfully bright.

Kith hadn't tried the effect often. His Divine Mentor card was simply too useful when it was internalized, guiding his movements and boosting his powers. However, the rare few times he had, it left an impression. The summons could more than just boost Kith's own physical capabilities. It could also be expended, whereupon it would move at supernatural speed to the chosen position, imploding in a burst of blinding light.

In bright daylight, the burst of light was enough to leave you momentarily blinded and disoriented. Following a few seconds' darkness? The sensation felt like the light of the sun itself! Yet, even before the light had fully faded, Chase was scrambling back on his feet, trying to gain his bearings.

Around him, loud cries preceded struggling shapes hitting the packed soil of the dirt road.

With dots everywhere in his vision, Chase saw what they were dealing with. They were small, human-shaped—as long as said humans were child-sized—with wide, bat-like wings, the sharp teeth of carnivores, and held long, pointed weapons in their thin claws.

The nearest had impacted just a few feet away from him. With one arm lying at an awkward angle, its legs drummed on the ground in obvious pain.

Chase slid knees first over the soil and brought down his dagger fast and hard several times, stabbing the creature in the neck, the throat, anywhere exposed. "Grimbolds!" he shouted. "Take the downed ones out now."

Grimbolds were a pest, rather than actual monsters, usually. The smallish creatures were omnivores, ravenous, mean, and utterly without self-control. They were known for descending on solitary homesteads, stealing and eating anything that wasn't nailed down. They were not above taking out the occasional traveler, stealing away unattended livestock or even children.

They were *not* known for attacking armored people. What little brains they had helped them avoid the most dangerous encounters.

As Chase scrambled to the next downed grimbold and impaled it through the ear, he heard a loud *whoomph*, followed by Cilia's strained voice. "These aren't wild. They're Guardians of Light. They'll fight to the death."

Chase cursed, as he looked around to find his next target. About ten feet away, one grimbold knelt, clawed hands pressed hard against the ground. Chase charged at it with a wild swing, but the small pest managed to take off, screeching furiously at the bleeding wound near its heel. As it disappeared upward, wings flapping franticly, he noticed that, true enough, the claws and eyes held a glowing light, proving exactly who'd sent the bastards.

From above, movement alerted him to an attack, and he flung himself back, watching the dart embedding itself into the soil right in front of his nose. It glistened with something disgusting.

A brief glance confirmed his thoughts. Their reprieve was over. "We go defensive! Circle up!" he shouted and ran for where Liam stood back-to-back with Cilia.

Liam...did not look well. Blood dripped from a deep wound in his back. From the looks of it, the only reason he was even standing was that a heal from Sera managed to close most of the wound. Still, he looked drawn, and his movements were sluggish. His face looked grey, too.

"Poison!" Chase shouted, realization coming to him too late.

A glow centered on Liam, covering him head to toe, as his Cleansing Fire card activated. The glow burned from within, then dissipated. A second later, he blinked, as if he were coming to his senses.

From above, the enemies hovered in a swarm of claws, teeth, and menace. Screeches and shouts drowned out most noise, as the pests communicated in their own animalistic language. There were at least two dozen of them still alive, even with the first handful down.

Chase came to a conclusion. The Protectors were nearby, and there was no way they hadn't spotted what was going on by now. They just needed to fend for themselves until they made it back over to help them. "Fully defensive!" he shouted. "Sera. Liam. Kith. That summon of yours, Kith. Take a side, fend them off. Cilia, in the center. If they cluster up, throw a stake into their midst. That should keep them divided. I'll ruin their day."

"Switching to Dark. They're Lightborn. We'll want to weaken any effects," Sera shouted. A second later, a dark flash from her right arm announced that she'd switched to Blessing of the Night that would double their own buffs and halve any Light effects.

With a growl, Chase made a decision, going with Steps of Brilliance and Race of Life over Sticky Fingers and Nights of Criffhaven. The group of Protectors was less than half a mile away. Mobility and a quick boost would see him through this...he hoped. The nine additional Agility also wouldn't hurt.

There was a split second of indecision, as if the beasts wavered, their questionable inborn intellect combating whatever drew them to attack. Then they descended, in a whirlwind of claws and throwing weapons.

They made it almost halfway. That was when a stake, flung by Kith, greeted the foremost grimbold in the center of its sunken chest. Right afterward, a circle of darkness exploded outward from the creature, covering anybody but the outermost creatures in shadows. The creatures on the edges continued their dive, but the ones emerging from within the effect arrived rattled and confused, half of them veering off with the rest, acting with anything but coherence.

Even so, five or six arrived in one concerted wave. They flung darts ahead of their assault and dove to charge the defensive circle simultaneously, gliding to spot the best point of attack.

Chase knew what he had to do. He didn't like it, but he knew it. He burst into a sprint. The grimbolds ignored him. With his trajectory, he'd cross their path, but far under their dive. There'd be no way for him to jump up to them.

Good thing he didn't have to.

Activating Steps of Brilliance, he climbed into the air. He placed the three steps at a steep angle, taking him nearly ten feet into the air. From the tallest step, he flung himself forward and up—straight into the path of the descending beasts. He arrived, dagger-first, driving it deep, deep into the side of the leading attacker.

To say that the grimbolds were shocked would be the understatement of the century. Two veered off. Another flailed defensively as it continued its descent, hitting nothing but air. One folded its wings protectively around itself which, one might add, is not an excellent survival strategy if you're flying close to the ground. The one Chase stabbed looked down at him, pain and confusion warring in its gaze. Then the eyes rolled up in its head and it dropped like a stone, Chase with it.

Having forty-three Agility was amazing. It allowed him to run at a speed unmatched by any non-wielders, perform movements that looked inhumanly elegant. Unfortunately, it did not help defy gravity. Having embedded the dagger deep in the body of the grimbold, Chase's legs continued dipping underneath the beast. He fell toward the ground, back-first.

He twisted his body to avoid falling flat on his back. That didn't do anything about the ground coming closer, fast. It did allow him to land on his side and roll end over end, instead of hitting dead center on his back or even his neck.

Chase picked himself up with a groan. He stood, slowly, painfully. Somehow, he'd managed to keep hold of his dagger *and* avoid stabbing himself. *Well done.* He turned his gaze on the others. The two grimbolds who'd continued their attacks were down. Liam raised a gore-dripping truncheon as he searched the sky for his next target. Kith pounded another beast into the ground, hand axes rising and falling with finality. Sera was off to the side, stabbing both weapons into the neck of the still-squirming grimbold that had crash-landed outside their circle. She rose, then pointed above Chase and said something.

He didn't hear it. However, he very much noticed the form that struck the freshly formed shield around him and bounced off. Chase shook his head, senses coming back to him. "Right. Enemies everywhere." He dropped down, finishing the stunned grimbold, thanking Sera in his heart for switching to her Cry for Blood card, allowing her to both shield and heal them.

The others returned to their defensive positions. Now, the grimbolds circled them from above, in a wide, bestial tornado comprised of claws and malevolence.

Liam tossed his own stake, hitting one of the beasts, which tumbled to the ground with a nasty, crunching impact as the circle of darkness burst into being high up in the air. This time, the rest of the monsters adjusted quickly, moving lower to simply avoid the shadow-covered area.

Chase cursed. He saw the Protectors in the distance. They were definitely moving back now, shouting something he couldn't hear. He flung his own stake, hitting one in the shoulder.

It didn't help. Seconds later, their circle reformed. Darts started to rain down on them from above.

Cilia plucked a dart out of her shoulder, hissing in pain. "I'm poisoned!"

Sera yelled, "Hang in there. I can switch to Tongues of Pride to cleanse it, but not for almost an hour."

Chase used his throwing daggers. Cilia flung her fire droplets. A few of the small shapes fell out of the sky. Yet, it was too little, too late. There were still at least eighteen of the small bastards flying around, attacking from a distance.

First Sera, then Kith cursed as darts hit them. Fortunately, the poison was weak and slow-working. However, if they didn't do anything, it *would* bear them down. The Protectors were still too far away to save them.

Chase prepared for another use of Steps of Brilliance. He might be able to cause some confusion up there, even if he wouldn't be able to make a huge difference, buy some time.

He moved too late.

With a muttered curse, Kith broke out of their defensive circle. Something flashed on his chest, then he *yowled* at the sky and flung first one, then the other hand axe at the whirling pests. They both hit an enemy. Where they struck, the enemies didn't react as much as implode. One hit a grimbold in the chest armor, another in the throat. Both folded up on the wound and dropped to the ground without a single twitch to show they'd ever been alive.

For once, the Furyborn lived up to the core part of his racial name. Unarmed, bleeding, and scuffed, eyes whirling with deep, tempestuous colors, he shouted at the skies, *"You want to test me? I'll take you all at once!"* He circled around, taunting the fliers one after the other, empty hands reaching out for any takers.

With what little intelligence the creatures had, they had to react. Whether it was the taunts, the kills, or the solitary, unarmed enemy standing outside the defensive circle, they whooped and screeched as they went for the kill.

The others stood frozen for a moment, wide-eyed at the suicidal choice. Then the silence broke.

Sera spoke first. "I'll shield him." A shimmering shield came into existence, and broke moments later, as a dart struck the surface and pinged off. She cursed.

The others reacted all at once. Liam started forward, only to be shoved aside by Kith's summons. The lumbering shape had by now grown to at least twice its original size. It gleamed from within, in lines and streaks, like a much-mended vase lit up from within by a candle. It was surely close to bursting. Yet, it thundered in a straight line after Kith.

Chase realized the game. He cursed. *"He's playing bait. Stupid bastard. We follow him, use the confusion. Take out those we can. Sera, Liam, keep him alive. Cilia and I do what damage we can."* That said, he grasped his dagger and sprinted off to follow his insane brother through the tempest of enemies.

There was a reason Kith never was picked to play bait, back when they lived in Isarn. Although he was strong enough to move past most obstacles, he didn't have the Agility to avoid them that Chase did. Also, his Toughness wasn't high enough that he could weather strikes and keep moving, like Liam did. Only, now, he didn't have a choice. The orange-haired Furyborn could only barely be seen beyond the layer of armed grimbolds dipping and diving to take him out.

Chase burst past Kith's summons. The big, malformed, fleshy shape fell forward, another limb forming to keep it moving, while its flailing arms managed to glance off a diving grimbold and send it skittering across the ground. Watching the blurring, diving mass of forms ahead, he could barely see Kith beyond (though his defiant shouts rang out past the infernal screeching). He timed his approach with a grimbold passing by low to come in behind Kith, slashed its wing, jumped into the air, and formed two platforms to take him higher. Then he leapt.

Another grimbold had just begun its turn as Chase arrived. His soft leather boots weren't made for battle. They were more effective for moving silently and running fast. However, for landing with both feet on the *neck* of the small flying creature, they did the trick. Its head whipped back at an angle that couldn't possibly be healthy.

Mid-air, Chase flailed at another grimbold, but the damn thing stayed out of his reach. Instead, he rode his fleshy transportation down to the ground.

The impact was ugly. Not painful, really, just...ugly. His one foot still rested on the creature's neck, and with nearly his full weight on top of it, the grimbold's windpipe didn't so much cave in as burst into goo.

Chase refused to acknowledge what was dripping down the top of his boots.

Around him, signs of his friends trying to make an impact were everywhere. The bulk of Kith's summon was ambling forward still, now blinking, in clear signs that it was about to explode. A wave of warmth burst with a whooshing sound not far above him, as Cilia hit with yet another of her precious fire droplets.

He only had eyes for Kith.

Ahead of him, the cloud of enemies was lessening. Now, he could see Kith's form, half-hidden by whirling, bestial shapes.

Kith should not still be alive.

The grimbolds had finally unleashed their trump card. As a unified entity, the tiny shapes had started to glow from their claws. Chase watched in horror, as one of them landed, waddling forward to strike at Kith's unprotected back.

Kith turned with unnatural grace. He kicked the child-sized creature in the chest, flinging it backward. As it fell, its claws grazed his legs. The shining claws opened up deep grooves in his pants leg and the flesh underneath.

From the tattered looks of his clothes, it wasn't the first time he'd been struck. More like the tenth. A light arose on Kith's leg, and the blood stopped welling up as Sera's heal struck. The next two attacks were already inbound, however.

Through gritted teeth, Chase realized it wouldn't last. There was no way Kith would be able to hold. Perhaps...just perhaps, the two in tandem would be able to make it last. With a heartfelt cry of frustration, he created three platforms, ran atop the air in a five-foot height, nicked the wing of a swooping grimbold and scared away one more, before landing right behind Kith. "Incoming!" he shouted.

Kith nearly punched the lights out of him. Instead, he turned his wheeling strike into a rolling dive, evading an incoming attack and emerging into a defensive stance a few feet away from Chase.

The young summoner looked entirely unhinged. His eyes were wild, he was *covered* in blood, and he panted open-mouthed with an emotion mixed somewhere between battle frenzy and something darker. He ducked to his knees, then leapt immediately again, almost parallel to the ground, his unprotected head crashing straight into the legs of an unprepared grimbold. Blood trickling from a fresh scalp wound, he shouted out in laughter. "Join the fun, then? I hope you can keep up!"

Chase bit down a nasty response, lashing out at a grimbold and making it weave away unsteadily. "Keep up? I'll show you how it's done!" Then he focused on staying alive.

For a while, the world devolved into one of chaos, of winged death on all sides, and, more importantly, of pain. Even with his Steps of Brilliance helping him perform quick, unrivaled movements, even with Kith taking half of the attention, there was no way that Chase could avoid all the damage. He received a nasty slash across the back, and one glowing claw laid open half his left arm lengthwise. Several darts struck him, sapping his Strength and Agility. The pain was transitory, however. Only moments after the wounds arrived, they would start closing, a sign that Sera was on healing duty. Once, a shield even emerged from above him, saving him from an ugly mid-air collision with a grimbold that decided it would do better as a missile. He stabbed down at the stunned beast, ending its life before moving back into the dance.

Because it *was* a dance, a dance involving him, his enemies, and death. Only once before had he been engulfed in as chaotic a situation as this, with the gleam skippers. There was a rhythm to it, a motion that allowed him to survive the worst of it, to stay a step ahead of annihilation. There was no overview in the dance, no idea what was happening in general. The only consistently perceivable presence was Kith, who, even without the boosts that Chase got, somehow managed to stay afloat, laughing maniacally through the blood and pain.

At some point, a loud explosion of light and sound announced the demise of Kith's summoned creature. Pain-filled screeches told the story that it didn't go alone.

Chase was too busy trying to survive to pay it much attention.

The end arrived as a gust of wind. Chase dove out of the way as it came, interpreting it as the whooshing sign of an incoming enemy. He dipped, rolled, and came to his feet in one flowing motion, slashing out with his dagger and finding...nothing. Spinning around, he saw the remaining grimbolds more than thirty feet away. They whirled through the air, out of control, buffeted by a targeted wind. A third of the remaining creatures were forced to the ground.

"So few. What happened to the rest?" The thought came unbidden to Chase's overwrought mind. There were less than ten of the beasts left, and most of them looked hurt. Then a salvo of arrows hit one of the remaining beasts, and Chase's brain finally caught up. *The Protectors. They'd arrived. They...were safe?*

Kith didn't look safe. He looked a mess. His clothes were tattered, practically falling apart on him. He still moved as if he were mid-combat, confused at the lack of attacks from around him. With a glazed look, his gaze met Chase's, his eyes rolled up in his head, and he fell to the ground like a punctured pig's bladder.

"Kith!" Sera's voice rang out. She sprinted forward. A flash enveloped her, and Kith's fallen body shone once again. Another flash followed hers.

Chase turned at a loud thump behind him, only to see Liam's body hit the ground as well.

CHAPTER 42

"Whatever it may look like, the towers do not care for fanatics. Believers, yes. Not fanatics. Fanatics blind themselves to reality, hoping to make reality adjust itself into their dream. Believers accept that reality will not adjust itself, and will work to reach the dream." There are a few fanatics out there. Overall, however, I would agree. The towers do an impressive job of being pragmatic about their situation and adjusting where necessary. (Page 5.)

When everything looked like it was coming apart at the seams and half their number were down, Cilia kept her cool. While the Protectors finished the remaining grimbolds, she checked on Liam, reassured herself that he wasn't badly hurt, but had overextended himself using his One Heart, Opened card. With a shouted, brief conversation with Sera, she learned that he was going to pull through, and that Sera had just healed what she could. Then, she moved on to cover their tracks.

Chase felt drained. Part of it was the stress and the near-death scenario. A larger part were the wounds, and the poison he could still feel burning in his veins. Yet, as the poison burned and sapped him of attributes, he recognized it didn't actually *hurt* him.

Sera took care of him. She checked his condition, healed him, and cared for him and the others.

Meanwhile, Cilia went to handle the conversation with the Protector team, smooth out any surprises and ensure they wouldn't get searched, revealing their cards, until they'd had the time to switch back to Light or Elemental cards.

When their rail-thin caretaker returned alongside Cilia, however, he looked more disturbed than either of them. "I insist. The healer teams of the towers are beyond reproach."

Cilia snorted and waved at where Kith was slowly getting back to his feet. "That's a waste of time. We have experience. We've been through this before. Nobody's badly hurt, and our healer assures me she's cured all the wounds already. At this point, we just need rest. Honestly, I'd rather hear about this attack. What happened to that cart out there? Does this happen often? It felt like an ambush!"

Chase smiled inwardly, approving of her switching the attention away from them. He wanted to join the conversation, but honestly didn't feel up to more than listening in.

"No. This was anything *but* normal." The man, formerly distant and derogatory, seemed genuinely disturbed. "These were not just Guardians of Light. They were armed and armored. This…okay, you didn't hear this from me. This is one of the safest combat tests outside the towers. Those stealth attacks earlier? They weren't even Guardians. They were summoned creatures, summoned and kept in check by one of our own. We had everything under control. It was meant to give you an appreciation of combat out here and the dangers. *Nobody* sees actual combat on the first day. Especially not what seems like targeted attention like this. And the cart's owner ran away as soon as we approached him. Our rogue is trying to catch up to him, but it looked like he had some Agility-based cards."

The man shook his head. "I'm sorry, but the real rest is going to be a while away for your team. Once you get back, you're bound to be caught up in debriefs for a good long while. The higher-ups are *not* going to like this. If the Lightborn are targeting our fresh recruits, that's a change in attitude we need to adjust to."

Cilia waved him off with a sigh. "As long as we can sit down while they question us, that's all right. I'm guessing we won't need to harvest these for parts either."

"Right. Right." The gaunt Elemental pulled himself together. Then he snorted to himself. "Obviously, summoned creatures don't leave anything behind, but these do. And you *will* be compensated for this, if I have a say. Which I do. Real Protectors get a percentage of the loot. What you did today? That was the work of real Protectors!"

It took hours before they were back in the towers. First, they had to get the transport beast summoned back. It had managed to run quite far and wasn't happy about returning to where it had been hurt. The blood and gore probably didn't help. When they finally left, the area was thick with birds trying to earn an easy snack, while the Protectors were applying some concoction around that sent them flying.

The trip back was uneventful and blessedly calm. After an hour, Sera was able to switch back to her Light card and took turns healing everybody until their wounds had all faded away and the debuffs disappeared. In the end, the one closest to death had been, surprisingly, Liam, because he'd received that first nasty strike, which hadn't healed all the way, before he kept sharing his health with Chase and Kith to keep them standing.

Kith, of course, was crowing about his martial prowess, offering them all lessons on how to do battle like a "real man."

Right up until Cilia took him to task, expanding on the stupidity of attacking enemies without involving your team in what you were doing.

Weirdly enough, Kith seemed to enjoy her haranguing. He looked strained, drained, like a wine skin left unattended near a worker crew, yet smiled through it all.

After that, they did relax. The summoned creatures, obviously, hadn't granted them any Ænima. There wasn't any life force for them to absorb and apply, when the creatures weren't properly alive in the first place. The grimbolds, however, had. What the tiny creatures lacked in individual strength or toughness, they appeared to make up for in speed, maneuverability, and Ænima. All of them, including Sera, who'd only managed to finish off one of the blasted beasts in the chaotic frenzy of the fight, earned a Step.

They kept to their choices. Chase invested in Potential, Sera and Cilia in Mental Power, Liam in Toughness, and Kith... Kith had hit his fifteenth Step and third Tier. He saved his choice for when they came back, but enjoyed the +2 to Potential from increasing his Tier and put his free point into Agility to keep his combat abilities level with his summoning skills.

The air-aspected Protector, whose name they eventually learned was Gerhard, turned out to be right. Once they returned to the towers, they were brought directly before the resident healers, regardless of their protests. Apparently, recruits downplaying injuries to look tough was an actual thing. After that, they were exposed to several hours of post-action questioning, first separated, then as a group. Fortunately, they'd spent the time on the transport beast wisely, syncing up their explanations. It wasn't like they had a lot to hide, either—they merely didn't talk about the Dark cards they'd used.

The Protectors near them, fortunately, hadn't noticed their use of shields in combat. Cilia's stakes might have proved a bit of an issue, since the large globs of darkness hanging in mid-air couldn't really be explained away. Only, it turned out that Light crafters *did* have the ability to create something similar, messing about with the absence of light instead of the creation of shadows, or some such. The officials seemed rather interested in those—enough that Cilia might be conscripted to create stakes like that going forward. Learning how to create those, using Light crafting? Well, that would be a problem for future Cilia.

The officials reacted a lot more controlled than Gerhard, downplaying the importance of what had happened. However, they could tell that, beneath the surface, the administrators were anything but calm. Eventually, they were let off the hook and allowed to go back to their rooms. At that time, they were well past the point of exhaustion, but still all piled into Liam's room to talk. The hall guard on curfew duty allowed them to stay up and chat—apparently, this was entirely normal and accepted following the final test before the Culling.

"I can't believe we managed to fake our way through that." Cilia frowned. "If they aren't more suspicious than that, it's no wonder their Cloaks haven't managed to figure out what is happening."

"That's what you're upset about?" Kith snorted. "*I* can't believe we actually survived that! I mean, I'm just *too* good—"

"*Don't* you start again!" Cilia admonished with a raised finger.

"I, for one, can't believe that we made it," Chase said, through a yawn. "Seriously. Guys. We made it. We're safe. We've *definitely* blown past the competition and are way past where we need to worry about the Culling, and tomorrow, we'll be able to get in touch with the High Elementalist and hear what the status is. It'll all be fixed. In the future, all we'll need to worry about is dealing with the Cullings and nailing any tests, like regular suckers."

Liam smiled. "It feels like we should have a toast. Only, we're here without any form of alcohol. How is that okay?"

"I...feel like it would be premature to celebrate," Sera mused. "Yes, we made it past the ambush. Yes, we somehow survived, not least through Kith's impressive performance—precipitous though it may have been."

Kith wrinkled his nose. "I'm not sure what that means, but...be nice!"

Sera ignored him, a tiny smile playing on her lips. "However, I, for one, am not resting until we have confirmation that the High Elementalist knows and has adjusted to our findings."

Chase groaned. "Come *on,* sugar."

"No."

"Sweetie pie?"

"I said no."

"Honey butter biscuit?"

"That's just demeaning." She rolled her eyes. "Regardless of how much it hurts to say, we *are* keeping a guard shift tonight and we *are* staying alert until we know that we are in the clear."

"You make my sleep schedule cry!" Chase protested.

"Wait a minute." Kith frowned. "Why are *you* complaining? I'm the one who's going to be up. It's not like either of you are able to see through walls—unless you think you'll be getting a lot of information staring at the door."

"That's...amazing. Thank you for volunteering, brother!" Chase rejoiced, slapping Kith on the back.

"I. No. That's not what happened, here, man!"

"Kith nearly died today," Sera said with a tone that brooked no argument. "We are not letting him keep a solo watch the entire night. The guard out there did not seem to mind us staying up to chat. Meaning, first we are letting him pick his Tier-three cards. Then, tonight, we are all sleeping in here, and we will take turns taking a guard. I will start."

"Gods, you're hot when you're domineering like that!"

Kith arranged himself, sitting on Liam's bed, and closed his eyes. His smile widened, until it looked like his head was about to split in two. He chuckled and didn't stop, while the others exchanged looks. Then he tensed up, blood vessels standing out as energy passed through his body. He exhaled slowly, then wiped sweat off his forehead. "That was fun. First, the upgrade I got from hitting the third Tier. I could've chosen either Divine Mentor or Crescendo of Light for my Light cards, Shadow Master or Tainted Earth if I went with Dark."

Liam interjected. "Let me guess. Shadow Master. You want more of your Darchibald and Dorky or whatever you're calling the shadows now!"

"Darchibald is an *excellent* name. But no," Kith countered. "I do love Shadow Master. But if improving Shadow Master increases the number of shadows, I'm not sure I have the Mental Power to handle them properly. So, I went with Tainted Earth. It's Epic now. The Toughness drain has increased...and now I no longer need to summon it on soil."

The crew exchanged approving sounds, waiting for Kith to get on with it. Extremely conscious of his audience, his smirk grew increasingly annoying, until he finally burst out in laughter and held up his hands. "Okay. I'll behave. Here are the two new cards I got."

[**Coils of Shadow**
Rare, Dark summoner
Tier three
Active, long duration
This card, once tapped, summons a number of small, venomous dredge spitters, calculated as one viper per two Mental Power of the summoner. These vipers are hard to spot in the dark, but vulnerable to Light powers and effects.
"Who's a lovely danger noodle? You are, my beautiful hazard spaghetti." The Valniers head chef races toward disaster.]

[**Sacrificial Saints**

Uncommon, Light summoner
Tier three
Passive, long duration
Nearly all summoning cards are active cards, requiring a certain degree of manipulation on behalf of the summoner. The bright saints summoned by this card do not. These are erstwhile heroes, souls so suffused with the power of self-sacrifice, that they feel the need to continue their deeds in the afterlife. Activating the card summons a random number of saints, between three and five. Each saint will attempt to block one attack against the summoner, be it magical or physical. Bear in mind that some attacks may be too powerful to be wholly blocked.
"You would not get this from any other. I will never give you up, nor let you down. We are no strangers. You know the rules, and so do I."]

As Kith spoke aloud the effects of his newfound cards, Cilia's eyebrows narrowed more and more. With a sigh, he gestured at her. "Okay, Cil. Lay it on me."

She rubbed her brows before frowning. "I dislike everything about this."

Kith rolled his eyes. "Yeah. I got that. Could we—"

"These are *perfect* choices! What are you plotting?"

"I..." Kith spoke, before stalling. "You like them?"

"Obviously. The Dark card, together with your Shadow Master card and Tainted Earth, is going to make you a one-man ambush at night. You won't be able to use it in the towers or in open fights, but...it's not like you were able to carry it in the towers anyway." The small crafter shook her head. "You know I don't love your frontline approach to being a summoner, but that Light card might just ensure that you'll survive it. In short, I'm waiting for the other shoe to drop."

Kith opened and closed his mouth a couple of times. Then he slowly tilted sideways on the bed and grabbed Liam's bed covers. "I'm going to sleep. Cil just approved of my choices. This is officially the weirdest day of my life."

The others, following a short discussion, followed his example. Liam was asleep before the others had even finished preparing and putting down their bedsheets. The rest, marveling at his ability to snore like that within less than a minute, took longer. However, the long hours, stress, and sheer exhaustion took its toll and soon, Sera was the only one not asleep, listening at the door. The worst was behind them, and they only needed to keep their cool until they were in the clear.

CHAPTER 43

"Gerek Firetongue. One Was Legion. Carrinne of the Bow. She Who Talks With People. While we pride ourselves on having the highest quality of soldiers anywhere in the known world, there are those who undeniably stand out. Sometimes, they are the powerhouses, Tiers six or higher, those gifted from birth or those who've waded through oceans of blood to reach their pinnacle. They all have one thing in common. When the need was the greatest, these heroes stood up and delivered, despite all odds." Heh. Heroes. At least we have our heads screwed on properly. (Page 61.)

There was no need for keeping a guard, it turned out. The alarm made quite sure of that.

Groggy and confused, they came to, listening to the howling outbreak alarm announcing a monster flood.

Cilia, who'd been on guard and was listening to the guard outside through the half-open door, popped her head back in. "It's an all-Protectors-on-stations. An all-out attack. No more details at the moment, but we're supposed to stay in here—and keep the door shut."

For a full minute, the only communication lay in exchanged incredulous looks and yawns.

Then Kith said what they were all thinking. "There's no way this is a coincidence, is there?"

Chase shook his head. "This stinks worse than the Waves. There's Lightborn trying to take us out, and now somebody's launching an attack on the towers? Something's wrong."

"What can we do, though?" Cilia asked. "If the Lightborn determined that their spy program has been revealed and decide to go all out...can we do anything about it?"

Sera squinted into the distance. "Not that I can see. However, I believe we are missing something. Say they managed to kill us earlier. Would that change anything? Would they not be attacking right now?"

"Myeah, no. That makes no sense." Kith scratched his nose. "We've already delivered the proof."

"Unless the proof never made it to the High Elementalist," Chase added.

That caused them to freeze up for a moment.

Liam eventually said, "Even if it hasn't, they'd still have to take us out, right? The towers have stood for so long, the odds are pretty damn bad they'll be able to crush their defenses right now. Please tell me I'm not wrong there."

Sera smiled and put her hand on his. "You are not wrong." Her smile died as she came to a realization. "Mind you, that does not remove the risk that they will make the attempt again while everybody is out defending the towers on the front lines."

"Damn. This is the old yell and snatch switch-up yet again, only on a way larger stage," Kith said.

Liam stood and started to put on his armor. His smile did not look like his regular carefree, open expression. It was darker and held a grim promise. Hefting his truncheon, he said, "That's perfect. Because, whatever happens, in order to get to us, they'll still need to defeat us. At this point, I am *more* than ready to give them a Waves send-off."

They didn't go back to sleep. With all the noise and chatter from the hallway and the surrounding rooms, it looked like few people did. There was no doubting that they went above and beyond, getting properly battle-ready.

Kith also switched his Tier-one cards to Dark, allowing him to summon his shadowy companions to help him peer through the walls on either end of the corridor, granting him the chance to warn them should anything happen. Then, they subsided into a stretched-out silence as they waited to see what was going on.

At the end of a period of terse silence, Kith hissed, "Something's happening." He squinted at the wall before continuing. "The hall guard's been gone for a few minutes. I figured he was just patrolling, but I'm not seeing him. And now... I spotted Jonathan sneaking out of his room and up the stairs. That's not all, though. Tam's lurking about in the corridor."

"Tam? Pit's she up to?" Liam scrunched up his face in confusion.

"Looks like she's sneaking over to your room, Chase. She's...knocking on the door now. Looks nervous as anything."

"Why would anybody do that? What's she up to? Tam doesn't seem the kind to do anything she's not allowed to," Liam asked.

"Because they're part of it." Chase shook his head incredulously. "It's so obvious. She's a Furyborn, sure, but we only have her word that she met up with the others accidentally."

"What do we do?" Sera asked anxiously. "Do we capture her and question her?"

"No." Chase frowned, thinking hard. "We have no proof right now, nothing solid, and we don't know enough to incriminate them. We need something—anything—to prove they're traitors."

Kith grinned. "So, we spring the trap?"

"That's exactly what we do. I'll go play innocent, ask some questions along the way...and you guys are going to tag along at a distance and step in if they do try something stupid. This way, we'll have, not just the numbers we located, but also, finally, solid proof of traitors in the towers."

"I don't like it," Cilia said. "It seems precipitous. If they are doing this, what is to stop them from simply killing you outright?"

Chase beamed at her, a cocksure grin that felt liberating and *amazing*. After too much time waiting for the ball to drop, they finally had something solid. They could move on the offensive instead of waiting around! "Because they're not dumb. There's five of us. They're not going to just take me out if they can't get all five. That would just bring even more attention on them. They'll want to interrogate me, like they tried in the city."

"I love it!" Kith said. "I just checked Rowan's room. He's gone too. It's definitely an ambush! Now, I'll follow you through the grimbrothers—"

"Worse than Darkony. How is that possible?" Sera groaned.

"And we can all follow you at a safe distance," Kith continued, unperturbed. "When they try something, we'll be right around the corner, ready to turn the trap. Like you said, there'd be no point in killing you, when they'll have to try to hide their involvement tomorrow. You'd better get going, though. Looks like Tam's getting agitated."

Liam grunted. "Just one thing. Erm. You're right here with us. How are you planning on getting back to your room?"

Walking around outside the towers in thin air was nerve-racking. Doing it *at night* was somehow even worse. At least the gale-force winds they suffered at these heights were not as bad at night as they could be during the day. Chase made it to his own window, which he'd kept cracked open a bit for the very same reason, and flung himself in one desperate, fluid motion. He felt the platform under his foot dissipate the exact moment he swung his foot inside. He latched the window before grunting at the door, where he could hear subdued knocking. "Just a moment."

Ruffling his hair wasn't necessary. The wind had done a great job at that. Chase made sure his sleeve covered the sheath of throwing daggers and pulled his uniform lower to disguise the dagger at his belt. He opened the door, blinking as if he'd just been awakened. "What? Oh. Tam. What's going on? I thought we were supposed to stay in our rooms."

Tam nodded. Her unruly braids fell forward to cover the wild colors of her eyes. "We were. But the hall guard's gone. Something's going on. And…Rowan and Jonathan went first. We need you to come." The normally taciturn young woman was sweating and looked entirely disheveled.

Chase nodded. *Definitely a trap.* It was too blatant, though. "Of course. I'll go fetch the others."

"No," the young woman started. "You can't."

"I can't?" Chase folded his arms. "This better be good."

Tam lowered her voice. "It's what Instructor Swansong told us. Before she died. We were supposed to involve *only* you in our findings. I don't know why."

He nodded. "All right. Tell me then."

"I can't. We're supposed to tell you only in confidentiality. Come. We have a place prepared, where we won't get overheard."

Chase felt a roiling pit of rage in the core of his stomach. They *had* been involved with her death. It was a classic conman's approach. Start out with something that was believable enough the mark would go along with something they'd otherwise never do. He punched down on his fury, making sure his face showed nothing but earnest eagerness. "All right. We'll do this. But you'd damn well better have an explanation for this. The entire world's gone mad!"

Tam nodded. "You can say that again. This attack's been ongoing for, what, twenty minutes now?"

Chase closed his door behind him, making a *follow along* gesture behind his back for Kith to see. He made sure his dagger was ready and prepared for the use of his Race of Life, keeping alert for anything or anybody lurking to catch him.

They walked along the corridors. Throughout the towers, the howling alarm still rang. Intermingled with that was an eerie sound of silence. Once, Chase felt certain he heard a clash of arms in the distance, but couldn't be entirely sure. Had somebody or something made it *into* the towers? That sounded far-fetched!

As they passed through deserted walkways and eerie staircases, Chase recognized where they were going. It was the administrative rooms on the lower levels. At this time of the night, there would be a few hours where there'd be no one around before the cleaning crew arrived shortly after dawn.

He tried to address Tam on several occasions, but she hurried on, staying mostly silent, sticking to saying that Jonathan would explain everything and it would have to wait.

Chase didn't react further. He just followed along, preparing mentally for dodging out of the way of whatever they had planned. Hence, he wasn't prepared for Tam slowly ambling back to walk next to him and whispering, "I think you should leave the towers."

"What's that now?" Chase said, genuinely confused. *Why would she say something like that?*

The young woman gulped, holding up her hands in supplication. Myriad small scars stood out as white lines against the earth-colored backdrop of her skin in the semi-dark corridor. "It's just...this is dangerous. You saw what happened to Instructor Swansong. You should get out while you can. Take your friends and run. If you decide to do it, right now, you can still get out."

Chase stopped and faced the Furyborn healer. To his surprise, there was more than the usual walled-off expression. Deep within those colorful eyes was a sea of hurt, of pain...fenced-in and tamped down.

Right up the stairs and to the left, they would reach their goal. Chase made a decision to take a chance. Glancing about him, he believed he spotted the motion of a shadow a way back in the tunnel. Gesturing behind his back for them to come along, he addressed the Furyborn. "You don't want to do this, do you?"

"I...what?" Tam didn't meet his eyes. "I don't know what you're talking about."

"Of course you don't." Chase gave her a sad smile. "Tell me, why would you try to give me an out? We both know your friends are lying in wait for me. Is it just them, or are there others?"

Whatever else could be said about the taciturn woman, she was *not* adept at secrecy. The glance to the stairs spoke volumes, even if she caught herself. She flushed dark red. "You don't know what you're messing with here," she whispered.

Chase shrugged. "So, tell us. What the Pits is going on? You just tried to save me. That'll earn you whatever leniency I can possibly give you. But you'll need to spill the goods."

The whites of Tam's eyes were showing. "I... I can't. You don't—"

"No, I don't know. So, elaborate, dammit. Tell me what's going on. Obviously, you're working for the Lightborn who've been trying to kill us for a long good while. What else is new?"

"I...can't. They'll know. My family." Tam's mouth snapped shut and her eyes opened wide in terror.

"Oh, that's what it's like, eh?" Chase's mouth opened in a toothy smile that had nothing at all to do with amusement. Making sure that there was no way Tam could sprint past him, he turned and spoke aloud for his friends to hear. "Our friend here has basically admitted that they're ready to ambush us and tried to give me an out, only, they've got her family or something and are going to punish them, if she tries something. Is that about right, Tam?"

Tam didn't answer. The horrified, crestfallen look on her face as she watched the others following, armed to the teeth, was answer enough.

"Mess with a woman's family, eh?" Liam rumbled. "Can't say I like that much. What do we do?"

Chase faced the fear-stricken woman. "Well. Since our friend here isn't being overly helpful, it looks like we'll just have to stab her and be done with it."

CHAPTER 44

"Power. That is what it always boils down to. If the Lightborn had the power, they would topple the towers. If the towers were powerful enough, they would scour the lands of the Lightborn. Hence, true peace will only be found among equally powerful enemies." I got a headache trying to make that make sense. Though...perhaps, in some cynical fashion, it does. I wish it didn't. (Page 4.)

Chase entered the room right behind Tam. She walked to the left, allowing Chase to pass her by.

Nodding, Chase moved in, noticing Jonathan on the far end of the room. There was nobody else there, though. *Where was Rowan?*

Jonathan seemed very happy with himself. He sat on the small desk, smiling with his arms folded and some item lying on the desk next to him, nodules of magic swirling around it. Nodding amiably at Chase, he leapt off the desk and walked forward.

The tiny glance over Chase's left shoulder gave the game away.

Chase didn't think, merely reacted. With a thought, he activated Steps of Brilliance, giving him the purchase to push off sideways with all his might. He careened through the air, hit his shoulder on a chair on the way to the ground and struck the floor, bouncing once before flinging himself to his feet. "What the Pits?" he yelled.

Not a word erupted to be heard from Chase's mouth. Darkness smother them. They *had* actually prepared some sort of silence effect.

On his right, Rowan appeared out of thin air, a shimmering layer of light slowly fading away as he came into view. The look of surprise on Rowan's face from seeing Chase dodge faded into concentration, as he nocked another arrow to his bow.

Jonathan's smile grew bigger and more devious. He waggled his finger disapprovingly. Then he grabbed the item, a two-pronged fork of some kind, on the desk behind him and said something. At least, his lips moved. No sound arrived. Waggling his eyebrows, the Lightborn tossed the fork back on the desk and stood up. Light flashed on his left arm, as he slowly moved forward. The light covered the entirety of his body and formed a shimmering shield.

Together, Jonathan, Rowan, and Tam circled closer, tightening the net around Chase.

Then the door sprang open, and, after a moment of indecision, the others poured in.

What followed was a chaotic, weird, and surrealistic mess of a struggle. After a moment's confusion, the tables turned, as Chase's friends went from moving *into* the room to trying to keep the others from escaping. In the process, there was no quarter given, no tricks too mean to be used. Rowan loosed arrows at point-blank range, while Jonathan commanded a force of heavy light, rushing around him with the power of dense waves. Tam activated some card to boost her group.

Against them, Kith sent his shadows to cover Rowan's head and effectively blind him, while Cilia moved in, staff whirling to punish the archer. Liam, meanwhile, rushed in to face off against Jonathan, testing his strength and fury against the momentum of the bright, roiling waves. Finally, Sera and Chase cornered Tam, daggers and sword breakers stabbing at her from both sides.

The silence made the situation eerie and mystical, like it wasn't entirely real. Yet the wounds and broken bones were very much real.

After less than thirty seconds, Chase brought the hilt of his dagger down on the weird item, which looked like a twisted, half-melted fork made of glass beads, and sensed it crunch under the weapon. With an audible pop, his hearing was restored.

On the ground, Rowan and Jonathan lay battered and subdued. Kith and Liam were right next to them, keeping them covered. Kith was surrounded by a half-dozen splotchy, see-through figures. At the far end of the room, next to a beautiful wall painting now spattered in blood, Sera knelt next to Tam. A glow arose from her, settling around the fallen, blood-smeared Furyborn. She rose from the ground, shaking her head with a sigh. "Too late. She lost too much blood."

Chase rounded on the downed Lightborn with a furious scowl. "Dark blind you, what *was* that? Why would you try to kill me? Tam just said something about you working with Instructor Swansong...only, that's not right, is it? You were the ones who killed her!"

Rowan lay in the fetal position, cradling his broken hand. He stared at the floor with a faraway gaze.

Jonathan, meanwhile, was collected. One eye was closed from a hefty punch and his left leg lay at an unhealthy angle. He glared at Chase. "We didn't do anything. Nothing you can prove, at least." His gaze had a feverish gleam.

Kith scoffed incredulously. "You just attacked my mate out of nowhere. You got your friend killed. You're seriously going to lie there and act like you're innocent? I say we kill him and be done with it!"

"We are not killing anybody," Sera announced.

"Sera's right," Chase said. "We're not killing anybody. Killing is too good for this bastard. We're going to deliver him to the Protectors and then we'll wait to see what the High Elementalist says."

From the ground, Jonathan chuckled wickedly between gritted teeth. "Oh, you haven't heard from her? That is *so* strange."

"*What do you know?*" Kith shouted. He hefted his axe and brought it close to the downed Lightborn, growling. "Give me an excuse, you pampered backstabber!"

"Who, me?" Jonathan giggled with a half-demented sound. "I am an innocent recruit, set upon by a bunch of wicked traitors...ones with Dark cards, to boot!" His finger pointed, trembling, at Kith's sleeve, which had shuffled up during the fight, showing the underside of his Shadow Master card. "Oh, that *is* a fun development. Dark cards? Really? I thought those had disappeared from the face of Ordei."

He drew in a shuddering breath, then laughed—a long, disbelieving whoofed laughter. "No! You're kidding me! *You* are the ones behind that mess in Isarn! That's amazing! I heard the inquisitors were all up in arms about whatever passed down there, and here you are, hiding out in the towers."

"Stop talking nonsense. Tell us what the Pit's going on! Why did you attack us? Why are the Protectors gone? Does this have anything to do with the alarm? Are the Lightborn attacking?" Chase fired off questions, one after the other.

Jonathan settled into a resting position against a table, grimacing with the pain. His demeanor was one of horrible smugness. "How would I know? I think I'll just stay here and let you find the Protectors. See how you're going to explain away those cards. Though..." He chuckled wickedly. "I wish you luck finding a Protector right now."

"Earth ground me, I'm going to stab you." Chase groaned.

"I'll do you one better." Liam strode over and assessed Jonathan; then, with a strike as unstoppable as the turn of the tide, he carefully struck him with the palm of his hand, right below his chin.

With a clack of teeth meeting teeth and a spasm of limbs, the tall, handsome man slid to the floor.

Liam held up a hand, forestalling Sera's furious outburst. "Wait." He proceeded to walk over to Rowan, who hadn't reacted to anything so far. He looked at the downed man, sighed, then repeated the process with the archer. It took two strikes, then Rowan was out like a light. "I felt less good about Rowan. But Jonathan...he wasn't going to say anything worthwhile. I've seen that look on his face before."

"Let me check on them." Sera quickly rounded on the two Lightborn, checking their eyes, breathing, and pulse. "They are truly unconscious, and in no risk of dying that I can tell."

"Thanks, Sera. Light scour me." Chase cursed, scrubbing his face. "That barely gave us anything useful. Tam, you can wake up now."

Reluctantly, the Furyborn sat up from where she'd laid stock-still on the floor, faking her death. Her gaze shot to her two erstwhile compatriots.

Chase nodded at her. "I'd sugarcoat it for you, but I'm not going to lie. Things aren't looking great for you. Whatever your so-called friends have been planning, they're deep in it. But we've earned you a tiny opening. Congrats, Tam. You're dead in the eyes of those two. Whatever's going on, as long as you leave the towers, you can create a new life for yourself elsewhere. You'll probably be officially labeled a deserter, but that can't be helped. That, or you throw yourself at the mercy of the towers, and we'll speak up for you. Regardless of what you choose? Your old life is over. And if you want a chance at a new one, you need to tell us what's going on."

The lost look in the young woman's eyes grew. "I never wanted any of this," she breathed.

"Neither did we, mate. Yet, when the city guard's at your heels, you don't stop to bitch over the weather. You just run with it."

Tam exhaled a shuddering breath and shuffled over to sit against the wall. She blinked a few times, then nodded. "All right. Everything you've heard about us so far is true. I did join up with those two only a short while before we came here. Yet, there is more to it than that. I was the bodyguard for the young lord for about a month beforehand. It used to be a good job. He really isn't that bad a person. Then, something happened, and he...closed off, like how you saw him earlier. He didn't tell me much, when they started to pack for the city. Only that it was important I give it my all, and that my parents, back in Stradeburg, would be in trouble if I didn't do what he said."

"They threatened your family?" Cilia spat. "That's low!"

Tam shrugged, cradling her legs with her arms. "It is what it is. I'm a servant. I don't have much of a choice. Or, rather, I guess I do now, if I can get out of here." She chuckled darkly. "Jonathan will believe I fell, pursuing my calling. That should keep my family safe, I hope."

"Please continue. I don't know what's going on, but I think we're short on time here," Chase urged.

Tam spread her hands in consternation. "I don't know much. The young lord—Jonathan—had us join the ranks here. Sometimes, he would go off by himself, and would return with orders. I don't know who he was talking with, only that he almost always returned in a wicked mood after the fact. He had us spread a few rumors about you. Oh, and Rowan was the one who stole that sword and hid it in your room."

Chase groaned. "Really? That Dark-cursed *bastard!* No wonder we couldn't find anybody else to confirm that Ernest was the one who set me up."

Tam lowered her eyes. "He never said what the goal was. We spent most of the time training and learning, like everybody else. Only...a few days ago, something changed. He returned from one of his outings, filled with nervous energy, near feverish, it seemed. Then he started planning something with Rowan. I wasn't involved, though."

"Oh, come on. They didn't even let you in on what the plan was?" Kith exclaimed.

"No. They did not. They told me that we were going to lure Chase here, that it was time to take him out once and for all. Then, we'd take the rest of you, one by one."

Cilia cursed. "He, or somebody else close to them, must have intercepted our information. I am not sure. It seems risky. It doesn't seem like the secrecy would hold up in the long run, and the odds of them failing, one of us not falling for the trap..."

In a low voice, Tam spoke, braids falling down to obscure her face entirely. "I'm not sure he cared about long-term secrecy. He was fired up. Kept saying things were going to change now. Oh. One other detail. It would seem that timing was everything. Rowan was wounded on our outing and wanted to postpone, but it *had* to be tonight, for some reason. He did go on about that. This being the fulcral..." She trailed off. "I don't know the word."

"Fulcrum point?" Sera asked. At Tam's confirming nod, she furrowed her brow. "There is something we are missing here. If tonight is the fulcrum point of whatever plan the Lightborn have, and it has to do with whatever attack is out there, it will have to be bigger than just a batch of Lightborn cheating the system again."

"What else could it be, though?" Kith asked. "Tomorrow's the Culling, where we get our updated rankings and the time where all the failures get sent home...but that's about it. Besides, it's not like Jonathan was at any risk of being sent home. What else is going on that could be a big thing?"

"They tried to kill us," Liam mused. "Twice. That's a pretty big thing to me."

"Shut it," Cilia said. "I'm... No. If that's it, then..." She stared off into the distance, lost in thought.

Nobody said anything. Not even Kith.

After a full minute, Cilia exclaimed in a low, fragile tone of voice, "We're in so much trouble. They're after the damn decks!" Seeing their lack of understanding, she snarled, "What else happens the same day of the Culling? The new batch of recruits are taken in and tested. Do you remember what they said? This is the only time in the next two months that the decks will be available and unsealed."

Chase just stared at her, shocked with the momentousness of it. He tried to take it in. "You mean to say that all these years of preparation, of secretly having Lightborn gain Elemental cards—were for tonight? For them to strike and steal the Elemental decks?"

Tam spoke up. "If that is what they were plotting, I had no clue. But I can say, whatever happens was not meant to happen today. The young lord has been visibly upset at you several times over the past months. I believe that your group have managed to upset their planning."

"That...makes more sense." Chase gathered his thoughts. "I think I'm starting to see it. The attempt on our lives today. Or yesterday, I guess. If they'd managed to take us all out, they wouldn't need to set everything in motion. If we'd died, that was it. They'd already intercepted the information, and could return to their old plan, whatever it was. Only, we screwed everything up. So, instead, they're planning to take us out and...take off with the decks, I'm guessing? But they wanted to end us first, to make sure that nobody was going to give the game away before it was too late."

"That's it," Kith said. "If we died, the Elementals would probably figure out things in good time...but with the chaos and everything, it was not going to be until everything had died down and they'd already gotten away." He tapped his nose. "That's *smart!*"

"But where does that leave us?" Liam asked, visibly distressed. "In the middle of a goddamn war for the towers? Does that mean the Lightborn are going to *invade*?"

Sera started to pace. "No. If they were able to invade, they would have done so ages ago. The attack outside has to be a diversion. Yet, even with this massive a diversion—the alarm still howling and all—the towers are anything but defenseless.

They must have activated any Lightborn within the Protectors as well, to be able to make an attempt at the dome and the decks inside."

Tam gasped. "That explains this." She pointed at her shoulder, showing off a cheap-looking, white brooch. "The young lord insisted that I clasp this on my shoulder tonight. I wasn't sure why...but if that's the way they identify themselves and make sure they don't attack each other?"

"So, let me get this straight." Kith cleared his throat. "What we need to do, right this moment, is to rise up through the towers, something we're very much not allowed to do, finish off any traitors—traitors, who have built their strength for years upon years—and take out anybody trying to steal the decks, all without getting offed by any Protectors still doing their job around the place?"

"Sounds about right," Chase said drily. "Also, I'd bet we're running out of time. The Lightborn likely won't be able to keep up that diversion forever."

"Fury tear me a new one." Kith frowned, cracking his knuckles. "I liked it better when we were the only ones stealing decks."

CHAPTER 45

"The towers are beautiful, they say. Vast, and filled with wonders. They are entirely right. Before anything, however, they are defensible. Anybody trying to strike at our heart will find themselves in dire straits." Nice words. I do wonder if they've thought about more…underhanded methods. Have they been proofed against a heist? (Page 20.)

"**W**hy do they even *want* the damn decks?" Liam complained as they ran through the empty corridors. "With all the traitors they've got to have…how many people with Elemental cards by now?"

"Past a thousand by now, less the ones who have actually died and not just faked their deaths," Sera said. "Less than a third of those will have more than one card."

Chase huffed. "It's simple. They might have a thousand people with cards, but if they're found out, they're not getting any new ones. That means that they'll only know about the exact combinations they already have. On a huge scale, that isn't enough for them. Also, the real kicker? I'm not sure if it'll work for *any* secondary deck, but if they get the original Elemental deck back to one of the Lightborn Wellsprings? They'll be able to grant their people Elemental cards for all time. That, with their superiority in numbers, is going to be the end for Earth's Ward."

"Oh. I see." Liam didn't even have the decency to gasp for air as he ran, like the rest of them. He just loped ahead, entirely at ease. "In that case, why are we running down, instead of up?"

"Because, you half-wit," Cilia managed through gulps of air. "There's five of us. There may be hundreds of Lightborn here. We need help against them."

Their fists thundered on the doors up and down the student halls. One by one, upset heads poked through the doors and voices rose in a clamor, demanding explanations.

Before long, a single figure moved ahead of the rest of them, imperious gaze boring down on Chase. "What is the meaning of this? You do realize we were ordered to stay in our quarters, Darkborn?"

"Ernest." Chase greeted him with a nod. "Like me or not, have I ever lied to you or treated you in a manner that made you doubt anything I had to say?"

Ernest rubbed a hand through his hair, straightening out a tuft that was out of place. "That sounds like the opening to a lie if I've ever heard one...but no."

"Yeah. You're not going to like what's coming next." Chase stood as tall as he could, put his fingers in his mouth and whistled, a long, loud wolf whistle that caught the attention of all the tired students milling about in the hallways. "Attention!" he shouted. "The towers are under attack. And not just the monster wave. That's a diversion. At this very moment, invaders and traitors are marching through the towers above us, trying to steal the Elemental decks. We need to make sure that doesn't happen."

Shouts and questions arose. Ernest took up the gauntlet as spokesperson and waved down the noisemakers. "That is a massive claim. Do you have any proof?"

"No. Nothing tangible. I can tell you that Jonathan, Rowan, and Tam were part of it. They tried to kill us mere minutes ago. Tam is dead," Chase only twinged a little at the lie, "while the other two are trussed up, out cold in a classroom two stories up. But I have nothing tangible to offer you. I have facts and numbers I do not have the time to go through, and theories I cannot afford to lay out, let alone try to prove."

The water-aspected Elemental's gaze didn't shy from Chase's. "What do you *want* from us then? Sounds a lot like you're asking us to arm up and get ready to attack Protectors inside the towers?"

"No! Far from it. But we need to share this with the entire tower. We need you all to spread out, to wake everybody and alert them to what's going on. Regardless how many Lightborn there are trying to steal the decks right now, they won't be able to fend off all Protectors, if they just know what's going on."

"You want us to spread throughout the towers and the floors and tell everybody what's going on?" Ernest raised an eyebrow.

"That's exactly it. Now, if we're in the wrong, you'll have caused a ruckus, we'll get the blame, and we'll be tossed out on our asses tomorrow. If we're right, you'll have helped fend off the theft of the century. So, *please* help!" Chase looked straight at his former enemy.

Ernest Chalico stood razor-straight, pride and self-righteousness combined in one heroic posture. He looked down his nose at Chase. "You're telling me that regardless of what happens, I can only win? That sounds like a scam."

Chase grimaced. "Pits, no. Didn't you hear the part where the towers are likely teeming with traitors, ready to kill anything that moves? We learned one thing from Jonathan and his helpers. The traitors are using these brooches to identify each other. Meaning, if you spot one of these brooches, *run*."

Ernest's demeanor was unchanged, harsh and unflinching.

Chase grimaced. "If nobody is willing to help, so be it. But please—*please*—don't stand in our way."

The proud Elemental ran a hand through his hair before nodding curtly. "All right." He took a deep breath, then spoke up louder. "All *right*. You heard our fellow recruit. The towers are in danger. *Who will stand to protect them?*"

Chase had to hand it to Ernest. Not only was he able to rouse everybody but the most fearful recruits to help, he also helped adjust the plan to increase the chance of success with mere seconds of time to think and process the plan. Within a minute, the first recruits sprinted away, to wake up the recruits who'd been here longer than they had and share the situation with them. The remainder of those present had each received their target and were being prepared to move out. They agreed to use the rankings and assign the higher-ranked recruits to the higher floors, given that it would inevitably hold more danger, both with traps, hostile Protectors, and any traitors.

Within ten minutes, the last group of recruits sprang away at a measured pace that they'd be able to keep up for a long time.

Chase turned to Ernest, who watched the leaving people, looking properly satisfied with himself. "Thank you, Ernest. It would've been easy for you to make trouble and stop us. This— No. Just thanks."

"Pish. It is as you said. If you are wrong, I'll get front row seats to watching your ass get disciplined. If you are right? Who would I be if I turned down the chance to defend the Towers?"

Chase stretched out his hand, and the two shook hands. "It's appreciated. Now, where are you going yourself?"

The caster burst into a haughty laugh. "Oh, you *are* dim-witted. I just went out on a limb to support you. In which world would I not follow along to aid you, or halt you, if you are up to something underhanded?"

Chase took a deep breath. "Yeah. Okay. I should have seen that one coming. In that case, I need to show you something else, and you're *really* not going to like it."

Again, Chase was impressed by the proud Elemental. He might be a stuck-up bastard, but he rolled with the punches. Once he was past the initial "burn the heretic" response of watching Chase swap to his Dark Tier-three card and got an *extremely* abbreviated version of how they had them, he admitted it didn't change anything in the big picture. He realized there'd be a reckoning afterward. However, considering the time to come was likely to see the need for the Dark cards and Kith *would* be running with his shadowy summons engaged regardless, Chase would rather share the information beforehand than have Ernest figure it out mid-battle.

Finally, they moved out, fully armed and ready for anything. Chase even dipped into Sera's room and came out with the sword they'd hidden. Ernest didn't comment on the sword. Perhaps he was past caring at this point. Perhaps he just didn't recognize it.

They agreed upon the positioning before setting off. Liam was first. Then came Kith, alongside Chase, who'd help him avoid wiping out while he scouted the tunnels ahead of them. They would be the three to carry the brooches as well, to let any hostiles think they were some of theirs. Their trio would be followed by Cilia, bag of tricks at the ready, with Ernest right behind to lay on ranged damage with his ice knives. Sera would be backup, ready to heal any damage.

They started upward through the corridors and hallways of the towers. Everywhere, the howling alarms persistently blared out, muffling any nearby sounds. Knowing that the place was likely teeming with people, conditioned to stay hidden while monster attacks were ongoing, so as not to interrupt those who were tasked with handling the attacks, didn't help. It gave the whole scene a haunted, eerie look. Torches and magical lights still shone bright in their regular spots, yet the lack of the servants, workers, and roaming Protectors was decidedly disturbing.

They made it unchallenged a few floors up, reaching the level past the training grounds, without seeing a single Protector. Without a warning, Liam slid to a stop. Chase barely managed to slap a hand on Kith's shoulder, so they avoided colliding with his bulk.

Liam held up a hand, forestalling any questions. With the tip of his truncheon, he slid the half-closed door entirely open, revealing a body, slumped on the ground, as well as the smears of blood from where it had been dragged through the door.

Behind them, Ernest exhaled a barely audible gasp. Chase looked back at him, and saw him, white-eyed and grim-faced, unable to tear his gaze away from the body.

Seconds later, they were off again.

A floor later, Kith spoke up. "Ambush. One person on the left. Follow my lead." He hefted his axes and raced ahead of the others.

Chase barely saw the person. It was somebody leaning out beyond a corner, and only the glittering of their eyes betrayed their presence.

Kith went on straight, seemingly oblivious to their presence. Then he tensed, as if just then realizing they were there, before pointing at his own brooch and slowing down. He started talking to the other. "Seen any enemies? I—" Mid-word, he cursed and pointed ahead of the person, starting to sprint. Behind him, Chase and Liam followed, brooches also affixed near the heart.

The person behind the corner inevitably turned, lurching to see what was happening ahead. With Kith several feet away, they likely didn't seem at risk. The hand axe flying end over end to strike dead center in their mass proved them wrong.

Chase arrived only seconds after, his sword sliding through their chest until it hit the hilt. He was still in full conflict mode, ready to attack again, when he realized there was no point. The enemy was dead, sliding off the sword to hit the floor with a wet thump. He raised his sword in wonder, ignoring the blood liberally dripping off the blade. No wonder they'd been upset at its disappearance. It had barely registered the resistance of the boiled leather.

Chase shook himself and focused, coming to a knee beside the downed enemy. He—no, she—was a Lightborn, tall and lanky, awkward in death with her limbs askew in her recruit uniform. He thought he recognized her. The unlucky combination of deep pockmarks and short, matted hair seemed to spark recognition of a recruit in one of the classes ahead of them. Possibly a rogue. With a grimace, he unfastened the brooch and tossed it to Cilia. "For you. Soon, we'll be able to fake a full team. At least for a short while."

Behind her, Ernest stood up, wiping his mouth. His shocked gaze jolted from the brooch to Chase and on to the downed figure on the ground. He stood back up, finger pointing accusingly at Chase. "You *killed* her!"

"Better her than me," Chase answered drily. He fought down the pang of distaste in his stomach and prodded something on the ground. "See this? It's her dagger. Still wet." He fought down the desire to snap at Ernest, adjusting to a more reasonable tone. "Listen, Ernest. I get that you haven't seen a whole lot of ugliness. However, this is what you signed up for. It's *way* too early for you—but it's sink or swim time right now. If we waste our time trying to reason with enemies who're *actively* attacking the heart of your lands, we're not going to make it." He walked close to the Elemental, ignoring the waft of vomit. "So, tell me, Ernest. Can you manage?"

Ernest wasn't looking at Chase. His gaze was fixed, almost physically attached, to the downed shape. His chest rose and fell painfully fast. "I will."

Chase *felt* the determination, the desperate application of force of will, as the usually so self-important Elemental came face-to-face with something that shook his world perspective and adapted.

"I will." This time, the statement was deeper, more settled.

Chase reached out and clasped his hand onto Ernest's shoulder. "Good." Turning to the others, he remarked, "If we didn't already know, this is proof. They're out there. They're waiting. This one wasn't even a full Protector yet, which is likely why they had her waiting on the lower levels. I'm afraid things are going to get hot from here on."

That became the most correct prediction of the day. Hiding in the next stairwell were two other recruits, and, regardless of them wearing brooches, these two didn't bother to wait for the others to close before opening fire. Heavy earthen shards tore at Liam, and small, bright balls unleashed tiny, stinging bolts at them as he advanced, drawing their attention. Seconds later, one of Cilia's bracelets blinded them both, and their attacks grew more erratic. One fell to Chase's throwing dagger, while the other dropped to his knees, clutching an icy spike impaling his throat.

They continued moments later, after Sera healed Liam's minor injuries and Ernest stopped throwing up.

As they rose higher in the towers, resistance increased. They overwhelmed a trio of summoners holed up behind a barricade, with their summons sent out into different corridors to hold off any advancement. As Liam went toe-to-toe with the first summoned creature, the rest of their group sprinted past to close with the summoners. They died before their summoned creatures made it back from the other corridors to protect them.

Next, they clashed with a full group of Lightborn recruits Ernest recognized as being from one of the classes ahead of them. Once the lead fighter died, though, the rest surrendered, and Liam was more than happy to leave them unconscious and hogtied with their own clothes. Even as resistance heightened, so too did the evidence that the towers were fighting back. Twice, brooch-wearing Lightborn bodies lay abandoned in corridors. One looked as though he'd simply fallen asleep. The other looked as if he'd been chewed on.

So too did the noise change. On the lower levels, they heard nothing but the howl of the alarms. Now, they heard other sounds intermingled with the loud, overwhelming clarion call. Massive, magical impacts. Screams. Clashes of weapons against weapons.

For a few floors, their progress was relatively fast. It seemed they reached an equilibrium where the Protectors hadn't prepared to properly strike back yet, but the attackers weren't entirely settled either.

Around halfway up the towers, that situation changed. They paused, hiding behind a row of massive pillars.

Off to the side was a scenario where several archers and casters had entrenched themselves in a stairwell against a group of Protectors within the earthen section of the towers. An earthen ball rolled across the ground, ignoring gravity and the stairs, settling next to a caster, before exploding into a shower of sizzling acid. The caster fell to the ground, screaming, even as a muscular Lightborn caster flung a massive globe of something back down the stairs at the Elementals.

Chase cursed. "We need to move faster." Watching the confused looks on the faces of the rest, he elaborated. "I was working under the assumption we'd be fine with slowly working our way up there. As long as we removed their element of surprise and anybody guarding the exit along the way, we'd have them trapped in the towers, with no mode of exit, right? Wrong!" He grimaced, pointing at the stairwell, where an acid-spattered archer cursed at his bowstring snapping. "This is just one spot. Protectors will be fighting back against the intruders all over the towers. There's no way they don't have a backup plan for if they get the decks and get trapped."

"Light blind me," Ernest groaned. "You're right. Move on ahead. I will follow...as soon as I help the Protectors here along a bit." He put his back to a pillar and breathed deeply. His card flashed, and a shard of ice pulsated, building in his hands. The others raced past him, rushing up the stairs to the next levels.

Their first serious obstruction came three floors up. Not only were the five Lightborn defenders prepared and balanced, with a full group of what looked like hardened recruits, they'd had the time to create a proper barricade. Somebody among their group must have had earth-shaping forces, because the close confines of a corridor had been tightened further, to allow for a single, tight aperture into the hallway beyond. Two fighters, one wielding a spear, stood ready to intercept anything else, while smaller openings in the earthen barricades allowed a ranged fighter and a caster to attack with less fear of getting hit in return.

"Oh, great." Kith finished his explanation with a grunt. "They've also got a healer waiting a bit farther back. Either she's there to heal them, or they're already buffed to their eyebrows."

Chase took a deep breath. "Tight fit. Settled defenders. No way to force us in." He nodded, nostrils flaring. "Okay. I've got this one. Cil, I'll need one of your flashy armbands. Ernest, I'll be relying on you here. Are you up for it?"

"Me?" The Elemental looked at Chase, astonished. "Why me?"

"I'll need somebody who can act the role of a major pain in the ass." Chase grinned. "You fit the bill."

CHAPTER 46

"If there is one thing that we Elementals have per-fected, it's the tried and true. Where other nations leave things up to chance, we do not. We take what works, iterate on that and perfect the outcome. Known and well-rehearsed will beat unexpected nine times out of ten—especially if you have spent decades improving it." For once, something I disagree with wholeheartedly. Not improving your tactics and such. But rely-ing on it to the point of ignoring the impact of surprise, of im-provisation? That's the best way to ensure that you get sur-prised. That tenth time out of ten is going to suck. (Page 91.)

Ernest's ice dagger slammed into the wall just above Chase. Chase tore around the corner, Steps of Bril-liance activating to give him purchase to avoid a head-on colli-sion with the painted glass mural covering the entirety of the outside wall. Seconds later, another dagger followed, punching *through* a glass frame.

Ignoring the howling of the wind outside, Chase started yelling at the entrenched Lightborn. "Incoming! Cover me, dam-mit!"

As a response from in front, a spear burst into existence, tearing straight for him. Behind that, a pellet of hard-flung earthen missiles peppered through the air toward him.

Chase activated Steps of Brilliance again, creating two platforms mid-air ahead of him. His sprint took him up into the air, and he leapt, nearly brushing against the ten-foot ceiling. *"Cover* me, don't kill me, you Dark-cursed morons!" he snapped out. The brooch stood out on the heart of his recruit outfit.

For the briefest of moments, another bright spear built on the other side of the opening in the barricade. Then a shout went out, and Chase was too busy pushing himself sideways through the tight passage for anything else. Behind him, another spear hit the barricade.

He was roughly pulled inside, past the barricade, and im-mediately started babbling. "Thank the gods! They broke past our defenses. There's three of them. I barely—"

One of the fighters moved on, focusing on the corridor behind them. The other still held onto Chase. Behind them both, the healer's eyes stared right at him, eyes opened wide in recog-nition.

Chase recognized the look of somebody about to blow a scheme wide open. He opened his hand and let the item he clutched drop to the smooth tiles. Then he shut his eyes tight and grasped for the sword in his sheath.

The world exploded. Even with his eyes shut, he felt his vision blur and waver. When he opened his eyes again, he couldn't see anything but vague shapes and blurs.

In this case, blurs were more than enough to get by with.

Unsheathing the sword, he used the hand clasped painfully tight on his arm to guide his strike to where the fighter was. He stabbed up, and felt blood gush over his hand and arm. When the fighter dropped to the ground, Chase was already moving for the spear thrower behind the barricade.

Their fight dragged on longer than he hoped. Not because there was any doubt as to the result. Chase got the ranged fighter, and Ernest somehow nailed the caster with an ice dagger *through* the tiny opening before any of the enemies had adjusted their eyes.

Yet, even with just the two remaining against their group of six, and the end result writ in stone, the healer managed to activate two cards. First was a buff that increased the fighter's speed and power tremendously—enough to where he could almost match Chase for speed. Even close up and with a much more practical weapon, the spear-wielding brute might have ended up giving Chase some real trouble, if it wasn't for Liam making his way through the tight passage and Kith starting to blind the man with his shadow summons. But the moment the fighter died, the healer activated another card and fled. Said card was a horrible annoyance.

"I can't believe this is a *Light* card," Liam groaned. His mace tore down and snapped back up again, almost hitting him.

Sera agreed with a grunt. She let her staff fall, growling at the lack of any response at all. "I cannot believe this is something a healer would have. What is the helpful part of summoning thousands of cobwebs into being?"

Kith worked in a furious rhythm. Each hand axe rose and fell in a complicated, swift pattern, cutting just one or two strings of webbing at the time. "I. For one. Want it. Beats. Getting killed."

"Yeah, I guess. And at least it's not sticky." Liam groaned and rubbed his back. "I just wish we weren't on the receiving end."

In the end, Ernest and Liam worked side to side. Ernest's icy blade snapped through the hardened webs, cutting them with ease. Liam borrowed Chase's short sword and used his superior Strength to keep up with the weaker Elemental.

Maybe fifteen minutes later, Liam finally snapped the last strands of webbing and wiped sweat off his brow. "I'm guessing that's the advantage of surprise gone."

It was. Well, not entirely. They managed to catch a fleeing Lightborn Protector who arrived from a side path by surprise and overcome him without hurting him too badly. The Protector wasn't very forthcoming, however. First, he announced that they were about to go into the grinder. Then he spat in Liam's eye and dared him to do his worst.

Liam punched his lights out and stood up, stretching. "That wasn't very helpful, was it?"

With his eyes closed, Kith grimaced before turning to the others. "Unfortunately...it kind of was. That grinder he mentioned? It's real. We're about to hit it. I could explain it to you, but at this point it's easier to just show you."

They traversed a vast, empty courtyard filled with large statues, huge blocks of stone, and some foot-thick slabs of rock covering each and every wall. From the splinters lying everywhere and the myriad scorch marks, this looked like a training ground for casters. Beyond the courtyard, the stairs continued upward, sloping gently.

In their spiraling travels up the towers, they'd consequently gone for the most direct path. Of course, their knowledge about anything above the central parts of the spires was nearly nonexistent, beyond half-remembered snippets from their only trip up there, which definitely led to a circuitous route and precious minutes wasted. Right now, they were returning to the central tower after a short visit to the inner edges of the rougher-looking earth-aspected parts of the construction. As they climbed the wide, granite staircase, they noticed how the central dome capping the towers was now visible above them. Just a hundred feet higher, they could see how the constructions, formerly adorning outside of the mountain, *became* the mountain, as bridges of all four aspects converged toward the top of the tower.

Chase groaned. "I'd forgotten about this part. You're telling me they've taken over the main security checkpoint?"

Kith rubbed his hands over his eyes, nodding. "From the number of bodies strewn all over, it was more of an army bunker than a simple checkpoint, but yeah. That's exactly what I'm saying. They've managed to take it over, and there is just one opening!"

The first body lay sprawled on the steps ahead. It was a fire-aspected Elemental Protector. She lay unmoving, a few small puncture wounds on her back the only sign of what had caused her demise. She was the first, but nowhere near the last.

The earthen side of the towers led straight toward the fort. The defensive structure was more of a beehive with a single entrance than an actual fort. The structure was semi-circular as well, forming a sort of half-bubble tacked onto the surface of the mountain. A platform stretched all around the slope of the mountain, allowing bridges and stairs from the other towers to connect, but only a single gaping mouth allowed for entry, with arrow slits and gaping openings promising ugly things to any who would dare to attack. The area surrounding the platform leading to the entrance itself was an abattoir: Protectors sprawled in unnatural positions, torn-off limbs and pools of blood testament to their violent demise.

"I'm counting twelve dead. That's just *outside* the fortress, though. I can see inside for a few feet, and there are defenders right there, but then my shadows can't move any further. There's...some kind of shield."

"A card or a fixed installation?" Chase asked.

"Fixed installation, I'm guessing," Kith said. "I've tried having my shadows tour the premises, and it feels like it's at the very center of the place, affecting everything in a circle, or dome, or something. Also, it would make a lot of sense to have something like that permanently affixed in a place like this."

They all took in the waiting tunnel just ahead of them. It had an ominous presence, like the gaping mouth of a skull—if said mouth was constructed with perfect care, adorned with magical, gleaming lights, and strewn with openings like the eyes of a spider on the mountainside a dozen feet in all directions around the opening.

"What I *can* see, before that," Kith continued, "is that the inside of those walls next to the opening is hollow. It holds defenders, all with those damn brooches, of course. I count six of them...ranged and casters all, I'm guessing."

Liam grunted. "Any wagers on whether those will be all defenders waiting in there?"

Sera shook her head. "No. Our house guard were grilled in proper defensive fighting. Standard defensive tactics say that you would take down as many attackers from a distance as possible. Yet, fortifications should be kept in place, readied for a frontal attack. All, obviously, with the terrain defensive gates and similar to worsen the odds for any attackers and enhance your own."

Kith snorted. "He was being sarcastic, princess."

Chase clapped his hands together. "Focus. So, we've got ranged defenders and likely an inner defense that will be settled and ready to rip apart any close combat attackers." He pointed at the ominous opening. "None of us wants to go in there. But if we don't, and they get away with the decks...what are the odds they'll let us stay here? Even if they do, this is just going to lead to the armies of Light eventually invading the entire damn place."

Liam grunted. "I can't keep us all safe if we try this. It's looking like a slaughterhouse. Most of those out there are full Protectors." He pointed at the corpses scattered on the platform in front of the entrance.

Chase shrugged. "Obviously, we have the option of waiting it out. Eventually, the attack out there's going to blow over, or enough Protectors will push past from their defensive positions to help us attack here. Except...think of this as a job. Nobody in their right minds would attack something like this without having an alternative way out."

"Meaning, we do risk our lives. Okay. But I want to go first." The big man jumped a bit up and down, shaking his wide shoulders for the heavy chainmail to sink properly into place.

"Relax. Yes. We get to risk our lives. That doesn't mean we face this head-on. I said think of this as a job. How would you handle this? I can't see our earlier approaches working here. We'd be out in the open, and I'm afraid they would shoot first and ask questions later."

Cilia stretched on her toes, taking in the abattoir before her. "It would seem that their outside range is around eighty feet, down to about thirty feet. That is where all the dead are, except that guy in the heavy armor a few feet from the wall. Speculation: I would wager that they have explosive blasts—"

"Really? Was it the missing limbs that tipped you off?" Kith snorted.

"Focus," Cilia snapped. "Explosive blasts, that they dare not use once enemies get too close. On top of that, closer to the walls, the archers who must be there, judging from the arrows, are left with awkward angles. There are all the other strangely shaped openings in the walls, presumably for poison, boiling water, and the like. However, I would not believe that those will be usable without numbers or preparation *they do not have.*"

"That's a damn fine point." Chase scratched his neck. "Meaning, if we make it to the walls, we aren't safe, but we'll be a lot less exposed. What's our status on crafted goodies, Cil?"

"Bad. We used a *lot* yesterday, and I didn't think I would need to replenish more straightaway. I have two shadow stakes and a single blinding bracelet left. I have a double handful of fire droplets, but that is all." The normally self-controlled woman looked like she wanted to hit something, bad.

"Not your fault, Cil. Nobody predicted something like this. But still, that's not nothing. With two stakes and Kith's shadows to blind some of the casters on the other side of the wall, we can probably make it to the walls safely. With the fire droplets and Ernest's ice attacks, we might be able to make short work of some or most of those lurking right inside. That still leaves us on the other side of a well-fortified position, with Light knows which defenders inside and no way to touch them."

"Do we know that, though?" Sera mused.

"What was that?" Chase asked, confused.

"Do we know for certain that our skills are unable to affect those inside?"

Cilia perked up. "Of course! Cards and crafted items always have hard limits on what they can and cannot do. It will be the same thing for that shield. We have no idea what it can repel and what it can't."

Liam blinked. "Why do you sound so damn *happy* about that?"

"Because I am, obviously. It means that we get to test it, and soon we will know exactly what we can and can't do. Then we can get to work on how we're going to break this nut apart."

Ernest had been pretty quiet on the way up, doing his part in the attacks, yet mostly observing and trying to deal with his world being turned upside down. "What in the Pits are you doing? Forget that. I'm not blind. Are you actually saying that you think you can crack this, with just a few minutes of preparation?"

"Not yet," Chase said, gaze drawn to the yawning opening like a lodestone. "However, that's the thing. This place? It's prepared for defense, against invading armies and such. We don't care about armies, proper ways of fighting, stuff like that. We just want to win."

"In this case, though, that's the same thing! You're trying to break your way into a defensive position meant to fend off carded invaders, with just a few minutes to prepare."

"Yes and no. First off, they're not likely to have full-blown defenses in place. Second, we don't care about invading. We just want to slink past. It might end up meaning the same damn thing, and it might not. We'll know in a bit."

They put their heads together and came up with a number of important details. For one, the magical shield was *right* behind the defenders lurking at the arrow slits. It was definitely constructed like that on purpose. Any defender who was under magical attack from the outside would be available to stay inside the defensive parameter of the shield, and then back out to retaliate. As to why it didn't cover the entire thing, Cilia sarcastically remarked how clever it would be to have a magical shield in front of a mage.

The exact properties of the shield soon became clearer. Chase untucked his sling and shot a stone inside the entrance tunnel—to no effect whatsoever. Meaning, there were no physical properties to it, and it only affected magic. Not only that, but when he launched a single fire droplet into the tunnel, it entered with no issues, and exploded into fire inside the stone hallway. Another one, launched to strike the wall right *next* to the shield, exploded as well, only for the tongues of magical fire to be extinguished upon contact with the shield.

Cilia hmphed. "Meaning, it will cut off any magic seeking to enter. However, any magic starting *inside* will work just fine...except for any that touches the barrier, of course." She frowned. "Would you be able to activate a card *within* the circle, but from the outside—like Kith creating a summon, but from the outside?"

"Oh. I actually believe I know the answer to that," Ernest said. "The activation of a card is, in itself, magic. As such, anything that might block magic standing between the wielder and the place they are attempting to activate it, would cut it off entirely. I know, because we had a room magically protected against eavesdropping, yet, the ceiling wasn't protected, so—"

"That's not the worst," Chase interrupted. "Keeps anybody within the shield from activating cards that influence stuff outside the shield. Kith. Tell me what you can see about the tunnel itself. I remember only parts from when we went through last time to get our cards. It had a bunch of defensive positions, I think? Plenty of possibilities for Protectors to hunker down and punish us at a distance?"

Kith nodded. "Yeah. The entrance starts out narrow, then widens out farther on. Basically, think of it as a reverse funnel. Thin at the beginning, so we'll have to enter single-file. Then it widens out, allowing the bastards on the other end to attack us all at once." He knelt and outlined a large cone shape on the ground. Around midway on the shape, he made some slashes on the outside of either side of the cone. "Here. Around halfway, we have a handful of apertures on either side. Openings large enough for a defender to hide in, ready to lay down the hurt on anybody intruding." He pointed to the far end of the cone. "Here, at the end, we have some even uglier details. Barricades, around waist high, for ranged defenders to hide behind. I couldn't see much because it's too far and the light is dim, but there was definitely movement down there. I think I did spot the glint of an arrow once or twice."

"So, the moment we enter, one by one, we're going to see ranged attacks? And if we try to press on, we'll be attacked from both sides at once?" Chase was silent for a while. Then a large grin started to build on his face. "I think I'm starting to see how this should go. Ernest. You are going to be our secret weapon!"

"I...am?"

"Oh, you better believe it!"

CHAPTER 47

"There is a difference between being a true patriot and a supporter of a cause. The difference lies in the lengths the person will go to in order to support his beliefs." He then proceeds to lay out how Earth's Ward is better for being filled with patriots. Which is nice. However, patriotism, as we have seen, also brings with it zealots and close-mindedness. (Page 21.)

Chase laid out the plans. Then Cilia laid into *him* for being a suicidal moron. A few minutes later, they came to an agreement and were readying themselves. Their enemies, at this point, obviously knew that they were on their way and would be entirely prepared to rip them apart.

Ernest, still looking shell-shocked from how fast things were proceeding, did agree with the plan. He was currently standing a dozen feet away from the others with a look of concentration on his face.

The others kept their attention spread between him and their target. The single, too-tight opening in the circular, threatening construction loomed, ready to swallow them all.

"The casters are talking about sequencing," Ernest said. "Arguing, rather. One of them says he wants to use his Light Bomb card first, before the archers engage, and the other insists he should use his Rain of Stars first, because, and I quote, *the remnants'll be easier for you scrubs to handle.*"

"That sounds like an absolute darling," Kith drawled. "I'm guessing, and I know this is wild speculation, that Rain of Stars is what has the surface littered with body parts out there?"

"You are likely right," Sera agreed, ignoring the gore. "I know Light Bomb. It was a common caster choice in Isarn. Area of effect with both blinding and minor damaging effects."

Ernest ignored their discussion, keeping his attention fixed on the dome. Finally, he turned around, a strained look on his face. "Looks like they're decided. We can expect a Rain of Stars first, then the Light Bomb, followed by the archers trying to pick us off. Kith, was it? Have you spotted the casters? They must be close together for them to bicker like this."

"They are," Kith said. "Third and fifth opening from the left. They're hiding just to the side of the openings, so we need to lure them out."

Cilia nodded. "That will be our first target, then. Take them out, or at least shake them up. Then we move, with Kith's shadows to keep an eye on them. Once we hit the shield, you all know what to do."

"Hit 'em hard!" Liam grunted, clenching his truncheon like he was throttling somebody's neck.

"Fast and disappointing." Kith chortled. "Just like Liam with the ladies. Ow." He rubbed his neck where Sera slapped him.

"I can't believe you people ever made it into the towers."

"Neither can we." Chase grinned. "Standards must be slipping." He rolled his neck, then jumped up and down on the spot. "Everybody ready to risk their lives?"

Chase felt the smooth sensation as Sera's Blessing of the Night activated. It was a subtle effect, doubling his current Race of Life and raising his Agility to a total of forty-three. Of course, that wasn't as important as the effect that halved the efficiency of enemy Light effects. Still, Chase cherished the sensation that made his step feel smoother, his reactions tighter, more willing to do exactly what his mind demanded of them.

He looked over his friends, his family, and felt a momentary pang of love and adoration for them. The fact that they were willing to risk this with him to try to earn a real future together. He expressed that love in the only way he knew how. "Listen. If this blows up and we all die? I want you to know this. I'm blaming you all from the afterlife."

Chase jogged from the safety of the stairs, just peeking out above and at the platform leading to the dome and the forbidding entrance. Increasing his pace, little by little, he raced, then sprinted, moving straight for the entrance, as if he were trying to break through by sheer speed.

"Incoming!" Kith's shout went up from behind him.

Chase knew what that meant. Namely, that he was about to be blown right off the damn mountain, probably in pieces. He activated Steps of Brilliance, crafting three steps that arched up and to the right, allowing him to run through the air and away at a steep curve that should be entirely impossible. His knees protested as he took the steps, ignoring any distractions. He sent a gracious thought at his past self for training as hard as he had. If he'd tried a maneuver like this with less Strength, Agility, or Toughness, he'd have ended up with a broken ankle. Instead, he soared through the air in the exact opposite direction of where he'd been running a second earlier, arms outstretched ahead of him protectively as he curled into a ball.

His evasive maneuver succeeded. He managed to evade the center of the blast by nearly two dozen feet. Even so, the blast nearly killed him. He was mid-air when the glowing missiles landed and the concussive forces blasted him, sending him careening through the air out of control and landing badly, skidding across the ground in a mess of cartwheeling arms and legs.

"Get up, get up, get *up!*" Kith's insistent voice reached him through the haze of pain.

He scrambled to his feet, started to run again, before re-orienting himself and changed direction to race the right way.

A glance at the dome told him that they'd struck true. A single one of Cilia's shadow stakes managed to strike dead center between the casters, enfolding the entire area in a globe of shadows. It effectively blinded both casters. It wouldn't last for more than maybe twenty seconds total—the duration and efficiency of her crafted items went up along with her control, practice, and Mental Power—yet, it should be enough for them all to reach the entrance.

Chase caught up to Sera, and took her over. She was the last in line, as they raced after Liam. Arrows whizzed everywhere, startled by the sudden appearance of a small group of attackers.

The Light Bomb impacted. The caster must have decided to take a chance and cast it blind. Fortunately, it landed off to the side, and they were ready for it, mostly. Cilia stumbled for a moment, crying out, yet Ernest caught her shoulder as he ran, and Sera's Blessing of the Night card shielded them from half of the effect.

Chase's short sword lashed out at an incoming projectile, catching it on the flat side. The glowing arrow burst into a dozen smaller fragments, tearing into Chase's arm and shoulder, even piercing the leather armor in places. With a desperate toss of his head, one of the fragments managed to nick his eyebrow instead of piercing his eye.

Behind the wall, the other archers were waking up to the fact that they were under attack. Cards activated and arrows came increasingly close to the charging group. Fortunately, most seemed to focus on Liam, who, with his heavy armor, clay-covered front, and massive shield, simply churned onward. One bright shape surrounding Kith was struck dead-on by a projectile and faded into nothingness.

They reached the opening in the dome. Ahead of them, they knew, the heaviest concentration of enemies waited, ready to unleash hell on them the moment they stepped past the shield, just a few feet in.

For a few blessed moments, they were relatively safe, as the angle to the defenders near the arrow slits was too steep for them to keep attacking, and the defenders were waiting for them to come closer. Yet, they knew it was just a matter of time before they would be in firing range again. Liam pulled to the side, allowing Sera to move ahead of the pack and launch her payload.

Chase had wanted to use Squall Sling for this. It would allow him to propel any thrown item with extraordinary force and accuracy—however, changing to that would mean losing Steps of Brilliance and the option of changing to Sticky Fingers later if they ran into a protracted battle.

Hence, Sera was next in line. Her Strength was high enough that she could throw far enough, and her Agility was twenty-three, allowing her decent accuracy.

The blinding bracelet sailed through the air, down the corridor to where their enemies were waiting. The group collectively held their breath, waiting for the defenders to shoot it down, for a defensive function to activate and burst it apart, or for it to hit the walls and detonate prematurely.

It was a perfect throw.

The bracelet landed on the ground, nearly fifty feet in, halfway between where the melee defenders were waiting and the protective fortifications hiding the ranged defenders.

As one, they clenched their eyes shut.

The dark tunnel ahead of them erupted into a blinding explosion.

Even before the explosion had faded, Liam barreled forward into the corridor, shield held high.

The rest of them followed on his heels.

They burst through the shield, and any active effects on their cards simply winked out and died. The hall lit with small bursts of brightness as cards flashed into being and they enacted their plan.

Liam thundered ahead of them, ready to take any hits and keep going. To increase his defensive capabilities as much as possible, he swapped to Draining Ward, increasing his Agility with every single arrow that hit his armor or shield. On top of that, he had his Become the Clay card active, adding further defense and making enemy weapons stick to him. He half looked like an earthen golem, if those were stalwart, furious attackers.

Next came Kith. His shadows were down and out for the count, and the Divine Mentor card was still on cooldown. The bright shapes of his Sacrificial Saints hovered around him, ready to save his life. On top of that, he carried a surprise in store for the defenders. With a flash, the ground—the wonderful, fortified tiles that the earth-aspected Elementals loved to use for their defenses—tore apart, letting the Tainted Earth crawl out to paw at the defenders.

The Tainted Earth wasn't overly strong. It was exceedingly hard to kill, though, its oozing, expanding form ignoring most types of non-magical piercing and blunt damage. Also, above all, it was distracting. Its ooze-like blobs of arms soothed out to reach all ranged and casters nearby, grasping, draining, tearing.

Cilia, Sera, Ernest, and Chase ran right after the other two. They let fly as they sprinted, missiles sailing from their hands at every other step. It was the rest of the fire droplets, now reaching out to burn, hurt, and, above all, scare away the melee defenders. They held nothing back at this point, throwing everything they had. Ernest let his ice knives fly, as fast as he could pull them together, as much for the threat of them as for the damage.

For the defenders, the change had to be horrendous. One moment, they were looking down at an empty hallway, everybody ready to defend for the single attacker who'd be able to squeeze in at a time. The next, they were half-blinded, fire burst out everywhere, and there was *something pulling at their knee!*

The defending Lightborn, though battle-hardened and tough, were not working in their regular teams. As such, their teamwork already wasn't much to speak of. On top of that, they were in an uncertain situation, handling a defensive position they were unused to. The result was exactly what Cilia expected.

Arrows whistled through the air followed by a single fiery lance. Light flashed ahead of them, as the defenders used cards to cleanse, to heal, to buff themselves, or attack. Yet, their accuracy was off, and they were fully distracted by everything going on at once.

Liam hit the first pair of defenders like a caarnath running amok. His shield took the heavy spear strike dead-on, and, once he passed the aperture, his truncheon slammed out with a vengeance at the defenders, forcing them to reel back.

On his left, Kith followed on his heels. His left hand axe shot out to hook a shield downward, before the right slammed down—once, twice—and the defender fell.

They didn't stop to make sure he was dead. Liam didn't even finish his own opponent. He just kept on sprinting, while, behind him, the others ran on, one on each side to keep fending off the melee defenders.

Chase spotted a robe in the distance rising behind a barricade, flung a throwing dagger and heard the repressed cry. Then he swerved to avoid an attack from the spear wielder Liam had battered, nearly getting skewered. Instead of dealing with him, he kept running.

On his left, Ernest was the same, continually flinging ice knives at any enemy in sight, and running as fast as he possibly could.

The entire experience was like an advanced, chaotic version of the obstacle courses in their Combat Training. Attackers were everywhere, clamoring for their attention. However, where they, during the training, were taught to never leave any enemies behind them, here they moved as fast as possible, keeping up the pressure. One large, blindingly white orb with four hands and four weapons manifested in the center of the tunnel, yet they flowed around the summoned creature, deflecting or taking its attacks to keep on moving.

It worked. It was far from perfect and definitely not painless. As they emerged through the tunnel on the other side to reach the wide, spiraling staircase that would bring them the final several hundred feet to the pinnacle of the tower, they were all still alive and running, if somewhat the worse for wear. Behind them, they left a series of stunned, wounded, and shocked—but mostly alive—enemies.

They didn't pause to celebrate. Instead, they ran up the stairs as fast as they could. Liam, grunting, pulled an arrow out of his shoulder near the clavicle, and nearly sagged with relief as a flash of light washed over him, stopping the blood from flowing freely.

Behind them, the defenders kept loosing arrows at their retreating backs. The summoned orb flowed after them, but at a slow, ponderous pace. A few of the melee defenders ran out of the tunnel, but halted, turning to discuss with the other Lightborn as they ran on.

Ahead and above of them, the staircase continued, at least thirty feet wide, with a waist-height guardrail the only thing between them and the mile-high drop below. The wind howled past them, pushing at them, proving beyond a doubt that there were no shields, magical or otherwise, to keep them in, should they step outside the rails.

"Status?" Liam grunted, as his faltering pace picked back up. He carefully moved his arm as he ran, nodding to himself. A short sword was stuck halfway into the thick clay on the arm.

"I think one of my ribs is busted. Otherwise, good." Kith gasped for air. "Also, surprised. The magical shield was one-sided. I have my Tainted Earth coming up behind us, slowly." He dislodged the sword from the clay and showed Liam, who chuckled good-naturedly.

"Good," Sera simply said. Blood flowed from a superficial wound on her scalp.

"Alive," Cilia commented. She limped but wasn't falling behind.

"Fan-frigging-tastic," Chase said, voice pitched higher than usual. "I can't believe that actually worked!"

"But...it was your plan! You people are insane!" Ernest's right arm looked thinner than usual and was glowing slightly, probably the lingering effect of some debilitating card effect.

"It's a classic dilemma." Chase huffed, running backward up the stairs to see whether he could spot any delayed pursuit. The only thing he saw was the Tainted Earth slowly falling behind as it tried to keep up with them. "When people are hired as protectors and guards, they often don't know if they're allowed to leave the premises, even if they're robbed. What if the store's robbed while they're chasing after the culprits? Of course, here, it's even worse for them, given that they know there's likely to be other Protectors incoming soon, and them leaving would mean abandoning the defensive advantage of the tunnel." He took a deep breath, surprised that he was barely even winded. He'd have to thank Boneridge for being as mean as she was, if they survived. "We'll need to keep moving, though. They're sure to send somebody after us once they are able to think straight, even if it's just the summoner and a couple of ranged to take us down from a safe distance."

They did just that. Liam made a judgment call, used his Cleansing Fire card to fully heal, then swapped over to One Heart, Opened and used that to share his health with Kith and Cilia. Liam barely showed it on his face, when he took over some of the wounds of the others.

Chase speculated aloud as they ran. After the constant exertions and stresses of the past hour and more, Cilia, Ernest, and Kith were too winded to speak in more than short bursts while running. "We have one real issue now. With Kith's shadows on cooldown, we're going in blind. Meaning, I'll be the one to scout out ahead, see what is going on."

"Chase," Cilia started, but he shook his head.

"I'm sorry, but it has to be done. We need to know what we're up against, and I'm the most evasive of us and the fastest. I'll try to be careful."

They assented in short succession, and soon, Chase raced ahead up the stairs as close to the wall as possible, trying to avoid making too much noise. There was but a half mile or so to go, and he knew, just *knew* that anybody clever and unscrupulous enough to plan and pull off an attack like this would have some sort of defenses protecting them as they stole the decks. At this point, with his Toughness barely keeping up, he managed to pull ahead of them quickly.

Using everything he'd learned in the past few months, and his Mental Power enhanced by the precious potion, Chase kept his gaze focused, scrolling over every inch of ground as he progressed, knowing that any sign he missed could be what killed him. Even so, he nearly didn't catch it.

If they hadn't been part of the active training in innumerable sessions so far, he definitely would have missed it. Yet, the tiny hazy area near the wall of the many steps of the circular staircase gave it away. It was one of the many common traps they were exposed to on a regular basis. An air-aspected creation, basically a short, round base the size of a caarnath dropping, as well as a barely visible motion-activated trigger, yet with everything but the trigger hidden behind cleverly applied air magic. It was not one of the most feared traps in training, given that it rarely killed or crippled, but let loose a powerful blast of air to knock people off guard. Positioned as it was right next to the wall, however, the burst of air could definitely kill, given that it was likely powerful enough to knock anybody off the stairs, guardrails or not.

Chase halted for a second, considering his options. Then he removed the dagger from his sheath and put it down, leaving it on the ground with the tip of the blade pointing at the trap for the others to see. Then he moved out near the edge, keeping a healthy distance from the damn thing.

Of course, it wasn't the only one. A dozen steps farther, another trap lurked, this one a classic earthen blade trap. Chase debated his approach. He could either wait for the others so they would be able to pool their resources and bypass the traps together, or take his chances, range ahead and figure out what was in store for them.

Chuckling, he leapt the next trip line and carried on. Like he was going to slow down just because of *danger*.

The pinnacle of the towers was equally breathtaking as it had been the first time Chase laid eyes on it. Mystical, overwhelming, and impressive, it surely must have been the ultimate of human craftsmanship and magic combined. Today, however, that wasn't the only thing to make Chase's breath stick.

Right next to the entrance to the dome itself lay two bodies: the ceremonial Protectors who'd stood outside the dome. Both were dead, shredded to pieces in a display of savagery and violence that made Chase reconsider his approach for a second. Yet, that was not what truly made him pause. There were two additional details.

One was the light churning within the dome itself. Chase couldn't see from out here, but it looked like a buildup of earth-shaped, unclean dirty brown and yellow colors, clashing with clean blue and white, spilling out the entrance as if within, the aspects of the Elements themselves were doing battle.

The other was what lay in front of the entrance: a wide, open bridge, the naked approach granting anybody the time to appreciate the grandeur of the dome. The first time they'd been here, Chase had barely noticed it, the beauty of the broad bridge fading before the brilliance of the dome itself. Yet, today, he couldn't *help* but notice.

When people spoke about the Pits, they usually had the generic images in mind that the Church of the Circle talked about. A hedonistic place, where armies of the Dark frolicked in dark, demonic rituals, bestowing harsh and protracted suffering upon those poor people to make it down there, before locking non-believers in demonic servitude for eternity. How exactly that would work in practice, given that the Pits would keep growing forever, was one Chase had always wondered about.

Yet, he'd learned that the vision of the Pits differed, based on where in the world you were. The Elementals, for instance, carried images of the different aspects in their depictions. Churning magma pits, acid baths, frozen wind scouring the skin of the suffering, and so on.

The image right in front of Chase *very* much looked like a picture of an earth-aspected corner of the Pits he'd spotted on a mural in a chapel of the towers. Whatever the surface of the bridge in front of the dome was usually like, now it had transformed into a bubbling, demented tar pit, black and brown churning over the top of the surface. He didn't know what it was—whether it was a trap unleashed, a summoned creature, or some activated card. However, he knew, beyond a doubt, that if he put a leg down into that roiling, moving, bubbling mess, he wasn't going to pull it back up again.

For a moment, his gaze pulled back to the stairs behind him. Would it really matter if he took the time to wait for the others? Helped them dismantle the traps so they could attack this together? Surely, they'd be able to find some way past this?

Only, ahead of him, the colors were still alive. Yet, even as he'd frozen here, undecided, he felt certain he'd been able to spot the bright colors dimming, getting drowned out by the sickly yellow-brown colors.

Chase cursed and ran. He approached the bubbling mess, activated his Steps of Brilliance, and ran over the wide mess in long leaps. Edging closer to the dome entrance, he swept his gaze over the huge doorway, cautious for any traps that might lie in wait for him, before he finally stepped through the opening to the dome and took in the scene before him.

Caution long forgotten, the words spilled from him. "Instructor Boneridge? What the Pits?"

CHAPTER 48

"It all started with one person. A nondescript earth-as-pected crafter, who refused to cave. Somebody who would not give in to the pressures of the Lightborn. Somebody who stood up and said, 'Not a single step further!'" Somebody could argue they have a serious issue with hero worship. Somebody probably should. (Page 7.)

As the scene unfolded in front of him, Chase took an involuntary step back. The colors intensified ahead of him, portraying the ongoing struggles of powers. The Elemental decks of the towers, vaunted in their promise of knowledge and powers, were there for the taking, protective sorceries and mechanics disabled for the benefit of the new recruits. Well, *nearly* all sorceries. A wash of intense, cold colors preceded an oppressive storm pressing down on the Combat Training instructor. She, in turn, gritted her teeth and flexed, with an inaudible shout, pushing back against the forces arrayed against her.

Because it *was* their instructor. Instructor Boneridge. The strong, muscular she-devil who seemed to take as much comfort in grinding them down as she did in building them back up again. She stood tall against the swirling blades of aerial death trying to push down on her, seemingly keeping them back with nothing but her mental presence. Arrayed at her feet were piles of Elemental decks, all awhirl with arcane forces. Meanwhile, her regular instructor robes were literal tatters, hanging off her, betraying her cards. All five of them. She was a power of magnitude stronger than anything he'd ever faced before, except for Arnault. Near her, corpses lay: four Lightborn, undignified in death, slashed to death by the aerial blades that the instructor ignored.

"Instructor Boneridge!" Chase yelled again, this time a lot louder. His mind was running on overdrive, reassessing everything he knew, trying to take it all in. He knew two things above all. He couldn't allow her to abscond with the decks, and...he needed to stall. There was no way he'd be able to take her on by himself.

She turned around, glacially slow to his vision. Her eyes were bloodshot and cold, ready to murder. Her muscles bulged and she panted heavily. Her eyes glazed over and she blinked. "I...know you."

"Of course you do, Instructor Boneridge. You've helped us all train to survive any dangers. What's going on? How can I help?" He wasn't a moron. He knew she was the culprit here. Only, perhaps he could confuse her, stall...

The woman's gaze went through a series of expressions. Shock. Dismay. Shame. Finally, cold, empty weariness. "How did you make it up here? You must have left any number of Lightborn behind."

Chase shrugged. "They're still down there. I crept past them. Assess the situation. Adapt a strategy that doesn't get you killed. Overcome. Like you taught us." Her eyes were clear, now, and her hand crept to the brutal mace at her waist. He clearly wasn't fooling her. Abandoning half the pretense, he beseeched her, "What are you *doing* here? Stealing decks? Working with the Lightborn? Have you got any idea what this looks like?"

Suddenly, she looked *very* weary. "Kid, do you have any idea how old I am?" She didn't wait for a response. "I am sixty-three years old. I have lived through every iteration of trainees in the towers, since the very beginning. You're young. You don't get it. You will never understand what it's like, watching those you care for grow up, sacrifice everything they have to feed the monster of a war that never changes."

Chase felt the conversation slipping out of his control. "I agree. I don't get it. *Help* me understand! I thought that the towers were growing in power. That they were taking back control from the Lightborn, edging toward a foundation where they would be able to stand tall against anybody?"

"Hah." The single word held so much scorn, she practically spat it. "Spoken like a true water-aspected. Growth. Those bastards. They would count anything as growth. An administrator who owes them a favor. Some tiny concession, in trades, grains, or allowances to our armies. You talk to me about *growth* when our recruits and Protectors bleed and suffer every single day, simply to maintain a status quo for the damn bureaucrats! I'll tell you what it's like. *They would keep us embroiled in an eternal war, just to play their games!*" That last part, she bellowed, her hoarse voice thundering out, lashed with rage, fury, and so much hurt.

"So...you are going to sell them out to the Lightborn?"

Her voice grew cold, her eyes distant. "You misunderstand. Still, your words are more exact than you would know. I am going to sell our decks to the Lightborn. That will allow them to add Elemental cards to any Lightborn soldiers, learn all our secrets. It will undermine the very foundation of our strength." Her voice was tired. So very tired. "Finally, our leaders will have no choice but to surrender. We will be annexed by the Lightborn, our culture subsumed. Finally, we will have *peace*."

As she was talking, the bright forces protecting the remaining few decks had expanded. Now, the instructor rolled her shoulders, growling in concentration, and the force surrounding her grew to shove back on the bright, sharp winds trying to push her back.

Chase could see where she was going with her complaints. He couldn't really argue against it. She might be right, and she might be wrong. He would have to have access to vastly more information than Chase did to gainsay her—and even so, it wouldn't matter. With her being as deeply immersed in the process as she was, watching recruits and Protectors train, work their hardest only to suffer and die in the defense of something she considered a lost cause? It was as close to mental torture as she could possibly come.

Blinking, Chase came to a realization. "Wait. You...tried to get us killed? That behemoth! You weren't stunned or anything—you were faking it."

She slowly turned back to Chase, sickly light dimming around her. Regret filled her voice. "Yes. I saw a chance and tried to get rid of you. It was a bad plan, but the only one I could see to complete without making myself seem suspicious." She growled, "I was not made for this cloak-and-dagger subterfuge *crap*. I was made for conflict! If they'd listened to me and focused on building our strength instead of all this diplomacy, whispering in corners and subtle power changes, we could have had *real* power. *Real* heroes. Now, all we have are shades and copies, mimicking the forces of old, trying to live up to something that we no longer hold." The earth-aspected powerhouse looked at the few pillars still holding decks and sighed. "I realize you're stalling. I don't know what for, and it doesn't matter. Make your choice. Stand against me and die or stand back and survive."

Chase laughed. It was a sardonic laugh, filled with little actual humor. "I don't really have a choice. The Lightborn are already after me and mine. If you get your way, and they win? We're as good as dead. In short, if you don't give me an alternative, I'll have to stand against you."

"You would attempt that? You are Tier three, and I know all your cards. Please, don't. I have no desire to see you dead. You're just a rogue with some talent at distraction, evasion, and training. I was made for *battle*." She pointed at the back of the huge domed chamber. "The vaunted *High Elementalist*"—she imbued the words with so much scorn it sounded like a curse—"will tell you what your odds are. Or she would, if she were strong enough to stand up to me."

Chase hadn't seen her. It was no wonder. The High Elementalist was only barely visible at the far end of the large space. She was cocooned in what looked like a large gemstone built of compressed air. The gemstone surrounding the woman, as well as the pedestal holding one of the decks, was riddled with cracks, yet still held.

Belatedly, Chase realized that the pressure emanating against Boneridge came from her. Still, if the threat was supposed to teach him his place and make him back down, it had the exact opposite effect. Because now, he realized how he could actually win this thing. He wasn't alone. He had somebody on his side, and more backup to come, if they made it past that huge, bubbling trap out there. This wasn't a case of him against insurmountable odds. It was more a case of him having to avoid getting killed, running away and evading her, while everybody else did the work for him. Running away...that he could do! "Instructor Boneridge?"

"Yes."

Something flashed on her left leg, and her entire visage changed. Where, before, she'd been bulky to the point of dwarfing most male Protectors, now her shape changed, becoming rougher, more angular. Her skin also received a different color, more earthen in tone. *Some sort of armor?*

"Thing is, Instructor, you were pretty much my favorite teacher here. I mean, you were an absolute raging *bitch*—but you were even-handed about it and didn't play favorites. A guy can respect that sort of approach."

"Get to the *point*." Her voice reverberated weirdly.

"All I'm saying is, if you'd actually asked for help? For somebody to fight against the Lightborn, for somebody to rise up and become those heroes, those powerhouses you seem to be looking for? We'd have loved to give it a shot. Only, now, we'll never know. Because *you sold out your own*." Chase watched the words hit home.

Her eyes tightened and nostrils flared. Then her left arm and right leg flashed at the same time, as she went on the offensive.

Chase went into evasive maneuvers. He ran away from her, aiming to put a pillar between the two. Then he activated his own two cards. He kept Steps of Brilliance, for now, but swapped both his second and third Tier for his Dark cards, activating both Nights of Criffhaven and, with just a moment's hesitation, Free of Perdition. Nights of Criffhaven didn't give anything immediately. In fact, it lost him the damn Race of Life boost he already had. Now, it would, hopefully, allow him to survive the fight to come, letting him grow increasingly more agile as the fight progressed—doubly so if...no, *when* Sera made it into range. Free of Perdition, however... Chase's body changed as the card kicked in and his Toughness expanded to match that of the instructor. He felt more solid, more grounded, and filled with an endless well of stamina. It was no surprise that the second part of the card didn't activate—he didn't have the Mental Power to replace the instructor's Toughness with his own.

She attacked, and suddenly, he had no time to marvel at the changes. Her mace glowed, a trio of brilliant rocks floating around the steel-studded tip of the weapon. On top of that, as she dragged her foot across the tiled floor of the dome, it carved up a furrow of tiles, launching them at him with unerring precision.

Chase managed to avoid most of the tiles, deflecting one with his sword, but one of them struck his arm, making blood spray from the impact.

During their attacks, she'd managed to switch their places, putting herself between him and the exit. She halted, deep voice laced with confusion. "What was that? That should have broken your bones. I know your limits. I've seen your cards. *What was that?*"

Chase laughed, taunting her. "Oh, come on now, Instructor. Like you're the only one around here who has secrets? I'll give you a little hint." He slowly bared his left arm, letting the tiniest hint of the edge of his card become apparent. "Surprise," he sang. Nights of Criffhaven gave him his first tick upward in Agility.

"Dark cards." Her words were a mix of incredulity and confusion. "You're just a recruit. How in the blistering nethers of the Pits have you— Are there— Are we under attack? Are the followers of Dark back to take what they lost? But..." She trailed off, momentarily confused, even as the whirling cold winds gained purchase and pressed down on the earthly energy around her.

Chase spoke earnestly, without further attempts at humor. "Listen to yourself. *Are we under attack?* When you're pressed, you know that you're part of the Towers. You don't want to do this. You don't want to give it all away to the damn Lightborn. You really think they'll keep up their end of the bargain? Or are they just going to run roughshod over Earth's Ward and finally eliminate all of you? I will tell you where I got these cards. Just, please, let's sit down and talk it out. We'll figure out something."

The look of her coming to a decision was a physical thing, a process that almost hurt Chase to look at. Something in her eyes died, even as her face hardened and shut off. There was a scary lack of emotion in her voice, as she eventually spoke. "No.

I have come too far, done too much, to balk now. For now, the most important—the *only* important—thing is to ensure that the towers stop their endless spirals of death and destruction. That means releasing our decks." With that final comment, she launched into her next attack.

For an eternity, it was all Chase could do to evade Instructor Boneridge. The vast dome surrounding them soon felt cramped and way too small, with the instructor following right after him, death in her eyes. He gave up any pretense at a real fight, and went all out on evasion. Several times, he tried to escape back out the opening. If he had empty space at his back, he'd be able to pull her away from the decks, back to his crew. Together, they'd be able to take her down.

Only, she didn't take the bait. Whenever he started moving too far away, she'd move back and make headway on attacking the High Elementalist. She would not let herself get distracted. Not only that, but the difference between the two became wildly evident. During a lull in the battle, he checked out his attributes.

> Personal Info:
> Name: Chase
> Title: Dark/Elemental/Light rogue
> Step: 18 (Tier 3)
> Strength: 16 (+1 Tier bonus) (+5) = 22
> Agility: 20 (+9 Tier bonus) (+8) = 37
> Toughness: ~~17~~ 54 (+1 Tier bonus) (+5) = 60
> Mental Power: 15 (+1 Tier bonus) (+5) = 21
> Potential: 26 (+1 Tier bonus) = 27

His Toughness was incredible. He'd never imagined reaching such heights, not even with Sticky Fingers. It felt like he would be able to take a sword to the stomach and keep going, run forever. Either the bulky Elemental had a buff that raised her Toughness to insane heights, or she'd trained to the point where she was practically invincible. Agility-wise, he definitely had her crushed. However, it didn't help him much.

Her technique and experience left him outmatched and reeling at every turn. On top of that, the two combat-oriented cards she'd engaged left him constantly at peril. The swirling missiles surrounding her—clearly magical maces—could be unleashed at a thought and be sent soaring against him, and they regenerated after a while. On top of that, she was able to mold anything—the tiles, the pillars, anything earth-oriented in nature—with a mere kick or punch, sending it flying at him.

One misstep, one bad judgment call, and he'd be history. If it weren't for the added Toughness granting him additional stamina, strengthening his skin and very bones, he'd likely be dead already.

Chase fell to the ground, his sword clattering across the, now ravaged, tiles. He spat a mouthful of blood, rolled, and fought back to his feet, ready to force his wounded limbs into acquiescence.

The marvelous room had transformed. Furrows were torn into the formerly pristine tile work. Pillars had toppled. At one point, she flung a head-sized boulder that smashed a gaping hole in the side of the building. At the far end, the High Elementalist was still keeping up the defense of the solitary deck she held. However, the cocoon looked laughable compared to the strength of Boneridge, and worse, the instructor was keeping up her onslaught even as she slowly tore Chase apart.

He panted, watching blood drip from his hand with a distant, mesmerized sensation. He was being killed, he realized. His Nights of Criffhaven card was finally starting to feel noticeable. Even though it felt like forever, it had only been five minutes, as proved by the boost from the card. He wouldn't make it further.

The instructor clearly realized that as well. She looked at him with dead eyes, momentarily filling with something that could have been pity. "Last chance," she rasped. "Give up. Or die. You can always run away."

Chase considered it. He seriously did. For just a second, he nearly caved. They could always flee again, take to the countryside. Only...it wasn't just him. It was his family. Was he going to force them to go into hiding, for his own survival? "I could," he admitted. "Only, it's not about me. It's about what I'm willing to give up to make sure my own people can live a good life. *Which you should know.*" He watched the words impact her like a physical blow. Then he felt a sensation, like dipping your head in a barrel on a warm day, or a playful finger running up your spine. It was relief and reward both.

Chase grinned, tasting the blood in his mouth. His gait felt lighter, like he was floating on air. The boost to his Agility wasn't too much. Just an additional six points. What it meant did make him feel better than the increase itself. "You're too late. We're about to show you just what family can do, when we fight for one another."

As one, they looked to the entrance and the roiling, churning trap that the instructor had left on the bridge. They watched—one in elation, the other in grim shock—as the team crossed the bridge *on top of the Tainted Earth*. The poor summoned creature was clearly hurt by the passage and fell apart into a dirt-colored mound of mud seconds later. Yet, it made it, spilling the group safely on the other side.

Chase shrugged. "Sorry. You might think that you're doing what needs to be done for your own. But so are we. And we all have Dark cards. Give up now. I'll see to it, somehow, that you don't hurt what you're trying to protect."

Instructor Boneridge cackled. There was an edge of insanity in there. "It's sad. If only I'd had more people like you training—more heroes—I wouldn't have had to do this. There is one thing you have refused to learn, however. Always make sure you have an exit."

Chase prepared himself for an attack, readying himself to dive out of the way.

Instructor Boneridge turned on her heels and ran...straight for the decks she'd managed to secure. She scooped them into a backpack and kept running...straight for the wall. The place where she'd already made a hole in the wall showed the night sky ahead, brightening slightly with the impending dawn.

Chase, confused, started to follow her, but didn't understand. *Surely she wasn't going to kill herself?*

Just before she reached the wall, she transformed. One moment, she was the sturdy, blockish shape that her card had changed her into. The next, she changed into a massive, ten-foot-tall boulder rolling straight for the wall at speed, and smashed its way through, right out into open air.

Behind Chase, his friends were coming up to him. They looked the worse for wear, clearly having dealt with pursuit, traps, or both on their way to close with him.

Sera raised a hand at him, relief and joy beaming at him, as she ran.

They didn't understand. How could they? That boulder...it had to be summoned to protect the instructor! She was tumbling down the mountain *right now!* When she hit the ground, if she survived, she'd be able to make it out of the city unhindered and meet up with the Lightborn. She hadn't gotten all the decks, and definitely not the original deck, which had to be the one the High Elementalist had cocooned herself around. Still, it would be a major blow for the Elementals, and would mean the end for them. A protracted, agonizingly slow end.

Gritting his teeth, Chase held up his hand to greet his family, his friends. It would double as a farewell, too. Then, with a pain-filled grimace, he sheathed his sword, turned around, and flung himself out of the hole in the wall.

So many things went through Chase's mind at once. Weird, irrelevant details. Surprise at the strength of the winds buffeting him about. Thoughts about just how stupid he was. The realization that he'd forgotten about the defenses that were supposed to be on the outside of the walls. A burst of fire behind him was likely one of the defense systems of the towers trying to burn him to a crisp, yet he was past it before it even activated properly. Yet, it all paled at the look of the steep mountainside maybe a mile below him, coming closer, much too fast.

Part of his brain processed how the boulder struck the same mountainside, didn't break, and kept rolling. Most of it was drowned out by the overwhelming litany of "I'm gonna die!"

Finally, so far beyond sheer panic that it felt like he'd already died, his head found some weirdly detached sensation—a sense of calm, as if this were happening to somebody else and he was simply here as an observer. His body adjusted, almost by itself, arms and legs extending. He bent his arms slightly at the elbows, extending them in front of him. Then, he allowed his legs to bend back until his feet pointed upward. Suddenly, he found, he was able to steer his body by adjusting his balance. It was tricky, and he almost overextended a few times, yet his Agility allowed him to make the most minute adjustments—and he found himself angling forward. Oh, he was still going at a pace that would kill him many times over. The only difference here and now was that it looked like he'd be able to do it just beyond the expanding slope of the mountain itself.

For a few seconds, he simply concentrated on angling himself as far forward as he could to avoid crashing on the steep mountain. Far below him, his mind briefly noticed, then forgot about, the boulder striking the mountain, hurtling into the air past the wall and out into the city beyond.

The fact that Chase had his Steps of Brilliance card still active had seemed like a saving grace when he leapt off the dome. Only, now, hurtling at a speed he'd never reached before, he realized that if he were to create a step below him to halt his downward progress, it would break his legs and *still* send him to his death. Some calm part of his mind, though, told him that this wasn't at all unlike the mudslides back in Isarn—how kids playing at the outskirts of town would sometimes, during the heavy seasonal rains, fling themselves down a slickened, nearly vertical mudslide that would only even out a hundred feet further downslope. It wasn't the hit that would kill you. It was the angle.

Watching the courtyard below the towers come inevitably closer, he created the first platform at a steep angle while angling his body to prepare. He hit it, feet-first, flexing in his knees to avoid hurting himself. Nevertheless, the pain almost sent his knees up into his stomach, and *did* send his free-fall into a spiral. He dropped at least a hundred feet more until he managed to level his body slightly in the air. Then he tried again, this time even steeper, trying to compensate slightly for the switch in his body weight. This time he only allowed himself to hit the platform for a split second, creating another one farther down with almost the same angle. There was almost no shift in his speed, yet, on the third platform, he managed to use the tip of his toes to fling himself farther forward, take a bit more of the weight and acceleration off.

The next trio of platforms came slightly less vertically. Chase was still hurtling down at an uncontrollable pace, but these three attempts to break his fall were slightly more controlled...more rushed, ultra-fast actual steps than the earlier attempts that seemed more like trying to sprint down a wall mid-air.

Little by little, three platforms at a time, with only tiny, second-long pauses to adjust his aim in between...twenty seconds after the dumbest decision of his life, he was not falling anymore, but on a solid spring mid-air at a forty-five-degree angle. Yet, he was, miraculously, surprisingly, in *control*.

Chase spared a split second to look far up and into the city and spotted her straightaway. Well, not *her*. However, the immense plume of dust and the weak screams past the huge walls surrounding the towers, that could be heard from half a mile away, couldn't be anything but her.

With a last, controlled set of platforms, Chase hit the ground a couple hundred feet past the tower area, and set off running. As he did, he switched his Steps of Brilliance to Sticky Fingers. For the second time in his life, he was going to go all out because of a woman. Only, last time, it had been to save somebody, with his team at his back. This time, it was to save his team and the entire fire-charred Elemental stronghold, and there was nobody here to save him.

CHAPTER 49

"Mercy is a luxury. So are principles, politics, and limitations. Yet, at some point, they become necessities. At times, I ask myself if we, as a nation, have toiled, in the name of survival, for so long that we have forgotten to ask...at what cost?"
That went to a dark place. It's something I've considered as well. So far, we have yet to cross any hard lines. Yet, are there any limits we would not cross to protect our own? Sometimes, I wonder. (Page 101.)

Chase sprinted through the streets of Earth's Ward. It could have been a reason to grow nostalgic, really. To think of that first intense arrival to the city. To consider how his only real outings to the city had been punctuated by running and fighting for his life. Yet, at this moment, he was way past that. He didn't even dare wonder at the absurdity of having survived the mile-high drop. The second he hit the ground, arms and legs propelling to maintain his equilibrium, he activated Sticky Fingers on a gawky teenager who stood with his mouth wide open at his sudden appearance. Then he hunted.

Two minutes and eight attribute increases later, Chase located the impact crater. The building had been a pottery, he decided. The amounts of shards, smashed clay, and elaborate, vivid colors strewn from the building and into the street itself was evidence of that. Now, it barely constituted a building. The second story had a boulder-sized hole straight through it, the roof was a thing of the past, and it looked like the proximity to its neighboring buildings was the only thing keeping the edifice upright. Chase tried not to look too closely at the number of very still forms sprawled around the wreckage. It would appear some potters started their work early.

Across the street, he found where her wild descent had finally stopped. There, a—thankfully empty—jewelry store now lay open to the elements. Chase stuck his head inside the wall, noticed the handful of enterprising go-getters who were busy using this chance to help themselves to the merchandise now freely available, then saw the remnants of the stone ball. Buried halfway into the next wall, the layer of solid earth that had helped the instructor survive the fall had been slammed around badly during the descent, with large planes cracked off or showing damage. Yet, it had made it, and now lay cracked in two like an egg. There was blood inside, betraying the ungentle descent...but no instructor.

Stealing a point of Agility from one of the looters, he burst out of the opening again and looked around. *Damn it. Which way to go?* Chase spent a second orienting himself, trying to locate where he was. He *thought* he had a decent idea, but his attention up in the air had kind of been drawn by...well, not plummeting to his death. Nevertheless, the sun was starting to grow in the sky, and at least he wouldn't have to run in full darkness.

There was one other piece of good news. This early in the morning, fewer people were out and about. That meant, it would, theoretically, be easier to find her. *Theoretically*. A cloak, a change of clothes, catching a ride inside a caarnath-drawn carriage—there would be any number of possible venues that would make it harder for Chase to find her.

Only...this was her backup plan. More like, the backup plan's backup plan, considering they hadn't originally planned to attack the towers just yet. There was no way she'd planned for this from the get-go, unless she had some serious suicidal predilections.

Chase took off. He was closer to the eastern gate than any of the others. With everything going on, he had to count on Instructor Boneridge trying to finish her job straightaway, instead of hiding out somewhere. She'd have to know that the chaos following the theft of decks would be monumental.

He found her three minutes later. She limped down the street, covered in dust and blood, ignoring the shocked looks she got by passersby. Her gaze was locked on the distance, where the eastern gate could be spotted. Yet, she wasn't done. With staggering speed, her head shot around to fix on the noise that came from Chase's pounding feet.

With all his considerable Agility and every instinct ingrained in him by countless times of needing to avoid being spotted, he acted immediately. He flung himself into a side alley and activated his Heart card.

It felt like it had been ages since he'd last used it. He'd used it once or twice when he and Kith were investigating the towers, but not in any life-or-death situations. Nothing to See Here remained a core part of himself. Staying in the background. Being inobtrusive. Back in Isarn, the card had failed, often as not. Often, he was already exposed when he tried activating it. At other times, his Mental Power was simply too low compared to the people he wanted to avoid getting discovered by.

This time, heart pounding, with his back toward a wall in the side alley, his Heart card activated perfectly. There was no outcry, no pointed fingers. Nothing. He waited for a few seconds that felt like hours. Then he glanced around the corner, and watched the traitor amble off down the street again. Chase followed her.

There was a trick to following people. Okay, there were several tricks, several different ways of approaching the task, of trying to make it close to a mark without them discovering you in the process. It also depended on what you wanted: whether you were learning their behaviors, doing a snatch and dash, scoping them out, or simply looking for dangers. Today, Chase was working with a very specific mindset: what to do, when you need to catch up to a suspicious mark without them noticing.

The best approaches were out. He didn't have the time for a proper disguise, didn't have any backup for distractions, and Nothing to See Here would be running out any moment now. Also, learning her patterns and behavior ahead of time was, obviously, out. Hence, there were only the remedial options, which were...not the best. Still, he made do.

People, in general, were absolutely self-absorbed. They noticed little about their surroundings and tended to remain focused on their own purposes alone. However, there were certain things that attracted the eye. Rapid movements. Others fixedly attempting to look away, when they really are trying to follow you. Certain stiff movement, betraying that you've been caught out. The more paranoid a mark, the more likely they were to notice these things and take a second, closer look.

Chase knew all this. Hence, the first thing he did was dump the tunic of his recruit uniform. It was bloodied and torn-up enough that it would attract attention by itself. Then he snatched a large hat from a passing cart to hide most of his face. Finally, he spotted a busy official who was walking in the right direction, faster than Instructor Boneridge, and put himself square on the opposite side.

Instructor Boneridge was not looking good. In fact, her looks were damaged enough that several passersby spoke to her. Her answering snarls chased them off. Her head swiveled around to anybody who came near her, and she looked ready to kill.

When the official he followed came closer to taking over the instructor, he let him move farther ahead...following, but at a distance.

The official, who strode ahead with a no-nonsense gait, passed by Instructor Boneridge with only a few feet to spare.

She turned on him with a hiss, and the official shied away like she was a rabid dog.

Chase, meanwhile, abused the momentary distraction and silently moved up on the other side. Once he was within ten feet of her, he unsheathed his short sword and *struck*.

She nearly caught him. At the last moment, she pivoted—a clumsy, jerky movement—and her arm shot out at chest height.

Yet, at that point, Chase was positioned a lot lower. His entire body extended as he put his weight on one foot, lunging with the sword. Even as she turned, the blade hit the back of her ankle above the shoe and bit *deep*. There was some resistance there, other than the flesh and muscle, but Chase ignored it, pushing hard. Then he tossed himself backward, out of her reach.

A stone shot out and caught him in his midriff. He retaliated by stealing a point of Toughness from her and distancing himself even more, ignoring the sensation of something digging into his stomach.

"You! How did you…" Her leg buckled under her, and she dropped to her knee. "How are you alive?" she finished hoarsely.

Chase got his first really good look at her now. She still carried the backpack, now secure on her stomach. Whatever card she'd used to harden her skin was still in effect, yet there was some serious damage there. Her left arm dangled unnaturally, and one side of her face looked cracked and slightly off-center, like an amphora imperfectly mended.

"Told you I had to stop you, didn't I?" Chase flung his head back and yelled, "Protectors! Somebody call the Protectors!" Directed at her, he continued, drawling, "That's the first time I've done that where it wasn't a distraction, I don't mind telling you that."

Her hand shot out and carved into the street. A furrowed stack of tiles and dirt sailed out at Chase at speed. He dodged the missiles, granules of dirt partly ruining his vision. With a twinge of pain, he recovered, only to have to dive away again to evade the next attack.

Around them, early risers and businesspeople fled the streets, some shouting curses, others yelling for the Protectors.

Chase retaliated with a Sticky Fingers, grinning at the point of Agility that left her. "You're done, Boneridge. Seriously. Make it easier for yourself."

She limped a few, halting steps closer to the gate that beckoned, maybe half a mile away. Her gaze shot back to Chase, lost. "You don't know what I've done."

"Oh, I have a few ideas how bad it is," Chase shot back. "Only, at this point, you'll have to admit it backfired. There. Can you hear the whistles? They'll be here in a second. If you really love the towers, you will give up and make the rest easy for them. *Because you are done.*"

Whether it was the buildup of pain and injuries or that final realization, Chase didn't know. Yet, that broke her. The solid, seemingly unbeatable fighter sank down to the earth, even as tears spilled from her. Her eyes fixed again on the gate and didn't leave.

Chase didn't allow his eyes to shy away from her. Alert for any betrayal, any attack, he kept up using Sticky Fingers any chance he got. All around them, whistles started to blow, then grew louder as Protectors came closer to their positions. Finally, the first Protectors became visible farther down the streets and Chase allowed himself a tiny, shaky huff of laughter. The comedown from his boosts this time was going to *suck*!

The Protectors didn't make things easy. Of course they didn't. Chase was a Darkborn, dressed in what could, with some examination, be recognized as recruit garb, while Instructor Boneridge was clearly a Protector from the towers. Yet, the decks in the backpack, still huddled on her chest, were not easily explained. In conjunction with the ongoing attack and the apparent lack of information coming from the towers in the latest few hours, the decision was, unsurprisingly, to lock them both up and kick the issue further up the chain of command.

Within the next half hour, Chase was chained alongside Instructor Boneridge, questioned, and tossed in a caged wagon...again, alongside Instructor Boneridge. They were then, with much ceremony and dozens of Protectors, ferried back to the towers. After that, he was separated from the instructor and introduced to more questioning and a seemingly endless row of demands, questions, and claims.

He probably didn't help his own case. Chase stopped using his cards, and, with the conflict over and done with, his attributes returned to normal. He crashed and crashed *hard*. Fortunately, his base attributes had grown since the last time, helping him weather the aftermath a tiny bit better. (Meaning, he didn't entirely pass out.) Also, he hadn't reached quite the same heights as when they rescued Sera back in Isarn. Still, him holding on to his head and groaning like a gapweed addict probably didn't help him look believable.

His latest stay was a cell, somewhere in the earthen side of the towers. The cell was clearly enforced, both magically and physically, with just a tiny, slitted window that allowed him to see the naked corridor and the Protectors right outside. The single, hard bed, however, was increasingly alluring, and he had to fight to stay awake between the rounds of questioning.

The heavy door slid open silently. Chase spotted two figures right outside. One was Professor Brookwatch, their World Knowledge teacher. The other was...Cilia!

Chase's heart pounded. His befuddled mind threw up increasingly unlikely scenarios. *What now? Was Professor Brookwatch part of the attack as well? Was Cilia being tossed in with him?*

The teacher said something Chase didn't catch. Cilia nodded at her, then turned toward Chase and did something absolutely wonderful.

She smiled at Chase. Cilia smiled—a heartwarming, reassuring smile at odds with her usual look.

The door closed again. Within a minute, the exhaustion won. Chase slept.

CHAPTER 50

"We do not forget. This is a direct quote from the first High Elementalist, Faleena of the Wings. Earth's Ward is a temple built entirely to necessity. We bow to pragmatism and worship everyday needs. Yet, we do not forget what brought us here in the first place. We do not forget the Lightborn." I knew there was a reason I liked the place. (Page 12.)

"This is most uncommon. Yet, everything about this day has been uncommon. As such, I believe that it is only fitting."

Chase only half-heard the sentence from the High Elementalist. Most of it was muffled by the heavy hugs from his teammates. He'd only just been escorted to this room, though they'd at least had the grace to take off his chains. To his surprise, what waited wasn't yet another interrogation session with increasingly high-ranked questioners, but his family, free and looking cleaner and healthier than he could have hoped.

Finally, they emerged from the group hug, though Sera still held onto his arm tightly, like she couldn't entirely convince herself that he was real. Cilia, standing well back from the hug, gave him an awkward smile.

"These are your own chambers?" Chase asked. The rooms were large—not palatial, but definitely of a higher quality than their recruit rooms, with heavy, well-worn furniture and what looked like remnants of her work all over the place.

"They are. I never hold audiences in here. Yet, these are anything but normal circumstances."

Chase felt something curl up tight in his chest. His battered brain made a tenuous connection. "That doesn't sound promising. You're not going to commend us officially, then?"

"Perceptive. Your teachers did agree about that. Also, temerarious. Most people would be more roundabout in asking for something as touchy as that." The air-aspected Elemental looked a lot better than when Chase had last seen her. Her hair was immaculate, back to bobbing about her head in a controlled, mesmerizing circuit, while her dress, covered in living, bobbing tassels of cloth, was more subdued than the times they'd seen her on official business. "No. I am not going to commend you officially. Not now that I know who you are, according to the Church of the Circle."

"Oh." Sera's single word said it all.

"Yes. Oh! Fugitives, then, who have stolen cards from the Church in Isarn, killed inquisitors, and harmed and killed a great number of Lightborn military personnel." She delicately waved her fingers. "The official reports go on to list any number of other offenses, yet I am inclined to believe your version of the events. If I listened to *their* version, I would be, at the very least, kicking you from the towers, and possibly investigating what the Lightborn would pay for your return. That is what we have on the one hand."

She raised the other, balancing them evenly. "On the other hand? You have saved our towers. You have, at a massive risk to your own lives, uncovered a plot to sell us out to the Lightborn and seal our fate as, at best, another subsumed territory, our culture relegated, our cards restricted. You have delivered to me the main traitor, who has revealed a, I do not hesitate to admit, *disgustingly* extensive number of sellouts, traitors, or opportunistic mercenaries in our midst." She kept raising the second hand and lowering the first, putting the scales out of equilibrium. "As such, I would be inclined to embrace you, reward you, and accept you among our ranks to be lauded as future Protectors."

"But?" Chase guessed.

"Just so. But you put me in a dilemma. Embracing you? It would mean war. Not just our present skirmishes and protracted stalemate. All-out war. Obviously, the fire-aspected among us are clamoring for this. So are a number of my air-affiliated brethren, and, surprisingly, some of the water-aspected who see this as stepping all over the legitimacy of their diplomatic arts. However? It is not the wisest path set before us. With everything that has happened, one thing stays true, even truer than before. We do not have the power to strike at the Lightborn. War or not, we cannot strike back efficiently at them. Instead, using this attack, and their underhanded attempts at stealing our powers, we can use it, let them save face, while we milk it of all the concessions and admittances that we can in the process." Her eyes were apologetic, but warm and sparkling.

Chase wanted to vomit. All of this, and *this* was how it ended? Being sold out when they'd risked everything for them? Kith had been right. They'd been wrong in trying to become legitimate. They should've run, found a way to carve out a place for themselves instead. Only...why did all the others look like they knew something he didn't? Pits, Kith was *smirking*!

He gave up on figuring it out. The day had been too long already. "What am I missing here?" he demanded.

The High Elementalist smiled. A wide, toothy smile that showed all the warmth of a huge feline who wanted nothing more than to snack on your entrails. "We do not forget!" she exclaimed. "Do you really think I am going to send you back to our *enemies*? I would, of course, if it were necessary to the survival of the towers. Even so, you have presented me with the juiciest of possibilities. A Deck of Darkness? Finally, after all this time, having somehow escaped the clutches of the Lightborn inquisitors? And you have made it *here*? There are many words for how unlikely this development is. Many would call it fate. I call it...a chance to be grasped!" She held up a singly, stately digit, requesting patience.

"Before we continue to the future, I should enlighten you on exactly what you have managed. Without a Wellspring of your own, there is no chance for you to know. Yet, in your specific situation, it is only logical for you to be aware." She tapped her lip, then nodded to herself. "Had our traitor escaped with these decks? It would have spelled trouble for all Elementals. Any Lightborn absorbing either of the decks and creating a Wellspring would be able to grant Elemental cards to anybody. The Wellspring would also earn other gains, yet... that is inconsequential. The point is, that the Lightborn would have access to our cards. *For as long as the one absorbing the deck lives.*"

Chase considered this, then thought to the way Arnault's deck had fallen to the ground upon his death. "Meaning, if they'd beaten you and taken the *original* Elemental Deck..."

She nodded. "The first situation spelled possible doom. This would be the certain death of Earth's Ward. The deck would stay with them for all eternity, while our own would dissipate with the end of the wielders' death."

Chase tried to take in what that meant. They truly had the only Deck of Darkness in existence then, since any other wielders were likely to be long dead. He searched her eyes. Despite the fervor, there was no cruelty there, or at least, none that seemed guided at them. "So...what are you planning? Whatever you're about to do, you clearly want to do it off the books or we wouldn't be in here."

She nodded. "Let me answer that with a question. You have defied the Church of the Circle. You have made a mockery of their nobility. You have kicked the Lightborn traitors in the teeth. If you could ask for a reward...what would that be?"

Chase searched his heart. He didn't have to look long. That part, in spite of all that had happened, had not changed. "A home! We've talked about this. The towers...they could be a home to us."

The High Elementalist took a deep breath. "Spoken just like Faleena of the Wings. Yet, that is the one thing I cannot grant you."

Chase grimaced. "Because of the Lightborn. Because of the Church."

"Exactly. However, if you believe that I am going to send you on your merry way, you are very mistaken. I believe that you and I can come to an agreement, that will culminate in us both obtaining our heart's desires."

He blinked and looked at the others. They were looking entranced at the High Elementalist as well. Whatever they'd talked about, this was news to them as well. "Well...you truly have our attention."

"First. You have the ability to grant Dark cards to people."

It wasn't a question. Still, Chase assented. He saw no reason to prevaricate at this point.

"Did you know that, centuries ago, before the schism between Dark and Light, before the aspects fell out, most cities of a certain size held all five decks? If you passed the tests, you could freely gain cards of all kinds!" She smiled, as if that had any logical connection with what they were talking about. "I would ask you to grant cards to a hundred Protectors of my choosing. Not only would that strengthen the towers, it will create another, secondary deck, that I would ask for you to leave here with us."

Chase cleared his throat. "That...is quite the ask."

"It is. That would be entirely to the benefit of the towers, and grant you nothing, except perhaps a tiny boost to your Title. Yet, I would not send you away unguided. In fact, I would send you with aid. And with a mission." She walked to an ornate chest and pulled out something. A battered, torn and dirty, old backpack. The High Elementalist knelt before them now and opened the backpack. "I would have you try to reclaim those old times. I would have you try to rebuild just that. A refuge. A place, with access to all kinds of cards, where anybody would be able to go and earn access to any sort of cards, unimpeded by the nobility and tyrants of this world." She extracted something from the backpack and laid it in front of them. It was a deck. A multicolored, glorious thing, sparkling with all colors of the Elements in perfect balance.

She settled back and watched them evenly. "Am I being altruistic in this? Of course I'm not. If you choose to do this? You will eventually be painting a target on your backs. However, we are not the Lightborn. We take great pains in using the decks to the fullest, knowing how they work. Our historians know even more. For every deck you absorb, your Wellspring, when you eventually build it, will be stronger, be able to grant better Titles to all takers. Your growth will be explosive. Your foundation stronger than any other on Ordei."

Hoarsely, Chase asked, "But...we're still just us?"

"No. Elementals have survived alone against the Lightborn. Yet, we are not a solitary blaze in the night. We have always entertained talks with the Furyborn. There is a...degree of trust between us, if not outright cooperation. This, I believe, can be the peace branch to finally set into stone the necessity to work together for a better future, for all Ordei."

Eyes gleaming, she stood and paced back and forth in the large, open room. "Let me put this straight. Even if you aren't going to entertain this, I will let you go. You have helped the towers, and, besides, you have caused so much trouble for my enemies, I have no doubts you will continue doing so. But if you *do* believe this worth a try? You will officially be let go from the Protectors as having failed, your ranks redacted to look like you were culled. Unofficially, we will outfit you, we will equip you and grant you the introductions you need to reach the Furyborn. You will have a way to contact us on the sly. Then, if and when you secure a deck of Fury, we will talk.

"If, eventually, you should manage to find a place to establish a Wellspring with all decks, we will be ready to help with anything we can. And I mean *anything*. At that point, we will be able to put our full support behind you." She shrugged, suddenly looking old. "Others have suggested—insisted, really—that we take your deck for ourselves. Fortunately, your honor and behavior convinced everybody that this would be too much like acting like the Lightborn, taking what we can simply because we have the power to do so. This...it's the compromise we came to. It's a gamble. You might fail, get crushed underfoot by the Lightborn. You might end up proving a short-lived distraction that can help our nation gain a much-needed break. Or, eventually, you might help us crush this unholy stalemate of constant conflict and help us build a better world. *What do you say?*"

Chase, wide-eyed, blinked at the momentousness of her offer, at what it might entail. He looked at the others.

Liam, beaming with pride, nodded eagerly. Kith had one eyebrow raised mockingly, as if to say "Like this is even a question?" Cilia faced him, even-keeled, decisive. Sera's eyes were filled with so much, all of it good.

He had to fight back tears. Eventually, he managed, "Looks like we'll be aiming to build a home."

EPILOGUE

"What is our purpose, you ask? Nothing but freedom. Unfettered, sweet freedom. To be what we want, to move as we want, to spread the Elements all over Ordei. We will not rest before then." Kith would make so many dirty jokes over this. I find that I approve. The freedom to act and move as you would want to? That is something worth fighting for. (Page 16.)

"Are we really doing this?" Liam's voice was doubtful and skeptical. He looked at the door, through which the High Elementalist had just left.

She had told them to settle down and take their time to talk things over, do what they needed to do. Currently, they sat on the plush couches around the tiny table that held the shimmering Elemental deck.

"Choosing our cards? Try to stop me, big guy!" Kith drawled.

Liam rolled his eyes. "First off, you don't want me to try, twigs-for-arms. Second, you damn well *know* that's not what I mean. Are we really going to...you know. Go to the Fury lands? Try to build a goddamn town or something? Stand up to the Lightborn empire? That doesn't exactly sound like something that's good for our health."

"If I may?" Sera asked.

"Of course you can," Chase said.

Kith snorted. "Well, you *would* say that. Typical situation. A wench comes along—"

"Finish that sentence, and I will show you just how violent nobles can be," Sera snapped.

"There we go." Kith grinned, completely unabashed. "She found her courage." In a stage whisper, he said, "Sometimes, they just need a tiny nudge to get them going."

Cilia slapped him on the head.

Sera bowed to Cilia. "Thank you. Now, I know I have not been with you forever. However, I do believe that I know you quite well by now. Your actions show who you are. You care about your family. You care about your friends. And you have trouble sitting still, especially when things are not like you believe they should be."

"Sounds like you're making us out to be some sort of heroes." Liam snorted.

"Gods no. You are way too self-centered for that." Sera laughed. "But neither are you villains. You could have easily sat back and let everything play out this night. We had done our part in unraveling this mystery, had we not? But no. You decided we should face off against countless enemies because you thought the trained fighters of the towers would not get the job done."

"That is *not* at all what happened," Chase said.

"I imagine you'd remember it differently." Sera laughed again. "How do you remember aiding Gunnha back in Isarn?" She shook her head and waved off the protestations. "Let us be realistic. We have ticked off several important people. Creating our own home, with the aid of powerful friends? It sounds like the best of all worlds. A place where we can ensure that nobody takes advantage of others. Where nobles cannot take advantage of their lesser." She shrugged. "If we get ourselves in trouble? We run again."

Liam barked a laugh. "Do what we want, and be ready to run? Count me in!" He squatted over the glowing deck still placed at the center of the small table. "Hard to believe that people will kill for this, isn't it? It *is* shiny, though. Want to do the honors?"

Chase nodded and reached out to touch it. The tingling sensation buzzed up his arm, energizing him.

[You have located an Elemental Deck. As the holder of a Deck of Darkness, you have the option to accept cards from it or bond with the deck, absorbing it. Which do you choose?]

[You have bonded with an Elemental Deck. From now on, through you, anybody may share in the Elemental gifts. In addition, any Wellspring you create will be strengthened, carrying attributes and granting bonuses born of Dark, Light, and the Elements.]

The deck faded away into nothingness, multicolored light circling around Chase. He felt like he could wrestle a caarnath. Climb the towers. Take a hit from Liam. "I am *never* going to get tired of that sensation." He shook himself like a dog. "It's done. We're ready to pick cards. Who's up first?"

"This time," Cilia spoke up quickly, "we do it right. We discuss what we need as a whole beforehand. *Then* we leave it up to each of us to ruin that choice." She looked straight at Kith, who mumbled something under his breath.

"Let's do me first." Liam rubbed his hands.

"Okay then," Cilia said. "What have you got? Your current Tier-one card is either the Dark life sharing one, the attack that gives you trample, or that Elemental clay defensive one, while your Tier-two cards are Cleansing Fire and Draining Ward, right?"

He nodded.

"That means right now, you can mostly go fully defensive if that's needed, with some healing and cleansing powers. I think it's clear what you need," Cilia concluded.

"Speak softly and carry a big-ass hammer?" Kith grinned.

"Just so. Additional damage."

Liam looked at everybody, then nodded. "I will say I could've used some added damage when we climbed the towers. Big attack, it is." He reached a hand forward toward Chase.

Chase took it and sent a tiny burst of energy his way, allowing him to access the cards. By now, this part was second nature. Sharing powers with anybody demanded just a tiny mental nudge. It was usually *slightly* more overwhelming to be on the receiving end.

This time, though, Liam started to laugh through the roiling energies and opened his eyes after just a few seconds. He rolled his shoulders. "Well, that was easy. My new card is titled, very appropriately, Earthen Might."

[Earthen Might
Common, Elemental fighter
Tier two
Active, very short duration
Sometimes, the best way to end a conflict is through instant, overwhelming force. How you decide to apply said force is up to you. For a brief window of time, the fighter's Strength is doubled.
Short cooldown
"Yeah, I guess I'm a bit scrawny. I 'unno. I think I can take you in arm wrestling. Care for a tiny bet?"]

Kith whistled. "Yeah, that'll do. What's your Strength now?"

"Twenty-four."

Sera coughed. "I thought it was a bit lower? Impressive! That card would bring you nearly to fifty in Strength. That would overpower every single fighter in our class for a moment. Also, I wonder if my boost would still work on that. We can play around with that. I agree, however. Amazing choice. As your Strength grows, so will the utility of the card."

"Who's next?" Chase asked.

Liam cleared his throat. "That would be me again."

Chase's jaw dropped, then he laughed in astonishment. "You sneaky bastard. That's why your Strength improved. You reached the third Tier?"

Liam beamed. "During our climb. Fifteenth Step, baby!"

Kith's fists pumped the air. "Well, what are you waiting for? Our chances for survival just skyrocketed. Find out what you earned!"

Liam nodded. "Of course, the new Tier gave me an upgrade to one of my cards. I already improved Become the Clay to Rare. The layer of clay is doubled, but the weight remains the same."

"Not bad, not bad. That should help you survive just about any regular weapon. But what about the *new* cards?" Kith wheedled.

"Okay then. Let's see." The big Lightborn closed his eyes and concentrated. His mien softened to a blank expression, constantly changing as he processed his choices.

The others followed as he went exploring. Surprise. Dismay. Elation. Focus. Disgust? Finally, a long, full-body shudder went through Liam, as Dark, Light, and Elemental colors swirled through him.

"That is never going to become any less unnerving." Liam shook himself like a dog. "Okay. Here we go. Three new cards. Dark, Light, and Elemental."

[Ravenous Shadows
Uncommon, Dark fighter
Tier three
Active, very short duration
Some cards only need a single thought as you activate them, then you can forget about them. This card does not. Upon activation, it smothers the wearer in a layer of magical shadows that absorb a level of impacting magical attacks for a brief while. Once this duration has passed, any consumed energies are converted into a Strength boost with short duration for the fighter.
Medium cooldown
"You don't fight fair. But that's okay, see if I care. Hit me with your best shot!"]

Kith frowned, then nodded. "Good choice, mate. That Become the Clay thing will protect you from physical attacks. This one should help with magic...only, you'll have to join me in Mental Power training. Looks like timing's going to be a bitch with that card."

Liam sighed, but nodded. "Figured as much. My Light and Elemental choices were more about making sure we'd be able to go the distance."

[Convince the Unbeliever
Uncommon, Light fighter

Tier three
Passive
This card consists of a passive and an active element. The passive element is a weak, but constant self-heal. The active element engages at the start of any conflict, granting a +1 to the wearer's Agility for every minute, maxed at +5.
"I say to you again. My beliefs grant me the strength needed to persevere. Is that all you would send against me?"]

[Unleash the Elements
Common, Elemental fighter
Tier three
Active, long duration
Activating this card adds an Elemental aspect to your attacks. For every attack made, another Elemental aspect is added. When all four Elements are engaged, their power grows with each successive attack.
"My power is no match for yours, esteemed Protector Erfwen? Give it time."]

"I thought about our fight with the behemoth and what I could've done against Instructor Boneridge." Liam grimaced. "My issue was that I had nothing really powerful to bring to bear. This should help."

Cilia slowly nodded. "Well chosen. If we are in a drawn-out fight where we need to stall, you can choose Convince the Unbeliever, go defensive and self-heal, even share your health with us with One Heart, Opened. If we're up against something truly tough, you can engage Unleash the Elements and your attacks will keep growing more powerful."

Chase added, "Yup. And if you need immediate power, Earthen Might will do the trick."

They shared looks. Kith spoke first. "You go ahead now, Sera. I actually have some thoughts on your pick."

"Oh, this'll be good," Cilia murmured.

He rolled his shoulders and ticked off on his fingers. "Your Tier-one picks are Blessing of the Night, which works wonders increasing all other buffs, and that Light heal you have...and the tongue thing that can give fire damage."

"Tongues of Pride *is* a weird name," Liam added.

"Focus," Cilia scolded.

"Tier two is that Dark card that lets you shield, heal or buff and then that Light buff where you decide who gets it and which attribute. So, the way I see it, you have excellent healing powers and boosting powers, right? Even a bit of utility, if we hit an enemy that's weak to fire. What you need, though, is something to save *your* ass. Damage, personal shield, whatever. We can't always be there to save your butt, and it's time you admitted it."

Cilia glared at him. "I'm annoyed at having to agree. Sorry, Sera. He's right."

A series of nods from the others, and Sera succumbed to the group pressure. She closed her eyes and lost herself to the process. It took longer for her, but eventually she blinked and grimaced. "Okay. I'm sad to say that there are no huge surprises from me. I reached Step fourteen, however, so there is not far to the third Tier. As to my new card... This isn't perfect. But I believe I like it."

[Unexpected Spillage
Uncommon, Elemental healer
Tier two
Active, instant
A battlefield is like an ocean. The waves go low and high. Sometimes, they act exactly as expected. Sometimes, you find unexpected lulls and towering waves coming from out of nowhere. Upon activation of this card, the healer may transfer one hundred percent of the force of an incoming attack, magical or physical, made on the wielder or anybody grouped with the wielder, to another being within range of the card.
Short cooldown
"Stop hitting yourself. Oh, who am I kidding? By all means, keep it up!"]

Chase gawked. He shut his mouth with an audible clack. "Okay, fair. I see what you mean. It won't save you if you don't see the attack coming, or don't have time to react. Also, I guess it wouldn't be any good for many smaller attacks. But still...this would let you take a direct hit from that inquisitor and funnel it *all* back on him? That's insane!"

The others quickly piled on to agree.

Cilia added, "Also, the way it's worded, it looks like any upgrades could increase the percentage of force that's redirected."

"Wait. So...a tiny cut could kill somebody?" Liam asked.

"Nothing so drastic, I assume," she responded. "But yes. That is the theory."

"Wow." The big guy sat back in the comfortable couch, blinking. "That's amazing. So...how about you, Cilia? Any plans?"

"Yes and no," she said. "I have a bit of an issue. My cards are quite decent. Being able to manipulate Fire, Light, *and* Dark puts me in a league of my own. On top of that, the card that allows me to blend aspects easier and A Hint of Permanence have me prepared to craft something extraordinary that will *last*. Except, the past two months have proved beyond a doubt that my knowledge of leatherworking is way behind the curve. The best for me would be to stay here and craft, uninterrupted, until I could become a *real* Protector."

Chase frowned. "You know, that's actually not a bad idea. I'm sure we could come to an agreement with the High Elementalist. We could leave you here and come back for you—"

"Stop." Cilia held up a hand, shaking her head. "Like I'm going to let you go off and get yourself killed without me to guide you. No, what I really need is something that helps me shore up those shortcomings, and do so while we're away."

Chase smiled. "Whew. I didn't exactly relish the thought either. I agree with your theory, though. Any other thoughts?" He looked at the others. "No? Okay. Elements preserve you, I guess." He held up his hand.

Cilia emerged with a shudder. "I am *never* going to get used to that sensation." A tentative smile emerged. "I think I got what I wanted."

[**Ritual of Fire**
Uncommon, Elemental crafter
Tier two
Passive, Activated
Crafting by itself can be draining, both on willpower and stamina. Now, however, you can decide whether you want to sacrifice your energy for improved results. Once activated, this card will continually siphon small traces of stamina from the crafter to remain working. While in effect, for the purposes of crafting, the crafter's Mental Power is increased by fifty percent.
"Donande-tak, donande'tek, eru menthala-ze...damn. Candle blew out. Lousy second-hand candle makers. Kill 'em all when I rule the world."]

"Fifty percent!" Sera breathed. "Yes. That should very well do it. Of course, it will be draining on you, but with my boosts, we can make it work." She hugged Cilia, who, to everybody's surprise, hugged her back.

"My turn? My turn!" Kith cracked his knuckles. "Now, I know what you're going to say." He changed his pitch to sound like a bad copy of Cilia. "You need something big to defend yourself." Waggling a finger, he continued. "That's not happening. I can defend myself. I have the Sacrificial Saints to take any stray blows, and we *know* that the big lug will be there most of the time." He cleared his throat. "Right now, I have my shadows, my Divine Mentor, and the insect swarm for the first Tier, my

Tainted Earth and that ugly bugger Crescendo of Might for the second, and Coils of Shadow, those lovely snakes, and Sacrificial Saints for third. That's got me with plenty of stalling power, decent defense, amazing scouting and ambushing, and some acceptable melee damage. The way I see it, either I'll want something to boost *all* my summons, or something for ranged damage. Thoughts?"

"If you're not going to listen, why ask for our input?" Cilia scolded. She exhaled heavily and conceded, "If that is the path you want, either choice would be logical, I suppose."

"That's all I wanted to hear." Kith bumped his fist with Chase's and closed his eyes. Moments later, he opened them again, dancing a small dance with his shoulders. "You guys. This...is going to be amazing. We're not entirely there yet, but..." He chuckled and recited the details of the card.

[...Twice the Fun
Rare, Elemental summoner
Tier two
Passive, permanent
Sometimes, you crave something new and interesting. Sometimes, the best choice is simply more of what you already have. This card, when chosen, will double the number of summoned creatures for up to two other cards.
"You think my summoned squirrels underwhelming? Wait 'till I show you...more squirrels!"]

"That's...absolutely ridiculous! I love it!" Liam half-laughed. "Sure. Right now, it's not going to change *that* much. But if...when you hit the fourth Tier and manage to upgrade it? Maybe even fifth? You'll be able to swarm them!"

"Right?" Kith held his hands up. "Please keep me alive until then!"

"Depends if you keep waking me up with those damn shadows of yours!" Chase growled. "What about your third-Tier pick?"

Kith blinked. "Oh. A second."

This time, Kith's jaw dropped almost immediately. He gritted his teeth through the transformation before turning on the others, breathing, "This is *ridiculous*."

[Fiery End
Uncommon, Elemental summoner
Tier three
Instant

Sometimes, in order to obtain your goal, you will have to make sacrifices. Summoned creatures are a means to an end. This card can ensure that the end in question will not be yours. Upon activation, any summoned creatures of yours explode in a violent conflagration, doing fire damage to anybody caught in their vicinity, proportional to their size and mass.
Long cooldown
"Outmaneuvered? Outmatched? One could see it that way. Only, why do you believe I have spread my summons this far out?" The last day of the city Acs Epilium.]

"Darkness take my eyes," Chase breathed. "So, first you get to double your number of summons, then you blow them up?"

Kith shrugged. "Yeah, well, again, I'll need more Tiers for it to be really effective, but the long-term prospects are pretty insane."

Chase nodded, eyes wide. "No complaints on your choice, mate. I guess that only leaves me? Let's see. For Tier one, I have my Sticky Fingers to net me added attributes, Steps of Brilliance for walking on air and Squall Sling, for a bit of ranged help and maneuverability. For Tier two, I have more Agility with Nights of Criffhaven for a slow, huge buff or the Light Agility buff for a smaller, instant buff. Tier Three is...Free of Perdition to steal a *lot* of attributes at once, and Spoils of the Undeserving for improving through training." He scratched his neck. "I guess right now, I'm fast, adaptable, and...if a fight drags out, I'll likely win it. Also, my attributes are growing to a decent level. What do I need then?"

"Damage." Liam and Kith said it at the same time.

They laughed, and Kith spoke up. "Yeah. No discussion there. If you can do some real damage right away instead of those butterfly kisses you call hits, that would help."

"I hear you. What else?"

Sera smiled. "We trust you. You have been able to surprise us and everybody else. Pick something good. A bit of defense would be nice, to keep you alive."

Raising his eyebrows, Chase nodded carefully, then entered to make his own decision.

[You have walked the Steps and reached the second Tier. Through the Elemental Deck, that grants you the right to choose a new card.]

Chase took in the choices. He was offered two Uncommon air cards: one a centralized force effect to himself, and the other a group buff, adding air damage to any melee strikes. The former was too close to the effect from Squall Sling, which was higher-ranked, and the latter...they had so many buffs already.

That left three cards, all rare. The first looked mostly to be a utility power.

[**Among the Raindrops**
Rare, Elemental rogue
Tier two
Active, medium duration
Upon activation, this card will start continuously summoning puddles, guided by the wielder, within a thirty-foot radius of the wielder. The puddles of water have a twin effect, both working only against enemies. First, they have an oily, slippery effect and will make it hard to keep one's balance. Second, they have an acidic effect, causing ongoing damage against any exposed skin or equipment.
Long cooldown
"Your fancy power is to make me stand in a puddle of water? Hah. Wait. Why are you laughing?"]

Chase ignored it. He had enough utility powers, and the damage would likely be inconsequential. He took in the final two cards, both rare, both damage powers, seemingly in direct opposition.

[**Razor's Edge**
Rare, Elemental rogue
Tier two
Active, instant
Fine control is all that you need. Sure, casters will burn entire fields with their fire waves and such—but that's just compensating. It's easier to backstab somebody with a small, hidden dagger than a two-handed axe. This card, upon activation, lets you magically fling a small, rapid, magically imbued razor blade, propelling it in a straight line for up to thirty feet. It does very high damage.
Short cooldown
"Ah. That is an impressive giant sword. Well, I got a razor's edge. With a razor's edge."]

[**Fiery Grenades**
Rare, Elemental rogue
Tier two
Active, instant
Sometimes, what's needed is chaos. And you won't find anything finer for that than the fiery grenades. Upon activation, you gain

three fiery grenades for you to throw. The caltrops will cause high damage in a radius if they hit anybody. If they do not hit, the grenades will remain on the ground for up to a minute, whereafter they will self-detonate.
Short cooldown
"You know those silent, nice surprises? These are the other kind."]

That was a tough decision. Both of these would do the trick, really, and help him cause some ranged damage. Sure, he'd have to throw the caltrops by hand, but they would cause a bit of area damage, where the razor's edge likely had a tiny area. He considered, then reconsidered. Both of these would help with ranged damage. But ever since the start, their strength had not been in overpowering strength, but the power to persevere, to grow, and outlast any enemy.

At this point, Chase already felt confident that he'd be able to match almost any single opponent in Agility, if not in skill. If he were able to take the entire *area* around himself and adapt it to the advantage of him and his friends? They would be able to outlast any enemy, direct damage be damned. Sighing at the inevitability of his friends' disapproval, he picked Among the Raindrops.

Chase took a deep breath and dove straight into the third-Tier choice, taking in all the choices. Then he looked at one of them again, re-examining it for any hidden traps or surprises. Finally, blinking in amazement, he made the selection before the deck changed its mind and realized just what it had offered him.

[Winds of Change
Rare, Elemental rogue
Tier three
Passive, Permanent
Versatility is a way of life. You understand that. Most don't. However, being able to surprise others with a vast array of abilities at hand may win you the day. This card is passive, remaining in effect whenever equipped. For as long as you have it equipped, you may switch freely between all other cards. There will be no limitation except a thirty-second cooldown after switching a card from each separate Tier.
"You hear that, you gods-forsaken bastard? It's the wind. It's blowing with the winds of change."]

For most people, this would be bad, verging on horrible. Spending a Tier-three pick for that, instead of something that would give you outright power? Not a chance! For Chase, however, who already had three cards for each Tier and was about to visit the Furyborn for yet another selection, it would allow him to switch cards on the fly without limitations, always able to adapt to the situation and ever-changing nature of the battlefield.

With a happy sigh, Chase opened his eyes and looked at his friends, who stared back at him expectantly. He bared his teeth at them in a grin so wide, it stretched the corners of his mouth. "I don't know about you. But I feel ready to take on the world!"

The end of Theft of Decks book 2, in the Theft of Decks series.

CARD OVERVIEW AT THE

END OF BOOK TWO

Chase:

[Nothing to See Here
Heart card
Active, short duration
The attention span of the average person is a fickle thing. What will keep you interested one moment will seem dull and unimportant the next. Sometimes, to get from one to the other, all it takes is a nudge. For a limited time, become less interesting to anybody around you. Those with higher Mental Power than yours may be less affected or unaffected.
Medium cooldown
"Now, to all those watching, I would love to extol upon you the forty-eight virtues of clean living. The first..."]

[Sticky Fingers
Legendary, Dark rogue
Tier one
Active, instant
Stealing is such a *clumsy* endeavor. Too easy. Anybody can steal a purse. This card allows you to go a step further, carefully manipulate strands of Darkness to grasp onto the key attributes of a mark, temporarily making them your own from a short distance.
There is a minuscule chance of the increase becoming permanent.
Short cooldown.
"You lost what, ma'am? Your Agility? Oh. Perhaps I can help you find it near my virility and hairline?"]

[Steps of Brilliance
Rare, Light rogue

Tier one
Active, instant
This card grants you the option of creating three palm-sized plat-forms wherever you may choose. These platforms are visible *and* tangible only to yourself, unless faced up against an adversary with much higher Mental Power than yours. The platforms only last for a short duration, but you may constantly create up to three platforms.
"I saw him, once. His was not the power of flight. No, it was a lot more unnatural. He moved like he did not belong in this world." A bystander, about the Acrobat of Virn.]

[**Squall Sling**
Rare, Elemental rogue
Tier one
Active, instant
This card allows you to create a localized brief burst of concen-trated air from your hand. This will allow you to add increased impetus to thrown items, deflect incoming strikes, or even change your direction mid-air.
Very short cooldown
"Out-throw Kargar the Giant? Kargar laugh! Kargar... HOW YOU DO THAT?"]

[**Nights of Criffhaven**
Uncommon, Dark rogue
Tier two
Active, medium duration
Some rogues go for the throat right away. Others like to drag out the fun, bleed their enemies and make them truly realize their defeat before they have even lost. This card, once tapped, grants you a slow build-up for as long as you remain engaged in hostilities. Every minute you remain engaged in hostilities grants you an additional temporary point to Agility, to a maximum of +15. After fifteen minutes, you have five minutes at the maximum boost, following which the buff is deactivated.
Long cooldown
"Stop trying to hit me and hit me!"]

[**Race of Life**
Uncommon, Light rogue
Tier two
Active, medium duration

This card, once tapped, grants you a small boost to Agility. It can be used several times a day, making it perfect for those who often need to work in bursts.
Medium cooldown
"Some people say that life is a marathon, not a sprint. Some people are wrong. Life, the way I see it, is a marathon of sprints. And we should plan accordingly."]

[Among the Raindrops
Rare, Elemental rogue
Tier two
Active, medium duration
Upon activation, this card will start continuously summoning puddles, guided by the wielder, within a thirty-foot radius of the wielder. The puddles of water have a twin effect, both working only against enemies. First, they have an oily, slippery effect and will make it hard to keep one's balance. Second, they have an acidic effect, causing ongoing damage against any exposed skin or equipment.
Long cooldown
"Your fancy power is to make me stand in a puddle of water? Hah. Wait. Why are you laughing?"]

[Free of Perdition
Rare, Dark rogue
Tier three
Active, medium duration
Tapping this card allows you to forcibly swap one of your chosen attributes temporarily with that of another living creature in short range. For a brief while, become as strong as an indomitable rager, as swift as a sky hare. If the target does not resist the effect, they will also see their attribute score temporarily replaced with yours. The effect remains until the cooldown runs out.
Medium cooldown
"How did you do that? Those skinny arms? It cannot be. 'The Beast' Sinclair has been brought low!"]

[Spoils of the Undeserving
Rare, Light rogue
Tier three
Permanent, passive
In this life, all good comes to those who earn it. Some people, though, are able to adjust the tendrils of fate, carve off more for

themselves than what they actually deserve. With this card, the wielder will improve their attributes through training at a triple pace compared to others.
"You can tell me, man. What potions are you on? I want some."]

[Winds of Change
Rare, Elemental rogue
Tier three
Passive, Permanent
Versatility is a way of life. You understand that. Most don't. However, being able to surprise others with a vast array of abilities at hand may win you the day. This card is passive, remaining in effect whenever equipped. For as long as you have it equipped, you may switch freely between all other cards. There will be no limitation except a thirty-second cooldown after switching a card from each separate Tier.
"You hear that, you gods-forsaken bastard? It's the wind. It's blowing with the winds of change."]

<u>Kith:</u>

[Cost of Life
Heart card
Medium duration
At what cost power? This is a question many ask themselves. You do not need to. You know the price. Whenever you need to, you have power, right at your fingertips. Upon activation of this card, your attributes are doubled for the full duration of the card, with no instant detrimental effects afterward. The only detraction? Every activation will cost you a year of your life force.
Long cooldown
"It whispers, does it not? That pulse, that promise, of strength and power, right at your disposal. You need only reach out."]

[Shadow Master
Rare, Dark summoner
Tier one
Active summon, long duration
This card allows you to manipulate your own shadow, split them into two shadows and order them around at a distance like they were your own summons. The augmented shadows are magically strengthened and enemy eyes cannot pierce them. The summoner may at any time choose to see through the shadow's

eyes and speak through the shadow's mouth as if it were his own body. They can only be destroyed by magic or Elemental damage. If destroyed, there is a 12-hour cooldown for the next summon.

"It flew, I tell you. His shadow burst from his body, walked right up to me and mocked me. Threatened me. I seen it!" Careem. Denizen of the slums of Veriten.]

[**Divine Mentor**
Rare, Light summoner
Tier one
Active, medium duration
This summon brings forth a divine entity from the heavens. Internalized, the being will aid the summoner, increasing all their attributes and improving their movement speed. It can also be expended, guiding the entity to a chosen position before making it burst in a blinding light.
Long cooldown
"Behold, oh mortal. I am you. Only better, bereft of this fragile shell of yours. Follow my guidance, if you can."]

[**Apian God**
Rare, Elemental summoner
Tier one
Active, medium duration
The queens are commonly recognized as the highest ranking in a beehive. However, with the use of this card, you summon something else: an apian god, controlling hundreds of tiny air-aspected summons. They are not as large as regular bees, but still cause tiny amounts of stinging air damage.
In addition to this, depending on the Mental Power of the summoner, nearby regular flying insects may recognize the natural hierarchy of the apian god and join in the attack.
"I. Summon you. Into. Beeing!" The Court summoner finally snaps.]

[**Tainted Earth**
Rare, Dark summoner
Tier two
Active summon, medium duration
This card allows you to awaken the soil anywhere you choose. It cannot be used directly on rock or crafted surfaces. When you tap the card, the earth grows to life in a shallow puddle of

tainted earth. The earth is extremely adhesive and hard to re-move. It can move, but only slowly. When touching skin, the soil drains enemies of Toughness at a slow rate. If destroyed, there is a 4-hour cooldown for the next summon.
"What's that? Get it off. Get it off!"]

[**Crescendo of Might**
Rare, Light summoner
Tier two
Active, short duration
Most summons are brought into the world with the desire to keep them present and active for as long as possible, given that they are the tools with which the summoner interacts with Or-dei. This summon is the exact opposite. It comes with a time limit and the express desire to create as much damage as possi-ble while it can.
Medium cooldown
"I am reading its mind right now. 'Rend, tear, kill!' Are you sure this is a being of Light?"]

[**...Twice the Fun**
Rare, Elemental summoner
Tier two
Passive, permanent
Sometimes, you crave something new and interesting. Some-times, the best choice is simply more of what you already have. This card, when chosen, will double the number of summoned creatures for up to two other cards.
"You think my summoned squirrels underwhelming? Wait 'till I show you...more squirrels!"]

[**Coils of Shadow**
Rare, Dark summoner
Tier three
Active, long duration
This card, once tapped, summons a number of small, venomous dredge spitters, calculated as one viper per two Mental Power of the summoner. These vipers are hard to spot in the dark, but vulnerable to Light powers and effects.
"Who's a lovely danger noodle? You are, my beautiful hazard spaghetti." The Valniers head chef races toward disaster.]

[**Sacrificial Saints**
Uncommon, Light summoner
Tier three
Passive, long duration

Nearly all summoning cards are active cards, requiring a certain degree of manipulation on behalf of the summoner. The bright saints summoned by this card do not. These are erstwhile heroes, souls so suffused with the power of self-sacrifice, that they feel the need to continue their deeds in the afterlife. Activating the card summons a random number of saints, between three and five. Each saint will attempt to block one attack against the summoner, be it magical or physical. Bear in mind that some attacks may be too powerful to be wholly blocked.
"You would not get this from any other. I will never give you up, nor let you down. We are no strangers. You know the rules, and so do I."]

[Fiery End
Uncommon, Elemental summoner
Tier three
Instant
Sometimes, in order to obtain your goal, you will have to make sacrifices. Summoned creatures are a means to an end. This card can ensure that the end in question will not be yours. Upon activation, any summoned creatures of yours explode in a violent conflagration, doing fire damage to anybody caught in their vicinity, proportional to their size and mass.
Long cooldown
"Outmaneuvered? Outmatched? One could see it that way. Only, why do you believe I have spread my summons this far out?" The last day of the city Acs Epilium.]

Liam:

[Heart and Hearth
Heart card
Long duration
From the heart comes that which we love. It provides life, love...and heat. For a while, your body will emanate a comfortable heat. Enough that anybody within your close surroundings will feel the difference.
Long cooldown
"Come close, love. Do you feel this? This, from my heart to yours."]

[One Heart, Opened
Uncommon, Dark fighter
Tier one

Active, instant
This card grants you a short-term Life Share ability. At your choice and direction, you may drain your own health and divide it among others, healing their wounds. Be warned that there is no upper limit here. If overused, you will drain your own heart's blood.
"I…did say I would give you my heart, did I not? Last C—" Final words of Shadow Knight Georgius Micael.]

[**Waterfall of Light**
Uncommon, Light fighter
Tier one
Active, instant
There are those fighters who advocate for technique, know-how, and weapon control to save the day. They tend to ignore one detail: with enough power, everything else falls at the wayside. Tapping this card causes your next attack to gain Trample. The attack will be very difficult to deflect or block, and has a medium chance to stun the enemy or knock them prone.
Short cooldown
"Rise, good sir. I was merely delivering a point. Get up…please." The chevalier earns his exile.]

[**Become the Clay**
Uncommon, Elemental fighter
Tier one
Active, short duration
For a short while after activation, the outermost layer of your skin is converted into magically thickened wet clay. The clay will make it much harder for any attacks to pierce and may cause weapons to get stuck. The layer is heavy and may make it harder for you to move if you do not have the Strength to handle the weight.
Medium cooldown
"Give that back, you stupid, filthy weapon thief." A master duelist is defeated.]

[**Draining Ward**
Common, Dark fighter
Tier two
Passive, permanent
Many fighters believe that the pathway to victory means not getting hurt. Amateurs. Veterans know that the only thing that counts is being the last one standing on the bloody field of victory. This card works on your currently worn armor and adapts

it in two ways. First, it grants the armor a minor increase to its protection. Second, anybody who scores a hit against the wearer on the armor sees their Agility drained by a point.
"Hold on. A second. I've stabbed you. Three times. Why are you. Getting faster?" The death of Squire Ulrien.]

[Cleansing Fire
Uncommon, Light fighter
Tier two
Active, instant
When activated, this card sends a wave of purifying power through the body of the wielder. It cleanses the body of most diseases and hostile effects, while also granting the wielder a weak healing effect.
Medium cooldown
"Who's ready for the next round? I can keep this up forever."]

[Earthen Might
Common, Elemental fighter
Tier two
Active, very short duration
Sometimes, the best way to end a conflict is through instant, overwhelming force. How you decide to apply said force is up to you. For a brief window of time, the fighter's Strength is doubled.
Short cooldown
"Yeah, I guess I'm a bit scrawny. I 'unno. I think I can take you in arm wrestling. Care for a tiny bet?"]

[Ravenous Shadows
Uncommon, Dark fighter
Tier three
Active, very short duration
Some cards only need a single thought as you activate them, then you can forget about them. This card does not. Upon activation, it smothers the wearer in a layer of magical shadows that absorb a level of impacting magical attacks for a brief while. Once this duration has passed, any consumed energies are converted into a Strength boost with short duration for the fighter.
Medium cooldown
"You don't fight fair. But that's okay, see if I care. Hit me with your best shot!"]

[Convince the Unbeliever
Uncommon, Light fighter

Tier three
Passive
This card consists of a passive and an active element. The passive element is a weak, but constant self-heal. The active element engages at the start of any conflict, granting a +1 to the wearer's Agility for every minute, maxed at +5.
"I say to you again. My beliefs grant me the strength needed to persevere. Is that all you would send against me?"]

[**Unleash the Elements**
Common, Elemental fighter
Tier three
Active, long duration
Activating this card adds an Elemental aspect to your attacks. For every attack made, another Elemental aspect is added. When all four Elements are engaged, their power grows with each successive attack.
"My power is no match for yours, esteemed Protector Erfwen? Give it time."]

Cilia:

[**Death of Distractions**
Heart card
Active, permanent
The Hand of Liberty keeps everything in check. Even distractions. Those pesky, tiny outside influences and sensual bombardments that constantly derail our thoughts, leading us to reduced productivity, minimal output, and any number of mental irrelevancies. This card can be activated at will, without cooldown. It will activate a small area of perfect control around the card holder, preventing anything auditory or olfactory from entering.
"Yeaaargh." The death of the scribe. He never heard the goblin sneaking up on him.]

[**Manipulate Darkness**
Uncommon, Dark crafter
Tier one
Permanent, passive
This card opens the gates, allowing you to manipulate the Dark aspect within you and, eventually, add them to your crafts in myriad ways. Manipulating your aspect will drain your stamina.

"From my soul to yours. A little shadow, a little mischief, to blanket the world and erase the tedium." Poet-crafter Erudian Nightstone.]

[Manipulate Light
Common, Light crafter
Tier one
Permanent Passive
This card opens the gates, allowing you to manipulate the Light aspect within you and, eventually, add them to your crafts in myriad ways. Manipulating your aspect will drain your stamina.
"Some people hack and slash to spread Light into this world. Not us. We, my dear, create." World-famous Light artist Everam Witteras.]

[Manipulate Fire
Common, Elemental crafter
Tier one
Permanent, passive
This card lights your inner furnace, allowing you to manipulate the fire aspect within you and, eventually, add them to your crafts in myriad ways. Manipulating your aspect will drain your stamina.
"Feel that? That rage, that wonderful heat. 'Tis yours, with but a thought. Feel it warm your soul."]

A Hint of Permanence
Uncommon, Dark crafter
Tier two
Passive, permanent
The quality of your creations is decided by the deftness of your fingers and the accumulated wealth of your expertise in your chosen trade.
The grade and power of the aspect you pour into your creation is defined by your Mental Power, your concentration and mental fortitude, and your expertise at applying it to your crafting process throughout the protracted creation period.
However, one thing holds true. The longer a crafted items lasts, the better it is. People remember the eternal, the items holding permanent effects. With this card, your Mental Power sees a medium increase when attempting to craft long-lasting items or items with permanent imbues.

"Might is right. Knowledge is power. Yet, permanence outlasts them all."]

[Apex of Growth
Uncommon, Light crafter
Tier two
Permanent, passive
There are few ultimate truths as a crafter. One of the rare exceptions is this: Aspects do not blend well. This card ameliorates some of the natural imbalances existing between the different aspects, making it easier to craft items merging powers from different aspects. Any difficulties from crafting items with conflicting abilities or powers still remain.
"Take the cold control of Liberty. Add a splash of unbridled Fury. Mix in the pure decadence of Darkness. Oh, my friends. This sinful concoction will be unforgettable."]

[Ritual of Fire
Uncommon, Elemental crafter
Tier two
Passive, Activated
Crafting by itself can be draining, both on willpower and stamina. Now, however, you can decide whether you want to sacrifice your energy for improved results. Once activated, this card will continually siphon small traces of stamina from the crafter to remain working. While in effect, for the purposes of crafting, the crafter's Mental Power is increased by fifty percent.
"Donande-tak, donande'tek, eru menthala-ze...damn. Candle blew out. Lousy second-hand candle makers. Kill 'em all when I rule the world."]

Sera:

[Look Deeper
Heart card
Instant, short duration
With a touch, the card wielder can pit their Mental Power against anybody, disclosing information about them. The higher the difference in Mental Power, the more information is disclosed about a person's Step, class, current active effects and cards, even their attributes.
Medium cooldown
"Sire. I regret to inform you that this cad has used his Mental Nudge card to influence your decisions." A merchant loses his head.]

[**Blessing of the Night**
Rare, Dark healer
Tier one
Passive, long duration
Once tapped, any attribute increases on you and group members in range are further boosted. Any active card effects of enemy Lightborn are halved.
Long   cooldown
"You dare come into this, my domain, and challenge my superiority?" The king of Fury is brought low.]

[**Warmth of the Circle**
Rare, Light healer
Tier one
Active, instant
This healing card is not the most powerful of all heals, granting a medium effect heal. However, it has an exceedingly fast effect and leaves the recipient with a small boost to Toughness that has a medium duration.
Medium cooldown
"This sensation. There is a joy here, a lingering trace of something divine. I thank you, Priestess, for this gift."]

[**Tongues of Pride**
Uncommon, Elemental healer
Tier one
Active, long duration
Once tapped, this card grants two effects. A weak fiery layer comes into being, adding itself to your weapon, as well as any allies' weapons in range. You will have weak fire damage added to your attacks. Finally, it carries a minor cleanse ability, continually working against any lower-Tier poison or debuffs used on allies.
"You ask me to bring the heat? Really? That is ironic." A Plague Knight falters.]

[**Cry for Blood**
Uncommon, Dark healer
Tier two
Active, short duration (effect instant)
Tap to place marker on a chosen enemy. If that enemy dies while under the influence of Cry for Blood, you drain his life force to be redirected to a place of your choosing as one of the following:

—One-person heal, instant.
—One-person physical shield, medium duration.
—One-person increase to Toughness, medium duration.
The effectiveness of any heals, shields, or increases is determined by the enemy's Toughness.
"Do not cry, love. You may die. But I will use your essence well."]

[Spark of Divinity
Uncommon, Light healer
Tier two
Passive, long duration
Sometimes, it is less about the power of the boost than the adaptability, being able to apply what you want and where. Tapping this card allows you to select an attribute. You can then select to either apply it to a single person for a medium increase to said attribute or your entire group for a small increase. Also, for the full duration of the boost, you may change your selection.
"Ah hah hah, Lord Agravon. You have grown stronger since last we met. Allow me a second to adjust. It would not do for me to fall behind."]

[Unexpected Spillage
Uncommon, Elemental healer
Tier two
Active, instant
A battlefield is like an ocean. The waves go low and high. Sometimes, they act exactly as expected. Sometimes, you find unexpected lulls and towering waves coming from out of nowhere. Upon activation of this card, the healer may transfer one hundred percent of the force of an incoming attack, magical or physical, made on the wielder or anybody grouped with the wielder, to another being within range of the card.
Short cooldown
"Stop hitting yourself. Oh, who am I kidding? By all means, keep it up!"]

Reviews

Anybody who's ever spent any time with me knows that I'm a simple creature. I prefer my beers liquid, my whiskey in a glass and my metal as extreme as humanly possible.

Yet, according to several police officers, I need to *pay* for my alcohol. The injustice!

You've already done your part to help me there, by buying my book or reading it on KU. I salute you. Now, if you're actually an angelic enough person that you're willing to help me more, (And of course you are, if you're reading the back matter, you absolute saint.) there is one thing.

Review mah book! Or somebody elses. Preferrably somebody amazing, like Rachel Ní Chuirc. Or Brian J. Nordon. Even Jez Cajiao's. Be sure to use long words – they confuse the hell out of him!

But seriously. That's the best piece of free aid you can give to writers like us. Review our books, tell the world exactly why you love them. We don't care about eloquence. But we do love you too!

Thank you so much.

-Lars

Patreon!

Okay then, now for those of you that don't know about Patreon, it's essentially a way to support your favorite Cheetos-smelling, sweatpants-wearing lunatics, otherwise known as writers. You can sign up for a day or a month or a year, and you get various benefits for it, ranging from my heartfelt thanks, to advance access to the books and art and more.

At the time of me writing this, the Patreon readers have access to a good deal of the final book of World of Chains which is available nowhere else.

https://www.patreon.com/Moulder666

Theft of Decks 3

Survival was just the beginning. Time to get FURIOUS.

Chase and his crew of outlaw card-wielders had it all figured out: Earth's Ward keeping them safe, promises of glory, and enough latent power in their decks to carve their names into legend.

But when an army of religious zealots marks your cards—and your head—for "cleansing," even friends in high places won't keep you breathing.

Their last shot at survival lies in the Furyborn lands, where their only hope is to convince a tribe of bloodthirsty isolationists—famous for turning outsiders into fertilizer—to part with their most sacred possession: a legendary Fury deck.

Simple? Not even close. Easy? Don't bet on it. Fun? Well, one out of three ain't bad...

By Lars Machmüller

Coming soon to pre order!

Arise Alpha

By Jez Cajiao

When you steal a hundred grand from some very bad people, the best way to survive is to stay small and quiet...

Possibly its not to save a pair of drowning girls, not go 'viral' on social media and certainly not to let the local police take your passport, trapping you on a small 'party' island in the middle of the Mediterranean Sea.

But Steve isn't the average guy, he's ex-military, ex-enforcer and ex-human. He's a one-man nanite fueled nightmare for those that cross the line, and he's decided that it's time to clean up his act. He's going to make up for the things he's done, and save 'the little guys'.

It's a nice fantasy, but even he has to admit, it's really just a justification, because he's a very bad man, with horrifying abilities, and he's only just learning what he's capable of. He needs a reason to not go to the dark, and if that's hunting down the creatures of the night and beating them to death with their own femurs?

Well, he's just the man for the job.

Stolen money. Greek Islands. Werewolves and Enforcers...
What could possibly go wrong?

<https://mybook.to/AriseAlpha>

Quest Academy

By Brian J. Nordon

A world infested by demons.
An Academy designed to train Heroes to save humanity from annihilation.
A new student's power could make all the difference.

Humans have been pushed to the brink of extinction by an ever-evolving demonic threat. Portals are opening faster than ever, Towers bursting into the skies and Dungeons being mined below the last safe havens of society. The demons are winning.

Quest Academy stands defiantly against them, as a place to train the next generation of Heroes. The Guild Association is holding the line, but are in dire need of new blood and the powerful abilities they could bring to the battlefront. To be the saviors that humanity needs, they need to surpass the limits of those that came before them.

In a war with everything on the line, every power matters. With an adaptive enemy, comes the need for a constant shift in tactics. A new age of strategy is emerging, with even the unlikeliest of Heroes making an impact.

Salvatore Argento has never seen a demon.
He has never aspired to become a Hero.
Yet his power might be the one to tip the odds in humanity's favor.

<u>Buy on Amazon</u>

Knights of Eternity

By Rachel Ní Chuirc

When Zara awoke in chains she thought she'd gone mad.

She was Zara the Fury - mistress of flame and fear. Her name was whispered across the land, from ramshackle taverns to the royal court. Even the heroic Gilded Knights thought twice before crossing her path.
She was feared—*respected.*
Now she was curled up on a dirt floor on her fiancé's orders. Valerius, leader of the Gilded, mocks her cries for help. And the kingdom is on the brink of war over the missing Lady Eternity...
But that wasn't why Zara thought she had gone mad.
The reason why is that the last thing she remembered was blood, an arcade screen, and the gun that changed everything.

But no chains can hold the Fury, and when she gets out? The world is going to *burn.*

<u>Buy on Amazon</u>

<u>Scarlet Citadel</u>

By Jack Fields

Gormon Hughes is 19, thin as a broom, and has—not for the first time in his life—been swept into the path of trouble. Poor, recently heartbroken, and indebted to the sort of people who file their teeth into needle points and devour wriggling bloated spiders for fun, Hughes sets his sights on salvation.

That salvation is the Scarlet Citadel, a wealthy organization of pageant fighters, monster hunters, and secret keepers. With the aid of strange oracles, rare good fortune, and a unique power that bubbles like champagne in the core of Hughes' being, he must join the Citadel and advance himself.

But the ladder of progression is harsh and dark. The rungs are slippery.

And falling means disaster...

<u>Buy on Amazon</u>

Facebook and Social Media

If you want to reach out, chat or just tell me my book was horrible, you can always find me on either my author page here:

https://www.facebook.com/groups/357145749698735/

OR

Legion recently set up a new Facebook group to spread the word about cool LitRPG books. It's dedicated to two very simple rules;

1: Let's spread the word about new and old brilliant LitRPG books.
2: Don't be a Dick!

They sound like really simple rules, but you'd be amazed…

Come join us!

https://www.facebook.com/groups/LITRPGLegion

I'm also on Discord here: **https://discord.gg/gyRkEgesH5**

In short, hit me up. I'd love to chat!

<u>Legion</u>

This is my first series with the Legion Publishers! It's run by Christine Cajiao and Geneva Agnos, who are also kind enough to let Jez Cajiao prance around in his underwear, where he can hurt nobody else.

It has, so far, been an absolutely enjoyable experience. You are welcome to reach out and ask if things have changed since I wrote this, of course. My safe word is **Jez is the nicest person in the world.**

They're taking on new authors, as we speak. So, don't be afraid to reach out.

Apart from being good people, I like that they have everything out in the open. Their contracts aren't hidden behind layers of legalese, you can find them here:

<u>https://www.legionpublishers.com/legioncontract</u>

If you want to reach out and ask any questions, get an idea of the support they offer, and possibly become part of the family? Just tap the link and fill in the form:

<u>https://www.legionpublishers.com/contact-and-submissions</u>

<u>Recommendations</u>

I'm often asked for personal recommendations, so if this book has whetted your appetite for more LitRPG, please have a look at the following, these are brilliant series by brilliant authors!

The Ten Realms by Michael Chatfield

Wandering Inn by Pirateaba

The Daily Grind by Argus

Quest Academy by Brian J. Nordon

Wandering Warrior by Michael Head

Calamity by Rachel Ni Chuirc

Codename: Freedom by Apollos Thorne

God of the Feast by Kevin Sinclair

Rise of Mankind by Jez Cajiao

<u>LITRPG!</u>

To learn more about LitRPG, talk to other authors including myself, and to just have an awesome time, please join the LitRPG Group

<u>www.facebook.com/groups/LitRPGGroup</u>

Facebook

There's also a few really active Facebook groups I'd recommend you join, as you'll get to hear about great new books, new releases and interact with all your (new) favorite authors! (I may also be there, skulking at the back and enjoying the memes...)

https://www.facebook.com/groups/LitRPGlegion/

https://www.facebook.com/groups/GamelitSociety

https://www.facebook.com/groups/LitRPG.books

https://www.facebook.com/groups/LitRPGforum/